Only The Wind Is Free | The Future Is Ours

ONLY THE WIND IS FREE | THE FUTURE IS OURS

MARGARET GRAHAM

BCA

LONDON · NEW YORK · SYDNEY · TORONTO

This omnibus edition published 1991 by
BCA
by arrangement with William Heinemann Ltd

Only the Wind is Free © Margaret Graham 1988
The Future is Ours © Margaret Graham 1991

CN 8829

Printed and bound in Germany
by Mohndruck, Gütersloh

CONTENTS

Only the Wind is Free

To my family

CHAPTER 1

Little Annie Manon was come home. Standing on the wind-whipped dune, lifting her face towards the lightening sky, she welcomed the North-East bite. She thought of the Wassingham she had known, the black streets of her childhood that seemed a million years away now.

The sand stretched clear and clean, all blemishes swept away by the tide before they had a chance to settle. God, she thought, who'd believe the pitch-black was creeping down to this beach last time I was here. She shook her head. Where did they dump the coal dust now she wondered – or had the miners been tidied away also, rationalised as though they'd never been?

But they had been there all right and somewhere the workings would be standing; stark and silent perhaps, but you could not wipe away completely years such as those or the memories that lingered.

She shivered, remembering the sound of the disaster whistle cutting through the loudest noise, bringing fear into every kitchen in the pit villages. Bet would slowly and quietly lift the latch and stand, helplessly watching the hurrying women, shawls hastily wrapped round greying faces and bowed shoulders, their breath white and thin as they struggled to go faster still. Please God, please God, not one of mine this time but none of this showing on their rigid faces and Bet hugging to her the certainty that it was not her pain this time because she had faced that long ago.

Annie could still feel the rough-textured dress of her step-mother as she clutched it, pulling it to one side so that she could also see, but not hear, for never a word was spoken on the long private walk to the pit-head. She was to nurse those miners in later years and she could never be professionally detached in the face of their grimy courage and determined humour.

Annie had been called a bonny lass then with her dark hair and eyes; though the eyes were not so dark really but hazel, deeply set under arched brows that cast a shadow. Like her ma, she was hinny, she had been told. Annie frowned with the effort of remembrance. The gnarled hands of Bet had always repulsed her. How coarse and vulgar she had seemed against the slight refined frame of her father. Annie sighed. How cruel children are, she thought, condemning so easily with no mercy given, even though they knew it was being asked.

Poor Bet, no wonder her hands were distorted; whose wouldn't be, hulking great kegs up to the shop from the cellar, corking and uncorking barrels for a trade that increasingly failed to give them a living. She remembered the smell of beer, the darkness of the small one-roomed store which sold cigarettes as well as Newcastle Brown. It was set in a street which was indistinguishable from the other back-to-back terraces which made up most of Wassingham. A village which had grown into a town after a station had been built and yet more pits had been opened. The pit wheels were always there against the skyline and the slag heaps too, though hardly noticeable because they were so familiar. And there was the smell of the coal which overlaid everything.

Their father's shop was a sorry remnant of the chain of wine merchants, the ownership of which should have been handed down from her grandfather to her da and his brother, Albert. Instead her father and uncle had been forced to sell it all piecemeal to settle the debts of a business which had been destroyed by the war. Her father had then leased one back from Joe Carter for the privilege of having something to call a job.

Those First World War years had ended more than one life she knew, broken more than one heart, but perhaps you only really cared deeply about your own particular grief. The rest were merged into a greyness against which the matt blackness of the pain stood out sharply and unavoidably.

She settled herself down, spreading her Harrods mackintosh on the sand. She did not want to return yet to Tom. She wanted to remember how it had been before she left; never to return until today. Her own hands were work-worn now, the wedding ring slipped easily up and down between the swollen joints on her right hand. Ruby Red of the left would never dance for anyone again. She smiled and stroked its crookedness, shaking aside the pain.

Leaning her head back, she let the wind sweep the fine hair where it chose. Her profile was strong and saved from prettiness by a chiselled nose. The lines of ill-health ran deep to the corners of her mouth and the sallowness of her skin owed as much to that as to the heat of her war years. Laughter had carved its path also. Maybe, she mulled, it was the laughter that carried her through, but only so far for it had then cracked and dried, it's husk blown beyond her reach.

She nestled deep into the mohair sweater which was too large for her slight frame but that was how she liked it; her cuffs were undone as well. The restraint of tightly buttoned clothes was unbearable to her. Strange that, she thought, remembering the long summers when they strolled in the spent warmth of the evenings, smoking and eating vinegar-soaked chips. Strange to hate such restraint when I so longed for it as a growing girl. Eeh, Annie, no one'll mind if you's late, we'll get others back first or they'll be for it else.

Tears threatened even now, so many years later, glinting like the coins they had bashed and filed from scraps of lead pipe before the fair. She laughed deeply in her throat. That was class she thought, remembering Don and Georgie choosing the stalls round which to loiter; the ones with the overworked taddy on whom they would then all surge, Tom, Grace and Annie at the front because they were smaller.

She picked up a handful of sand and let it fall through slightly parted fingers. The wind blew it back against her body. It was a good gang, she reflected, but one which yet another war has done its best to scatter. Annie sighed as she traced her salt-dried lips with her forefinger. In the beginning though, there were just the two of us, Don. And you are the one who stayed, deep down in your guts, stayed where you were and what would our da have thought of that, she pondered wryly. She could never forget her father's chronic need for his children to climb back up as he had failed to do.

Annie allowed herself then to remember the first time she had consciously seen her father but by then he was already wounded beyond endurance, with his youth long away and joy a distant memory. It was 1920 and she was 7. Don was 9.

The air had been sharp on her chapped face, much as it was now, and it had stung the roughened lips still wet from licking. The salivary warmth had eased the misery for a moment but as the wind whipped it dry again it hurt even more. She hunched herself deeper into her coat and wished Don would hurry. There was no way of ducking out of the cold here by the school gate. The railings were as dull as the iciness all around and their chill sank into her back as she changed from foot to foot, dragging her socks up with the toes of her boot. She grimaced at the thought of Aunt Sophie having to make yet another pair of garters. I don't know where you find holes to hide them in Annie, she'd say, I really don't. And you standing there the image of your bonny mother so's I don't have the heart to scold you.

Annie was glad it was Friday because Don would be here again, home from Albert's for hot scones and buttered toast. She wished he hadn't gone to live with their uncle. It was strange how things and people always seemed to disappear eventually and she rubbed her nose on her sleeve.

First it had been the light and pretty house on the hill that had gone. One day when she was 3, the light had simply fled and shadows had filled the rooms as the drapes were drawn across the windows; they were pink like plums. Everyone had spoken in whispers. Jane, the nanny, had red eyes and there had been a quiet emptiness until she and Don had moved in with Aunt Sophie but before that her father had come and gone from the big house, dressed in khaki with a black band on his arm. She knew now that he had come to bury her mother and that after her mother died, the house had too. Did the house always die she wondered, and shivered as the wind suddenly blustered down the street.

The cables were grinding up the slag-heap which had been created behind the school. She could hear the clang as the buckets emptied their waste when they reached the tipping gear.

She and Don had clambered into a black taxi when they travelled from the big house for the last time and Sophie's arms had hugged them to her. Her coat had been black and smelt of damp and they had passed the station and a church with no steeple, down street after street until they were at Sophie and Eric's, backing on to the railway line.

It was when she was 6 and Don was 8 that Albert had come for Don. She had thought her brother would stamp and scream and not leave as she would have done, had she been taken from Sophie and Eric's and put in that smelly old shop a good mile across town. But Albert had said he would give Don sixpence each week for running errands and he had laughed and gone.

The wind blew again bringing the noise of the cables nearer it seemed and then died away and the mist crawled in up the street. Again she searched the road for Don and she wanted someone but did not know who.

In the failing light she first heard, then saw her brother. Eeh, it was grand to see the lad but he was walking with someone, holding his hand and at this she frowned. Aunt Sophie had told her that, even though she was old enough to start school, she was never to talk to strangers and here was Don, for goodness sake, holding this big, strange hand. She faltered as they came close, unsure of what to do.

'Hey, Annie,' Don called. 'Guess who this is?'

He puffed out his chest and tried to look big. She bit back a retort and flicked the hair out of her eyes with a quick nod of her head. Eeh, you'll catch it when we get home, Don Manon, you see if you don't she thought to herself. She held the railing behind her. It was so cold it hurt her hand as she looked from Don to the man. He was not very big, she saw, and he was thin, so thin that he looked even smaller in the heavy brown coat. He squatted before her, his tired hazel eyes the same height as hers now. He held out his hands and said.

'It's me, little Annie. It's your da come home for good.'

His hands drew her towards him and held her close. Dear God, he thought, neither of my children know me and I would have passed them in the street. Annie's body was stiff against him and the brown serge hurt her chapped lips and she hoped she would not have to leave Aunt Sophie now that this man who was her father was home.

There was no colour, not even the grey of evening to help the long walk home. The hand which held Annie's was not warm but it did protect to some extent the painfully reddened wrist, which was grand. All the time though, she was aware of the soft slapping of the worn brown leather glove into which her da had pressed her other hand. Don had looked away as the warmth, someone else's warmth had stuck, clammy, to her hand. She had seen the snigger though. Just you wait, she thought, you daft beggar. Just because it doesn't bother you. You'd go and roll in the muck heap given half the chance. Her skin crawled with distaste; it was as bad as sitting on someone else's warm seat. She half closed her eyes, holding her hand taut within the glove.

Maybe if she held it quite still the sodden heat would pass her hand and seep out through the top without touching her. Then, so long as the sides of the glove did not touch her skin, it would be all right. In fact it wouldn't be so bad if it was someone she knew. She sighed.

'Are you liking school, Annie?' her father asked quietly, at a loss to reach these children, aware that already there was a distance between him and this quick-eyed wary child whom he had last seen when she was barely 3. She had changed little; there was still the chin which tilted in something short of defiance when she was uncertain but the voice was Mary's. He felt the pain tense and leap at the sound of her reply.

'Yes, Da.'

Somehow in the last four years he had imagined the child but not the voice. The sound destroyed the nervous unreality of his mood, hurling the cold dark evening and the remnants of his family before him. Despair hung poised to swoop but was held at bay by the memory of his daughter's stiff embarrassed body awkwardly allowing his earlier embrace. A glimmer of feeling emerged as they silently trod the cobbles and his corrosive grief was given reason to pause.

Annie stared steadfastly at the ground as that old cat Sadie passed by. That did it; now the whole neighbourhood would know that Annie Manon was walking with some strange man. She dreaded a new round of whispers and furtive stares like those that had made her cringe with unhappiness when she had joined the school. Somehow these people were not like her or perhaps she was not like them since she was the one who had spoken differently and had struggled to understand the words which corkscrewed out so fast it had left her gaping. She smirked with satisfaction as she recalled how geordie she had quickly become and now was even as tough as Nellie, that gormless great gertie from Lower Edmoor Street.

Bye, that was a great day, the day she tripped Nellie into the steaming pile left by Old Mooney's rag-and-bone mare. She giggled softly as she pictured that face smeared with it. She had laughed so hard she'd wet her knickers but it was half fright as well because she hadn't meant to; she'd just turned at the end of the hoop run and her foot had caught Nellie's ankle. She had half thought she'd be killed by the great lump but Nellie had run off crying and Annie had been slapped on the back and given a jelly baby by Bert, the toughie of the street, and no one, but no one was given anything by Bert. She had nipped off the head first, then the legs and saved the body till last. After that she had sounded and looked the same as them and she was glad.

Even Sophie and Eric had seemed different in their own home to the people they had appeared to be on their visits to Annie's old house up on the hill. Without her hat and coat and in the compact terrace Sophie had been fuller and she smelt of lavender and Eric of the colliery smithy where he heaved and banged at glowing metal every day, singing in his deep voice the music of Gilbert and Sullivan. The difference was a good one, Annie thought, for the house always bubbled with talk and fun and Sophie would grasp her by the waist and lift her, tight and close and laugh into her neck so that she could hardly breathe for shrieking and Eric read her stories each evening before she slept. They made her body feel loose again like it used to before . . . but she wouldn't think of that now.

Sophie was watching for them, unalarmed at their lateness since Archie had written to say that he was coming home and would be in Wassingham, today. She had not warned Annie at his request and by now the headache which had been nagging all day stretched from her shoulder to her eye.

She moved to the fire and stood with her back to the heat which eased it a little but the tension that had knotted her muscles drove her to the window once more. The tears were close again and she clenched her mind against them. There had been so many shed over the last four years and now was not the time for more. But, Mary, my dear girl, she could not prevent herself calling silently, if only it hadn't happened, if only you were here now. What in God's name is to become of them?

She chewed her nail. I couldn't even manage to keep them together for you, your pigeon pair, and Don has grown away from us as I feared he would, once Albert had his way. She

11

wondered yet again if she could have fought harder at the funeral to prevent Albert from persuading Archie to allow him to take Don when he was 8, but he seemed so determined, almost obsessed by a need to have one of Archie's children. Was it just that he wanted a messenger boy or did he really care for his nephew? Somehow Sophie doubted this.

She rubbed her face with her hands, trying to shake the past from her head and moved first to the fire to add more coal, and then to the window searching with strained eyes through the mist and, dimly, they came, three figures emerging so sparingly from the dark of the street that it nearly broke her heart.

The years since 1914 had made a mockery of so much shining promise, she thought savagely, and there is absolutely nothing I can do about it. Her impotence drew back her tension, her headache increased, but she drew herself straight and moved to the front door, spilling the light into the thick darkness and drawing the now recognisable figures into its beam.

Annie blinked, warmed by the promise of familiarity and the scones which she could smell even as she crossed the stone step that clicked against her father's shoes as he followed her into the glinting hallway.

'Go through, Annie love,' Sophie coaxed as she kissed the hair which was cold and hung with minute droplets of evening chill. She pushed the thawing child gently from behind, only patting Don on the shoulder and smiling. He had told her last time that he was too old for kisses.

Annie, relieved that tea was as usual in the kitchen and not in the starched and strange front parlour, hurried past. She grinned and, shrugging herself free of her coat, flung it and the now lifeless leather glove onto the airer by the range and lolled kneeling against the guard. Her cheek pressed against the linen towels and the smell of boiling was still deep within them. With her face protected from the heat her knees and feet roasted themselves free of numbness until the itch of chilblains drove her further back to the chair in which she usually sat.

She glanced quickly at Don who had taken her place. His thin face was blotched with cold and his brown eyes were half closed. His light brown hair was dry now and flopped down towards his eye. She reached for the winter-green from beside the clock on the mantelpiece. Its tick was loud close to, but once back in her seat at the table it became lost in the hiss and spit of

12

the fire. The mirror above the fire reflected the gas lamps which spluttered on the walls and the pictures of Whitley Bay that Eric had found wrapped up in old newspaper on a train.

'D'you think,' she pondered, her voice muffled as she drew her leg up and pulled off her sock, 'I should let a claggy skunk like you have any of this?' She held up the winter-green and dared him to reach for it. She hoped it would gain a response and it did.

'It's that or a damn good clout,' he murmured, scratching his throbbing toes and making a lunge.

'Now, now, Don lad,' she taunted him, her voice full with laughter, her mouth rounded into posh. 'Is that any way to treat a young lady especially when her father is outside ready to save her.'

She rolled her eyes and clutched her hands to her breast and was helpless to beat off Don's attack which came and soon they were both tingling with suppressed laughter.

Don tossed it back for her to put away, as Annie knew he would. Bye, she'd get the beggar one day she vowed, happy that he was here and that, for this moment, he was as he had been before he went to Albert's. She leant her mouth against the knee she liked to hug. The smell of her skin was pleasing to her and she resisted the temptation to make a bum of it between her fingers. He might walk in.

In the pause they heard the lowered voices in the hallway and it drew their eyes to one another.

'D'you remember him, Don?' she whispered. 'And why is he here?'

Don shook his head, his finger to his lips. 'He says he's come home,' he mouthed. 'I hope so, then I can live back home.'

Annie nodded. So perhaps he didn't like it at Albert's after all. She was pleased. The winter-green was interfering with her sniffing and making her eyes water. Reluctantly she pulled her sock back on and allowed the leg to drop. She settled back into the chair, sitting on her hands and feeling warm all over, with no gaps at all. He seemed old, she mulled. It wasn't that he was different to the man she had imagined for she had never thought about him. She watched Don put more coal on the fire and didn't want this moment to pass. There was something so certain about the heat, the smell of winter-green. Something so certain about scones and Don rubbing his hands free of coal marks. It wasn't exciting but it was the same as last Friday and the Friday before. The dresser was up against the wall, the rag mat was by their feet. The walls were still cream, the scullery was through the brown door.

She looked at Don. 'But where is his home?'

Don shrugged, pulled his socks back on and searched in his pocket.

'Give over Annie, they'll tell us when they want us to know.' He held out the smooth Jack stones. 'Come on, I'll give you a game. Best of three and if I lose, I'll get a pennyworth of chips tomorrow and you can have a few.'

'You're a tight one,' she accused and smoothed the table cloth which she had rucked as she had turned her chair. Her back was now to the fire and it felt good. 'Don't you like it at Albert's then?'

'It'll do,' he said as he tossed the ball, 'but he's the one who's as tight as a mouse's whatnot. Won't let me have any sweets unless I pay for them.'

He was feeling the table cloth now.

'The stones will lie steady but it gives the ball a low bounce,' he remarked.

'Well, I think it's lovely.' She looked at him. 'Is that why you want to leave, because he's a skinflint?' Hoping that he would say that he missed her.

'It's like this see, if we've got a da, why not live with him. It's right isn't it, then I won't have to work for me pocket money.' His voice was impatient.

Annie sat back in her chair watching as he threw up and grabbed three pebbles. She couldn't see at all why it was right to live with a man she didn't know.

'But . . . ' she began.

'This is the one they used for the vicar,' Don interrupted. 'The tablecloth, you daft nellie.'

He threw again and Annie said nothing, knowing that he did not want to talk about it. It was finished as far as he was concerned and Annie wondered whether he really had feelings or just bounced like his jack ball was doing.

She heard the click of the front-room door and thought how wonderful it would be to be able to melt into invisibility, slide under the door and sit close to Auntie Sophie, rubbing her face against the softness of her jumper. She wondered if someone would feel an invisible stroke or would it be as light as gossamer. She frowned.

'What's gossamer, Don?'

'Don't talk daft, Annie.' His small blunt fingers were steady as he readied to catch the last stone. His nails were dirty from the coal and she hoped that he would wash his hands before they had tea. She traced the pattern of the satin stitch which edged the table cloth and it was smooth and raised and cool. She eyed the bare corners of the table; the cloth had never been put round that way before. So, an extra place must have been laid and there it was, at the end. It would be Uncle Eric at one end, and him, her father, at the other. She fidgeted and folded her arms across her stomach holding her breath knowing it was coming but unable to prevent it. The rumble escaped.

'For Pete's sake, Don, hurry up,' she snapped, a blind anger sweeping over her but he just laughed and dug her with his elbow.

'Still as noisy as an empty barrel,' he sniggered, handing her the stones. 'Your turn and let's have some hush while you're at it. Eeh, I'm right hungry, what are they doing in that room anyway?'

Sophie had closed the front-room door behind them. The fire was still well built up and Archie stood before it, rubbing his hands in its warmth. He turned and stood quietly looking round the room as though familiarising himself with a place he had once known but had now forgotten.

It was lit by a small table lamp which left the corners in darkness. The antimacassars showed up clearly against the dark maroon of the settee and chairs. There were just two occasional tables, one which held the lamp and a photograph of Annie and Don; the other, set to the left of the settee, held several; one of Eric in uniform before his injury, one of Sophie and Eric on their wedding day. The other was of his own wedding with his cousin, Sarah Beeston in attendance. He looked away quickly, away from his Mary, back to Sophie.

'This room's hardly changed at all, my dear,' he said after a moment.

Sophie smiled. 'But we have.'

They looked at one another and were comforted. She sat and beckoned Archie to the other fireside chair. He sat down carefully as though he were a person who had been ill.

'It was all such a rush last time,' she murmured. 'It was difficult to . . . ' she paused, searching for words, 'to approach the future.' She gestured helplessly. 'I didn't know how to help you.'

'Sophie, it's all right. I've sorted things out a bit now, made some plans.' He paused. 'They've grown so much. Don's a real lad now, though it'll be good to get him away from that shop.'

Sophie nodded, her eyes darkening. Archie continued.

'It was a mistake. Albert is not the one to look after children. I was wrong to agree but he seemed to want it so much, but that's in the past now. And Annie, well Annie's so like Mary isn't she?'

He leant forward resting his elbows on his knees, his hands clasped tightly. Sophie watched the taut face with concern. The fire's half-light accentuated the shadowed eyes.

'Damn it Sophie, I still find it so hard.'

He pressed his fist to his mouth, his eyes dark and years away. She leant across and held his other hand, saying nothing, letting the minutes drift by along with her thoughts. She knew now that he had come for the children and logically, emotionally even, it was right that he should. Dear God, he had little else and he was a good man, but how broken was he, she wondered anxiously. She pushed the thought away to the back of her mind. Eric was still talking of Australia; it had been their alternative should the worst happen and there could be nothing worse than losing Annie. They had the money saved and they would go, go as soon as Annie was gone.

Her headache was throbbing and there was an ache which filled her throat, one which she knew would spread this evening and which would always be with her no matter whether they were here or in the heat of a new land. I must not think about this now, she told herself. I will think about it in small pieces, that way I can bear it. She forced her shoulders down, taking deep breaths, composing her body into a calmness which was essential for them all.

She wished Eric would come home soon, his shift must be nearly over. It would be so much easier if he were sitting on the settee, his hands held loosely, his eyes gentle and calm.

'Tell me about your ideas, Archie,' she prompted. 'Will you stay in the army for a while. I never expected you to stay in after

16

the armistice. You could have been back two years ago. It seems strange?'

Ignoring what was really a question, Archie explained that he had finally left the service. 'There was,' he added awkwardly, 'the chance to rent back one of my father's shops.'

He brought out his pipe, knocking it against the hearth before he unfolded his tobacco pouch carefully, just as he used to, Sophie noticed. The pungent moist smell was one she had not thought of for six years. It had always been their Christmas present to him, a two ounce tin of Player's Navy Cut.

He pushed the dark shiny fibre neatly into the bowl before lighting it, relishing the absorption of the task but knowing that he must speak to her of the things he had arranged. How to tell her that in what he planned there was no disloyalty to her dead sister since he dealt only in practicalities these days. Since the war had seen fit to pass him along to the end he had to exist but his survival made him bitter.

There was that time when he should have died, the day there was no wind to blow the gas across. The day he had been called a murderer by someone whose hand he could still feel clutching at his leg. He ran his hand over his face, snapping the shutter down. Would he never shake off that voice or this tiredness which now dragged at his heels. Though it must drag even more for those who stood on street corners, filling in empty days in this land fit for heroes. He, at least, had a job to go to now and it was all comparative anyway, he told himself briskly. For God's sake though, it was hard not to think of the good years but the love of my life is not here any more so let's get on with the next bloody lifetime.

Sophie was startled when he spoke, he had been silent for so long.

'You see Sophie, this shop is owned by Joe Carter who bought it off us when we had to sell out. He's had enough and wants to lease it.'

'But what about the children?' she interrupted.

'I'm coming to that.' He smiled nervously. She was so very much like her sister. 'Elisabeth Ryan housekeeps for him.'

'So you'll employ her?' she interrupted again.

'Not exactly. You see it'd look bad, her being young and with the lad.' He finished in a rush. 'I've asked her to marry me.'

Sophie was stunned, then perturbed, at a loss for words.

17

She eventually asked slowly, 'But do you love her Archie?'

He drew on his pipe, tilting his chin as he exhaled. Her blue eyes were confused as he explained.

'No, I don't love her and I doubt that she loves me but without Joe she's homeless. Not many want unmarried lasses with bairns these days; there aren't that many men around any more. I want my children with me, then maybe I can make sense of things, and I can't have them without help. Let's just say we need one another.' He looked at her seriously. 'Barney, her fiancé, was killed at Ypres in '15. I was there but later.' His voice tailed away.

Sophie shuddered thinking of Eric's leg which had been saved even though he had been in a Somme shell-hole for thirty-six hours after being shot. They said it was the maggots which had kept it clean, free of gangrene, but she preferred to consider it a miracle. A shaft of compassion for the girl went through her. At least she'd been lucky enough to have her man return and if Elisabeth had a child of her own she would know how to care for the children. She found it helped to concentrate her mind on the facts.

'When will you take them?' she asked, meaning when is my Annie to leave me.

He stood up. 'I thought a week on Saturday might suit us all, I'll have a word with Albert about Don. I can get moved in by then and Elisabeth has agreed to marry me that morning. Don't want to close the shop longer than necessary; can't risk losing custom. I must get on my feet you see.'

She saw his hands clench and unclench at his sides and nodded though suddenly she was unable to sympathise with his reduced circumstances because a violent spasm of outrage had gripped and held her. She fought to keep it from her face but she wanted to scream at this man for taking Annie from her, just because he was her father. And it was this word which cut through the anger and made her shoulders sag and her lips tremble. She forced herself to rise calmly, banking the fire carefully and repeating that word – father – because of course Annie was not her child. Annie was Archie's. Replacing the shovel, she turned towards the door, still unable to meet his eyes but she repeated the question she felt she had a right to ask and which he had not yet answered.

'But why have you stayed away so long?'

18

Her hand was on the doorknob; she would not pass through until she had an answer.

Archie paused a moment. 'I couldn't come earlier,' he pleaded in a whisper, fearful that the children might hear the conversation, now that they were so close to the door. 'I had to sort something out first, have something to offer the children.' His long slender fingers sought her understanding. But inside he knew it was nothing so honourable, just a long blank series of weeks, months, years, where responsibilities were ignored, buried beneath the noise of ghosts. He was ashamed that it was still without any real interest that he had finally come to take up the pieces. It was simply that there was nothing else to do; he was finished as a soldier; the shaking and the nightmares were too bad. Now he needed to cling to something which belonged to him, to try to find a measure of peace. Therefore he had come to claim his family and rent his shop.

Sophie waited but he said nothing more.

'Will you tell them your news or shall I?' Her voice reflected her troubled doubts. Every breath was difficult now.

'Perhaps we both could,' he replied, laying his hand on her arm, delaying their entrance. 'And Sophie, I will never be able to thank you enough for taking Annie in for these four years. There is a spark in those eyes of hers which makes me feel,' he searched for the right word, 'interested. Heaven alone knows what would have happened to them both without you to sort it out.'

'Your cousin, Sarah, helped a great deal you know. She's always been there, should I need her and she has, without fail, sent the children Christmas and birthday presents. I thought you should know.'

Archie smiled. He was not suprised. Sarah, the daughter of his father's cousin, had always been a good friend to Mary since their marriage and to him as well.

Sophie continued. 'One thing I haven't yet done, although Annie asked so often in the early days, is to tell her how Mary died. She never mentions it now but one day she may hear from someone else.' She paused. 'Perhaps you should be the one, not some spiteful gossip.'

Glad that she had found the courage to say what she had long felt, but not hopeful about the result, Sophie opened the door into the hall and then walked through into the kitchen and the throb of young life met them instantly, softening the tightness of their faces.

'Anyone for scones,' she called, smiling love as Annie won the last game of Jacks and Eric's voice called from the yard.

CHAPTER 2

Betsy leaned against the iron mangle, arching her back in an effort to relieve the ache which dragged at her body. The washroom was the last to be swept, scoured and polished and now the copper shone and she longed to run her hands over its round shine-splashed shape; it looked so warm to the touch.

The ceiling was free of webs which had cocooned spiders all through the long winters but the drab green walls would never look as sparkling as they really were. The sun shafted in from the skylight but it was still dark in this basement section of the house. She could hear, but not see, passers-by as they hurried to where they were going. She straightened, rolling each shoulder in turn, proud of the stiffness of hard work and reached for the shawl which had been flung aside as the sweat had pricked then run down her back when the scrubbing-brush and hearthstone had whitened even the back step. She clicked at herself and said out loud:

'For Pete's sake, bonny lass, they're only a couple of bairns arriving, not the princes of the land.'

'Aye,' she answered laughing at herself, 'but they're to be my bairns so they're better than the King himself.'

She winced as she dried her hands on her coarse apron, the sacking rasping and scratching her work-reddened and swollen hands. Her eyes were pale blue and her lips full and red. Her hair was brown and curled at the temples, the rest was drawn back into a bun and she tucked in the pins more securely. Her hands shamed her and she pulled her cuffs down, the same cuffs that she had nervously pulled this morning at the service. Thank the Lord there was no photographer she thought, and was relieved to see that they contrasted less against the blue cotton than they had against the stark white of her arms.

She traced the raised veins with a puffy forefinger and shook

21

her head. Barney had kissed them and called her the Queen of Sheba and promised her rings for her pretty soft fingers. Well, that's a long time ago now she thought and it should have stayed at fine words but it had not so that was that. The clock in the upstairs hallway chimed but the number was too distant to register so she hurried up the steps, through the kitchen, then on up into the hall.

'My God,' she gasped. 'Four and the buns still not in and they'll be here soon.' Her hands flew to her hair. She could feel the thick damp strands hanging heavy with sweat on her forehead, released from the bun by her rush up the stairs. Her nose and cheeks felt greasy with the shine of labour and there was no tea ready.

She felt her body begin to shake and the hot waves of panic and fatigue swept her first to the stairs leading to the bedrooms, then to the front door until finally she rushed back down to the kitchen.

'Calm yourself, girl,' she urged. 'Just get them buns on. Tom will do at Ma Gillow's for a while longer, then when they come give them bread to toast on a fork, bairns like that.'

She looked in the pantry. 'There's the ham and pickle, they can go on the plates now. And talking to yourself is the first sign of madness.' She carried plates and breadcrumb-coated ham back to the table. Grey ash lay thick where there should have been glowing coals in the grate. The oven set into the left of the fire held barely any heat now and the hotplate on the right was only warm. Betsy shovelled coal on gently, trying not to spurt the ash up into the air only for it to settle on her polished and wiped surfaces.

'Just a few for now,' she breathed, then held up an old newspaper to try and provoke a draught. It was no good. 'Oh God damn it,' she swore and rushed to open the outside door, the paper flapping in her hand. At last there was sufficient air to try and suck the flames up the chimney and what did it matter that the cold raised goose-bumps on her flesh if only the coals roared enough to heat the oven. At last they did and before the newspaper could yellow with the heat she pushed it back into the kindling box, grimacing at the blackness of her hands, the smudges on her apron. She rushed to shut the door, confident that the fire would burn quickly now. She added more coal, still gently, then stood momentarily at a loss.

22

'Come on, get 'em washed, then do the bliddy buns. And don't you swear like that,' she aped her mother, scrubbing her hands then rushing and spilling flour and water, almost in tears. The bowl was already on the table but the buns were soon too wet and stuck to her hands as she tried to mould them.

'More flour, that's all you need, hinny,' she soothed herself but her voice was shaky and high in the chaos. 'That's right, take a deep breath and then bang them in the oven.'

The smart of the oven heat on her tender raw hands made her gasp and two of the buns lurched on to the flag-stoned floor whilst she saved the others only by steadying her arm against the open oven door. The searing white pain brought everything to a stop. The spreading whiteness of the dough at her feet barely registered and tiredly, mechanically, her panic cut through as though sliced from her by a cleaver. She slid the tray, hard and real between her thumb and forefinger, into the dark of the oven. The door clanged shut and carefully she slotted the latch home.

The earlier satisfaction had vanished and her arms ached with a weariness that seeped throughout her body and emptied her mind of even her nervousness. She pulled her coat from the back of the chair and slumped into its clammy heaviness and sat looking round a kitchen which was, from now on, her own. She felt no elation.

It would all have been so different but for the war. Then she would have married Barney and had Tom. Done things the right way round, her mother had hurled when Barney had died, and soon after his son was born. Look at the mess she had just made of a room she had spent hours cleaning and polishing; what a talent she had for little messes; and yes, her mother had said that too. Her hands lay throbbing one upon the other and the harsh pain of the tightening burn across the softness of her upper arm was almost a comfort. It was something which belonged to her and on which she could focus. She had been burned before and knew the course of the pain and that was all she wanted to know at this moment. Her head hung to one side and she lifted her shoulder to rub her cheek and that caress was better than none.

Barney Grant had been a strong young pitman but how gently he had led her to the slopes of the slag after he had arrived home on leave. She pressed her cheek closer now, deep into the cotton of her blouse and she could feel the heat of her skin and she remembered the smell and the feel of the body of her man.

Again and again they had promised that they were different, that lovers who opened their mouths to one another and knew such pleasure in one another could not be touched by war, by death. But his eyes were deep with thoughts that were his own, that he would not share and later he had cried and worried for her in case there should be a bairn, my bonny wee lass he had whispered.

She had laughed then because next week they were to marry and no God would defy her love. And he had nodded and kissed her hand fit for bloody diamonds he had said again.

They had all been recalled the next day in a rush for the next big push. His mates had told her he had felt nothing but she knew it had been raining, raining, raining because that's what the papers had said of Ypres and he hated the rain on his face.

He wasn't found for days. Wipers was such a stupid name for a grave she thought and wished she could have cleaned the mud from his eyes and carried him home, warned him and, in time, shown him his son.

She stared dully at the fire. Here she was then, living in the same house where she had worked since she was 14 but now it was to be with a man who had today given her a name and a family, not just a job. She should be grateful but her scream for Barney sounded so real that she snapped upright and could not tell whether it had pierced the air or just her mind. The fire was solid red now, God knew how much time had passed, she must be mad to sit as though life was a holiday. She pressed her fingers to her forehead, nervous at the thought of Archie coming home before all this was straight, but she had to fetch Tom, she was already late.

Betsy straightened her coat, drew the latch and the cold of the early evening caught her again. It cooled her even as it caught in her throat and she reached for the bairn's blanket. He'd need it over his face in this chill, then she'd just have to be back in time for them to arrive. Yes, that was it, be quick and there was nothing to worry about she urged herself, thinking as she went that he was such a cold one there was no knowing how he would take a mistake. God, she thought as she undid the gate, what I wouldn't give for a cup of tea.

24

Archie led the way up the four steps and fumbled for the keyhole.

'The shop is over there,' he told them over his shoulder and Annie nodded though all she could see were dark forbidding shapes in the dim light. She grasped the peak of one of the railings which lined the steps to the front door and through the thickness of her glove she could feel the flakes of old paint first stick into it and then give way beneath her restless thumb. The tip of the railing was not as sharp as had first seemed and it had flat edges which swept to a modest point.

'D'you think if you fell on these they'd go right through you?' she asked her father. 'I mean so they come out the other side.'

He was on the step above her and seemed not to hear. His back was towards her, his face pressed close to the keyhole.

'Don't be daft Annie,' mocked Don. 'You'd have to be right tender and skinny to have them go through. Most people would have 'em stick halfway through and they'd wobble about with their eyes popping out.'

'Until you knocked them off in three throws,' Annie retorted. 'Hey, that would make a good fairground game. Roll up, roll up, knock off the gentleman with the funny hat and win yourself a – a what, Don?'

'Clip round the ear if you go on like this,' he whispered, nodding his head and pointing it towards their father. They sniggered together and tried to count the railings from the bottom to the top even though the gloom made it difficult. Archie looked at them in confusion. They had forgotten him and he was glad for he hadn't known how to react to their extraordinary conversation. He could not remember discussing impaled bodies with Albert as a child, far less attempts to dislodge them once they were 'set up' as these children of his had suggested. Mind you, he and Albert had never been close enough to discuss anything. The key was by now in the frozen lock though it was stiff to turn. Peering closer, working it backwards and forwards, he muttered:

'I'll have to get Elisabeth to oil this thing. It really is too slack of her.'

Annie wondered why he didn't just breathe on it instead of bellyaching about what other people should have done. He's got a pair of hands hasn't he, she thought, and in her irritation could no longer be bothered to count the railings.

She moved her toes inside her boots, her feet ached with the cold but her toes were empty of feeling and seemed heavy in their numbness. She rose and fell, pressing all her weight on to them and longed to squeeze their cold dampness between warm hands. She felt Don close to her, his breath showing white as he blew on his hands. The door loomed large as they grew accustomed to the dimness and Annie's eyes hurt as she struggled to follow the shadowed bulging shape hanging on the door which minute by minute seemed to sharpen and move even as she looked.

Well, she thought, fancy having a great big claw knocker on your door and then spending all night fiddling with the keyhole. She stood staring hard, until the knocker disappeared in a blur of cross-eyes and she felt triumphant at reducing the bunched brass to nothingness. As the door finally swung open she began to move with it. Don felt her sway and shook her arm.

'Don't be stupid,' he whispered in her ear and Annie felt the sniggers rise and shake her shoulders. Oh no, she prayed, don't let me start again else I'll never stop and she wondered where the giggles were coming from.

'Come along then,' their father directed, standing in the dark of the hall and the laughter drained from her and she held back. Why should she go first to be swallowed up by this strange dark house? Don could, the canny beggar. She twisted from his grasp and stood sideways, her eyes refusing to move until he had passed. Her feet curled in her boots for a better grip and her legs braced for battle.

'Come along Annie,' her father ordered shortly. 'Ladies before gentlemen. Donald is quite right.'

Annie raised her chin in a fury of frustration which contracted her scalp but she could do nothing but obey. It was two against one. Turning she squelched hard down on Don's foot, twisting as she did so and sailed in on his indrawn breath of pain and surprise. That'll teach you, she thought, you canny little squid.

Inside there was no wind and it seemed much warmer and very quiet but for a loud tick and there was a strange sharp smell mingling with polish but no scent of cooking or arms outstretched. She stood quite still, her heartbeat loud in her ears, not wanting to move unless it was to touch something definite, to lean against something solid. She felt no friendliness about her, just thick space which could hold endless horrors. She longed for the noise of trains clattering beyond their eyes but not their ears at Wassingham Terrace and the pigeons scattering in their loft as the cats screamed.

Here, in the dark, the ache was swelling. Closing her eyes, Annie tried to remember whether she had missed any black dogs on her way here. There was only the brown one she was sure but still she had held her collar until she had counted a hundred. She had not trodden on any cracks either so surely her wish would be granted. She'd also prayed to God each night, twice, but he had seemed to be deaf for quite some time. Nonetheless her father might just change his mind or even drop dead so that Sophie could walk over and take her back.

It would have been just bearable if Sophie and Eric had stayed in the town just half a mile from this shop but to pack up and go to the other side of the world seemed like the end. There would be no more stories from Eric, no more hugs and tickles from Aunt Sophie, no more drawing on the kitchen floor while Sophie and Eric held hands and talked at the kitchen table.

Sophie had said that she and Eric were young enough to start a new life in a new country and must go straight away. She'd said how she was 29 and Eric was 30 and if they didn't go now, this minute, perhaps Australia would be too much for them. Annie had never thought of them in terms of years before and 29 seemed very old. It's the same age as Sarah Beeston, Sophie had said, but Annie was not interested in other people, only in Sophie.

'Come on in Annie,' her father's voice called and as she turned she remembered the feel of Don's foot beneath her heel and her hands went still and her fingers filled with splintered ice. Oh no, she'd broken her good luck, just when she'd done nothing wrong but everything painfully right since that day in Sophie's kitchen.

Her lip stung between biting teeth and she wanted to drop to the ground and beat it with her hands because now there was no way back to the old life. She wanted to screech to Don, to pummel him with her fists and hurt him as she was hurting. Why did you get at me and make me do it? Why didn't you leave me be, she wanted to shout, and the hate spilled out from her eyes and Don was shocked and she was glad that someone else was feeling pain. Then in turn she was shocked and frightened because she did not want the hate to remain. He was all she had if Sophie could not come for her and she didn't want to be alone with just this dark angry hole left where people had once been.

'Elisabeth, Elisabeth,' her father called into the darkness but there was no reply. 'That's strange,' he murmured almost to himself and the children stayed still. 'I think we should go down to the kitchen and see how dinner is coming along. Get your bearings first though.'

He had already lit the gas lamp and now blew out the match; then shook his arms out of his coat, helping Annie with hers when he had finished. The elastic, which ran from one glove through her sleeves to the other, caught on her cuff and she had to scramble to free herself. She looked up at him. What big nostrils he had and why did he call tea dinner and dinner lunch she wondered. She sighed. And he had not called them bairns since that first day; it made him seem very far away. But now that the smell of the gas lamp was nudging at her it seemed, together with the light, to bring the house to life and that was a surprise for it had almost been as though nothing existed beyond the darkness.

The light showed steep stairs rising with a dark glossy conker-coloured bannister which curled and stopped like the doormouse and she could almost believe she was Alice. Ahead of her was a passageway with a strip of carpet laid on black and white tiles. It ran into the hall and was the same carpet which was laid up the middle of the stairs. It drew her feet far less than the stone of the pavements. She was feeling better now that the front door was shut and the Gladstone bags were lined up at the hall-stand. Now there was no decision to be made. She was here and must stay.

She looked round the dim hall and across to the clock which stretched from the floor to way above her head; much higher than the hall-stand which was now lumpy with coats. She followed the brass pendulum as it swung from side to side disappearing and reappearing with a regularity which calmed her. She had never seen anything like it before but the deep sure sound of the tick, unchanging and predictable, made her feel that here was something that would never surprise, never shock and she was comforted. She tried to reach fifty strokes in one breath. It was five o'clock.

28

The eruption of sound hit her full in the face and the bone buttons of her cardigan were pulled harshly on straining thread and she jerked back her shoulders in terror. Then, hickory dickory dock her mind raced and she laughed. You'll not catch me again she challenged and it was to life she shouted.

Turning to Don, she drawled. 'Don't fret bitty bairn, it's only a grandfather clock.'

Don caught her tone and cursed himself for leaving his mouth hanging. 'Course I know that,' he snapped but they both knew he hadn't. He had been peering up the stairs, his back to the clock and the noise had been like a clap of violent thunder without a source.

They followed Archie down the passageway, Annie carefully treading on her toes to avoid the pattern. Don's hiss of irritation as she veered into his path was a small price to pay for catching up on some luck. It was dark at the end of the passage and the door to the basement was shut. Annie pulled Don back against the wall. His head was well into the wallpaper above the wooden rail which divided the bottom paint from the flock wall-covering. Hers was part in both and they grinned at one another. She needed him and she had made him feel big again and their anger was gone.

When their father closed the basement door behind them there was silence again and it was cold and dim. The light from the gas mantle outside the kitchen door was the merest glimmer but there was now a smell of baking which was gentle on them. Archie was relieved, this was an important moment for them all and he had feared problems.

'Come down these steps carefully now,' he instructed, guiding them to the rounded wooden hand rail. 'The ground drops at the back of the houses so the basement is at garden-level whilst the front door is at street-level.'

Annie loved immediately the long-grained smoothness of the rail and tried to stretch her hand round it, finger to thumb but failed. She laid her hand lightly on its surface instead and had double value by running it backwards and forwards as she followed the darkness of her father's back. He smelt of hair oil and she thought of his voice which she decided she liked, though it was different to everyone else's that she knew. It had a pattern which kept nudging at a shadow in her mind. She wished he would call them pet or hinny though, since it sounded like love.

As he opened the door, the light burst out at them, warm and tasty, and she and Don followed him quickly through. There was no one there. The fire was low but still red hot, almost clinkered and the table was covered in flour with a bowl in the centre. A boiled ham lay on an oval dish. The floor was smeared with white trails and plopped against the hearth were two dough lumps and the kettle was bubbling its head off on the hotplate.

She looked at their father who just stood there, saying nothing but feeling something because his face was pale and his top lip had thinned. She moved closer to Don who looked nervous in the mounting tension. Annie looked at the white blobs and then at Da; they were the same colour and hysteria rocked inside her.

'Well, I dare say there's a perfectly reasonable explanation,' he managed and picked up a tea towel from the peg to lift the kettle on to the table. The steam made his hand red and wet but the rattling ceased and suddenly it was quiet.

They all stood there staring in silence at the black kettle as though it was the most interesting thing, Annie thought, since Ma Henry's teeth fell out when she sang 'God Save the King', last Empire Day in front of the flag-pole. Why doesn't he just get on and make us a cup of tea like Eric would have done? She changed her weight to her other foot. At the sound of running footsteps in the yard, she stepped back; the door burst open and Betsy spun to a halt. Her laboured breath was loud in the room and she held Tom close, glad of his warm weight against her body, glad that she had a shield against the group.

The frost had turned her nose red and her face white and her hands were still swollen with cracks of deeper soreness opening. More hair had fallen from her bun and hung loosely over and around her face and there was a drip teetering on the end of her nose. Annie shrank as it dropped on to the bundle in her arms and widened and sank into the worn blanket. She saw that it was not a baby but a child with holes in its boots.

'I'm sorry, Archie,' Betsy gasped, her breath still shallow and fast. 'I fell behind and then had to fetch Tom from Mrs Gillow.' She drew away the blanket as the child began to squirm and pull to one side.

'There now, Tom,' she soothed. 'Say hallo to your new brother and sister.'

Betsy smiled and drew two chairs close to the fire and then Tom's which was cut down.

Annie smiled at Tom as he sat on the small chair. His eyes were a deep blue and his hair as brown as the bannister upstairs and she'd never seen that colour eyes with dark hair before. Tom ducked his head and looked at her under his brows. He was smiling.

'Come on then, pet,' Betsy coaxed Annie. 'Come on and sit by the fire. And you lad.' This was to Don. 'Are your toes frozen? Then warm them gently or you'll start chilblains.'

Annie moved to the chair nearest the fire taking advantage of the fact that Don was further away and unable to get there first without pushing and shoving and he was hardly likely to do that with her father standing there looking as though he had sucked a lemon. Her Da still hadn't said anything and she stretched her legs to the warmth, trying to ignore the tension he was creating. It made her feel as though she had a clenched fist in her stomach. Betsy leaned past her and shovelled more coal on the fire and the noise was welcome and familiar.

Don stepped to one side as Betsy crossed the room to the guard which she had moved against the wall as she cleaned. It was heavy and the strain showed on her face as she attempted to drag it back to the hearth.

'Don't want you falling on to the coals,' she said in a voice taut with effort.

Annie looked at Da; he was gazing into the fire. She looked at Don, he was looking at his feet, so Annie rose and moved to take the other end and together the two of them brought it back to the fire. By then Don was sitting in her chair, as she knew he would be. He did not move as Annie took her end past him, brushing close to the oven. Breathing hard with the effort she let it drop down, now that it was in position. She heard the thud as it hit Don's boot and she smiled, knowing that she had judged it to a nicety and that it was heavy enough to bruise a toe, even through thick leather. She heard his gasp and trod on his other one as she stepped over him to what should have been his chair.

'Oh dear,' she said, as he hugged his foot. 'Chilblains?'

'Chilblains, did you say?' asked Betsy as she hung her coat

31

up on the peg at the back of the door. She had noticed nothing but Tom had. He buried his face in his hand and tried to stifle his laughter. Annie grinned at him and winked, he was a bonny lad with his eyes so full of warmth.

'We'll have a winter-green party, shall we later?' Betsy laughed. 'Or at least when I've sorted out something to fill your bellies.'

She glanced at Archie who had stood silent since she entered and ran her hands over her apron, remembering too late its black smudges. She smiled nervously at him, moving over to collect the kettle from the table and realised that she must have left it on the range while she fetched Tom and flushed. Oh God, it must have been bubbling its bloody head off, she thought.

He was looking at her flushed greasy face and eyes which were smudged beneath with shadows and he turned from them and left the room.

Betsy stood and looked at the closed door and listened to his tired footsteps as he climbed back upstairs and knew he would be going to his study. She also knew that she had not fancied the flash of distaste before he had left and it hurt. What had she done that was so terrible, why had he made her feel like a gormless slaggy?

'Mam,' called Tom, 'Your buns is burning!'

Annie and Don helped her as she rushed to open the door and snatch them away from total disaster. As she tipped them onto the table, bits broke and Annie looked sideways at Betsy, her mouth rushing with saliva at the hot sweet smell and Betsy nodded and they both laughed. They were spicy.

'They're not half good,' Don said and Annie agreed as she pressed some into Tom's mouth, watching Betsy wash her hands, and felt a slackening of tension. She had a thing about snot her Auntie had said.

'How old is Tom?' Annie asked, sitting back in the chair which, this time, she had managed to reach first.

'I'm 5,' Tom replied. 'I've got ears and a mouth, you know.'

Annie laughed then, loud and long. Her feet were against the guard and not yet burning. The smell of mashed tea was thick and her hands, round the mug Betsy handed her, felt in place. Betsy's eyes were kind, she thought, but had the same blackness beneath as Aunt Sophie's. She felt sorry for her; it must be hard to be old and have sore hands with no one to pour cream on to cupped palms and no one to put the stopper in or stroke coolness into heat.

She had tried to do it herself once but the cream had run all over the table as she upturned her hand putting the top in the bottle. She ran her tongue along her teeth wondering if her da would do it for Betsy and the thought of him stroking anybody seemed daft. She remembered the look she had seen on his face and shook her head. She was glad he had left because the stiffness had gone with him. He looked as though he had moved from sucking a lemon to finding a nasty smell under his nose, especially when he looked at Betsy, but she didn't really smell, she just looked sweaty.

Anyway, Annie thought, holding the toasting-fork, Betsy was full like Sophie and spoke kind words with laughter in them. It made her feel floppy and her jaw sagged. Maybe it was going to be all right after all.

CHAPTER 3

Archie sat in the cold of his study. It was not heated in any way, though there was a fireplace set into one corner. He did not notice the temperature but sat in the mahogany carver chair which had remained, together with the desk, when he had leased the premises from Joe. Bellies, he thought. It was too much. This room was naturally cold set as it was on the north side of the house and, now that it was evening, he had automatically drawn the curtains across the window when he had crossed to the desk, not completely though, because he never liked to shut out the light altogether. It was a relief to eliminate some of the down-draught from the ill-fitting sash-windows. He had hung the curtains himself as they were ones which Sophie had given him from the attic where she had been keeping them. Bellies. He tore his hands through his hair and made himself think of other things. The curtains.

They were ones which Sophie had rescued from the sale of the house on the hill and they were his and Mary's first purchase for that house. They had chosen a heavy damask drape. Oh yes, he remembered now how he had explained to Mary when they had been delivered to the house that damask was the name originally given to a rose from Damascus, hence the colour, whilst she was a rose from Wassingham. It sounded trite now in retrospect, but she had lifted her hand to his cheek and stroked him. She was so soft he could hardly feel her touch though the heat of her reached him.

The maids had hung the curtains that day in spite of the fact that they were really too heavy for that achingly hot June, the one that blazed just before the world went mad. At least, he recollected, the farmers were able to reap their harvest in time to feed the troops who were quickly blasted away, so more came to eat the supplies the others were no longer hungry for and I was one of them. Balance and counter-balance, he thought, picking up the paper-knife on his desk, that's what most things amount to. He ran his fingers either side of the blade.

The ivory handle, carved in the image of some long forgotten Indian god was as cold as it always was. It was too dark by now to see clearly but he knew its contours intimately. It had been his father's, made from the tusk of an elephant that he had shot himself when on one of his frequent forays to the Raj. Archie had always refused to go; he couldn't bear the heat and he wondered whether Albert had ever been asked.

His father had not liked Albert; not from the same mould, he had grumbled, can't think what went wrong there. Just like your mother's father, like a pot of cook's gravy. Thick and slow. I wonder if Albert noticed, Archie pondered, but dismissed the memory as unimportant to him. Blood sports had disgusted him but the knife had always appealed. It was so impervious to human warmth, to friction. So totally detached.

He turned in his chair, running the blade gently down the curtains. His ivory against her damask, his pale cold skin against her soft warmth. It was too much. He flung the knife on to the desk, burying his face against the faded worn curtains as she had done but that had been on the day when they were vibrant and new.

It's so beautiful, all of it, she had said, her voice muffled by its folds, and he had reached out, taken her shoulders, feeling her flesh beneath the light cotton day-gown and had drawn her to him. I love you so much he had murmured, his mouth in her hair, then on her neck, his hands seeking and finding her breasts, full now with her pregnancy. He could remember still how she had leant into him, pressing her laden womb against him and he had felt her down the length of him. The sounds of the summer which had filled the room through the open windows had disappeared and all that was left was her; hot, soft, urgent, leaning into him, her unborn child thrusting against him as though in protest.

I love you, I love you, she had whispered. My cool ivory blade. I want you in me and she had coloured then, hiding her face in his shoulder, embarrassed at speaking words like these in the daylight, in the drawing-room with Annie curling and turning deep inside her.

He had gripped her black hair which hung loose down her

back, pulling her head so that her face lifted from him, kissing the damp strands which had caught on her forehead and finely boned cheeks. Some swept across her half-open lips and he had kissed her mouth and then her body.

He stirred in his chair, rose and paced the floor.

She had tapped a heat in him that he had not known existed. From the moment he had seen her in his father's office, she had stirred in him a response that no one else ever had. He could at last relate to another human being. Her cool ivory blade she had called him because they both knew that this ivory could only be warm near her source of heat.

He drew the curtain back so that he could see out over the dark yard and then the passageway which ran down the rear of the terrace and looked for the stars but there were none. She had risen to the big house, moved up from Wassingham as though it was natural to her. There had been no bellies from Mary. He felt the pain and then his breath grew shallow and he fought to control the rising panic that increasingly sprang from nowhere. He knew he must push all thought of her away. He must breathe deeply, steadily. Pull into his mind the image he had built of his life from today. He repeated his words in time with the slow breaths he forced himself to make. Cling . . . to . . . the . . . image . . . he . . . had . . . built . . . of . . . his . . . life . . . from . . . today . . . Again and again he said it until his hands which had been gripping the arms of the chair became gradually less tense, his breathing more normal. His mind uncoiled. How much time had passed this time, he wondered, feeling drained.

It usually worked. It had worked when they went over the top, following the white guide-tapes. It had worked when the whizz-bangs fell too close. It worked during the long nights without her, sometimes. He would have liked to thank the captain who had shown him how it was done but his head had disappeared when he'd been on his third breath. They'd heard the shell a fraction later. And of course there was the gas, but even the breathing couldn't help with that.

I was the only one who could have helped with that but I did not. I went ahead and gave the order. He flinched then and bunched a fist, bringing it down sharply on the desk, against the edge because he wanted it to hurt, wanted it to stop. He put his head on the desk, rolling it backwards and forwards waiting for the trembling, which would have built up in his body by now, to explode into his hands and when it came he thrust them between his thighs to contain them. It was quite a little routine now he thought. I'm really becoming quite good at dealing with myself and my rather peculiar habits.

His breathing was becoming normal and his hands were still enough now to light the lamp on his desk. The wick burned blue then yellow and the smell of oil pervaded the room. Gas did not reach above the ground floor so at least he was spared that reminder.

Calmer now, he was able to think of the children and determined again that those four years which took everything else were not going to rob him of the people his children should have been. They were not going to be guttersnipes, they were going to climb out of this shop, back to the top with him and that would include Betsy's bibelot, but my God, there were going to be some changes. God blast it – bellies!

Archie Manon was not going to have a wife behaving like a damn skivvy with buns all over the floor and hair all over her face and street-talk falling from her sloppy mouth. Next it would be the children if it wasn't already. The work was going to be hard, why else did he marry her, but there was no way she was going to look as though it was. He lowered the wick now that it was burning steadily. Barney would no doubt have been happy with bairns, bellies and buns, but there was no way he would ever accept it. He flung himself back in the chair. Damn the hospital, damn their incompetence. How dare they take my Mary from me and he bit on his hand to save himself from calling aloud.

He finally heard the repeated knocking and, forming a tight smile, he rose and walked towards the door. His movements were deliberate and he paused momentarily before he opened it, preparing himself to face the present. It was Betsy.

'I'm sorry, my dear,' he murmured, his voice level, controlled. 'I remembered I had to sign some papers.'

She nodded, not believing him.

'Tom is tired now, Archie,' she apologised. 'Shall we eat without you?' She no longer wore her apron and her hair was newly brushed and coiled.

'Not at all, I'm on my way now but just one moment.' He turned and doused the lamp, replacing the paper-knife at right angles to the letter-rack before returning. He held out his hand to guide her down. 'But perhaps we could be a little better organised in future.' It was not a question but a command and one he gave without even looking at her.

Betsy had expected something of the sort but still the gall rose in her throat and she burned with anger. He had said nothing of her hours of effort and she turned to say as much but his face was closed to the subject and she lost her thoughts in a mesh of clumsiness. Perhaps, she thought as they entered the kitchen, perhaps she could draw nearer when they spent their first night as lovers.

Lying as far under the hot bath-water as possible Betsy felt tea had been better than she had feared. The children had eaten well though they'd been sent to bed early by Archie, and Betsy smiled, grateful for his eagerness.

The air was cold and she soaked a flannel in the water and laid it across her breasts. They were still firm despite feeding Tom and she stroked them and thought of the pleasure a man's hand would bring. It was hard to imagine Archie beneath his well-behaved clothes she thought. Barney's body had been broad and scarred blue from the pit but his skin had been smooth and smelt of sweat. She remembered the weight of his body and the gentleness until they had both wanted something stronger.

The water was cooling and she felt nervous. The nightdress clung to her imperfectly dried body as she slipped it hastily over her head, holding the feeling of abandonment and joy tightly to present it to her husband. What did it matter that it arose from her dead lover?

The fire hissed and flickered in the bedroom with urgent tongues and the room felt strange to her; she had only cleaned it in the daylight as Joe's maid but now she belonged here and could sink into the mattress and open her mouth beneath his. She longed for it, for the grasp of a man's arms after so long. The clinging together, the end of loneliness and shame. She was to be a wife at long last, half of a pair and she was grateful to be made complete.

Archie lay quite still on his side as she edged into the bed. Betsy trailed her hand towards him beneath the sheet and it grew cold as it passed over the emptiness between them. He felt the rustle and then the hand. It lay in the slight hollow of his buttock and his body became rigid at its touch. His eyes moved rapidly in the dark and gently he took it and placed it alongside Betsy's thigh, then rolled over on to his back, closer to her and she held her breath in anticipation.

'My dear,' Archie said quietly. 'You and I have both had our difficulties during the past few years and I think we both have cause to be grateful to have found a partnership that fills both our needs. I feel however that there is one area in which I need not trouble you. After all, neither of us wants more children do we?'

He patted her hand.

'I think it is more important for us to concentrate on providing the right atmosphere within the family. I should prefer that you do not use the vernacular with the children since it won't sit well when we move back to the good side.'

Betsy lay in the dark, loose with shock, her tongue heavy and enormous with grief in her dry mouth. Yes, she wanted more children. Yes, she wanted to writhe and cling to a male body. And what the hell does the vernacular mean. She understood neither him nor his words but she said nothing and moved not a muscle and finally Archie turned towards her again.

'I mean I would rather a standard of manners and language was maintained. Belly is really a word I would prefer not to hear in my own home.'

The fullness in Betsy's throat hurt and she had to breathe cold air through tightening nostrils until they were too full with the mucus of tears. Then, through barely opened lips, she spoke and did not recognise the sound of her own voice.

'Yes, Archie, I understand.'

'Goodnight Elisabeth.'

She turned on her side away from him and, carefully, she cried silent tears for her 22 years and the countless more that were yet to come and there was a coldness in her now, a despair which soured her youth.

CHAPTER 4

Annie hung on the bar which divided the allotments from the wasteland at the back of the lanes, near to her father's shop. The rust was gritty beneath her hands and smelt of old money. At last her balance was perfect. She released her hands and opened her eyes, lifting her head slowly, savouring her success, smiling though the bar pinched her breath up into her throat and her stomach was pushed into her back. The sky was dusty blue and everything shimmered in the heat.

'All right Annie, we know you can do it, get yourself down here now. Eleven's too old for that sort of thing,' Don ordered.

She flipped over the bar, the air rushing through her body so that her face screwed up with ecstasy. It was pleasure mixed with pain and she did it again.

'Hey Annie,' called Tom. 'If you do that too often the blood will rush to your head and burst all over the ground, and I'm not clearing it up.' She laughed and stayed where she was. 'And you're showing everyone your knickers. There'll be a long queue soon.'

'Don't be daft Tom. Who wants to see these bloomers? But just think, if they did, we could charge a penny a look and save all this work.' She pointed to the lead coins which she had finished in record time so that she could be free for the bar

They laughed at her, Georgie, Tom and Don as she stood brushing red dust from her clothes, then bent again over the piping. Don and Georgie chiselling then banging, while Tom just hammered. He'd have to wait until he was 13 too, Don had told him, before he could use the proper tools. Nine was too young.

Grace had not been able to come today but would be at the fair this evening and in spite of Don's protests they were doing enough coins for her too. Tom had flared at Don that it

40

shouldn't matter if Grace was there or not. They were a gang weren't they and Annie had kissed his thin cheek. They loved Grace, her and Tom did, but she loved Tom more. He was a like a puzzle piece. He fitted her exactly.

Bye, it was grand here in the sun she thought, but hot, very hot. When they had arrived, Don, of course, had grabbed the shaded area created by the corner of hawthorne hedge that ran round the whole of the allotment. The only other area of shade was along by her father's shed where they had found the hammer and chisel but nettles grew three feet high in this spot and Georgie had not let them beat them down to make a cool work area. Might see a Camberwell Beauty he had said and besides, the butterflies need nettles more than we need shade.

Georgie was now sitting by the rows of lettuce which were yellowing and limp from too much sun whilst Tom still sat where she had been, next to the young leeks which had wafted a strong smell as they worked.

Her da would need to water them tonight, when the sun had gone down, but most likely it would be Tom or her again as usual. She looked along the rows. There wasn't much in this year; the patch was mostly overgrown with weeds, though the runners had gone in as always. Her da liked runner beans but without the stringy bits. Shame really that it was so neglected. It was like everything else round here now and she reached down and pulled at some weeds; the ground was too hard and would not release the roots. Georgie looked up and smiled, his mouth turned up at one side as it always did. His brown hair was too long and it fell over his eyes. He flicked it back. His teeth were white against his tanned skin.

'You're always brown,' she called. 'Where do you get your tan from? Been taking the sun by the sea, like the royals?' She thumbed her nose and strutted about doing a regal wave.

Tom giggled and Georgie threw a handful of grass he had torn from the verge. It fluttered to the ground before it reached Annie, lying in a loose circle.

'A cloak for me to walk on – how kind,' minced Annie and the laughter continued. She felt a sense of delight.

'Get on with the work,' Don growled. Tom glanced across at him.

'She's only having a bit of fun,' he protested. 'And she doesn't act like a lady that often.' Annie shook her fist at him.

41

'Well, she's not doing it on my time,' ground out Don, his head still down. He ran his fingers round the rim of the coin, making sure it would pass without comment tonight.

Annie gazed at Tom. He raised his eyebrows, then they both mouthed, 'Bloody Albert!'

'Hope it's not catching Tom,' Annie called.

'This Albertitis, you mean,' he replied. They both turned to Don and stared. 'No, we'd have to work in Albert's shop every Saturday and the old man's not going to have us over the doorstop. We have to help Betsy in ours for nothing. Good thing we like it, ain't it, Annie.'

Don looked up and glowered at them both.

'Get on with your work.'

'I've done my share,' challenged Annie, 'and Tom's doing fine. Just keep your hair on, will you, or you'll be polishing your head in the morning. Anyway, it's just because you're the eldest you throw your weight around.'

'Only by two days,' chipped in Georgie and Don returned to his coins without a word, forgetting everything but the need to finish the job.

Georgie sat back on his hunkers, wiping his forehead with the back of his hand. His coins were perfect and Annie was intrigued that those broad hands could produce such precise work. He had worked quickly without seeming to, always calm, always accurate. She watched as he half closed his eyes against the sun and cocked his head to one side.

'I'll show you how to hang by your arms from that bar, turn inside out and dangle if you like.' His voice was soft.

She moved closer, blocking the sun and casting her shadow over him, her eyes alight with interest.

'When?' she asked.

He half smiled. 'Whenever you like,' he replied, looking directly up into her face, able to do so now that she stood as a shield between him and the sun. She could see that his eyes were almost black with small yellow flecks, like a cat's. Tom moved near to her, his small shadow cast over Georgie's neatly stacked coins. Georgie pulled a long stem of grass from a nearby clump, eased it out of its shaft and chewed the moist white shoot. His smile grew into a grin and she responded but did not know why she felt so pleased.

'Will you show me too?' asked Tom, his small face eager. He

moved up against Annie and she put her arm round his shoulder and pulled him close.

Georgie continued to chew for a moment while he studied Tom and through his eyes Annie saw Tom as he now was; very thin and pale, though without rickets yet, thank God. She hadn't noticed how gaunt he had become, how gaunt they must all have become but it looked worse on Tom because he was younger. She took out the last of her bread and dripping from her pocket and made him eat it. Hunger seemed always to be with them these days.

Georgie smiled. 'I reckon you're just too young Tom, but I tell you what; I'll take you to the hives, shall I? Down by the beck. Show you the bees, you'd like that.'

'You would and all Tom,' agreed Annie shaking him slightly, aware of his disappointment, wanting to make it all right for him. 'Bring your pencil and draw it. There's the beck and that willow and the shape of the hive. Georgie'll tell you all about bees, he's good on insects. I know, we'll make a day of it. I'll do a picnic for you and Don. What do you think? We'll ask Grace, she'll like a picnic.'

'Oh aye, Annie, that'd be . . . '

'Oh God,' Don broke in, 'not old fatty.'

Annie turned to him. Why could he never be easy? She felt anger growing. He knew she couldn't stand to hear him start on Grace. She felt hotter as the anger took her over, made words spill out.

'Why d'you have to be so mean?' she hissed. 'You know she can't help being plump; she's made that way and she's nice with it an' all.'

She strode over the uneven ground in a hurry to reach him, in a hurry to fight him, to make him stop it once and for all. She stood above him, hands clenched, waiting. Georgie reached out and held Tom back as he moved to follow. He was squinting against the sun now that Annie had moved. 'Stay here with me lad, it's between them two, I reckon.' Tom tugged against him but Georgie held firm so he stood and they both watched.

'Look at me Don Manon and stop poring over your bloody money for a minute.' Annie waited but he ignored her, banging with his hammer at the lead. 'Don, look at me.' She moved closer but still he ignored her and a great swamping rage cut out the banging, cut out the sun and she grabbed his hair.

'I'm not bloody Betsy and you're not me da so don't start treating me as though you are.' Her voice was low, her hand clenched his hair tighter.

Don slapped her hand away, still without looking up. She grabbed his hair again and pulled. 'Lift your head and look at me,' she shouted.

This time his slap caught her leg and she almost went down but did not. She still had his hair and at last his head was forced up as she pulled again. His eyes were watering with the pain, his face was red and sweating and full of anger.

He lashed out at her leg again, the crack echoed across the allotment. Tom struggled in Georgie's grasp.

'She's doing fine bonny lad, she's all right for now.' But though his voice was still soft, his eyes were narrowed and alert, and there was a set to his face. His legs were tensed to spring, though he still squatted like the miner he would become.

'I'll kill him if he hurts her,' Tom cried, still tugging away.

'You won't need to Tom, because he won't hurt her. I won't let him. I won't let anyone ever hurt her.' His voice was still quiet but there was something in it that allowed Tom to relax, to stand and wait.

Again Annie withstood the slap and tightened her grip. 'Grace is not fat, she is clever. She is just big for her age – got it. And don't ever let me hear you say that again, and don't let her hear you either. You made her cry last time.' She was speaking slowly, clearly, her face close to his. She could feel his breath on her cheek, see his eyes staring into hers.

'You're a cruel boy sometimes Don Manon and when you are I don't like you.'

She released him and still he said nothing, just glared. As she turned he tripped her. She sprawled on the ground and smiled, she had known he would and she had let him. It made him think he was even but she knew he would not call Grace fat again. She scrambled to her knees and looked at Tom. He would understand that she was all right. He always understood her but would Georgie? Would he think she had been defeated? She looked past Tom to him and he winked.

'For God's sake sit down and stop causing a draught,' he said and suddenly laughter played around the group again. The atmosphere was broken and Tom and Don began to bang again.

44

Annie sat down shaking inside, upset by the sudden fight. She raised her face, eyes closed towards the beating sun and felt the heaviness of her hair as it dropped on her back. She shook it until it brushed against her shoulder. Forget it she told herself and made the last few moments squeeze into a black box she kept at the back of her mind. She was sheltered from the slight breeze by the blackberry bushes and the allotment shed and the heat drew the creosote out to hang heavy about her face, stinging her nose with its sharpness. Her breathing was slower now, the trembling in her hands was less. She made herself look out over her da's patch to help push back the last few moments. The beans were setting bright red flowers and she could hear the murmur of bees. Yes, it would be nice to go to the hives. She lifted heavy lids and could see, or almost see, minute insects which flickered full of lightness and then were gone. The soil was baking drier with each day and she rubbed warm dust into the cracks which ran everywhere at her feet and would probably stretch down to Australia soon. Was it as hot with Aunt Sophie she wondered, but her last letter had said their winter took place during our summer. She sighed but was not unhappy with her life. It had settled into a pattern, though there was no money any more and men out of work all around.

She stretched her arms and felt loose again. The winter seemed long ago and she was right glad to be free of the liberty bodices and rough wool stockings. She squirmed at the thought; it was like living in a cinema seat for half of your life. She rose and sauntered beyond the bushes, flicking at the straying brambles with a split birch twig. They'd soon be picking the berries which were now only green and hard to the touch.

The pain from Don's slaps was receding. Her heartbeat had slowed again. The clicking of a cricket and rustle of unknown life was close and loud. Beyond that were the distant sounds which reminded her of the world beyond the allotment but nothing was real today except them and their work because he, the Lord and Master, their father, had allowed them to stay out late at the fair tonight and had actually given them each tuppence, even Tom, which was a bit like the second coming. He was tight with Tom though she made sure the lad had half of everything of hers.

She reached down and eased a ladybird off a blackberry stem

on to her hand, watching it until it opened its wings and flew to its burning home. She would go straight for the boats tonight, she decided. They thrust you higher the harder you pulled at the rope thronged with ribbon rags. It hauled your arms as though they would come straight from their sockets and lifted you half out of your seat, or at least they did last year but she was bigger now.

Annie hugged herself and grinned. They must have been minding their manners or something to go again this year with things as they were, but Don was right, tuppence wasn't near enough, not if you wanted to win a coconut and skewer out the sweet milk or stay on the painted horses for another go. Mind you, they could make you sick if they went on too long dipping and rising, round and round.

Yes, Don's idea of the lead coins was a good one but she felt again the sense of unease at the gap which had begun with his year spent at Albert's and had become even greater as the years passed and she did not know why. He was her brother but she could not get close any more. It was as though he was slapping her away all the time.

She watched as they worked and gradually the thrill of passing the coins pushed everything else to one side. She was half excited, half terrified and wondered if they would get caught and that was what was so much fun. Bye, just think of the row if that happened. Da would go even paler.

The shadows were lengthening across the allotment now and she called. 'Come on, you lot. That's enough. If we're late for tea we've had it.'

'Dinner you great daft dollop,' Don hissed, looking tired now and she wanted to put her arm round him and hold him to her but she daren't. 'Right, we're coming. Make sure it's all clear. Go and look and wait by the corner, Annie. Now listen, Tom, not a word to your mam about this or you don't come tonight and for God's sake be quiet. Make sure you're the same Georgie.'

Georgie threw a lazy salute and ambled along watching the ants as they scurried in and out of the cracked soil.

At the corner with the street in sight, Annie heard them coming and would have done a mile away, she thought. She stood, arms akimbo, a breeze lifting her hair and dropping it as quickly; it was refreshing. She watched as they came in single file round the edge of the last three vegetable plots, dry earth puffing up with each step, covering their boots so that they had no shine left as they reached her.

'It's no good, you'll have to wrap them in something. You sound like a load of brass monkeys, jingling about like that.' She could barely talk for laughing.

Don glared. 'Will you shut up with your daft remarks. Go on then, find us something.' But there was nothing here or further down by the entrance to the street so they retraced their steps hoping that no one was watching from the houses which faced the plot. They searched for old sacking in the shed but there was only dried disintegrating newspaper that crumbled as they touched it. There wasn't even a dock leaf with its moist expansiveness.

'You'll just have to keep your hands in your pockets and stifle the noise until you can belt up to your rooms. Will your ma be in, Georgie?' Annie asked.

'O aye, but she'll not notice over the noise of the bairns.' The grass stem was still in his mouth. 'Go on Don, you'll be late,' he chivvied. 'We'll meet in the usual place.'

Annie ran on, turning to look at them following her. She held out her hand to Tom and clasped his free one. It was hot and sticky. She was laughing so hard her stomach banged against her ribs.

Betsy turned as they stumbled in the door, the laughter making her long to be out with them and ten years younger.

'Just look at you,' she scolded, turning Annie round. 'Your skirt is filthy and screwed up in your knickers. You've dripping round your mouth. You're worse than Tom and he's no bleeding angel.' She turned to Tom. 'And you can wipe that smile off your face, that's nothing to be proud of.' Tom straightened his face and Annie saw Betsy smile as she turned away.

'Come on now, all of you, clean up and then sit down, your da will be here in a minute. Come on, Don, don't hang about outside, and leave that door open, it's too hot as it is with the fire on. Get your hand under the tap and sort yourself out.'

Don caught at the door as it swung shut and pulled it open again. The water spluttered as Annie twisted the tap. She waited for Tom to wash first then held her hands under the spurting water.

'Go on with your pocketful,' she mouthed under cover of her splashing. She was thirsty and her tongue ached with the thought of a cold clear drink but she knew she would have to wait until she was clean before Betsy would allow it.

Tom was on his way and Don moved with him.

'I'll just nip upstairs for a moment, Betsy.' He was nearly at the door, having side-stepped round the laid table when he stopped dead-still as their father entered.

Tom sat down in his seat, he had been just behind it, gripping both pockets.

'Come along, Don,' their father said. 'Sit down or I shall assume you don't want to finish your meal in time for the fair.'

Annie's eyes widened and she half turned, splashing water down the front of her dress. Don was stranded halfway to the door and had to return to the sink without rattling and giving everything away. She coughed, again and again and Don bolted over to the sink, gave himself a quick splash and moved, stiff-legged, to the table.

'For goodness sake girl, have a drink. Don't stand there looking helpless.'

'Sorry, Da.' She reached for the enamel mug and filled it. Avoiding the black chip she looked over the top to see if Don was safely seated. He was. 'I should have had a drink earlier,' she tossed at Betsy and scuttled to her seat as she caught the look in her step-mother's eye. It would be a clip round the backside if she wasn't careful. She pressed her leg against Tom's as she sat down.

Betsy looked at Annie and then at Tom. His wide-eyed look betrayed him. Just like his da when he's up to mischief, she thought. Ah well, let them have some fun, thinking all the time of the unpaid invoices she would have to deal with this evening and the partnership papers that Albert was coming to sign, though what good it would do to pool their meagre profits she could not understand. If there was no work, there was no money for traders. Even those in the pits knew they could be working today and not tomorrow so were being canny with the pennies, especially with wages going down, not up.

She shivered, looking at the rashers she had put before the family and worried about the future. For the moment they were just about fed and clothed. But for how long? She sighed. It must be time for another of Ma Gillow's readings. Maybe the tea leaves would be clearer this time. She lowered herself heavily on to the chair and played with her meal; the fat had congealed and a thick whiteness coated the bottom of her plate and she had little appetite.

'Your knife is not a pen, my dear,' remarked Archie.

Automatically Betsy shifted her grip, no longer stung to a retort. At least the bugger had been right about one thing she thought; she wouldn't know what to do if she had a string of bairns hanging off her skirts as her mother would have said. At least she did not have to suffer a husband's beer-breathed Saturday night demands and Archie's pale hands on her body. Betsy wiped her forehead with her arm. The thought of her belly full with Archie's child made her feel sick.

She stretched back in the chair. Her hands were swollen and aching again from the beer kegs and they would be worse tomorrow and the next day and for as long as she had to drag and hammer and cork hop-reeking barrels.

Again Archie broke into all their thoughts.

'I'll just get along to the study and make out Bert's invoice. He's coming along later to settle.' He rose. 'Now, be in by ten all of you and no mischief.' He looked particularly at Annie before leaving and laughed at Don who said:

'As if we would.'

They all watched as he reached the door. He seemed to hesitate, then passed through. Betsy pursed her mouth in frustration; wouldn't we all like a study to hide in, she thought, but at least this time he'd given her lad the same as the others. Annie and Don nodded to Tom to follow as they slipped from the table and made for the door.

'Before you go, please make sure you wrap those lead bits in cloth,' Betsy had spoken softly, smiling as she caught the clink when they stopped abruptly.

Annie swung round, her mouth open.

'And don't think you were the first to work out that fiddle.' Betsy laughed. 'Just make sure you're not the first to be caught.'

Don and Tom dodged out of the door. Annie remained, looking closely at Betsy who stood with her back to the light but there was enough from the fire for her to really see her and she was shocked. Her step-mother was not really old, she realised. In fact she was young where the lines hadn't dug in and spewed out wrinkles. She must once have been a child and laughed in the sun, and pity twisted inside her and drew her across the room, back to the bowed shoulders and cruelly worked hands.

Betsy was now looking at her with gentleness in her eyes. Annie touched her hands which were like the sausages in Fred Sharpe's window, blotchy and glistening. How could Betsy bear to leave behind the things that she and Tom knew. The smell of blackberries as they burst, ripe segments between thumb and forefinger, the pink mice from the corner shop. Leave them behind for this. She thought of the cooking, the washing with arms deep in water again and again as she dollied and scrubbed the same clothes week after week. The house was a prison to be escaped at all cost and so was the shop with its smell of beer and a man who never looked at you as you cleared up behind him.

'How can you bear not to be free?' she asked looking up into her face.

She allowed Betsy to place her hands on her shoulders and pull her into an apron which smelt of bacon.

'Nobody is free,' she replied. 'We all have our place and you have to make the best of it.'

Betsy was comfortable to lean into, Annie realised with surprise.

'Come on, Annie,' called Don through the door, his tone strident with impatience. 'We'll be late.'

Annie stayed. She felt that if she went now she wouldn't quite keep this moment, wouldn't be able to find her way back to it.

'I said, come on.' Don called again.

Annie pushed back from Betsy's arms then, thrusting away the feeling that this was important, then was gone, but not before she said. 'I'll be different, I'll be as free as the wind.'

Betsy stood empty, now that she had gone, but still aware of the warmth where she had been. I love her, she nodded to herself, but there never seems enough time to show her.

Archie sat in his study, arms loose and hands dangling. It was cool in spite of the heat of the day and little of the soft evening light penetrated, though the street sounds were a constant murmur and he welcomed them. There was noise but nothing discernible, nothing he had to note or which demanded his attention. That was why he liked the prints on the far wall. Framed in mahogany they were so discoloured that the views were merged into the paper; totally indecipherable. His pipes were set in their stand, each in order. The paper-knife at right angles to the letter-rack. His chair was placed in the middle of his desk and the whisky was in the decanter; all could be reached without conscious thought.

The decanter stood out now like a jewel and he treasured it as such with a sensuality which was usually reserved for a smooth-skinned woman, but that was because Mary had given it to him. It was all that he had left of her now.

He set his lips as he turned to the invoices and went yet again over the last four years' trading. It seemed impossible to make any headway, there simply wasn't the money any more with the depression biting harder.

If only the war hadn't happened. It had destroyed overseas markets for the old industries because other nations had been forced to produce their own coal and steel, and now, where could the North sell their wares?

He went over all the alternatives for his own survival again, knowing that this was what he was fighting for, not any longer his dream of middle-class status. Perhaps with a family partnership one store could keep the other afloat.

To merge with Albert went against the grain somehow, though. He took a pipe from the rack and filled it, tamping down the tobacco. He did not feel easy with the man though, for God's sake, he was his brother. Was it unnatural he thought to dislike Albert, to feel nothing but irritation at his surliness; at the way he pressed close in order to use his larger size to intimidate?

Above all, was it normal to resent entering into a partnership of equals when he had always felt superior? His father had encouraged that of course, grooming him to run the business whilst sending Albert into one of his shops.

He should have objected then, told his father it was unfair on Albert, but he had not. He enjoyed too much the position of power and Albert had never objected, never complained. Even when they were at grammer school together and Archie had always beaten him in the exams, he had never appeared to register the fact. They had just grown up ignoring one another.

Albert was like Betsy, Archie thought, not aware of anything very much.

The irony was, of course, Archie sighed to himself, his father had groomed Albert to succeed in the world they now found themselves in whilst he was sinking rapidly. The golden boy was going under and, what's more, he doubted if he really cared.

He struck a match and sucked until the vapour entered his mouth and the tobacco was alight. He kept his hand half covering the bowl and turned to the window. He knew he needed more customers but where were they to come from. There were so many men on street corners making their woodbines last all day and not having a beer at all as they wondered when the air would be filled again with the noise of the pits, but there was no more work here than in the docks. At least the bloody war had kept the men off the streets, he had heard a vicar say to his companions as they waited to cross the road in Newcastle the other day. Makes it untidy for you does it, he had wanted to say. Should have finished a few more off, should I, while I was out there. As his hands began to tremble he clenched them between his thighs. His pipe was still gripped between his teeth but he had forgotten, he was falling back into the darkness again.

The trouble was that he had known nothing about gas, he pleaded silently, he had just been sent along to fill a gap. But had he known about wind? He nodded to himself. There was no excuse, he had known about the wind. God damn it, everyone knew about wind. The bloody generals knew about wind. How there had to be wind.

The shuddering in his hands was violent now and this was transmitted down the length of his legs. His pipe was cold. He had told them though, he had told H.Q. There was no wind. He had shouted it over the sound of the bombardment which preceded the attack. He was sure he remembered shouting but it had made no difference and he had obeyed the order. His eyes were open now, his head jerked back, he drew in deep breaths, he could hear again the murmur of the streets in place of the scream of shells, of men. He knew a lot about gas now.

His hands were finally still, he was too tired now to even relight his pipe, which he placed on the desk in an exact line with the paper-knife. He heard faintly the sound of the fair organ as the breeze blew up from the wasteland and he envied his children who lived every moment joyously. What did they know of 1924 and the way things were coming apart at the seams?

The shadows deepened in the room and he leant over and lit the lamp, hearing heavy footsteps on the stairs and knowing that it was Albert and he was not alone, for there were lighter, quicker ones in his wake. That would be Bob Wheeler who was coming as witness. He was a good man and worked at the colliery in the office but spent most of his time on union affairs. Archie had only met him once, briefly, but had liked the man. There was an intelligent look about him.

Albert didn't knock, just came straight in as Archie rose. He covered his irritation by reaching for his pipe and striking a match. He waved to a chair while he relit his pipe.

'Not late, am I,' said Albert. It wasn't a question. He was late and relished the fact, it was clear from his voice which had more than a hint of belligerence, Archie thought.

He turned to the man who waited in the doorway while Albert slumped into a chair. He was small and wiry in a well fitting but old dark blue suit. He held his hat in one hand and smiled as he waited to be invited in.

'Come in,' said Archie, bringing another chair up to the desk. Albert grinned.

'You know Mr Wheeler, don't you, Archie? I brought him along like I said. Equal partners at last, eh, Archie!'

Archie felt his face tighten. He nodded and turned to Mr Wheeler.

'Good of you to come. Sit down, won't you.'

Wheeler's handshake was firm but there was a slight tremble as he took the whisky that Archie offered. War, Archie wondered?

He poured one for Albert.

'Bit more in that, Archie, this is a celebration.' Albert leaned forward and grinned again. His long face looked heightened with pleasure. His large body still seemed as though it had been tipped into dirty clothes but there was an air of expectancy about him, almost a lascivious pleasure.

Archie forced himself not to visibly recoil as he poured more Scotch into his glass and listened to Albert.

'Wonder what the old man would think of this then. You and

me equals. He'd turn in his grave and I don't see you laughing all over your face either Archie, me lad.'

Archie was surprised. So, he thought, I've underestimated you, all these years have I, and now the question is, how deep is the grudge, for he felt sure that there would be one. He felt curiously detached; not worried, not frightened since there was little anyone could do to hurt him any more. He just felt surprised. He watched as Albert settled himself back in his chair, his shirt open at the neck, his chest hairs crawling up his neck. He really did despise the man. He turned to hide his eyes.

'Let me take your hat,' he suggested to Mr Wheeler but he refused.

'Call me Bob,' he said to Archie.

'Right we will then, Bob,' Albert said, annoyed by this instant familiarity, knowing that Wheeler had for two years preferred to stay on formal terms with him. 'Let's have another drink then, Archie.'

There was sweat on his upper lip; this was not his first drink of the day, thought Archie, but then it isn't mine either. He poured another for Albert but Bob had drunk hardly any yet. Archie noticed the tremble of his hand as he took another sip. It must be the war, he thought again.

But it was not the war, though Wheeler had been through that too. It was merely a family trait passed down from father to son along with all the other failings Bob Wheeler's mother had listed on many occasions, always with a smile. Wheeler's father would snort in reply and his son grin. His mother knew really that the hours spent discussing the latest leader in the newspaper were not wasted. After all, it had helped Bob to form an articulate argument.

Together they read under the dim light of the oil lamp in the cold front room of the small house, well away from the airing washing and the endless mashed tea. His mother might have swiped at his head with a towel when he was too lost in thought to shift himself to help her but it was as much her wish as his da's that their son, Bob Wheeler, should get some learning under his belt and go into the offices of the colliery not the darkness of below ground which had stifled his father's urge to improve their lot, and the lot of their fellow workers. He had been too physically broken within a few short years but from those offices they knew that their son would keep a clear head and a vision beyond the blank coal-face. Bob Wheeler frequently thought, though, that vision was one thing and progress quite another, for how could you get blood out of a stone? It was satisfying trying nonetheless.

And that was it, he was completely satisfied with his work to the extent that he never missed not having a wife or family of his own, even now with his parents dead. His mother had died of flu the doctor said, but Bob felt it was a broken heart after his father had died of black spit. What he did miss, though, were his conversations with his father and he wondered whether this man, Archie Manon, might prove to be something of a substitute. He looked as though he saw beyond the confines of the Wassingham streets.

'Business any better with Ramsay in power?' Bob Wheeler asked.

Archie stirred, about to speak but it was Albert who replied. 'Business would have been better if the mines had stayed under the eyes of the government,' he grunted, settling himself back in his chair. 'Bloody stupid handing them back to the owners with exports down. The wages come down and that makes my business difficult.' He pointed to Archie. 'We were saying as we came along that the owners did all right out of the war, not like the rest of us.'

Bob Wheeler caught Archie's eye and they exchanged nods.

'Where are these papers then?' Bob asked, and took them from Archie as he passed them over. 'Shall I stick my name under both of yours as witness? Is that the idea?'

'If you don't mind,' Archie pointed to the area with his finger. 'The owners have iron and steel interests as well, I think you'll find, Albert. They sell cheap to the plants and get even better profits from their iron companies as well as exploiting the miners. What do you think Bob?'

Bob twisted his pen round and round, his long face thoughtful. His hair which was greying at the temples had receded slightly giving him a broad forehead and an elderly air but Archie guessed that they were much the same age, about 40. His brown eyes matched exactly the colour of his hair but his moustache was more red than brown.

'I think you're right Archie.'

'How come the South is getting all the new industries? After all the unions supported Ramsay's campaign and most of the strong union men are up here. Why can't the chemicals and radios come North for a change?' Albert slapped the table. Scotch had spilt down his chin.

Archie had to admit to himself that Albert had a good point. Chemicals had come on greatly during and since the war and there was talk of the small companies merging to form Imperial Chemical Industries to make them more efficient but that would not take place up here, there was no doubt about that. If only they had brought the car industry up North. The steel works were up here after all and so were the men. It was crazy.

'I know why,' Albert cackled and answered his own question. 'They're afraid our lad's will get to like the feel of clean hands and light work, then they'd have no bloody coal or steel at all.'

His face was very red, his eyes now bloodshot and ugly. He breathed Scotch across the table at Archie. 'Ain't that right Archie? But then you never liked dirty hands did you? Had to keep 'em clean up in that hoity-toity office at the top of the heap. Didn't matter that I got mine dirty in that poky little shop, did it?'

He was beginning to slur his words and Archie felt his face flush with embarrassment at the scene that was developing. Embarrassment and guilt because it hadn't mattered to him that Albert got his hand's dirty, but for God's sake, he was not his brother's keeper.

Albert had not finished. It was as though a dam had burst and he could not haul the words out fast enough.

'Mr Wheeler's big too, you know, in the union. Works in the office of Bigham colliery but is rising faster in the union. Clever to juggle the two like that. But I was forgetting, you're not big any more, are you, Archie, you're just like me now. You and your bairns are just like me. Especially Don.'

At last Archie began to feel a stirring of unease. The children, he had forgotten the children when he had decided he could no longer be hurt. He tried to gather his thoughts but Wheeler coughed and looked at Archie.

'I quite enjoy the work you know, but it's the union side that matters. The men need more than they're getting on the dole.'

As he spoke, Archie let go of his children. He would return to them later, but now he would listen to this man who he felt held something he needed: a possibility of companionship.

'They need something more than soup kitchens, there's nothing for them to do, nothing to remind them that they are human beings.'

He accepted another tot of whisky from Archie.

'They need something else.' He tailed off in thought.

Archie was glad that Bob Wheeler had scooped the conversation out of the scene that had promised to develop and now Albert seemed to have lost his thread and was slumped quietly in the chair.

'I was thinking before you came of that problem,' he sucked at his pipe, prodded the tobacco with a match. 'I used to arrange football behind the lines – I wonder if . . . ' he looked out of the window. 'Yes, I wonder.'

Silence fell momentarily, Albert slurped the last of his drink, then slapped the glass back on the desk.

'Partners now, Archie.' His voice was slower and he was lisping. He thrust the papers over the desk to Archie.

Archie did not look at them, just longed for Albert to go now, but if he did, so would Bob and he didn't want an end to the discussion which seemed about to begin. The air in the room was heady with tobacco smoke which mixed with fumes from the oil lamp, whose wick had not been burning clean.

'You want to trim that you know,' Albert said. 'Get that lad of yours to do something to earn his keep.'

'Were those the children we passed as we came down the street?' Bob asked, as Archie eased open the lower sash-window. Immediately there was a breeze and the sound of the fair increased.

'That's right,' nodded Albert. 'Off to the fair, were they Archie?' He gave him no chance to reply but turned to Bob with a truculent face. 'What's the government doing then, you never said. Bloody Labour in and nothing's changed.'

Bob Wheeler appeared to be marshalling his thoughts for he said nothing for a moment, but his face became set in bitter lines.

'I'll admit Ramsay's been a disappointment. He's more set on joining the establishment than doing much for the likes of us but I suppose, in all fairness, he's sensible to take it steadily. Labour's a new party and after the revolution in Russia people are afraid of the same thing happening here. Perhaps he doesn't want the country to think that's what the Labour party is, a bunch of revolutionaries in disguise. Remember too, Albert, that his is a minority government so he needs to persuade the Liberals to support him if he wants to change things, and that's easier said than done. Remember they're a bosses' party.'

'It's hard to explain to the miners though, isn't it, Bob,' Archie said gently, 'especially when they threw their weight behind Labour in these elections?'

Bob nodded. 'You're right there. It's not too bad because some coal's still selling abroad at the moment so let's hope that goes on. It'll keep the job situation stable though it's pretty poor I grant you.

Archie nodded. Albert seemed to be asleep, thank God, his head was slumped on to his chest. 'Once the German and French fields are back in full production though, we're in trouble.'

'Exactly.'

'And if we go back on to the gold standard?'

Bob looked up in surprise. His face took on a look of respect. 'Then, my friend, the North is in deep trouble. If the external value of the pound is raised, exports will fall even further. Production will decrease, our men will be out of work in droves. We need customers for our coal. If there aren't any customers, why should the owners pay miners for coal they can't sell?'

'What about the modern pits?'

'They're not up here though. Nottingham should survive. They've the latest machinery and high production from good seams. Good seams and good conditions mean good working relations. They'll be all right down there but up here it'll be a different story.'

And so the talk swayed between them through another glass of Scotch until Albert woke.

'Wages still going down, aren't they,' he spluttered 'and talk of another strike an' all. Christ, if that happens . . .'

'Then,' said Archie slowly, 'perhaps we've done the right thing to come together at last Albert.' He felt the need to reconcile himself with this man.

'Clutching at bloody straws, I reckon,' grunted Albert, and Archie wondered if he meant the partnership or his own deeper meaning.

'It's new owners we need,' urged Bob, 'one's that'll put money in and stop shoestring mining that kills and maims.' He was still with his miners, Archie realised, a long way from the partnership he had just witnessed. 'Owners that will give a decent wage and invest to improve efficiency and safety. State control and ownership must come.'

He stopped himself and raised his hands. 'Sorry, my hobby-horse. I forget where I am somethimes.' He smiled at Archie. 'Well, I wish you luck with the shops. Who knows you could be founding a business which the children will take over and expand. End up employing some of the poor devils round here.'

He pushed himself out of his chair. 'I must get off to a meeting now. Are you coming, Albert?' He looked to see if he was ready to leave.

'Aye, we'll get off now.' Albert rose without looking at Archie. He lurched towards the door and was through it and on his way down the stairs without a backward glance.

Archie watched and bit his lip. Bob walked on ahead of him, stopping in the doorway. He smiled at Archie.

'I enjoyed our talk,' he said.

'And so did I,' agreed Archie. As the door closed, he said again, 'And so did I.' He smiled and cradled his amber glass. He felt as though he had touched something interesting for the first time in a long while tonight and because of that he pushed the unease that Albert had evoked into the background.

So much of the time he felt shut away, he mused, shut away to one side of the life that went on around him. But sometimes life almost touched him as it had done just now and during the meal when he had decided he would go to the fair with his family. But the children had seemed so preoccupied, he had felt an intruder. Lethargy had claimed him and it had all seemed pointless again. He felt invigorated now though, his horizons had widened. Just so long as the gold standard stayed a fiction, maybe they could still pull through. And how he had enjoyed meeting Bob Wheeler.

There was a further knock at the door. He finished his drink, savouring the heat of its passage. He wondered what on earth Bert would be offering as a pay-off for his debt this time. Surely not the pony again? From now on, he was determined that credit was not going to be extended beyond a repayable sum for anyone. After all, exports had improved slightly, as Bob had said, but maybe not for long.

Annie was gloriously weary, her skin was singing with pleasure and a good tiredness, the lights were busy behind the crowds of people who were still milling as Don and Georgie took Grace to the toffee-apple stall. She had met them at the entrance to the fair and Don had not spoken out of turn once. Annie and Tom had wedged themselves up against the edge of the firing-range, waiting. Annie flexed her spine on the sharp edge of the upright.

'Give us a scratch, Tom,' she said and squatted down as he was doing. 'Have you had a good time, bonny lad?'

'It's been the best day of my life, Annie,' he told her, his eyes solemn. 'And I didn't have no trouble with me coins, did you?'

She laughed. 'Not even a sideways look.'

They stayed on their hunkers, Annie drawing her skirt up so that it was squashed between her thighs and calves; better that it was creased than became too dirty sweeping the ground, she reasoned. They clasped their arms round their knees and waited for the others. The sounds were raucous and indistinct but if she relaxed she found that bits floated to her as people passed; private soppy love-words that sounded right on a night like this. The cracks from the rifle stall melted in with the general muddle and all she could see were legs; heavy-booted men's and stocking-covered or barelegged women. She had not noticed how much people moved their feet when they were supposed to be standing still. She nudged Tom and pointed to one pair which seemed to be wriggling like a pair of stung ducks.

'Reckon he needs a tiddle,' she whispered but Tom couldn't see past two sets of heavy ankles.

'As long as no dog comes along who needs one too,' groaned Tom and she laughed.

Annie peered at the barrier of mottled hefty hair-covered legs, grimacing at the bulging and knotted blue veins, then up at the face. Bye, if it wasn't Mrs Maby from Sophie's road, aye and with her eldest, Francy, and if she isn't a fast one I'd like to know who is, Sophie had always said. She was about to pull at the uneven hem but preferred to lean back and let her ears pick up their talk. There was little flow as yet but their heads bent forward.

'Hasn't he grown, that young Don,' Mrs Maby was

mouthing loudly to her companion. 'Eeh, he was nought but a bitty bairn when she did you know what.'

'I don't know what, Mam. Come on, tell us?'

'Well, you know, the mother. Mary Manon it was, did herself in she did. The baby died you know, soon as it drew breath. Well, some do, some don't and her in that posh nursing home an' all. They should have known better than to leave things like that unlocked.' She shrugged her head into her neck and clicked her tongue. 'They say she went off her head and took poison from the medicine cupboard. Burnt her guts out, they say, with acid. I mean, it's not right, is it, with those two bairns at home. That little Annie Manon was only a wee one. Sight too fanciful she was, that Mary. Should have thought of others. They say he's a ruined man now, taken to drink he has, but then he's lost his wife and all his money. I mean, look at that Don, looks like a ragamuffin, and them so posh once.' She sniffed. 'I hear he gives that Betsy a dog's life. Taken to drink she has an' all. Not right, is it? Still the mighty shall fall they say and bye, he's come a cropper.'

The legs shuffled away, mingling in with the stream of passing revellers, but Annie did not watch them go. She just sat with her eyes fixed on where they had been, sensing her mind floating high above her body and away, taking all her feelings with it and leaving her stuck in the ground amongst a world which seemed to have slowed and become silent. Tom had gripped her arm, his hand was stroking her face. She reached for it and held it tighter and tighter.

She looked up and saw Don there and knew he had heard it too because his face looked still and thoughtful. She tried to stand but couldn't and Tom pulled her up. She was stiff and her feet tingled and hurt with her weight. The toffee-apples dangled heavy in Don's hand and he did not notice as Grace took them from him.

'We'll go home now, shall we Annie,' Tom said and Georgie nodded at him and pushed Don before him. The lights had lost their colour and people their faces as they walked free of the place. The noise pursued them and she wanted to swat it away so that she could think but when they had moved out of its sphere no thoughts would stay in her head long enough for her to grasp and shape.

Their footsteps sounded hollow as they approached the back

and they did not notice Georgie and Grace leave. The only light in the street was from their kitchen; all else were back in the spinning light and frantic music. Annie felt a spurt of rage which tensed even her eyebrows; the bloody bugger couldn't even unbend enough to come out on a night like this, be a real father. Too afraid of getting his spats dirty. Well, she hated him, hated them all, hated her for dying, hated the legs with blue veins. Oh God, oh God, I want me mam, she wanted to shout, I want me own mam. She cried then, tears that raced hot and sharp and shook her body so that Tom was frightened. He kissed her hand, again and again.

'There now, there now,' he soothed. 'It's all right, I'm here, I'm here.'

And she knew she would always love him for those words but the pain peaked again and she tore from him, from Don who tried to stop her and ran, ran through the years, into the house past him and her and up to her room, way up across the rag rug into the high bed with its patchwork quilt. Her hands held her head and she rocked and moaned through the jagged slashing hurt and still there was no colour.

Archie had looked up with a start when the door banged open, as the latch snapped up and Annie hurtled through, her face contorted and her limbs swinging wildly. He started after her but turned, grabbing Tom's arm as he ran in behind her and made to follow. His face was white and drawn.

'For God's sake, boy, what's happened?' he demanded. Betsy had risen and rushed to turn Tom's face to her. His eyes were confused and he looked from one to the other, unable to speak. He shook his head.

'Donald, what's happened?' asked Archie urgently as Don came in, putting out a hand to stop Betsy following Annie until they knew more but she looked past him to Don who stood in the doorway. His face was pale too. Betsy shook free of Archie and gathering up her skirts ran after the child, her heart thumping with fear; Annie had never cried in all the time she had known her.

Her legs were heavy as she reached the top landing and she put out her hand to steady herself and draw breath. It was dark here and the wooden boards creaked beneath her feet as she placed one foot before the other, the dark unnerving her. She felt along the wall until she reached the oil lamp on the sill and, striking a match, lit it. She could hear the frantic sobs and putting her hand to the doorknob called to Annie.

'Can I come in, pet?' She waited but, receiving no answer, went in regardless. The landing light shed a dull glow into the room but it was not enough to pick out the girl. Perhaps it was as well, Betsy thought. Problems were sometimes better spoken out loud to a faceless shape. She sat on the edge of the bed, the quilt soft beneath her; she could feel its seams with the fingers which supported her as she leant over to Annie. Her own mother had made it before she died of the flu in '19 and she could picture the colours in her mind. Annie had it because she liked it so much and that had pleased Betsy.

'Now, my bonny lass, my little Annie, what's the matter?' She lifted the crumpled body on to her lap and sat crooning and stroking the damp hair away from the hot wet face. The sobs gradually stilled but Annie said nothing; her eyes felt heavy and it was as though she was almost asleep and then the wracking sobs began again. They seemed to have a life of their own and she was a small voice inside this strange frantic body, apart from it but linked to the noise and leaping shudders. She wanted to escape from it, to leave all the distress here, in a little heap, while she walked free, back to the allotment and this morning, back to the time before the lady with the ugliness of the blue-veined legs and loud words. Back she would go and then come this way again, remembering nothing of what had happened.

Archie came to the door and looked helplessly at Betsy as he came across and sat on the bed.

He sighed and shook his head. 'Annie, I'm sorry that you heard about your mother's death in the way that you did. I should have told you long, long ago but I couldn't bring myself to. There seemed no need, you never asked. But I should still have told you.'

His eyes met Betsy's across the head of his daughter and hers were narrowed in deep distress. She held Annie closer, wanting to berate him for his selfishness. He should have heeded her and Sophie earlier instead of putting the world to right in that study of his. And he was filled with guilt for neglecting such a task.

He reached across and took his daughter's hand, a gesture which seldom occurred. He had forgotten how soft and small the hand of a child was. He rubbed it between his thumb and forefinger, angry at himself.

'Your mother went away to have her baby, Annie, but it was poorly as many babies are and it died. It was another daughter. Your mother became ill. It was septicaemia which affects not just the body but makes the mind rage when it's in the throes of fever. One night, when the nurse was elsewhere, she found a cupboard and taking a bottle, drank it and died that night.' His voice struggled to keep steady as he relived what had happened – was it only eight years ago – it seemed an eternity, one long day following another.

'It could have been that she was thirsty and just wanted a drink. What is certain though, is that it was a mistake which was purely the staff's fault. I've hated nurses ever since.' He ended in a low voice.

He leant forward to stroke his daughter's face. She seemed so small, so defenceless that he lifted her from Betsy and held her close to his body. She smelt of today's sun. Don came to the door and Archie lifted his head and beckoned him, drawing his sturdy body to his side. There were tears on Don's face.

'I can remember her with her pretty face and her laugh; she was always laughing and singing. Then it ended, she went away and never came back.'

Tom had crept into the room and now stood by his mother, his eyes never leaving Annie.

'I know lad. I came home when it happened but once I was back I found the longer I stayed away, the more difficult it was to return.'

Annie stirred. 'But Fatlegs said she burned, Da, and if she didn't burn then, she will be burning now, won't she?'

Archie stiffened. 'What are you saying Annie?'

'Well, if she killed herself, she'll go to hell, won't she and if we want to see her again we'll have to do it too. All that light that was in her face will be clouded behind the fires of hell. I want her but I don't want hell.'

Annie was surprised at breakfast. The table was laid and Betsy and Tom were sitting quietly. The tea vapour was drifting lazily from the spout in the middle of the table and there was the humid richness of its flavour throughout the kitchen mingling with that of freshly baked bread. The loaf was on the table, crumbs scattered beyond the breadboard and the knife glinted as it lay half-on and half-off the smooth but scarred wooden platter.

'Sit down, pet,' Betsy said, a smile on her face. 'Your Da has slipped out for a moment, with Don. They'll be back in a minute. How are you this morning?'

Annie sat down. 'All right, Betsy.'

She didn't want to talk about last night. She had pushed it into the black box she kept in her head for thoughts that should not be seen again. She would just turn her head away if they crept out, or push the lid hard down. The sky looked blue across the yard; it was going to be another good day and the school holidays had just begun.

She winked at Tom. 'What shall we do then, Tom? How about finding some jars and catching the minnows down Bell's beck, or slinging a rope to the lamp-post and having a swing?' Her throat felt sore when she talked and she didn't feel quite the same as usual but it would get better. She would make it get better.

Tom's face lit up. 'Eeh, that'd be a grand idea, Annie, but you've got a . . .'

'That'll do now, Tom,' broke in Betsy sharply.

Annie looked from one to the other as she sank her teeth into the spongy whiteness of the bread. She had peeled off the crust, eaten that first and kept the best bit until last. Good thing her da wasn't here to see it or else there'd be a do. She sat back in her chair, feeling tired. There was no sound, not even the hissing of the range since Betsy had allowed the fire to die down. She used the gas cooker a lot now, did Betsy, but not for bread and that pleased her.

Don lifted the latch and called to her. She looked at Betsy who was grinning and Tom who was wriggling.

What's the matter with the daft great things she thought; the silly beggars are up to something. Warily she followed Don out into the shady cobbled yard where despite the cast shadows it was still much brighter than inside. She stood bemused just outside the door and her father led the pony to her.

'This is for you Annie, just for you. It can go in the stable when we've cleared the rubbish out. Bit smaller than a dray, I know, but come on,' he beckoned her, 'come and take him.'

Annie stretched out her hand and she felt the hot air from the

65

pony's black, dry nostrils gust in short spurts into her palm and the softness of his lips as he nibbled sideways then backwards and forwards across her stretched fingers.

She looked at Don. 'But what about you?' she asked.

He held out the leather football and grinned.

She turned to Da, then to Betsy with a question clear in her eyes.

'Your da took it as payment for a debt,' she offered. 'He wanted you to have something special. It's a Shetland, that's why he's so small and he never was a pit pony so he's still got good eyes.'

'He's lovely,' Annie said burying her head in the hollow between his neck and shoulders, drinking in his musk.

Betsy and Archie nodded as they turned. The shop should be open by now. The pony's mane was long and coarse and Annie pulled Tom over and lifted him onto the felt saddle.

'I expect I'll look a right nellie with me legs dangling to the ground,' she muttered. 'But I'm right pleased with you, lass. Black Beauty, that's what I'll call you.'

Don stopped bouncing his ball. 'Don't be so daft, she's a he and it's black and white.'

'I'll do what I like,' she retorted. 'And what's more, I'll sell his doing's at the allotment for a penny a bucket. You and me'll go into business together, Tom, how'd you like that. Will you come in too, Don?' She looked at him.

'Not bloody likely, kid's stuff, that is.'

But Tom grinned, 'I'd like it right enough, Annie.' He was glad she was with them again, but he could still see the hurt at the back of her eyes and it made him want to hug her.

Don looked across at them and laughed, loving the seamed leather in his hands. He tossed it into the air, letting it bounce on the cobbles before he kicked it against the stable wall. Thank God the hysterics were over, he thought. She was like his ball, tough and always bouncing back.

Annie thought, maybe it won't matter one day, any of it and the hurt will go and let me forget.

'You and me will share her, Tom,' she whispered, leading the pony forward. It wasn't right that Tom should have nothing – again. After all, he had lost one of his parents too, but no one ever thought of that.

CHAPTER 5

The broom handle felt sweaty as Annie swept the corner of the kitchen, six weeks later.

'You'll knock up more dirt than you sweep away at that rate,' complained Betsy. 'Do it proper, girl, for God's sake.'

She pushed Annie to one side and took the broom.

'Here, like this, see.' She used long slow strokes. 'Don't slap it about.'

The trouble is, thought Annie, you've got great big arms with muscles like Christmas puddings and I can hardly raise a bump. She stood behind Betsy and jacked up her arm, prodding the raised muscle. It was hard but small. The best things come in little parcels, she consoled herself.

Betsy stood back to admire her handiwork. 'There you are, now try and do it like that. I know your da wants to make a lady of you, but I reckon he'll never do it with things as they are. It's best you learn how to clean; there's always a living there.'

Large circles of sweat were spreading underneath her armpits and it was not just her apron but her clothes that were grubby, Annie noticed. She looked down at her old flowered dress, cut down from one that Betsy had been given, and was grateful that at least Betsy made sure she was clean. She touched her arm lightly.

'It looks right good, Betsy,' she said and took the broom from her. It was heavy and she was tired but then she was still having dreams of fat blue-veined legs and flames that leapt higher than their house in a place of awful darkness. She shook herself and brought the broom towards her slowly. She didn't hear the knock at the door but felt the push as Don shoved past to reach the door.

'You two've got cloth ears, I reckon,' he said, and, as she

turned, Annie saw Betsy put the beer that she had been drinking behind her back and glare at him.

The door had been closed to stop the dust from swirling and, as it opened, the dirt lifted and caught in her throat. She coughed but needed water to clear her throat. Betsy poured it for her and passed it across before she could reach the sink. She doesn't want me to see her booze, she thought. They must be daft if the pair of them don't know I can see how much they tipple, and all day at that.

Georgie was at the door. She smiled at him.

'It's a right good day for mating,' Georgie said as he stood in the doorway. 'Let's go up the beck.'

Annie gawped, then spilt her water. It splashed on to her dress and she brushed at it with her hand, Betsy's jaw had dropped.

'What the bloody hell are you talking about?' Don gasped, looking back over his shoulder to see if the others had heard.

Annie smirked at him. We did and all, she thought.

Georgie laughed. 'Get the kids, Don. I promised Tom I'd take him to the hives and it's a real scorcher today. The queen might just take it into her head to be mated.' He called in, over Don's shoulder, to Betsy, 'I've never seen that, Mrs Manon, you know, and it might just happen today. It's bright enough.' He was swinging his da's bait-bag backwards and forwards in his hand.

Betsy nodded, suppressing a smile. 'Well, I can think of worse ways for a load of bairns to spend a summer day.' She looked at Annie and cocked an eyebrow. 'Worth a picnic anyway, lass.'

Annie looked from her to the sun which streamed in through the door. It was warmer out than in on a day like this and yes, to be out, away from the smell of boiling dishcloths and dust that puffed up into your mouth and nostrils, yes, that would be a belter. She looked at Don who was pulling Georgie towards him, speaking quietly in his ear. She knew he was about to get his ball and pile down to the end of the street with Georgie for a game. She held her breath but Georgie shook his head.

'Just call the bairns, Don. I promised Tom and we're meeting Grace at the end by Monkton's.' he turned as Don shrugged and slouched into the passage to call Tom.

'You've got some butties then, have you?' called Betsy after Georgie.

'Aye, Mrs Manon,' he called and settled himself on the edge of Beauty's water-trough to wait. He always looks comfortable thought Annie, even on that.

Annie held Beauty's reins loosely as they strolled along the street behind Georgie and Don. Chairs were set up outside front doors for the women to sit on later, whilst they did their mending and gossiping. The leather of the reins was hot and she wanted the air to get between it and her, to stop it going soggy. Tom rode and held their bread and dripping tied up in an old tea-towel and it didn't look that clean, thought Annie, but who cares. She looked up over her shoulder at Tom who beamed down at her.

'Ain't she grand, Annie. It's only taken her a few weeks to settle down, hasn't it?' He patted the pony's neck.

Grace looked over Beauty's head at Annie. She had been late and had run to catch them up. She was still panting slightly in the heat and her freckled cheeks were tinged with red, her auburn curls were damp.

'It's not as though she was a bundle of fire when she came though, is it, Annie? If she settled down any more I reckon she'd be asleep.'

Annie chuckled and ran her hand down Beauty's face to her nostrils which puffed and snuffled in her palm. 'Later you can have your apple because you're a right little cracker.' She crooned into her ear which twitched in response. 'Don't you take any notice of your nasty Aunty Grace. Just wants a ride, she does and it's too hot for us big 'uns on you little 'uns.' She heard the giggles of the other two. 'We'll just get one of Georgie Porgie's little bees to sting her backside, shall we, darling, then she really won't be able to sit on you.'

'Did you hear that, Georgie?' Tom shouted. 'Annie wants one of your bees to do a nasty on our Grace and there's no way I'll be putting bicarb on that sting!'

They were passing the last of the terraced houses which fronted directly on to the cobbled streets.

'Mind your head on the cage, Tom,' Annie shouted, and he ducked beneath the canary which Old Man Renton had put out to hang above his door. It was singing, though it stayed in the shade of the cover which was half over the cage.

'It must be grand for the birds not to have to go down in the pits any more,' said Tom. 'Do they miss it, do you think?'

'I don't know about that,' said Annie suddenly oppressed by the houses which seemed to press in on her, to trap her in the heat and dust, to make everything seem dark. The coal-dust covered the bricks and the cobbles, bringing gloom with it.

It was a relief to reach the wasteland with its space and grass-hillocked ground. Grace's uncle tethered his goats here, but there was only one today.

'Did the others go into the allotments once too often then and eat the prize marrows?' Tom asked, shifting in the saddle to look around. The clip of Beauty's hooves had changed to a soft thud as they crossed towards the lane which led through the trees to the meadow and then the beck. It was still some way off and shimmered in the heat.

Grace shook her head. 'Not this time, Tom. Me uncle's been laid off an' all. They've sold off the billies for meat. They need the nanny to feed the bairn. Me aunty's gone dry.'

'Anyway,' she added, 'the billies don't half pong.'

Annie grimaced at the memory. 'I know,' she said. 'I used to kick the ball up here with Don before he had his good one. If there was a wind . . .'

'And I always thought that was you, Annie,' chipped in Tom.

They laughed and let Beauty stop to crop at the grass. The noise of tearing grass and clinking bit added to Annie's growing sense of freedom. She turned to look back at the streets they had left, cut off from the world as though someone had sliced through them with a knife.

'You'd have thought someone would have curved 'em round a bit, or dotted a few to make it look nice, not just plonked 'em here.'

'It's to do with the owners of the pits, I reckon,' Grace said. They both looked round as they heard Don and Georgie call them from far ahead, then returned to looking at the town.

'They just stopped building when the miners had enough houses,' Grace continued. 'They didn't care what it looked like, didn't think the likes of us needed anything nice.'

The older boys were racing back towards them and Don panted up to Annie. He stopped and caught his breath.

'That stupid pony's supposed to make it quicker,' he gasped, and began to bounce the ball at Annie's feet. The dry earth flew over her sandals. She kicked it away and as he scrambled after it, Tom said:

'No, she's supposed to make it better, and she does, Don.'

Don scooped the ball up, flicking it underarm to Georgie who fielded it with his hand and then dribbled it away from the others.

Don strolled back until he reached the pony, then glared at Tom. 'I've told you two that it's a boy, a bloody boy.' His thin face was screwed up.

Annie pulled up Beauty's head, clicking with her tongue to move on. 'She's what we want her to be and so she's a girl.' They were moving forward now at a leisurely pace. She tilted her chin and looked at him sideways. 'Anyway, clever clogs, tell us why they just stop the houses like that?' She waved her hand towards them.

Don turned back to look. 'I don't know what the hell you're talking about.'

'They just stop,' Grace said, 'that's what we're talking about.'

Tom was standing up in the stirrups to look, wobbling in time with Beauty's stride. 'They're so ugly. Someone's just dumped them there, in the middle of nowhere.'

Georgie was walking with them now. 'It's on top of a seam of coal and that ain't nowhere to the bosses,' he said softly. 'They'd get the workers here by giving them a roof, then the poor sods couldn't leave if the wages got bad because they'd lose their houses as well.'

'Good idea, that,' grunted Don and sidestepped round Annie to take the ball off Georgie. 'Come on Georgie, race you to the lane.'

Annie watched them go. She would have liked to run too, but Grace would have found it too much.

Tom called softly. 'That's not a good idea, is it, Annie?' His face was troubled.

'Nay, lad, you'd think some of them would go away now wouldn't you? They can call their homes their own these days you know.' She looked over her shoulder again. 'There's something that keeps them all together, I reckon.'

'Us all together, you mean,' Grace corrected her.

But Annie knew that was not what she meant. She looked back again and still she thought of the town and its people as

71

them. She wished she did not. She wanted to feel that she belonged somewhere and then she looked at Tom and felt a surge of warmth; here was an us, she thought.

Even across the unbroken wasteland there was no wind, and there was a hush because the pit wheels were idle, over on the other side. They couldn't even hear the bleating of the sheep as they grazed on the grass-covered slopes of the older slag-heaps. Poppies sagged in the heat at the side of the grass track and Grace said she would pick some on the way back, but Tom said they would die and that he would paint her one instead. Annie saw that the boys had reached the lane now and were about to disappear into its darkness. Tom had seen too and wriggled free of the stirrups.

'I'll get down now, Annie, and give the old lady a break. I want to run a bit and Georgie said he'd show me how to blow on grass and make it whistle.'

He was already throwing his leg over the saddle and was on the ground and away before Beauty could stop. He flung the picnic over his shoulder as he ran.

'Crumbs for lunch,' Annie said, laughing, and slipped round the front of the pony so that she was walking with Grace. She slipped her arm through the other girl's. Grace always smelt nice and she let her look at her arithmetic in class. It saved her getting caned too often by that old witch Miss Henry. Old Dippy Denis had never hurt them and he'd let Grace come up a grade into his class even though she was a year younger than the rest. She'd be 9 now, thought Annie, but she's better than the rest of us. Quick at her work, but not a swot.

'It was a shame about old Dippy,' she said to Grace who nodded.

'I wonder why he did it.'

'Me da said it was the war.' Annie remembered her da's hands when he'd heard about it and how they had started shaking. 'When the lorry hit the playground wall and the bricks came down he must have thought it was a shell. That's what me da said anyway, and the boys who stood and watched must have looked like Germans.' She saw again how Dippy had thrown himself on the ground in the playground, screaming, then crawling towards the bricks, then on to the boys who had stood rooted to the spot. He had grabbed at two but had not had time to kill them.

72

'He's still in the loony-bin, isn't he?' Grace asked, fanning herself with her hand. 'It's so hot.'

Annie thought of Dippy being locked in a dark room with bars away from the sun and the sky and the birds. He had been 26, her father had said. There were so many years to live, she thought, shut away.

She said. 'He looked so kind. When they took him away there were tears all down his face. It was raining but I know they were tears.'

She looked up at the sky. It was so blue with light white clouds. War could only happen when it was grey and wet. People could not fight on a day like this, no one could do anything but feel this feeling. She drew a deep breath. This feeling that she thought perhaps was joy. Sophie had always called her a joy and delight and a day like this sounded like those words.

She looked sideways at Grace to see if she felt it too but Grace looked uncomfortably hot. Some of her curls had stuck to her forehead and cheeks. She walked over on the sides of her feet as though they hurt. It was a shame she would never put on a swimsuit, otherwise they could have had a swim in the beck. Betsy had told Annie to put hers in with Tom's, but she had not. She knew Grace would be upset. She said it was because her skin was so fair that she wouldn't strip off, but Annie knew it was because she felt fat and ugly. But she wasn't, she was lovely. Grace pulled her blouse in and out trying to get cool and, as they entered the lane, Annie snapped off a beech twig from the hedge that ran along between them and the fields of corn. She found one with plenty of leaves and handed it to Grace.

'Fan yourself with that, bonny lass.' She dug into her pocket and fetched out a piece of apple. It was warm and covered in bits, but Beauty wouldn't care. It was cooler here with the branches locked into one another over their heads like fingers creating a church and steeple. The birds were louder than she had ever remembered, caught as they were in this tunnel of leaves. The boys had slowed and were not far ahead now and, as they approached, they heard the screech of Tom's grass whistle.

Georgie had stopped altogether and was peering into the hedge off to the left. Annie saw him beckon to Tom and together they bent down. She saw that Tom's face was still but his eyes were dark with concentration. She pulled Grace with her and they trod softly up behind.

'Get a look at this then, Tom,' Georgie was whispering. 'See the hind legs?'

It was a bee, its head deep into a cornflower and pollen stuck so thickly to its back legs that it seemed impossible that it could ever fly. But it did and soared out and up, past Tom, who flinched and then Georgie who did not move a muscle.

'It might have stung you,' hissed Annie, pulling at Georgie, frightened for them both.

He turned and shook his head. 'Suicide for them. They only sting if there's no alternative. They can't take their sting out again you see. It's a once and only weapon. Protection of the hive is what it's all about, deep inside their heads, I reckon.'

Annie had not heard death mentioned since the fair six weeks ago. How strange to think that it could be discussed so casually by other people.

Georgie strolled forward, on to the meadow with Tom. Annie and Grace brought Beauty, Don had gone before them. 'They fan themselves like you to keep cool you know, Grace,' Georgie said. 'With their wings, in the hive.'

'Clever, aren't they, Georgie?' marvelled Tom.

'Do the others miss them when they sting and you know . . .' Annie faltered.

Georgie dropped back to walk beside her. ' 'Spect so, but it's life really. It's happened, it had to happen.' He paused. Grace had walked on to be with Tom. Beauty was swishing her tail to be rid of the flies. 'A bit like your ma really. Perhaps she felt there was nothing else to do and the rest just have to go on. Just like the bees.' He coloured now, and took her hand in his as they walked, squeezed and was gone. She watched him catch up with Tom who was chasing Grace with a spider.

No one had spoken of her mother since that night and she was glad now that someone had. Her face was relaxing again and she allowed herself to notice the birds above her and the corn which waved in the slight breeze that had now appeared. Bees could die and still the sun came out. She wouldn't think about people yet but she could still feel the heat of Georgie's hand around hers.

The hives lay across the other side of the beck in Mr

Thompson's land. He owned the meadow too, the one in which they sat and which ran up to the beck. He had said Georgie could bring them all today.

'We come all the time anyway,' boasted Don. But Annie thought it was nice not to have to post a look-out for once.

She was sitting on the bank of the beck with her feet flopping in the water. Tom was in his swimsuit, the one that Betsy had knitted before her hands had slowed her up too much. He had brought a jam jar tied round the neck with string; it had made red marks on his hands where he had wound it round so that he could hang on tight as the water tried to tear the jar from him. The beck was not more than a foot deep here in this hot dry end of the summer but already his costume was sagging with the wet and he looked like a sack of potatoes.

'Caught any yet?' she called.

He shook his head but did not look up. His legs were so pale they could do with a good dose of sun and she wished she was in there too but down at the deep pool which lay beyond the willow that hung in the water just by Tom. Instead she pulled her dress up over her knees and lay back on the grass next to Grace. It was rich and warm and green. She turned over, pulling herself further on to the grass with her elbows, then lay on her face, breathing in the freshness.

Grace spoke lazily at her side. 'Me mam says that's what they get the consumptives to do. Pure oxygen, me mam says. The grass eats our breathings out and spews back good pure stuff. Gives you rosy cheeks, me mam says.'

'Someone should bottle it then,' said Annie, too lethargic to speak clearly. 'Give it to the miners with the black spit.'

'Me mam says they can do that, in the hospitals.'

Annie raised herself on her elbows so that she could peer out through the high grass across the meadow. There was a sheen of yellow from the buttercups; black-eyed daisies sat in wide clumps. She could hear the thud of Don and Georgie's boots as they kicked the balls and their shouts as they gave directions. The plop of Tom's jar sounded behind her as he scooped it out and back in again when he had checked on a catch.

'Your mam talks to you a lot,' she remarked to Grace as she turned on her back, flinging her arm over to shield her eyes. She saw red spots dart themselves across the inside of her lids and hoped Grace hadn't heard the note of irritation in her voice.

'She wants me to get on, see,' Grace said, stirring at Annie's side. Annie knew that Grace was too hot but could not imagine ever feeling that way herself. The heat oozed into her and she loved it.

'What will you do then, Gracie, when you're grown?'

'Me mam wants me to go into the library I reckon. It's clean and quiet with a nice sort of people.'

Annie laughed out loud. 'It's quiet right enough, Gracie. Remember being chucked out for giggling when Don got the hiccups.' They both lay back grinning. 'But what do you want, Grace?'

Grace flapped her beech twig, the air stirred over Annie too. 'Seems good enough to me,' she said. 'But what about you, Annie?'

There was a scrabble of stones and then a splash and Annie was up and over to the water before Tom could cry out his fear, but then she saw that he wasn't going to. He was sitting up grinning, water dripping from his hair into his face, his body drenched.

'I think I'll do a wee while I'm here, Annie,' he called and splashed her as she stood on the bank laughing. 'I should have brought the soap and saved meself the trouble of bath-night.'

Annie splashed him. 'Come on out for your bread when you've finished poisoning the fish, you little toad.' She turned and waved to the other two boys. 'Come on, you two. Or we'll eat the lot.' She was ravenous.

They all lay on the grass, close to the water looking over at the hives where there were a few bees hanging in the air. Tom had taken his pad from Beauty's saddle-bag and was drawing.

'So what about this mating you wanted me to see, Georgie.' Annie peered closer at the other bank.

Georgie pulled at the grass about him, throwing it up into the air and letting it float down. 'It's the queen, you see, she mates once in her life on a sunny day. I've never seen it happen.'

'But you've been coming for years to help here, haven't you?' Grace asked.

He nodded. 'But I've never seen it.'

'Well, you won't from here, will you,' mocked Annie. 'Their private and personals are a bit too small.'

Georgie laughed. 'It's not like that. Hardly anyone has seen it. She leaves the hive on just the right day, circles over it so she'll recognise it again and flies way up.' He pointed with a grass stem. 'Then the drones come out after her and the lucky one does it there, right up in the air.'

Annie looked up into the sky above the hive. White-streaked clouds seemed miles above them.

'Lucky old drones,' Tom murmured.

Don said, 'Well, I hope he thinks it's worth all that flapping about, that's all I can say.'

Georgie looked at them sideways. 'Aye, it needs to be a bit special. It's a dance of death really because his gubbins breaks off inside her when he's done and she drops him off dead, on her way back down.'

'That's disgusting,' protested Grace, her face screwed up. She stood up and made her way down the shallow bank into the stream. She pulled up her skirt and paddled. Her thighs were dimpled and wobbled as she moved.

Annie pinched Don as he started to giggle and frowned at him. He turned his back on her.

'I'll tell you something,' Don leered at Georgie. 'She's got to be something for them to chase her around like that with the big black nothing at the end of it.'

Annie wondered at the way death seemed to poke its nose into everything, or did it just feel that way to her at the moment?

'Is she,' she asked at last, 'is she something special?'

'Aye, she is that,' answered Georgie. 'She's a whopper.'

Again Don looked at Grace and sniggered. Once more, thought Annie, and I'll pull your bleeding hair out.

Tom had put his pad down and was looking out across at the hives.

'How though,' he asked, 'does one of them get to be so special?'

'It's just luck, lad. The queen lays her eggs in small and big cells. The ones in the big cells are fed with royal jelly when they become larvae and the first to become a bee kills the others, the rival princesses, and becomes queen.'

He showed Tom how to make a daisy-chain.

'And so,' urged Annie, 'what about the old queen?'

Georgie looked up, 'The queen has to leave the hive and find another. That's when they swarm. She takes some of the bees with her.'

'That's what I like to see, the women doing well,' Annie

called to Grace who laughed and nodded. Her hair was wet from the water where she had been dipping in her hand and patting her forehead.

Georgie looked out from under his brows. He looked like the tailor of Gloucester, Annie thought, with his legs crossed and his fingers busy making slits in the daisy stems to thread through the next link in the chain. Tom was too clumsy to continue with his and turned instead to his drawing.

'I'll do something that takes a bit of skill,' he muttered putting his finger under his nose and thumbing it.

Georgie punched him lightly.

'It's only the queen, remember, who has a life of luxury. The workers are all females. They work their guts out in the hive, cleaning and feeding the growing kids and all the drones of course who have to be fit for their only use in life – to fly up to the sky for that big moment.'

'Quite right, too,' said Tom, 'they know their place,' and he braced himself for Annie's slap, which came.

'But don't they ever get out?' Annie persevered.

'Oh aye, they're off out after nectar or pollen, like the one we saw, then they rush back to roll their sleeves up to make the honey and wax.'

Annie was red with anger and flounced up to join Grace in the stream. The pebbles hurt and she wobbled. 'Just like Betsy it is. Work, and nothing else. It's a bloody disgrace.' She raised her voice so that the boys could hear. 'It's a bloody disgrace, I tell you.'

'Calm down, hinny, you'll stampede the pony,' drawled Georgie.

'Never,' called Don. 'Never will that pony stampede anywhere. Just look at her.'

'It's a him,' snapped Annie, and scrambled out of the water and marched away across the meadow, away from the hives. She picked a bunch of black-eyed daisies.

'Only take a few from each clump,' shouted Georgie. 'Helps them to make up their numbers.'

'Can't you think of anything but breeding?' she retorted and their laughter restored her humour.

She collected a few buttercups, then saw the smoke from a train as it appeared and ran along the track way off into the distance. She could hear it surprisingly well and wondered where it was going; what the world was like away from here. I had forgotten, she thought, that there was anything apart from the streets, from the pits. She looked around the meadow. I must come more often and perhaps one day I will get clean away from here.

'Come on, then,' called Tom. 'Let's see who likes it and who doesn't.'

Annie wondered what he meant and then remembered the buttercups hanging limply in her hand.

Yellow bounced off all their throats and they licked again at the remains of the bread and dripping and pretended it was butter. She threw the buttercups on to the water and watched them float out of sight.

Grace dried her legs as she sat down near Tom. Don had moved along the bank and was trying to play ducks and drakes with flat pebbles but the water was too fast-flowing. Tom was drawing a picture of the willow tree and Georgie had finished his daisy-chain.

Annie turned from them and looked across towards the train but it had gone. The oaks at the end were absolutely still, there was no breeze at all.

'Did you see any clover?' Georgie asked, as he rose to his feet. He came to her and tossed the chain over her head. It was so long that he looped it over her a second time.

'Better than pearls any day, lass,' he said and strolled away, head bent, searching. He stopped and called her over. Crouching he pulled out the clover petals from the plant between his thumb and forefinger and sucked the moist white ends. She moved over and watched as he did it. He pulled out some more and handed them to her but they loosened and showered to the ground as she reached for them.

'You do it,' she said.

She wanted to watch his strong brown fingers against the soft pink and white and see how he had not bruised them at all. He held it to her mouth and she sucked. She was not sure if she could taste the clover at all but she had felt his fingers against her lips and her tongue had caught the essence of his skin.

'It's nectar,' he said. 'The bees like it.'

By four the mating had still not burst into the air and Annie felt a disappointment as sharp as Georgie's. Don was restless and paced round Georgie who dug into his bait-bag and brought out a jar sealed with muslin.

'It's honey-comb,' he said and untied the string around the top, peeled back the muslin and, using a spoon from the bag, levered out a piece of honey-dripping comb. He gave it first to Annie and she felt her face flush. He smiled, then passed pieces round to Tom and Grace. Don and he shared the last. The white comb was waxy and stuck in her teeth. The honey was sweet and sticky. Some had dripped on to her leg and she scooped it up with her finger and licked it. Tom looked at a piece of comb he had saved. 'It's perfect,' he said. 'Look at that shape. It's quite perfect.'

Don took a mug of water from the flask, though it was luke-warm by now, and swallowed.

'There's got to be money in this,' he said and Annie sighed.

'Sorry, Don,' Georgie said disappointing him. 'It's too cold up here really. You'll have to make your fortune elsewhere. Try the horses.'

Don strutted about. 'I reckon I could be a jockey.'

'Well, you're small enough,' chipped in Grace, and Annie was glad that she had got her own back on him. She had thought Grace had seen his earlier sniggers. He was small enough an' all, she thought – that's a good idea of the lad's.

'There's money in riding,' he continued, ignoring Grace. 'You get to hear of all the best tips.'

'You've never ridden though, Don,' Annie pointed out. 'Would they take you d'you think and what'll Da say? He wants you to do something important or take over the shop when it's doing well again.'

'Well, it won't go well, will it, the pair of them drinking all the stock. And don't you or Tom go telling him before I'm ready.'

'As if we're likely to try and talk to him about anything.' She glanced at Tom and he shrugged. 'If it's what you want to do though, we're at your side, aren't we, Tom?'

Tom nodded. 'It'd be a grand life, Don, all that fresh air.'

Annie saw that he had, in his drawing, draped the willow fronds in the water, though they stopped just above in reality. His version was better.

'Hold it up a minute, Tom,' she instructed and put her head on one side and studied it.

'He'll be an artist when he's older,' Grace said. 'He can come and hang his pictures in the library when I'm in charge.'

Tom beamed and put his pad down, tearing out the sheet and giving it to Grace. 'You can put it on your wall if you like.'

'Queen bee then, is it, Annie?' Georgie teased.

She looked at him, then the others, then out over the stream, seeing the way the water eddied round the boulders and sucked at the bank as it went on round the lower bend. Then she grinned and twirled her daisy-chain at Georgie. 'With these pearls, what else could I be?' She let them drop. 'But I'm telling you, I'll be off to another hive and things will be a sight different there, just you wait and see.'

'A revolution,' grinned Georgie.

'And not before time,' breathed Annie. 'The women will live a little, just you wait and see.'

And then it happened.

Over beyond the beck, in the baking heat, the bees left the hive in a long meandering trail, round and round and then up. High into the air, towards the sun.

'Georgie,' screamed Tom, but he had already seen and in one lithe movement was up and on the bank, standing still, his head raised as he watched. Everyone watched, for what seemed like hours. Annie strained to distinguish the queen and her lover, who would soon be cast to the ground. She winced at the thought of dying at the peak of love, plunging to the ground, the children safely made but never to be seen by you. She stood with her hands clasped as the bees settled back into their hive and only the sentinels remained, buzzing like always above.

No one moved and still no one spoke until Georgie sighed and turned. 'That was something I shall never forget,' he said and his mind was on his face and that was something that she would never forget.

She moved her arm round Tom who had come to stand with her. The shadows were lengthening rapidly. The willow cast itself well over to the other bank. She squeezed him to her as Georgie and Grace packed up their picnics.

'Remember this,' she whispered fiercely. 'Remember that something happened here today that someone really wanted.'

She looked again at the hives. 'It shows that things can go right, bonny lad.' She felt wonderful, full to her throat with success.

'It's been the best day of my life, it has,' she said.

CHAPTER 6

Annie sat on her knees beneath the bedclothes pulling on her liberty bodice whilst trying to keep the blanket hooked on to her thin shoulders. Bye, it was freezing, the bodice felt cold, damp and prickly and too small which only added to her irritation. At 13 she was still wearing the same one she had worn at 11. Oh God, the thought, I shall have to stick me legs out to get me stockings on, but she was a suspender short.

Throwing on a blouse and wool jumper which had thinned at the elbows she wriggled into her skirt and, bracing herself against the chill, slipped out on to the rug, its knotted rags knobbly beneath her feet. More by feel than by sight she hunted, but it was no good; she lit the oil lamp and there beneath the bed it lay amongst dust which lifted and floated before her probing fingers. The rubber was dry and cracked. As perished as I am, thought Annie, as she clambered into her boots, fingers stiff with cold.

There was a heavy dust hanging all over the house these days; it seems as dead as the rest of us, she sighed, and peered out of the ice-frosted window. It was going to be a mite cold out on that football field she thought as she scratched and filled her nails with ice. Serve the silly beggars right!

She stamped downstairs to the bathroom, thankful as always that Joe had a bathroom put in when he was living here. It was cold but at least she didn't have to break the ice in the privvy, though the torn-up bits of paper were no silk stockings on her bum.

She was reluctant to start the day; another Saturday, another pie-day and Tom not even here. She kicked the bathmat. He was only supposed to be at his Aunty May's on Wednesdays but it looked as though it was creeping into Fridays too. She missed him. Missed him pushing past her to the basin in the morning, missed his chatter and his smiles.

He was thinner these days, so maybe it was as well that May, Betsy's sister, asked him more often. Poor bairn, at least his aunty fed him up good and proper, brought a bit of colour into his cheeks, and he liked being with May's boys, especially Davy. He was older than Tom but good with him. She bit her lip as she thought of the two more in his class who had gone down with consumption. She'd heard Betsy telling Ma Gillow in the shop last week and the anxiety she had felt then clutched at her again. She rubbed her face violently to chase the thought away. Yes, he must go more often to his aunty, much more often; she would make sure of it because Tom must be kept safe. She reached for the towel which was already damp after Betsy.

'Get down here, Annie, for God's sake,' she heard Betsy call and leant against the basin, glad of the interruption, a new train of thought.

Thank God it was for the last time; this match, these pies. Next Saturday she'd be able to go to Grace's to read her comics. She'd take Tom too and Grace would be sure to share her liquorice with them, she always did. Grace was lovely that way. Tom would buy some pink mice too, now that he'd taken over from her on the manure round. She was glad she'd passed it over; at 13 she was almost a woman and muck sales didn't fit in with that. She straightened herself and undid the plait that she now slept with every night. Yes, there were some waves, not many but a few. She put her shoulders back and looked at her chest but there were still only the smallest of bumps. Grace was enormous and even her shadow wobbled when she walked.

She hoped Tom wouldn't cram all the mice into one pocket again. They had come out in bits last time, all over Grace's floor. Her da had roared with laughter and given them money for another two pennyworth. He was never cross, Grace's da wasn't. Even when his stump was swollen and new after his leg had come off in the coal fall he had still smiled but there had been new deep lines round his mouth.

It was strange when he lost his leg, she thought. When the siren went Betsy and me were washing and never thought it was him. You're always frightened it will be someone you know but you never really think it will be. The siren had gone on and on that morning and they'd seen the women pass the door, shawls over their heads but without their usual faces. They were blank and empty and there had been Grace's ma but she hadn't seen them. The women never saw anything until they knew their man were safe, or not.

It was the week after they had been to the beck and seen the mating but it wasn't warm then, or did it just seem as though it wasn't. She tried to remember but could not.

'Will you get down here, girl.' Again she heard Bet call.

'Coming, Bet,' she shouted. 'Keep your 'air on,' she added but more quietly; no good looking for a clout she thought.

She rubbed her teeth with the flannel. Bye, they'd had some good laughs, her and Grace, even after Georgie and Don had become too old for the gang although it wasn't quite the same with just the three of them. She thought of the time her da had bought a load of manure off Sid at the allotment and come home tutting at the way some of the neighbourhood children earned themselves a few extra pence. Sid had been her muck man, selling it off for her but she was the one with the shovel heaving up steaming blobs from the road and Beauty's stable. Her da would have killed her if he'd known.

She squeezed the flannel dry and hung it over the edge of the basin, then tried to find a dry bit on the towel which was worn to a thread. It hurt her chapped hands. She envied Don away in Yorkshire, galloping across the wide moors he had told her about. It must be good to be a boy, to get away.

It was strange where her da found the money to drink so much, and Betsy too now, breathing heavy breath into her face all day. It made her repulsive and what's more she didn't half clout now. At least Da never became slobbery, just quiet, deathly quiet as though there was a wall drawn up around him. She sat on the edge of the bath, first putting the towel beneath her, the iron was cold enough for her to stick to, she grinned. What did he do in that study all day she wondered, except booze.

He had started going in there when 'Churchill's returned to the gold standard,' he had groaned. She remembered him coming in and saying that. It sounded so silly, what the hell was a gold standard? Let some silly old fool return to where ever he wanted, she thought, I'm making me tea if you don't mind. Then he had rushed off to see the glorious and good Mr Wheeler who she had shortened to God but that was no loss because he was never in the shop now, Annie thought, her right foot arching and stretching. Good for slim ankles Grace had said.

'For the last time, get down them stairs or I'll belt you.' The call came louder this time and she went down now, slamming the bathroom door behind her.

Archie heard her as she passed the study. He threw down the pen with trembling hands, his letter to Joe finished and took another drink, feeling the heat as it burned down his throat. The trembling improved. His shoulders hunched as he pored over the figures yet again but the answer was no different – he was finished.

Albert had been quite right to bow out of the partnership a year ago, no point in them both going down but it still grated, especially the look of supreme pleasure that had for one brief moment lighted Albert's face when he had sat back and listened as Archie told him he was near to ruin and needed the bolster of the partnership more than ever. Albert had shaken his head and said that he was sorry, he must think of himself and that he was sure Archie would not keep him to an arrangement which would destroy both their father's children. That would mean total shame for the family name.

Archie remembered wanting to put his hands round Albert's neck and squeezing until the veins bulged on his forehead and his bloodshot eyes blazed. But the man was right, of course; it was logical that one of them should survive.

This year, 1926, had been the crunch for the business, that and Churchill's gold standard budget of the year before. The General Strike, though, that was what had ended it for him. It might have been over in a few days for the rest of the workers but the miners stayed out for months. They starved, so he starved and it had been little better when they had returned to work, for wages had been even less, if indeed there had been a pit left open to take the men.

And Bob had said last night that this was a picnic compared to what was to come. What was it he had said? Archie gulped at his drink as he tried to organise his mind, it was difficult for him to hold the thread of his thoughts these days; he knew it was the drink but was glad because he did not want to be able to think coherently. Now, Bob had said that Europe, including Britain, would be in trouble if they had to repay their American war debts. That our economic well-being depended on America's economic stability. If that went, debts would be recalled, world trade would slump, industry would collapse and he seemed to sniff that this could be a possibility. He was usually right, but then it really wouldn't matter, would it? 'Would it?' he said aloud and smiled, cradling his glass in his hand, feeling the cut patterns in the crystal. He finished his drink, picked up the letter addressed to Joe and smiled again. He ran his finger round the rim of the empty glass and it rang, a low continuous note. He withdrew the stopper of the matching decanter and poured a large drink and pondered his success and failures.

A good thing to come out of the last few years had been the football team and through that had begun his friendship with Bob. Sport had worked as a morale booster during the war when, well behind the lines, on yellow gorze-flecked land, his platoon had kicked a ball and forgotten for a moment the hell and concentrated on a victory of smaller proportions. It had worked here too. He had approached Bob with a plan and the men Bob sent had warmed to the idea of victory also. The team had become important to them and had pushed the lack of a job into the background for an hour or two and the pies he provided had kept their hunger at bay for just as long.

His friendship with Bob had grown through their efforts to set up the matches and it had satisfied a hunger of his own. A hunger for conversation of a kind he had known before and during the war. Every week they met either here or at Bob's home the other side of Wassingham and discussed things other than the declining money in the till or what he wanted for tea, as Betsy increasingly insisted on calling it. Almost as though she was challenging him. Into the small hours they would talk about world affairs and matters which took him beyond the confines of his life. And so Bob had kept his starvation at bay, he thought wryly, but now he could no longer help the men with their's, for there was no money in the till to pay for the pies which were served at the end of each game and he, Archie Manon, felt that now was as good a time as any to hand over to someone else.

The whisky was slipping down smoothly now and his hands were quite steady. Might just as well drink the remaining stock as pour it down the drain he thought sourly, aware that his thoughts were becoming increasingly disjointed, his movements more clumsy, but that was comforting.

He looked at his son's photograph set in a wooden frame standing behind the decanter. I wanted so much for you, Don, he thought. A racehorse owner, not a stable lad and so much more for Annie. A better education, more opportunities to see another life, to move from here and make something of herself. It's all been such a waste of time. He saw that his glass was empty again and refilled it and sat, elbows resting on the table until even bitter thoughts became blurred and slipped away before they could dig in and spiral into his brain.

Annie knocked on the door and, turning the handle, entered. He was just sitting there, his face towards her, his eyes fixed on where she was but not seeing her.

'Da,' she began, then louder, 'Da, Ted's come for you, they're waiting outside to go to the field. Betsy called up to tell you.'

He frowned with the effort of concentration and leaning forward said clearly and distinctly:

'I can do nothing more for you, Annie. I have nothing that will help you make your way in this world except to say, for God's sake, girl, marry above you and get out of here. Never marry down.'

Violence made him spit and Annie watched the bubble rest on the shine of his desk and wondered how much he'd had and it wasn't even breakfast.

They heard Betsy call up from the basement door and Annie said, 'Come on, Da, let's find you a piece of bread before you go.' She moved before him down the stairs, impatient with this man and his never-ending misery, but knotted up inside because of it.

Betsy stood by the brass fender which no longer shone, with arms folded as Annie cut a hunk of bread and handed it to her father. He passed out of the door, taking his coat off the hook as he went, looking at neither of them, and Annie thought that once he would rather have been seen dead than in clothes that were as torn and dirty as that coat was. The tea was stewed and coated her teeth with bitterness.

'He's been at it again,' she said and Betsy nodded but was too tired to care. She pressed her hand to her breastbone, her indigestion was bad again she thought.

'Come on girl, give us a hand with these pies or they'll never get cooked and hand me some of that magnesia while you're at it.'

She was mixing the pastry, and flour clouded the table as she pummelled, her sleeves rolled above her elbows. She pointed with a flour-covered finger. 'For God's sake, next to the salt.'

Annie reached up and passed it over, tying the apron round her waist. It was warm in here.

''Ere, take over from me while I get this down me.' Betsy moved to the sink with the magnesia.

Annie plunged her hands into the mixture. She hated the way the lard slipped through her fingers, then clung to her as it became pastry.

'Though God knows it's the wives and bairns who need it as much as the men but who are that lot to give a monkey's.' Betsy elbowed her to one side and the bitterness in her voice penetrated Annie's thoughts of Grace and the new dress, the one she'd worn to school on the last day of term. Must be nice to have men in the family who were in work. Grace's brothers were all in the same pit as Georgie, Grace said.

'Still,' Betsy continued. 'if they don't have the men to feed for one lunchtime at least it's one more helping for the kids.'

'But not a hot slice of meat and potatoe pie though,' replied Annie, as she washed the carrots and potatoes under freezing water, then chopped them. 'You're right, Betsy, it's a bloody disgrace.'

The clout knocked her to one side. 'Don't swear. You're nothing but a bairn and bairns don't swear.'

The back door opened and Tom walked in. Annie knew that he'd heard the crack as Betsy's hand had caught her head. 'Not growing another cauliflower, are we, Annie?' He was smiling but his eyes were angry as he turned her head, lifted her hair and checked. 'All right, bonny lass.' He turned and glared.

'You shouldn't do it, Mam.' But Betsy ignored him. Annie ruffled his hair, her ears ringing. He was nearly as tall as she was now.

'Go and sit by the fire and get warm. We'll be out taking these little bits of heaven to the men soon.'

He grinned and passed her the towel to dry her hands, then walked over to the table. His jacket was torn at the pocket and his scarf was too thin to be of much use. It was so discoloured that its stripes were indistinct. His boots clumped as he crossed the floor.

He stuck his fingers in the bowl and rubbed it round and licked it.

'Bring those tats here, pet,' Betsy called to Annie. It was her way of saying sorry, Annie knew. Tom winked at her. 'The women will make do with their smithering of dripping and be none the worse for it,' Betsy continued.

'But . . . ' Annie retorted.

'And take your jacket off, Tom,' Betsy called to him. 'You'll not feel the benefit when you go out. And you Annie just get done with your mithering, there's nought you and I can do about it.' She wiped her hands down her apron which was stretched taut round her body which seemed to get fatter by the day, Annie thought.

'I'll stoke the fire, Mam,' offered Tom.

'Right lad, we'll need the gas and the range today.' The rolling-pin crunched her swollen hands as it travelled beneath them, thinning the pastry. Annie saw the tears fill her eyes as she lined two tins with lard. She left Betsy to finish, to fold the pastry into the tins, load in the vegetables and a few scrag-ends of lamb and seal the edges. She held the oven door as Betsy put one in the range. The other was put into the gas oven.

Betsy stood up and sighed, stretching her back.

'I'm off to the shop now. Can't leave it locked all day,' Betsy called, as she left the room. And can't go on much longer without a beer, thought Annie, as she and Tom sat on by the fire.

'Did you have a good time, Tom? Was May good to you?'

Tom sat on her right, his legs splayed as he relaxed in the heat. He had hung his coat on the end of the fender but it was beginning to smell of burning.

'Move your coat, Tom. Keeping it warm is one thing but it'll be a puff of smoke in a minute.'

He nudged it off with his foot and kicked it on to Betsy's chair.

'Oh aye, May's right good to me. So much to eat. Here.' He struggled to bring from his pocket a piece of apple pie. 'It's a bit squashed, but good.'

Annie laughed and ate it. 'You should go there more often.'

89

She looked at the fire as she spoke, not at him. The heat thrown out made her shield her eyes.

'I'd rather be here with you, trying to keep your ears out of trouble.'

'Don't be daft, I've got too much to do without bothering with a scruffy little tyke like you.' She leant across and pinched his leg gently. 'You must go more often Tom. I'll see you do.'

Tom said nothing and neither did Annie. It was nice to sit here and have nothing to do for half an hour she thought, though she should really be washing the dishes; but she made no move to do so, just wriggled her toes and enjoyed the heat. We'll have to get up to the slag-heap again soon and try and sort out some bits of coal.

Betsy came in when Annie was feeling her lids drooping, her hands heavy. Her face was flushed and her lips slack from the drink. She tipped the pies from the oven on to the trays. Annie nudged Tom and pointed to his coat. She took hers from the peg.

'Get these off now and no messing mind.' Betsy threw the towel on the table and sank into her chair. 'And shut the door behind you,' she called as they left.

They carried the weighted trays out over the yard, past Beauty who stamped in her stall, and down the back alley; the steam was white in the colourless chill although the pies were covered by two layers of boiled white cloth to retain the heat.

Annie turned down Sanders Alley halfway down the street. They had passed no one yet this morning. It was too cold to go out unless you had to.

'Where are you going, Annie?' called Tom, as he stayed, uncertain, at the mouth of the alley. 'You're going the long way round.'

'We're going this way today, Tom,' Annie ordered, her voice tight.

He took a step forward, then stopped. 'But it's too cold,' he wailed.

'Just do as you're bliddy well told,' she shouted, her shoulders bent under the weight of the tray. 'We've got things to do today, Tom, important things you and I. It's time you learnt a few facts of life, a big boy like you.'

She continued, knowing that he would follow. His tray was

the smaller of the two and would not be too much for him on this longer route.

They moved through the alley into Sindon Street with Annie stopping at different doors while Tom's eyes widened in horror until Annie was finally ready for the field. Tom had not spoken at all. When they arrived they put the trays on the frost hard ground. A frost that had whitened and stiffened black smutted grass that crunched beneath their feet. There was no one else watching the game and there were no pitch marking but the men cheered and slapped when a goal was scored between two old coats. The final whistle was blown by Archie and Annie turned to Tom.

'Go home, Tom. Now.' The sky was grey and pressed down on them. They could hear the laughter of the men as they gathered together, shaking hands.

He hesitated, his eyes travelling from her to the men, who were now ambling across the field towards them. They looked big and were getting nearer. Fear made his legs feel weak. He should stay with her, he knew he should.

'Go home,' she repeated, shouting at him. She pushed him from her. He was crying now, silently. He turned and looked towards the football field then to her. He should stay, she looked so small here on the big field with men closer and closer looking like dragons breathing smoke as their breath met the cold air. God, he was scared, too scared.

'Go,' she said, turning from him to wait for her father and then he fled. His feet turned on the frozen ground but he didn't stop. He ran and ran, hating himself but not going back. She heard him but did not take her eyes off the men. Her feet were very cold but not numb yet. She wriggled her toes and transferred her weight from one foot to the other.

Her da was feeling the cold too, she thought, watching him walk towards her, rubbing his hands, his scarf wrapped up round his chin. She saw him stop and wait for the men, herding them towards the trays.

'We're ready for this, aren't we, lads?'

'Right enough, Captain,' the men laughed and blew on their hands.

Makes him feel big, Annie thought. Captain this and Captain that but I suppose he hasn't got much else so who can blame him. She could smell the booze on him and all around him and he was a good five feet away. The men stood round her now, their breath blowing white; they blocked out the light and hemmed her in. She stepped back, out of the circle.

'Come on then lads, take a slice and let it warm you.' Her da pulled aside the cloth.

The bits of bread and dripping were very dull, Annie thought. They didn't steam like the pies had, like the men as they turned to face her. They looked cold like the air and the ground; like her feet; like her father's voice as he said:

'What's the meaning of this?'

Annie set her feet and braced her shoulders, her small breasts sore in the chill wind. The men seemed larger now.

'The meaning is that it is just not fair,' she blurted. 'You run around chasing a little ball and having hot pies when the families have this muck while they're stuck inside four walls. They cook and wash and never get out of the rut. It's like a bliddy hive.'

She stepped back as her father moved. He stood still.

'If you don't like this, why should they?' she challenged.

There was a dog barking over by the coats which had made the goal. It pulled one along, tossing it, then barking again. The slag-heap in the distance was grey with frost. No one spoke.

Annie turned back to her father, her anger under control but her resentment still present. 'Who's thought to give the women anything like this? Don't you think they have longings too?'

He was looming above her. His face was red and there was sweat on his nose. He found his voice at last. 'That is enough, more than enough.' He had his hand up like a bloody policeman, she thought. 'Go home to my study and I shall see you there.'

She stood for a moment, there was more to say but she could no longer find the words. She pushed her head down into the bitter east wind and left, but twisting her head she called:

'I told them that you men had decided to do a swap. It wasn't their fault.' Her words were whipping back in her face; her face felt frozen with the cold.

'It wasn't their fault,' she shouted again.

'Go home,' her father replied and she knew then that he had heard.

Betsy was sitting at the table as she opened the door. Tom leapt to his feet from his chair by the fire and rushed to her;

putting his arms round her. His warmth pressed into her. She held him close.

'It's all right, bonny lad. It's fine, everything's fine.' She stroked his hair. He might be tall for 11 but he was all skin and bone.

Betsy had heaved herself out of the chair, her mouth working soundlessly, then she shrieked. 'You bloody little fool!'

Beer froth was lying on her lips. She slopped the jug she held in her hand and beer ran over the table.

'What did you want to go and do a thing like that for? When will you think before you act? You've made him look a fool and he'll lather you.'

Tom clung tighter to Annie. 'I'm sorry,' he wept. His voice muffled. 'I should never have left you.'

Annie took him by the shoulders, pushing him a little from her and looked into his face. 'I've told you everything's fine and when have I ever lied to you? He's not cross.' Her gaze was steady, she shook him slightly and looked over his head to Betsy. 'Tom should go to May's tonight, Betsy. He could do with a good meal after today.'

Betsy looked at her, her hand resting on the mug that now stood on the table. She looked confused and beer had splashed down her bodice; she dabbed at it. 'Oh, perhaps you're right,' she said abstractedly, her anger gone as fast as it had come, tiredness taking over and making her slump back into her chair. She didn't want him to go, he was her son but there was not enough food any more; she always felt hungry and if she did, he did.

She looked through bleary eyes at Annie and Tom standing there and saw the red welt on Annie's cheek that was still there from that backhander this afternoon. She knew she shouldn't do it, but Annie was his child – that bugger who lived up those stairs and had brought them all to this. She would have been better off with Joe; at least he knew how to run a shop and would Archie listen to her if she tried to help? Not bloody likely. She wanted to hit him, to slap his pompous face but she couldn't and all the time she had this anger inside. The drink helped, but it made her even more tired. Life was too much of an effort. The kids were too much of an effort, they got under her feet, they never stopped wanting, and when the rage got too bad she had to hit, had to shout, had to drink even though she

93

could see that it made Annie cut off from her. She had loved her once, loved them all once. She supposed she still cared for Tom but inside there was only this anger.

'Can he go then, Betsy?' Annie's voice interrupted her.

She sipped at her beer and enjoyed the taste. She waved her hand at Tom. 'Get on over to May's then,' she said.

Tom looked up at Annie and she winked at him, wiping his wet cheeks with her hands. 'Go on, Tom, and bring me back some apple pie as a present in the morning.'

After wrapping him into his jacket and shooing him out of the door, she went on up the stairs to sit on the study chair for the two hours it took for him to come home.

She had tucked her feet beneath her and wrapped her coat around, glad of its extra layer in the bitter room. She realised that she had never just sat before in this place, which was essentially her father's den where stale tobacco had threaded into the curtains and lined the walls, and she felt an intruder. It made her sit upright in the chair, stiffly uncomfortable and nervous in case he should come in and find her lolling as though at her ease.

So little sunlight reached this spot and today was worse than usual with its grey cold cloud. She wanted to set up the oil lamp, to throw some of the shadows back into the deepest corner, but dare not. She felt she must make as little impression on this room as possible, rather like her attitude to her father over the last few years. He was there, around the place but not of it. She swallowed; never before had she directly involved herself with this man and she felt small and vulnerable and friendless. She sank her chin on to her chest and wondered what Don would say when he heard as he undoubtedly would, for in this neighbourhood it would be round like wildfire, and a letter would be sent. Maybe he would tell Georgie, but would he remember their day at the hives and understand? She didn't know because he was too busy with his grown-up life to see the kids who used to be the gang.

It was silent up here; there were no sounds drifting up from the alleys. It was not drifting weather, she thought with a sigh, and ran her hand along the top of the desk. The green leather square which slipped into the sharp edged mahogany top was warm in comparison with the cool shine of the desk. Papers were everywhere, some in piles, some just scattered as though abandoned. There were two photographs, one of her and one of Don but none of their mother. I wonder what she looked like, she pondered. There was nothing to give a clue to their father except his pipes and feather cleaners.

She looked more closely at the papers before her. They were a jumble of figures which held no interest for her since they did not speak to her of the man who was her father. Leaning forward she poked her finger under the corner of the nearest stack and laying her face sideways against the desk she could see spidery writing stalking across the paper. Lifting the top sheets she started a landslide and slapped her hand down on the top. The desk was damp where her breath had skated across the surface. She wondered why her father had been writing to Joe about coming back to take over in the event of 'my demise'. Demise was an odd word, she thought, and wondered what it meant.

When is the man coming? she sighed, then whistled tunelessly through her teeth. The waiting seemed endless. She wondered if they would go to the pantomime in Newcastle this year, probably not after today's little effort, she thought, especially with things being so bad. But it was such a delight, so bright and exciting, with Betsy in her hat, her stockings held up instead of rolled down round her ankles and Happy Harry in his spats and striped trousers.

Suddenly she longed for Tom to be downstairs waiting by the fire for her. She rubbed her nose harshly. No tears, she had promised herself long ago; they did no good.

Then she heard her father on the stairs and rising, she edged away from the chair to stand next to the wall, her hands pressed against the cold plaster and her chin lifting; she chewed the inside of her mouth. The door opened slowly. He said nothing to her as he entered the room and she wondered whether he had remembered her. He sat heavily in the chair looking only at the papers which he tidied absently, not acknowledging her presence in any way. She waited, fascinated by the small pale hands which first patted the papers into squared layers, then fingered a pipe, the wide-bowled one; and after he had drawn the pipe-cleaner through he prodded tobacco into it, lit a match and sucked until it glowed red. She had never seen this private ritual before and felt as though she was watching him clean his teeth. She fidgeted.

'So, you chose to make your own judgement and then to act on your decision.' He finally turned to her, leaning forwards, his elbows on his knees. His pipe hung from his right hand and glowed weakly. It was the only warmth in the room.

'If you ever interfere in my life or that of the neighbours again, I shall take strong remedial action. At thirteen years of age you know very little of the real world, so do not presume to act the adult. Is that fully understood?'

Annie nodded, one look at his face which was drawn tightly to a point made his meaning abundantly clear. And how could he say all that without drawing breath; she was amazed.

'You'd better come over here, take your coat off and bend over.'

Annie blinked. She really had not believed it would come to this and her cheeks burned. Stiffly she walked to where her father pointed, taking her coat off and letting it drop in a heap on the floor, a gesture of defiance which he ignored.

Archie took the wooden ruler from the drawer, his hand shaking in spite of the drinks he had taken throughout the day.

'Bend over,' he repeated, keeping his voice impersonal with an effort. She was so small, looking 9 not 13 and she was thin, her buttocks outlined against her skirt and her vertebrae ridged beneath her sweater. He took a sharp intake of breath and briskly delivered three strokes and Annie said nothing, just retrieved her coat and slouched into it, turning to face him. It was not the pain but the embarrassment. She hoped he had not seen her suspenders while she was hanging head down with her backside in the air.

'Have you anything to say to me, Annie?' Archie asked.

'I still think it's unfair to the women,' she said, determined that she was not going to apologise.

And at this Archie felt tired and his distress from the punishment churned deep inside.

'Maybe it is, but you are a child and it is not up to you to change patterns which have held good for generations. There is a great deal that is bitterly unfair but you, of all people, must know that we have enough to do to survive without you throwing pebbles in the pool. As it happens, this time the men were amused but maybe they would not be again and we need their custom. If you want to change things then change them for yourself, not for other people. And Annie,' and here he paused 'you must make sure you do change things for yourself. Get out, get up that ladder. Now go and have some tea.'

He would have liked to draw up the corner chair for her and really talk to this child who saw beyond the confines of her world to things that should not be, but felt constrained. She would sooner be away downstairs, warmed by the fire.

She started to speak and he leant back and looked at her quizzically.

'Are we going to the pantomime this year, Da?' she asked, wanting to talk about patterns and life and themselves but knowing that here was a man who had no use for her chatter and none of the need she had for company. She wanted a reason for not turning to the door and stepping out into the gloom of the landing that led to no one she wanted to be with and nowhere she felt at home. But she had only been allowed into this room for punishment and she knew that here there was no place for her either.

Oh Annie, my little love, Archie thought, thank God you have no thoughts to torment you, no loneliness to plague you, just your wonderful zest for life, the love of tomorrow and he desperately wanted the brightness of her youth, now and in the future; the nearness of her small warmth and her interest. But he tried to restrain this intrusion into his daughter's life and merely nodded at her request and again when she pleaded that they should all be together for the trip, Don too.

There was a silence between them, her hazel eyes looked up into his.

He could bear it no longer. 'I love you, darling child,' he murmured, so softly that Annie could only guess at what he had said. She leant forward to try to hear again and he reached out to her and kissed her soft cold cheek. Annie wondered again what he had said.

He dropped his arm from around her. As he had feared, the time had passed when he could expect love from his family and he knew that the blame was only with himself.

'Off you go now,' he said, patting her. 'Find Betsy for some tea.'

Annie went, feeling that something had slipped from her, something important and she couldn't quite see what it was. Silly old fool, she hissed, hurt and angry as the door shut behind her leaving her cold and alone. He doesn't care whether I'm alive or dead; all he cares about is his bloody shop and his booze. Well I just don't give a damn. He can drink himself sodden. I just don't care about you any more, she hurled silently at the door. You and she's just as bad as one another, her with her beer in her tea mug. You with yours in that posh glass. You must think I'm daft, the pair of you, if you think I don't know what's going on and she flung herself down into the kitchen to find it deserted with practically no fire left.

It'll be me to make the tea again, she thought. Bet's in the shop and she'll be too sozzled to turn a hand to anything. She opened the door into the passage that led up through the basement into the shop. Bet was sitting behind the counter on the high stool, her hand resting limply round her mug, the earthenware jug to one side. Annie saw the jug was nearly empty and thought of the clumsy evening ahead of them as Betsy slipped and slumped around the kitchen.

'Shall I do the tea then?' she asked, her voice indifferent and hollow in the deserted shop.

'Aye lass, I'll be a while yet.' She did not look round and Annie did not expect her to. What closeness there had been had become submerged somehow during the long grey weary days, weeks and months of depression and despair.

'May doesn't mind having Tom, does she?' she asked over her shoulder as she began to leave.

'No, God bless her,' murmured Betsy, her lips so stiff with beer that some trickled from the corner of her mouth and she lifted a distorted hand and wiped it back on to her tongue. 'It's the best for him, I reckon, with things as they are.'

She half turned, tears brimming, her breaking heart clear in her eyes but Annie refused to notice. She forced herself to feel revulsion since it did not hurt as much as pity. She thought, as she left, of Betsy's buttocks and sagging thighs planted on top of her seat, her legs wide apart, her feet lolling on their sides, straining against dirty brown shoes. At least her da kept himself a bit neater, she thought.

It'd be one pennyworth of chips tonight and a piece of fish, no one else would be in a fit state to eat. She felt weary and had a pain and that night Annie had her first period. She came down from her room, her cardigan wrapped round her shoulders, held together with a hand small with cold and touched Betsy who was slumped face forward on the table, her snores rattling her gaping lips and blowing across the pool of saliva that had oozed casually from beneath her tongue.

Annie shook her again, shivering in the cold of dead embers. It was no good. She stood, frightened and in pain, not wanting to go upstairs again to the smell of the oil lamp. For a moment she held her cardigan together with her chin, the knitted rows scraping her skin and awkwardly piled some kindling on top of paper and began the range for the kettle. The gas stove would be quicker but did not give the same warmth and it smelt funny so she put some coal on and knelt as it took hold. Somewhere she knew there was a hot-water bottle and that, pressed to her stomach, would ease the ache.

The kettle was singing gently now as she looked round the room. The dresser was bare of all but a few plates and the door dragged as she opened the cupboard which was full of old sheeting but right at the rear of the pantry she found it. She scraped her knuckle on the stopper but, as she filled it, the heat became a balm. Betsy stirred and Annie called to her.

'Betsy, I've come on, what do I do?'

'What's that you say?' Betsy reared up, her eyes glazed and heavy. 'What's that you say, my pet?'

She reached for Annie who stepped back out of reach of the flailing hand.

'It's me, Betsy, I've come on and I don't know what to do.'

She hated it, every bit of it, having to expose herself to this woman, to anyone, in this most secret of things and her face was hot with humiliation.

Betsy shambled to her feet, leaning her weight on one hand and pushing off from the table towards Annie.

'It's a bloody shame, that's what it is, and you such a bit of a bairn.' She crossed her arms. 'Now don't you go mucking in the lanes with any of them boys. Just you keep yourself to yourself or it'll be trouble and this house has enough of that as it is.'

Annie backed away towards the sink.

'I just need something to wear, Betsy, that's all.'

'Well, you'll have to make do, same as me.' She staggered to the linen cupboard and pointed. 'There, see that pile of old rags, not the sheets, those at the back. Take 'em, use 'em, wash and boil 'em then use them again. Now, I'm off to bed. I suppose he isn't in?'

Annie shook her head as Betsy nodded towards the door.

'Put the guard up and some ash on that fire,' she slurred heavily towards the end and left the room.

Annie looked at the rags bunched in her hand. Da might come in at any moment and she crept out of the door, her boots slopping at her bare ankles, up the dark stairs and into a bed grown cold. Safe, clutching the stone bottle, her head beneath the blanket, it seemed very lonely up on the top floor. It wasn't fair that Tom had an Aunt who loved him. She felt for the Australian Christmas card which had arrived this morning and told of the baby Eric and Sophie were so proud of and which they had named Annie.

She beat the mattress, crumpling the card and hating the child who had taken her place and her name. She thought of her body, bleeding and sticky and railed at it for taking the child's body from around her thoughts and feelings and replacing it with one which would soon be really adult, not just pretend. She lay quiet, hearing her own breathing. Tom would be here tomorrow and maybe Don and she thought of the scarves she had knitted. It was Christmas Day in the morning.

Archie sat in Bob Wheeler's front room. It was a long walk across town but he had felt the need to stretch his legs and see his friend. Bob lived near to the Bigham colliery because, he said, he liked the sound of the pit wheel.

The two men had been silent for some time. Bob had found the suspension of the seven-hour shift and less pay a poor Christmas present, he had said. It was a poor reward for a strike which started as a general one and ended yet again as a miners 'down tools'. His face was set and he looked back over his years in the union and despaired. Archie asked:

'Why didn't you go ahead and strike in 1919 when coal was booming and they desperately needed you? With unemployment so high you had no bargaining power this time. It seems all wrong.'

Bob shook his head. This is what he had been awake thinking about for the last three nights. He had moved the clock on to the landing in the end because the ticking had drummed '1919' again and again. He had feared all along the General Strike would fail. It was the wrong time. 'You don't need to tell me that, man. We thought we'd get the support of all the workers, but the essential services continued. The country kept going in other areas with the volunteers and the government did well with their propaganda.'

'Didn't the TUC support you properly?'

Bob laughed. 'As much as anyone could do in conditions of such low employment. But it was more than that. They were worried, Archie, I think, especially after the *Mail* published a leader saying that a general strike was almost the same as revolution. The Council want respectability in order to be able to negotiate with government in the long term. They don't want a revolution, I don't know anyone that does. Changes, yes.' They both nodded and Bob leaned forward and poured whisky into Archie's glass and added more to his own. He must put back that clock, when he was sleeping better. It had been his mother's.

'Anyway, after a few days, Samuels arranged a meeting with the TUC to end the General Strike and they arranged terms, but they were bad terms. The workers came out with nothing, just less pay. And you know what, Archie?' He leant forward and pointed with each word. 'There were no miners' leaders there. The Council wanted the strike ended because they knew nothing was to be gained by it so we were on a hiding to nothing, but the miners were bloody livid. They'd been baton-charged by the police in Newcastle and all they were getting for their pains was another hiding, so they stayed out for another seven months, not that it did them any good. They came out with less pay, just like the others, only they'd starved for seven months to earn it. The whole thing was bloody stupid.' He was talking to clear his own mind, running through the events of the past few months, trying to make sense of it all.

Archie held his glass up to the fire, tilting it so that he was looking through the liquid at the flames. The fire was set in a blue-tiled surround which was matched by the curtains and chairs. It was a plain room but spotless. Bob had good neighbours, he had told Archie, and the wife came in to run a duster round from time to time.

'So why did they decide to strike now not in '19 when there was full employment and the country needed coal? There were stockpiles this time Bob.'

Bob nodded, throwing his hands up in despair. 'I know, I know, but the government were withdrawing their subsidy and the miners were told they'd have a drop in pay and longer working hours again. It was desperation and anger I suppose, anger over 1919.' He stopped.

Archie said again, 'But you didn't strike then and got better conditions.'

Bob took a deep breath. He remembered those times vividly. He'd come back from the war and his da was ill but not too ill to take an interest in what was going on and they'd sat up late talking, hoping for public ownership of the mines. His da would have died happy then, but it didn't work out that way. 'Yes, we got better hours and wages but we did not get public ownership, which was the main demand. Look Archie, Lloyd George arranged to set up a commission under Sankey if the miners postponed their strike which they did.' He was speaking clearly and slowly as though to a schoolroom of children, thought Archie, but he felt it was Bob's way of controlling his feelings.

'The Federation and the owners agreed to a compromise at an interim stage of the inquiry, hence the hours and pay and then public ownership or state control, whatever you want to call it, was considered and – glory be – Sankey came out in favour. But, and it's the biggest "but" you'll find, the government betrayed the miners and refused to accept the recommendation.

'Under the owners, you see, the profits are not ploughed back into the industry to increase efficiency and safety. There is no security. There is no attempt to set up other industries now that coal and steel are in decline.'

Archie knew all this but he let his friend continue. He seldom spoke as such and it would do him good.

'The men are bitter, Archie. It's something they'll never forget, never forgive. Betrayal ruins trust forever, it will affect relations between the government and the miners for a long while yet.'

'And how do they feel about the unions now? Surely they'll feel let down. First it's the government, then the TUC, or maybe that's how it will look in their eyes?'

Bob rose and walked to the window. It was snowing. He drew the curtains and returned to his seat and smiled at Archie.

'You're right. They'll see that in conditions of high un-employment there is little the unions can do. Membership will

102

fall off, dues will lessen so there will be a decrease in financial support and even weaker unions. It's a vicious circle.'

He saw that Archie's glass was empty and refilled it. 'It'll be a white Christmas anyway, the sledges will be out tomorrow.'

Archie nodded absently. 'Will the government leave it at that? Allowing prevailing conditions to curtail your power?'

Bob smiled. 'That's the interesting one of course. They're preparing another bloody Disputes Bill, trying to stop us striking, supporting each other. We shall just have to wait and see whether it leaves us toothless. Labour will not be able to oppose it in the Commons with its small party.' He sipped his drink. His throat felt dry from the long discussion. 'I would like to see the day when even the middle classes will have unions. That and better employment figures. That will give us conditions for a concerted push, a better world.'

Opposite him, Archie nodded his agreement, his mind dwelling on Bob's last words, and then he felt the familiar feeling of panic come to him here, in this safe front room. He made his movements slow and careful as he raised his glass and took a drink. He tried to stop the words which were forcing themselves out into the room but it was no good.

'I was once in a concerted push, you know,' and he laughed, but it was not a humorous noise, 'or rather should have been.'

Bob Wheeler had been deep in the problems of the unemployed, chasing them round in his mind and he took a moment to grasp what Archie was saying. He sensed then the giving of a confidence, one that he feared might ruin the tenor of their friendship based on a comfortable, somewhat detached atmosphere of political discussion which never grew intimate. He looked at Archie rather more closely; he was drunk but that was nothing unusual. There was something else though now, something which darkened his eyes, pulling him back to another time and place.

Bob was attempting to defuse the situation. 'I was always at the back of the big push you know. The transport columns never got to the front. They were shelled though.'

Archie seemed not to have heard and Bob knew that he had lost him for now. He had seen it and listened before to those who had never quite left the war behind. The fire leapt in the grate as he leant forward and put on a log. He liked log fires and had one every Christmas Eve. There was a small Christmas tree by the window, lit by the glow from the gas lamp. The pine smell filled the room and presents for his neighbours lay amongst its branches until tomorrow when he would take them next door in time for Christmas lunch.

He waited.

Archie said again, 'Or I should have been.' He looked up as Bob pushed a log further on. The flames curled round and began to blacken the wood.

'It was all a bugger. Best forgotten,' Bob soothed quietly.

But Archie was not to be dissuaded.

'The barrage had started in the evening. We were to attack the next day. You see, they liked to soften up the Germans first, but all it did was warn them we were coming and shake the ground so the trenches began to crumble. I was sent with my platoon to replace the sandbags and shore up the trenches. We worked all night.' His voice was measured and too slow. He was not seeing the fire but the wet earth. 'It had been raining you see, raining for days and Ypres is heavy clay. We couldn't dig deep trenches because of that so we had had to build up the traverses and lay duckboards because of the mud and if you fell off you drowned. The water couldn't run away you see, it just went on making mud, inches, then feet, and they wanted us to go for a big push.' His laugh was sudden and harsh. 'Bloody mad they were. You couldn't walk in that mud, let alone storm the bloody huns. No man's land was a marsh by then.'

Bob handed him a drink. 'Come on, Archie, have this and where's your pipe?' But Archie couldn't hear him, couldn't see the drink.

All he could hear was the noise of the whizz-bangs, the machine-gun fire. He felt his hands beginning to shake and he put them between his thighs. He did not have time to breathe deeply, there was too much to say.

'I was to take my men over in the first push at dawn. The sun rises in the east, but of course you know that. Just for a few moments as dawn came up we could see the Germans before they saw us, and in those few precious minutes we could get out and over the top and maybe not get killed.'

Bob took a swallow of his Scotch. Archie was rocking backwards and forwards, but Bob was not alarmed; it was a familiar pattern with other friends, other survivors. He waited, hoping that when it was over Archie would not regret his confession because Bob now knew that this is what he was about to hear.

'Gas is dirty soldiering, you know.' Archie was talking in a conversational tone now. 'Dirty soldiering. The noise was getting worse. It was still dark but there wasn't long to go until daylight, until we went over. I was by the signal dug-out. If I hadn't been there, it would all have been different. Captain Mollins called out: "Manon, get down to the gas company, they've lost their officer. Shot through the head. Let off the gas. It's got to go before dawn. We want it on the Germans and clear of no man's land by the time we get over. Get on with it, man."'

Archie's voice was no longer calm, its pitch was higher, the strain was in every word.

'I slipped as I turned to him. My sergeant held me up. The mud was greasy beneath my hand and I was on my knees. A shell hit the trench further down, the barrage was still blasting away, the noise was horrendous. Mud flew over us. "But sir," I said "there's no wind."'

Archie was shaking, he was wiping his hands as though to free them of mud, but they were shaking too much so he put them between his thighs again.

' "Do as you're bloody well told, Manon. We need that gas. It's five o'clock already, man. We're going over at six." He was shouting, his face pushed towards me but I could only just hear him against the crash and scream of the shells. I pushed back towards the gas enclave, climbed over the collapsed trench to get there. There were bits of men in it. I trod on a leg. The gas team were waiting. The shells from our battery were falling short, landing around us. There was flying mud everywhere. It was impossible to think.

'The sergeant was struggling with the valve on the gas cylinder. "Give me that," I said, and took the spanner, it was icy. The rain had stopped and there was a mist so I knew there was definitely no wind. I sent a runner back, Bob. "Tell him there's no wind," I said. We were pushing back the sandbags all the time. They were being shaken down as fast as we replaced them. My sergeant was killed by a sniper, shot through the eye. The runner came back. The captain had said, "Get it off now," so I did.' Archie was quieter now.

'The cylinder discharged all right, but the gas fell back into the trench. It's heavier than air you see and there was no wind to blow it across.'

Bob nodded but Archie did not see.

'It fell back and the company stampeded, struggling to get their gas masks on. Why didn't they put them on before? Why hadn't I ordered them to? God knows.'

He was shaking and rocking. 'They stampeded over the top but they weren't the only ones. The push had started too soon, we had lost our advantage of the light and the Germans put flares up and could see us all.

'The wire wasn't cut in front of us. My mask was on, I don't know how. I was alright but those who had survived the gas were being cut to ribbons on the wire, shot to bits and hanging like rag dolls a few feet in front of the trench. I was cutting it, trying to cut it, tear a way through when I felt a hand on my leg, pulling at me. It was my corporal drowning, yellow-faced in the gas, his buttons already tarnished green.

' "Murderer, murderer," he bubbled. Someone from further down the line was screaming. I trod on him, Bob, ground him into the mud, anything to get him away from me, and then a shell exploded, it must have been near. Knocked me out but didn't kill me. God damn it, it didn't kill me.'

All he could hear were the screams and the guns. He looked at his hands and rubbed the palms and Bob could see that they were crossed with white scars. He reached across and held Archie's wrist. Forced him to take a drink, guided it to his mouth. The frenzied shaking had ceased.

Bob looked keenly at Archie. 'It happened all the time, old friend. It was a nightmare and no one was to blame in that chaos.'

Archie smiled but it was without humour. 'I've said that a thousand times, Bob, and it just doesn't bloody help. I killed a lot of people that day and I wonder every night, I wonder, if it wasn't because I just wanted to kill myself. I'd just returned from burying Mary and wanted to die, so did I let off that gas deliberately?'

There was silence in the room except for the ticking of the clock on the mantelpiece and the crackle of the fire.

'No,' Bob said gently. 'No, you didn't, and it's best not to think about it. Life is very strange and we do the best we can.

That's all, we just muddle through.'

Archie seemed exhausted, perhaps a little more at peace with himself, but Bob was not sure. He watched him as he slowly collected himself.

'Anyway,' Archie said in a voice which betrayed his tiredness, 'it's over with now, and yes, maybe one day we will get middle-class unions. Baldwin really would go demented if he thought that was on the cards. Who knows, Bob, maybe one day you'll have Labour back in. You should think of that, think of big-time politics for yourself.'

Bob silently applauded Archie's attempt to regain the thread of their earlier conversation. 'No, Archie, I'm too old for that particular game. Not enough fire in the belly. I've too much to do here anyway, too much everyday trouble in the area.'

A silence fell, a companionable silence, and Bob was relieved that, if anything, the relationship had been improved by the glimpse into a private hell.

Their glasses were empty and the fire was dying. Archie looked at the clock. 'It's very late. You must get some rest.' He looked at Bob earnestly. 'It's good that you have much to do. That's the way it should be, my friend. Thoughts of tomorrow.' As he rose he nodded. 'Yes, that's as it should be.'

They moved from the front room into the hall which was lit by a solitary gas lamp. Archie took his worn coat and hat; Bob helped him into it. His scarf was still hanging on the hook and Archie took it and wound it round his neck while Bob opened the door.

The snow had stopped and there was only a light sprinkling on the ground. The night air stabbed at their lungs and Archie lifted his scarf across his face.

'Have a good sleep, Archie,' said Bob, touching his elbow.

Archie stood looking out across the street. 'It's the dreams though, Bob, the faces, the voices. They make strange bedfellows these days and there's too much noise in my head to find answers to them or the problems of the shop.'

He shrugged and began to walk down the street, his feet unsteady on the slippery cobbles. He turned back to Bob. 'Today, my little Annie did what I should have done; did as she thought right, and I punished her.' He paused, 'Thank God these children at least won't know the feel of a war.'

He moved away, lifting his hat to Bob.

'Merry Christmas,' Bob called after him and watched until he reached the corner. He closed the door. He did not know what else to do.

CHAPTER 7

The tram-stop was a bare one hundred yards from their shop and the morning was crisp and most houses were quiet. It was Boxing Day. The tram rattled to a stop and Archie pushed Annie and Don, then Tom and Betsy before him on to the platform. He might be without his watch, but who cared. Today was special. Today his family was going to Newcastle, to the pantomime, and Donald could redeem the damned watch any damn time he wished. He, personally, had no need of a watch any more. He felt euphoric, as though the decision he had made had drawn every line stronger, every colour brighter and the years were shed and the minutes savoured.

His gaiety was infectious and the children scrambled on to the bench laughing, pushing and poking. Betsy and Archie settled themselves opposite. Betsy had borrowed powder from Ma Gillow to hide the meandering red veins in her cheeks and nose. She'd begged a coat for the day also though she still had no gloves that would fit over her knuckles, so instead she kept them bunched in her pockets.

Annie was wedged between Don and a stranger whose heat penetrated and touched her. She tensed, stiffening against the sway and lurch and fought away from the pressure of the unknown body which pressed closer to her than her closest friend Grace would ever dare. The woman had thighs that should have been hanging in the butcher's but which instead nudged against her and her floppy bosom pulled at the buttons fastening her coat. She had a sweaty face and perspiration lay along the line of her scarlet lipstick which was sticky and had gathered into a lump at the corner of her mouth. Annie wondered how she ate without clogging up her innards.

She laughed inside, grinning up at Don, winking at Tom. It was so wonderful to be actually going to the city, going to the

Empire to see Peter Pan just when she had thought that nothing bright would ever break the long grey winter.

She dug her hands deep into her pockets, regretting that Don's Christmas present of pear-drops had split their bag and seemed fluffy to the touch, but then who would see in the dark of the theatre?

Don was quiet, she thought. He had changed since he had left home. It wasn't just that his hair was short or his voice deep. He seemed further from them than ever now that he was away so much, even when he was this close, and she felt she hardly knew him. She had noticed Betsy and Da sitting either side of the basket so as not to squash themselves buttock to buttock. She bit her lip; her father was so neat today and small beside Betsy who was doughlike and spreading. Jack Sprat had nothing on this little lot she thought.

She looked past Don to Tom.

'Stop picking your nose, Tom,' she whispered, reaching across to slap his hand. 'Don't think you're too far away for me to get at you.'

'Weren't picking,' he mouthed as he leaned forwards. 'Just itching it, that's all.' He tucked his hand beneath his legs and hunched his shoulders. 'It's good, isn't it, Annie, altogether like this.' His eyes were alight and his grin was broad.

Annie wanted to put her arm across and toss his hair and press him to her. He was such a bonny lad with his smile that always seemed to be waiting to plaster itself all over his face, if it wasn't already there.

She nodded. 'Yes, lad, that it is.'

He looked so much better for having wrapped himself round Aunt May's Christmas pud and had brought her back a bit an' all. It had hardened as the suet set but had been rich and sticky.

The tram windows were steamed behind their heads but she could sense the darkness of the station terminal as they arrived. It had blotted out the midday sun. The bustle and noise of the station, as they stepped down, confused her; it seemed to be all around, swirling in a senseless pattern, opening and closing around them as they stood while their father decided which way to go.

'Come along,' he called, sweeping foward into the mêlée, and she reached for Tom's sleeve, tugging at him and running along behind her father's hurrying back. If they missed the train, oh, she couldn't bear to think of it. Instead of swanking in the new school term, there would be nothing to tell.

'I'm not going to disappear in a puff of smoke,' he panted. 'Let go of me arm, Annie, I'm all at an angle.'

But she wouldn't, she was too excited to hear him.

Archie turned, still walking, his face red. He looked again at the chalked boards. 'Come on, Annie,' he called and took her hand. 'You must keep up with us, we haven't time to wait for you both '

They all broke into a run as a train steamed and roared to a spark-spitting halt and the steps were a blur as they raced up over the bridge, then down the other side. The hoarse smell was everywhere. As they approached, the train doors lurched open and swung, slapping against the sides. Annie saw her father and Betsy climb aboard. She sucked more breath into her lungs.

'Come on, Tom,' she shrieked. Don was urging them on. He stood with one foot on the platform, one on the train.

'For God's sake, get a move on,' he bawled and, as they arrived, he heaved at her elbow. 'Bloody girls,' he hissed. She shut her eyes over the yawning gap between platform and train.

'Get Tom, too,' she cried, her voice high and seeming to come from the top of her head. Doors were being slammed the length of the train and finally they were all in.

Their carriage was empty but for them and Annie threw herself on to the seat, heaving a sigh of relief. She pulled Tom down beside her and they laughed and couldn't stop. The seats were prickly and dark red and the paintings of the seaside which were screwed to the wall above them looked dull and uninviting. She tucked her coat beneath her, gasping at the lurch and stagger as the train set out for the city.

There were arms with ashtrays between each place and Annie screwed her nose up against the smell. Black-tipped matches were piled up in the dead ash. A lipstick-tinged cigarette-end had been ground out on the floor. She had heard Georgie telling Don about women like that, it was a sure sign, he had said. If one of them girls up the market is standing smoking in broad daylight with thick red lips, you can lay a penny to a pound she's on the game. Common as muck they are, he'd said. She'd asked what 'game' was and they told her to wait until she was grown up, then they'd tell her. They never had.

The countryside had a smattering of snow but most of it had thawed yesterday. There had been so little anyway and she was rather glad because Tom would have wanted to go sledging and she couldn't bear the cold. It seemed to be racing past; the cattle in the fields looked unreal. In the distance she could see a farmer as he laid down straw by a water-trough. He seemed from another world and she wondered if people in the train had felt the same when, or if, they had seen a group of children in the meadow by the beck that day so long ago.

The picnic buns were still warm from this morning's baking and, long before they drew into the yawning Newcastle station, Betsy passed round chicken which oozed and hung out of tangy rolls. Even Don looked wide-eyed at such luxury and Annie thought the world had gone mad.

'Thought black pudding would be the height of it,' Tom murmured as he held his and just looked.

She looked at her da who smiled and Betsy who nodded and then she sank her teeth into the soft white meat and lifted up her shoulders and hugged her elbows to her sides. She could hardly breathe through the pleasure.

The taxi her da pushed them into, when they came out through Newcastle Station, was so tall they could almost walk into it. There were three small seats which flipped down behind the driver and she and Tom sat on those while Don tried to choose between sitting high up between Betsy and Da or low down with them. Annie knew it was no contest and was not surprised when he squashed in next to Betsy and smiled down on them as though he was Lord Muck.

The Empire was bright and like Christmas had always seemed as though it should be. They stood across the road and watched the crowds as they spilled into the foyer. Annie could not believe that she was actually going through the front and could look the red-uniformed commissionaire in the eye. She nudged Tom and he winked, his shoulder bracing back as he moved closer in the noise of the traffic, the smell of exhaust and the clatter of horse-drawn carts. There was not one pony as small as Beauty, he thought.

'It'll be great to go in the front way, bonny lass,' he whispered and Annie laughed, glad that his thoughts had found their way through to hers. She could feel in her mind the weight of the exit bar at the flea-pit which she had so often heaved up to let the others in. Six for the price of one was good going. Georgie, Grace, Tom and Don and whoever had tagged along that day. Today though, there was to be no ducking as the usherette came down the aisle. Maisie had known who had passed her torch as she stood in the doorway into the cinema and who had just appeared but she had only found them once. Today they could forget it all and just be there, maybe even have some chocolates.

Inside the shell-shaped lamps were pink, the curtains were a vivid red that soaked up the light in patches and was dark and bright in turn. Excitement hummed and was echoed deep within Annie and her hands felt limp with satisfaction. She turned to her father and smiled.

'Thank you, Da,' she said.

He nodded, handing her the binoculars, but with these she could only see parts of the whole and she preferred to be without detail and soak in the buzz and laughter. The chocolate was passed. It was already soft and stuck to the roof of her mouth. She sat perfectly still to let it last. There was its stickiness around her mouth and on her hands until Betsy licked her handkerchief and wiped around her lips and it smelt of her breath until Annie dragged her sleeve harshly across her face. She grimaced at Tom who tried to jerk his head back but Betsy scrunched his hair in her hand until she was done. He shuddered at Annie and leaned nearer.

'We need one of those, then she won't do it.' He pointed to Don's straggly moustache. 'That means they've dropped, you know.'

'Shut up you little –' Don growled, not daring to call him names so close to his da.

'I'd rather have me mouth wiped,' answered Annie. 'They'd stick me in the circus if I had one of those.'

Archie ignored these exchanges. He was training his glasses on the boxes which held calm ordered well-dressed families. All the excitement seemed to come from the well of the theatre and the cheap seats where they were sitting. The orchestra were in the pit, tuning their instruments. It wouldn't be long now.

The heat beat against Betsy and she ignored the bickering between Don and the others. Her dress was too faded and stained to remove her coat so she had to endure the next few hours in it. She opened the collar and let her hands hang as far from her body as the seating would allow. It was good to be away from the shop and Wassingham and Archie looked young again and eager. That was it, she thought, he looked eager as though he knew of a secret joy. He was still such a strange man, so stiff and alone. Her head felt heavy as the lights dimmed and her thoughts trailed away. Her hands were eased by the warmth and she was comforted by the lack of pain. Her chin dropped to her chest.

Annie looked at Betsy. As long as she doesn't snore, she thought. Please God, don't let her snore. She looked along the row beyond her father to Don and saw him unwrap the muffler she had knitted for his present. She had noticed how he had run his fingers between it and his skin a thousand times since he had wrapped it round his neck but hadn't removed it until now and that was kind.

She knew the wool was rough because she had pulled out one of her sweaters to make them and they were all like wire wool. She had thought boys skin was hard and they wouldn't feel the prickling as she did. After all, they were always going on about being so tough.

Tom still wore his but outside his coat. He said he liked to be able to swing it up over his nose and let it hang down his back to keep out the cold air. He had given her a bag of pink mice when he had returned from May's late last night but he had painted her a Christmas card earlier and she had put it on the mantelpiece with the ones from Grace and Sophie on Christmas morning. Sarah Beeston's had arrived the week before and Betsy had put it away for her to open on Christmas day. The package had been soft and it was gloves again, as she knew it would be and they fitted too, they always did. They were dangling on the end of her elastic and she stroked them. The wool was so soft. Bet had stayed in the shop all Christmas Day, empty of trade though it was, and her da had stayed in his study, unspeaking. Both had been drunk.

But now the music was heaving and barking as Mrs Darling settled the children into bed and Annie watched them in their warm bright bedroom being kissed by their parents, tucked in by the dog, Nana. She soared with them when they followed Peter out through the window to Never Never Land and clapped, clapped, clapped to save Tinkerbell's light and life.

She booed the crocodile, screaming with laughter when Tom stood up and shouted his warnings.

At the end she hated the lost boys for returning to real life and called, 'Don't go, don't go,' when Peter asked her, for it was her he was asking, not really the whole audience. Asking whether he should return or stay with Tinkerbell and the treehouse and his freedom. She clutched Da's arm. 'Don't let him go,' she beseeched and he put his hand over hers and said, 'I won't my love. Everyone has a right to be free.' And he had kept his promise.

The trip home was full with quiet and the smog held the pantomine close to Annie where she hugged tight the thought that Peter had stayed. She looked at her da through lids heavy with sleep as the train thundered away from the glowing clouds back to the shadows of home and was glad that he had saved Peter for her. Tom had fallen asleep against her and she moved him slightly to ease her arm.

Don had waved them goodbye at the station to catch the Yorkshire train and Annie had seen Archie grip his arm but had not heard him say, 'Happy New Year, my boy. I have always loved you both, look after my little girl.' She had seen him turn and then Don was gone but not before Annie caught his expression of contempt. Too much booze making the old fool maudlin, it had said.

Betsy woke, her legs stretched out across the bed. No Archie as usual, she thought. He'd be still asleep over his desk in the study. She stretched, her hands playing with the brass bedstead and thought how she loved this bed when it was hers alone. Her limbs could sprawl and her body lie loose on its back unlike the nights when Archie was here. Then she was rigid, careful not to cross the empty space between them, her head motionless on the hardening pillow, tense in case she should irritate her meticulous husband. It wasn't so bad when she'd had a wee drink, then she slept and the more she drank the more she slept. Softened the edges it did, gave her a sort of pleasure. She felt good this morning, no headache, no sour taste from too many gills of beer. She had energy, she was new. Bye, they'd have to go into town more often.

She dressed briskly. In the bathroom, the water was crisp, too cold to wash. She tapped on the study door as she passed but there was no reply. Up and off early on some business no doubt and she was relieved. She thought of the cleaning up she would do this morning, then later she could take the two bairns out for a change. Last night had made her feel excited and energetic and she smiled to see that Archie had laid the fire and the table was ready for breakfast. He must be feeling good too, she thought, and wondered if this could be a new beginning.

The hose that was attached to the gas cooker ran past her up the stairs and she looked at it, her hand still on the doorknob. Her feet felt heavy as she turned for the stairs noticing now how neatly it was laid against them. Up, up she went, seeing the fibres of the carpet clearly but not seeing them at all.

There was a gap under the study door as there had always been and the hose fitted beneath with no noticeable flattening. How could she not have seen when she passed, was it just a moment ago? Her breathing was shallow, rapid.

'Archie,' she called. 'Archie!'

She rattled the door. 'For God's sake, answer. Let me in.'

But there was silence as she knew there would be. She hammered on the door and then it opened at a mere turn of the knob and the ugliness of the gas filled her face in a rolling wave. She shut it again and leant on the door, rubbing her forehead backwards and forwards against the panel. It was cool; so cool. You bloody bugger. Oh my God, you bloody bugger, how bloody could you. She beat her fists on the door, her mouth working and her rage growing but she did go in again and she did open the windows, her hand across her nose, gagging against the drowning mist and she did look at his body, upright in the chair except for his head which hung on his chest but she did not touch him. The gas was still writhing out of the grey flaccid hose but it was silent which was how his death had been, she thought bitterly.

Upstairs Annie half lay on Tom's warm body. She was glad he had crept in as he usually did when the cold had sucked the warmth from his feet. She slept better when he was here; when he wasn't at his Aunt's. She pulled the blanket over her head and sank back into the underground treehouse and the lost boys. It had been the most wonderful Christmas of her life and she still felt the thrill of a world she seldom saw. The lights, the size, the gaiety, and she wondered if the people there knew of the world the sparkle did not reach. Tom had said he would shout loud enough one day so that everyone would know; paint it on canvas for them to see. Good with his hands Tom was. She drifted, seeing daubs of yellow, red and green slashing from dark to light.

Through the warmth she felt the clumsiness of Betsy's feet as they banged against the stairs, heard her shout and the hair on the back of her neck rippled. Betsy could not run! The landing was cold when she reached it and she stood looking at Betsy as she came towards her and saw the words slowly fall from the working mouth and she wondered if she could push them back, stream after stream, hand after hand but she knew they would just keep escaping though they would not reach her ears. She would not let them do that. Betsy pulled her hands away from her ears, jerked her, held her between strong hands and then Annie could no longer escape.

'Finally gone and done it, he has. Joined your bloody mother,' shrieked Betsy. 'Bloody well stuffed himself with gas, d'you hear. Didn't care a bloody monkey's did he?'

'What do you mean,' Annie shouted, wanting to be heard above the noise.

'Bloody killed himself, hasn't he.'

Annie's scream was loud and went on and on. Tom was there now, pulling at her, pushing at his mother. He had heard what Betsy said and it couldn't, no it couldn't be true. Annie's face was ugly, her mouth was open. This wasn't happening. It couldn't be happening. 'Look at Annie's face!' he shouted at his mother, 'What's happening to her face?'

Annie held him back. 'Get away from me, you bitch. He wouldn't do it. He wouldn't do anything so ugly. He was too neat. He wouldn't leave me for her.' She screamed again and could see herself from a great height; she was as ugly and distorted as he must be and she wondered if she would ever fit together again. And she saw and remembered throbbing bulging veins and heard the grinding fairground music. She refused to see the body and so did Tom.

Don came home the day after it had happened. He walked in the door and came to her. She was sitting by the fire, her hair was uncombed, she didn't speak, just looked up as the door opened and he walked in.

'So, the old fool left us all sitting in the middle of a right bloody mess, didn't he,' he said, sitting down beside her. He had red eyes, Annie saw, but hers weren't red. The pain still wouldn't explode into tears, just sat in her body and tore her apart. She reached for his hand and he held hers. He had put his bag down by the chair but had kept his jacket on.

'Where's Betsy?' he asked.

'Round with Ma Gillow. She said she needs a good cry and someone to read the tea leaves for her.' Annie laughed, then shook her head. 'Poor Betsy. There's no money but there is a ticket for you to get his watch back. It paid for the pantomime.'

Don stood up letting her hand drop. He walked to the sink and poured himself some water, then threw the mug back into the sink.

'No money at all?' he asked, turning to face her, his face dark with anger.

'None. He wrote to Joe suggesting that he came back and took on the shop, using Betsy as housekeeper.'

'Well?' Don said, walking to and fro behind her, still thin-lipped, still raging, she knew, because he hit the back of the chair every time he passed with his fist.

'Joe says yes, but not me and Tom.'

Don came and sat with her. 'Well, I can't have you,' he said. 'I've got me job to think of.' He stood up again and this time walked through to the shop and poured some beer. His voice was distant but she heard him say. 'Can't you go to Albert's?'

And Annie felt more anger to go on top of that which was already filling her to the brim. 'I am going to Albert's so Betsy says. Apparently he's the nearest relative. Sarah Beeston wanted me but Albert said I was to go to him. Betsy said she'd trained me well enough to suit him.' She tried to stroke through her hair with her fingers. It was like rats' tails.

The door opened again and Tom came in carrying a tray, 'May sent you this, Annie.'

She looked up at him and smiled as he took off the cloth covering a steaming bowl of broth and brought it to her.

'You're like a little old man, Tom.' Her voice sounded strange to her, thin and flat.

'Remind me to put me shawl on next time,' he said, passing her a spoon. He sounded tired and sad.

'Don's back.' She took a sip though she was not hungry. She felt she would never want to eat again. The spoon felt heavy.

Tom looked up as Don came through. 'Glad to see you, Don.'

He smiled but looked at Annie in query as Don glowered back.

'He's just heard there's no money,' she offered.

Don came and propped himself up on the fender. 'So where are you going, Tom? Your Auntie May, I suppose?'

Tom nodded. 'I wanted to go with Annie.'

'I told him May would do a better job of looking after him. He wouldn't want to go to Albert's.'

Don drank his beer. 'He's all right you know. Don't know what you all go on about. He knows how to make money, not like . . .'

He stopped, aware that Tom and Annie were looking at him. He leant over and took the spoon off Annie. 'Let's have a bit of that,' he demanded.

'Only a bit,' said Tom. 'She hasn't eaten for ages.' Why did Don always come and shove his weight around? Couldn't he see Annie wasn't right. He was almost as tall at 11 as Don was at 15 but he was no match in weight. Don looked him over as he spooned another mouthful. Annie felt the tension between them.

'Let her have it,' Tom said, squaring his shoulders.

Annie's hand felt heavy as she reached forward and touched Tom's arm. 'Do you think May could run to a bit more for Don? He's had a long journey remember, he's tired and upset. Just pop round the corner to her, there's a good lad.'

She smiled at him and he looked at her, nodded and left. It was what she wanted but he was also scared.

Don grunted as he left.

She ate what she could before she passed it over to Don to finish up. 'I'm going to bed,' she said and did not come down again except for bread and dripping until the day of the funeral, though she did go into Tom's room whenever she heard him crying and she hugged him and told him everything would be all right. Think of the day at the beck – wonderful things do happen, she would say wishing she could believe this herself.

But he was the only da I had, Annie, he had wept, and she had almost felt the pain burst out of her into tears but it had not done so. Still there was this harsh blackness which choked her and which was shot through with great gusts of rage. She had patted him, hoping that, in May's husband, Tom would find a father who would treat him like a real son. She sent him over there after that.

She did not see Don until the funeral. He stayed with Albert and earned himself a bit of money helping in the shop, and she would not think of that.

Betsy called her down on the morning of the funeral. She polished the sideboard, dusted the table, flapped the curtains a little free of dust. Tom helped her put in the middle leaf of the table and they carried through the food and it looked like a feast. But the smell and sight did not tempt her to eat. She felt as though she wasn't really here, as though she was floating above it all but couldn't escape.

CHAPTER 8

The funeral was simple. It was cold and wet and Annie knew her feet were soaked and frozen standing in the earth at the edge of the coal-black hole and she felt grief give way to anger yet again. The graves looked pathetic, she thought viciously, just the two of them side by side in this poky corner to one side of the consecrated ground. Well, she hoped they were happy now, the two of them, wherever they were, because they'd sneaked themselves out of this beggar of a life very nicely thank you.

What about us, her mind challenged the yawning darkness as the coffin was sunk deep into the ground but she was suddenly too tired to work out any answers. She stood apart from the others, shoulders hunched and heard words solemn and deep-spoken by a vicar who could not say God, only Gond. Fancy choosing a man who stumbled over that word, she thought. His words went on and were licked away by the wind before they could settle. She preferred the silence which fell as they turned from the grave, from her parents and walked back through the narrow streets past neighbours who took off their caps and lowered their eyes. Another victim of the bosses, they thought and looked to the pit wheel in the distance which was still and quiet and had been since the owners had closed down the mine. They squatted down oblivious of the drizzle as the mourners arrived at the shrouded house. The ham tea was laid out in the dining-room.

Coats had been hung in the hall by Annie, and dripped on to the black and white tiles. Umbrellas, the few that there were, had been shaken and set in the stand. Sarah Beeston's was grey and stood out against the black of the others, and the clock just went on ticking, thought Annie, as she moved past it and through into the dining-room. A room she had never sat in before.

She slid into a chair, set round the polished dark table. The clink of glasses and murmur of voices washed over her. Tom squeezed her leg and she covered his hand with hers. Albert sat across from her, his face satisfied and for once not dour and bitter. Like the cat with the bleeding cream, she thought.

There were people she didn't know. God was there, of course, in the shape of Bob Wheeler who looked pale and stroked his moustache continually. Grief was on his face and Annie was strangely pleased that he mourned his friend. Next to him was Sarah Beeston. Annie had not known her as she climbed out of the taxi. She had arrived just in time for the service and had slipped into the back of the church and Betsy had nudged her. Thank your da's cousin for the gloves before she leaves, she'd said. She was tucking into the ham all right, saving herself a dinner when she got home, thought Annie, and my word, gets on well with God doesn't she. Sat at his right hand too. The vicar would like that, sat at the right hand of Gond the Father.

She put Tom's hand from her gently. 'Get on with your food,' she said quietly and rose. He was pale and shaken but wanted to stay next to her, so he rose also but she put out her hand to stop him, so he sat again and saw that the laughter, the smiles were growing now that the sherry was out. Annie could see Don swigging his back. He had been quiet at the graveside but now he was laughing with Albert and she wanted to bang their heads together but moved instead to the musty faded brocade curtains which had once been green, she knew, but now had no colour. Like the streets outside and the slag-heaps beyond and the distant laughter behind her. She gripped the curtain, dug her nails deep into it. How could the lost boys have come back to a world like this when they could have been free forever?

'Annie, bring the decanter over, pet, let your Uncle Albert have some of your father's whisky. Been a bit of a shock for the poor dear, hasn't it?'

Automatically Annie turned to fetch the whisky. Betsy looked flushed, her eyes were still red-rimmed. She had cried and howled and Annie had been surprised at her grief. It had a fierceness about it which was almost savage, more like a rage that had burst and could only be forced back bit by bit. Perhaps it was an overpowering anger and who could blame her. She had borrowed a dress from her friend, Ma Gillow, who lived on the corner and was here, stuffing her face as a reward. Bet's hands were permanent claw sausages in this weather and she was struggling to cut her ham. Annie moved across and did it for her. Poor bloody woman, she thought.

'And what about you, Joe dear? Will you have a sup of Scotch?'

Annie stood straight again, putting the knife on to Betsy's side-plate. She felt the anger stir again.

Yes, what about you, Joe dear, thought Annie. Coming back to get your feet under the table again are you, just as he planned. Nice and neat, Da, you were always nice and neat. Little letters to little people, but it's gone wrong and we are to go to places we don't like. There are some things you can't organise you know and other people's lives are one of them. One day I'll pay you back for what you've done, just you wait and see.

Betsy slapped her. 'For God's sake, hinny. Pass the decanter.'

It had been moved down here from his study and stood on the newly dusted and polished sideboard. The rich clean smell of polish lingered. Annie still had it on her hands from the waxed cloth. Not beeswax, Georgie Porgie, but it still looks good.

'It's all that's left of his good stuff,' minced Betsy to Ma Gillow. 'Wedding present, not ours of course, his first.' She pursed her lips and pressed her breasts up with her arms.

Annie felt the weight of the crystal solid in her hands and observed with mild interest the speed at which it dropped on to the floorboards. The nuggets of shattered glass exploded about her feet and were pretty as they reached the corners of the room. A room which was so beautifully silent now that she was able to watch the spreading stain loose it's amber tone and merge into the darkness of the floorboards in perfect peace. Tom flung down his napkin and left the table which was now beginning to seethe with outraged mutters.

'Don't worry, Annie.' He took her hands and understood her look of satisfaction as she stepped over the remains. He squeezed her hands.

There Da, she shaped. There is nothing left of you but a mucky floor and you never liked mess did you?

Her eyes were dry as they had been since his death and left Tom and looked beyond him at the table as she moved towards the door. Ma Gillow's mouth had fallen open. Albert was taking more sherry. Don was glowering at the loss of the family heirloom, she realised. God was still stroking his moustache and Sarah Beeston met her eyes and nodded her approval.

She started up the stairs. No loose ends now, Da, eh. There's even the redemption ticket for Don to reclaim the watch, but what about the running sore that twisted and clung throughout her body and wept with no sound. She walked along the passageway to the bathroom, looking curiously in the mirror at a face which had not changed. It was the same as last week and it should be so different.

Next morning her limbs were still heavy and her face was still stiff as though it had never been used. Even speech was an effort. Annie stood in the yard and heard no sounds beyond the yard gate, not the laughter that was pitched high by the crisp snow which she had watched falling throughout the night nor the scrunch of boots as they packed soft whiteness beneath their concerted march. She heard only the snuffling breath of the pony and saw the white vapour disperse gradually into the vast space beyond their two figures. The sun was bright and sharply etched the gables and the water tub, like one of Tom's charcoal drawings. The ice was loud in its breaking and reared sharp-pointed before settling in patterns around the rim. There were several shards, clear as diamond splinters, in the tin which was used to ladle water into Beauty's trough.

It had been difficult to pass from the crook of warmth against the pony's side not because of the cold but because her feet would only move if dragged forward by a demand she found she was reluctant to form, but the restless shift of Beauty's weight forced her.

His coat was dry but not unyielding and she stood again with her arm along his mane, her face pressed into his smell and his snorting and bubbling filled her world and she found a satisfaction in the sweep of his neck, the stretch of his throat as the water protested and swirled but was drawn in nevertheless. Even the ice was gone and all that remained was a long slick of saliva which hung from the left side of his mouth as he raised his head but this too lengthened and snapped as he coughed and shook.

'Bit cold was it, my pet?' she murmured. 'Sorry, lass.'

And she felt her voice begin to shake and at last there were tears in her eyes, then coursing down her cheeks. She should have warmed the water and she hadn't and now she wept, racking sobs which she knew were only partly for the pony and mainly for that lonely, wretched man who had been her father. In spite of herself she could feel his despair as it must have been, his hopelessness, but to leave her, to leave them all as he had done was not a clean death. She could not grieve for him properly because it was ruined by anger at his wanting to go and leave them all behind to continue a life he had found unbearable. She gripped Beauty's mane, gulping in air. Trying to stop. I am in despair too, she cried, but I want to go on living, fighting, getting out of here to something better. I just don't understand how you could do it. The pony pawed the ground and moved backwards, unsettled now, and Annie lifted her head from his neck, sniffing hard, forcing herself to smile, taking in a deep breath until the shuddering ceased. It seemed to take forever. She rubbed the pony's nose.

'I'm going today, Beauty, going to Albert. Tom'll take care of you. Probably do him good, give him something of his own. His Aunt'll let him come on his way to school. He'll want to see Betsy anyway.' Her lip trembled again as she remembered how Betsy had wept when Tom had left; she had leant on the door and sobbed a moaning sort of crying that went on and on until Annie had left the room. She knew that Tom had been crying too, from the set of his shoulders as he passed down the street, walking next to the cart that took his bed and mattress and a bundle of clothes. May's was only two streets away but to Betsy it must have seemed like the end of the world.

Again Annie felt the confusion of feeling, the pain that gave way again to rage this time because her da had killed himself and she and Tom had nowhere to live. He should have made sure Joe would have them before he did it. Then Tom wouldn't have to leave Betsy and she wouldn't have to go to Albert who couldn't wait for her to start, which filled her with foreboding because she had always felt he loathed her guts.

She heard the knocking on the gate and hid her face against Beauty as it opened. She did not want anyone to see that she had been crying.

'What are you doing there, lass? It's your death of cold you'll be catching.' Ma Gillow hurried on past. 'Come on in, for the love of God.' The kitchen door slammed behind her and her footprints were clouded by the scuffing of her long black skirt.

'Silly old fool. She's a witch you know, Beauty. Wears long skirts and reads tea leaves. I reckon the greedy old fag just fancies food and drink she hasn't paid for.'

She felt shaky still but more in control.

The back door opened again. 'Will you get in here now, Annie. Albert doesn't want no germs in his house and that's all you'll be taking him if you stay out there much longer.'

Annie heard the words but let them carry past her and disappear into a sky she now saw was blue. How strange to see that she thought. It was like seeing Grace's mam's primroses in the window-box telling you that spring had come. The streets wouldn't tell you in any other way.

'If you don't come in here, lass, I'll come out there and belt your hoity-toity backside. Thirteen and she thinks she's a bloody princess. It'll be the Prince of bleeding Wales she'll be escorting to the races next.' Raucous laughter greeted this sally and Betsy slammed the door again. There'd been more in Betsy's mug than tea this morning, Annie realised.

The long mane hairs caught round her fingers as she moved away and Annie was glad at their resistance to her going.

'I'll be back one day, my love,' she whispered.

They were bunched over the table as she had known they would be. Elbows planted and hands possessing steaming cups which they dropped their heads down to in a way which would have tightened her da's mouth but here her thoughts snapped shut and she fought against the sweat which seemed to swamp her body and the trembling which laid her open. Why couldn't Tom be here? Why couldn't Don have stayed a little longer? Don't think, don't think of anything except this minute. Look, there's Betsy staring at Ma Gillow.

She had passed her cup across and now her lower lip hung red and full and looked as though it would drool as it often did and Annie hoped it would not since the bread was just beneath her and she had not eaten yet. Quickly she slid on to the chair opposite Betsy and moved the bread but Ma Gillow was too close so she moved the chair further to the end, bringing the loaf with her. There was no hunger in her but it was important to prove she was untouched by sorrow. The bread was dry and her throat small but no one was watching anyway.

'What do you see, then?' Betsy breathed. Ma Gillow rotated

126

the cup, tilting it away, then setting it down. She pursed her mouth.

'Times is hard,' she announced and glanced at Betsy who sat back in her chair.

'You don't need to see that in the tea leaves, just step outside that door.' Betsy shifted with irritation. 'What about something special?'

'Nothing special today, Betsy lass,' she said flatly, pouring herself another cup.

Betsy pulled at her lip and wiped away a streak of ooze. She looked round the table. 'Well, what about Annie here? What about the skivvy job with Albert. Keen to have her he was, thank God. That Sarah Beeston didn't like it but he's family, you see. Is she going to do well? Tell you what, see if the School Board'll find out she's left before time. Should have done another two terms by rights but she's a big strong girl, ain't you, lass? Here, take another piece of bread.'

She broke off a piece of crust and pressed it into Annie's mouth. Annie felt sick.

'Give the lass a mug of tea, then we'll see.'

It was just half a cup and easily finished. Anything to be left in peace, Annie thought.

Ma Gillow looked at the leaves, turned the cup about and checked again. Her face was puzzled.

'Oh aye, she'll do well,' Ma Gillow murmured. 'Won't be with Albert mind. It'll be with your Tom, it will.'

But it was to Albert that Annie first went. Into the kitchen with its rank odour of damp and unwashed dishes and then systematically through the rest of his house which was behind and over the sweet-shop, for that was all he sold now, that and cigarettes. It was a shop that smelt of nice things. Liquorice that could be unwound from its shoelace packet and rewound round fingers. Good for bowels, Betsy would have said and nodded her approval. Sherbet which frothed and stung the tongue on lazy allotment afternoons. Victory cough-drops which burnt out the back of your throat making it impossible to cough or even breathe. No wonder they worked, Georgie had gasped one winter. They clear out the cough by burning out the whole of your inside. Nothing left to make a cough, is there?

The smells did not creep beyond the thick oak door which divided the shop from the house. Here there was a parlour along from the kitchen. It would only need a quick flick since the curtains stayed drawn to keep out the cold and Albert grunted that he never used it anyway. The outside privy was quite another matter though and the torn newspaper strung on an upturned hook broke through the grey apathy.

Skinflint, that's what you are, she seethed inwardly. Black ink on me bum as well as chilblains! He was no longer with her but had passed back through the kitchen without a word and then on through the door which opened on to cupboard stairs which wound up to the next floor. There was no light and no carpet and Annie felt her way up following the squeak and creak of his boots. We'll be a pair of Wee Willie Winkies up and down these stairs, holding a bloody candle, for there was no gas up here and she hadn't yet seen an oil lamp.

'Here's where I sleep and I likes it clean,' he wheezed.

It was a bare room looking out over the street with yellowed net curtains suspended halfway up on a horizontal wire. Nothing much else, just a bed and a chest with an oil lamp, thank goodness, and a hairbrush on top, though from the look of his thatch he wouldn't be needing that much longer.

Annie wondered how long the long-stroked strands would stay swept over the balding patch once a wind got up. She was standing close to him and disliked the old man smell which lingered wherever he was.

'Your room's up those stairs. I'll have tea at six when locking up's done, me supper's at nine and breakfast is half past six. I like it in a warm kitchen, mind.' His stare was hard and then he was gone.

There was another door on the half landing which, when opened, showed a further set of stairs. The plaster was crumbly beneath her touch and damp with spots of green and black mould, thicker at the bottom than the top. Tom would think this was one of his abstract masterpieces, she thought.

Annie quite liked the room with its small window which overlooked the street and a ceiling which followed the line of the eaves and ended halfway down the walls. Like her uncle's room, there was little in it, not even a net curtain or a chest. Not that anyone would be peeping in up here unless they were very desperate, she thought, or blind. The bed was small and not made up, but so what, she shrugged. Her bag took little room and she could put her da's watch on the floor. She had not wanted it but Don had left it in her room. It'll get nicked at the stables, he had said. She wanted nothing of her father's she had raged, but its usefulness overrode her anger and she was ashamed that pain could accommodate practicalities with such ease.

He was waiting for her in the kitchen, sprawled out in front of the fire in a chair. He kicked with his foot towards the coal-bucket. 'Put some more coal on and then fill the bucket.'

She leant over and dug the rusty shovel into the coal and tipped it on to the fire. She was aware of him watching, grinning. His lips drawn in a hard line which slightly opened over long yellow teeth. Like one of those pub dogs, she thought, but there was no smell of booze on Albert. So that makes a change, she thought. She began to pick the bucket up but Albert said:

'I'll have a cup of tea first.' She washed her hands, which were still winter raw, in the sink that had green slime beneath the tap where it dripped.

'There'll be no pay for you of course.' He was tapping his knee. 'Your keep and sixpence every two weeks. That's more than enough spending money for a bairn of your age.'

She wouldn't look round, she told herself and set her shoulders in a straight line.

Albert watched her. 'You'll get used to being a skivvy, looked down on wherever you go.' He licked his lips. 'Look at me when I'm talking to you.' His voice was rough, violent suddenly, and Annie turned, making herself do it slowly.

He was looking at her with a look of satisfaction.

'Looked down on all me life I was, by the likes of you and your da. And look where he ended up. Down the bloody spout leaving everyone to sweep up his messes.'

'I'm not one of his messes. I'm me own person,' Annie retorted hotly, her back to the sink. He surged forward in his chair, his face ugly. A strand of his long hair slipped off his pate. She gripped the draining board, determined not to flinch. Bloody old fool, she said to herself, trying to control her fear. He was so big.

'You listen to me girl. You're my person now. I bloody own you. And what would he think of that, the blue-eyed boy, the father's pet.' His voice was grinding the words out. His finger was stabbing the air but he had come no closer.

'He had brown eyes, and I'm me own person,' Annie repeated, not understanding his hatred. He's barmy, she thought. She rushed on, 'I can go into service anywhere I like. I don't have to stay here. I'd have a starched pinny an' all.'

He laughed at her then and sank back into his chair. The room seemed lighter all of a sudden.

'Oh no, you slaggy little bitch. That you can't. Not at your age. You should be in school, so no one would touch you with a barge-pole. You'd better wake up to the fact that no one wants you. Joe don't and Sarah bloody Beeston can't. I won't let her, you're mine, see. You're mine to clean up me mess. At last it's my turn, you see, and I've waited a long time for it too, one of his brats skivvying for me.' He was shouting now, leaning forward with his hands between his knees. They hung down with big knuckles.

'You wait then, just wait until . . .'

'Just get me tea, for God's sake,' he interrupted, and pulled himself out of his chair. She braced herself for a blow but he pushed passed her and opened the door into the shop.

'Bring me tea out to the shop,' he grunted, 'and remember to keep your mouth shut. You've got more wind than sense and you'll have to learn to keep your place like the rest of us had to, all but your bleeding da.' He slammed the door behind him.

'I'll make good and sure none of me precious sixpence goes into your till, anyway, you miserable old bugger,' she hissed, but not loud enough for him to hear. She felt better for fighting him but there was no doubt who had been the winner. So, she thought as she filled the kettle, her da had rattled the old misery's cage good and proper and it looked as though she was going to have to pay the price. Her stomach tightened and she was afraid.

That night, when she was in bed and the chores were finished, she let the tears come again. She had decided, before she left for Albert's, that she would only cry in bed at night. That she would live her life in sections until the pain had eased and was not a constant ache which covered everything in a dull grey. She would keep her da in the black box with the blue-veined legs, tight shut it would be, right at the back of her mind.

She had been pleased to fight her uncle. She had been pleased to feel frightened because it meant that she was not dead inside. The house was quiet, there was no rustle from a bedroom that had been Tom's, no hug goodnight from him. She drew the bedclothes over her head and thought how, on her Sunday off, she would go to Grace's and they would fetch Tom and walk and talk, but not about her da. They would walk past the church along the graveyard and listen to the bells as the ringers practised. Annie forced herself to think of the sound which was one that she loved, but which Grace said drove her da mad, which was a shame because they lived just round the back of the church.

She felt her limbs going loose and stretched her legs down into the cold part of the bed. If I live from Sunday to Sunday it will be all right. As long as I see them Sunday, it will be something to hang on for.

Her jaw was slackening now and sleep would not be far off and she wondered whether they would see Don again soon. He had said not to bank on it, he had a lot of rides coming up. He might write.

CHAPTER 9

'I'm off now, Uncle,' she called behind her, expecting no answer and receiving none. The spring evening was fresh but milder than it had been for what seemed like years. It was Sally's party and she hoped her hands were not too red and chapped, but in any case her cardigan was too big and the cuffs sat low on her hands hiding her wrists. She liked it better loose than tight and the stars were making her feel good to be free but how would it be meeting the others after all this time? She had seen Grace of course but no one else. She had not wanted to see them after the funeral and even less when she was up to her elbows in Albert's dirty drains but Sally had seen her in the corner shop and insisted she come. Nice that was, Annie thought. She'd always been a bit flighty at school but she had been kind.

Come over Friday, Annie, she'd said, we haven't seen you for, what is it, four months. Most of the lads will be there but not too many girls. Scared, I expect, or their mums are anyway, can't think of what, she'd giggled and nudged. Anyway, no one sitting at home to make a prig of you, is there, Annie, and Annie had smiled at the bobbing yellow curls as they minced away but wondered at the ache the words had caused.

Sally lived a mile away and the evening was fading fast as she walked through the streets. She could hear the shouts of children in the back alley and had to dodge a group of boys as they kicked a ball.

There was noise but not much light coming into the yard from Sally's kitchen window. Annie dropped behind the privy, changing her boots for the sandals she had carried in newspaper. She stuck the boots in the corner where they were hidden by the shadow and walked on feet that felt as though they were bulging grotesquely between taut straps. Her feet and legs were bare and she hoped no one would notice feet that were puffing out of shoes a size too small and being rubbed red by the straps.

She had not noticed she had grown so since last year. She certainly hadn't got much of a bosom or a bum yet. From the back or front she still looked like an errand-boy, or so Ma Gillow had said when she came into the shop for two pennyworth of glucose drops the other week. For the indigestion, she had offered, as she poked her nose further into everything.

At her knock, the door opened. 'Come in, lass.' Sally pulled her in and shut the door. Her long ear-rings were dangling nearly to her shoulders, Annie thought, and matched her red dress and red shoes. Sally was laughing to someone over her shoulder and pointed Annie to the table which held some beer and lime cordial. 'All right, I'm coming,' she called to the boy who was tugging at her arm. She raised her eyebrows at Annie and giggled, 'He's so impatient,' and turned from her and was gone into the bobbing shapes which circled and flowed and filled the room.

The room was lit only by a low oil lamp but the heat was oppressive. Her feet throbbed and her eyes took in no one person but filled themselves with the hissing phonograph, and the movement which had swallowed Sally completely.

She edged sideways to the table wanting to choose the lime but the jug was full so no one else had. She poured a beer. She stood with her back against the wall which ran on from the sink and smiled, feeling her face widening and stiffening. She held the glass with both hands to stop the trembling and still it was as though she had not entered, for the movement continued unchecked and bodies flowed amongst it, their mouths working but the sound milling with the greater noise through which laughter threaded like the pink silk borders on Auntie Sophie's antimacassars. Annie fixed and held her smile while she brought the glass to her lips. Aunt Sophie; why had she not thought of her for so long? But here was warmth like those days which were now blurred and distant.

It wasn't so bad at Albert's now, she thought. He had stopped his shouting and seemed to have accepted that he couldn't make her cry so he just made her work harder instead and that seemed to satisfy him. He didn't hit her now, just took away her sixpence if she cheeked him, so she didn't. Just kept her mouth shut and hated him. She did not cry every night now, either. It still swept over her like a storm but far less often and she had worked out how she could snatch an extra moment with Tom when she was supposed to be fetching a drop of dripping from the corner shop. She'd rush to the school and they would walk home to May's together, her arm would rest on his shoulders, but only just, for he seemed to have sprouted and thickened since he had been there. It was amazing what six months could do, she thought. They would laugh or be silent together and she would tell him she was all right, as happy as he was at May's.

When they arrived at May's he would plead for her to come in and May too, but she never did. It looked too warm, too happy and she was afraid that if she saw what life could be like then she would cry in front of him.

She looked down at the beer, away from the circling laughter, and took a sip. It was sour and harsh and stung her throat and she felt the retch begin but pressed the cold glass hard to her lips and forced it down, feeling the sweat break out under her arms. She pressed her elbows to her sides. For God's sake, don't lift your arms, bairn, she ordered herself, mimicking Don, you'll bring down the wallpaper. It made her laugh and the tightness at the base of her neck softened and she felt her body ease. The music seemed louder now and the sink she leant against was cold and her smile became easy and meant but still at no face which sought her out.

Figures whirled past, some very close together, but still moving in time to the music. Snatches of conversation escaped to float past her.

'They'll get in this time. There'll be a Labour government, you mark my words,' merged with soft dance-time. 'They'd better, things won't improve under this little lot. We need improved dole if more bloody pits are closing and the shipyards.'

She hummed to herself to drown the talk which was the same, day and night, on every street corner where men squatted on their hunkers or stamped from foot to foot in the cold. 'Nothing else would matter in the world today, we would go on loving in the same old way,' she mouthed the words now. Not tonight, no politics tonight.

'Burns your tonsils out, Don used to say.'

The boy was broad and shut out the dancers from her. In the dim light she saw large black eyes with lines which deepened as he smiled at her. He was tall now for a Geordie, not as wiry as most, and his voice had deepened, but not changed. His smile still turned up on one side.

'You've grown, lad. I would hardly have recognised you.' It was Georgie. He reached forward and stroked her cheek with one finger. She wanted to be like a cat and wind herself round his hand.

'I'd have recognised you anywhere, hinny. You've barely grown at all.'

Try telling that to me feet she thought and forced more beer down to prove that she was nearly 14 and was glad when the noise hid the explosion and Georgie's handkerchief dried her eyes and dress. Then she could breathe again.

She laughed before he could, but he did not. People danced to a quickened tempo, they jostled closer to her. Georgie moved to shield her.

'Takes time to get used to, beer does. Come and have a dance.'

He smelt of the mines. It was a hard smell and Annie was surprised since it was all that was strong and big and adult to her. His hand was hard, unlike the hand that had beaten coins and created daisy-chains when summers were hot and Annie knew that time had passed, years had passed, but inside she felt just the same, just as far away from everyone. His arm was loosely round her waist and his breath was faintly beery on her forehead and she could think of nothing to say.

She had not danced before but she had watched and now followed his slight sidesteps tensely. He had hairs on his upper lip which were downy and his neck was thick and she liked his collar with its top button undone. She could feel that his chest was warm beneath his shirt and she was proud to be dancing with Georgie and felt her flesh melt in a way which was peculiar to her. She wanted to flow all over and into him but that was just plain daft. Still Georgie had not spoken but his head dropped on to the top of her hair gently, and he pulled her closer.

'You're such a bonny lass,' he murmured and she felt the tingle through each of her limbs. Should she say something?

She did not know. She could see and hear the other dancers but they did not intrude.

'It's been a long time since you were in the gang, bonny lad,' she replied and shook her head when he asked if she had seen Don. 'I see Grace and Tom every week though,' she said. 'Don has a lot of rides and rides are money.' She raised her eyebrows and they both laughed. She barely noticed the pain in her feet when he walked her home still in her sandals because she felt too ashamed to collect the boots from their hiding-place.

The bed was cold but she could still feel his head on hers and you're a bonny lass, he had said. On the way home they had held hands and she would not wash that hand just yet in case it removed the feel of him. Georgie had kissed her softly and gone, his face wet from the drizzle and until then she had not realised there was any. He had said nothing about seeing her again but she wondered what had filled her thoughts before the shape of his face and the sound of his voice had soaked into every space of her being.

In the morning, the sun was shining though it was a bitter grey dawn and Albert wanted his egg.

'We'll be needing some more coal soon, Uncle,' she said as she poured his second mug of tea. He did not look up from spooning out the runny yolk with a jagged piece of crust. It dripped on to the plate, hardened and darkened.

'I'll need to go out later for a bit of sugar, Uncle.'

'Don't be long about it. I want me dinner on time and there's work you can be doing. Take a walk up to the slag later. Pick out some coal.' He threw down his spoon. 'Just hope this new idea of that flabby fool Baldwin will stop the strikes now. Business is bad.' He pointed his toast at her. 'Longer hours and less pay, that's all they got for their troubles last time and when their money goes down, so does mine.' He pushed his chair back. 'High time they brought in something to stop their nonsense and thank God they've done it. Trade Disputes Act, they call it. High-faluting name but it'll stop sympathy strikes and reduce picketing. That'll sort the buggers out.'

As he rose he said, 'Can't beat the owners, you remember that. And what am I?'

Annie said as she had done many times before:

'You're an owner, Uncle.'

'And what's an owner?'

'An owner is a boss.'

'And what do bosses do?'

'Hire and fire, Uncle.' And stuff their bloody faces with eggs that'd be a bloody banquet for most of them round here. Her face was set. She would never look at him because she knew it made him feel as though he wasn't winning.

'Just you remember that. If you want a job, you have to do as you're told. That's one lesson we should all 'ave learnt by now.' He pulled out his handkerchief and wiped his nose. He dropped it on the floor, watching it as it fell. 'Boil that up today.'

He pushed past her to the door. 'You're lucky to have such a tolerant boss, Annie. Work, that's how you survive these days.'

She shook her hand at his back as he shut the door. And lending money out and adding on a power of interest, you bloody old skinflint. Don't think I don't know all about it. You're a blood-sucking scrooge. She picked up the handkerchief with the shovel and poker and heaved it on to the fire. It might mean a clout but it would be worth it, to show him he didn't treat her like that. Today it didn't matter anyway.

The boots were still there in the corner, the newspaper was soggy from the thawed early spring frost and fell away as she lifted them but she did not put them on although her toes were numb, neither did she hurry as she walked back from Andover Street and shopped at the corner near Wilson Terrace. Georgie lived near here and just maybe she might see him when he came off the midday shift.

The walk home was long because he was not to be seen although the whistle had blown at the pit for the shift end. The sandals found new areas to rub and she tottered into the yard, the sugar heavy in her hand and he was there, leaning against the shed rolling a Woodbine, his face black from the pit, his cap on the back of his head. Annie knew her nose was red and her legs mottled by now without stockings. She was joyous and ashamed.

The yard broom had slipped down the wall by the corner of the privy and she set it back in its place. The mortar was crumbling between the bricks and flakes fell where she had disturbed it.

'The pit needed pudding and pie today, then,' she called and marvelled at these words which came from herself and sounded quite calm.

He moved from the wall, settling his cap more firmly on his head.

'Never change, our little Annie, do you?' he drawled.

This time she could not answer because the words would have found no way to squeeze through the swelling in her throat. Our Annie he had called her.

'Here, try this then.'

The finished cigarette was thin and flopped in the middle with tobacco straggling from either end. It was still damp from his lick down one side and smelt like her father's pipe. The taste though of the dark brown shreds was sharp and bitter and when he lit it the paper flared, her mouth opened and it dangled helplessly from her lower lip quite unalight. He reached out and between strong square thumb and forefinger gently peeled it off her lip without tearing the skin.

'Like this, pet,' he said and placed it between his lips which were pink on the inside but otherwise dust-covered to blend with his face. He lit it with a match picked from amongst others, red-tipped and pale-stalked. The sulphur scent lingered long after the hiss of striking until the mellow breath of lit tobacco replaced its odour. He was the most beautiful creature Annie had ever seen.

'Now breathe this in as though you are sucking them corn stalks we used to pick up peas.'

Sharp and burning was the drawn breath but his lips had held it as hers were now doing so heaven was in every puff.

'Where's me bloody lunch and put that fag out of your mouth or I'll belt your behind, you lazy little strumpet.'

The door slammed behind Albert as he withdrew his head and the noise of the back alleyway came alive and the yard looked small again.

He grinned and lazily pushed his bike to the gate.

'See you, bonny lass, and don't burn his bread and cheese.'

How had she never noticed his eyes were brown and his lashes as thick as the hedgerows along by the beck?

Before he rode away, he turned. His face no longer smiling. 'You tell me if he ever hurts you, Annie.' He hesitated, his foot on the cobbles, steadying the bike. 'I won't have anyone hurt you.'

The days passed in a rapid pulse of waiting and being with him. The summer evenings were lazy and long and the fish shop had a lamp-post which had known Tom's swing-rope and now knew their shoulders well. Around their feet the crumpled paper blew and she failed to notice when a scattered sheet would catch against her legs until tugged further by the breeze. Until nine at night she was Albert's, after that she was Georgie's and the gang's. Albert had said she could do whatever she liked and Annie had been deflated; she had expected a battle but he had merely shrugged. Your da wouldn't have liked it, he had grunted and turned again to his paper.

When Georgie was on late shift she still passed along Mainline Terrace on shoes bought from Garrod's used goods shop and lolled and laughed but did not soar and felt tired when she was the last to be dropped at home because no parent would be breathing fire and threatening damnation of bairns of 14 walking home late with lads of 16 at well past the time decent folk were in their beds. Aye, but when the lad was there, then was the time for flights of pleasure as rough hands held hers and arms which thickened daily with twisting muscle lightly pulled her to him and she was special.

The hours merged into softly breathed air and mirth which melted one girl into one boy and they strolled with occasional words the longest way to the door, then long, closed-mouth, breath-held kisses left her yearning and bereft to see him go. Annie knew he was her summer sun and the only reason she drew breath and that no one in the entire world had felt as she did.

On Sundays, they would collect Tom and Grace and stroll to the beck with Beauty. She was too small for any of them now but still kept Tom in liquorice and pink mice with her manure and nuzzled Annie as she lounged on the bank. Sometimes Georgie would have some honeycomb and they would lick and suck the honey. They watched one day as Georgie and Mr Thompson smoked out the bees to lift the combs and Annie had never known such fear for another person as when the bees attacked their covered figures. Later she had dabbed bicarbonate of soda on Georgie's arms where he had red stings up to the elbows. He had brought it in a screw of paper and she used the hem of her skirt, dampened in the beck to whiten the lumps. The swellings were large and angry but he had never referred to them again that day.

Life's too short, he would always say, it's for enjoying, Annie. There's so much to look at, to find out. And he would kiss her and Tom would look at Grace and they would raise their eyes and pull a face.

Tom always brought his pad and would sketch and draw the changing season or the fly agaric toadstool which grew under the birches, marking in the white warts on the scarlet cap, and which Georgie explained he must never eat because of the poisons it contained. Or the speckled wood butterfly which Georgie showed him on a sun-spotted leaf. Or the foxglove with its tuber-shaped flowers drooping on one side of the stem only and which Georgie told him contained digitalis which doctors used to heal hearts. Tom had said that Georgie and Annie should have a bit of that since their hearts seemed to be all over the place.

Grace pulled a face when he picked her feverfew for her headache and made her eat it. Her headache disappeared.

Summer turned to autumn and winter sharpened the air. Grey overlaid blue warmth but Annie saw only sun and butterflies dancing. She answered an advertisement for a housemaid now that she was 14 but was refused because Albert would not give her a reference. She would go on trying always though, in spite of his rantings. You're mine, I've told you once, he had growled, and she did not tell Georgie what had been said but instead allowed her thoughts to fly high above the cracked ice of the lavatory pan and the soda fumes as she prodded and plunged with the long-handled brush.

I bet he even looks a cracker with his trousers round his ankles and sheets of newspaper in his hand she thought and pulled her sleeves down as far as she could to stop the chapping as the wind tore into every crevice.

But winter passed, then spring and summer waned into a gentle August and she was pleased when he rolled up, with quick deft fingers, his shirt sleeves and she saw his strength. The movement of his muscles held her eyes and quickened her breath and tears seemed close but why they should hover and return she could not understand.

'Tell you what,' he said, as they walked home late one night. 'On your birthday we'll go as far from here as we can and not come back until the end of the day. How's that then?'

Annie had forgotten there was anything else apart from these streets.

'Will we walk then or go by train?' she asked. 'Shall we take Tom?'

He squeezed her to him and she fitted in with his stride.

'No, this time we won't take Tom,' he said. 'And you just wait and see where we go and how we go. That's part of the surprise.'

'Great God almighty,' she gawped. 'There's no way, no way, my lad, I'm getting on that.'

He laughed as he pushed the cycle at her, propping his own against the wall of the yard. They were standing in the alleyway at the back of the shop. 'You'll get on and bloody well like it. I'll hold the saddle, you just peddle and steer.' He put down his bait-bag because he had brought the picnic with him.

'Peddle and bloody steer,' she panted, as they went down the alley for the fifth time, rushing past back gates, dodging the central gulley. It was coming but he had to start her on the saddle and push her fast or it was without hope. One hour later, they were ready to go.

'Just follow me and do what I do,' he told her, bringing his bike alongside. 'And don't fall off because the beer's in your basket and I'll tan you proper if you break it!'

They laughed and he bent forward and kissed her cheek and was off. She followed. It was good but the cobbles rattled her teeth and made the beer chatter. His jacket was flying wide as he turned yet another corner and jumped off, putting out a hand to steady her halt. They were surrounded by piles of coal waiting for shipment to the ports.

'Into the station now, we'll put the bikes in the van.'

Annie remembered the steaming of that other train, but here the sun was shining and the gap between platform and train held no fear for her. She held his arm, pulling him to a stop as they walked down the platform to a carriage.

'Tell us where we're going, Georgie.'

'We are going to the seaside.' He grinned and kissed her face and loved her.

She remembered the colourless pictures on that other train and her heart sank.

The train jerked and spat and roared and pulled and stopped and left them on the quiet Northumbrian coast. The bikes beat into the wind and her hair whipped across her face and she saw more sky than she had dreamed existed and forgot the pictures.

The pale white sand ran out from the creeping blackness of the coal-spoilt beaches and swept round the endless sea in a curve that was clean and quiet. The waves left bubbles as they ran away from her feet which clenched at the sand; the sea, determined in its greed, plucked and sucked from beneath her. Her legs stung as the salt dried and Georgie stood smoking back at the couch-grass-tipped dunes. She knew no haste because this moment had been here for ever for the sea and would be here long after she had left. Waiting, always waiting; the sea, the wind, and the shriek of the gulls too, proved how little anything mattered as it rolled and swept away every imprint.

'Look, Georgie,' she called, trailing and pulling through soft shifting sand until her calfs dragged and her breath rose in pants. 'There's no sign of me down there and I've only just turned me back.'

He was down on his hunkers now and his eyebrows were raised.

'They throw the tiddlers back, you know. Just not enough meat on you, lass, to do more than just tickle it a bit.'

She was nearing the dune now. 'I'll show you I have grown enormously since last year.' She drew herself up in the wind which dragged her clothes tight against her form. Her nipples challenged by the cold stood proud on small firm breasts and she laughed down into his eyes, her hands on narrow hips, half child, half woman and Georgie felt a thickening in his throat.

He turned to watch the white caps behind her and pulled on the Woodbine which burnt fast as the wind rushed in gusts around them. Annie could smell the smoke but not see it. It was snatched and thrown into nothingness and she tipped her head back.

'Wouldn't it be wonderful, Georgie, to be like the wind. It's just as it is, no memories to carry with it, no rules to heed. Just free.'

'Come and sit down, you daft fool. Wrap yourself round this ham roll, it'll do you more good than standing there catching your death. Some memories are good. I need mine.'

The hollow-sided dune was quiet after the buffeting wind and surging water and Annie felt the tightening of her skin as her feet dried. Holding the roll in one hand, she scooped sand up in the other and let it fall through her fingers and then lay back on one elbow.

'But what about the bad things, how do you stop them creeping back?'

'You don't. You just clobber them, see them for what they are and throw them out again. You don't run away from them. Have some beer.' He passed her the bottle and she took just a sip. He was watching her.

'What if you can't do that?' The beer had left a thick warm taste.

He tilted his head back and took a drink. His throat was bulging up and down. He wiped his mouth with the back of his hand, then looked at her.

'Then you learn to do it.' He dug the bottle into the sand to hold it firm, then leaned forward and rubbed her feet until there was warmth. He was never cold. In all the time she'd known him he had never felt cold, she thought. She watched him as he lay on his side like her, propped up on his elbow.

'Does your mam scrub your back, Georgie, when you get home from the pit?' She couldn't look at him while she asked, she was too conscious of the line of his body, the way his leg lay partly on hers.

'Aye, and me brothers an' all, them that's in work that is.'

'Do you like the pit then, Georgie? Don said he'd never go down but that was me da telling him.'

The gulls were wheeling above and Georgie threw the remains of his roll far down the beach and they shrieked and clustered around it.

'I don't remember me ma or da ever talking to me about it. The pits are there, the slags are there, getting higher every year, slipping further down towards the houses in the wet. Each day me da went to the pit, me brothers went and so now I go and every evening so far we've come back. We've been lucky. It's all just there, Annie.'

He reached over and stroked her arm and her softness amazed him yet again.

Annie persisted. 'Well, do you like the pit then, Georgie?'

And he said all he could for the moment. 'What's liking got to do with anything, our Annie? The pit's there, me da was a pitman, I'll be a pitman, our kid'll be a pitman. There's nothing else round here.'

Annie felt the thudding shock in her stomach. Georgie looked at her with his smile hooked up at one side but his eyes anxious.

'How'd you like to scrub me back in front of our own fire then, bonny lass?' He ran his finger slowly round her lips.

She caught his hand and pressed it to her mouth.

'When?' she said, her voice muffled.

'When you're 16, if the old skinflint'll let you go, but then I'll just have to make him.'

His voice was soft, he was laughing, his brown hair was lifting in the slips of wind which dropped before being forced upward and through the pale dry green grasses on the encircling sand-solid slope and then his eyes became dark and the laughter left them. His mouth was still, his hands were gripping hers.

'I love you, little Annie. Shall we be together, you and me?'

'Yes,' she said and sat within the curve of his arm.

The day sped by in thoughts and words and skin held close together and his hands were firm not rough as he stroked the length of her body and she was not cold without clothes and there was no mark of coal on his. But there were scars where jutting rock had torn and sliced into the hard muscle of his back or the rounded curve of his shoulder and she kissed the raised and shining wounds.

His scent was sweet and strong in the curve of neck and shoulder and grew stronger as beads of sweat pricked up through his skin and his breath grew short and rapid. She had never seen a naked man before and the sense of his power made her pull him closer, ever closer, feeling him against her, his heat, his strength, until he threw himself away. And Annie lay alone and cold, his weight pinioning her arm into the shifting sand while the other chilled without the warmth of his body. Her body, so unhidden, lay open to the sky. She wanted to moan because it was unfinished, incomplete. She curled up to watch his stillness.

'Put your clothes on, hinny.' His back was to her, his voice was strained.

She pulled her arm free and still with no words pulled on first her pants, then her stockings which were warm with the same hole in from this morning and her dress whose button-holes seemed clearer than before. The third one had frayed so that the stitching hung limp and useless from the bottom end and finally her cardigan which was smooth and wrapped her away into herself again.

She sat with her hands clasping her knees, her face pressed hard down against them and they tasted salty, not of herself as they should. Her mind would hold no thoughts and her mouth no words and all she could hear was the roaring and threshing of waves which followed no pattern.

He was beside her now, his arm around her shoulders, his head on hers and their tears came quickly as her face pressed into his neck.

'We don't want a bairn yet, you're no more than one yourself, my little Annie. We must wait.'

The sun lowered itself enormously into the sea, red with effort, as they pushed the bikes on to the road and the uncertain dusk helped them to see each other's presence but not their eyes or mouths which still trembled. The train was crowded with last-minute returners so still they had time to pause and fit each fragment of themselves into a whole that felt something like it had once done, only better.

'Race you home, our Annie,' Georgie called as they left the station and, closeted by the street lamps, they laughed again and sang again and then lapsed silent for the lights were on in Albert's kitchen and they stood still, for he was always asleep when they returned.

'I'll come in with you,' he said and took her arm but before they reached the door it opened.

'And what time do you both call this for coming home?' It was a woman's voice. 'Come in this minute, Annie, and I will see your friend here at ten o'clock sharp.'

Annie hung back. She could picture the grey umbrella in the hall-stand on that wet funeral day. Georgie looked at her, confusion in his eyes.

'It's Sarah Beeston,' Annie said. 'She gives me gloves.'

He reached past her and took the handlebars. 'I'll come in with you, pet.' He spoke firmly.

'No need for that,' Sarah's strong voice answered. 'I've never been known to eat people and I doubt whether I shall start now. It would probably give me fearful indigestion at this time of night.' She had appeared full in the doorway now, standing quite still. They could not make out her face because she was standing with her back to the light.

Georgie touched Annie's hair with his fingers, then cradled her head against his hand. She leant into the caress. 'Will I see you tomorrow?' she asked, not wanting him to move from her side. This he sensed and turned back to the figure in the doorway.

'I'll be coming in with her, if that's all right with you.' He was already taking the bikes and propping them against the side wall.

'Very well,' Sarah said. 'Come in both of you.'

She spun back into the house and light fell out into the yard. Annie took Georgie's hand, lifting her eyebrows and shrugging at his silent question.

The fire was banked up in the kitchen and Sarah Beeston pointed to the chairs around the table and sat in one at the head. Georgie took his cap off and stuffed it in his pocket, steered Annie to a chair and took one himself.

'Now,' said Sarah. 'Here's tea. I was just pouring one for myself. Your uncle, Annie, I am pleased to say, is now in bed, though there will be more to discuss in the morning, I am quite sure.'

She sat back, her calm eyes watching them as they watched her. Her suit was black with a straight skirt and she had a white blouse on that had no frills but she was not pretty, neither was she ugly. She was strong, decided Annie and her apprehension grew. The mug was hot between her hands. She took a sip.

'It won't do, you know, Annie, all this running riot until the early hours. In fact none of this will do.' She swept her hand round the kitchen.

It looked clean enough to Annie. She had a clout if it wasn't. The fender was shiny, the sink was clean with no trace of slime. The table was scrubbed. There was mould on the walls at the bottom but that was because Albert would not pay for any whitewash.

'It won't have to for long,' Annie answered, adding to herself – and what business is it of yours anyway? The steam wafted into her face as she sipped. She looked over her mug at Georgie and smiled.

Sarah's eyes were steady as she looked at them both. They seemed painfully young, as of course they were. Annie was just 15 and Georgie, for that was the name her informant had given her, could not be more than 17. Well, she thought, I wonder what our Annie has decided she's going to do with her life, because she was very sure it was not what she, Sarah, intended and so she asked her.

'And why is that, might I ask?'

'Because we shall marry when I am 16 and leave anyway.'

Sarah watched her sit back, pleasure at her statement evident on every line of her face and body. She knew it was not unusual for early marriages up here and in the mining communities of Wales, just as the areas bred young militants, but this girl was not going to be one of those young brides. She, Sarah Beeston, who had watched from a distance her childhood turn into youth and her youth into blossoming womanhood was not going to be held back from putting this girl into an arena where she could choose what sort of a life she wanted rather than one which seemed the better of two evils. Thank God for Bob Wheeler who had written to her, as she had asked him to, at the funeral. Tell me if there seems to be a problem she had said, when she was baulked yet again of taking custody of her cousin's child. Don, she had decided, was well able to look after himself. He had seemed to know precisely where his future lay when she had spoken to him at Archie's funeral. With himself in the main, she thought, and everybody else could go hang. She shook her head again at the suspicion that he and Albert were pretty much alike.

She had always thought that Albert was as he was because of the favouritism shown to Archie but Don had had two parents who doted on him and it appeared that still his God was himself and damn the rest. Perhaps therefore it was after all a family trait that reared its head whatever the circumstances. She wondered if it was inherent in Annie. It would be interesting to find out because, if it was, she felt sure it was in a form that would encourage survival of the spirit, but not at the expense of others.

She had called in on Betsy before she came here. She had been sitting by the fire sewing whilst Joe had been doing the books at the kitchen table. It had seemed that at last that poor unfortunate woman had a modicum of contentment, but was the loss of a son too high a price she wondered? Betsy had made her a cup of tea. Sarah looked down at the one which was in her hand; she felt full with the liquid and longed for the Earl Grey which Val made at home in Gosforn.

She had explained to Betsy what she intended for Annie and

147

Betsy had nodded. Annie deserves better than Albert, she had said, with a hard look at Joe who was oblivious as he reckoned up his day's takings. Take her away she had said to Sarah. I couldn't do anything for her, maybe you can.

So here she was now, she thought, and focussed again on Annie. Marry, indeed. Not yet, not while she still had breath in her body.

'I think not, Annie. I would like you to come and live with me in Gosforn, go back to school and have the opportunity to make something of yourself.'

There was a stricken pause and Sarah saw shock in both their faces.

'I'm bloody not coming with you.'

Georgie sat and waited.

'Albert and I have decided that you are to come and live with me and somehow I shall produce something that your poor father would have been proud of.' Sarah poured herself another cup of tea, not because she wanted one but because the scene she had had with Albert still made her want to castrate the man.

He had allowed her in, though he had recognised her immediately and no doubt remembered that she had been against him taking Annie after Archie's death. She had bowed then to the fact that he was a closer relative and that it might be better for Annie to remain in an environment she was familiar with after such a bereavement. And indeed Annie did seem inordinately attached to her step-brother which Sarah could understand. She herself was no advocate of blood ties automatically ensuring compatibility and the fact that Tom and Annie had chosen to cement a close step-relationship through choice not expectation was altogether laudible. That relationship, Sarah had felt, would help her more than anything. The fact that she now had a boyfriend did not bode so well, especially as Albert was allowing the child to run riot as well as mistreating her.

Bob Wheeler, God bless his upright soul, had discovered all this for her. He had been attached to Archie and had always felt in some way responsible for his death, though why, Sarah could not imagine. He had taken it upon himself to write with regular reports of Annie's well-being and had become concerned at gossip and rumour which seemed to indicate neglect and perhaps violence. Sarah had received the last of these yesterday, had arranged leave from her job in the solicitor's office where she worked and driven over.

Albert of course had blustered and created but Sarah had seen his type before. Out of my way, she had said, as he tried to prevent her coming further into the house, or I shall get the law on to you.

His mouth had fallen open, she recalled, and what a mouth it had been. Very few teeth and what there were would not invite closer examination.

This child that you have living with you, she had begun, stripping her gloves off and sitting by the fire, in his chair, she hoped. I shall take her with me tomorrow, you have done quite enough damage.

She remembered his mouth, opening and shutting and the abuse which had been hurled from it had been quite entertaining.

That's quite enough of that, she had said. Annie is to come with me now.

She can't, he had said, moving in towards her. She had learnt self-defence years ago and had been totally unperturbed. Albert was a bully and would not attempt any violence on a grown person she had been quite sure, and if he did, she would make short work of him. He had quite a beer paunch on him and looked flabby.

She had allowed the tirade to go on for quite some time; it so often defused a situation, she felt. It was amazing how many aggressive husbands, being sued for divorce, entered the office and then left, mild as lambs, after expelling a great deal of hot air.

Albert, of course, had not wanted Annie to leave. She's mine, she remembered he had kept saying. But, Sarah Beeston had said, she is nobody's but her own. She is old enough to leave you and if you make a fuss I shall call the police and explain to them that you initially employed Annie as an under-age servant, and what is more, subjected her to considerable abuse, is that clear? She had stood up at that point and he had actually stepped back.

In fact she was not too sure of her rights in the case but how was he to know that. She would check when she arrived back at the office.

He had told her to get out and she had said certainly not, not until Annie was home, then they would both remove themselves in the morning. It would be an uncomfortable night on a chair for her, but she had known worse. But now, back to the matter in hand, she thought.

Annie had been looking at Georgie, drinking him in and he had kissed her hand and smiled.

'Me da gave me nought to be proud of,' she said. 'He was a bloody fool who stuffed himself with gas to save getting on with it.' Annie was fighting for her life now, her fists were clenched and she was standing, leaning forward, her chin tilted, spitting out the words at Sarah.

Sarah applauded her courage, aware that, inside that rigid body, a heart thought it was breaking and who knows, it might have been.

'Sit down, Annie, let me talk to you both.' Sarah stirred her tea and her voice was gentle; she was moved by this child more than she cared to show.

Georgie was waching her closely, she saw, and he put out his hand and held Annie's arm. 'Sit down Annie, let's hear what –' she saw him hesitate. 'I'm sorry, what do I call you?'

'Sarah,' she said. 'I am Sarah Beeston.'

'Let's just hear what Sarah has to say, Annie.' His voice was soothing. Sarah felt the atmosphere become calmer and was aware of Georgie's power.

'Now listen to me. You have no choice but to come, Annie, because Albert has agreed. You could, I suppose, go and find a job elsewhere but I doubt whether Albert would give you a reference.' She knew that she would have to convince Georgie if she was to succeed, so she continued. 'Naturally, if you still want to marry when you are of age, we shall reconsider. In the meantime, I am offering you the opportunity to be free to make a choice about your future. Here there is no choice.'

'But there is . . . ' cried Annie.

'Hush now, pet.' Georgie turned back to Sarah. She could see the fear in his eyes, the pain. His voice was still steady but it was only through a desperate effort, this she could tell.

'Things are going to get worse in the pits.' Her eyes were steady as she talked directly to Georgie. 'You know as well as I do that coal is not being sold as it once was, that more pits must close; that you can no longer strike effectively for better conditions, with the Trades Disputes Act in force. You are in work today, Georgie, but your pit might close tomorrow. Unemployment benefit is low. MacDonald's Labour government won't do anything to improve that.' She held up her hand to forestall his protest and silently thanked Bob for his political information. 'They might want to but they can't. It's obvious. The Liberals and Conservatives will combine against them to thwart it.'

It was what was being said in every pub, on every street corner and Georgie could only nod and affirm the truth of what she said.

'There's a depression coming that will make the others look like a picnic. The North will suffer as it always does. With luck you would both manage. But is that what you want? Just to manage? I want to get Annie out. I do not want her to breed children with rickets and consumption, and neither do you, I am quite sure.'

Georgie was hurting, probably more than he had ever done before, but she had to go on.

'Neither do you, Georgie.'

Annie broke in. 'I love him, I want him as he is. That is the life I want for myself,' but already she was remembering that train at the beck and the life outside and hated herself for the glimmering of wanting, of needing to go.

'Just for a while, Annie,' Georgie was saying, 'just for a while.' He was raising his voice to get through to her. Shout at me, Georgie, she was thinking. Shout at me so I don't hear this other half of myself. She gripped him, afraid that he would see her conflict, afraid that he wouldn't.

Sarah was watching them keenly and saw Annie's face and knew that it would be all right. The talk went on, back and forth, loud then soft, until Georgie said, 'I'll come at ten o'clock.' Georgie was speaking now to Sarah and she nodded, placing her tea mug down. She did not enjoy another's pain.

His voice was deathly tired and Annie wanted to stop the clock, stop everything because it was going too fast. Too fast to think. Too fast to go back to the beginning and start again. She rose as he kissed her and told her he would be here in the morning and that what was said made sense. He said that it was time he left Wassingham to sort something out for himself and that he would come back for her when he was ready, and she was ready. He seemed not to care that Sarah was there and kissed her hard and held her close to him. Then he turned and left without saying goodbye to Sarah, desperate to be gone before he could change his mind and drag Annie with him.

Annie walked to the door but did not open it, just stood facing it.

'I belong to him,' she said.

Sarah sat silent for some moments, not trusting her voice because she remembered the sparkling wedding of cousin Archie and Mary. The christening of this lovely child, for she was lovely, just like her mother; and intelligent. And for that reason she had to give her all that she could.

She finally said: 'I want to provide you with the opportunity to be free to make a choice of belonging with someone, but never to someone else. Perhaps one day you will be glad and now we shall wash up the mugs and we shall leave at 10.15 in the morning.' Her voice was firm. 'You must say your farewell to George when he arrives at ten, but before that perhaps it would be an idea to see Tom and Betsy, and perhaps Grace.'

Annie was too tired to wonder how Sarah knew so much about her.

She still stood facing the door.

'We belong together you know. I will marry him. I'll make something of myself and then I'll marry him.' She half wanted to go to that world out there; she knew that now and knew also that Georgie had known and had made it easy for her, but still she could hardly breathe for the love of him, and the pain of separation would be another ache to put into the black box. Was there no end to being torn apart? she wanted to cry.

Sarah nodded to herself. She had depended on a short sharp action. It had proved successful.

CHAPTER 10

Tom sat in the corridor outside the headmaster's study. His legs were set firmly on the floor and his hands lay in his lap, just touching. He felt the damp heat where finger met finger and put them instead on either thigh. At 13 he felt too large for the chairs which were short-legged and small-seated and, since this morning, he felt too old for school. The brown of the corridor paint was unrelieved by even a timetable and would look a good deal better for a few of me paintings, he thought. You could get a good run of them down there, though the light was poor. He found that he could think like this, just as he would ordinarily, but all the while, underneath, there was the great deep gouge of Annie's going running like a silent groan. He felt tired and unreal as he allowed those few minutes to rise to the surface; it was as though he could not leave the memory alone.

He heard again her call to him as he turned the corner to cross into school, just a few hours ago. Tom, Tom, she had called, and it sounded torn down the middle with jagged edges and he had felt the hairs lift on the back of his neck. She was at the head of the alley, off to the left of the gates, standing with one hand against the wall as though she needed its support and he had been unable to move towards her.

His feet had stuck to the ground as though they had taken root like the gnarled oaks up on the start of the hills behind the town. He had thought of their brown-sinewed strength because he could not bear to look across at her standing there with such pain running down her face in streams of tears. His breath had beaten in and out through his mouth as everything around him stopped. Her tears were rolling down her cheeks past a mouth which was white like May's dough as it lay in the bowl and Annie never let him see her cry. He had stood and watched her and her eyes were on his as she walked slowly over the road, her hair lying in unkempt strands, unkinked by overnight plaits.

She had begun to run when she was halfway across and he watched as she favoured one foot.

He had let her come right up to him, still not moving because of the great weight which was settling in him. He had felt her breath on his face as she said she was leaving today.

He looked at her boots then, not at her eyes, not at her mouth which was saying the words again and again. Slowly, as though they hurt her throat, the words kept coming but he would not look at her. Would not listen. It was her boots which had held him; cracked and scuffed.

You should tie your boots better he had said, stooping and grasping the flapping ends. You should tie your bloody boots better, then you won't get blisters. He had pulled the laces savagely until they cut into his hands, telling her again and again that she should tie them, while she told him each time that she was leaving in a voice that stabbed and twisted in his chest so that he could hardly breathe.

Don't keep saying that, he had shouted in the end, but she did. She told him that she was leaving for Sarah's in Gosforn this morning. That she did not want to go but that a piece of her did and she hated herself for that. He heard her but he would not listen. He had felt her pulling at his jacket until it lifted taut from his shoulders; he heard his bait-tin fall to the ground.

He had tugged and tied a bow, then a double and then he had felt her hands in his hair and she pulled until he could stand the pain no longer and lifted his head as Don had done in the allotment that day and he smelt again the leeks and saw the sunshine and the lead coins. And could not bear that she should leave him here. Then finally he had stood.

You've never come to see me at this time before, he shouted, blaming her, hating her. His voice had been loud and fierce and she had taken his head between her hands and there were still tears running off her face on to her faded dress but no sound of crying from her and finally he listened as the bell sounded in the yard and the children filed one by one into the school. She told him that she was going and with whom and when.

He watched the rope left swinging on the lamppost as it ground slowly to a halt. He saw the women come out of the open-doored houses with brooms, sweeping the dust into the road. He saw the cages emptying at the top of the slag, churning up the black slope behind the streets, up and up just as they had done yesterday and the day before and he wondered how they could when Annie was leaving.

He had looked at her then, her dark hair and thin face with dark patches beneath her hazel eyes, hazel like the nuts which lay on the ground on the paths leading to the beck, and knew that nothing could be the same again if she left him, but he lifted his arms which felt heavy and clumsy and pulled her to him and the wet of her tears and her warm breath were against his skin as she told him everything. He rocked her and himself and his tears were gulping gasps whilst hers were still silent.

It's this big black gaping hole in me belly, he had said, to think of you gone from here and he saw that the women had finished their sweeping but that the cages were still travelling and dumping the slag.

He stroked her tangled hair and soon there were no more words from her and he brought out his handkerchief, tugging at her hair as she had done, but gently.

Lift up, bonny lass, he had said, or you'll be going to school with a bald head and you'd need to polish that every day and she had laughed and wiped her face in the white linen as she swung from him and leaned back against the wall.

She had looked up at him and smiled saying that it was the choice. Yesterday it was all so certain; she was staying here, each day was the same and, in time, she would marry Georgie.

He had stood sideways to her, his shoulder rubbing the wall, listening as she explained how suddenly last night nothing was sure, there was this chance and she wanted it but wanted to stay here too, to stay here with everyone.

Sitting in the school passageway Tom felt again the warmth of the two pennies he had jingled in his pockets and the heat of his legs through the trousers. He had asked what Georgie said and she had looked at him then with all the pain he had ever seen in her face, as much as on her father's death, or the day of the fair. Georgie, Annie had replied, made it easy for me but I could still have fought but I didn't and her voice cracked and her lips trembled too much for her to say more and then he had gripped her chin and made her look at him, telling her that she was brave to go and that the world did not stop at Wassingham; he and Georgie would come to her at Sarah's. She was to go, to get out and he meant it, however much it hurt, he meant it. He had not cried as she had pulled him to her, kissed his eyes, his cheeks, his lips then torn away, running from him back up the alley, still favouring her foot.

He shifted on his chair and pressed hard down with his hands. He must not cry here, in the corridor. He focussed on the cracked linoleum, covered in smeared mud, stabbed with studded boots. The headmaster had still not called him in and he wanted to be back in the classroom, busy, not sitting with time to think. The chair was digging into his thighs where the wooden frame stood above the sunken cane. He sat on his hands, trying to lift himself level so that he was more comfortable.

What did the old man want, he thought, pushing Annie slowly back to a manageable depth. The Head, Wainwright, couldn't know he'd been late because Mr Green had cornered him the moment he entered the school and sent him to the art room to do the pictures for him. He smiled wryly at the term 'art room', for it was an old store-room with poor light and a few tables and paints.

It couldn't be the lateness then because Mr Green would not have told on him. He liked Tom too much. He sighed as the bell rang in the playground to call in the others for afternoon school. It went on and on, like it was the start of the second coming. That Nobby Jenkins loved his bit of power and leant into the bell like a miner leant into a rock-face and bye, he was giving a good shake today, thought Tom, and that was because Nobby knew there was someone outside the Head's study. Other people's trouble gave that lad strength in his elbow. It'd be the same when he started in pubs. He'd throw his beer back at the first spot of scandal and still be licking his chops for more.

Tom stirred. He'd make no pitman, that grubby little misery, and he looked at his own hands and nodded. Maybe he did like to handle a paintbrush but he was good and strong an' all. No nancy boy like Nobby liked to make out; his voice had broken already, hadn't it?

They were coming in from outside, slipping into the classrooms lying either side of the corridor. He nodded at those who waved and those who glanced at him furtively, crossing his arms and extending his legs. He wasn't nervous, not after this morning.

One boy slipped out of the line leading into Mr Thomas's room.

'You all right, man?' It was his friend Ben. They were to start in the pits together in February. 'Has he seen you yet?' His blond hair had a centre parting and was cut very short.

'Awa' with you Ben. If I'm held up here, tell me Auntie May I'm at the library.' It was a lie she would easily believe. His aunt was used to him catching the worms in that book place, as she would say, and he would laugh as he always did and say that one day he'd bring her one home, a book worm that is. And she'd shriek and say he'd get a dose of liquorice if he ever did that and Davy, his cousin, would wink and grin.

Ben nodded. 'What've you done, man?' he asked.

Tom shook his head. The corridor was empty now. 'Nothing, I've been painting all morning. Get along with you Ben or you'll be here next.'

'Take care now, lad, he's already thrashed Sam today,' Ben said and scooted back into his classroom.

The headmaster was a cruel bastard, Tom thought. It was no wonder some had looked sideways at him as he sat here. It was said he'd been sent back from India after he'd lost his position at a mission school or that's how Green had put it to another teacher when Tom had been busy in the art cupboard. The sun had addled his brains which was why he was so short-tempered. The man hated it in the North, Green had said, the cold, the squalor, and blamed everyone but himself for having to be here.

It was quite silent in the corridor now, not even the murmur of the teachers' voices from behind the doors and then the headmaster's door opened and Mr Wainwright called, 'Get in here, boy,' in a voice as cold as the wind that whistled through the town when it was coming in from the east.

All Tom could see was a yellowed hand on the door and a starched cuff. Well, our Mr Wainwright, he thought, you'll need to soak that hand in vinegar for a while if you're ever going down the pit, but then you'll never do that like the rest of us, will you?

He stood up and walked into the study, his boots clumping on the wooden boards, until he reached the square of patterned carpet, and then becoming silent. The headmaster was sitting behind the desk now, and his paintings were spread out before him. He said nothing to Tom, just sat there looking at him.

Tom stood still. Yes, he thought, even this way up they're good. It's the colour. Maybe he wanted to put them up in here? The room was certainly dull and needed some brightening. Even the carpet which had once been many-coloured was a mixture of browns except for the beige thread which broke through to the surface where feet had worn a path. The walls and the wooden filing-cabinet were brown also and there was not even a brass fitting to relieve the monotony, only a wooden handle.

Tom looked back to the pictures, then to the man behind the desk. He sat back in his chair, his hands steepled under his chin. His eyes were a pale slate-grey from which it seemed all feeling had been washed long ago. They were sunken in dark hollows. There were deep lines that ran from his nose to the corners of his mouth and his lips were set in a thin line. Behind him, Tom could see the deserted playground through the window. A ball was caught in the corner where the tall wall ended and the railing began. The sky was clouding over, making it look colder than it was. He looked back again to the headmaster, waiting for him to speak, but he just sat on, looking Tom up and down, his face twisted with distaste and Tom wondered again why he was here. And then the man moved. He pointed a long finger at one of the paintings.

'What have you to say about this then, boy?' His voice was cold and his face barely moved as he spoke.

Tom thought, the man's gone daft, can't he see it's a bloody painting. He cleared his throat. 'It's a painting. Mr Green asked me to do two for the class wall.'

'And this is what you produced, is it?' He paused. 'How dare you.'

Tom felt confusion stir within him, overriding the churning darkness of Annie.

'Don't you like it, sir?' He looked at the painting again. It had been done from the heart, for her, and he thought it was the best he had ever produced.

He saw the headmaster rise and lean forward, resting his weight on his hands. 'Don't take that attitude with me, boy.' Pink was beginning to tinge the sallowness of his cheeks, spittle settled on the desk.

158

Tom kept his face still. Thank God he missed the painting, Tom thought, but these silent words were just a device to gain time for some understanding and he found none. He looked at the man who stood across from him and did not know what he meant.

'I don't understand you, sir. Is something wrong?'

The man picked up the painting, shaking it at Tom. The paint had dried hard and thick and a flake fell off. Tom jerked forward, his hand outstretched but the headmaster pulled away from him. All Tom could see was what he had painted. A small child on a freezing cold playing-field holding its hand towards a girl with a tray of steaming pies. She was holding back a pack of men, their breaths clouding the air, whilst she gave them to the child.

'This is what is wrong, Thomas Ryan.' The headmaster was holding the painting with one hand and pointing with the other.

Tom felt his thoughts become disjointed, broken up. There was nothing wrong with the picture that he could see, the colour was good, the perspective correct.

Wainwright's face was jutting towards him, ugly in its anger.

'Don't think I've forgotten I had your cousin Davy Moore here at school before you and had nothing but trouble from him and now I see it rearing its ugly little head from your direction.' His eyes had narrowed and his forehead was etched with deep horizontal lines.

Davy, thought Tom, he's been in the pits for four years now, what's he got to do with anything?

'What is, sir, what's rearing its head?' Tom was confused. Davy didn't paint, never had done. He was good at his work though but even better as a union man. But he wasn't a painter.

Wainwright was talking as though he was a river in full flood. '. . . I shall stamp it out boy. I shall stamp it out.'

Tom watched the reddening face of the headmaster and felt at a loss.

'You and your kind will try to bring the country down to your level if you can. Marx, Engels, don't think I don't know what you rant about in your lodges and your halls. Kier Hardy is your idol and it should be God! God!' He was shouting now. 'God and Empire!'

Tom just stood there, listening but not following, his mind a

159

maze of images that wouldn't stand still. The man was moving too fast and Tom did not know in what direction he was going.

'Well I hear your cousin has just been thrown out of another pit for his rabble-rousing and so now you think you can try it here, do you? Well, not in this school, you don't, not in this school.'

The headmaster was still shaking the painting and minute flakes of paint were lying on his desk, on his papers; one had fallen on the covered inkwell. Tom saw that the man's fingers were grey from the paint where he was holding the paper.

'I can see what you're trying to say, boy, say all over my walls. Well, you won't, see. This is seditious propaganda, a dirty bolshevik slur.'

Tom looked at his painting again; he could only see Annie on a cold bleak day.

'It's people like you that have driven people to ruin, driven people like me to ruin. Given natives ideas above their station. Louts, that's what you all are, louts.' His voice was vicious now and his eyes were staring and then he stopped abruptly, breathing heavily. He wiped his hand across his face leaving a grey trail. 'I demand an apology from you.' His face was hard, his words clipped and loud.

Tom stood quietly, he looked again at the painting and wondered how far Annie was from Wassingham now and how far Wainwright was from bursting all over the room. He was pulsing with rage and Tom still did not know why. He shook his head at the man.

'I can't apologise for painting that,' he said, feeling tired and miles from this room.

Wainwright seemed to stop breathing as he looked straight at him and slowly tore the painting through once, then twice, then again.

Tom swung back to this room as the pieces scattered on to the desk and one fluttered to the floor at his feet. Blood filled his face, his eyes, his ears. That was Annie who had been torn and she had been torn enough. He moved one step forward.

'That was my sister you tore,' he said, his breathing rapid now and his hands bunched. He wanted to smash his fist into that yellow face, into his ribs and belly. 'It was only a picture about sharing, about something that happened a long time ago.'

Wainwright moved round the desk towards him. He was bigger than Tom and he was shaking.

'That picture,' he snarled, 'was of a seditious nature, an encouragement to revolution which I will not have in my school. I've heard your cousin's call for redistribution of wealth and he's put you up to this. I know your type, Tom Ryan, and I don't like them. I've been watching you, waiting for you to start, like he did.' His breath was sour in Tom's face.

Tom drew back but Wainwright held him fast.

'It's about a girl and a few bloody pies, man. That's all,' he hissed.

And now the headmaster pushed him over towards the chair in the corner.

'It's about far more than that, don't take me for a fool. But I'll sort it out, don't you worry, like I wanted to do with David. Bend over that chair.'

The headmaster was rolling up his sleeves now, grunting as he did so, grinding out these words, 'You can tell Davy Moore from me that I don't want his bolshevik propaganda in this school. There is no room for anything but the Empire here, boy, and I want you to remember that.'

Tom gripped the back of the chair as he felt the first searing stroke across his back; up high, near to his shoulder blades.

Christ, he thought, what the hell is happening here? What the hell has happened today?

Tom felt the next and the next. 'I still don't know what the bloody hell you're talking about,' he hissed, turning his head.

'Another five for lying and another five for swearing.'

The pain was like a knife slicing across Tom's back. He could hear the stroke land and feel it through to his belly. And then the fury came again, pushing aside the shock and he rose and wrenched the cane from Wainwright's hand. The headmaster was red in the face and sweating. His sleeve had half rolled down.

'If I knew what you meant I could answer you, man,' said Tom, his voice not much more than a whisper. 'But I'll find out what it is that is ranting through your crazy mind and tearing up my pictures. I'll find out and then I'll do something about it.'

They were both panting, facing one another. Tom broke the cane over his knee and threw it into the corner, then moved to the door. He heard his feet clump as they hit the wooden boards after the silence of the carpet. He could feel his shirt sticking to his back and knew he was bleeding. He left the room and shut the door quietly. He didn't know whether Wainwright had tried to stop him, he couldn't hear him, or anyone. He walked to the art room and painted the scene again. He would need it when he arrived home and asked Davy to explain to him what there was to a painting about a girl giving a child a pie.

The front door of Aunt May's house was open as it always was when the weather was mild but Tom slipped down the back alley and in through the yard gate. He could hear Davy in the wash-house and knew that Wainwright had spoken the truth when he said Davy was out of the pit again. The afternoon shift was still underground.

He hesitated by the door; he could hear the water run off Davy's body and on to the floor and the clang as he put the empty bucket down.

Then he saw May standing in the scullery.

'Come in here, lad, and have a piece of bread.' She waved him into the kitchen where there was bread on the table and blackberry jam which she had made from the overflowing buckets that he and Grace had picked with Annie and Georgie.

The fire was blazing in the hearth, cooking the stew for tea and heating the irons for May. She had moved to the far end of the table by the pile of linen and her face was red from the heat of the fire. She spat on the iron and thudded it into the stiff white clothes, rubbing backwards and forwards with all her weight.

He loved the smell of heat on linen and sat down, careful not to lean back against the chair while he spread the jam straight on to the bread. It had set something splendid this time, he thought, and wiped a drip off the jar with his finger and sucked it, not thinking of the pain; easing himself back into this room which he loved.

It was naturally dark in here with the small window and the stairs which spiralled straight up from the corner to the three bedrooms upstairs but it was dotted about with vivid patch-work cushions and rag rugs. Brass reflected the fire which shone warm on the fender and on the horse brasses which hung down the walls. The cat was sleeping on Uncle Henry's chair and some of its ginger and white hairs had already settled on his trousers.

May changed the irons on the hot plate, holding them in a thick white cloth. She looked at him as he poured a mug of tea.

'One for me, boy,' she said, 'or don't you think ironing's hot work?' She threw the cloth at him and he caught it with one hand but the pain from his back snagged as he began to laugh so he just poured the rich stewed tea and added a drop of milk. There were no brown sugar crystals today, which definitely meant Davy was out of the pit again. Sugar always went back into the cupboard when they were one pay-packet less; to make sure there was some for Christmas, May would always say.

He looked up at her and she pointed with her head to the sideboard. 'Put it on there, bonny lad.' She watched as he rose and walked with care round the table and put the mug on the wooden mat he had painted for her.

He knew that she was watching him and wanted her to ask, not to have to tell. He always thought May should have been a farmer's wife. She was as big as his mother, her sister, but not pale and flaccid as she was. May was firm and pink with the same blue eyes as his, the same eyes as Davy, though the other boys, Sam and Edward were brown-haired and brown-eyed like their da. May's hair was like the corn, but with white shot through it. He had once said how pretty she was, how few lines she had, not like his mother and that was the only time she'd slapped him. It had been a real slap too. I would have them if I'd had your poor mother's life, she had said. But Tom had turned away from her. His ma had given him and Annie away so she wasn't his ma any more.

He turned back to the table and sat down and then she said:

'Trouble is it, you've been having with your back?'

She spat and the iron sizzled. She leaned into her work again, backwards and forwards.

'I was thrashed today,' Tom said. He felt tired. 'She's gone, you know.' But he knew she would already know, word went round like a slag fire that hit the surface. 'She's gone and I did a painting and the bloody man thrashed me for it.'

May folded the clothes carefully, making a neat square of the tablecloth she had finished.

'I know she's gone, lad, but you'll see her soon.' Her voice was full of kindness. 'Now lift up that shirt, lad, let's be seeing it.'

He felt a flood of relief. She would soothe the hurt, which did not pain him like that black hole which had grown since this morning, but the soothing would help that too and make him feel less alone.

He hung his jacket on the hook and then tried to ease the shirt from his back. It was stuck to the flesh. May tugged her apron straight as she moved round the table towards him.

'Give it to me,' she said and turned him round. She just held his shoulders, didn't lift his shirt or even tut.

'Get sat down again,' she ordered and her voice was carefully flat. 'I'll get Davy in here.'

She bustled past him, not looking at him, out into the yard, banging on the wash-house door.

Tom lay his head down on the table. He was so tired, so bloody tired and the pain from his back seemed to go up to the top of his head and down to his legs and the ache for Annie was everywhere that the thrashing wasn't.

Suddenly Davy was there before him, crouching down and lifting up his head. Tom felt as though he had been asleep but his eyes had not been closed.

'That's a rare old belting you've had, my bonny lad.' Davy's eyes were smiling but there was a blackness behind them. He stood and took the bowl of lukewarm water from his mother and the cloth and sponged the shirt free. Blood reddened the water darkly and Tom tasted the blood in his mouth from the lip he was biting. He must not cry out in front of a pitman and he forced the sheet of pain to lift by talking.

'So you're out of the pit now, Davy?'

There was a soft laugh from Davy, whose lean dark face was transformed. He was a miserable-looking devil, May always said, until he smiles and then the sun comes out from where it's hiding and we all have a bathe in it.

'Well lad, how word gets around.'

May snorted as she piled up the linen and carried it to the cupboard. 'Less talk and more work and this wouldn't happen my lad. More money than sense it is. More mouth than sense if you ask me. What's the point of setting the world alight if we have to put the sugar back in the cupboard?'

Davy dug Tom in the ribs. 'The kettle's boiling again,' he said, 'rattling its top off.' And they both laughed.

'We'll find out how you got your lugs on to that news later, our Tom, but I want to find out how you picked up this little masterpiece.' He was wrapping round greased clean flannel and the heat was taken out of his back and he felt the tension ease in his neck. He liked the feel of Davy's hands, quick and firm, as they passed the strip of sheeting round and round his body. It made him feel like a bitty bairn again.

Davy stood up. He groaned and Tom wished he had thought to stand up. Pitmen hated to crouch; they spent all day doing it and their backs were creased for life.

'You'd like the pattern on your back, Tom,' joked Davy. 'Stick it up on the wall, you would, boy, but I'd like to know the name of the artist if you don't mind.' He was carrying the bowl back out to the scullery and May called for a sprig of thyme to be put in the stew.

Tom watched him as he lifted the lid and followed the steam as it puffed out up the chimney. He took a sip of tea and poured some into Davy's cup as he sat down. The smell of thyme wafted now, faint to begin with but increasing to a pungent thickness.

'It was that bugger Wainwright,' he said and saw May return to the room and stand with her hands on her hips. She had taken down a string of onions from the hook by the pantry and they rocked across her full thighs. He went over the scene for them; it was vivid still but full of colour and there had been none in that room apart from his pictures.

'He said that, did he,' remarked Davy at length. 'I think you've just been thrashed for another man's work, Tom lad. He's wanted to belt me often enough and never found the excuse. Called me a guttersnipe radical.' He patted Tom's knee. 'Me mam's right, I've more mouth than sense.' He sat back in his chair.

'It was a good painting was it, lad? Worth the cane-work?' he asked.

'The best I've done,' said Tom. 'It's in me jacket.'

At their look of surprise, he added: 'I painted another before I came home.'

Davy laughed and signalled for him to stay put and fetched it himself, raising his eyebrows as he studied the painting. Tom felt again the cold of the field, the fear of the panting men, his own breath rasping in his chest as he ran and left her. Now he'd had his beating too and the aching felt a little better.

Aunt May took the picture from Davy and said: 'Re-distribution of wealth, isn't that what Wainwright said?'

Tom p. ested. 'It was Annie sharing out the pies.'

Davy laughed and slapped him on the back before he remembered, 'Sorry lad, I forgot. I wouldn't mind taking this for a poster though because that's what it is right enough. It's a good one boy. Your Annie had the right idea.'

'Davy, lad,' warned May, 'don't start the boy off on your ideas. See where it's got you, on the blacklist. No pit'll have you now.'

Davy shrugged, his face closed and no longer smiling. 'Someone's got to say something.'

'Leave it to the unions, Davy,' his mother said as she cleared the jam from the table and gave him the knives and forks to put round. She waved Tom back into his seat. 'You,' she commanded, 'sit down and don't listen to this man. Eighteen and he thinks he knows everything.'

She flounced out to the kitchen and began to chop up the leeks.

'Why are you out then, Davy?' Tom asked.

'Oh, the overman kept giving the best seam to his mates. It's piece-work in these pits you see, Tom, or if you don't, you soon will when you go down. And those in the better seams get pickings; more money. Should be done by ballot, by luck, not by favours. I told the overman, see, and he had me out.'

Tom looked at him as he finished laying the places and perched himself on the fender.

'Why didn't you leave it to the union then, Davy, like your mam said? You're a union man.'

'Because since the General Strike, the unions have no teeth, man. Now the owners can use the workers to get rich and get away with it more than ever before, and the overman can flex his muscles and do us rabble-rousers down, as your Mr Wainwright called us.'

Tom narrowed his eyes as he remembered the headmaster. 'I don't want to go back, Davy. He's a bully.'

Davy looked at him firmly beneath his brows. 'You'll go back and stay until you leave to go to work. You don't let bullies chase you away. Look at your Annie, she stayed with that bloody old bully Albert and now she's free of him, thank God. I wonder if she'll go on giving away pies to people?' And he laughed.

Tom smiled and wanted to put the ache back where it had been, well below the surface.

'What did Wainwright really mean by redistribution?' He forced himself to listen to the answer, to keep his mind on things outside himself.

'Sharing boy, that's all it means.'

'But why did he belt me?'

'Because, I suppose, one way of doing it is to tax everyone harder on their incomes, that would take more from the rich, spread it about a bit. Makes those with money right mad to think of it. It's sharing, like I said.'

'And who were Marx and that other one then?'

Davy laughed. 'No more questions, get on with your tea. You'll learn soon enough when you're working.' He lounged out to the kitchen. 'I'm just off to see someone about a heavy right arm, Mam,' he said and May just nodded.

'A warning, that's all my Davy.' Tom saw him nod.

He took a sip of his tea but it was cold.

May called through the door. 'What about going to see your mam, tell her about Annie?'

'She'll already know,' he replied and May shook her head.

'She'll like to hear it from you.'

He shook himself into his shirt and then his jacket. 'Maybe I will, Aunt May, but I've to go and tell Grace first.'

'Putting your girlfriend before your mother then is it?' She stood in the doorway and grinned, shaking a spoon at him. He dodged round her.

'I'll be in for tea,' he called, avoiding her blow which never landed.

He walked down the back alley, his hands in his pockets since it looked more grown up and did not jog his back so much. His girlfriend, Aunt May had said, and he wondered how Grace would take to that, her in higher school and him a year younger. But soon he would be a working man and she would like that. He felt as though he had changed today, grown up. He would not see Betsy, of that he was more sure than anything, because it was her fault that Annie had gone and he hated her even more now. If she had fought Joe and made him take them both he would not have gone to May's and she would not have gone to Albert's. They would have stayed together and Sarah would not have needed to come . . .

CHAPTER 11

At ten-thirty prompt, Sarah edged the bull-nosed Morris away from the front of Albert's blank-faced shop, leaving the chattering groups to disperse once the novelty of a car like this, driven by a woman, for goodness sake, had been talked to death. Georgie was not there to wave to Annie.

He had arrived at ten and had stood quite still, in the doorway of the kitchen, his cap held loosely between slack hands. He had looked at Annie steadily and her eyes had held his and had answered the question they held from the deepness of her life.

Worldlessly he had turned and leant against the wall, one foot wedged against his bike. He had taken out his cigarette paper, rolled it round tobacco teased along its centre while she had stood close enough to touch the length of her body against his as he licked and lit the cigarette. She breathed in the scent of sulphur as he sucked in the smoke. She opened her lips as he slipped it from his mouth to hers and she felt his moisture as she had done before, so long ago and they remembered without words those months and weeks and every minute between then and now.

He had not kissed her but had cupped his hand about her cheek and laid his face against hers. I've still to teach you to hang by your arms on that bar, he had said, and she had whispered, I'll love you all my life, my love.

And now she was gone from him, leaving him and while Sarah peered through the windscreen, steering the car clear of tram-lines, she looked back as the juddering cobbles changed to asphalt and the car climbed the hill out of the town. She could see the slag creeping ever nearer to the houses which looked as though they were banked against the black advance. She could hear in her memory the whine of the cages which were swaying as they lurched and climbed steadily higher up the coal-dust mountains to discharge at the peak a dense choking black cloud.

She looked to the front, to the hill which was unfolding as they, in turn, climbed and wanted to wrench at the door handle and fling herself back down to Wassingham while she still had the time because, once you left, you never came back, never truly came back. The crest was drawing nearer, the car engine was groaning, then it hesitated, as Sarah changed into a lower gear. Now, her mind screamed, now, but the crest was here and they were over and the world was in front of her in a burst of light. Sweeping fields and trees flicked past faster and faster and her knuckles were white on the door handle. She turned and looked back but now could only see the hill, not the town which clutched Georgie and Tom in its grip. It's too late, she told herself, and the tearing inside seemed quieter. It's too late now, she repeated to herself.

It took two hours to travel to Gosforn through rolling countryside that was dotted with pit villages and ironworks that belched foul smoke onto sprawling mean streets. Sarah pointed over to Newcastle on the left but Annie could see nothing of the city with its bright lights and theatre drapes, just grey smoke bulging from pencil chimneys into a late August sky. She could not yet speak to this woman who had stirred her into betraying Georgie, betraying Tom.

Sarah's house was not joined to another, none of the houses were, Annie saw, and the light seemed to pour through the gaps lightening the whole road.

There were gated front gardens which ran down to the pavement and Sarah's was shielded by a clipped privet hedge. The car jumped as the engine died.

Sarah set her hat straight and gathered up her bag.

'Take your things then, Ann, and you do not need those sandals any more, they are far too small.'

'I'm keeping them,' replied Annie as she clutched them to her and slammed the car door. She lifted the latch on the wooden gate and walked up the path to the front door past the privet hedge which sported pollen-heavy flowers and separated this house from the neighbours.

Inside, the brown and white tiles looked crisp and cold and

her boots clicked loudly as she walked along behind Sarah, past the hall table. She stopped to look at the large gong which stood by it. There was a brush on the table and a few letters stacked in a neat pile. She put her cardboard suitcase down and brushed her hair in the mirror. It was still the tangled mess it had been this morning.

'I usually brush my coat with that,' said Sarah gently. 'You might find it full of fluff.' She stood in the doorway to another room and Annie hurriedly put the brush back.

Sarah spoke again. 'That table is walnut, it has a nice grain hasn't it? Incidentally we ring that gong twice for meal times. It's a bit like a race and goes back to my father, I suppose. Once means on your marks, twice means it's on the table and things are going to get a bit frosty if you are not waiting for it.'

Annie looked along the passageway which went on past Sarah, down to a closed door. She looked back again at the brush and felt the heat from her reddened cheeks. It all seemed very strange and she felt so alone.

'Come along, my dear,' Sarah beckoned to her. Once inside the room, it seemed slightly darker than the hall but not much because the windows were large and stepped out from the room. The air was heavy with beeswax and the dark red chairs were like train seats, but not quite so prickly. Annie sat upright, her skirt tucked under her knees to stop the irritation.

'I remember using a dog's brush once to do my hair, when I was in a strange house,' Sarah said, removing her hat and putting it on the table next to her fireside chair.

Annie did not answer. She watched as Sarah smoothed stray hairs back into place. Her hair looked smooth enough now, she thought, and shining as though it was a copper that had been burnished. It was short with crisp waves. Sarah sighed and sat back.

'It's so nice to get home . . .' And then she stopped and frowned. 'I am sorry, Ann, that was tactless.'

Annie sat as she had been doing. She was not going to show this woman that she had felt a flush of longing, a loosening of tears; that she wanted to run back down this light street, down the miles of road and then over the hill that led back to the pits, to the streets, to the people she knew.

'Me name's Annie, not Ann,' she said.

'But I think Ann is more mature,' Sarah replied and walked

171

to the window. 'Tomorrow,' she continued, 'we have an interview at a school nearby. It is one of my choice since I know the Reverend Mother quite well, we play bridge together and, of course, it was my old school. She is prepared to accept you and coach you for your examination, old though you are. There is a bicycle in the shed for your journey to and from school and school uniform can be obtained from a shop in the centre of town. We will equip you there if there is a successful conclusion to the interview.'

There was an anger growing in Annie.

'I'm not living with a gaggle of bloody left-footed penguins.'

The prints on the wall were of the sea. Grey and blue they were, not a drop of colour anywhere. Georgie would look for birds, Tom would check the perspective and Don would wonder how much they would fetch. There was a white marble clock on the mantelpiece with a gold slave hanging all over the top of it. Bet he had a shock everytime it chimed, thought Annie, and pictured their father's clock which had made her jump but she was not going to think of Wassingham until tonight.

'You are quite correct,' Sarah was saying. 'You are not. You will be living with me and leaving any excess of religious zeal that you may acquire within the walls of the convent when you depart at the end of the day.' She paused as she looked at Annie who was watching the clock creep towards one o'clock; anger was mixed with helplessness now.

'It's a strange clock isn't it, Ann?' She did not wait for an answer but went straight on. 'It's one my father brought home one day, quite why my mother and I could never understand. It's perfectly hideous, don't you think, but it keeps excellent time.'

Annie looked at her, then back at the clock.

Sarah spoke again. 'My father was a shopkeeper too, you know, so it runs in the family.'

Again Annie just looked at her and then back to the clock. She would wait for it to chime and then she would not be able to run out of the house, back to Georgie. Once it chimed she had to stay here, as long as it chimed before she could count to one hundred. As she finished fifty, the clock reached one and a chime rang out, and she sat back in her chair, on her hands to lift her clear of the bristles. She had to stay now, she thought.

She had to stay because the clock had chimed before one hundred and it was not her fault that she was still here, it was the clock's; but was the clock enough? She felt herself begin to sweat.

She looked again at Sarah, who was watching her closely. Through her confusion Annie saw that it was a nice face, quite old though, she must be in her middle thirties.

'These nuns, Ann,' Sarah resumed, 'are neither penguins nor left-footers but are a protestant order with an excellent academic record and reputation.'

'I've not understood a word you've said.' Annie moved only her lips as she spoke, her voice was terse.

'That, my girl, is precisely why you are here,' Sarah riposted and enjoyed Annie's fleeting grin. 'Any other points you wish to discuss?'

'Can I have me dinner?' Perhaps if she was rude enough, Sarah would send her back. If she did not, then she, together with the clock, had decided for her.

She felt the sandals on her lap, the cracked straps that had dug in at Sally's party, that she had not worn since but that she would always keep because they brought every minute back sharply the moment she saw them.

'You may have your lunch. If you insist on asking for dinner when I'm quite sure your father explained the difference to you, you will, presumably, be quite happy to wait until eight this evening.'

Her hands sat in her lap and her face stayed still round her eyes and all Annie heard was the deep tick of the clock.

'You'd better show me the kitchen then,' she said, unable to think of a retort. 'I'd better get on with it.'

Sarah looked at her more closely then and there was movement across the brow.

'Come with me, Ann, there are some things I must show you and others I must explain to you.'

Annie followed her through the tiled hall to the door at the bottom which led into the kitchen. An elderly plump woman in a red apron was putting some cold meat and hard-boiled eggs on to plates. The white was blue next to the yolk and she could smell it as she entered. The meat safe was tightly shut, its cream paint was chipped and one piece was hanging. Annie pulled it off as she stood next to it.

'Ann, this is Val who helps me to run the house. Val, this is Ann, my ward, who will be living here as I've already explained to you, from today. We have prepared the back bedroom for her, haven't we? It gets so much sun we thought you'd prefer it, my dear.' Sarah looked at Annie and smiled. She turned back again to Val. 'Lunch in half an hour, I think.'

Val smiled at Annie and her eyes squeezed to slits above round cheeks. Her arms were pink and dimpled and there was no sign of any bones. Annie followed Sarah from the kitchen to the bedrooms, up a staircase with a turned banister and more prints on the walls. So, thought Annie, she hasn't sent me home, and she didn't know if she was relieved or not.

Sarah turned towards the back of the house and opened a dark panelled door on the left of the landing. She did not go in but stepped back and urged Annie forward. She was still clutching the sandals and her hands tightened as she walked into the room.

'This is your room, Ann. You will hear the gong in just under half an hour. We will be ready to sit when we hear it the second time. The bathroom is next door to your room. You will find a few things in the drawers. I bought them for a fifteen-year-old but a few sizes smaller would have been more apt. A clean pair of knickers every day please and also a bath. There is a linen-basket in the bathroom. I know little about godliness but cleanliness is just plain commonsense.' She pointed to the bathroom.

'Incidentally, in this house there are no servants. I work as a legal secretary at Waring and James, Solicitors, in order to keep myself. Val works in order to keep herself. Ann Manon will work in order to one day provide for herself. In this house we are all members of a household which will only thrive if we all play our parts. We are all people in our own right, no one should have to suffer another.'

Sarah shut the door quietly and perhaps went downstairs but the carpet was so thick Annie could not hear.

She had not understood the last part of Sarah's speech, for that was what it was, Annie decided. She talked as though she ate a book for breakfast every day.

The sun had filled the room with warm light, her suitcase was on the carpet by the bed. It was a carpet which ran to the walls and her feet sunk in with each step and when she removed her boots she felt the softness beneath her soles and the tufts which rose up between her toes. She traced the swirling pale blue pattern with pointed foot and ran her hand along the smooth sleek quilt. She had not known such comfort existed.

There were no gas lights, just a switch on the wall. She flicked it and the light came on and she knew that this was electricity because it was so quiet.

She stroked the quilt again and wondered if this was what silk was like and sat on top of the bed which sank effortlessly beneath her weight. The curtains were pulled back and the polished window-sill held a vase with just one white rose.

Annie walked across and the rose smelt thick and rich, caught against the leaded window. She looked closer at the tight corners; they must be a pig to clean she thought.

The garden was grassed with rose-bushes edging a lawn that looked smooth enough to lie on and she stretched herself instead full length along the carpet, her hands running to meet one another, collecting carpet fluff which lifted before her passage. The bed was high and beneath was an enamel potty.

She felt a surge of excitement and then, as quickly, it was overtaken by a despairing panic, an encompassing sense of loss, of guilt. She wished she could cut it out of her mind and just enjoy all this but she could not, so sprang to her feet, anxious to move, to push back feelings with action and slipped on to the landing and into the bathroom.

The bath was encased in rich mahogany with a step in the side. The basin had a mahogany cupboard underneath and there were toilet rolls on the shelf. She touched the bath taps. They were brass and heavy and beautiful and the water gushed out steamy hot. The toilet flushed at the first pull. There was dried lavender in a bowl on the window-sill and she picked some out with her fingers and smelt the long-ago scent of Aunt Sophie.

She had scattered lavender heads on the window-sill and picked them up in a fever of anxiety in case Sarah should come in, then smoothed the bowl over but could not remember whether it had been flat or heaped and felt her face flush and tears come to her eyes. Then the gong sounded. The better-get-going gong and she splashed water on her face and was glad that she had not let the tears really come and redden her eyes;

so that they would see. She dried herself on the white towel that was so full of pile she could have slept on it.

The table was not laid with a cloth but with table-mats backed by cork. She sat down where Val showed her and they waited for Sarah who, by rights, thought Annie should be frozen to the marrow since the second gong had gone and Val had brought the food to the table already.

'Did you like the room, my love?' asked Val as she unrolled her napkin from its ring and pointed to Annie to do the same.

'It's the most lovely room I have ever seen and the carpet is so thick and enormous. There's no wood around the edge at all.'

She heard Sarah's laugh as she entered and sat at the end of the table and knew that if she had known Sarah was there she would never have said what she had. Here was someone stronger than her, who had power over her like Albert and Annie found herself thinking that at Albert's at least she had worked and received some small payment which was different to here. Here there was all this just given to her which took away her right to anger, to argue. She was beholden now and it felt all wrong. She couldn't fight back and this would have to be changed if she was to stay. Her name was Annie, not Ann.

Sarah was dishing up the thinly sliced meat; pink ham and something else but she didn't know what.

'Ham and beef for you, Ann?' Sarah asked and Annie nodded. She had no idea what beef tasted like but it had to be good for only the wealthy ate it.

'You must be very rich,' she said, as Sarah passed her the potatoes.

'No, and one does not discuss financial matters at the table and I should leave the parsley on the potatoes, Ann; it's rather nice. Potatoes, Val?'

Annie put back the spoon and looked at the green bits which were spread all over the waxy white of the vegetable.

'Where do you sleep, Val? Up in the attic?' she asked as she picked up her knife and fork.

'Val does most certainly not sleep in the attic,' Sarah broke in. 'Her room is opposite yours and just the same, and your knife would really be more comfortable if you don't use it like a pen.'

Annie altered her grip. Albert had eaten like that and she had forgotten what her father had always said.

'I didn't have a nice room at Albert's.'

'Look, Ann, you really must accept that we are all equal in this house, it is just that our tasks vary. One day you will be an adult earning money and you will find that equality is not usual for women but it should be. It's something worth fighting for. Last year we were at last given the vote at 21, something to thank Baldwin for but it took far too long.' She paused to wipe her mouth and Annie wondered whether she ate a book for lunch as well? Perhaps that's where she had been when they were sitting waiting for her, stuffing herself with the latest book from the library. She grinned to herself. She must tell Grace that, she thought, when she comes to see me and she felt happier at the thought. Wassingham was not too far after all.

Sarah had put down her knife and fork, and was leaning forward on her elbows. 'Just remember that you might need to stand up and say, this is not what I want, but you must know what it is that you wish to put in its place. It is not enough just to be dissatisfied. You have to have an aim. Can't stand woolly thinking.'

After dinner Annie left the house through the kitchen door to check on the bicycle as Sarah had suggested. Down past the roses with their warm heavy scent to the shed which stood behind the green waxed laurel. The garden was bordered by a red brick wall which beat back the afternoon heat and sheltered the garden from the wind. The latch was stiff and it was dark inside. The smell was of dust and old sacking, of creosote. The bike leaned up against the wall, black with spokes that were slightly rusted.

She moved towards it over floorboards that were springy and creaked and touched the handlebars. The rubber grips were worn through to the metal either side. She felt safe in here, with the same smell that had been in her da's shed, the same creosote thickness around it. It made her remember that she was still in the same world as Georgie and Tom, as her old life. That some things stayed the same; that she was still Annie, not Ann. She moved to the window which was sectioned into four panes. Val had said the shed was ash, like the greenhouse on the other side of the garden. Seasoned ash she had said and Annie had pictured the trees with their pale grey bark and late leaves and remembered Georgie as he had pointed to the ashes past the hives and she saw again the purple flowers which came before the leaves.

She ran her finger along the frame. The creosote had stained the grey to dark brown. She could miss him here, in private. She could let the pain come and think of his laugh as he held her on the bike, his hands as he stroked her body on the sand, miss his voice, his eyes.

The glass pane was dirty where dust had collected at the base and her finger came away grey, not greasy-black from the pit dust. She peered through the window out to the wall and above it there was sky, pale blue sky with clouds streaked and still. There was no slag mountain, just clear air. She felt a racing panic, an urge to run, to get free, to be back again in Wassingham.

She moved past the bike, past the window to the door then back again, to the end where there were dry dusty sacks stacked one on top of the other then sat on the floor, her arms clutched round her knees and she rocked herself, her head down, remembering Grace and her dimpled legs and her soft arm which was good to hold. Remembering Don when he had given her Da's watch, remembering Tom when he fell in the beck and did a wee. Yes, she would remember that and Georgie, looking up into the sky at his precious mating bees which no one could see but which everyone could picture.

She put her mouth to her knee and smelt her skin. She would think of that day when things got bad. She would think of holding Tom and making him believe that sometimes things would work out. She lifted her head to the window, shrugging her hair back out of her eyes. Yes, that's what she would do and what's more she'd make bloody sure they worked out and what wasn't going to was being given everything for free; it made her a prisoner here, it tied her tighter than rope would have done. She leant back against the wall, her hands clasped loosely now and watched a tortoiseshell butterfly at the window, caught in the square beams of light. The dust was tumbling around it, caught too, and she pushed herself suddenly from the floor and quietly cupped the tortoiseshell in her hands, edged open the door with her arm and threw it gently into the air which was bright and hurt her eyes, then walked along the path leading to the greenhouse and opened the door.

The humid heat made her flinch, it seemed to spray out at her as she moved amongst the tall staked tomato plants and felt the weight of the red fruit in her hands as she crouched and sucked in the fresh smell. They were so glossy red, with dew caught on the leaves. Condensation streamed down the inside of the glass although it had been whitewashed against the heat.

'Lovely, aren't they,' said Val behind her.

Annie spun round and up, knocking a tomato off and watching as it fell and split and the pips oozed out on to the dark rich peat.

'I didn't mean to,' she said, backing off.

Val smiled. 'It doesn't matter, my dear, they're so ripe they are ready to drop on their own. Pick me some, there's a love and I'll get on with the lettuce. Bring me the basket when you've done, dear.'

The basket was large and Annie did not know how many to pick; whether to pick them with the green bits or not. So she did four with, four without.

Val was over by the vegetable patch. One row of lettuce had gone to seed and she was bent over feeling the hearts of the rest.

Annie waited beside her while she pulled up one, then another. Rich dark soil clung to the roots, even when Val shook them. Even have better soil than we do, Annie thought. It's not bloody fair and she remembered the dry thin soil of Wassingham that baked as soon as the sun shone.

She watched as Val threw the roots into a wooden-sided bunker which had no top and stood next to the vegetable patch.

'That's my compost,' explained Val. 'Must have a compost or you don't get the goodness. Mustn't waste anything in a garden you know. If you take out, you must put back.'

She smiled as she put the lettuce into the wicker basket that Annie still carried. 'A few radishes now, I think.'

She stooped and pulled up several red orbs and laid them on top of the lettuce.

'I used to sell me pony's plops,' said Annie. 'Manure's good for the garden too, you know.'

She stood as Val moved along to the chives and knelt by the bed. 'I like to be able to pay me way, you know. Makes me feel better.' She waited to see if Val would understand.

Val looked up, her face was red now from the heat, then

down again as she picked a few more thin chive shoots. At last she said:

'Why don't you go in and talk to Sarah, Ann. She'll understand. I promise you she'll understand. Give us a hand up now.'

Annie moved and grasped her elbow; her fingers sank into the warm flesh as she tugged. Val took the basket from her and Annie did not want to let go of that arm but she turned and walked from Val to the house, her chin up, her fists clenched, looking for words which would tell Sarah she was strangling her, not setting her free.

Sarah was reading the paper in the sitting-room and Annie did not knock but walked straight in, her boots loud on the wooden surround.

'I need to talk to you,' she said.

Sarah looked up and over the paper, then laid it on her lap. 'Yes, Ann.'

'That's just it, you see,' Annie blurted out. 'Me name's Annie but you can call me Ann because I haven't got any choice. You keep me, pay for me food and school and I don't earn it so you can tell me what to do, even change me name if you want. I can't let that happen. Me name's Annie and I want to earn me keep or I can't say what I think, I can only say what you think.'

Her hands were down by her side and her chin was jutting. Her eyes had not left Sarah's face while she had spoken but in the silence that followed she looked away; at the fireplace, at the lamp with a shade made of coloured glass sections, at the photograph beside it of women wearing hats and veils and men in funny trousers. They all wore long slats on their feet and it was snowing. She hadn't said all that she had meant and it had come out badly. She had wanted to be calm and talk as Sarah did but she didn't know how.

Sarah had her finger to her mouth, she was frowning and Annie clenched her hands but stayed standing still.

'Please sit down.' Sarah pointed to the chair opposite. 'We're both tired you know, we've been on the road for quite a long time this morning and your uncle, I'm afraid, is a most difficult man.'

Annie did so. 'He's all right but I worked me way there and

got sixpence as well. I never felt beholden to him.' She was leaning forward, her elbows on her knees.

Sarah smiled ruefully. 'Oh dear, Annie. You are quite right of course, but I am your godmother you see and so I do have a certain right to act *in loco parentis*.'

And what the hell does that mean thought Annie and was about to say as much when Sarah laughed.

'I'm sorry, you must make allowances, Annie. I'm not used to children you see. What I mean is that I can undertake, in your case, the role of parent but,' and she put her hand up as she saw Annie about to interrupt, 'you are quite right. I am not your parent. Therefore, if you feel as you do, we must remedy the situation.'

'Do you mean I can earn me keep then?'

'I consider that you will earn your keep if you work hard and find a career that is worthwhile.'

'Or marry Georgie,' challenged Annie.

Sarah paused. 'Yes, we did agree to that, did we not, but marriage does not necessarily mean you do not have a career.'

'But I still need to earn me keep for me own sense of being me.'

Sarah sat back and looked steadily at Annie, then to the window. She nodded. 'Very well, I accept your point but I shall have to sort something out. Can you give me a bit of time?'

Annie sat back, her hands under her legs against the prickles. 'As long as it's not too long,' she insisted.

'I promise,' Sarah said and smiled.

Success surged through Annie. She would be a person who had rights and that was what she had wanted. She breathed a deep sigh and smiled at Sarah. It was the first one that they had exchanged. The clock was approaching four o'clock, the fire was laid for this evening.

'Is that you?' she asked, pointing to the photograph. 'What are those things on your feet?' she asked when Sarah nodded.

'Skis for sliding upright down snow slopes. You must try it some day, you'd enjoy it, I'm sure. It would present a challenge.' Sarah moved over and picked it up and passed it to Annie, who noticed for the first time that there were lines under her eyes, grey in her brown hair.

'How old are you, Sarah?'

Sarah looked at her and laughed as she turned to sit down.

'I'm 38 and Val is 45 but you mustn't ask anyone else their age. It is considered rather rude.'

Annie nodded and looked again at the photograph. 'You look young here, but very thin.' She looked more closely at the photograph. 'So very thin. Were you ill?' She was thinking of the boys in Tom's class with consumption, but not him, thank God.

'No, not ill. Shall we just say that I had been having trouble eating. It was called the cat and mouse game, Annie, and one day I shall tell you more about it but now, now I think it is time I sat and thought carefully about what we should sort out to solve our problem. Can you for now go and help Val with the salad, Annie?'

Annie nodded, rose and left the room. She stopped outside the door and went back in.

'Thank you, Sarah,' she said and Sarah smiled. 'I'll ring the gong from now on, shall I? That'll be a start.'

And Sarah nodded.

That night, Sarah lay in bed too tired to sleep, too full of the change in her life. The curtains were not drawn since there was a full moon and she could never bring herself to waste the strong colourless light which lit the bedroom, bringing no detail but an awareness of shape.

She shook her head slightly at what must be almost an obsession with waste, much like Val's with her compost but then she'd been with the family for thirty years so was as imbued with tradition as she was. It was her father of course. Waste, I cannot abide waste, she heard him say with a clarity of remembered sound that startled her. And the vividness of that particular scene that was so long ago took her unawares.

Her father had entered the sitting-room, the same one that Annie had stormed into today in those dreadful boots. Must do something about those tomorrow, Sarah reminded herself. Yes, he had entered the sitting-room rather later than usual dressed as always in his black suit and starched collar which was his uniform as manager of the hardware store. Hardware was an understatement since Mr Mainton, as the town always called her father, never Martin Mainton, had built up the store into more of an emporium for the owners, a complacent and rich family called the Stoners.

Sarah frowned as she fought to remember what she and her mother had been doing and then sighed with recognition. Embroidery. Her mother was explaining that embroidery should be as neat at the back as at the front since it was somewhat like underwear. Seldom seen but always clean and tidy, and they were laughing gently together.

Waste, I cannot abide waste, he had said as he had come rushing in. She had never known her father to walk, it was beyond his capabilities. They had looked up, not startled because they were used to his fads but a little wary, especially her mother who had suffered recently under the burden of producing meals which her father had decided would stimulate their 'flushing systems' as he had called it.

What now, her mother had said in that voice. With a flourish, her father had produced two bicycles. Exercise and freedom, freedom to enjoy the countryside, the beauties of which are being wasted by you. You have energies which are being wasted, he had finished and had stood there beaming.

The next day, she remembered they had obtained split skirts and were soon traversing the country lanes and indeed they found freedom. She and her mother had travelled for miles stopping for picnics and talking. Talking about the dreams and aspirations of her mother, her frustration at wanting to do so much and not being able to within the confines of a provincial society and marriage, though her father had been an enlightened husband. Sarah had spoken of the suffragettes; it was 1910 and she was 19 and her mother had applauded their efforts, their bravery.

Her father had relished their adventures and was proud of their independence though their neighbours were somewhat shocked especially the Thom sisters next door who played the piano at the picture house in Gosforn. But Sarah had always thought they were, in reality, envious. What would they think now about this girl living with her, because they were still next door, though no longer at the cinema.

That summer, her parents had determined that their daughter should be equipped with skills which would enable her to weather the rest of her life, good or bad. All they could afford was a secretarial course but it was the best. Sarah sighed with satisfaction and pushed herself up on to her pillows. The moon was half obscured by fast-moving clouds, much as it had been so often when she was driving ambulances during the war. That was another of her father's fads. Both his women should learn to drive. A waste of potential he had roared and pushed his wife into the driving-seat. She had hated it but Sarah loved the feeling of power.

She had taken a job in London, staying with Aunt Jesse, her father's sister, and it was there she had become involved with female suffrage. She had worn green and purple rosettes; marched and spoken at rallies, been punched and pushed by hecklers for her pains as she left the halls. There had been spit down the front of her jacket when she had returned from one meeting. She had thrown it away and cried in her room, unable to bring herself to wipe it away.

When she was a member of a group blocking a road near Trafalgar Square, she had been arrested. The cobbles they were sitting on had been cold in that winter of 1912 and she remembered how they had been told by their leader to go slack when the police picked them up and threw them into the van but she hadn't expected the pain and the bruising as she hit the studded floor of the vehicle.

Aunt Jesse had come for her in the morning but she was charged with causing an obstruction and breaking the peace. The sentence was three months in prison. She had gone on hunger-strike like the rest, like her friend Norah, but they had been kept in separate cells and Sarah moved in the bed as she remembered the fear of dying, the hunger, being alone and then after days or was it weeks they had come and pushed the tube into her nostril and down her throat. She thought her nose, her throat, her chest would burst and then finally it entered her stomach. Each day they had done that, pouring liquid, not much but enough to keep her alive and each time, when they had left her and she had still not screamed and struggled, she had been proud of herself but had lain in fear hour after hour until they came again.

They had released her early to build up her strength. Her father had collected her and taken her to Aunt Jesse. He had been pale but still bustled. Val had fed her up and said she would sit in the streets with her if she didn't stop. No, they need you, Val; if I'm not here, you must be, she had said. They had wanted her to come back but she had to stay in the district and would not have run away anyway, or would she? When she was fitter, the police came for her to finish the sentence and her father did not ask her not to go on hunger-strike again, nor did her mother. He had kissed her and said that freedom must be worth a great deal and he couldn't ask her to go against that but he had aged, and his mouth was trembling and she had turned from him to the policeman frightened that she would cry and beg to stay. Look after me, Papa, she wanted to cry, hold me, send them away.

She had starved again and the tube had come again and the pain and weakness until her sentence was finished. Until the next time she was arrested and the cat and mouse resumed. It was a very effective form of fear, she reasoned now from the safety of age, that cat and mouse game of the government's, but it didn't break them, just killed a few, like her dearest Norah. She felt a thickening of her throat at the thought of the tube going into her friend's lung instead of her stomach.

At last in the early spring of 1914, her father and mother had sent her to Austria, skiing, for fresh air and good food and to keep her from the streets too she suspected. There had been relief at boarding the ship, then the train, leaving the battle because they had asked her to, just for a while. That way it was less like desertion.

Then war had come and the campaign had ceased for the duration and women were given jobs, useful jobs and she drove an ambulance and was glad it had come and she no longer had to suffer.

Annie should be told one day because, throughout it all, her father had supported her financially and had not regretted one penny. He told her so when he and her mother caught flu after the war, just before they died. After she had sorted out the little matter of Mr Beeston her life had settled into its tranquil lines and again she settled herself more comfortably on the pillows.

And now she had Annie, a child who had burst in on her life when she had spun into Wassingham to sort things out after Bob's letter. She had not known definitely whether she would be bringing her back but what she had found in Wassingham was waste and the well ordered life in Gosforn would just have to accommodate this awkward spirit, this child who was not a child. It would be interesting, to say the least.

She was sorry that Archie would not be able to see his daughter develop but in her heart of hearts she also knew that she was supremely relieved. For if he were here, she would not have this repeat of her relationship with her parents. A repeat of the knowledge and caring that would be passed on again. A repeat of love, for that is what she was already feeling for this child.

CHAPTER 12

Annie felt strange in her stomach two days later when August had changed to September and Sarah drove through the large wrought-iron gates, past dark full-leafed bushes, which lined the gravel drive, and up to the entrance of the convent school. Sarah told her that the grey stone building had once been a hunting lodge in the days when Gosforn was a small hamlet, before it had grown up into a market town and a dormitory for Newcastle.

She looked at the sloping gardens beyond the shrubs which Sarah said were rhododendrons from the foothills of the Himalayas, wherever they were, thought Annie. She made her hands lie still in her lap as the car crunched to a halt though she felt as though she was trembling all over and she had a tightness in her chest. The engine died and the car jumped.

'Out you come then,' Sarah instructed and they stood together at the bottom of the three wide steps which led up to the studded double wooden doors. The building seemed to be falling over and would crush them at any moment, Annie thought as she looked up to the turrets which lined the roof, but at least that would mean she would not have to go through the next few minutes.

'Of course, rhododendrons are at their best in early summer,' Sarah continued as she took her arm and nudged her up the steps. 'Large glorious blooms, so much better than the original purple of the wild ones.'

Her gloved hand reached for and pulled the bell chain and Annie's legs felt uncertain. She turned to look out over the drive, down through the yew hedges set in squares which lay in front of the school. They were cut as sharp as Val's bacon when she scissored off the rind. There were flower-beds within their squares with a path running from the drive right through them down to the empty playing field which Annie could see at the bottom.

It looks like a bloody mansion, she thought, not a nunnery. And where were all the girls, because that's all there were. Boys were not allowed through the gates, Sarah had said.

They could hear the bell peeling deep inside the building and Sarah turned and stood looking across the grounds with Annie.

'It is rather lovely isn't it?' she said. 'I was here as a girl and very little has changed, only the length of the hems.' She laughed. 'Mine was down to my ankles and just look at yours. Mother Superior would have had the vapours.'

Annie looked down at her grey pleated skirt, ending well above the ankles and smoothed it over her hips. It was so soft and light, but warm too. The vest she wore did not itch at all. She had not known you could be warm but comfortable. She ran her finger round her neck, chafing against the collar but she liked the grey and red of the tie against the white of the shirt. She wasn't sure about the red cardigan since it seemed to drain her of colour but Val had said that a few games of hockey would soon bring the roses into her cheeks.

She had not known what hockey was and Sarah had shown her an old stick, told her that the object of the game was to get the ball into the other team's goal and that you bullied off for possession of this ball when the referee started the game. You'll enjoy it, she had said, but Annie had thought it sounded ridiculous.

Sarah rang the bell again and Annie half hoped that no one would hear and they could go back to the house again. She could not say home, not yet, not ever, she determined. Home was Georgie. But she would not think of him now, he was for the darkness and her bedroom.

'It is nice, Sarah,' she replied, waving her hand at the gardens, looking again at her shirt, feeling that everything matched, even the grey blazer with its red piping. This had never happened before and she grinned in spite of herself. She'd have to change out of them when she arrived back this evening. Sarah had decided that they would keep hens and that it would be her job to feed, clean and collect the eggs. They should be there, at the house by four and the men were erecting the coop and wire run this morning. If Val had anything to do with it, it would be done in record time. Bye, thought Annie, I bet she could pack a punch.

The door swung open and Annie spun round. A nun in a dark blue habit and a white wimple stood there smiling, just like a penguin, Annie thought.

'So nice to see you, Sarah, let me take Ann in with me, shall I, and we'll meet you at four o'clock.' She had a pink and white face with full lips and a wide brow over pale blue eyes and looked as though she had washed with a scrubbing brush, she was so fresh. Annie smiled at such a neat dismissal of Sarah. That's one in the eye for her she thought, for getting them to call me Ann and opened her mouth to correct the nun. There was no need.

'My ward's name is Annie, Sister Maria. We do so much prefer it to Ann. It was my mistake, I'm afraid.'

She was smiling at Annie, her blue hat set at an angle on her head, matching the coat which had a silver brooch set in a leaf on her lapel and Annie felt her shoulders relax, her stomach feel better. She stroked her hair which she had plaited this morning and adjusted her school hat. It would be good to see Sarah at four o'clock.

Sister Maria stood with her on the top step as the Morris swung round and crunched back down the drive. Sarah tooted and the sound was out of place in the quiet of St Ursula's and Annie knew that it was Sarah's response to Sister Maria and she grinned.

The nun led the way into the high-ceilinged entrance hall. She didn't walk, she glided, Annie decided. It was as though she was one of those little wind-up fat people that rolled along a table with no feet, just wheels. She cocked her head to check that black shoes appeared at the front of the habit and they did. Perhaps it was the wimple that made them move like that; it was so starched it looked as though it would crack if it was jogged at all.

Sister Maria turned, her smile kind and reaching her eyes. 'We'll have a quick look round the school, Annie, and then we'll slip you into your class. Is that all right?'

'Yes, thank you,' Annie replied, looking round the hall which was wood-panelled except for a mural of the crucifixion with drops of blood falling from Christ's hands. Below, on a walnut table, larger than Sarah's, was a vase of russet chrysanthemums. She moved over to touch the petals and could smell their scent all round.

Sister Maria touched her arm and brought her to a halt.

'You must address the nuns as Sister, Annie, and as a sign of courtesy the girls never turn their back on us.'

Annie swung round to her, her face flushing red. She bit back a retort and said, 'Yes, Sister,' but thought, I'm the Queen of the Nile, because it was just like royalty. What would Tom say to this then? She had received a letter from him this morning telling of the Wainwright episode. I'll be a right little bolshie next time I see you, he had said, and she put her hand in her blazer pocket and touched the lined paper which held his pencilled news.

They moved down to the corridor which led from the entrance hall and she had to quicken her pace to keep up with Sister Maria's glide. Her patent leather shoes were catching the light from the windows which ran down one side of this end of the corridor. They were the first shoes she had worn and were so much lighter than boots that she felt as though she had bare feet and they didn't rub anywhere. On the other side of the corridor she saw that there were notices pinned on to cork boards. Hockey and drama stood out in bold red print but then Sister Maria spoke as they rushed on.

'We have put you in with the younger children since you are a little behind, Annie, but never fear, you will improve and at the end of three years you will undoubtedly have your school certificate.'

Annie stopped, her shoes forgotten, her face twisting, her eyes suddenly full. Sister Maria stopped and turned, her hands clasped together under the sleeves of her habit.

'But, my dear,' she said, 'there is no need for the other girls to know. You are so lucky, oh so lucky to be *petite*, so delicate. How they would envy you if they knew.'

But it was not that which had taken the breath from her chest and brought blood to her face. Three years, three years echoed round her head and she wanted to rip the clothes from her, throw them to the ground and run back to the caustic air and noise of Wassingham, back to Tom and Georgie. She had not asked Sarah how long all this would take and now she knew she felt that it was not bearable.

Sister Maria took her arm and they walked together down

the corridor which had lost its windows now and merged into a large dark area which was criss-crossed with stands spiked with pegs, covered now in blazers and hats.

'You will leave your hat and blazer here when you arrive each morning.' She shook Annie slightly as though she were aware Annie wanted to run, to leave here. 'You will come, won't you, Annie?' She looked closely into her face and Annie stared blankly back, deep inside herself. But hadn't she decided that first day that she would stay, Annie told herself, so stop making such a bloody fuss. If she shouted at herself loud enough, it might stop the panic which seemed to swoop and drench her with ice, then fire and leave her so much alone. Sister Maria shook her again.

'You are going to come, Annie?'

And this time Annie nodded, her chin tilted. 'This is my peg is it?' she asked hanging her things on the blunted hook, and was surprised to find that her voice sounded quite normal.

The Sister smiled and patted her arm, then showed her which one to hang her shoe-bag on and also mentioned that she would need a hockey stick, skirt and boots.

Well, thought Annie, that means more work from Sarah or I shall be playing in me bare feet.

'And along here, Annie, is the chapel.' Sister Maria still held her arm as though she was afraid that Annie would turn and run but she wouldn't, not for three years anyway.

'Services are held in the chapel daily. I gather you are not confirmed so we shall have to arrange that.'

Annie raised her eyebrows. We will, will we? she thought. I'll have to think about that.

The chapel was painted cream and there were wooden beams up into the roof and thick long ones that spanned the width of the chapel and held the lights which hung down on black metal rods. It was so light and calm, Annie thought, not like the one which had buried her da. Here the windows were large and light streamed in. The pews were light wood and smelled of beeswax. The altar was simple with a white altar cloth and a metal cross, which shone green and red from the light which dropped through the stained-glass window.

Sister Maria was ahead of her now, pointing to the choir stalls, the pulpit and the lectern which was a gold eagle with a beak which could catch someone a nasty nip if they fell asleep during the sermon, Annie thought.

'We embroider the hassocks ourselves, with the help of you girls of course. Do you sew?' Sister Maria was moving back towards her now. The air was heavy with more chrysanthemums. They were in every window and either side of the altar; orange, purple and yellow.

'No, just a few buttons and repairs,' Annie said, touching the back of the pew. She had not moved down the aisle yet. She had seen Sister Maria cross herself and she could not remember which way round she had done it.

'Well, you'll learn quickly enough. We have a competition coming up which you would enjoy.' Her voice was not Geordie but more like her father's and Sarah. It sounded pleasant, not high or low, and if she sang it would be a comforting sound.

Sister Maria stopped halfway up the aisle. 'Shall I teach you to genuflect, Annie? Would that make things easier for you in here?'

Annie stood still, confusion clouding her thoughts.

'The sign of the cross,' Sister Maria added.

Annie sighed with relief. It was not going to be too bad here and she copied, with her right hand, Sister Maria's movements.

They left the chapel and passed along polished floors and gleaming cream-painted corridors which murmured with muted voices as a door opened and closed and another was left ajar. Three doors on, they stopped.

'This is your class, Annie. I'm sure you will be very happy but, when you see Mrs Beeston, please ask her to buy you another pair of shoes. Patent leather is not permitted in this school, but, for this week only, we will make an exception.'

As they entered the classroom which Annie had noticed was opposite a conservatory, the lesson stopped and the girls rose in unison and Annie wondered how much another pair of shoes would cost.

'Slip into that place, Annie.'

She pointed to a space at the end of a long bench which was attached to a desk of the same length. Annie was aware of turning heads as she passed between the rows and slid into place. It was indented with Christine loves John and Sandy loves Sister Nicole. The girl next to her passed a sideways look and smiled. She did not look very much younger, none of them did, thought Annie, and why did the Sisters object to patent leather shoes? They were so beautiful.

'Shows your knickers it does. The patent leather reflects them, or so they think,' Sandy told her at break. 'Gives the old girls a thrill and they get palpitations.'

'Do you love Sister Nicole?' Annie asked her. The milk tasted thick and made her thirsty. Val had given her a flapjack for break and she shared it with Sandy. They sat in the playground on a wall which was wedged thick with other girls. The crumbs fell on to her skirt and she brushed them clear, anxious about grease. She did not want to have to ask Sarah for another one, there'd be enough jobs to do after today as it was.

Sandy's cheek bulged with flapjack and she waved her hands and pointed to her mouth and Annie grinned. 'Don't rush,' she soothed and was glad that Sandy was red-haired and had freckles because she reminded her of Grace except that she was skinny and her hair was more orange than red.

'Oh, I loved old Nicole last term. This term it's the gardener, he's glorious. Watch out for Batty, she's after break and squeaks the chalk and makes your teeth ache, then throws the board-rubber if you daydream. So you keep your head up and go to sleep with your eyes open or it's the conservatory for you. That's the punishment block you know.' Sandy picked at a tooth with her tongue. 'Lovely grub. Did your mother make it?'

'No, I live with my guardian and the housekeeper. She made it.'

'Oh, I live with my ma and pa, deadly dull and Ma will fuss so. Much more exciting to be different like you. Are your folks dead, then?'

'Yes,' Annie said, not wanting to open the black box by speaking of them. 'How old are you?'

'Dreadfully old for the class. I'm nearly 15 but we've been abroad and I got frightfully behind.'

'Yes, I've lost some time too.' Annie paused, then rushed on, not wanting to explain further, 'I'm 15.'

Sandy grinned and squeezed her arm. 'Good, someone to talk to at last. Jenn is another girl who's older but she's away at the moment. Got a bit of a tongue on her but she's all right, I suppose. When we go for the garden walk, which we do every day after lunch, we can make up a three.'

'A three?'

193

'Oh yes.' Sandy tapped her heels against the wall. 'Have to go in threes, pairs create unhealthy friendships or so the old girls think. Wish they'd let us have a few healthy ones instead like a stroll with the gardener or something.' She roared with laughter and dragged Annie up. 'Come on, the bell's going to go. Let's get to the front of the line then we can grab a desk at the back. Batty's aim isn't so good then.'

It's a different world, thought Annie, as she moved across the playground. It's so easy and most of her would love it in time but there was still the sharp ache for lost alleyways and windswept dunes.

She felt in her pocket for Tom's letter and wished there had been one from Georgie too.

That evening, Annie stood by the chicken-run, her fingers hooked into the wire. The hens were jerking about the run and already the ground was scratched near their coop but she loved the noise of the clucking, the glossiness of their feathers, the shine of the cock's tail.

Sarah stood by her, with her arms crossed, her brown cardigan matching her skirt.

'I thought we should get the cock, then you can hatch some chicks and sell them, or keep a few more layers, whichever you prefer.'

Annie felt a rush of relief; she had not been able to tell Sarah about the shoes or the sports kit and this would make it easier. Sarah went on:

'I've been thinking about the shoes we bought, Annie. I do feel that it would be more economic to keep those for home and buy some sturdy ones for school. Your feet have practically stopped growing so they should last for ages. Would you mind very much if I asked you to help me in this way?'

Annie kept on looking at the chickens and nodded, her back to Sarah. Thank God, thank God, she thought but there was still hockey to sort out and if Sarah was economising? She chewed her lip.

Sarah continued. 'I have some hockey clothes which a friend of mine has given to me. They used to belong to her daughter. You will no doubt be needing some this term.' She was looking down at her and Annie felt her gaze. 'And there's my old hockey stick.'

'You must be a witch,' she said as she turned to look at her.

Sarah laughed with her head right back and put her hand on Annie's shoulder where she allowed it to lie. Annie wanted it to, for a while.

'No.' Sarah shook her head. 'Not guilty, Annie, but I had a look at the uniform list when I arrived at the office and realised we had made some mistakes.'

'So, is it true then, about the economising?' Annie asked, ready to draw back from her hand, to think of more work she could do. She wanted no charity.

Sarah felt the movement and said, with no hint of laughter now. 'Absolutely, Annie. Good strong shoes as they suggest will be far more appropriate and last so much longer and I really have been given the sports kit. Now get those chickens fed and come in and settle down to some homework before dinner.'

'Where's Mr Beeston?' Annie asked. 'Sister Maria called you Mrs today.'

Sarah looked surprised, then amused. 'Let's just say I lost him, shall we?' She stroked Annie's hair and turned to go but stopped. 'I wonder what Tom would think of these?' she murmured. 'Shall we ask him over and Georgie?'

Annie gripped the wire tighter. She kept her voice level as she replied. 'Oh yes, and Tom will come but Georgie won't, not until he's ready.' She pressed her lips together in a straight line and turned again to the chickens.

'Well, what about Don?' persisted Sarah.

'That's an idea. I've written to him telling him where I am but he's very busy. When men leave home they build other lives, don't they?' Sarah nodded at her. 'But I'll write again and ask him. It'll be good to see him, after so long. Hope he hasn't grown too much.'

At Sarah's quizzical look she explained that he needed to keep small for riding and Sarah nodded, laughing at the hen which was pecking near their feet. Then she walked down the cinder path, stopping to pull at a few stray weeds, then a lettuce.

'Make it two,' Annie heard Val call from the kitchen window. The Thoms next door were bringing in their washing from the line and called good evening to Sarah. There were birds in the apple trees down by the greenhouse and the sound of bees as they snuffled the fallen apples. Georgie had always said fallen fruit made them drunk and lazy and that's when they would sting you more easily, forgetting that they would die.

She opened the gate to the run. It felt wobbly but was safe enough; it swung shut behind her and the bowl was half full of feed. The hens were pecking at the ground, brown and plump, lifting their feet as though they were about to burst into a dance with their eyes beady and swivelling. She threw corn to them and watched as they chatted about and chanted in excitement and one came jerking across while she squatted. She held the hen round the neck and stroked it and was surprised and disappointed that it was not soft all through but hard as though there was a brittle cage just beneath the feathers.

'Never mind, bonny lass,' she breathed. 'Just you do a good job laying and we'll get along fine. Who knows, you might get a bairn of your own.'

It was nice to talk in the words she had used in Wassingham because slowly but surely she already felt herself sliding over to the language of Sarah and the people who lived in this tree-strewn town.

She let the hen go as it pecked her and rubbed her finger and laughed. 'Any more of that and you'll be in the pot,' and waved her hand at Sarah as she called her in for homework.

'Ruddy slave-driver she is,' called Annie to the cock and threw him the last of the corn as she headed back to the house.

The smell of sponge pudding wafted from the kitchen window and her mouth watered. It was still strange to have meals cooked for her, it made her feel guilty but pleased. The house had a paved area by the dining-room, under her bedroom and held wrought iron chairs and a table on which lay Val's book from this afternoon. Annie stooped and picked it up as she passed. It was *The Modern Compost Guide*.

'Annie, do come along,' called Sarah. 'Val has some ginger beer and cake here for you and then you must do some work.'

It was going to be hard to be unhappy here but she felt that the others should be sharing all this, that laughter should not come without Georgie, but it would, she knew that now and she also knew he would understand.

CHAPTER 13

Tom's hands were cold. It was November. Annie had been gone for nearly three months and, this Sunday, Grace and he were walking out of Wassingham, along the road to Bell's farm. It was a walk they had often taken when the four of them were together but now, just two of them remained. Georgie had left last month and Tom still did not know how to tell Annie.

He had come round to May's last week when Tom was having his tea, knocked at the door and while Tom stood on the backstep wiping his mouth on the back of his hand he had said he was off. He had a suitcase which was bruised at the corner and ripped where the cardboard had softened too much. Tom had grabbed his arm and stepped out into the yard, shutting the door behind him and the light went with it, so that he had been unable to see Georgie's face.

Are you going to her, man? he had asked, but Georgie had shaken his head. Not yet, our Tom, I'm off to see if there's something better away from here and you'd do well to think on that too, Tom. The pit's hard, Annie doesn't want it for you, you know that, but Tom had shaken off words about himself, it was Georgie who was going, Georgie he would miss.

What about going to Don? he had said. You and he was mates, he'd get you a job in the stable.

Georgie had laughed and picked up his suitcase. I'm going further than that lad and higher. Down south, I think, that's where the jobs are. May had called through the door that his tea was getting cold and Davy had come out then, the light had shone too bright and they turned away. The tin bath was propped up on one side of the wash-house and threw a long shadow down the yard. Come away in Georgie, Davy had said, there's enough for you too, but Georgie had said no and punched Tom lightly on the arm. Take care, bonny lad, and then he'd turned and walked in his measured stride to the gate and was gone. They'd listened to his boots on the cobbles and Tom had pictured the sparks striking from them.

As he and Grace walked round the bend the wind was blowing from the east, harder now than it had been and he grasped his sketch-book more securely under his arm and hunched his shoulders, turning up his collar.

'Oh, so you're back with me then,' Grace said from his side, poking at his arm. 'If I had a penny, I'd give you one for 'em.'

'For what, bonny lass?' he said, grinning at her.

'Just for your thoughts, so that's quite enough of that.'

They laughed and he pointed to the path leading off the road up over the sparse farmland where sheep grazed.

'Come on,' he said. 'Let's go over the top of the hill. It's a better view and we'll sit in the usual place while we have our picnic.'

And I can help you over that too, he thought, as she nodded and they turned towards the wooden stile.

'Give us your bag.' He took it and put it with his by the end of the hawthorn hedge. 'For God's sake, mind yourself on the thorns,' he called, as he grasped her arm. The hedge was stripped of leaves now and the thorns were eager to snag their skin.

'Don't know about keeping in the sheep,' Grace said, as she stepped up, 'but there's no way I'd try and get through that lot.'

She was still plump, our Grace was, thought Tom, as he watched her teeter on the first bar, and he gripped her harder. But she'd grown, bye, she'd grown and had breasts like any he'd seen in Botticelli's pictures, or he thought she would have beneath her clothes anyway. Her body must be creamy and dimpled and that hair, free of its plait could curl all about her shoulders and her back and he would paint her one day with one strand between those breasts. She was so nice too, was Gracie, like Aunt May. Plump and kind with blue eyes like cornflowers that grew in the meadow down by the beck. And teeth that were even and white. Her freckles were soft beige.

'Give us a hand then, you daft dollop,' Grace called, one leg half over the top bar. There was no step up this side, the wood had fallen clear. He kicked it to one side then came behind her and levered up her buttocks and she shrieked and tried to slap him but he dodged and said:

'For God's sake girl, I'm doing you a favour. Get yourself over, will you, before you break me bloody back.'

But he grinned as she scrambled over and jumped down the other side. She was flushed and panting and pulled her dress down where it had hitched up above her knee.

'You can get yourself over, and the bags,' she stormed and stalked across the grass, her head up, her hands busy trying to tuck stray curls back into the curves and hollows of her plait.

Aunt May had packed bread and cheese and a flask of tea and the bag banged against his side and against Grace's which hung over his shoulder too as he caught up with her. As he took her arm, she sniffed then glanced sideways at him. He grinned, then so did she.

The farm was half a mile away now, he reckoned. It was strange coming here on their own. It had always been a race to the top with the other two. Georgie always won, he was second, though Annie had beaten him twice and Grace had insisted on walking with the bags. She said it was undignified but they all knew that she didn't like the wobble of her body and loved her for it.

The oaks near the road were the only trees on which leaves remained, though even they clung in shrivelled clusters and would come down if the wind increased. The sheep grazed all around them as they walked and those in front moved away as they approached. Tom liked the farm, liked the walk to it, the picnic in the hollow on the far side of the hill and the view from there which he had sketched again and again. Each time it varied; the cart was not there or had a different load and the sky behind was blue or grey or flecked with rain. He patted his pocket. Yes, they were still there; the pencils Annie had sent with her last letter. She'd been to Woolworth's, she'd said, where everything was under sixpence.

They were breasting the hill now and the wind snatched at their breath as it whirled across from the sea over to their right, but too far for them to see. There were no sheep up here on the top but rocks showed through the scant soil and the wind tugged at what grass there was and pulled and pushed at the dark spiked gorse-bushes that almost, but not quite, reached the crest. The farm lay at the bottom.

Tom looked at Grace, at her hair with its escaped curls leaping and flicking about her face and reached across and pulled the collar of her thick cardigan up round her neck. They dug heavily into the ground with their heels as they began the descent.

He took her hand loosely, wondering if she would pull away but she did not. He tightened his grip and she did also and then they looked at one another and smiled. It was not so bad after all, thought Tom, coming back here without Annie and he whooped into the air, scattering the sheep and making Grace laugh.

He pulled her faster and faster until they were running and she was with him and laughing and not pulling him to stop. Leaping from hillock to hillock, avoiding the molehills and the sheep which thudded away from their path until the breath bounced in him and they were taking great gulps of air and laughter. He lost his footing half way down and dropped her hand as he rolled over and over, seeing the grass, the sky, his sketch-book as it flew from his hand, his bait-bag as it leapt as he rolled. Over and over he went until he fetched up on the flattened area that was theirs. He lay flat, his arm out, his bag and Grace's flung over his chest, laughing and panting until gradually he was able to heave himself up on his elbow and look for her.

She was running along the hill, not down it, chasing the loose pages from his pad which the wind was sucking and blowing into the air, turning them about and letting them swoop, but always too far for Grace to reach.

'Leave them, Gracie,' he called. 'Leave them and come on down.'

He watched as she turned and cupped her hand to her ear. Her skirt was blowing up over her knees and tight against her legs.

'Leave them,' he called again, then beckoned her with exaggerated hand movements and she saw and came down but not running now, though she was laughing. He could see that and hear her.

'Oh, you great daft thing,' she said. 'No wonder Wainwright gave you a belting. I'm surprised he didn't expel you for breaking his cane.'

She sat down next to him and they edged up so that their backs were against the slope.

The sheep were tearing at the grass all around them, calm again.

'Our Davy had a word with him, or so May said, so he only stopped me from painting, but Mr Green lets me take paints home with me so it doesn't matter that much.'

Grace shook her head and reached for her bag. 'It's as well you've got Davy now. He's taken over from Annie.' She brought out some bread and dripping.

'He'll not do that, nobody'll take over from Annie.' His voice was devoid of laughter now. It was hard and firm. Grace looked at him sideways, sinking her teeth into the crust, it was tough and with her fingers she tore a piece and chewed it.

'Not even me?' she asked, looking down at the farm this time.

'Don't talk with your mouth full. It's common.' He slapped her leg and pulled a face. 'You're not me sister, are you? I feel something different for you.'

He felt the ground cold through his trousers and brought out from his bag an old knitted baby blanket. 'Lift your backside and stop being daft.'

He put the blanket beneath her and she handed him what was left of his book. The pages were askew and out of order. 'All that's left after the wind had a look.'

'Never mind lass,' he said leafing through them, straightening the pages. 'I'll do the farm again. They were just sketches of the yard.'

'Have something to eat, for God's sake,' she said. He looked at her bread and dripping and handed her some of his cheese that he had dug out of May's parcel. The wind was far less raucous where they sat sheltered by the slope behind and it seemed unnaturally quiet. Even the rooks settled along the branches of the elms around the farm were silent as though bowed in sleep.

'You're on dripping then? Are the boys out of work again?'

Grace nodded. 'All but young Frank and he brings in a pittance. Me da's getting right fed up and me mam wants to know how she can feed a family on a few shillings a week. That's why I'm starting at the library next week. At least I'll bring in a little.'

'Do you mind?' asked Tom, taking some bread from her and laying some of his cheese on it before passing it back.

She shook her head. 'It's what I want. It's stupid staying on when I know what I want.'

Tom nodded and lay back, his arms over his head, listening to the sounds of the sheep; there were no insects to buzz and click in his ear at this time of year.

What was it Davy had said last night when he had sneaked him into the snug with his mates? He frowned as he went over the scene, trying to capture the flow which had rolled round and across the table.

He could still taste the beer which had bulged down his throat and the excitement of being included and what Davy said had made sense, all that about families needing an extra allowance from the state to make sure that no one starved. Frank, Davy's mate, had been right too when he'd said that would be a chance for the owners to drop the pay again.

Tom sat up and stared down at the farm, not seeing it, not hearing Grace as she told him to sit still, for God's sake, she was trying to have a sleep. She settled down again, pulling her cardigan tighter round herself. He took off his jacket and put it over her.

Aye, it had been interesting right enough and it had been grand to see Davy's face when he'd suggested that along with the allowance the unions should press for a decent basic minimum wage so that the bosses couldn't try that trick. Tom grinned to himself as he recaptured the look of surprise on Davy's face, surprise which changed to respect but after all they were only ideas which Davy himself had taught him. Davy had gone along with that but had come up with an even better idea himself; that the allowance should be paid to the women so there was no way the bosses could carp that it was supplementing the men's wage packet. Tom looked across at Grace. It wouldn't half help her ma, an idea like that, help everyone, especially up here, whether they were in work or not.

Davy still had no job but he was talking about taking one at Lutters Pit. There was talk of the owners opening it to get what they could out of the bottom seam. It was better than nothing, Davy had said, when May protested and Uncle Henry had banged the table. It was danger money Uncle Henry had shouted. That pit's been closed too long, there's too much water to weaken the props and loosen the coal.

Tom had said to him later that night that he should go away

like Georgie, like his brothers, but he wouldn't. Who would help with the union if he went, he had replied? He was in line for union representative and someone had to stay.

Tom turned now and looked down at Grace. 'Our Davy says, if you start at the library, get 'em not to black out the racing in the papers will you?'

She laughed. 'Tell him I'll bring round the dailies after work if you like but I can't stop them blacking the runners. Can't have men on the dole finding a bit of pleasure in gambling, can they! Anyway, your Davy likes coming into the library. It gets him out of the house and he can find more facts to cause trouble with.' She poked her tongue out at him and grinned. Aye, the lad liked the library right enough, and tinkering with his old motor bike which he refused to sell however much he needed to.

The farmhouse was bordered by outbuildings and today there was washing on the line and a dog lying over the back doorstep. The cart was slewed at right angles to the barn, half full of sawn logs; its wheels looked as though they were growing out of the mud which covered the yard. There was an old plough rusted in the lee of the barn, almost grown over with nettles. He took out his pad and drew in sweeping lines.

'I had a letter from Annie today,' he said.

'Another,' replied Grace. 'I had one too last week.'

'Aye, she told me. She sent me the pencils and another pad. The hens are laying well and now she sells some off to the old sisters who live next door. Their cat got stuck up the monkey-puzzle tree further down the road and they had to get the fire service out. Caused quite a stir.'

Grace smiled and moved her arm arcross her eyes as she lay back, almost asleep.

He still missed Annie, he thought, though it wasn't such a raw ache and it helped have Grace to walk with on a Sunday, though she hadn't let him kiss her mouth yet. He chewed his lip as he wondered how he was going to tell Annie that Georgie had left.

'Does she know Don's back?' Grace asked through lips heavy with sleep.

'I wrote and told her,' he replied. 'I dropped into Albert's the other day to see him. He looks well enough and has taken to the shop like a duck to water.'

Grace clambered on to one elbow. 'Can you pass us the tea then, Tom?'

He unhooked the cup from the top and poured the brown milky liquid, took a sip first, then handed it across. 'There's no sugar, Grace.'

She shrugged and sipped.

'I had a letter from Annie.'

Grace laughed. 'You've just told me that.'

He put his pencil down and balanced his pad on his knee whilst he dug the blue paper from his pocket. It was written in pen and the ink was black. 'She talks about Betsy. I'll read you that bit if you like?'

Grace was looking at him quizzically and nodded when he looked at her. She tucked her hair behind her ear and adjusted his jacket over her legs.

He smoothed the pages and looked through the first one, then put it to the back and stopped halfway down the second page.

'Here it is,' he said. ' "I've been thinking about your mam, Tom. Just imagine how it must have been having to slave away for me da, putting up with all the work, the booze and the misery. Looking after Don and me as well as her own bairn and it wasn't until the end that she belted me, when her hands were like balloons and the booze had got to her.

'She must have felt so beholden to Da because he had taken you too. That's why she could never say what she felt, never stand up for herself, so she got drunk and angry. Then he killed himself and left her with the mess and nowhere to go. At least Joe gave her a job and some money so she can pay May for your keep. She couldn't keep us, you must see that. How could we have lived in some poky room on a pittance she picked up skivvying?

'I feel bad about the way we didn't go to her. We should have done and I'm going to write to her. I think you should go and see her Tom, I really do. She loves you and what else could she do?

'See you when you come next week. Is Grace coming too? Thanks for telling me Don is back. I've written to him at Albert's. I hope he's all right there. It worries me to think of him with that man but he always seemed to like him.

'All my love to you, Tom." '

He handed the letter over to Grace and looked again at the farm. The farmer was out now, loading more logs from a pile by the cart. He used his hands and never seemed to pause between swinging the logs through the air and picking up more.

'Will you then?' Grace asked, when she had finished reading through it again.

Tom shrugged. 'Maybe, maybe not.'

He took up his pencil again and shaded in the side of the barn.

'Did you know she paid towards your keep?'

'Oh yes, me Aunt May told me when I was going on one day, just after I moved in.'

He tore the page out and handed it to Grace. 'What do you think of that?'

He was drawing again, this time trying to capture the farmer in action. It wasn't working and he threw himself back and watched the clouds as they scudded darkly against the grey sky. It wouldn't rain though, the clouds were too high.

'I wonder what me da was like,' he mused. 'Poor old Barney.' It was hardly his fault he'd been killed in the war but what would he have thought of Betsy palming off his son. He thought of his mother, blowsy and overblown and he could not imagine, did not want to imagine, her locked in passion with a man; that gross body all panting and eager. He shuddered and flopped over on to his side, pulling at the grass.

He remembered her clouting Annie, shouting at her and at him, again and again. She was ugly, in the same way that the woman with the veins at the fair had been ugly. Her hands bulged and he didn't want to go and see her, didn't want to go and have to be touched by her. Annie didn't understand. Betsy was not her mother, she was his and had given him away. He wasn't interested in whether she felt beholden, she should have kept him.

Had Annie, he wondered, forgiven her father yet for killing himself? He, Tom, had because Archie had not been his real father. Oh yes, he had been upset, he had grieved but he had forgiven him, but he doubted whether Annie had, whether she ever would. He remembered her saying that she hated him and could never forgive him. Well, he wasn't about to forgive his ma. It was the same thing, he would write and tell her or perhaps he would keep it all inside. It was better there.

He felt Grace's hand on his shoulder. 'Me da knows who your father was, you know. Barney Grant he was, their family came up from the Welsh mines years ago. He had a lovely singing voice me da says. Blue eyes and black hair.'

Tom saw the breath from the nostrils of the sheep grazing nearby. He turned over and said sharply.

'Is that all he knows?' So his surname should have been Grant should it. He had often wanted to know his name.

'That's all he'll tell you.' She sighed and stroked his face. 'He thinks you should go and make it up with Betsy too. He says it's not right for a boy to hate his mam.'

Tom stood up, brushing his trousers free of grass. The farmer was hitching the cart to his horse now, urging him to the track which led eventually to Wassingham. Tom stooped and packed the flask away, offering it wordlessly to Grace before he did so. She shook her head, watching him anxiously. His mouth was set in a thin line, his brow was furrowed in a scowl and his movements were rapid and sharp, almost violent. He was seldom angry and she felt the tears come to her eyes.

She stood up and he snatched the blanket from beneath her, shaking it. The grass flew up and into her eyes; she buried her head in her hands and tried to blink the dust from them. Tom saw and dropped the blanket, brought her hands from her face and lifted her eyes.

'In your eyes is it, Gracie? I'm sorry, lass.' He dug into his pocket and with the corner of his handkerchief slipped out a piece of grass which was in her eye, then lowered her lid over the bottom one until at last it was clear and the tears had stopped. His face was close, his eyes concentrated on hers as he searched for stray grass and dust. Then, satisfied, he said:

'I'm not a boy any more, Grace. I feel a man and I'll be doing a man's job in two months. I can't change how I feel.'

He dropped down and secured the clasp of his bag.

'Won't change,' Grace corrected.

He stood up now and took her by the shoulders. The wind was whipping the hair across her face, he felt the cold through his jumper.

'Can't,' he shouted. 'If I could, I would but I bloody can't. I love me Auntie May but me mam broke me heart when she sent me away and then Annie went and that was her fault too.'

Grace pushed him away from her and slapped him then, hard across the face and red marks came almost immediately.

'Annie, Annie, Annie. All I ever hear is bloody Annie. I'm here too but for all you care I could be one of them sheep cropping the bloody grass.'

She was red in the face with rage and he felt the heat and the pain from the slap and kissed her hard on the mouth, pulled her against him so that her warm soft body was pressed to his. It was his first kiss and he had not known that lips were so soft and he wondered whether he should breathe or not. He did not.

At last they drew apart but he held on to her arms.

'I'm telling you for the last time Grace, you and Annie's different. She's me sister just as much as if Barney had been her father. We're part of one another. I love her, she loves me but when she's not here I feel as though half me bloody heart's gone too. If you went, I would probably feel that the other half had gone. But don't bring Annie up again like that. It's different, what I feel for you both.' He was shaking her now and she nodded and then smiled.

'Don't forget your book,' she said as a page began to blow away again.

He raised his arms and galloped after it, stamping his foot hard down on it.

'I'll take you out for some chips in February, when I'm working,' he shouted as he came back with it bunched into his pocket. 'Until then, you can take me.' He grabbed her to him and kissed her cheek, then picked up the bags and made her wear his jacket as they set off back up the hill.

'I never did get the farmer right,' he murmured as they turned and watched the cart disappear round the hill. 'I can't get me figures to come alive somehow.'

'Annie wants you to go to art school you know. She's frightened of the pit for you and so am I. Look what it did to me da.'

'It's not going to get me, bonny lass. Maybe one day I'll go but it'll take money you see. Anyway, there's time enough.'

'And you'll see your ma, will you?'

She felt him tense and saw the muscle in his cheek jump.

'Maybe,' is all he said. 'Maybe.'

CHAPTER 14

Annie was smoothing down her new blue dress which slid over her skin and hung soft from her shoulders. She turned before the long mirror which was screwed to the inside of the mahogany wardrobe in her room and then she heard Tom's voice.

'I should stay here in the hall,' replied Sarah. 'It is somewhat improper to visit a young lady in her bedroom.'

But his steps were nearer and she faced the door, hiding her laugh in her hands.

'You lovely boy,' she cried and ran to him. His dark jacket was prickly and his chin rough as he held her tight and swung her clear off the ground.

'Aye, but you've grown,' Tom laughed. 'In three months you've grown, bonny lass. And in quite the right ways too.'

She held him from her and grinned.

'Don't be improper,' she mimicked Sarah and minced from him with one hand on her hip. 'Come on, is Don downstairs?'

She grabbed his hand and moved towards the door but he pulled her back. 'On me back then,' and her laugh jogged in her throat as he reared towards the stairs with her on his back and then on down, past the prints. She leant her head on the back of his and felt his warmth as he spun to a halt on the bottom step. Don was waiting, his elbow on the banister, his eyebrows raised.

'Not made a lady of you yet, then?' he drawled and she flung her arm round his neck and kissed his cheek. His moustache was very bushy now and she wondered how he ate without it getting in the way.

'I sometimes feel that day will never arrive, Donald,' called Sarah as she came through from the kitchen with an apron on.

She had been cutting egg sandwiches for tea and Annie could smell them from here.

'She hasn't got ears, you know,' Annie whispered to Tom. He hitched her further up his back. 'She's just one big flap that picks up everything.'

Don frowned and Tom laughed. Annie knew it would be all right. Sarah liked to be teased.

'I don't think we wish to go into my anatomy just yet awhile, Annie. Why don't you go into the garden and see the hens?' Sarah smiled and walked back to the kitchen and Annie winked over at Val who had come to the door and was laughing.

She dug her heels into Tom. 'Come on then, get a move on.' Tom edged out through the back door, still with her on his back and then he galloped down the garden, past the rose-bushes which were stunted with pruning and Annie felt the air jogged from her and the garden tipped and lurched. She waved wildly to the Thoms across the fence and turned to look back, beckoning to Don.

'Hurry up,' she called and her voice sounded as though she was rolling over cobbles.

He didn't see her as he talked through the window to Sarah in the kitchen. Tom dumped her by the wire but still kept an arm round her waist as he struggled to regain his breath. She held on to his shoulder and he kissed her cheek. Her hair was loose and kinked, almost curly and he touched it.

She grinned. 'I put it in lots of plaits at night. Sandy, one of the girls at school, taught me that little trick. It's better than just a few. Do you like it? She's nice; red-haired and blue-eyed but not plump like Grace. Couldn't she come, Tom?'

She'd said it all in one breath and her face was wistful as he shook his head.

'She's working tomorrow, bonny lass, and her Frank was in a fall in the pit, so she's home nursing him.'

Annie gripped his arm. 'Not bad is he, not like his da?'

Tom smiled and squeezed her to him. 'Just a bit of a knock. The coal fell behind him and he had to be dug out so he was bloody lucky. She sends her love.'

Annie bit her nail. Suddenly she was back in Grace's kitchen, laughing as Tom spilt his pink mice all over the floor, back in the dark streets, the beck and on the moors. Back where the wind tore through her hair on the beach, back where slag-heaps

209

loomed wherever you looked and coal-dust coated the trees. Then Tom slapped her hand from her mouth, lightly, but enough to bring her back to the light and the cleanliness of the garden and the hens, but part of her still called for the past while the other sank back into the space and light of the present.

'Don't bite your nails, hinny. It's a disgusting habit, or that's what our Gracie would say.' He was smiling at her, his blue eyes deep into hers and she knew she would be all right if she could still feel his arm round her, see his pictures as the years went by. All right if the pit didn't get him and fear clutched at her and she banged the wire to attract the hens towards them.

'We'll feed them in a moment,' she said, 'when Don gets here.' Anything to put that image from her mind. She looked round for Don again.

He seemed to have been a man for years and years she thought. Above and away from the two of them, always busy with his own plans, never needing them, seldom writing when he moved away. She felt like a fly Beauty's tail would want to swat when she was around him. He was old, he'd been old for a long time and she couldn't find ground between them that she could walk on and reach him. But she loved him. He was her brother.

She watched Tom as he squatted by the wire and stuck his finger through, waggling it to attract a hen. 'She'll think it's a worm and nip you,' she laughed, pushing him so that he nearly fell over.

He stood up again, taking his cap from his pocket and slipping it on to the back of his head. He moved his shoulders as though his back ached and suddenly she remembered.

'Your back,' she gasped. 'I must have hurt you when I was having me ride. Here, let me have a look.'

She darted behind him and held up his jacket and the shirt with it and her skin went cold as she saw the raised red scars. She heard Don strolling up the garden behind her and turned.

'Look at this will you, Don. I'd have bloody killed him if I'd been there.' Her lips tightened with rage and she touched Tom's back with her fingertips.

Don had walked on past and was clucking through the wire at the hens.

'Teachers have a job to do,' he said. 'Tom's like you, all mouth. He probably asked for it.' He twanged the wire with his finger and moved further down to see the cock which was pecking at corn left over from this morning.

Annie felt the old irritations rise up as she tucked Tom's shirt back. She wanted to slap Don's face, push it into the wire so that he had red marks and then tell him he had too much of a mouth on him and begged for it. But Tom winked at her. Albertitis, he mouthed, his hand up and she nodded and shrugged. Nothing had changed, she thought, between them all, but wished that it had. She pulled a face at Don behind his back.

'If the wind changes, you'll stay like that,' Don said without turning his head and her eyes widened at Tom and then they started to laugh and she moved up to Don and put her hand on his shoulder, hoping he would stay next to her and talk. Tom nodded quietly at her and she showed Don her best layer. He moved from her to take some corn and flicked it through the wire. Her stomach tightened and she looked away, not at Tom, not at Don, but at nothing until she was able to smile again through lips that were stiff.

She gave them bowls and watched as they took in the corn and spread it about, laughing at the hens that pecked and chattered and pushed to reach the choice piles, leaning on the wire while the weak sun fell on her back. Don had let her touch him for a while at least. She would not tell them yet of the card she had received this morning from Georgie saying that he had left Wassingham and was in the Army now. That he would come for her later and that he loved her and always would. She had left it under her pillow and would allow herself to look at it and feel it again tonight and until then would not think of him being where she could not imagine him, not see him sitting or standing in a place she recognised.

The wire lurched as Tom slammed the gate behind them and screwed the wire shut. He stood next to her and looked back at the house. The winter sun was low and he pulled his cap further down over his eyes and took out his pad while Don walked over to the greenhouse. He sketched in the french windows of the sitting room, the flagstones and rose bush in the tub which was pulled close to the house for frost protection.

'I need colour really,' he murmured and Annie looked over his pad, shading her eyes as she studied the house again. He had caught the essence of the place.

'It's lovely here,' Tom remarked. 'Are you happy?' Looking at the house not at her.

Annie moved to the laurel tree and picked at a dark leaf. 'It's too early to answer that. I love the comfort, the ease. It's electricity here.' She heard the pride in her voice. 'But it's still strange, still as though I'm not really here.' She was going to continue but Don called over.

'How much do you make on the eggs then?' The cinders were wet from yesterday's rain and did not move beneath his feet but stuck to the soles of his boots as he came towards them.

'Enough,' replied Annie and waved to Val as she came to beckon them in to tea. 'Coming,' Annie called. 'Race you in, Don.' She grinned at him, willing him to run with her, but he shook his head and walked with his hands deep in his pockets towards the house so she walked beside him, pointing to the vegetables and the shed which was full of garden furniture, as well as her bike.

'Well, you have done well for yourself then, haven't you,' he murmured before they reached the kitchen and she wanted to tell him that she would, somehow, make it up to him one day. She would give him his share of her good luck.

As they entered, Sarah handed Don the tray of cups to carry through to the sitting-room and Tom left the sketch of the house on the table and pushed the trolley, taking over from Val and making her go before him into the room. It clattered as he pushed it and the smell of scones was strong because Sarah had covered over the egg sandwiches with a bowl.

'Annie's eggs are beautiful but they are rather ripe when hardboiled, don't you think?' Sarah asked as she settled down by the teapot.

Annie watched as the boys took a sip of tea and had to bite her lip to stop laughing out loud. 'It's Earl Grey,' she explained. 'I like it now.'

Sarah looked up from her sandwich. 'I'm so sorry, would you prefer Indian?' She had flushed with embarrassment and Annie wished she had said nothing because underneath Sarah's poise there was an uncertainty at times, one that was usually to do with her. She wondered, not for the first time, how she would cope if her home was invaded by a girl from a different background who endlessly upset the routine.

Tom had shaken his head but Don nodded. 'Tastes like soap.' He pulled a face.

'I said you'll get to like it,' Annie snapped and took his cup to the kitchen and made another pot of tea.

'How did you manage to leave the horses then, Don?' she asked on her return, her voice friendly, her face stretched in a smile which was too broad. She was sorry for snapping, sorry for Sarah, annoyed with herself.

'Just take a look at me, Annie. I've grown you daft thing. Too big for the horses now.'

'So how long are you at Albert's?'

She noticed how he poked his scone into his mouth all in one whilst she had cut hers into quarters. The butter dripped out of the corner of his mouth and ran in a greasy trail to his chin. There were crumbs in his moustache. She passed him a napkin to wipe his mouth but he opened it and tucked it in the open collar of his shirt and the butter ran under his chin. He wiped it with the back of his hand.

'He's going to make me a partner. I'm in your old room.'

'But how could you go in with him?' Annie protested. 'How could you even think of it? He's a money-lender and he charges the earth.'

'So what?' He reached for another scone. 'There's more out of work, so more'll need to pawn or borrow. We'll do both.'

Tom put down his knife. 'Well, you set your rates too high for the likes of Grace, you know; the likes of anyone round our way. We're struggling with things as they are. They're our people you know, Don. We grew up with them and you're making mint out of their bad luck. We should be working together to try to sort it out, not gaining from it. They don't like it, Don. It'll lead to trouble.'

'We run the shop as well,' Don was sitting back now, sipping his tea, smiling as he savoured the rich brown brew. 'Don't forget that. And how is our Gracie these days? Still a wobble a minute, is she?'

Annie put her hand up to stop Tom who jerked forward. Tension had leapt into the air, sparking between the three of them as it had always done, but louder now, more serious than just the squabbles of children and Annie did not want his anger growing and souring her family. She loved them both.

Silence fell whilst Don sipped, his eyes cold on Tom, who glared.

Sarah cut in, her voice crisp and clear. 'So things are bad, are they, Tom?' And Annie settled back in her chair though she knew that trouble had only sunk to just below the surface and was ready to rear out, spitting, at any moment.

Tom explained that work was more difficult to come by because coal was just not selling; that poverty was increasing; that Grace's family was finding it harder, like all the others and that the miners couldn't do anything, they had no power now. Annie looked at the scones dripping with butter on the doily-covered plates, the sandwiches and the cakes, at the two pots of tea, and the dark streets seemed far away. It was easy to forget that Wassingham had rickets and consumption, bare feet and starvation.

Sarah had lit the fire when the tea had been poured and the heat was reddening Val's cheeks as she sat with her hands on her lap near the hearth. Her eyes were nodding shut and Annie let the conversation wash past her now, thinking that soon, as it was every day, Val's head would be on her chest. She knew also that later she would sit with her sewing-box darning over the wooden mushroom or altering dresses or making napkins out of old tablecloths and that Sarah would read the paper until nine-thirty when she would make the cocoa and call Annie from her homework.

Life had a gentle pattern these days. School with Sandy and Jenn and the walks round the gardens, then Val and Sarah. It was as though she had been ill and was slowly recovering, slowly finding herself whole again, but she must not forget what life was really like.

The sharpness of anger broke in on her thoughts and there were her two brothers clashing again. Don sat upright and stabbed his finger at Tom, speaking with scone in his mouth.

'Albert's got a right to make a living like everyone else. He's all right. You just want a revolution, you and that Davy of yours. He's always stirring things, he is. What's wrong with making a profit?'

'You shouldn't make a profit at the expense of your neighbours, that's all I'm saying. Don't do it, man, don't follow that old bugger and go against your own. You're too good for that.'

'He's not an old bugger,' Don stormed and Annie looked to Sarah who was not remonstrating, just listening. Val had her head up now.

Don continued. 'He's giving a service you know and if you treat him proper he's all right to be with. He's me uncle after all, me da's brother. He's family, isn't he?' There was a hard set to his face now.

'Our Annie treated him proper,' Tom was shouting now, 'and look what happened to her and it was because he was your da's brother he did that. He told her that an' all. You're on the wrong side, Don.'

Annie felt a knot tightening in her stomach again, her hands gripped the arm of the chair as the voices went through her.

Don leant forward. 'Our Annie rubbed him up the wrong way if I know anything about her. He didn't have to take her on, did he?' He jerked his thumb at her and Sarah went white. Val was poking the fire loudly.

'For Christ's sake,' hissed Tom and put his hand on Annie's arm.

Don stabbed at Tom again. 'If you don't like the facts of life, boy, why don't you get out, like she's done, like Georgie, and have your revolution somewhere else? You've got no one to keep you in Wassingham. I've got me uncle.'

Don turned to Annie now, ignoring Tom's sudden silence. 'Gone in the Army, Georgie has, did you know? I heard from his mam when she came in.' He put up his hand as Tom began again. 'To buy some fags it was, not to borrow, so keep your holier than thou shirt on.'

Annie nodded, angry at him for throwing Tom's family in his face, angry at him for throwing Albert at her as though he was a saint, wanting him to stop making her feel as though she deserved to be belted and screamed at, wanting them both to think the same way, to stop quarrelling, to stop what she feared had become hate. Wanting most of all for him to stop talking about Georgie, but needing to hear more.

'He'll be all right, will Georgie. Uniforms bring in the girls, they do, and he'll be all for getting his leg over if I know him.'

Tom was on his feet now, his face white. 'Well, you don't know him do you, so that's enough.' But Annie pulled him back down although she felt cold with shock and everything seemed impossibly far away. Don did not know about her and Georgie, so it was not his fault, none of this was his fault. It was because of Albert that he was like this and was it, she wondered, something about her that inflamed him?

She watched as Sarah patted her mouth with her napkin with a hand which shook. How strange, Annie noted with detached surprise; she had never seen that before.

'That's quite enough of that language please, Don,' said Sarah in a voice as cold as ice. 'You've obviously been around horses too long.'

Annie stroked butter on to a teacake, then cut it carefully in half, then quarters, watching as the butter flowed over the knife. Tom was sitting stiffly in the chair beside her; she saw that his fists were clenched, that he was breathing quickly. No one was speaking. The fire was crackling though and Val used the brass tongs to put two logs either side of the grate.

'Could you help me with my embroidery, Tom?' asked Annie desperate to break the tension. She put down her plate and looked across at Val. 'Could you pass it from there please, Val?' Her voice sounded strained, high-pitched but it was better than the silence.

Strung across a frame was the hassock material. Annie nudged Tom. 'I have to enter this competition.'

'What's the prize?' asked Don, drinking his tea again.

She ignored him. Tom rose and took the frame from Val.

'I can't bear the flowers as they are. I want something different, Tom, but it must be easy.' She laughed and slowly felt as though she was more in touch with the room. Sarah was looking at her, smiling her approval.

'Something Art Deco do you think?' suggested Tom, sitting down again, keeping his eyes on her work, away from Don.

'Art what?' queried Annie and Sarah cocked an eye at Tom.

'What do you think of Art Deco then, Tom? I'm not sure myself.'

'It's different right enough, but I like the geometric lines.' He turned to Annie, his face less red, his eyes concentrating on his thoughts, not flashing with frustration as they had been. 'Makes me glad I did a bit of geometry at school. It grew out of the Art Nouveau movement which showed that art could be used in an industrial age and Art Deco tries to unite design and industry. They say that it can enter into the design of anything, even a cinema. So why not a hassock?'

'A hassock's not industrial,' objected Annie.

Sarah laughed. 'But why not borrow the idea? It would shake Sister Maria up a bit.'

So, guessed Annie, you still haven't forgotten the first day of school, and laughed, but made sure that Sarah thought it was at the idea of Art Deco hassocks, not at her in this instance.

Tom had taken out his pad and was drawing a rising sun design but Annie told him it had to be a flower motif, so he altered it to a sunflower. She passed it to Sarah.

'Could I do that in satin-stitch and cross stitch?' She grinned at Tom and then, stiffly, at Don. 'It's all I can do.'

Sarah passed it to Val for her opinion.

'Should be fine,' agreed Val. 'As long as she keeps it tidy at the back, she won't disgrace herself.'

Annie heard Don grunt and showed it to him but he did not react. She took back the design and heard Sarah ask Tom why he didn't go into textile design. 'It would combine art with manufacturing.'

And bring him out of the pits, Annie thought, and watched the lad as he leant back and looked at Sarah, his expression thoughtful.

She looked around the room, then at the curtains and then the wallpaper. 'Hey, what if the curtains and the wallpaper matched. That'd look good. What do you think Tom?' She felt a stirring of excitement.

Tom grinned. 'It's a good idea. Does anyone make them like that?'

'No one round here anyway,' Val commented.

Sarah leant forward. 'Make them yourself then, Tom.'

Suddenly the room was alive again, full of ideas and thoughts and words, though Don would still only sit and drink his tea. The fire died down as the time strode past and Tom said, 'What do you think, Don? Would you want to come in too, if we could get it off the ground?'

'It's funny,' said Don, 'bloody funny. There you are, shouting your mouth off at me because I lend money and here you are, you and Annie, talking of setting up a little capitalist empire.'

'No, Don, that's just what we've been saying,' Tom enthused. 'We're thinking about a cooperative. Then the men share the profits; if productivity rises, so does their money.'

Annie took his arm and pulled him back into his chair.

'Just a minute, Tom, remember that day at the beck when I said I'd lead me swarm out? Well, if I came in with you I'd want half the work-force to be female.'

She looked at him in triumph as Sarah and Val laughed and nodded. Don settled himself against the back of his chair and said, 'That's the end of that idea then, Tom.'

Annie lifted her chin. 'Just why is that?' she asked.

'The men wouldn't wear the lower wages. If you employ women, the wages would have to come down to match theirs.' Tom was tapping his fingers on his knees.

'That's no problem,' said Annie airily. 'You bring the women's up and they have same share of the profits.'

Tom and Don burst out laughing. 'There'd be a riot from firms elsewhere,' Don argued.

Tom nodded. 'We'd be setting a precedent. The unions wouldn't like it.'

Annie would not give in. She was determined now. Here was something she could build up. It would get Tom out of the pit eventually and maybe Don would come in and get away from Albert, be closer to them. There would be a place for Georgie and for Grace and for all those women.

'Then they'd have to lump it. Look at Sarah, why should she be paid less for doing her job than a man would? She has to keep a house. If I don't marry, I would have to. It's not fair, is it, Sarah? Surely you can see that Tom.'

His face was thoughtful and she could see that he was trying to sort it out. 'You can't be a socialist and not care about the women too,' she insisted, and listened as the talk swirled round the room again and soon the scones were finished and the cakes too.

Then he nodded. 'You're right. Of course you're right. We'll make the women equal.'

And he took a cup of warm tea from Sarah and gulped it down, his mind busy, and Annie was thinking that she would find Georgie and bring him back. They could go to the Lancashire mills for the cotton. Then Don said, 'You'd need to go to Art College, wouldn't you?'

The words cut across the excitement, the thoughts of the future, and the dreams disappeared, but then Sarah said, 'That's no problem. I will fund the Art College training.' Annie looked up at her and Tom spun round. His face had fallen into hopelessness but now was alight with hope. He looked at Annie, then back at Sarah. She leant forward and switched her table lamp on and it threw the light on to her face and showed her enthusiasm.

'Oh, so it's a paintbrush you need, to get anything round here, is it?' Don sneered. His eyes were on his cup and Sarah kept her face still as she turned it to him in the hush that had fallen again. Annie felt the sweat break out as she heard his words.

'No, Don, you do not need a paintbrush. I was intending of course to give you the same start as I would give Tom. In that way, all three of you will be equal.' Her voice was carefully expressionless and Annie flushed with shame for her brother and despair for herself.

Sarah rose. 'Come with me now to the study. I'll sort something out for you now. It might make the partnership you speak of with Albert that much more businesslike.' She smiled at Annie. 'It will be two years at least before Tom is able to go to College and we have plenty of time to sort his affairs out.'

Annie sat on as they left the room. Val and Tom cleared the tea things and rattled them out on the trolley and tray. The fire flickered lower and she did not think to replenish the logs. It was right of course that Don should have the same from Sarah as she had had, but now her task would be to find the money to repay her guardian for all that she was to give to her brothers or there would be no freedom for her. It would be like Betsy all over again.

Later, long after they had left and she was in bed, with Georgie's card in her hand, held against her body, she cried for him, wept for his strength. Georgie was her rock, the only one stronger than her. He had taught her, loved her, shown her a world that she had not known existed. Taken her by the hand to see the marsh marigold, the rowan berries ripening in late August. Made her look beyond her mere existence; to push thoughts from her head so that they did not absorb her energies, to enjoy the moment. What was it he had said? Push those black memories away, they don't have to stay inside your skull unless you want 'em to.

She needed him, needed his body, needed his strength that

had steadied her and then coaxed heights of passion from her. She knew he would be back, but only when he had brought himself up to the level that Sarah had determined for Annie. Only then, when he could match her, not need to take from her, would he be back. That was the love she missed, the love of someone she did not feel responsible for.

Don's whispered request, as he left, made her writhe again; the feel of her da's watch as she had given it back to him, as he had asked, made her feel a repeat of the anger she had felt.

It wouldn't get nicked from Albert's, he had said, pocketing the watch, so there was no longer any need for her to hang on to it, and now she forced the anger she felt away from him across to her da because it was a watch he should still have been wearing but he had killed himself, hadn't he. He would not make her angry at her brother for something which was his fault and she cried again as she tried to push the black memories back into the box, but it was too late now, they were out again and she wondered if they would ever give her any peace and go away completely.

CHAPTER 15

The marigolds were growing spindly in the beds and their bulging green seeds pulled the long stems down into the path; their acrid smell would be stronger as the sun rose. Annie dead-headed them as she went past, then segmented one in her pocket using her thumbnail and, pushing her bike, bumped down the steps through the gate and out into the road.

She was early for school today, deliberately so, and she did not ride the bike but pushed it along until she reached the lamp-post beyond the Miss Thoms; then she propped it up by the kerb and leant against the street lamp, unfolding Georgie's letter which she had already read twice since it had arrived after breakfast.

Here, on the pavement, with people walking past and lorries braking and revving as they came round the corner she reread every word, slowly savouring the shapes and lines, seeing in them his face as he bent over the paper, his hands as they fashioned these words, hearing his voice, even though he was so far away. It was two years since she had seen him. Two years since she had left Wassingham.

April 1931

My dearest Annie,

I never thought I would be writing to you from the North West frontier of India when I last wrote. It will take a good few months for this to reach you because letters from here travel by foot, mule, train before they reach the sea. Is your summer nearly over?

221

I am hunched round the fire with the snow falling all around. It is freezing hard and we have been marching all day in the column out from the fort to keep an eye on the Pathans. These are mountain people who enjoy a bit of fisticuffs between themselves and the odd raid into the lower farmlands. We are supposed to keep them in order. Some hope!

They like our guns so will be trying to take them fairly soon but they won't be successful.

We are also here to check the passes and make sure that Russia is not about to invade India but the officer here says that the bolshies are probably too busy with their own problems to be starting any nonsense like that. I expect Tom could tell us all what he means by that.

I'm a lance-corporal now which isn't bad for 19. I got me first stripe soon after we landed in India, so have just helped our lads to build a stone wall, which is called a sangar out here, before reporting to the sergeant. He's set up a machine-gun inside it and of course ourselves.

The hill we have climbed today is rather higher than the one we used to race up to get to Bell's Farm and you would need all the vests you could find to survive. I can't see you climbing in our gear. The brown woollen shirts would prickle you to death and on top of that the jerseys scratch through them. Our shorts go as far as our knees and the footless hosetops, socks, puttees and the boots would drive you mad, they're so tight.

We sleep out in the open, though some sit up round the fires, preferring the warmth to a good night's kip. I don't mind it too much, Wassingham could be pretty bad – remember? But if I were here with you neither of us would notice the snow, even if it fell for a million years. I've missed you so, my bonny lass, my darling. I think of you every night, every day. Think of you with Val and Sarah, think of you sitting on your wall with Jenn and Sandy. Think of you lying in bed and I want you so much it hurts. I can picture your friends but wonder how wrong I am. It must be grand to have a break from the hard graft of life and you must enjoy it, you must try not to spoil it by worry over the boys or missing me.

Tom is right, you know, when he says that Don is asking for trouble with his money-lending. His interest rates are far too high from what Tom says when he writes, but he'll talk some sense into the man so don't let it get to you. The idea of your own business still seems to excite Tom and at least it will get your bonny lad out of the pits won't it, which is what you want more than anything, isn't it?

I wonder, though, whether the business is what you really want. You sound so interested in your work at the hospital but Sarah's right to say it's too much for you. Little hinny, you must take care. Don't work your guts out just to pay her back for Don's money. She doesn't want it and even if you feel you must make it up to her there's all the time in the world to do it.

You mustn't worry about me out here either. We are really sent out from the fort to push off boredom and it is just a bit of a ramble so you can imagine that it suits me grand. The hills are covered with the holly-oak scrub with leaves that barely rot when they fall, so we march through inches of them. Their acorns don't ripen for eighteen months either so new growth is slow here. I want to get down to the Himalayas which should be our next posting and will then see the rhododendrons you talk of having at the convent. It will make me feel nearer to you, my little lass.

I think if it was warmer you would find it good here. The views take the breath from your chest and the wild life is the sort you only read about in books. Yesterday I saw a leopard and we hear the wolves at night. The Hindu Kush mountains are too large to be real. I will bring you to India one day, but not here; I will find a place I love and that is warm and clear and it will be there that we will have our honeymoon.

It will make the time go more quickly to think of

that day, but I don't know how long it will be; there's quite a way for me to go before I have a chance of becoming an officer because that is what I intend to be; for you and for me.

I thank God, the real God not Bob, that Sarah took you out of Wassingham when she did. The depression, what we hear of it, sounds bad. Tom tells me a bit, but not all. He's in work, he says, but not Davy yet, though they're both up on soap-boxes shouting their mouths off most of the time from what he tells me. If we had married and still been there, what would have become of us?

I have to write these long letters my darling, there is so much spilling out of me, so much I want to say to you, but what I want more than anything is to see your face, feel you in my arms, kiss your lips. But it will be a long time yet and I will say what I always say to you; you must be free my love, free to make other friends, take other lovers, because life is too short to be wasted and to turn down love.

Just remember my sweetest darling that I love you more than life itself and that, in the end, I will be there to teach you how to hang by your arms from the bar. I didn't on that day of the fair, did I? I will always regret that.

Sweet dreams, my bonny lass. Thank you for your precious letters which I keep with me all the time, though some are so well read that they are in pieces.

I will write again, my love,

Georgie.

Annie smoothed the letter in half, then quarters and put it in her inside pocket. She was still in the stinging snow, amongst scrub holly-oak, still standing dwarfed by the mountain range as she pushed her bike out into the road and on towards school. She rode up the drive past the rhododendrons which had been beautiful in June, a month ago.

She would like to see them growing at the foot of a mountain, but only if it was with him, with her love, and the ache which his letters always brought burned through her and she wanted to walk and run anywhere so long as it was without people. She wanted to lie on a warm meadow bank or on a windswept dune and think of him, urge him to come home, will him to come back to her. But today was Wednesday and she was here, at school, and it was piano with Miss Hardy. She shrugged Georgie up into a corner of her mind, pushed him until he could barely be seen, be felt, until she was in bed tonight, free of interference and climbed back into the convent and her life today.

The music room was across from the main building in what used to be the old hay loft above the stables. Marjorie Phelps was in before her and the notes flowed melodically through the brown door behind which the old bag would be sitting, smiling like the Cheshire Cat because some little nimbled-fingered princess of the keyboard was putting pianissimo where it belonged.

Her leather music-case flopped along her thighs as she sat on one of the two chairs which lined the small waiting-room. She was tired today, she always was on a Wednesday because Tuesday evening she was at the cottage hospital. It had been Sundays only at first but Sister Newsome had asked her if she could come in on one evening as well to read to the patients. It calmed them before their operations Sister Newsome had explained, her purple sister's uniform crisp and her buckle large and glinting.

Annie had been pleased because her duties should have been just tea-making and plate-washing in this part-time job she had seen advertised in the local paper. This small sister though, with her laughing eyes and brisk, but kind efficiency, had begun to ask her to roll bandages, sit with ill patients, play with sick children with shorn deliced heads. And Annie loved it; loved to watch the nurses as they changed dressings, fought for a life. Loved to watch Sister Newsome take charge of a crisis or just run her ward from day to day. She envied her authority, her competence. Yes, she had been pleased but it made her tired. She would not stop though because, as well as loving it, she needed to be able to give Sarah those few shillings each week.

She looked at the door opposite and a pulse flickered in her throat at the thought of the next half hour. That Sarah should think piano-playing a useful asset in later life was absurd. Even Jenn's mother had let her stop and she was very much a drawing-room devotee.

There was no noise now, no flowing scales, no fluid arpeggios. The door opened.

'Oh dear, come along in, Ann, and very well done, Marjorie. One would wish all one's pupils were such a joy.'

You're no violet yourself, you know, thought Annie as she squeezed passed the small round woman with gold-rimmed glasses and moles on her pale dry skin.

She slid on to the stool and pumped away at the scale of 'C' as Miss Hardy first stood behind her, then moved to sit down on the chair at her side. The metronome gained on her as usual and the sharp pencil jabs began.

'Evenly, Ann. How often do I have to say it? Have you practised at all?' The metronome continued to tick.

Annie yawned; it was slow and deliberate because one knuckle was oozing blood slowly and it hurt but she would not show that she was affected.

'I suppose you have been out gallivanting with all and sundry and paying no attention to your work.' Miss Hardy was sitting bolt upright on a chair next to Annie. She could see the movement of her plump thighs each time her rhythm broke but it was the fidgeting broke it. The piano had a dark glossy varnish and was wedged across the corner of the small room. The window was to the right of Miss Hardy and through it Annie could see the girls as they walked from the tennis courts to the changing-rooms in the school. They trailed their tennis rackets in loose hands and clouds hung motionless in the pale blue sky beyond the school vegetable garden. A row of runner beans was beginning to sport heavy red flowers and she smelt the scent of leeks from long ago and felt Don's hair as she tugged his head up to hers and wondered yet again why he went on provoking the neighbourhood and knew that it was because there was more money in it for him. He was a fool, a bloody fool and he wouldn't listen to her but Tom had said he would make sure he got through to that thick skull before an iron bar did. Tom was growing up fast, she thought, older than his 15 years but the pits did that to a man, so did a woman and as she stumbled over 'Sunshine after Rain' she grinned to think of him and Grace and was pleased.

'This won't do, you know, Ann.' The pencil jabbed again into the back of her hand. 'Two mistakes in that piece and no heart at all.'

Miss Hardy flicked over the pages of the book, her gold charm bracelet rattling as she did so.

'Try this one and remember the "F" sharp.' She pencilled round the note with a flourish.

Annie stumbled over the 'F' sharp as she always did; somehow her fingers just did not make that lift to the black note cleanly. Miss Hardy's voice was rising nicely, she thought, a little earlier than usual perhaps and she braced herself for the tirade. Annie knew she provoked this woman, always had done and she felt it was something to do with Sarah but did not know what.

'I blame the home of course.' Miss Hardy was rocking in sharp movements and Annie was ready for the jab when it came. The kettle was boiling on the small table in the corner and Annie noted that the outburst was rather more powerful than usual. She lurched into an arpeggio, also in 'C' and the kettle was allowed to continue boiling; the lid rattled and Annie could see the cup out of the corner of her eye and wished Miss Hardy would have her usual tea-break. It always calmed her down.

'I suppose,' Miss Hardy went on with her voice like a coiled spring, 'it's boys, making you tired, making you rude and obstinate.' She jabbed again and Annie felt the first stirrings of anger.

'Now "The Skater's Waltz", if you please.' She reset the metronome. The tick was faster.

Still the kettle rattled. 'Shall I turn off the kettle, Miss Hardy?' The steam was drifting across the ceiling now.

'You see, I do not go out at night.' Miss Hardy was staring at her, her glasses glinting and her face screwed up as though she was about to cry.

'I live with my friend, hardly ideal, is it? We don't really get on but it's better than being alone. No men left you see, all killed you see. It's not that we were unattractive, you know, it's just that there was no one left from the trenches.' Her voice was shrill and unpleasant. 'It's not out of choice that I'm teaching, spending hours with girls like you who do not wish to be here.' She was shaking now and Annie left her seat and turned off the kettle. 'We're all wasted women aren't we, dried up, all wasted.' Miss Hardy was ranting now.

'Well most of them are nuns,' Annie replied.

'Not just here, you obdurate girl,' she raged on. Her face red now, her breathing rapid almost as though she was choking. Jenn said she got like this when she'd had a row with her friend.

'Stupid, stupid girl, get out of here. I refuse to teach such impertinence, such appalling lack of talent.' She sat straight-backed, her lips pursed. 'And there are those that throw marriage out of the window as though it were of no value. Trollops and scarlet women as you know only too well.'

Annie looked at the woman, at the sweat that lay in a sheen on her top lip. This was a new line, she thought.

'Divorce is a sin, and to think that she was once at this school and now sends you here. It's a disgrace. I saw her fetch you yesterday in her smart little car. I hadn't seen her for years until then and she looks so young still; it's not fair.'

Annie felt her jaw set and picked up her music book and placed it in her case; anchored the metronome so that there was silence in the room and left. She was sure that she would never touch a piano again.

'How was your day?' Val asked her over dinner.

'Is Georgie well?' Sarah spoke before Annie could reply.

'Yes, he is, Sarah,' replied Annie as she cut up the beef which she had come to accept as normal. 'And yes, Val, it was interesting.' She kept her voice carefully neutral. 'Miss Hardy went barmy.'

The runner beans were stringy; Val must have cooked the edges again. Keeps you regular, all this roughage is what she would say if you dared complain.

Val looked up, then laughed while Sarah wiped her mouth carefully with her napkin. 'Would you care to improve on that remark?' she asked.

'After she started to prick my hands she went off into hysterics about not being married and those that were pushed it out of the window and became scarlet women. That divorce was a disgrace.' Annie drew a deep breath and grinned. 'And that she would never teach me again.'

Val banged down her knife and fork. 'Well, I never did, and

she was at school with you as well, Sarah; always a mouse though, never any admirers.'

Sarah rang the school after dinner and said that Annie would no longer be continuing with the piano since it would appear that she had no appetite for the subject. Another victim of the war, she had sighed, and Annie half knew what she meant. She would write to Georgie tonight, he would be glad her piano lessons were over.

'Should I know about divorce, Sarah?' she asked as her cousin poured the after-dinner tea with a steady hand. The cups were the white bone china which made the tea taste quite different.

'I was married during the war but my husband left me two years after the armistice.'

It was simply said and there was no tremble as she passed Annie her cup. Her face was quite calm, though her voice was very careful.

'Why did he leave you?'

'I suspect because I failed him. Now finish up your tea and do your homework or is it time for another letter to Georgie?' Her smile was gentle as Annie nodded and told Sarah all his news.

The drive out to the country was unexpected and so had been Annie's excellent end-of-term school report. She had felt a smile grow and stay as Sarah read it to her.

'We both deserve a treat, especially as the conservatory has seen you only once this term,' she announced. 'Look, one punishment mark, that's all. Come on, put your jacket on, we're off for some lunch.'

They pulled into a country inn with a sweeping drive and a garden at the rear with a small patio on which tables were set; more spilled on to the lawns. Red and white cotton umbrellas shaded diners from the sun. As they sat down, Sarah pointed to the river running slowly past the bottom of the terraced lawn.

'I'm told they catch trout here, but so far I've never seen any signs of success.'

Annie sat back. They had no umbrella and the sun was hot. She raised her face and all she could see through closed lids was a blaze of yellow which distanced all sound. She thought of Georgie showing Tom how to tickle trout and how Tom had told her that the beck was now so dead with black sludge that the fish were gone.

A man's voice said 'Good afternoon, Sarah. How are you?'

Annie shaded her eyes and looked in the direction of the voice. The back of the inn was a glaring white, with dark beams sharply exposed and much nearer, standing by their table was a well-built man, rather like Georgie except that he was fair and had a pale moustache. Georgie was clean-shaven, or had been when she last saw him; she must ask him whether he still was.

'Very well, thank you, Harold,' Sarah was replying. 'You haven't met my ward, Annie Manon, have you? Mary's child, of course.'

Annie felt a quietness sitting on Sarah who turned to Annie.

'This is Mr Beeston, Annie. Shall we order?'

The tables were filling up now and Annie looked at Sarah as she sat against the sun.

'May I have chicken salad, please?' Annie asked. It sounded quite normal and Sarah ordered the same. The man smiled tightly and left.

Sarah said nothing as they waited for their meal, just smiled with her mouth until Annie asked, 'Why did you come?'

Sarah did not answer immediately but sat thinking quietly, then said, 'Oh Annie, I don't know really. A need to beard the lion in his den perhaps. To assure myself that I have a full life which gives me great pleasure, especially now that I have you. I suppose it's a laying of ghosts and besides, my dear, they do have such excellent food.' She turned and thanked the waitress as she brought their meal.

They both sat back in their chairs and Annie did not taste her food, she was too busy with her thoughts. A laying of ghosts, Sarah had said, and she envisaged her own ghosts as they trampled through her room at night. Don who seemed intent on stirring up hatred, Tom who sank down into the pits each day and had so far come up each time, but for how much longer? She almost hoped he would lose his job like the rest of the poor buggers. She thought of Georgie and wondered if he had moved to the Himalayas yet, of her father who had begun all this. She stirred restlessly. She was still not free of memories and fears and remembered how she had clung to Betsy and told her that she would be free, would not be like her. Annie rubbed her eyes; thank God she had written to poor Betsy, but she had not heard back because Grace said she could no longer write with her hands as they were.

Sarah spoke again. 'I rather fear I emasculated poor Harold. I had changed you see from the girl I was before the war when he knew me through my family. I had wanted female suffrage and I fought for it. I then drove an ambulance during the war. I was financially independent even before my father and mother died. I was a person in my own right and I thought we married on that basis. What I did not realise was that he had in his mind this picture of me as I was when I was your age and living in Gosforn; an age when I did not even know he existed other than as a friend of the family.' She sighed and then continued. 'He, poor man, had a vision of me soft and malleable. He'd had the bad war that everyone had and came home to a wife that he soon found threatening.'

Annie looked at her. 'Threatening, what do you mean?'

Sarah laughed. 'I mean that I was independent in thought as well as means. I didn't need him in those ways but what he could not understand was that I loved him dearly and needed him emotionally. I was distraught when he left and I lost the child I was carrying.'

Annie felt a flood of feeling; she wanted to rush round and hold this woman tight and instead she covered her hand with hers and looked at the face which seemed softer now than when she had first known her, her hair was in gentle waves round her face, her clothes were less severe.

'Did he know about the baby?'

Sarah nodded. 'Oh yes, he knew, but he didn't care. I repulsed him with my personality, I suppose, and that is something that I hope will never happen to you.'

She gripped Annie's hand and looked hard at her.

Annie smiled, her face was older she knew, more mature and her hair suited her cut shorter. Her eyes were more considered in their glances. She felt absolutely sure, as she said:

'Georgie would never treat me like that. He would know I needed to be free.'

'But it might not be Georgie, Annie. It could be so long before he is back that you find someone else.'

Annie shrugged. 'It might be a long time and there might be others before he comes but it will always be him in the end.'

'Oh my dear, don't be too set on that. You should always

remember that choice is going to be there for you. It is a great freedom.'

'Freedom to me is leaving all the darkness behind, forgetting everything you want to forget, releasing yourself from responsibility for others being, oh, I don't know, unmarked, I suppose.' Annie leant forward, a frown drawing up between her eyes. She could talk to Sarah now, trust her because with her job, with her hens, she felt almost without debt to her; almost but not absolutely, but that would come. But here she sighed. There was still the business course after her exams to be paid for and she felt a flash of frustration as Sarah laughed and tapped her hands. A slight wind was drifting up from the river and the frill of the umbrella on the next table was wafting in the breeze.

'That freedom is a dream, Annie.' She gathered up her handbag and smoothed down her skirt where it had creased as she sat. 'Come along, it's time we were on our way. I do so enjoy tipping that pretty little blonde thing at the till.'

They walked arm in arm in the weakening sun to the counter, the breeze chilling the coffee of those who still remained.

'Thank you so much, Mrs Beeston.'

Sarah smiled sweetly. 'Another culinary delight. Do give my compliments to the chef, Mr Beeston.' And she walked past, her eyes full of something which looked like defiance, Annie thought.

CHAPTER 16

Tom shut the backyard gate behind him and joined the stream of men walking down to the pit. It was a warm morning and would be a fine day, not that he would know about it until this afternoon when his shift was finished. He sank his hands deep down into his pockets, his boots making the same noise as those walking in front and behind. Uncle Henry was on the afternoon shift at the same pit and was still asleep and Davy had started work at Lutters Pit yesterday; he too was on the late shift but if Tom and Henry had been able to do anything about it he would still be going to the library and kicking a ball around with his mates.

It wasn't that they didn't want him to work; they did, anywhere but bloody Lutters. Tom kicked a stone hard against the wall as he turned into the cobbled street that led down the hill to the pit. That Lutters wasn't safe, he knew it wasn't safe. It had been unworked for far too long but Davy had insisted. It was the only pit that would take him with his reputation and the means test that the government had just introduced to try and cut down money given to the long-term unemployed had made him take the risk.

Tom nodded to two of his mates, shambling on past him.

'See you tonight then, Tom, at the meeting.'

He nodded. He would be there because they needed to talk more about this new test but before he went there he had Don to sort out.

He pulled his scarf round his throat and stuffed it down inside his jacket. He didn't need the warmth of either now but he would when he came up out of the heat and dark when the hooter blew for the end of the shift.

There were too many curtains still drawn on the houses he passed, too many men still in bed, still without jobs. Too many starving bairns and again he thought of Don. He'd have to go and try and knock some sense into the bugger. Annie had spoken to him but he just called her a bloody bolshie. Tom scowled as he passed through the colliery gates and rubbed the back of his head. If what he'd heard in the pub was anything to go by, our Don was going to get told good and proper about overcharging on loans but it wouldn't be with words.

He'd been with his back to the next table with Davy arranging the meeting for tonight since it was no good leaving it to the union rep; he was a flaccid little tyke who kept out of everyone's way. Even if there was an accident you had to chase round after the little bleeder to make sure he got to the hospital to deal with the owners' offer of compensation, if there was one.

Tom waited by the cage door, his head down. He didn't want to talk, he wanted to think. But it wouldn't do any good, he had said to Davy about the meeting. There could be no strike; they had no clout with the unemployment and low union funds. But at least the men could talk and that was better than nothing, Davy had argued.

They'd heard the men behind them then in the snug, saying that they were going to get Don. Bad as a blackleg, one of them had said. The sort of bloody bugger that'd do our job when we were out on strike. We'll get him, we'll beat his bloody head in for leeching the blood out of his own people with his bloody rates. Tom had not been surprised; he had been expecting something of the sort. The cage was up now and it was no easier today than when he had started to go down two years ago. It was still the same iron cage lined with wooden planks blackened by inches of dust that stank raw and filthy even before you plunged down into the black heart of the pit.

Don was forgotten, Davy too, as he crushed up against the next man, his bait-tin digging into his hip. He clenched his nostrils against the smell of coal and looked away from the last sight of the sky to the back of the man in front and waited, his mouth dry with a fear he could never conquer, a hate he could never master.

Then down they went, screaming through pitch-black cold rushing air and his legs felt as though they would never catch up with the base of the cage but stay forever two inches above it as it plummeted down the shaft. The cold made his skin crawl and always he wondered if they would not slow but instead hurl against the shaft end in a tangle of wreckage and shattered bodies but, at last, there was a slowing, a stopping and his legs felt firm again as though they were at last bearing the weight of his body.

Dimly lit by lights every few yards, the main seam throbbed with men, the smell of coal, the rumble of the trams as they were pushed back with coal from the headings to be taken to the surface. There was the hammering of the picks as they heaved and tore at the face. In each tunnel, in each hole, miners attacked the face.

Millions of tons of coal pressed close on top of the workings and Tom removed his jacket in the heat. Their boots clumped and they edged sideways where the heading narrowed, careful always of the tram-lines and their cargo which could take off a foot. The men pushing the trams did not look up, their heads were down into their shoulders, their bodies streaked in black sweat. In the narrow entrance to their heading, away from the lights, they felt their way along, their lamps scything through the darkness, cutting a beam in which the black dust danced.

Tom was bent double now as the seam reduced in size and then he crawled, with Frank, Davy's marrer, who had been put with him today, going on ahead, until they reached the face.

Frank was quick with his pick, hammering with short sharp blows while Tom heaved the broken lumps. They worked in silence changing jobs to ease the tearing muscles of shoulders, back and stomach, lying down and throwing the pick-head deep into the coal and, when straining thighs could take no more, they squatted. And however much coal was moved, more was always there, waiting.

It was there above him too, Tom knew. Hanging there with its miles of height and weight. It grew grass on the top and grazed sheep but hung waiting over the ants of men which picked and irritated its great bulk here below. It had chosen not to fall yet, not on him but he was reminded each day that it was only waiting as a fine coal-dust spewed down all the time and lay in every crease of skin, every pore; filling nostrils, mouth and lungs. Oh yes, Tom ground out, as he heaved at his pick and pushed back the coal to Frank, kicking the slag to the sides as he worked, you remind me you're there, you bugger. Even when I eat me bait, when I drink me tea, you're there crunching in me teeth, reddening me eyes, falling in me cuts.

He never counted the hours, just lay, crawled, squatted and picked at the coal, grabbing a sip of tea now and then; smelling the coal, the excrement, hearing the rats and he longed for the end of the shift, longed for the end of fear and screaming muscles. He tore his shoulder as they edged and crawled back towards the main seam when they had no more strength and it was, thank God, the end of the shift. He felt the tear but could not see the blood; it ran down his back and dripped on to the ground as black as the sweat which joined it.

His legs always shook as they walked down the main heading which was brick-arched and busy. But there was soon to be air, air and light and the coolness of a breeze. The clean, clean air; until tomorrow of course. He breathed and coughed, breathed and coughed as he slumped towards home, towards the water which would sluice him clean; his body and his mind.

May had set the buckets out in the wash-house as Tom had done for Davy and Uncle Henry, and Frank and Edward before they had gone to the Midlands and the factories.

Inside the wash-house, he could feel the stiffness of his clothes as he dropped them on to the floor. He leant against the inside of the door, the trembling still in his limbs, his arms too tired to raise the buckets. Let me be for a minute, he moaned to himself. Just let me be, I'm so bloody tired, so bloody scared. He stood naked, his head thrust back on the door and felt the roughness of the wood against his shoulders and buttocks. He fingered the raised untreated grain, traced it up and down and slowly the panic subsided, slowly the steam from the buckets looked inviting, looked normal. He took the first and poured it over his head, his body; gasping as it covered his face and then on down his chest and back. He lathered the soap and, still standing, ran it over his face, the whole of his body, eager now to remove the taint of the coal. Another bucket, another soap and then another so that the water slopped over his feet before running across the floor into the gutter which ran to a drain in the corner.

He scrubbed until his flesh felt raw and at last the coal was nearly gone. He could see his own colour, his own flesh and now he stepped into the bathtub, easing himself down into and under the water, his hair floating, his muscles easing into looseness.

'I'm ready, May,' he called and waited as she came from the

kitchen. Much thinner now she was, but still a smile, though with Davy at Lutters it didn't reach her eyes. Her scrubbing was hard across the back and shoulders, as it had to be, and the knots between his shoulders eased and he saw the blackness float past his hips and cover the water right up to the edge of the bath.

'There you are, bonny lad. A bit of a soak and then a cup of tea.'

She shook her wet hands at him and he dodged and ducked and laughed. He was always surprised when he laughed because he felt sure that just one more day in the pits would dry all the joy into a black dust.

The water still had some warmth and he ducked himself down for one more minute then he would sluice himself and climb into the clothes that May had brought and put on the chair which no one would sit on because it was rotten.

He wondered what it would be like to have Grace scrub his back, her plump soft arms holding one shoulder so that she could have purchase with the brush and the thought of her hand on his body made him flush with heat. They had kissed of course and he had felt the weight of her full breasts in his hands but always through clothes. He had never felt her flesh, her blue-veined flesh, never run his finger from her throat to her nipple and kissed that luscious softness. He dreamt of it more and more because soon he would go to College in Newcastle and then on down to London for three years. Would she come too?

He stepped out of the bath and held his breath as he poured the last bucket over himself. It would be cold by now and perhaps it was a good thing, he thought grinning.

And then he stopped. Oh God, he had to go to Don and his face set and he was glad his body had thickened with muscle.

He walked from May's, through Beckworth Alley, up past the school and down the alley where Annie had stood when she had come to say goodbye. His boots were noisy in the streets and alleys where children hung about at the back of yards, too thin and tired to play, some just squatting as they copied their fathers, doing nothing. Men were on street corners, propped up against lampposts and Tom walked past quickly, nodding as they said they'd see him tonight at the meeting. He kept his eyes lowered, ashamed of their redness which showed he'd had a day's work and they hadn't.

It made him angry and his jaw was clenched when he came through Don's backyard. He moved past the privy and into the kitchen. Don would be there doing his books; he was always there in the afternoon while Albert took over the shop. People slipped in the backyard; men with their caps drawn low over their heads, women with their shawls across their faces, barely able to repay the interest let alone the loan.

He realised that he hadn't locked the gate and he wanted no interruption for what he had to do this afternoon so he turned as Don looked up, turned without a word and walked back sliding the lock across and entering the kitchen again.

Don had half risen from his chair. 'What the bloody hell do you think you're doing? I've a business to run, Tom.'

He was resting on his hands which had gone white where the wrists had creased with his weight but his face was tanned by the sun and Tom felt a further spurt of anger that his own had the pallor of a pitman. He stood there facing Don, his cap folded in his hand, then took a chair from the hearth and set it opposite. The kitchen was dirty; there were dishes piled up in the sink and green slime where the tap had dripped. He sat down. Albert had not allowed Annie to have visitors so this was all new to him. There was a low fire in the grate and a kettle was on the hob but not boiling yet, a broom was propped against the wall but the floor was dirty with bits of paper screwed up and scattered around.

Don was watching him. He had a wooden box and a ledger written up in pencil on the table. His hair was too long and falling in his eyes, his mouth was pinched and he turned a pencil round and round between his two hands.

'Well, what d'you want? A bit short, are you?' Don laughed.

Tom felt the heat rising in him, the heat of an anger which was years old.

'No, I'm not, bonny lad, but you're about to be.'

Don looked at him and put the pencil down. 'What d'you mean by that?' His face was wary.

Tom told him then about the conversation he had heard in the pub. Explained that the men were in an angry mood, that the means test was pinching and they wanted to get back at someone and that Don would be that person and it looked as though it would be soon.

Don flicked a pencil across the table and lounged back in his chair.

'Don't be so bloody daft,' he sneered. 'If they were after anyone, they'd be after Albert.'

But Tom shook his head. 'Nay lad, it's you they want. You grew up with them, remember. You're young and greedy and that's what they don't like.'

His words had become hard; he realised that he wasn't afraid of Don any more. He had always been, he knew suddenly, and had let Annie do the fighting, but not any more. She was worried about Don and so was he.

Don said nothing, just tapped the table and then rose and propped himself up against the fender.

'You're asking me to drop the interest rate, is that it?'

Tom nodded. 'If you drop by quite a bit, Don, word would get round by the end of the day and you'd be safe. I could spread it about at the meeting tonight too, if you like.'

Don was pacing in front of the fire now. 'Well, I don't like. I don't believe a word of it,' he said. 'I think you're making every bloody bit up. You just can't stand me getting on, that's it, isn't it? Annie's been rabbiting on as well and I reckon you're both jealous because I'm going up you see. You've come to put the dampers on; that's what Albert's been saying and I reckon he's right.'

Tom leant forward. 'For God's sake, man. I've come to warn you. I'd get a good belting if anyone knew. I don't want to see you getting hurt, that's all. I want to see you doing the right thing by everyone and I want to see you getting on, of course I do, but not like this.'

Don moved to the door, holding it open.

'I told you, I don't believe you so you can get out and leave me to get on with my life and you get on with yours and your bloody stupid politics. Just stop siding against me, the pair of you. It's like Albert says, you both hate me.'

Tom rose, his cap was still in his hand and he stuffed it in his pocket. Don looked tired he saw, tanned but tired.

'Don't be bloody stupid, no one hates you and I'm not going Don, not until you bring your rates down. I'm not having you beaten up by anyone but me and I'll do it if you don't give in any other way. That way you'll still have your head on your shoulders, not a bloody smashed eggshell to hold in your hands.' He moved towards Don now. 'For God's sake,' he ground out, 'don't be so stubborn. Annie's right worried about you, you know she is.'

Don was still holding the door. 'The pair of you can sod off together. You always were together weren't you, always. You on the inside, me out there somewhere.' He flung his hand wide. 'Now bugger off home, Tom.'

He moved out into the yard, towards the gate. The shadows were thick today in the light of the sun and Tom took off his jacket and flung it on the ground.

'Don,' he said softly. 'We care about you. We don't want you to be hurt. For God's sake, you're family, man.'

Don turned, his face red and hands bunched. 'You don't care, you and she don't care. Thick as thieves you've always been. Haven't wanted me around.'

Tom walked towards him. 'That's not true.'

He searched in his mind, looked back at the years which had gone. 'That's not true, man. You were older, had your own friends; you had Georgie and then you went to Yorkshire and, by the time you came back, there was no home left. We were all on our own. Think about it, man. We both care for you. I keep telling you, that's why I'm here.' He stopped and drew a deep breath. 'But you're not that easy to love, Don. You shrug us off. You're a bit like Albert, you know. He's made you like this. He did his best to get back at Archie through hurting Annie and now it's you. You're going to get hurt now. For God's sake, I wouldn't be here if you weren't me brother and I cared.'

There was a pause and then Don said slowly and clearly, his mouth thin-lipped. 'But you're not me brother, are you? You're a bastard.'

Tom knew he would say it, knew that Don would throw it in his face at some stage but he did not move, just looked and said quietly:

'I'm your brother and I'm not going to have someone come and bash your bleeding head in, so are you going to lower your rates?'

Don shook his head and they stared at one another and then Tom moved quickly but Don was quicker and the blow caught

Tom on the side of the head. Here was another, hard into the stomach and Tom felt the breath go from his body and was surprised at Don's strength; at his speed. He stepped back quickly. It was not going to be as easy as he had thought to stop the bloody fool from meeting a few men on a dark night.

He closed and they slugged punch for punch, their breath mixed in harsh pants and the yard reeled round them as they pushed and punched from wall to wall. Tom's lip was bleeding and he had blood on his shirt but Don's was worse. His nose was pumping blood and Tom backed off.

'Come away now, man. That's enough.' But Don came after him and the fury that was in both of them exploded and they knew nothing but darkness and blows and grunts. They went down, their arms round one another, their fists still punching into sides and backs.

Tom's knuckles were bruised and one hand was caught between Don and the ground and he feared for his painting and reared up with his body, punching Don to the jaw, until he rolled over and then was able to snatch out his arm, then he grabbed Don's hair and pulled him back to lie flat beneath him.

'Lower your bloody rates will you, man,' he shouted, his breath coming in gasps.

Don just looked at him through swollen eyes and Tom's heart broke for this man who had always been his brother and the heat left him. He released his hair and instead gripped Don's shoulders and shook him.

'For God's sake, Don lad, I don't want you bloody killed. Can't you see that? We care, of course we care, that's why I'm here.'

He sighed at the blank look in Don's face, the lack of response and he clambered off him, dusting his trousers down with hands that trembled. His legs were weak and his lip was swelling. He ran his hands through his hair and looked again at Don, then reached down with his hand. There was no movement from Don, he just looked back up at him and then, as Tom dropped his hand he raised his.

'Give us a hand up then, lad,' he said through lips that were swollen. His clasp was strange to Tom. He had never held Don's hand in his before and he pulled him up, helped him back inside to the darkness of the kitchen and his chair. Neither of them spoke and the air was loud with laboured breath as he moved to the sink and poured them both a drink and hoped to God that Annie never heard about this.

'Don't tell Annie about this, Tom,' said Don, mirroring his thoughts. 'She'd give us both hell.' He looked at Tom and winked, if that swollen lid could wink and Tom tried to laugh but his chest hurt too much so he just slumped down in the chair and they sat for minutes in silence.

'What'll you do Don, lad?'

Don sat hunched forward, his hands between his knees and said nothing for a while. The fire was out now, grey and lifeless in the grate and Tom was too winded to riddle it back.

'Since you've asked me so nicely, I reckon I'll lower the interest rate.'

Don's voice was thick and Tom smiled, then stopped. His lip was too painful.

'And I'm right sorry about what I said,' Don went on. 'I get clumsy, living here. I forget about people.' His movements were slow and painful and Tom nodded.

'I know, it's all right, but we didn't want you to get hurt, see. We're all family, aren't we?' They looked at one another and at their own bruises, shrugged and laughed. Tom could not remember the last time they had laughed together.

Don rose stiffly and took a towel from the fender. 'Come here then, lad, and I'll do your face, then you do mine. We'd best get a bit of cold on these before we both look like footballs.' He dabbed at Tom's lip and his cut brow, then handed the towel to Tom who did the same to him.

The afternoon turned into evening and they sat at the table, cold cloths pressed against their faces, talking of the years gone by; the horses on the moors which galloped so smoothly that you did not know you were on one, the early morning exercise, the feeling when a race was won. They talked of growing up, of Betsy who Tom had still not seen. They talked of Archie and his death, of Annie's continuing bitterness. Of Sarah and Georgie and now Don knew and would never again talk of him as he had. They also discussed Albert and Don said he liked the old bugger and thought he could turn the business round and the old boy at the same time. It was worth a try.

He wouldn't come to the pub with Tom.

'Another night,' he said as Tom opened the gate. 'You'll not get me involved in your crazy ideas,' and as Tom left he called: 'Thanks, lad, and how about you doing as Annie wants and make up with Betsy?'

Tom waved back but did not go to the pub because, as he approached from Enderby Terrace, the disaster siren rose above the town, wailed and tore through the early evening air and he ran, ran back down the street, his ribs hurting but he did not notice. He ran and the breath jogged in his chest like a knife but he knew he must keep on because it was Lutters Pit, Davy's pit, and he could see the coal which was above him this morning piling down on top of the men, on top of soft flesh, grunting and grinding the life from them.

It had been Davy of course, it had to be him, May kept saying as they carried him back to the house much later when the bodies had been dug out. She washed him, wiping the dead blood from his ears and nose and mouth. Henry had straightened him out while Tom stood at the side of the front room watching and felt the fear and grief building up as though he were a dam. He remembered Annie screaming and shouting when her da had died and he wanted to hang back his head and do as she had done.

He turned from the house, walking at first, past the drawn windows that lined the streets like dead eyes. The town was in mourning but that wouldn't bring him back, bring his young body back, whole and strong, bring back the light in those blank eyes that looked just like houses. He walked quicker now; he wanted to reach her, to feel her hold him, to cry and weep and have her make it better.

His boots struck sparks as he moved over the cobbles; his feet were heavy and the night seemed black as pitch but when he lifted his head it was a deep blue and the stars were out alongside the moon.

He was nearly there now and he began to run, thrusting open the yard gate, past the stable and in through the door, his hands finding the latch as though it was yesterday. And she was there, gazing into the fire, her arms plump where the sleeves had been rolled up, her hands motionless on her lap. He stood in the doorway and the tears were coming now, loud shaking sobs.

She had turned at the noise of his entrance and moved to take him in her arms.

'Oh Mam,' he wept. 'Our Davy's dead,' and felt her hold him close and he sank into her warmth.

CHAPTER 17

Tom changed gear as he roared Davy's motorbike, which May had said he could take, up and over the hill as he left Wassingham that same night. It was midnight but he had to get to Gosforn to see Annie and tell her about Davy, tell her that things had changed now, that the future was to be different. He pushed up the goggles and wiped his cheek with his finger where the sweat and grime from the road had started to chafe the cut that he had received in his fight with Don.

The villages he rode through were dark and quiet and the hedges of the road and the fields beyond stood out black against the navy of the sky.

He thought of his mam whom he had left just a few moments ago; of the feel of her arms as she drew him into the kitchen when he was desolate and in pain. The room had been brighter somehow than he remembered and he could not think why until he noticed the patchwork cushions on the hard wooden chairs, the bright tablecloth. Even his cut-down chair had a cushion and he had been surprised that Betsy had kept it.

She had taken him across to the fire, sitting him in her chair, stroking his hair. She had heard of course but listened as he told her again and again, in short bursts. It had all come out. Davy who was so quiet and dead and black, and later there had been Annie who had gone, a mother who had given him away. It all came out, bursting and stopping then coming again and his head had lain against her body and she had held him to her, rocking him, her apron smelling of clean boiling, not the greasy staleness of the days gone by.

He had said how he had wanted to come before but could never do it and she nodded, understanding him better than he did himself. Her hair was grey now and there were lines around her eyes and down to her mouth, deep as though carved with a chisel but the blotchiness of the booze was gone, there was no smell on her but that of baking.

She had made tea; thick and brown and they talked of Joe who was in bed and she had smiled at him as she told him of Annie's room which was now hers. Done up with me own money, she had said, and he had reached over and taken her hands, gently because he could feel the throbbing heat of their pain.

He had asked her not to give May money for him any more because he was earning now but she had shaken her head and explained how she wanted to, needed to, because she could not forgive herself for not keeping him and Annie.

Over cheese and bread he had told her how he liked the room and she had laughed and he had no recollection of hearing that sound from her before. As he leant into the bike to take the sharp bend which meant he was halfway to Annie's, he shook his head at the thought. But she had laughed and said that she had finished the patchwork before her fingers packed up for good.

They had talked of Davy again, so young, so much to give and he had felt lightheaded and restless, unable to sit, unable to eat and had put his plate down on the table and paced the room, touching the dresser, free of dust now, moving to the back door and looking out, up at the sky. He had heard Beauty in her stable, shuffling and stamping and had walked out into the warm night air and leant in, running his hand down her neck, stroking her soft nose.

His mam had been sitting as he had left her when he returned and asked her if she was happy. He sat at her knee on the floor with his legs crossed, his hands playing with the rag rug beneath him which was a mixture of blues and red worked into a soothing design. She nodded. The fire was hissing as a damp coal dried out and she explained that she was happy because she was her own woman now.

Is it enough for you though? he had asked. You're a young woman still and she had laughed in a great peal that made him smile even as he remembered it and told him that 33 wasn't young round their way and that, aye, it was enough for her since she had not known a man's touch since his father.

Tom had said nothing but had felt the shock run through him as he thought of Archie and the years of their marriage. She had gazed calmly into the fire, her hair neat in its bun, her floral frock spotless with its small round-edged collar.

She explained how Archie had not wanted a wife and that she was pleased now because it enabled her to remember Barney more clearly. He was a good man, your da, she had said, and had gone on to tell that he was a face-worker in the pits until the war and she would be eternally grateful that, when he'd died, he hadn't been the same as poor Davy stuck like a rat in a trap but in the open air though it had been raining and he hadn't liked the rain. She had stroked Tom's hair with the back of her hand. So like him you are, she had said, and, thank God, soon there'll be no more pit for you my lad and never another war.

She had sounded distant as though she was remembering things long gone which were still clear but only for her to see. He was a real bonny lad he was, Tom, strong but not tall; I wish you'd known him.

He had not asked her more then but he would another time because he was hungry now to know and see and feel his father. To know what he sounded like, know what he painted, what he drew because, as he had his father's body, he would also have his talent.

As he passed the first houses of Gosforn he throttled back to quieten the bike. His arms were shaking now from the vibration and from tiredness but his mind was racing still with thoughts and feeling and decisions he must make.

Annie woke to the sound of knocking but couldn't for a moment think what the noise meant, then she heard Val and Sarah calling.

'Who is it? Just a moment.' Then Sarah spoke more quietly to Val. 'Better fetch the poker.'

Annie leapt from bed into her dressing-gown and slippers, then on down the stairs. When Sarah opened the door, Tom stood there.

His face was grimy from the road dust with white patches where his goggles had been, his lip was swollen and his cheek cut. He wore his dark jacket only and she knew he must be cold. Pushing past Sarah who stood speechless in the hallway, her hair tucked up in a net, she pulled him in, feeling the trembling in his body as he clung to her.

'Davy's dead,' he said and Sarah gasped and Val moved up behind them.

'Shut the door, Sarah,' said Annie with one arm round Tom. She moved with him into the sitting-room as she would have done with one of the patients in the ward. 'Can we have some tea, Val, or perhaps cocoa would be better.'

She put on the light and sat him in the chair near the fire which had been banked up for the night and still gave off a little heat. Sarah sat down looking frail suddenly, while Val disappeared into the kitchen. Annie was calm as she sat on the arm of Tom's chair, one hand on his shoulder.

'I've been to Mam's,' he said. 'We talked and she helped but he was too young to die, Annie. It was that bloody pit; it had been closed too long and the maintenance had just not been done. God, if he were here now, he'd be slanging the bloody owner something shocking.' His voice broke but there were no tears. He punched one hand to the other then winced and Annie saw his bruised knuckle.

Val brought him cocoa and he held it between both those hands and sipped and talked while they listened and watched but said little until he was talked out, until he was tired, finally tired.

Annie still sat on the arm of his chair with a hand on his shoulder. The photograph of Sarah skiing shone in the light from the lamp next to it and outside the birds were beginning to stir as the dawn threatened to bring a weak sun to the early morning. It was four o'clock and she leant over him and gently touched his face.

'And how did you manage these cuts? Were you in on the rescue then?' He looked up at her, his lids heavy, his face drawn with exhaustion. God, he was so tired now, so bloody tired and still hadn't told her of his decision.

'Annie, I won't be going into business with you now. I shall have to take over from Davy,' he sagged back in the chair, unable any more to keep awake, to cope with the voices that were jumping in his head, clamouring to be heard.

Annie and Sarah fetched blankets down from the chest and pillows and together they made him walk to the settee, removed his jacket and boots and he was asleep before they closed the door. Annie went with Sarah to her bedroom, crossing to the window and looking out through the open curtains. The sky was lifting into a paler shade and against it the trees were grey not black any more and soon colour would be flooding into the garden, into the road which she overlooked.

She turned. 'It's a pig's ear, isn't it, Sarah?'

Sarah was sitting in the cane chair near the bed, her pink wool dressing-gown folded round her and the satin quilted collar turned up at the back. She reached to her neck and flattened it.

'That's one way of putting it, my dear.'

Annie moved to the bed and sat on the thick blue blanket which was still crumpled and thrown back just as it had been by Sarah when Tom had knocked. The floral bedspread was folded neatly at the foot of the bed as it was every night before Sarah went to bed; as hers was too.

'Of course it is the grief talking,' Sarah went on. 'He won't give up his art so easily.'

Annie had meant Davy's death but she pulled herself round to Tom's words. 'He won't give up his art, you can bank on that, but he means what he says. Our Tom always means what he says. It'll be his way of paying back I reckon, if he takes over Davy's activities.' She nodded because she understood.

'Oh I can see that, he was so very fond of the boy and it is such a waste, such a tragedy, but Annie, what about you, the business course you had decided to do?' Her voice was concerned.

Annie looked down at her hands as she drew the dressing-gown around her. She had made it at school during needlework and the seams were puckered and it did not hang straight but the colour suited her; a pale green which made her look a bit fatter, rather more of a woman. But what about her future, she thought, and felt a sense of release now, a release which would always be tinged by fear though. Fear for Tom working in the pit because she could not bear to lose the bonny lad, could not bear it if he died under that stinking mass of coal.

Sarah was frowning at her, her eyes concerned, her hands pressed tightly together.

'I'd like to nurse, Sarah.' Annie knew now that she had wanted this ever since she started work at the hospital. She picked some fluff from the blanket and rolled it into a ball between her thumb and finger which sprang back when she released it.

249

'But Annie,' Sarah protested. 'My dear, it is such hard work, so little money and you would need to leave us, to live in the hospital.' Her face had paled and her hand was across her mouth. Annie looked at the ball of fluff, she would not look at the face that went with that voice.

'I know all these things, Sarah, but I need hard work, it makes me feel myself somehow. It's all I've known up to now, you see. This has been a holiday for me, a rest to sort myself out. It's time I got back into the real world, a bit like Tom, I suppose.'

She looked at Sarah then. She was sitting back in her chair, her hand away from her mouth and lying casually on her lap and her expression calm. Annie knew the effort that it took and was more grateful than she had ever been to Sarah before.

'I don't want Tom to go back down the pits but I can't stop him. He must be free to make his choice.' Annie was picking her words extremely carefully. 'Davy's death has given me the freedom to choose too and nursing is really all that I want to do, at this time. I don't want to start the business yet.' She would not say that nursing would give her freedom from Sarah, from the burden of taking from her all the time. This would hurt the woman she had grown to love.

To be earning, instead of enrolling on a course which would cost Sarah money, was a luxury she craved. She was determined to lift herself up, to be somebody, as Sarah wished, but it had to be done on her own and nursing would pay her, give her lodgings and the responsibility for other people's well-being in a professional sense. She wanted to be Sister Manon, a person in her own right, and that was a kind of freedom.

Sarah had risen and come to sit next to her on the bed. She took her hand and smiled. 'If that is what you want, my dear child, then of course we shall pursue it.'

Her voice sounded almost as usual and any tremor could have been put down to tiredness. Annie put her arm round her.

'Thank you, Sarah.'

They understood one another and sat quietly thinking and remembering the calm of their time together, the ties which now held them. Sarah stirred herself at last.

'I think that it might be an idea however to keep something of an eye on our young Tom. What we don't want is a bad seam coming his way because of his socialist activities. I rather feel he could become a little extreme under the circumstances.'

'I know,' replied Annie. 'That's what I can't bear to think of. Imagine if he was hurt.' But she could not go on. Sarah patted her hand.

'I think I shall mention it when I write to Bob Wheeler,' she mused.

Annie jerked up her head. 'God. You write to God.'

Sarah burst out laughing. 'We correspond from time to time, my dear. But I'm not sure that he'd appreciate the promotion you've heaped upon him; he's an atheist after all.'

'But why do you write to him?' Annie protested. 'He's old and dry and Da's friend anyway.'

Sarah sighed. 'Don't be silly, Annie. He's been a good friend to you. How else do you think I knew that things were not as they should be when I came for you. Poor Bob thinks he was in some way to blame for your father's death; he feels he could have done more to stop it happening and we talked at the funeral, before and after the crystal decanter episode.' She nudged Annie who blushed but said nothing. 'I asked him to check up on things and he did. He's a good man.'

So Da, thought Annie, you've left someone else with a packet of grief too have you, a burden of responsibility and she remembered how her father had hated nurses and it made her decision even sounder.

'Please write to him then, Sarah,' she said. 'Tom'll need all the help he can get, one way and another.'

As Tom left for Wassingham that morning he dug in his pocket and brought out Da's watch. 'It's from Don,' he said. 'He wanted you to have it, to keep.'

Annie felt the cold of the silver in her hand and the chain flopped over her hand and swung to and fro. She looked at Tom who shuffled his feet and climbed on to the bike, his head away from her.

'We had a bit of a talk yesterday and he's seen sense about the loans and one or two other things.'

She looked at his hands again, at his split lip and cheek.

'He's all right, is he?' she asked.

Tom lifted his leg and brought it down on the kick-start; the engine roared into life. He nodded.

'He's fine,' he shouted. 'We're going for a drink next week.'
He looked suddenly bleak and she cupped his face in her hands.

'I love you, Tom. You must be careful, bonny lad. Careful in that pit and with your mouth at the meetings.' She was shouting to make herself heard above the noise of the bike and he nodded as he leant forward and kissed her cheek.

'You're sure about the nursing then, are you?' he asked in her ear. Sarah was on the step watching.

She nodded. 'I'll get me school certificate and then I'll go to Newcastle but you must keep on painting though you'll need a teacher. Somehow we must get you a teacher.'

He grinned and pulled at her hair and before he could go she pulled his hands to her lips. 'You must be careful,' she insisted as he slipped the clutch and pulled away from her.

'Be careful,' she called after him as he turned to wave and the smell of exhaust lingered where he had been.

CHAPTER 18

Tom clutched Grace's arm and pulled her through the back gate into the yard. Betsy had daffodils growing in a tub by the edge of Beauty's stable and they were bright with only a light covering of black smut. She was cool and her mouth tasted soft and clear and her lips pressed back and her body was hard against him.

'That's enough of that, you two, it's Sunday,' laughed Betsy from the kitchen door and they turned and waved to her.

'I know it's Sunday, that's why I'm only kissing her once, before lunch anyway.' Tom tilted his cap on to the back of his head and leaned over Beauty's stall, stroking her and bringing out the apple which had been stored in crumpled newspaper along with the rest since last autumn in May's cupboard. It was wrinkled and soft, a murky yellow, but Beauty ate it dripping juice into his hand which he kept beneath her mouth, letting her nibble and kiss him with her warm blackness.

Grace leant against his side, her head on his shoulder. 'We'll take her for a walk this afternoon, shall we?' she asked, stroking the pony's ear so that she twitched away from her. 'Up the beck. It's warm enough.'

Tom slipped his arm around her, pulled her even closer against him, moving his hand upwards until he could stroke her breast. Her nipple hardened and she moaned softly. 'I'd like that,' he murmured. 'It'll take me mind off tonight.'

Grace pulled away, her head up and her curls spinning as she stalked from him to the kitchen, her buttocks jumping beneath her yellow dress. Tom laughed and called:

'I'd like that even if I didn't have the meeting tonight.'

He watched as she shook her fist at him before disappearing in to Betsy.

He was nervous and leant on the stall with both arms, letting

Beauty lift her head and blow hot breath into his chest. Annie had said it was time he did it, time he gave the talk that Davy should have done six months ago but which his death had prevented. Betsy had agreed with Annie and promised him a lamb roast to put some iron in his blood.

He sighed and smoothed Beauty's fringe. The days in the pit stretched endlessly now that there was no stopping-point any more, no art school to make the minutes and hours seem an irritation to be endured temporarily. That fact had clouded his grief for Davy and made his anger sharper for, if he was to stay here and take Davy's place, he wanted the men to feel anger along with him, to fight for something better, to work in the bloody pits and be able to afford food for hungry bellies. He wanted those out of work to feel that they should be employed and, if they weren't, to have, as a right, enough to live on without losing their dignity. Davy had been right to make them want to talk, make them want to think and he owed it to the lad to take his notes and make them into words.

He felt soft hands slide round his waist and her breasts and belly press into his back and buttocks. 'Come away in, bonny lad,' Grace said. 'Your mam's ready to see your ugly mug, you know.'

Betsy was pouring out steaming water from the greens into the sink. She held the lid on and kept the gap to half an inch and Tom felt the damp heat as he kissed her and took the pan from her.

'Don't let them fall out, like you did last week,' Betsy scolded and he grinned.

'Taken the gravy water out first then, have you?' he replied with a wink to Grace.

'Teach your grandmother to suck eggs, would you?' Betsy sniffed and went back to stirring the thick liquid on the top of the oven.

Grace was laying out the knives and forks and Tom saw that there were spoons too.

'Having a pud today then, are we?' He tipped the greens out into the bowl.

'Aye, lad, thought you'd need a lining to your stomach if you're to be telling the lads what they should be thinking tonight.'

Tom sat down; there were three places laid, so Joe was out at

Newcastle again then. He was glad; he wanted his mother to himself. Joe was all right really but he was her boss, wasn't he, so it made for a funny feeling. Funny-looking bloke and all, he was, long and thin and jerked his head a bit like that cock of Annie's but at least he didn't crow. Just sat there looking as though he should have a drip on the end of his nose and always with a worried look on his face. Maybe it was his age, 50 was getting on a bit.

He smoothed the cloth with his hands, there was black dirt under his fingernails and a flick of green paint on his cuff. May would grizzle when she saw that but Tom guessed that she liked it really for it gave her something to do, something to pound at in the tub; take out her rage at the pits which had sent two of her boys away to the factories and crushed the breath out of the other.

'I'm not trying to tell the men how to think, Mam.' She brought the meat to the table and the juice of the lamb oozed from beneath the joint and the fat was cooked to a crisp. She smiled at him and passed the carvers.

'You do it, bonny lad, and get yourself sat down, Grace.' She pointed to the chair opposite Tom and sat down herself. She looked pleased, her mouth lifted in a smile and her blue eyes relaxed. Her hands were not so swollen today Tom noticed as he took the knife from her.

'Better are they?' he asked. Grace was putting the plates in front of him and, as his ma nodded, he cut the meat and lifted two slices on to each plate. It was pink in the centre and his mouth watered. He wondered if the rich aroma would float through the window and out past the back doors of the other houses in the street and the thought made him feel uncomfortable. There'd be no meat for most of the buggers today, he thought, or the next day or the next. The carvers had bone handles and they were well balanced.

The light of the fresh spring day and the sound of the birds as they came after Beauty's oats came in through the window.

'I thought Don might come,' Betsy said as she passed the mint sauce to Grace along with an extra potato, waving aside her protests. 'You've gone thin lass and you suit a bit of flesh, don't she, Tom?'

'Oh aye,' Tom said, but thought she's bloody marvellous whether she's thin or fat and remembered the first time they made love, up on the hill by Bell's Farm when it was so cold the grass had been like dry bracken but they'd not noticed. He felt the warmth of his longing rise in him and looked across the table, his eyes heavy with thoughts of her, and she kicked him and his ma asked:

'So where's Don then, lad?'

Tom swallowed past his throat which felt swollen, then forced down some lamb. 'He's off to Annie's, today. He said he'd like to come next week if that was all right. He's borrowed the motor bike and will be back tonight. If he's got a strong enough stomach he said he'd come on to the meeting, if only to give me a bloody good heckle.'

Grace laughed. 'I bet old Albert's right livid at his going across to Gosforn again.' She passed Tom some more greens and Tom helped Betsy to cut her meat.

She nodded her thanks and held her fork awkwardly as she ate her meal. 'There was bad blood between him and Archie. He won't want them two to be friends, I reckon.' Her lip began to tremble. 'I never realised how he was though or I never would have . . . '

'Hush now, Mam,' Tom interrupted.

'I never would have sent her there if I'd known he was so bad. I reckon he wanted them kids ruined to spite Archie, you know, and I should have seen.'

'Now, Betsy,' soothed Grace, 'eat your meal and forget all about it.'

'I can't really remember much about them days you see, it's all a bit of a blur, what went before and what went after.' Her cheeks were red and her eyes darted from one to the other.

'Mam,' said Tom firmly, shaking her arm and feeling its softness beneath his fingers. 'Mam, it's gone now. We're all fine and you should have seen the lad on the bike.' He was speaking loudly now making her listen and he saw her eyes focus on him and knew that he had her attention.

'He's bought himself a helmet and goggles and looks like something out of a horror story.' He laughed and Betsy did too. He felt Grace stroke his leg with her foot and caught her eye which was gentle on his.

'So it's working out, is it, sharing Davy's bike?' Tom nodded and wiped his mouth on his sleeve.

Betsy slapped his hand. 'Use your napkin and don't be a pig,

256

lad.' He raised his eyebrows at Grace and was glad that he had pulled his mam back to today.

'Them eggs you brought back from Annie's were beautiful and fresh. They're in the pudding you know.' Betsy cleared the table and gave Tom the cloth to carry the sponge from the oven to the table. 'She sounds keen in her letters about this nursing, but worried, lad; worried about the pits. She wants you to go on painting.'

'We all do,' agreed Grace, frowning at Tom.

He showed her his cuff. 'See, I've done some this morning already.'

'But Annie says you need a teacher and we reckon a correspondence course is the best idea.'

Betsy sat back at the table heavily and handed the spoon for Grace to dish up. 'Don't we, Grace? You, me and Annie.'

Grace grinned and nodded.

'And I've got the money,' said Betsy.

Tom shook his head. 'No Mam, I've some money from the pits.'

'I've got the money, I said,' insisted Betsy. 'Annie says there's one for six pounds. You send away to London and I'll pay.'

'No, Mam,' said Tom, his mouth full of custard and sponge, his words indistinct.

He winced as Grace kicked him. 'Let her, she wants to,' mouthed Grace. 'Or I'll not go to the beck with you.'

He finished his mouthful, the laughter welling up. Now there was a threat to be reckoned with. Betsy ate on, not looking up as Grace pulled the kettle on to the hob.

'Can you manage it then, Mam?' he said at last when his plate was scraped clean. 'Maybe a couple of bob.' He knew she'd be disappointed but he didn't want to ask her for too much.

She nodded and sat back in the chair with her arms folded. Tom grinned to himself to see her in Archie's chair. She was a strong woman now, his mam was.

'It's not right that you've gone into the pits for good. You should have gone to College and then on to this business with Annie. It's bad you know, the life down there. Your da wouldn't have wanted it for you.'

Tom sighed and pushed back his chair, carrying the pile of

plates that Grace handed to him. 'I know, Mam, but it's just something I've got to do. Maybe later Annie and I'll get together.'

Betsy nodded as she moved over to her seat by the fire.

'Aye, that you will. Ma Gillow always said it would be you and Annie together and so it will be; if not now, later.'

She tucked her head into her neck and smiled as Tom stoked the fire for her and sat down while Grace made a pot of tea.

'So me da wouldn't have wanted me to go into the pit, then?'

Betsy shook her head. 'Nay, lad, he didn't like it himself you know. His da was killed when a cage fell and my Barney couldn't forget that. He didn't like the dark either, or the rain.'

'So tell me more about him, Mam.' Tom was leaning forward, his hands resting between his knees. Grace turned and watched him, then brought tea to him and Betsy.

'How old was he when he died then, Betsy?' she asked gently.

'Nineteen he would have been, lass. Nineteen, that's all. He was the only one, you know. There were no other children.'

'So what was me grandma like then, Ma? Did she visit us?'

Betsy shook her head and sipped her tea, holding the cup between two hands as she had always done. Grace sat down next to Tom, lifting the cushion from his cut down chair as she did so, tracing with her finger the hexagonal lines of stitching. Tom watched the line of her face, her cheek, her chin and he reached out and touched her softly. Betsy nodded as she watched them.

'No,' she answered quietly, blowing the steam from the top of her cup. 'No, she never saw you, lad. She died not so long ago but didn't want to know me. I was a slag, you see. I'd had a bairn out of wedlock and nice girls don't. You were her grandson and she didn't want to know you even though both her men had gone.' Her face was sad but she smiled gently at him. 'But my mam thought you were a right cracker, she did, and then she died too, of the flu, you know.' She sighed and Grace put the cushion back in the chair. 'Joe cut that chair down, you know, lad. He's a good man in his way. Took me in, paid me he did, when lots wouldn't have done.'

'Aye, Mam, I know.' Tom replaced his empty cup on the table. The dresser against the wall was catching the sun, the blue and white plates looked fresh and clean. 'So didn't me da ever think of doing painting then?'

Betsy looked over her cup at him, her face puzzled. She stretched out her legs and leaned back in the chair.

'Now why would he want to do a thing like that, then?' she asked.

'Well, look at me. I'm like him, you said.'

Betsy rose from her chair, then sat down again. 'Tell you what, lad, take your young legs up them stairs, into your Annie's old room. Bring me down the picture that's on the side of me bed. Off you go now. Grace can hop up with you or stay here and keep me company.'

She smiled at the girl, at her copper curls and soft blue eyes and Grace said, 'We'll have another cup of tea, shall we, Betsy?'

Tom had not been up into the house since the day he left and it all seemed smaller somehow, the black-patterned hall floor, the turned banister which led on up to the study where it had happened. He opened the door and the room was empty. The old dark desk was gone, the prints were no longer on the wall. It was an empty room which did not even hold a ghost, just a vague memory of the man who had locked himself up in here so often, until the last time. The walls had been whitewashed as though to wash away the stains of the past and the northern light made his breathing quicken. He walked on into the room, stood in the centre, turned around judging the size, judging the feel. It was right, you know, just right, he walked swiftly to the door, and down the stairs before he remembered that it was to Annie's bedroom he had been going.

He walked on up as he had done for all those years. The stairs seemed dark when he was a child and his footsteps had always sounded sharp and cold but now there was a carpet on the stairs and at the top a large oil lamp which glowed as the old one had never done. He did not go into Annie's room yet, but opened the door into his own and there were the drawings he had done, still pinned to the walls as he had left them. His old cardigan was on the chest which had been at the bottom of the bed, but now of course there was no bed, for he had taken that with him, the day he had left. There was just a square section of black-painted floorboards surrounded by cracked linoleum. The little table which had held his oil lamp was spotless and there lay his jacks which he had left because he could not believe he was never coming back. He moved to pick up the stones, the hard ball, but then stopped, leaving the room as he had found it; as his ma wanted it.

He crossed the landing into Annie's room and this too had been whitewashed. The bed was draped in a new patchwork quilt in muted beige and purple colours, ones that picked up the rag rug exactly. There were flowers on the dressing-chest and he felt a tightness because Annie had never had it like this and thanked God that his mam now had some beauty, some peace.

There was a picture of a man's face on the bedside table. It was in pencil and he knew it was his da. It was his own face he was seeing but with darker hair. The face of a young man who had only been three years older than him, for God's sake, when he had died.

He picked the drawing up, brought it to the window. It was good, there was life in the face, in the eyes. It was easy for portraits to look like death-masks, the colour too heavy, the eyes blocked in, but this was good.

He took it down to Betsy. 'He was a lovely man, Mam.'

She held it carefully in her swollen hands. 'He said he'd buy me rings for me pretty fingers, called me the Queen of Sheba and afterwards I drew this.' She sat still, looking at the drawing, framed in glass, the mahogany polished until it shone vivid in the firelight.

Tom was still, quite still, watching her, watching her hands, hands that had once drawn this and could now barely hold the frame.

He gripped his own hands tight together, seeing again the design of the rug he had his feet on, the colours of the patchwork and he knew he should have guessed before. His mother, he knew now, had the soul of an artist, his soul and that she must have felt as he did when it was stifled, when life took over and snatched the dream away. One day, he decided, one day when he had done enough here, he would be an artist, then come back, he and Annie together, because they had much to do.

'It's good, Mam, so very good.' He said, 'Look, Mam, if I'm to get on, if I'm to be a painter I'll need another pound towards me postal course. Can you give it to me?' He wanted her to feel that she was making art possible for him.

Grace reached over and took his hand, squeezed it and nodded at Betsy.

'Aye, lad, I reckon I could.' Betsy looked again at the picture. 'D'you really think it's good?' Her voice was tentative.

'It's the best, Mam. It's the best I've seen.' He looked again at the face of his da and knew that here was the real man.

He took Grace's hand and pulled her to her feet.

'We'll go now, Mam, take Beauty for her walk.' But Betsy did not look up. She was gazing at Barney, running her swollen finger over the outline of his face.

As Tom left the room he stopped and turned. 'Mam, d'you think Joe would let me use the study for me studio? It's the light you see; the light is right and if I do the course, I'll need to get a folio together.'

He thought she hadn't heard because she sat so still and then she lifted her face to his and looked hard at him and said nothing.

'D'you think Joe would let me?' he repeated. It was as though she was making a hard decision and thoughts chased across her face too quickly to grasp and then she nodded.

'Oh aye, he'll let you.' But there was a strangeness about her and he turned to go back but Grace called him on.

'I'll pay him, Mam,' he offered as he stepped out into the light.

'No, bonny lad,' Betsy said quietly. 'I'll be the one doing the paying.'

The Lodge Meeting Hall was crowded and Tom slipped through the men, nodding to some, not recognising others. Smoke from cigarettes held in cupped hands rose into the air and stung his eyes. He edged between two groups and forced his way through to the platform, nodding to Davy's mates who were setting up the lectern. Frank patted his shoulder and he nodded, his mouth suddenly dry, his hands shaking and he put his notes down on the sloping stand as the men slowly noticed he was there and the talking became a murmur, then the murmur slipped off into silence.

The only light was on the platform now and he turned to Frank who nodded. 'Get on with it, lad,' Frank whispered, 'they'll not stay quiet for long, the bar's open.'

He turned again to the floor and felt too young for this. It should have been Davy; he was the one the men had come to hear and that was why they were suffering him, so he'd better do a bloody good job, he told himself.

'Davy,' he began tentatively, fingering his notes. 'Davy died just before he was going to talk about the means test; about what it means and his thoughts on where we should be going, what we should be asking our union to do for us. I have,' and he held up pencilled pages, 'his notes here.' His voice was stronger now. He put down the papers and leant on the lectern.

'We all know,' he said, 'that, because of the world depression, there is long-term unemployment and God knows when it is going to end, whilst here we are, up the bloody swanee without a paddle.' He waited for the whistles to die down, the calls and cheers to fall.

'What this has meant to us up here in the North is pit closures, no work for two thirds of us. That means that families cannot buy newspapers, or a stamp to post a letter, can't help a neighbour any more, join a sick club, pay subs to the union. People feel helpless.'

He was in his stride now, the words were coming quicker without any need to look at the notes. His voice was stronger and the trembling in his legs and hands was gone. It was still dark on the floor but he could see shapes, the glow of cigarette ends, the stillness of men listening and felt a surge of power, of enjoyment. The lectern edge was cool and hard as he gripped it again.

'Bairns have no spending money; we have nothing to give them. Their das have no tobacco or beer money; mothers have no dresses. There's not enough food to keep the family healthy or free from hunger that keeps us awake at night. There is not enough coal to keep us warm in winter and we are living on top of a bloody heap of the stuff.' He banged his hand in his fist and nodded at the calls from the hall, the agreement in their tone encouraging him to continue.

'So what have the National Government done, a government which I might add, brothers, is led by a Labour Prime Minister? Why, they have brought in the means test.' He bowed ironically and the catcalls were loud and he held up his hand to quieten the hall.

'The means test is a grand way of lowering the money paid out by the government and at the same time does a bloody good job of lowering the dignity of the unemployed. Who likes snoopers coming in, poking their noses into cupboards, telling us we have to sell grandma's best teapot? Nobody.

'The means test must go, Parliament must be lobbied, we must make our complaints loud and long. Get your unions to make them for you.'

He stood back and let the calls and the talk between the men on the floor continue while he took some water from Frank and sipped at it, asking him over the top of the glass how it was going.

'Good, man,' said Frank. 'You've got them thinking, got them talking. Just give 'em a burst of Davy's allowance idea and call it a night.'

'Aye,' agreed Tom and picked up the gavel. The knocking brought a hush to the hall again.

'But, lads, as we all know and as Davy knew, there is another problem. What about the low wages when we're in work? Work does not bring fresh milk. It does not bring butter. It will bring one egg if you're lucky and that doesn't keep our bairns well. So, you will ask, what do we do?'

'Aye, that's a question could do with some answering right enough,' called a deep voice from the well of the hall and was taken up by others, loud and long.

'Well,' shouted Tom, forcing his voice through the uproar. 'Well, we can stop having bairns but the bosses would like that less than a wage rise because their future workers wouldn't be produced.' He pulled a face and the men laughed. 'We need a decent minimum wage; we need state control of the mines so that our men are on the board and can make sure of safety, reinvestment, a decent return for our work. But, more than that, men.' He held up his hand for silence.

'We need an allowance, not just for the miners but for all the workers in the land above and beyond wages. An allowance that is paid out by the state to the families, a certain amount for each child. That would mean that, low wages or no wages, there would always be enough to feed your bairns.'

There were cheers now and he could feel the sweat running down his back and sides, running down his face and on to his open shirt-collar.

'What about the unions though?' a voice cried from the back of the hall. 'They won't back that idea, it might make owners pay less in wages if they thought we was all getting extra anyway?'

Tom smiled; this'll get them going he thought. 'Then it should be paid direct to the women, that'd settle that argument and give the lasses their own income.'

He watched as men turned to one another and the volume of argument and discussion grew louder and louder. They were talking and that is what Davy had wanted and, bye, he wished Annie had been here to clip back her ears at what he had said about giving it to the women. She'd have been right surprised, right glad, but it wasn't just for her he had said it; he'd done it because it made sense.

He turned and moved over to the chairs where Davy's mates were sitting. They were leaning forward and talking amongst themselves and he listened as he heard Frank say, 'I'd forgotten Davy said that.'

'Well he did,' Tom replied pocketing his notes and standing with his hands in his pockets. 'It makes sense you know. It'll be hard enough to get union backing for the idea but if you make it payable to the women it's different somehow. It doesn't affect their bargaining position so much, does it, when they come to negotiating wages.'

He looked as a smile slowly spread itself over Frank's face. 'Come over to the bar for a drink, lad.' He rose and took Tom's arm but Tom looked over at the men, milling towards the bar which had opened at the end of the hall, at the smoke and the dim lights which had now been lit and his legs felt heavy with tiredness. His head ached with the noise and it was as though a band was being drawn tighter and tighter and he shook his head.

'I'll get on back now, Frank.' He shook his hand, then the others. The grips were firm, the faces friendly. 'I'm tired now and me feet is killing me.' They joined in his laughter and he pushed down the steps, through the men, his back stinging with slaps and his head full of their arguments until at last he was out, into the cool air. He drank in the spring-laden coolness, felt the fine drizzle, relished the quiet once the door swung shut behind him.

He dug in his pocket for his cap, stuck it on his head and sauntered down the street which was dark with many windows boarded up and houses deserted, their tenants gone from them to the South, to anywhere which might give them a living. Yes, the men were arguing, talking; they would have more to think about tonight than how hungry they were, how they were going to last until the end of the week. His boots slipped slightly on the wet cobbles and he hunched his collar up against the increasing wetness.

He was not going home but to the pub where he and Davy had sat the night before he had died. Don had not been there at the meeting and he was glad really. He wanted to be quiet for a moment, to think back over this evening, to think back over Davy's words and check that he had said all that he had wanted the men to hear. Bye, it was a powerful feeling, that it was, standing there knowing that they were listening, knowing that they were chasing around in their minds for questions, answers and arguments. It was a bit like looking at a painting; sizing up the texture, the light, whether the artist had caught the moment, what he was trying to say. He shouldered his way through the doorway of the pub, undoing his jacket and easing the white muffler until it hung loosely.

'Just half a pint,' he said to the barmaid. His voice was hoarse and his throat slightly sore. He took the glass from her, sucking at the froth and taking a mouthful of rich brown beer, feeling it slip down his throat and soothe the rawness.

'You'd better watch yourself, young man. Speaking out like that could see you out of work. One of the Socialist League, are you?'

Tom knew the voice, low and measured and thoughtful but it was a long time since he had last heard it. He did not turn his head, just took a sip before saying. 'I belong to nothing, Mr Wheeler, and my business is none of yours.'

Bob Wheeler laughed. 'Two half pints, please. You'll have another, won't you, Tom? Revolution is thirsty work.'

Tom turned. 'Hardly revolution, Mr Wheeler, and aye, I'll have another drink.' The man had aged, he thought. His hair was now quite grey, his face thinner and his skin was dry and deeply lined.

'Let's sit down?' Bob waved towards a booth in the corner.

The pub was quiet but then there weren't many with money for beer these days, as I've just been saying, thought Tom ironically. The lights were muted and the curtains at the windows were drab and uneven though the table they moved to was spotless. Tom's glass left a wet ring.

'You remember me then, do you?' Bob Wheeler said.

'I remember when you used to visit Archie Manon.'

Bob nodded and brought out his pipe, filling and lighting it while they sat in silence. He had been waiting to speak to Tom, waiting since he had received Sarah's letter asking him to keep an eye. There had been little for him to do so far but if tonight was anything to go by this lad would need a bit of a rein on him, a bit of steering or no pit would touch him. He would be marked down as an agitator, a trouble-maker as his cousin had been. He sucked at his pipe looking over at the lad as he drew on his pint. Maybe he would side-track him with union business. Tom was a good-looking boy, heavy set with intelligent blue eyes and a manner much older than his 16 years. Oh yes, Tom Ryan, there's not much I don't know about you, my lad, he thought, and I daresay rather more than you know yourself.

He smiled to himself at the tone of Sarah's letter; it had been urgent and worried. Well, let's see what we can do about it all, eh? And he shifted in his seat, pleased to be involved again with Archie's family, pleased to be able to pay off his debt but perhaps it was more than that. Perhaps it was because he was lonely that he was prepared to become interested in this young man with the jutting chin. He had spoken well, there was no doubting that and he had caught the men in his hands, something that was hard to achieve.

'So, how many points did you make tonight, then?' Bob asked.

Tom looked confused; he had been thinking of Davy and the night they had sat here and had overheard the group who were going to duff up Don. It seemed an age ago.

'Oh, I don't know. Two main ones, I suppose.' He sat back on the seat and looked at Bob.

'That's what I reckon, lad.' He acknowledged Tom's look of surprise. 'Oh yes, I was there, a union official should know what the members are getting up to! It was good, lad, but leave it at one point each meeting and only up it to two if you must. People don't remember a great deal, you know.'

Tom leaned forward, his brows lowering, his face interested. He was going to learn from this man tonight and they talked then until closing-time and on some more in Bob's house.

It was strange, Tom felt, walking into the small two up two down that Archie used to visit; that he had visited the night before he had killed himself. He wondered whether Archie had sat here as they were doing, round the kitchen table with the fire glowing in the grate, the kettle heating on the range. The table was covered with a heavy wool cloth with darker tassels which caught on Tom's thighs as he sat down. A jug of beer frothed between them and Bob poured them each a mug.

'It'll keep us going until the kettle's boiled,' Bob laughed and Tom nodded and looked at the photographs on the wall to the right of the dresser which had only a few plates propped on the shelves. A man and a woman looking stiff in Victorian dress peered down at them and Tom could see the likeness between Bob and the man.

He pointed and asked, 'Is that your da then?'

Bob craned round and nodded. 'Yes, it is. He was a good man. Bought this house, though it took a lot to do it. He was a pitman, Tom, though I never was; I went into the office.'

'Me da was a pitman an' all,' Tom said tracing the weave of the wool cloth on the table. Bob knew already. He had done some ferreting about, as he had told Sarah, and found out quite a bit about Tom's background, about Barney Grant.

'I know, lad,' he said. 'I know that Barney Grant was a good face-worker, a good pitman.'

Tom sat up, his eyes eager. 'You knew me da then, did you?'

'No, not exactly but I knew of him.' He had found some of Barney's mates, those who had been in the pits with him; joined up with him. He'd found them through the union records and they had wanted to talk but mostly about the war and so he had let them, listening as they spoke of Ypres, which they called Wipers. They told him of the salient which guzzled up lives like a bloody great pig and the waterlogged trenches that never moved forwards. They told him too of the tunnels, one hundred or so feet deep, which the big nobs, as they called the Generals as they spat into the gutter, had thought were a good idea.

One of Barney's friends explained that the idea was to blow the Germans up. He was a cripple of 35 who had broken his back in the pits in '25. Survived that bloody mess, he had hissed, to lose me back in the pits; like that Barney, you know, but Bob did not know and had said so looking along the mean streets which converged on to the corner where they were all standing. The man had shaken his head in disgust. They needed miners, you see, he had sneered, miners to carve out the tunnels, build up the shafts and then lay the charges beneath the German front-lines so what did they do, they took us off the surface, didn't they, brought us down into the clay and put us to work, like bloody rats in a trap again.

They wanted to shift the Germans back off the salient, the man had grunted as Bob frowned, and they couldn't do it from the top so we crept along beneath them, quiet as bloody mice because they were tunnelling too. We lived down there, one of the other men explained. I can still hear the pumps as they kept the water out he had said with a shudder, but not the dampness, so you still coughed and your skin looked white in the lights but at least they had light and electric they were too. The other men nodded and one said that it was grand what could be done when the nobs wanted it enough, while the other cursed and became restless.

Bob had passed round Woodbines and brought them back on to the subject and learned how the men had lived and worked down there until the tunnels were long enough and deep enough and the poor buggers above them had been blown to bits. Went up like a bairn's mud pie kicked by a horse, the cripple had said, but Barney Grant didn't see it, did he. He was killed when the bloody ceiling fell in two weeks before. The man had hunched himself forward in his wooden wheelchair and stabbed a finger at Bob. Gone all the way from our pits, he had said, to die in a bloody frog's. They hadn't told Barney's missus, of course, not that she was his real missus but you know what we mean and Bob had nodded and he remembered their faces even now as they had walked away from him, not wanting a drink, just wanting a job. He had watched them as they walked down the street, all but the one who had told him the most. He was being pushed by his mates. They had all been at Ypres together; they were all out of work together.

He sighed and put his beer down, moving past Tom to the bread-tin, bringing out a loaf and some cheese from the dresser.

'Have a Scotch,' he said to Tom, hoping that he would not ask but knowing that he would.

'No thanks, I never touch it,' replied Tom. 'Tell me about me da.' His face was serious, his eyes steady.

'Have some cheese.' Bob cut some bread and passed it over

268

on the point of the knife. He moved a plate to the lad and some cheese. 'Tell me, when are you going to start your painting again?'

But Tom did not eat his cheese, did not answer Bob, so, in the end, the older man sat back in his chair and told Tom about his da. About his life as a pitman, about his marrers who had been with him until his death. Tom sat quietly while the fire dwindled and the kettle puffed its lid gently up and down. Silence fell between the men and Tom thought of his mother and knew that he would never tell her that Barney had not seen the sky when he died.

The hours passed as they sat at the table, the older man and the young one talking of Barney, of Betsy, Annie and Grace. Of Don and Albert, of the pits and what could be done. Bob had known Davy, known his thoughts and he grew now to know Tom's.

Tom heaped his bread with cheese as early morning came; some crumbled and fell and he picked each bit up, pressing it against his finger then sucking. It was a sharp salty taste and went well with the beer, and then the tea which they made an hour later. His muscles felt loose and he was leaning easily back in his chair. He must remember to tell Don how God had been made man; he would appreciate that, would that canny lad.

It was three when he reached for his jacket and shrugged himself into it. The next day he'd be for it with Grace; she'd be cold at his hangover when he came into the library after the shift to read up on Van Gogh.

'It's his colour, his fragmented impressionism,' he explained to Bob as he left his house. 'That's what I like. The life in his brushwork.' And Bob told him that he should not be wielding a putter's shovel alongside a palette knife.

'Grace says that he paints as though he has one of her migraines,' replied Tom as he waved to Bob from the street. 'I've got to stay in the pits. It's just something I've got to do for now but me mam's sorting out a studio so that's going to make it grand.'

As he walked back through the streets to May's, Tom pulled his jacket round him and shivered but it was not the cold, it was the thought of the black pit waiting for him.

Betsy lay beside Joe in the double bed that she had shared with

269

Archie. She was naked beside him, his hand lay on her breast, it felt cold and damp. She could still feel his weight on her as he had thrust his body into hers, kissed her with thin lips, his breath on her face, his tongue probing her mouth. She had closed her eyes and thought of her clean white room above, her patchwork quilt which would be too small for this bed and about her son who needed a studio; which he would now have.

CHAPTER 19

Annie was relieved that Sarah was coming with her to Newcastle Hospital for her first day. They drove in on roads lined with fields and copses which slowly merged into the spacious houses of the suburbs and then into streets lined with terraces clenched tight against clumps of factories which belched black smoke. Gulls wheeled over the hospital as they approached, flying in from the docks. The sky was lighter over there, as it always was by the sea, Annie thought, remembering the call of the gulls and the cold of the sea as it had dragged the sand from beneath her feet.

Sarah stopped the car at the entrance to the tall redbrick building. A statue of Queen Victoria looked over them to the town and the bedding plants had been cleared from around the plinth as it was September.

'So,' said Sarah as the engine jumped, then died. 'So one day they will put up a plaque saying that on September 1932 at two-thirty in the afternoon Nurse Manon began her career.' She laughed and laid her leather-gloved hand on Annie's arm.

Annie sat back, feeling the leather-seamed seat, seeing the dark brown wood of the dashboard, the pot-pourri that hung in muslin from a knob and which Sarah said would trick you into thinking the Morris was a new car with new smells. She remembered picking the oily lavender and the rose petals which they had then dried, together with the herbs.

'You'll feed the hens then, Sarah?'

'Of course,' Sarah nodded. 'And sell the eggs, taking the money towards Don. But I'd far rather send it to you, my dear. Remember that you get no pay for the first quarter and then it's only thirty shillings a month.' She was pulling her gloves from her hands, finger by finger.

'I'm fine. I've saved enough from the job and the patients' collection means that I can manage.'

'Come on, then,' urged Sarah.

The side entrance, where they had been instructed to assemble was signposted and Sarah's footsteps were brisk as they walked quickly past the trimmed lawns, down the path alongside the long-windowed building until they were there. The door was closed and Annie felt the same trembling, the same tightness in her stomach that had come on her first day of school. She looked at Sarah.

'Does this remind you of something?' Their eyes met and they smiled. But it was not the same, Annie knew. Today she was to begin her freedom.

'I'll be home on my first day off then, Sarah, if that's all right.' She leant forward and kissed her and Sarah's hand came up to her shoulder and held her close for just a moment and then she was gone.

Inside, the hall was lined with white tiles and there was a smell of disinfectant. Eight girls sat on a bench in the corridor and there was space for two more. Annie sat down and smiled at the girl next to her.

'I'm Annie Manon,' she said. 'From Wassingham.'

The girl, who was sallow-skinned and thin, returned her smile. 'I'm Julie Briggs from Whitley Bay and I'm scared to death.'

The girls laughed, all along the line, and leaned forward; words came slowly and then laughter joined them. Julie was 18 too, she told Annie, and had come over by train. She was the last of her family to leave home and the only girl. Her brothers were fishermen and married.

Sarah pulled on her gloves as she walked back to the car, skirting the lawns she did not really see and people who nodded and she did not acknowledge. The drive home seemed too quiet and too long whereas the three years with Annie had disappeared with a speed she would not have thought possible. She would not cry, could not cry while she was driving, but the loss of the child who had filled her life would always be hard to bear, too hard to speak of, even to Val. She wondered how she would fill her evenings, her weekends until that day off, the day Annie came home.

There would be no more hot cocoa at the end of each day with Annie, no more of her friends home for tea. Would Tom still come with Grace, or Don, now that Annie was not here?

She put the car into third gear to take the corner which led out from Newcastle. Her ward, her child was free now and she must be on her guard never to restrict that freedom.

Julie and Annie shared a room in the nurses' home and they prodded the beds and felt the stiffness of the blankets, then walked down green-painted corridors and stairs until they found Sister Tutor as they had been instructed. She was in a dark navy uniform and cap and wore a frown which looked as though it was never wiped away.

They wrote for the next two hours in a classroom cramped with desks and other girls until Annie's hand and mind were as jumbled as the room. There was an overwhelming smell of beeswax and the desks were sticky with it and a blackness formed on her cardigan.

The next day they were issued with pale blue uniforms and starched aprons and caps which crackled when they walked, but she did not glide as Sister Maria had done. Her heavy black shoes felt like boats and her feet at the end of that day were swollen and throbbing. Together she and Julie dabbed methylated spirits and talcum powder over the toes, the feet and up to the ankles before they crawled into bed, unaware of the heavy blankets, unaware of anything but the white-tiled corridors, the rows of beds, the sisters and nurses, the doctors and students, the dining hall, the mortuary, the Children's Ward. Unaware of anything until the call at five-thirty the next day.

For six weeks, they wrote and watched and listened in the classroom but did not see the wards again. Annie wondered if she would die of cold in her short-sleeved uniform, but each morning she hugged to herself the thought of the future, of the present, of her freedom.

She learned of leeches and smiled to think that Don could have used them after his discussion with Tom over the interest rates. Sister Tutor asked her to share her joke with the others and when she could not, she had to write out the lesson twice.

She learned about enemas, bedsores; about dangerous drugs which must always be locked. Suddenly through the open window the sound of the gulls seemed much louder and the whistle of the butcher's boy, the grinding of gears as a lorry struggled up the hill past the hospital. So simple really, she thought, a pin anchoring a few keys in a nurse's pocket could have saved a woman's life, not any woman but my mother. She had to copy up the notes she missed during that lecture from Julie that night.

They had no days off for those first six weeks or for the next four when they were on the wards at last.

The wards were large and white and smelled of disinfectant. Her feet swelled every night and did not go down by the next morning. She was in casualty when twelve miners came in and the enamel bowl shook in her hands as she washed and washed until the blackness was gone, leaving white flesh and red eyes.

She could see the blood then, but Sister drove her on to the next for washing and she smiled and talked soft words and pushed the thought to the back of her head that this could be Tom; this could be Tom. And so on to the next and the next and the next. Her apron was black and her hands too and later she scrubbed until they were red raw, until the smell of the coal and the sight of it was gone. But she could still smell it, see it as she cut clothes from a child who had hurt his arm, still smell it above the vegetable soup she served for lunch and that night she dreamed of dark tight streets, of pitwheels and slag-heaps, of allotments, of a shop, of a room with a snake which writhed and vomited gas. When she woke, in that moment before Julie's breathing was heard and the day had really begun, she knew that memory was still hers, that hate still remained. She was tired all that day and made sure that the black box in her mind was pushed tightly shut.

The week before her first day off she was moved to the Women's Ward. At six-thirty she took tea round, at seven she bathed and washed and combed hair. At eight she made beds, folding corners and putting on clean pillowcases with their openings away from the door. At nine she had a cup of tea and poured one in the small kitchen off the corridor for Julie who was on Men's further down.

'Guess,' Julie said, as she walked in, her hands behind her back. 'Guess what I have here.' Her eyes were dark with bags beneath and Annie knew that hers were the same.

Annie sat back in her chair, her legs up on the table, her ears pricked for Sister. 'Guess you're an idiot. Come and have some tea, we've only another seven minutes.' She checked the time against the watch that Sarah had given her when she was accepted for training by the hospital. 'Another eight minutes,' she corrected.

Then she saw the crumpled letter that Julie brought from behind her back but dropped and they watched as it floated to the ground, blue against the white of the tiles and the green of the linoleum.

It was from Georgie. Annie knew before she saw the writing, before she held it in her hands and saw the creases and stains from miles of travel. She tore at the envelope, ripping it open.

'Where did you get it?' she asked, not listening as Julie told her Sarah had brought it into the hall porter.

She searched now for his words of love.

June 1932

My dearest darling love,

You will be 18 by the time you read this and probably bossing everyone around in the hospital but I want you to know that I don't miss you any less with time, I just love you more and more. It is deeper and tucked down inside me but I am still seeing everything new here with your eyes as well as me own. I wonder, I do, if you would like the mountains which sometimes I can see as clear as day but which can get hidden by the thick clouds that clump together all of a sudden, here in the Himalayas.

How are you, my bonny lass, my darling girl? How are your feet? Tom says you soak them in vinegar like the miners do. He says it's a voluntary hospital supported by contributions from the miners mostly; have you had any in yet? If you have, try not to worry about Tom. Push it away, it can't happen, you love him too much.

It's hot here, the rains haven't come yet so it is a wet heat and I'm drinking lime juice until it comes out of me ear holes.

We've been down to the plains to Lahore which is

in a right mess. There's been a lot of fighting between the Muslims and the Sikhs and we're supposed to stand in the middle and calm it down, which I suppose is what we did. It's all a bit difficult, you know, here with the Indians. They want their freedom from us, (and I can't say I blame them) and I reckon there's going to be some fighting before too long; against us and one another. Anyway, I got me corporal's stripe out of it all, so now I'm waiting for me sergeant's but that could take a while.

Will you wait, my love? I don't mean miss out on things, just want me when I come, because I will come but it is all taking so long and I worry that you'll get tired and find someone else; a permanent someone else.

You would like it here today, my love. The geese and ducks have just flown over, heading for the water on the plains, and the bullock carts have been plodding by the station all day, but they always do. We have musk-roses which are white with a scent that your Sarah could put in her pot-pourri and make the Morris smell as sweet as a baby's bum. The whitebeams are trees which I really like. They are everywhere and have huge leaves which are dark green above and furry white below. There's a bitty fruit which changes to English autumn colours and the birds make right little pigs of themselves.

It was grand that the boys have sorted themselves out and that Don is back with you all. Who'd have thought that Bob was Sarah's flappy ears in Wassingham but I'm right glad he's keeping an eye on the lad. He needs a bit of controlling, you know.

I'll write again, my darling. I'm hoping to go to Kashmir because I'm told that it's beautiful, but before that we're off on exercises which will mean marches of ten or fifteen miles a day, so we'll both have sore feet.

I'll love you forever, want you forever, your soft skin, your beautiful face; my dearest darling, I miss you so.

Georgie.

Annie looked up at Julie. 'He still loves me.'

Julie smiled and took their cups to the sink. 'Sister won't love you if you don't get back, you know. It's the nit-round after the doctors.'

The medical students were crowding round the small man in a dark suit as he walked swiftly down the corridor and Annie pushed the letter into her pocket and slipped into the ward ahead of them and took up her place beside the senior nurse at Sister's desk. Mr Morton, the small physician, marched past, three of the medical students with him but the fourth stopped to tie his shoe lace in front of her. His blond hair was cut short and his neck bristled with shaved hair. He turned and winked and she blushed; his shoelace had not needed tying, she could see that now.

'Such nice legs, nurse,' he murmured, his wide mouth barely moving but his voice carrying beyond Annie to the senior nurse.

Annie flushed and he grinned, walking away now to catch up, his white coat flapping, a stethoscope dangling round his neck. Senior Nurse Wilson, her lips pulled into a thin line, pointed to the screens around the bed at the top of the ward near Sister's table.

'Try and leave your love-life outside the ward, nurse. There's a septicaemia case just come in. Doctor's already seen her so get on and delouse her and better stay with her for a bit. She's very poorly.'

Annie felt her hands grow damp. How poorly was poorly, she wondered.

The woman was lying still when Annie moved the screen gently, slipping through and pulling it closed behind her. She was yellow and thin, her face ravaged by illness, her eyes bright but not with health, with fever. Annie longed for the day when she would be able to take pulses and temperatures, give medication instead of dragging a steel comb through nit-infested hair.

She smiled at the woman. 'Hallo,' she whispered. 'I'm Nurse Manon, I have to check your hair, I'm afraid.' She wanted to think of Georgie's letter but knew that it must wait until tonight.

She hated it, hated the humiliation that they must feel. The lice she found were big and black and full of blood and Annie touched the woman's hand.

'What's your name?' she asked and had to lean forward to catch the faint words.

'Well, Mrs Turner, you're fine here, nothing at all on your hair, but I'll just run me comb through and put a bit of this stuff on just as a precaution.' She held up the brown bottle. 'We don't want you picking up anything while you're in here, do we?' It was a very small lie, she thought.

Mrs Turner's hair was dry and split, shot through with grey. She moaned as the comb pulled through.

Annie stroked her face with one hand. 'There now,' she soothed. 'This won't take long.' She squashed the lice between the bowl and her fingernail, hating them, wanting them to die for sucking what little blood this woman had and for forcing her to do this to an already ill patient. At last it was done and Annie smoothed back Mrs Turner's hair, wiping the tears from her cheeks where they had smeared as she had tried to brush them away before Annie saw.

'Oh, lass,' she whispered 'It's no job for a young girl. I'm right ashamed, you know.' She turned her face away from Annie, towards the tiled wall but the glare was too bright and she shut her eyes.

'There was nothing there, I promise, Mrs Turner. Nothing.' She put the bowl on the locker, covered with a cloth.

'Let's get you comfortable now.' She smoothed the sheets down and gently plumped the pillows, then sat. The woman was hot, very hot and Annie remembered that when she had been feverish with a heavy cold every touch had felt like a needle on her skin, so what must this woman have gone through just now.

'You'll soon begin to feel better you know, now you're here.'

Mrs Turner turned, her eyes were sunken and the lines around them were so deep it was as though they were coloured in with soot.

'Aye, lass, maybe I will. I lost the bairn see, lost the wee thing and now I've got the poisoning.' She coughed slightly and Annie held a glass of barley-water to her lips, holding her as she took a sip.

'I'm sorry about the baby, Mrs Turner.'

The woman smiled weakly. 'Thank God, you should say, lass. One less to worry about.' Annie laid her back on the pillow. She did not try to argue with the woman because she had not forgotten Wassingham; the cold, the hunger, the men on street corners.

Mrs Turner died at the end of her shift.

'Died just like that,' Annie told Julie as they ate their supper in the dining-room. 'There was this funny breath outwards; it went on and on and then she was dead.'

The cabbage was soggy and the fish dry and tough. It had been left too long in the oven again.

'No talking shop,' called a senior nurse from the other side.

Annie stood up and walked out of the dining-room, out of the hospital to stand by the grass. There was a rich smell of grass cuttings; it must be the last cut of the season she thought. For God's sake, it's the end of October already. She walked on past Queen Victoria who had her nose in the air. Well, it can't be the lobelia, they're not here any more, it's got to be me feet and she looked up at the plump shape and out through the gate over the town where the lights made the sky seem black above it. She stood with her arms crossed. That woman was starved before she came in, she thought. She died because she was poor, not because she had septicaemia. You don't die from septicaemia without a fight unless you take bloody poison or are starved. She said it again, challenging herself to shrink from the thought of her mother. She walked up and down and she felt the tears come down her cheeks and the heat of Mrs Turner as she had held her hand, the moan as she had torn the metal comb through her hair. There shouldn't be bloody nits, she shouldn't have had to go through that. She breathed in deeply and looked up at the sky wondering if she would be able to take the suffering that she was going to have to see over the next few years, but knew that she would. Above the glow of the town the sky was black and the stars were vivid. She wiped her cheeks and shook her head, angry now. These women needed work, needed money and one day she would do something about that, she and Tom together would make it a little better between them but not now because Tom had other things to do and so had she.

Annie caught the train to Sarah's on her first day off. The walk from the station was cold but the sky was a bright blue and the light seemed to fill the streets again, just as it had done when she had first come here from Wassingham.

She walked up the path, breaking off a leaf from the privet hedge, bending it over, hearing it crack clean, free from sap. Sarah held her close in her arms and Val hugged her and she took the bowl of corn that Sarah gave her and walked down the garden past the pruned roses, opened the wire gate and threw the corn to the hens, watching as they jerked, watching as the cock strutted.

The shed door opened easily and the smell of creosote was slight without the hot sun and she edged in past the bike, past the worn rubber grips to the window. She rubbed the glass, looking out into the open sky and leaned against the wooden frame. She loved it, she loved nursing. Loved the work, the girls, the being on her own, but she was glad to be back.

Lunch was calm until the doorbell rang and there were Tom and Grace, Don with a girl. Tom held her close, looked at her feet and said they were like bloody battleships. Grace kissed her and said how she'd grown. Don hugged her and gave her a bag of victory drops to keep away the germs and introduced Maud who was little with very curly hair and had Don right under her thumb.

Val laid more places at the table and Sarah laughed. They ate well and laughed and talked, then sat in front of the fire and Tom told them about Bob; how he had met him, how he was teaching him all about the unions and Sarah and Annie did not look at one another but at him and acted surprised. Don held Maud's hand and Tom winked at Annie. Grace asked about her work, about the food and they all laughed, Don too.

She told them about the Sister Tutor who had dragged them over the coals for the first six weeks, about the doctors who thought they were God but not about the blond medical student, William. She told them about the boy who had come into casualty with his head stuck in the potty but not about the child who had died of a congenital deformity and who she had carried in her arms, wrapped in a cloak, to the mortuary; you did not let the little ones take that last cold journey on their own, on a trolley. She told them about the woman who had produced a bairn when she thought she was suffering from indigestion, but not about Mrs Turner.

The train ride back was quiet after the talking and the

laughing and the hugs and kisses. They had asked after Georgie and she had told them about Lahore, about the heat, the fighting. She had not told them that he had said she was to live her life until he was back. The train pulled into the station. It was dark and the sparks flew up until they died and disappeared. She took the eggs and cakes that Val had made, the toffee that she and the others had boiled up in pans, then rolled and thrown at a nail Don had hammered into the door. Again and again they had taken the slack and thrown it and stretched it until it was ready. They had left it to harden while they had taken a last look at the hens, at the garden, then Tom had hammered it into pieces and they had taken some home with them but the rest was here, in this white box, for her patients in the morning.

The platform was empty by the time she had collected her parcels and climbed down from the step. She walked to the domed exit, through the dim lighting and the smell and huff of the trains and there was William, as he had said he would be.

He took her parcels but she kept one so that they each had a hand free to hold loosely. The night was fine and papers flew about their feet. Taxis waited in the ranks and they saw the glow of cigarettes in the cabs.

They walked back to the nurses' home and now everything was close to her after a day of distance, of waiting. They stopped at the pork stall on the corner and William ate a dripping sandwich which oozed and ran down his chin and Annie wiped it with her handkerchief. His laugh was light and easy and that was what she wanted. He took a piece of his bread and put it in her mouth, his hands were small and pale; he was going to be a surgeon.

He kissed her lips at the gates, away from the lights and she could taste the pork as his lips opened over hers. The parcels were in the way and she laughed and pushed him away knowing that she would see him again when they were on nights next week.

She was on duty at Christmas and sang carols round the tree and kept her hand in her pocket clutched tightly round Georgie's letter, the one that she had received in October. She smiled across at Julie, at William and knew that Georgie was safe deep inside her, quite safe from William or any other man.

Night duty was tiring because they had to work at lectures as and when they could during the day. As winter turned to spring, Annie took pulses, gave enemas, read temperature charts and spent two months in theatre. She took the severed legs to the chutes, mopped the surgeon's brows, watched William watching the specialists.

Tom and Don came to Newcastle with the girls and they went to the Empire, to the pantomime. Julie and Trevor, another medical student, came too, and William. The lights were still the same shell-pink, the curtains the same rich red. The binoculars were released from their stand on the back of the seat for the same sixpence. The seat prickled and Annie sat back and tried to forget her da. Tom pressed his arm to hers.

'All right, bonny lass?' he whispered and she nodded and most of her was, but still there lurked that dark hate that would not leave her in peace.

Tom wrote to her that week, wrote and asked her if she was all right now, asked about Georgie, about William, and she smiled and replied that she loved Georgie, she liked William because he made her laugh. She said that she wanted Tom to behave himself, keep out of trouble and sent him love for Grace and Don and Maud; for Don was still with this pale small girl.

Every other day off, she went to Sarah's but the others were for her and William. They walked in the parks, went to the cinema and sat on seats which flicked up the minute they were left. She screamed at King Kong and laughed at the silent movies that were still being shown.

In the summer, they went on holiday with Julie and Trevor to the Lake District and she shared a room with William. It was a small private hotel which lay on the banks of Windermere and had chalets which lay some distance from the hotel.

The hills across the lakes were not as high as the hills that Georgie wrote of and were seldom hidden by cloud. She was shy when William had locked the door, it was the afternoon of their arrival and the sun was hot. He turned to her, his hands stroking her face and she could feel the tremble in them.

He had blue eyes not brown like Georgie and soft hands, not hard like Georgie's and then she stopped herself. This was William and Annie and was quite different, quite separate from Georgie. He kissed her then, his lips soft, his eyes shut, his eyelashes casting a shadow on his cheeks. He was a good boy, Annie thought, as her lips pressed into his, from the South and different, but a good boy.

He undid her blouse and stroked her breasts as her nipples hardened; his breath was quicker now and he picked her up and took her to the bed.

'I'm a virgin,' she said as he sat down on the bed. He looked at her, traced the line of her cheek then her throat and her breasts and promised to be gentle. And he was, and afterwards she lay on the bed, wet with his sweat and her legs overlaid with his, looking out through the window at the water. There was a boat which seemed to be barely moving, the curtains were flowered and puffed out in the breeze. She turned and stroked his face and he kissed her hand.

She needed him, needed a man and a love that was light and happy and did not dig too deep.

They walked the next day, Julie and Trevor behind them, Julie's voice fading as they marched on higher and higher, avoiding the scree and laughing as Trevor slid down until he reached a rocky outcrop. Home Sister was a million miles away, Sarah was in Brighton with Val on holiday, and Wordsworth travelled with them as William shouted his verse and they hiked down to the lake and paddled in the cold clear water.

At the pubs where they stopped on their outings, the beer was heavy, the cheese flaky and it fell from their mouths as they threw back their heads and whooped with glee and Annie dug her hands deep into her pockets and let the wind whip her hair and swung into William's arms as he wished it, or she wished it.

They boated or made love as bees flirted with the heather and ladybirds plopped on to springy turf and hustled in and out of the shadows in a rush to find their way home before their houses burned and their children were all gone. Annie lay on her back and listened as William spoke of his home with its tennis court and the girl he would one day marry, the girl he had grown up with, and she felt a freedom which made her want to sing and shout from the mountain top because he wanted nothing more from her.

He told her about his mother who rinsed her hair blue and his father who was a stockbroker and had survived the crash of '29. She did not tell him of her father who had not survived, of the streets which were cruel and hard because these things were her memories, her problems and one day she would solve them.

She chewed the fleshy stalk of the long grasses and showed

William how to suck clover and flood his mouth with nectar and then wished that she had not for that was Georgie and she would not make love when he pulled her to him, the clover discarded in the grass.

The holiday was a release for them all, from the 67 hours she and Julie worked each week. The sun shone each day and they laughed on the train back to Newcastle.

Interim exams were just after the following Christmas in the January of 1934. Annie passed near the top though Julie only managed a scrape.

Annie spent some time in Male Surgical, nursing damaged miners, not just washing then. She checked for the redness of bedsores, eased dressings off burns and knew before she began each one that it would stick and cause the man to turn from her to hide his face. Once it was over there was no relaxation for they would go through the same process the next day. Then there was the shipyard worker who had fallen from twenty feet up and broken his back and the man with ingrowing toenails.

In Men's Medical, she nursed miners with black spit but most were sent home to die because their condition was too advanced. She would look into the sputum mugs and want to scream that it wasn't bloody fair.

Maternity was always busy with malnourished mothers at risk and underweight babies. The Children's Ward was full of bairns with shaved deloused heads who missed their mams and cried for them because the doctors would not allow more than a rare visit in case the child became upset. They called her Nurse and she liked the sound of it and of her feet as she bustled from bed to bed, knowing now that she was capable of caring for these people.

Georgie wrote in the early spring and she received the letter on the first day of June, just as she was leaving for Windermere again and perhaps fields and slopes full of daffodils.

March 1934

My darling love,
I've done it my love, I've made sergeant! We had a
real party, about as good as Christmas but then it

was better because the sergeants waited on us and the officers on them.

It is still quite cool here, the rhododendrons are in full flower, purple not red like the ones at your old school. You would love to see them, have you any at the hospital?

The lakes you wrote about sound like the ones in Kashmir but much smaller. I managed to get there on my leave, darling, and it's where we'll spend our honeymoon. We'll take a houseboat and spend two weeks just being together. Would you like that? Please say you would.

We've been very busy here, on exercises. It's so hot and the dust gets everywhere and your feet get rubbed raw. I'm right surprised the vultures don't come and have a go at us; they hover around though wherever we go, they're buggers and I hate the bloody things.

The trees are so lovely now. The leaves are sprouting on the oak, chestnut and walnut. Do you remember that walnut hall table you told me about at Sarah's? Well, it probably came from here.

My bearer is having a high old time because the snakes are always getting into the ghuslkhana, or privy to you, so when he sweeps out the excrement, and don't pull that face, they usually come wriggling out too. I'm very careful before I use it, I can tell you, hinny.

Now, my darling, listen to me. I'm worried about Tom. He's getting very het up about this Mosley and his blackshirts. Try and stop him taking it so seriously, won't you. I know there's trouble in Germany but I don't want our Tom in any bother in England. He tells me he wants to go to one of their meetings in London to tell the other side of the story. They'll be rough on him, bonny lass, if that happens. A mate of mine who's just come out from Blighty says that the blackshirts are buggers who like to put the boot in and his da says Mosley's trying to be another Hitler. Stop him, hinny, tell him to stay clear. I hope he'll listen to you and maybe Don. Get Sarah to ask Bob.

You work so hard at the hospital. I hope you're not too tired. I lie awake when we're on exercise looking up and thinking that somewhere you are under the same sky. I feel better now, pet, better because I can see an end to it all. It should be possible to become an officer, especially if I transfer to the Engineers. It's easier to come up from the ranks in that set up, me old sergeant says. I'll be applying and if I'm taken on I will be home to take my commission at Woolwich.

Don't hold your breath though because it will still be some time yet. Please don't write to me again telling me that you want me home. It is too hard to read that out here, when all I want is to be with you. I love you so much but you must see that I have to make it in my own way.

Please enjoy yourself and remember that I love you.

Georgie.

Sitting on the bed, Annie read it through again. Julie finished her packing and looked across.

'Still loves you, does he?'

Annie nodded. 'Oh yes.' I will never ask you that again my bonny lad, she thought, because she understood exactly what he meant.

'Does William know anything about Georgie?'

She shook her head. 'He knows precious little about me at all, that's the way I want it. I like him, I'm fond of him, but that's all.'

Julie shrugged. 'You could have him if you want him, you know. Marry a doctor, Annie, wouldn't it be great?'

Annie stood up and put on her coat before locking Don's watch in the wardrobe. She did not want it stolen while she was away. 'No thanks.'

'Why not though, Annie? You'd be comfortable for the rest of your life. I reckon Trevor's going to ask me if he passes his finals. He'll hear when we get back.'

Annie smiled at Julie, at her face which was still tired but fuller now; the sallowness gone and her cheeks pink. 'So you'll miss your finals will you? Just rush off and marry the boy?'

'Without a backward glance,' Julie said as they carried their cases down the stairs.

Annie wondered whether she would if Georgie came home, but knew she wouldn't. Knew she wanted to finish, to have that buckle on her belt and the full salary to finish paying Sarah, and then it would be time to force Tom into a college. She would be able to afford it herself then.

On the train they talked about the blackshirts, about the Nazis and William said that his father thought it might be a good idea if Mosley did well. It might get the trains running on time and sort out some of the slackers.

The train was passing through fields rich with green corn and the banks leading to the railway lines were sprouting green again through blackened stubble where sparks had set the grass alight the previous year. There was a farmer driving a team of horses which were turning over the earth. Rain had been forecast for the end of the week.

She looked at William as he sat back, his head rolling in time to the train's movements. 'What do you mean, slackers?' Her voice tightly controlled, she was aware that Julie had tensed and was looking at her. Trevor laughed.

'These buggers on the dole. You can always find work if you want it.'

Annie looked at him, at his curly black hair and red lips then turned back to William. 'You've seen them in the hospital, William. These people are hungry. They want work but there is none. It's not easy to move out of your area to find it either, you know that, and if they do go who's to say there'll be a job at the end of it. It's a big depression. These people are ill because they haven't any work.' Her voice was too loud, her words too slow.

William looked at her, his brow contracted with irritation. 'Don't shout at me, Annie. I know work is difficult to come by, but perhaps if someone like Mosley came in there'd be work. People would have to do as they were told. Look at Germany. There's full employment there or as good as. This Hitler's getting them all organised.'

Annie remembered last Sunday and Sarah sitting by the fire reading the paper, passing it to her and shaking her head over the brawling in the streets, the camps for the Communists and the Jews.

'What about their camps, what about the Jews? That can't be right. You can't think that is right?' protested Annie.

'That's only temporary,' William laughed, reaching for her hand kissing each finger. 'Once he's got things organised, all that will die down and the movement will become respectable.' She wanted to pull away from him, slap his face until it burned red but she caught Julie's eye, the fear and the pleading, so she said nothing more but wrote to Tom from the hotel repeating what she had said to him before but doubtful that it would make any difference. Then she walked in boots up the hillsides and drank beer and made love to William without enjoyment. She thought too often of the patients that these men thought were shirkers, of the people her brothers were and their friends. It was not warm this summer and she felt the breeze through her cardigan, felt William's hands cold on her flesh and no surge of wanting. She lay with him and beneath him noting when his passion spent itself inside her and that the lampshade and the cobwebs that hung from the ceiling and wafted in the breeze were not there last year. She saw the cracks which ran to the corners and the mirror that was not screwed on straight to the wardrobe door.

The weather broke on Thursday and storms lashed the hills and turned the lake into a stormy sea. They packed their rucksacks and took the train to Newcastle. William and Trevor found that they had passed their exams and Annie was glad for she wanted William gone from her. Trevor asked Julie to marry him and Annie was sad at the waste of a career.

There was also a letter from Bob to say that Tom was leaving on 6 June for London to attend a blackshirt rally at Olympia. She was on duty and could not intercept him at the station and she knew that it would have done no good if she had.

CHAPTER 20

Tom arrived too early for the train from Wassingham on Thursday and Bob waited with him. Frank had told Tom about the rally in London the week before. He'd said it would be a big one and they had arranged to go with two more from Frank's street.

Tom had told Grace while he sketched her by the beck where the wild honeysuckle was out and the shadows were sharp in the sun and the air was thick with scent. She had said he was a trouble-maker and all mouth, like Annie, only she had the sense to get out and stay out. She'll not come back, Tom, so don't go on expecting her too. She'd meant to hurt, wanted to hurt but he'd drawn her to him, kissed her, pulled up her blouse, stroking and kissing her breasts until she'd pulled away saying that she wouldn't love him any longer if he went down to London, but he knew that this was something she would never do.

'It's a matter of principle,' he explained to Bob as they waited for the train. Frank was over on the seats, playing cards with his marrers. 'No one objects to this man Mosley, they think he will bring good roads and trains that run on time.' Bob looked at his watch then and Tom punched him on the arm. 'Aye, Bob, we can put up with a bit of lateness, you know.' And they laughed. 'He's a bloody fascist. He's drilling his men and marching them through the East End. He's Hitler in England and look at what's happening over there in Germany. We could go that way, you know. Anyone who disagrees with the bugger would be squashed.'

Bob sighed. 'For God's sake, man, he's a nutter. No one will take him seriously, and besides, it's not your fight.'

Tom looked down the line but there was still no sign of the train. He moved from foot to foot. 'Look, Bob. This bugger dresses up his goons in black uniforms, then sets 'em on anyone who gets in his way and what happens? Sweet nothing. The cops just hold back the hecklers while he marches past or finishes his speech. He's got the support of the establishment, or some of them. It's bloody disgraceful, man.'

'So what are you four going to do then? Take the Fascist Union on single-handed?' Bob had a pink tinge to his cheeks, his voice was rising. There were very few people on the platform at five in the morning. The slag trolleys were tipping their loads behind them.

'I'm going to speak out, Bob, that's all, bonny lad, just speak out along with a lot of others.' He turned and whistled to Frank and jerked his head and then Bob also saw the train as it came round the bend, its smoke thrusting up into the fresh early morning air. He felt very old.

'So they're going to listen to a lad of 18 are they?' Bob called into Tom's face as the train steamed and screeched passed them to a halt.

Tom looked at him and laughed. 'I'm the one with the good lungs, aren't I, too young for the damage to have been done yet, no black lung for me, but ask Annie about the others.' He slapped Bob's arm. 'Thanks for coming, Bob, and for trying. It's just something I have to do. You understand eh, man? Annie does.'

Bob nodded as the door slammed shut and the train jerked out of the station. 'No one will hear, Tom,' he said quietly and waved as they passed round the bend.

Tom kept his eye on Frank as they left the train in London and headed for the underground; he was afraid of getting lost. The loudspeaker boomed across the concourse but he could not distinguish the words. At the top of each stairway there were men in blackshirts waving copies of their paper and calling 'Action! Action' and Frank grabbed Tom as he moved towards them, his cap low over his eyes.

'Nay lad, it's the meeting we're here for, leave it a while.'

They rushed down the steps past posters and toward the noise of trains. Litter blew round their ankles and up into the air when a train roared from the tunnel and it felt as though he was being sucked into its path.

There were over 15,000 people there, the papers said the next day, it was hot in the auditorium and they stuffed their caps into their pockets and shouldered through the crowds until they were halfway down the hall where they separated. Frank and he to one side, the other two, Jack and Sam, pushing their way through to the opposite wall.

Tom felt the sweat break out on his face and undid his jacket. The noise was so loud that he could not hear Frank when he spoke so the man leant forward and mouthed into his ear. 'Let's wait and see what the man in black has to say, shall we?' and Tom nodded but his mouth was dry as he watched the stewards in their black uniforms circling the hall, beating truncheons into the palms of their hands.

The stage was dark until the lights were dimmed in the hall and silence fell. Spotlights prodded the side of the stage then picked up the slim dark-moustached figure in a neat black shirt and suddenly the noise was deafening and Tom felt the mass of feeling sweep from behind, in front and all around him and felt a fear that drenched him, that was different to the pits because it rolled over him in sharp waves in time with the rhythm of the cheers and then the man spoke and it was as if he had waved a wand for silence.

He spoke for ten minutes until the first heckler interrupted, but a spotlight found him and the blackshirts moved in. There were more and more disturbances and more spotlights, more men in black and Tom set his shoulders as Frank tensed by his side.

'Sings like a bloody canary, doesn't he, this little man. What do you say to breaking his rhythm, Tom lad?'

Tom nodded but he wanted to run away far from the men who looked and listened all around him, their faces turned to the stage as though it was a god who spoke from the platform. He felt suddenly the cold of that football field, saw the trays which he and Annie carried, watched as the men came closer with steaming breath and then there was his own breath jogging in his chest as he had run, run as far from the field as he could go, leaving her, his Annie, there alone.

It was easy now in this hall and he drew himself up.

'What about democracy in this corporate state of yours, then? What about liberty, man?' His voice was loud into the blackness and he heard Frank's echo of his words and then the murmuring men around him moved as the spotlight found him, blinding him so that he held his arm across his eyes. He did not move or try to twist out of the beam. 'What about freedom?' he called and the stewards found him then, gripped him on either side and though he resisted there was no chance because there were four of them and thousands more besides and they were dragging him so that his feet could find no purchase.

There were faces and fists shaking at him, spit hit him on the face and still Mosley talked on and on until the sound stopped as the doors swung shut and he was in the passageway. Dark it was as they flung him first to one wall and then the other. The light from the solitary lamp which hung at the end of the corridor wall did not reach them here except for a stray glint on the large belt buckles and the gold tooth of the man who faced him. He was smiling.

It was the smile that crystallised his fear; he wrestled hard now against arm-locks which held him almost immobile. 'Oh Christ,' he groaned, as a truncheon broke his nose and pain exploded like a great noise. He could see nothing, not even the smile now as his eyes filled with the tears of pain, and so, as the fists and truncheons drove into his ribs and stomach, and grunts thudded against his ears, he reached back and brought out Annie standing in the cold, standing facing her da and the steaming breathing dragons of men. A boot caught his thigh and twisted him half round, knocking him free of the clasp which had held him upright.

The floor seemed no distance away but he hit it hard. He dragged himself up on his arms until they were kicked away and he tasted the blood pumping from his nose and mouth and again he hung on to Annie. The floor was linoleum, he knew that because of the feel and the smell and he curled up against it as the kicks developed a pattern of pain which swallowed him, leaving only his fear, and Annie. He knew he was weeping, he could hear himself, but he curled up round his hands and they were unhurt and that was his victory, you buggers. Me bloody victory and then he heard them laugh and then he didn't. Away and back they came and the light at the end of the corridor was there and then not and he was here and then not. On and on it went until he felt the hands as they lifted him by his coat and the sudden draught as the door opened and he was rolled on to the sun warmed pavement into the light June evening. It was over.

It was bloody over and then the boot crunched into his back and it was too bad even to scream.

Frank and the others found him after searching round the building inside and out where the police were arresting the demonstrators, not the blackshirts. They half carried him to the station and the train and laid him on a seat and Frank sat with him and held his hand and cleaned his face but the blood still came from his nose and mouth but not so much now. Tom smiled at Annie on the field, smiled at her as she stood and held out her arms to him. I knew you'd stay, she said. I knew you'd stay and face them with me, my bonny lad.

'We should have taken him to a London hospital,' hissed Jack to Frank but he shook his head.

'Nay lad, he wanted to get home, get to his sister's hospital so that's where he'll go.'

They sat hunched on the long journey back. They were bruised only, they'd been lucky. Tom moaned now as the train lurched round bends and scrambled over the points. His foot was burning inside his boot. He wanted it off, oh God, he wanted his boot off and his chest hurt. It hurt when he breathed as though knives were slicing through his lungs but it was his back that swamped him, that chased Annie away and then allowed her back as it eased. He held on to her face, held on to her voice and the feel of her hands as she stroked his hair and told him she would make the pain go away, but how could she do that, out here on this field with all these men around? He struggled to tell her, to push them back but then the pain came again.

Annie was asleep in the room she had shared with Julie before she had gone straight back with Trevor, back to the South to meet his parents and make sure he didn't trip over a Southern lily, Annie had thought wryly as she had waved them off and William too. She had kissed him, remembering the good times but unable to forget the things he had said.

She woke at the first shake. It was Staff Nurse Norris, her finger to her lips. 'Come to casualty, Annie. We have your brother in. Quick now, he won't settle until he sees you.'

It was Tom, she knew it must be Tom and her hands trembled as she put on her uniform, checked her belt and her shoes and ran down the stairs. Running is only for fire and haemorrhage, she chanted to herself; and Tom, and Tom. The wards were dark with just dim lights at the sisters' desks and she trod quietly past but still ran down the corridors and more stairs until she was in the glare of the white tiles, stretchers, screened examination-beds, drunks who lolled on benches.

It was Frank she saw first, his jacket creased and his boots loud as he paced up and down, his face grey with tiredness. He was large here and stood out strongly in the unsparing light. His jacket was rough as she gripped him, pulling him round, shaking him, saying:

'What's the matter with him, Frank, what's happened to him?'

Before he could answer, Staff came through from the screened-off bed. Her face was thin and she was older than Annie, nearly 30 someone had said and still unmarried.

'Nurse Manon,' she called softly, 'the doctor hasn't been yet, he's on his way. Your brother's conscious, on and off and he wants to see you. Keep him calm until doctor comes, there's a good girl. He's in great pain.' She smiled and patted her arm as Annie moved towards the screen, noticing where the red material was pulled slightly to one side of the frame and stopping to adjust the top. The trembling was back in her hands. She turned and Staff Norris smiled. 'Go on,' she said. 'He needs you,' but Annie was too afraid of what she might find.

The screen frame was cold in her hand and she held it as she slipped through and walked to the bed. He was still dressed but his boot had been sliced off with a razor and his foot was swollen and bruised and she could tell that it was broken, badly. His eyes were closed and his nose was also broken and his lips were swollen and bloody. She slipped open his shirt, checked his ribs and knew there was damage. She ran her hands along his legs and left his hands to last and they were untouched.

She held one and kissed it, stroking his hair, smelling the sweet scent of shock and knew that Tom was hurt, badly hurt and she leant over and whispered in his ear.

'Well, I leave you for a minute, bonny lad, and look at the mess.'

She watched as he struggled to open his lids and took a swab from the enamel bowl on the trolley and wiped away the trickle of blood from his split lip.

His eyes were on her now and she moved herself above him so that he would not have to turn his head.

'You're all right now, bonny lad. I'll make you better.'

He smiled.

'They were buggers, Annie,' he whispered.

'Aye, and you were all mouth, as usual.'

His eyes creased fractionally. 'Aye, like you.'

Then the doctor was there and Annie was sent away. She boiled the kettle in the small kitchen and gave Frank a cup of tea, then sent him back to Wassingham to tell Bob and Betsy. Then on to Grace and Don.

So this is respectability is it, William, she said to herself and was glad again that he had gone.

Tom was operated on immediately. His kidney was damaged and there was internal bleeding. It was removed. His foot was set and his ribs strapped. He was in Men's Surgical and Annie asked for and received a transfer to nurse him.

He was white against the pillowcase and was in the bed nearest Sister's desk. There were screens around and Annie sat with him checking his pulse every fifteen minutes and his blood pressure. His drip was set up at the head of his bed and she held his hand, talking to him, coaxing him back, telling him Grace would come. Betsy and Bob would be here. Don would bring Maud. Sarah and Val would bring toffee. She had to leave to dish out the lunches but his hand closed on hers and he whispered, 'Don't.'

'I'll be back,' she assured him and was, to sit with him through the afternoon.

Bob came with Betsy and they were asked to wait in the corridor. Annie left him again and again he said, 'Don't.'

Sister Grant waited by the ward door. 'I've spoken to them, Annie.' And Annie was grateful for the use of her name. 'But you have a word. They may see him briefly. He is very poorly, you know, my dear.' Her eyes were kind and Annie nodded.

Her head felt light and she was one step removed from everything, from all of them but Tom and was impatient to return to him; after all, she had said she would.

She pushed the door and Betsy was sitting on the bench with Bob beside her. Annie heard her shoes on the floor; they sounded brisk. There was a clatter from the sluice and she sat down by Betsy.

She had aged, had Betsy. Her hair was a little grey but there was something that wasn't to do with age in her face. It was fuller, somehow more complete. Annie took her hand. 'He'll be all right Bet, he's a fighter.'

Betsy nodded, 'Aye, lass.' She could not say more, her throat was too full and Annie put her arm round her and let her cry, looking over her shoulder to Bob.

His face was drawn, his eyes deep and he fingered his hat, round and round. 'It's his kidney, you see,' Annie told him as she patted Betsy. 'A broken foot and ribs and his nose.'

She smiled at Bob. 'That'll teach him to poke it in where it's not wanted.' She patted Betsy again as he nodded and tried to smile back.

'He'll be all right though, I promise you, Bet. I'll make sure he is.'

Grace came later that night and she and Annie sat by the bed but still Tom didn't really wake. All night they sat and next day Grace had to work or she could lose her job. Sarah came in the afternoon with Val and they stayed as Annie took round the tea. Don sat with him in the evening.

It was the next day when he rallied and took some liquid, but not much because of his kidney. Bob came and brought in papers which protested at the violence of the fascists at Olympia.

'At last,' he said and, in the weeks that followed, support waned for the blackshirts.

Tom was in hospital for ten weeks and they talked each day and each evening. Talked of the future and Annie told him she had had enough worry over him, that he was to go to art school now, do textile design and, if he didn't, she would break his other foot. He laughed at her and told that he had already decided he must do something of the sort.

She spoke to Sarah that evening, while Grace and Tom kissed quietly and sat together talking of bairns and art.

'He's agreed to go, Sarah. In fact he had already decided, so all our nagging won't be needed.' They laughed together. 'But it's the money.' Annie heard the strain she had been feeling transmit itself to her voice.

Sarah tapped her sharply on the arm. 'It's no problem, you know that. Tom hasn't had his share yet, has he, so that's that.'

Annie sighed. 'I know that, Sarah, but I can't begin to pay

you back for Tom until I'm qualified in 1935 and I still haven't finished Don's money yet.'

Sarah shook her head. 'It's no use me saying don't, so what I will say is that you can pay me back when you are able to. There's no hurry because we'll be jogging along for years yet.' Annie looked down the corridor, at the nurses who pushed trolleys or backed into kitchens and sluices, at a world that she felt a part of and turned to Sarah. 'If it wasn't for you, I wouldn't have had all this.' She leaned forward and kissed her.

'Nonsense. You would have made it happen somehow. And how's Georgie, while I remember?' She was embarrassed and tucked her arm into Annie's and listened to the news that he had been on exercises and had also written about the walnut trees and Sarah's hall table.

When Tom was close to going home in August and the ward was quiet with the lights low above the beds, Annie straightened his sheets and then they sat for a while, listening to the sounds of the ward, the coughs and muted conversations, the laughter. It was then that he told her of a conversation he had held earlier with Bob. He told her of her father, of the man who dragged at his leg, of the still air that made the gas fall, of his heartbreak over her mother and Annie felt her skin grow cold and she took her hand from his but he took it back.

'You must forgive him some time, Annie, for your own sake. Try and understand.'

But she could not because the hate was too strong. After all, her father had killed himself and left them as though they were nothing, but she didn't tell Tom that, just nodded and said that she would be qualified in two years, he would be finished in four, which took them to the back end of 1938.

'So you see,' she said. '1939 will be our year. We'll give you a year to produce some designs and earn a bit of money for capital. I'll probably be a Sister by then and will have saved a bit and in the meantime I'll keep my eyes on the administrative procedures and see how things are run.'

She put the thermometer in his mouth to stop him bringing up her father again.

'It'll be grand, lad, to do something for the people here. Give them an alternative to coal or steel. It's exciting, isn't it, Tom?' He shook his head and pointed at the thermometer and she laughed, taking and checking it. 'The rudest of health, my lad.'

She put it back in its container.

'And what about Georgie?' he asked.

She leant over him and tucked the sheets in around him. 'He'll be here when he's ready and I'll be waiting for him. He's the man I love, the man I'll always love.'

She reached over to turn off the light. He was looking better these days, the pallor was gone but he'd be weak for a while yet. London would do him good and Grace would go with him, though they neither wanted to marry yet and Grace's da didn't seem to mind. She pictured him laughing at the pink mice all over the floor.

'So, 1939 it is, then,' Tom whispered and she nodded.

'The back end,' she said. 'When the summer has gone and the nights are drawing in. It's my favourite time of year.'

Tom laughed. 'See you in September, Annie Manon.'

CHAPTER 21

Annie remembered Miss Hardy and piano lessons today. It was August 1939 and newspapers spoke of war over the Polish crisis but she could not believe it. There had not been war over Czechoslovakia last year so why should there be one this year? She shrugged the thought aside and walked towards the bus-stop which would take her from the Manchester Cancer Hospital where she now worked to the restaurant where she was meeting Sarah.

Don was to be married this afternoon in Wassingham and Sarah had promised to buy her an early lunch on her way back from the Lake District where she had been holidaying. They could then travel up to Wassingham together.

She took the lift up from the bottom floor of the department store and was shown to Sarah's table.

'My dear,' said Sarah, kissing her and patting the chair next to her. 'You look so well and I do like your hat.'

Annie smiled and touched the net with her fingers. 'And you're looking pretty grand yourself, Sarah. It takes a wedding to bring the smart ones out of the cupboard, doesn't it? I hope mine doesn't smell of moth-balls.' Sarah looked better for her holiday. She had come to the nurses' home when she travelled through, two weeks ago, and Annie had thought she looked tired. Her hair was now very grey and her skin was pale and translucent but she'll be 50 in two years' time, Annie thought, and wondered where the years had gone because, as she had reminded herself just last week on her twenty fifth birthday, she was no chicken any more. Sarah had sent her a five pound note and Georgie had enclosed a piece of Indian silver in his letter. She showed it now to Sarah, her face alive and full of hope. She knew it off by heart.

Central Provinces.

My darling lass,

Well, it looks as though it could be any day now. My transfer to the Engineers has been accepted and my C.O. is supporting my application for a commission. By the way, did I tell you his daughter is nursing in England?

Now it is finally happening, my commission that is, I can hardly believe it. The sergeants' mess is celebrating every night but I wish they wouldn't. My head won't take it and they might be in for a disappointment.

I'll talk of other things, it might be unlucky to go on too much about what I've dreamt of all these years which is coming home to you. If I get it, I'll be sent to Woolwich for my training, see.

I'm pleased to hear that Don has finally popped the question to Maud. She looks a bit like him from the photo you sent me; fairly small the pair of them but his hair looks as though it's getting a wee bit thin whereas hers is good and curly. I've sent them a silver tea-caddy.

Got a letter from Tom last month. He's loved his time in London, hasn't he; living the life of an artist and Grace with him too. A bit bohemian isn't it, not being married? Bet Wassingham had something to say about that. Grace seems to have liked her job in the library and feels good at sending her ma and da some money each week. Tom says he's about ready to start on the business but he has to finish this commission to paint a mural at a restaurant in Piccadilly first. Well, that sounds grand doesn't it. He says it will give him a bit of capital to go with the money you've saved. I've a bit too, remember, which can help you get started.

It makes sense to start in the small way you've planned and the idea of it has kept him at his art instead of blasting off to Spain or anything daft like that.

Bob must have missed him badly all these years but Tom says he's been right busy with the union, pushing for state ownership of the pits. There's still not a lot of work up there, he tells me.

It's grand to hear that things have settled down a bit in Germany but there's talk here in the mess that Hitler won't stop with Czechoslovakia. Will there be another war, Annie? It seems so far away here though we keep an eye on the Japs who seem to be pushing their way into China in the war they've started there.

We're exercising down in the jungles of the Central Provinces since Burma would be the way into India for the Japs and this is similar terrain, but maybe they're just game-playing.

There's a great deal of trouble in India. They want us out, though Gandhi is doing his bit to make it a peaceful independence movement. I guess that Tom would approve.

The butterflies here in the jungle are beautiful, very different to the Camberwell Beauties that used to settle by your da's shed, do you remember them, my bonny lass? There is one we call the Cruiser which is very fast and high-flying, it's a sort of yellow brown and there is a really beautiful one called the Swallowtail which has a flash of blue across its wings. It seems very nervous and hovers over the petals of the lush flowers you get in this steamy climate. It's bloody hot, sticky and humid and we go up to the hill-stations for a break. Darjeeling is the best. We ride horses up the trails and cool off a bit. I'll take you there one day.

Well, my dearest little lass. I will close now and will write again as soon as I have any news. I have kept all your letters, there seem to be so many but then years have gone by since I last saw you. I can't bear to think of that. I will love you always with all my heart.

Georgie.

Sarah passed it back, took out her compact and patted her nose with the powder-puff. She looked at Annie over the mirror, the back of which was studded with seed pearls.

'I've watched you all these years, my dear, laughing and flirting and learning. By the way, how is Dr Jones, such a nice Welshman?' But she did not wait for Annie to answer. 'You were always waiting for Georgie though, weren't you? How can you be so sure, my darling, that you are still right for one another, that he will ever come? I know he says he will, but after all this time, can it work?'

Annie picked up a knife and set it absolutely straight against the mat which was a view of the Manchester Ship Canal. The handle must be solid, it was so heavy, but surely it was silver plate? She listened to the strains of the Blue Danube and watched the cellist lean back and ease her shoulders. The mock palms were bright green.

'He'll come and we'll be right for one another, don't you fret.' She tapped Sarah's hand with her finger. 'He knows me, knows my family, the streets, the pits. He knows that you have a walnut hall table, that your bathroom is posh. That Tom lost a kidney, that Don loves Maud and is the only one who can handle Albert. I don't have to explain myself, that I'm not the posh person I sound now.' She lifted an eyebrow at Sarah who laughed. 'He knows me and I've never had to look after him, he looks after himself and I'm right proud of the lad.' Her voice was soft now and she had slipped back into Geordie and she didn't care.

Sarah beckoned the waiter and asked for wine. It had to be white and chilled and he brought the ice bucket and set the bottle back in the crushed ice after he had poured them each a glass.

'I'm just wondering, Annie, whether you love him because it's safe to love someone who's so far away, someone who won't try and get too close? I wonder if you're running away from anything?' Her face was quizzical.

Annie looked puzzled, her thoughts slowed down and she watched the bubbles in her wine break through to the surface.

'I don't know what you mean, Sarah.' She would not dig deeper into herself to try and understand her guardian; she did not want to disturb the black box.

Sarah smiled absently. There was a pause then. 'Did I do the right thing, Annie, taking you away from Wassingham, from him?' Her face was sad and tense.

Annie ran her fingers up and down the stem of her glass, then carved stripes down through the mist of the bowl. 'You've not taken me away, Sarah. No one will take me away, that's where I'm going now, back there for the wedding, back there with Tom, soon, to start my business. I couldn't have done that without you and I would not have known you, had you not come, and that would have been intolerable.'

She leant back as the sole arrived. It was fresh but the sauce was not as good as Val's. The mannequins were parading round the tables now, their backs arched and their legs going on forever. Sarah's face had relaxed and she was flushed after Annie's remarks. They smiled at one another.

'What about the war if it comes? Your business? Georgie?'

Annie took a sip of wine, it was dry and light. 'There won't be a war surely, Sarah? Chamberlain's sorting it out, isn't he?'

She thought of Dippy Denis who had been led away and locked up in a place she had always imagined would not have windows. Would he still be there, she wondered? No, there could not be another war, not after the last one. The lettuce that accompanied the sole was crisp, the tomatoes fresh. And besides it was the summer and she could never imagine war on a summer's day, with the sun out. It should always be wet and cold. Grey. There would be no war; no one wanted war. There were still too many damaged people from the last one, but she would not think of her da and his gas. She lifted her glass again.

Sarah had finished her meal and was studying her glass. 'But if Chamberlain should fail, Annie,' she persisted, 'would Georgie come back? What about the business?'

Annie frowned. 'I just don't know Sarah. I really don't. Georgie would still come home, surely, and I would stay in nursing, I suppose. They'd need nurses but it wouldn't last long, would it, Sarah, so we could start the business when it was over.'

Sarah was pleating the thick starched napkin that lay beside her plate. Her fingers were steady, her eyes on her work. 'We said that about the last one.'

'But it's different now, we have planes. It would be quick.' Annie did not want to think any more about it.

Sarah continued however. 'God forbid there is one but you

303

could travel with a war, Annie, you could join the military nurses, even pick up ideas for fabrics from other countries and give Tom a run for his money on design.' She smiled. 'It's got to be better than nursing here with that dreadful radium stuff dripping from needles stuck in those poor patients. Why you every transferred here in the first place, I can't imagine.

'Thank you,' she said to the waiter as he poured her more wine.

Annie laughed. 'Hardly dripping, Sarah, and we do manage to save some of them you know. But only some,' and her voice tailed away. She had moved to gain more experience and the pay was better which made Tom's fees easier, but she was tired of suffering now, too tired to stay in for much longer. She was ready to start on the next stage and Tom was ready too. There must not be a war, not when they had people to help and a firm to set up.

They took a taxi to the station. Doors slammed and whistles shrieked and the compartment was full with people as they left the city and the low cloud which seemed to hang motionless sucking all the light from the city.

'How can you live here, Annie? It's always so wet and gloomy.'

'I hope you're not becoming imprecise in your old age, Sarah. It is often wet but not always.' They leant into one another and laughed and then their hours were their own and Sarah slept while Annie felt the effects of the wine make her limbs easy and she watched cities merge into country. The noise of the train must be the same as any other but it seemed to rush and lurch and she could not sleep and then they were there and it was the same station they had flown across with Da to find the Newcastle train, but now it was small and she was helping Sarah as she stepped from the carriage to the platform over no gap at all. Sour coal was heaped high in the sidings outside the station as it had been when she last saw it, as it had been the day she and Georgie rode their bikes here for their day by the sea. The slag-heaps were bigger. Oh God yes, they were bigger and still the cables churned the carts up until they tipped more slag on to the top.

They took another taxi, this time to the church which was darkened by soot though the windows were lit by the lights inside. Their heels made sharp sounds as they walked to the

304

front and Don turned and smiled. He was sitting with Albert who was best man and whose face hung even more than usual from his brows. Always the same ray of sunshine, thought Annie, and squeezed Don's shoulder. He turned and grinned but he was nervous and had bunched his handkerchief in his hand and was kneading it.

'Like your hat, bonny lass, and like seeing you even better,' whispered Don and she was back again amongst the life they had lived together, one that she had avoided until now, but why, she wondered? She glanced at Sarah who nodded.

'Nice to be back, is it, little Annie?' she asked and squeezed her hand. Yes, thought Annie, and realised that the veneer of speech and polish was thin indeed. Sarah was looking along the pews searching for Val who had come up from Gosforn separately. There was a wave across the other side and there she was, in pale blue with her handkerchief out, sitting with Bob who was smiling.

'Oh dear, she'll cry,' she whispered to Annie who giggled and waved across to the plump woman.

'Tom couldn't make it after all, then,' Annie breathed into Don's ear.

'They're still in London. Tom's mural is almost finished but not quite.' He pulled a face. 'He'll see us when he gets back.'

The pews were dark brown and the hymn books wobbled in their binding. The blue stamp of St Mark's Church was faded on the flyleaf and she was glad that Don had chosen 'Eternal Father'; it was Da's favourite. She had not been inside a church since the convent and here, today, there were no chrysanthemums but dahlias; red, yellow and purple. There was no incense either to laden the air but Albert's stale smell was just the same. Thank God for Sarah's Chanel. Maud was late and Don fidgeted.

The vicar came out from the side chapel. God almighty, she thought, it's the same vicar who buried me da but without the dewdrop this time and then the organ stirred them and Maud arrived. The vicar still said 'Gond' and Annie wanted to laugh.

The reception was at Merthyr Terrace, at Maud's home, but the neighbours would have their doors open for the overflow as always. They walked along the streets and Annie talked to Bob about Tom and thought how much older he looked. 'It's the men,' he explained to Annie, 'still no work and now perhaps the war.' She talked to him of Grace and whether she and Tom would every marry; she did not want to talk of that subject, the one which the papers ran as headlines. It was the wrong time for war. This was to be her time; Tom's time.

The ham was pale pink on the table which was stacked high with plates and salad bowls and punch. Betsy stood near with Joe, hand in hand, and Annie kissed her and shook Joe's hand.

'Are you well, Betsy?' Annie knew that she was. Her face was relaxed and her eyes were soft and Joe laughed as Annie said, 'And your lad's coming back soon, then.'

'Oh aye,' said Joe. 'He's always got a room with us, they both have, Grace and him.'

Annie nodded. 'And how's May?'

Betsy smiled. 'Her other boys are back so she's happy. Made me a patchwork quilt for our bedroom. It's lovely, isn't it, pet?' Joe nodded his reply.

Betsy looked over towards the table with the drinks, then handed her glass to Joe. 'Get me a barley-water would you, pet?' He smiled and moved away.

Betsy looked up at Annie, almost shyly. 'I'd never have thought I'd be this happy, you know.'

Annie looked after Joe. 'Is it because of him, Betsy?'

'Aye it is, lass.' She paused and searched for words. 'I had to do something a long while ago that I thought would make me unhappy, but it hasn't. It was gradual, see, very gradual but I love him now. But I still keeps me own name and he still pays me for doing the housekeeping. I don't want to get back to being a skivvy, see.' She looked confused and defensive and Annie held her arm and looked into her eyes.

'You're right, Betsy, absolutely right.' The people were pressing round them and Joe was back with Betsy's drink and Annie thought of the way her father had treated Betsy and the old anger was back again, though it had never really gone and she swallowed it down as she always seemed to be doing.

'I tell you what, Betsy,' she said taking herself in hand telling herself that she would think about it some other time because, try as she might, it was something she could not throw out completely as Georgie had said she should. It just wouldn't go but lodged inside the black box, waiting. She shook herself. 'I tell you what,' she repeated. 'Tom and I will make you some matching curtains for your bedroom when we're in business, how about that?'

Joe shook his head. 'I reckon that might have to wait, lass. We'll maybe have a war.'

Sarah had found Albert over by the food. He was drinking beer by himself.

'Well, Albert,' she said planting herself in front of him. 'You didn't destroy Don, then, like you promised you would. It was the destruction of Annie though to begin with wasn't it, but they've both escaped. So Archie wasn't destroyed either, was he?' She hated this man for what he'd done to Annie.

Albert sipped his beer. 'Just an old dried-up prune you are, Sarah Beeston.'

She wanted to tip his beer out all down the front of his suit but just smiled.

Albert turned from her and looked at Don. 'He's a good boy, that one. He's not like his da, not a high-flier like the girl. He's been all right to me and I'll be all right to him, so let's leave it at that.' He moved from her, into the other guests, his eyes hooded and she heard him say into his beer. 'Like me own son he is. A good boy that one.'

And she felt moved and saw him as he really was, lonely and unsure.

Annie had moved on from Joe and Betsy, waved to May, talked to Bob and then saw Ma Gillow peering into her cup of punch. Good God, she's trying to read the bloody fruit, she thought, and felt the laughter well inside.

'She's trying to read the fruit then, is she?' and he was there, just like that, a glass of beer in his hand and her breath caught in her throat. 'You've changed a bit, bonny lass.' Georgie was so close she should have been able to sense him there, should have known he was within a mile of the place, and then he turned her to him. Tears were caught on the lids of her eyes and her lips were tight together and she could not see him unless she blinked and if she blinked the tears would loosen and weave downwards like the rain on the train windows.

'And where the hell have you been, you little bugger?' she said and he wiped his thumbs beneath her eyes and held her head between hands which were still the same only broader, stronger.

'Waiting for today, bonny lass,' he said and kissed her lips and eyes and hair and she heard no one, saw no one, just him as he held her and drank her in.

' Then Don was there, standing in front of them. 'I see you remember one another,' grinned Don. 'About time too, lad. She was turning into an old maid before our very eyes. Like the khaki, like the pips.'

She saw then the Sam Browne belt, the pips not stripes and felt his arm tighten round her and the hardness of his straps against her.

'Took too long getting them though, Don,' Georgie said, but Don was away again and his eyes were the same brown as he asked. 'Did I, hinny, did I take too long?' His skin was brown and his smile white and one-sided as it had always been.

'Never too long to wait, not for you.' She stroked his face and then the speeches began and the toasts were drunk in sparkling wine and beer was pulled as afternoon turned to evening and the dancing began but all she noticed were his hands as he held her, his arms round her strong and certain; his voice as he talked and his eyes as he listened, his lips as he kissed her. All she felt was her body wanting his, because her love was the same, only stronger.

Ma Gillow bumped into them as she wove her way through to the punch again. 'Told you you'd do well,' she smirked, 'but it should be with Tom. You mark my words, it will be with Tom.'

Annie laughed and Georgie grinned. 'It will too Mrs Gillow, just wait until the lad gets back up here.'

'But there's the war, isn't there?' And Georgie's face grew still.

Then Sarah came and smiled at Annie. She shook Georgie's hand and he leaned forward and kissed her.

'Thanks for looking after my bonny lass, Sarah. And for your letters.'

Annie felt her jaw drop and she turned to Sarah who had blushed.

'Yes, I just thought a few letters might help keep you both in touch. I do so hope I didn't interfere.' Annie laughed and kissed her cheek. 'You really are the most extraordinary woman and I love you so much.'

Sarah turned to Val who had come up behind them. She could not speak, just nodded and turned away. Val sighed and looked at Annie. 'She's waited a long time to hear you say that and I'm right glad you have but we'll get off home now. We won't be seeing you tonight, I dare say.' She patted Annie's cheek and they were gone.

Annie ran her hands over his uniform. It prickled her and his shoes were so shiny, Mother Superior would have had him straight in the conservatory, she thought, as they left two minutes later.

The streets were empty but still lit and they found his hotel room without ever feeling the pavements change to cobbles and the dry night to drizzle.

This time there was no fear of bairns, of passions which frightened and confused. They were not two children beyond their experiences but two people who talked and kissed and remembered their youth together; who spoke of their times apart.

The room was whitewashed and the curtains were soft pink. The light came from two bedside lights and the double bed was soft. He undressed her and kissed her shoulders as he slid the clothes from her body, kissed her breasts and her stomach, her thighs and she lay and watched as he unbuckled his belts and threw his clothes over the armchair which stood in the corner. His body had hardened since that day on the beach and he was tanned except for his buttocks which remained stark white. There were still the blue-ridged mining scars down his back that he would never lose.

'I've missed you so much,' she breathed as he walked towards her and his eyes crinkled as he stood by the bed and looked from her face down the length of her body.

'You are so beautiful. I hope, bonny lass, that you have been loved?' His eyes found hers and there was a question in them that demanded an answer.

Her voice was level and strong when she answered, 'Yes.' Because none of her men had touched the place she kept for him.

Her hands felt loose with relief as he smiled and nodded and said:

'As I have too, bonny lass, but it never touched you at all.'

There need be no lies with Georgie and that was something she had always known. He sat down on the bed and his weight made the bed lower and she slid towards him.

'How long will you be in Woolwich?' That was where he had told her he was posted.

'Not long, my darling. There could well be war.' She pulled him to her then, covering his mouth with hers, not wanting to hear that word here, in this room with his body so close to hers. She could smell his skin and it was the same as it had always been. His mouth grew demanding, his hands were feeling her breasts, her thighs and she stroked his back, his legs, his arms as they moved along her body and she loved his strength, his power.

'I want to leave the light on, my love. The missing has been so hard and I must see and feel every second of tonight because that's all we have for now.'

His voice was deep against her mouth and his breathing fast as she rose to meet him and she knew only the dark rush of years without him and his touch which was the same today as it had been so long ago. Evening turned to night and still they clung together, still their passion remained and had to be satisfied once more.

They did not sleep all night. His arms were round her, stroking her hair, telling her of the heat and dust, the beauty and filth. The memsahibs who drank tea and were fanned by bunka wallahs and looked down their noses at pitmen who became sergeants and sergeants who became officers. She told him of Manchester and Tom's progress, his limp and his tiredness. His talent and her determination that they would provide work so that her patients, or some of them at least, would recover from illnesses which should not kill but did.

'Will you be here, in England, for a while, my darling?' she asked as she kissed his fingers which had just teased her to such heights.

'I should be, if the war doesn't happen. I'm with the Engineers now, bomb disposal but there aren't any bombs, thank God, so we build bridges instead, or blow 'em up.' He pulled her close to him, breathing in her scent. 'If there's a war, God knows where I'll be. Maybe it will be back to India but it won't be for long and we can get married, my love, you can come back with me.'

Her stomach tensed, her back stiffened and she felt every breath.

'There won't be a war,' she said. 'There can't be war, not after the last one.' She turned to him, kissing him fiercely. 'No, we need not marry, not yet. There's no need.'

His eyes were closed and she kissed them. 'We are together now, there's time to make plans later.' She kissed him again and again and slowly his arms closed round her.

The next day he left on the early train which would take him back to Woolwich until he could see her again.

'If we were married,' he urged, 'you could come with me.'

But she shook her head. 'There's time for that,' she repeated.

Annie walked to the station two hours later and, apart from the click of footsteps which were her own, a Sunday silence cloaked the streets. The glazed lightless shop fronts seemed to hang and the scent of her home town was all around, the black dust lay on each sill, in each gutter. Suddenly the sky brought darkness and lightning clawed the clouds which rolled thick and black and the wind sucked air in great gulps and hurled harsh rain which poured down drains and swirled in the alleys. On and on it came, soaking through her coat. Her tongue tasted the savage cut of water and she could neither see nor hear until suddenly it was over and she was frightened and alone and calling for Georgie deep inside but he had gone and she had not left with him.

She transferred back to Newcastle on 1 September, wanting general nursing now. Evacuation had begun in the hospital of all patients who were not at death's door to make way for possible war casualties. Gas masks were to be carried at all times for all people and air-raid shelters which had been started at the time of the Czechoslovakian crisis in 1938 were finished. The parks were dug over with trenches. Light bulbs in the ward were painted and sandbags at the windows cut down the light. Sarah asked her for lunch on Sunday but all leave had been cancelled.

War was declared on 3 September and soon barrage balloons were flying over the Tyne. Annie nodded as the matron at the War Office building in the city asked her if she was prepared to give up her independence for the duration and two weeks later she was accepted into the Queen Alexandra's Imperial Military Nursing Service.

Georgie was still in England and they met in London before she received her posting.

His eyes were veiled as he talked about his movements. He had lines which cut deep round his eyes but they forgot the war, forgot their faded hopes as they lay together and drew closer than ever. They talked of Tom's marriage, the day after war was announced. They had called into Annie before they took the connection for Wassingham. Grace had clung to her and Tom had stood back and their eyes had met. Georgie saw her off on the train back to Newcastle. He did not know when he would see her again but he was meeting his CO in London and would give him her name because his daughter was joining the QA's too. Maybe the boss could wangle the same posting for you both, he'd said, and get you into a safe zone.

They had kissed and hugged and promised they would see one another soon, that each moment until then would be an ache.

CHAPTER 22

Annie's first posting was to a girls' boarding school in Oxfordshire which had been converted into a small military hospital.

As she was driven up the long drive by the army car that had picked her up at the station she saw that tents had been pitched on the sweeping lawns that led down to the line of oaks which designated the boundary of the school where it met the road. Oaks also lined the drive and there were two rows of drab military ambulances parked where the horses had once paraded outside the stables. There were steps which led to the hall and she returned the driver's salute wondering if he could see her hand tremble. It was the same feeling in her stomach and legs that she had experienced at the convent and the hospital on her first day but this time there was no Sarah and she missed her.

The hallway smelt of wax with overtones of disinfectant. Was there ever a hall that did not, she thought? There were Daily Orders pinned where timetables should have been and she followed the lance-corporal as he clumped on ahead of her up the wide stairs, his boots clattering where lightfooted girls had previously trod. She smiled to think of the army descending on the convent. Jenn and Sandy would have been in heaven. Where were they both now, she wondered? Sarah had heard that they were both married though she had not received letters from either for years now.

Her room was on the top floor; it had previously been a teacher's study, the lance-corporal explained as he clicked his heels and left her to unpack. There was another bed in the room but so far it was unoccupied. The window overlooked the side garden and beyond was the playing-field, just so long as there was no Miss Hardy they'd be all right, she grinned to herself.

There were flowered curtains at the window though the beds had plain blue covers. There were photos of old school hockey teams on the walls. The faces were blank as they stared at the camera with hockey sticks held to the right of the knees. It was all very proper.

Matron gathered the new arrivals into her office which was light and faced south. She was dressed as they would be when they were on duty, in a grey dress with a cape trimmed with scarlet and a white veil which fluttered in the breeze coming in through the window. Annie pulled down the jacket of her grey QA uniform.

'You'll have your inoculations today and your medicals,' Matron explained in a relaxed voice that was hard to accept after years of civilian hospitals. 'You are all here, bar one; a late arrival, I'm afraid.'

The medicals took an hour each and the inoculations were painless but made Annie wonder where she might be sent eventually.

They toured the wards; the orthopaedic with Balkan Beams already installed; the operating theatre, surgical and medical, and the burns unit. It was strange to see no flowers by the beds, just the statutory towel correctly folded for commanding officer's rounds each morning and the shaving kits.

'No nighties here anyway.' Annie murmured to the dark girl next to her.

The girl grinned. 'Cheer the men up no end if there were!'

Her name was Monica and she came from Birmingham but Annie already knew that from her accent. They had tea together in the Sisters' mess. Toast with butter and jam and thick brown tea. All the rooms were high-ceilinged with ornate coving. Grey cobwebs hung down and floated in long strands on the breeze. Well, as long as I don't have to get up there and waggle a duster about, it's not my problem, Annie thought and ate another piece of toast. She looked at the oil painting that Monica pointed out. It was of a woman and child and was badly in need of a clean.

Halfway through tea, Pruscilla Briggs arrived. Monica nudged her and pointed to the door. 'Your room-mate has finally arrived. Lucky, lucky you,' she murmured.

A blonde girl stood in the doorway, her suit straining over a large bust, her eyes wide and her lashes fluttering.

'Oh dear, I'm so dreadfully late,' she gushed to Matron who had risen to meet her. 'I'm so frightfully sorry but we lost our way,' she simpered, 'so daddy's adjutant and I decided to stop for tea in this dear little café to ask the way.'

'Well, you won't need any more, will you?' replied Matron crisply. 'Go to your room and perhaps your room-mate, Sister Manon, will be so kind as to show you round the wards. Your medical and inoculations will just have to wait now until tomorrow. The doctor will not be pleased.' She moved swiftly past Pruscilla who giggled helplessly and smiled at Annie as she groaned at Monica and moved towards the girl.

'Come along then, I'll show you your room first. Then we'll have a look around, shall we?'

Pruscilla chatted her way up the stairs but was quieter by the time they reached the fourth flight. She was plump and panting and her footsteps were quick and short, a bit like Mrs Tittlemouse's, Annie thought, not like Grace and Val who walked in tune with their size.

Her luggage was already there, all six cases of it. And I bet the corporal loved that, thought Annie.

'What will you do if we're posted, for goodness sake?' and then wished she hadn't asked as Pruscilla told her how Daddy would surely send someone to help if it couldn't all go on the train.

That night at dinner, a piper played in the gallery and there were candles on the table. Oak panels lined the dining-room and chandeliers hung above. Cutlery gleamed and wine accompanied each course. Pruscilla sat with Annie and dabbed her lips with her napkin as she finished her melon. 'Of course, I'm used to this sort of thing with Daddy being in the Army. CO of a station in India actually. I schooled in Devon but popped home for the hols.'

Annie laid her spoon and fork down as Pruscilla had done, neatly at one side of the melon shell, and was silently grateful for her unconscious guidance.

'You must find it a bit cold in England after that heat. I know someone who has been in India for years and finds it freezing.' She smiled at Pruscilla and Monica, pleased to be talking about Georgie. 'And you haven't a tan.'

Pruscilla fluttered her eyelashes at Annie, her eyes really

were remarkably blue she thought and moved slightly to allow the steward to remove her plate.

'But one doesn't allow oneself to become tanned. It's all too frightfully common, don't you know. And yes, it does get a trifle chill but one just has to bear this sort of thing for one's country, doesn't one?'

Annie took another sip of wine; trust her to be sharing with Pruscilla, and she sighed to herself. The piper had begun a lament.

'Mark you,' Pruscilla went on. 'Daddy's station is in the Himalayas so it never becomes as hot as the plains. They've been exercising in the jungles over the last year though where it's been humid enough to sprout orchids out of nothing, Daddy says.'

Annie fingered her glass. So she thought, the CO managed it, did he? Good God almighty. There was a steady murmur of conversation on each of the three long tables and the stewards in white jackets refilled glasses as soon as they were empty.

'My friend's name is Georgie Armstrong,' she said.

Pruscilla leant back in her chair and looked up towards the piper. 'I do wish he'd stop soon, I've such a headache. Yes,' she turned to Annie. 'I know Georgie Armstrong. A sergeant made up into an officer. Good man Daddy says, good body the wives say.' She tittered and thanked the steward as he placed fish before her and held the silver platter whilst she took carrots and small potatoes.

Annie wanted to tip it into her lap and turned to talk to Monica instead but Prue's voice continued. 'Georgie is being posted back, so the adjutant says. He's been seconded to Daddy's regiment from the Engineers. They'll need a bomb expert out there and someone to blow bridges if the Japanese come in through Burma.' She was eating her fish now, daintily.

Annie took just a few carrots and one potato as the steward stood on her left, waiting. She was no longer hungry. The candles were flickering along the table and the Sisters all looked alike in their grey suits with Matron at the head of the table. All at once the piper's wail was irritating and she felt alone and only wanted him, Georgie.

She began to eat her fish. 'I didn't know he was leaving,' she said.

'Oh, but neither does he, Annie. Not yet anyway.' Pruscilla

stopped and looked at Annie and her face sobered. 'Oh I say, is he rather more than a friend. I'm so dreadfully sorry. I would never have said. I never should have said anyway. It was a secret and I never know when to stop talking.' Pruscilla was red now, her eyes distressed. She seemed young, Annie thought and smiled.

'I'm always the one being told to stop talking, you know. Don't worry about it, Pruscilla, it will be fine.'

They talked in bed that night or Pruscilla talked and Annie listened. Prue had led a life that seemed identical to that which Georgie had described for the memsahibs over the years. There were the bearers who served food, dressed and fanned you, saddled horses, brushed hair, but Prue's mother had died when she was 16, six years ago, Prue had mused, and that had cast a shadow. I don't really miss her, she had said, because I didn't know her awfully well but one misses the guidance, you know. Daddy is a sweetie of course but fathers aren't the same. Annie did not reply but looked out through the gap between the wall and the black-out curtain at the moon which was large. The harvest would be in now and the winter would be here soon. Would she see him before he went back, she wondered? She didn't want to talk of her father.

Georgie came for two hours, three weeks later. She met him in the town and they had tea in the small café on the main street and he smiled when Annie said she'd met Prue. He was to go away, he said, but they would meet again soon, that the war couldn't last forever. That he would write, but then he fell silent and they couldn't eat but just sat with hands clasped and then walked through the town not noticing its black-beamed prettiness, just wondering and longing.

'I'd like to marry, my darling,' he said, stroking her cheek holding her close to him and his dark eyes were looking deeply into hers and again she felt the tension grip her body.

'Not now, my love,' she said. 'It's not the right time now.' Her words were strained and he said nothing but continued to look and his eyelashes cast a shadow on his cheeks. He bent his head and kissed her lips gently and held her head in his strong hands.

She felt a longing for him but something else as well and the pain which flooded through her showed on her face. He pulled out his cigarettes and lit one passing it to her and they stayed in the shadow of the overhung houses as they shared it. He kept his arm around her, holding her gently to him and kissing her hair and cheeks and she felt his breath on her skin and the tension slowly faded and she pulled in close so that she moulded into his body.

'I love you, bonny lass. I'll always love you and one day you'll be ready to come with me.'

She waved him away on his train, half an hour later. He leaned out, his broad shoulders stretching his uniform.

'I love you, Annie,' he shouted again and again as the train gathered speed and she replied, 'I love you, my darling.' And her tears were those of anger and despair and were directed at herself.

Pruscilla and she were assigned to the burns unit and there was still no way of removing a dressing painlessly or waving a magic wand and regrowing noses, faces and hands but there was plastic surgery, she told her patients, and when they were stronger they would go to a specialist hospital for treatment.

In the meantime she arranged with the manager of the local cinema that they should all go to see a film once a week but, he insisted, they must come in after the lights went out and leave before they rose. He didn't want to scare away his regular customers.

Annie felt Prue's hand on her arm as she made to protest.

'So kind of you, dear man. We, of course, do not want our patients upset by other people's ignorance,' Prue had replied and swept out with Annie in tow.

And so through the winter months they went to the cinema every Thursday evening, even when Annie was transferred to surgical and nursed soldiers without legs or checked the drains and drips on those internally injured. The black-out slits on cars were also reaping their reward and traffic accidents were high and many lives were lost that winter.

In the spring she received a letter from Georgie.

Central Provinces.

My darling love,

Well, I'm back here, bonny lass, back in the jungle and I can tell you this because I'm sending the letter back with a friend returning to England on sick-leave. Malaria is the curse out here.

Things are different this time, my darling. More serious. We seem to be learning a new craft and travel miles with heavy packs, track through jungles, lay charges and that's where I come in – I teach the others.

It's right noisy here, you know. There is always something moving above you or alongside and the monkey's chatter must sound like Prue from what you say.

We're living off the land and roast monkey is very tasty and the blood right good for quenching your thirst.

Burma looks as though it could be a ripe plum for the Japs with their oil refineries at Rangoon, and the CO (Mr Prue to you) says that if the Nips decide to take Burma, they're likely to come on into India across the border expecting the Indians to turn on us from this side and who knows, maybe they will.

Tom shouldn't be in the pits, you know, he should be checking on the surface. I know he's a good pitman and that's what they need but it's not right, I agree with you, not with his injuries. Good old Don getting a cushy number. That lad has the luck of the devil, clerk in a supply depot, well I'm buggered. Maud sounds well from what Tom says and Grace has taken to munitions work like a duck to water. There's more money there too, he says.

Sarah has written and says she liked the hospital when she visited you. She's a game old bird, isn't she, and loves you so much but it can't be as much as I do.

I must stop now, my darling. We will be together when this is over, won't we, my darling lass, and then I'll bring you to Kashmir. I must go, the plane is flying my mate out now. I love you. I always have and I always will, my own precious Annie. I miss you.

Georgie.

In May, Dunkirk fell and their days were long with a steady stream of shocked men with war wounds that gaped and maimed, and they worked until their eyes were black with tiredness but still Prue fluttered her eyelashes, but not at Annie any more because she had threatened to trim them while she was asleep if she continued to create that sort of draught around her. Prue called the British Expeditionary Force the Back Every Fridays and had her backside pinched by a major who could no longer walk.

It was their way of dealing with the horror.

In June, France fell and Prue was relieved that Paris had not been bombed, such a lovely city, darling, she had breathed as they sat in the mess. The art galleries are like no other. Annie had written this to Sarah who had replied that they must arrange for Tom to go after the war, which they would win of course.

July was busy in the wards. The Battle of Britain had begun and they saw the dogfights above and then the burns unit was busier than ever. Annie was transferred back to comfort the raw red heads which had once been young faces and took too many gins in the evening with shaking hands. Day after day there were new patients and the hours they worked were long and she grew thin but Prue did not. 'I never lose weight, darling. I never lose my appetite, that's the problem.' And they laughed together.

And then there was the blitz and the bombing of the provinces and the ports and Annie heard from Tom that they were tired but still all right, though the bombers came every night and sometimes during the day.

Prue and Annie took a train to London on their day off in the autumn when things were quieter and passed Peter Robinson's which looked strange with such a large chunk missing. There were gaping holes wherever they looked but still people worked and talked and laughed and there were lunchtime concerts in church halls and they went down into a crypt and sat with Londoners and listened to Chopin and Annie wished that Sarah could have been here. She would have sat, her head moving slightly with each stanza.

Georgie wrote from India. He could say little and there were great sections blacked out by the censor but she could tell where he was from his description of the cruiser butterfly and she thanked God that the Japanese were not involved in the war.

She worked on through the winter, thinking of the times they had been together, the love she felt for him, the ache that was always with her now he was gone.

Now there was extensive rationing but Pruscilla still did not lose weight and the Sisters' mess had a bet on that, by the end of the war, she would still be the same plump blonde, and made Annie promise to write to them and tell them all, wherever they were if they had won.

And so winter turned to spring, and May to June 1941, and they played tennis on the old school courts and Dr Smith taught Annie the backhand and pinched her bottom at the net. Prue threatened to tell Georgie and Annie laughed and chased her until they fell in an exhausted heap under the budding oaks.

The grounds were sweeping and bordered at the back of the house by magnolia trees which were tranquil in the winter and bore white waxed blossom in the spring and, lying beneath the largest in June, Annie could see patches of blue through the fresh green canopy of leaves which had taken the place of the flowers. She could hear the drone of planes and could never imagine a time when she would grow disenchanted by the sun. It drove the thoughts of the wards and injury to the back of her mind. It made Georgie seem nearer and Tom and Don safe and Sarah had written to say that, after seeing the blossoms of the trees when she was down last month, she would try to obtain one after the war.

But Sarah died while she was lying there, while she was relaxing and thinking of nothing, one arm over her eyes and her hand picking at the grass. There was an air raid as Sarah shopped in Newcastle, but she was unmarked and beautiful, Val said in the letter the orderly brought over to her as she lay there. It was another blast death to the rescuers but to Annie it brought the world to a stop.

The letter lay on the grass, discarded. She gripped a handul of grass, it was young and taut in her hands. Sarah couldn't be dead. She would not allow her to be dead. She needed her, needed her voice rolling out words as though she was a book, needed her kindness, her sharpness. Needed her visits as she passed to or from her holidays, needed her letters which told of Gosforn and the hens, told of Val and the Miss Thoms, told of herself. She had been her mother, so how could she die too, like the others?

The magnolia leaves were rustling above her, the sun played fleetingly over her hands which clutched the grass. No, she could not be dead; they had sat here together and enjoyed the sun just a few weeks ago, she could still hear her voice, see her smile. No, she could not be dead, not be cold, Annie loved her too much for that to have happened and what the hell was she doing shopping in Newcastle when the bombs dropped? What the hell was she doing taking risks for a yard of cloth? What did she want a yard of cloth for? Annie looked at the grass she had torn up, grass which hung from fists which were lifted to the sky. Oh God, if only she didn't know what a dead body looked like.

Sarah, don't leave now, not now, not ever.

There was another letter too, from the solicitor, and the envelope was stiff vellum; its edge cut her thumb and it bled but she did not feel it, just brushed the drops to a smear as she focussed on the typewritten words which must be read, Val had said in her letter, but which were an irritation, an intrusion. She wanted to think, to remember, but not to either, because how could she bear this loss? Why die over a bloody piece of cloth? Oh Sarah, why? Grass lay discarded on her lap now dark against her uniform, against Val's letter.

The solicitor informed her in black detached perfect lettering that she now owned the house and also a large capital sum including an account which had been set aside to receive her repayments for the loans Don and Tom had received. This was also hers now. Sarah had assumed that she would continue to maintain a position for Val, who had been comfortably provided for. Annie would not have thought to do otherwise but money was not what she wanted to clutter her mind up with now; it was Sarah who must fill it, who must stay with her, tight inside her, safe, well, devoid of a yard of cloth, devoid of dust on her dear cold face.

She went back on duty and changed the dressing which was overdue on the amputation and read aloud the letter that the blind pilot's wife had written, made tea for Pruscilla and herself in the ward kitchen, drank it while Pruscilla remained silent and watchful. She could not taste it and her hand trembled only slightly as she replaced the cup in its saucer, right in the middle, so that it fitted perfectly or was it a bit too much to the right. There, that was perfect, or was it too much to the left?

'Leave it, Annie,' Prue said gently.

Only that night when the moon was brilliant in the sky and had blazoned the stars into nothingness did she cry, standing at the window and gripping the frame, silently at first until Prue led her back to bed and then the sobs rasped deep in her chest and her fists beat the pillow which was wet from her mouth and eyes and the missing was deep and dark and she could now believe that she was never going to see her again.

Georgie's letters eased her pain a little over the next days and weeks and months, but only a very little. She filled in ward forms, ate at mealtimes, played tennis again but could not remember doing it. She never lay beneath the magnolia tree again because her comfort was gone and that is where she had last been. Sarah was gone and life would never be quite the same again.

They knew that they were soon to be posted overseas because they had been instructed to buy tropical kit and Annie was glad. Glad to leave England, to be nearer Georgie because she needed him more than ever now that Sarah was gone.

Annie took the train to Gosforn for her embarkation leave. The privet hedge still smelt of dusty yellow pollen and she took a leaf and bent it between her fingers and it snapped into segments; so autumn is with us, she thought.

The key slid easily into the lock and the brass doorknob shone as it had always done and the hallway was empty as it often was but it was an emptiness now which rolled off into the sitting-room because Sarah was not in the winged chair with her glasses low on her nose as she looked towards the door and rattled her paper.

Then the kitchen door opened and Val bustled through, her

arms pink and plump and warm as they held her close.

'I've put the tea on for you, my dear.'

But first Annie climbed the stairs, took off her grey suit, looked under the bed and there was the potty. She moved to the window, slipped the latch and leaned out. One last cut would do the lawn, the roses could be pruned and the air was still heavy with the scent of honeysuckle and baked bread. The hens were still in their runs and she smiled as the cock strutted backwards and forwards. Nothing has changed, she marvelled. But everything has changed.

There was boiled egg for tea, the warm brown shell of which peeled off to expose a fresh white and then a vivid yolk which welled orange and rich.

Annie leaned back. 'Are you able to give the Miss Thoms a few too, Val?' She dug her toast soldier into the yolk and chewed at it.

Val nodded. 'And they give me honey because their gardener has a hive.'

And there it was suddenly, vivid in her mind; the hive across from the beck, the black-eyed daisies in the meadow and the train that steamed away to God knows where. 'I wrote to Tom and Don and they are going to come over, Val, if they can manage it. Don's been called up and has landed up as a clerical private in the supply depot. Tom's in the mines again. Did they tell you?' She raised her eyes as Val nodded.

'They pop in from time to time,' she smiled. 'Worried that I might be lonely, I think. They're good boys. Did you know that the Miss Thoms have lent me their gardener as well, Annie? Kind of them but he drives me mad. Rake, rake, until I could scream. Why doesn't he just bung in a few seeds, that's what I'd like to know? I don't let him feed your hens, don't trust him to do too much. Bit old, bit dense, if you know what I mean.'

She touched her finger to her head and pulled a face.

'He says a girl like you should be tucked up in a little house with a few bairns hanging off your skirt but I say to him that, if I had to decide between that and being waited on hand, foot and finger, I know what I'd choose.'

Annie laughed. 'I do a bit of work too you know, Val.'

'Oh, I know that but you're an officer and officers don't do much, do they?'

Annie just shook her head and smiled. Her egg was finished

now and she took a sip of tea. 'Do you miss her very much, Val?'

Val sat down, easing her legs round and under the table.

'It feels as though she's still alive. I think I hear her coming down in the morning.' She reached over and cut some more bread. It was fresh and fell on to the board as the knife sawed through. Annie picked up some moist crumbs pressing them together and wondered if there would ever be a time when simple gestures did not take her rushing back to the past.

'Aye, I miss her, every day I miss her,' Val said in a calm voice. 'But it's not an aching. It happened and it was quick and everything is the same except she's not here but there again, she is, if you know what I mean. Life goes on, lass. I think of her and it pleases me. It doesn't pain.'

Later in the darkness of the sitting-room Annie felt the sameness and was comforted. She lay her head back in her chair opposite Sarah's and was grateful for the table at its side which held the same lamp, the same photograph of the skiers. The only difference to the room was the black-out and the empty chair, but otherwise so little was disturbed and Sarah's essence was everywhere bringing good memories. Death did not mean the end of everything as it had done before. It did not have to be ugly and wounding but calm and part of natural life.

Time passed and she rested her head on the back of the chair. Well, Sarah, she thought, tropical kit, iron kettle and a tent pole. What do you think it means? Where will I be going now? I'm a bit old for camping at 27, aren't I?

First though, the lawn had to be cut and as she rose the boys were there; Tom limping towards her and Don grinning as he came along behind.

'Had to come now, bonny lass,' Tom said as he hugged her. 'Got an early shift tomorrow and Don's on night duty. Grace sends her love and so does Maud but they're both working at the munitions factory so can't get away.' He held her at arm's length and smoothed back her hair. 'You look tired, bonny lass.' Then Don pushed him out of the way.

'Let me have a kiss then. She doesn't look so bad.' He hugged her and she liked the feel of their familiar arms around her.

She led them into the garden and watched as they took turns to push the lawn-mower. They talked and fell silent, laughed and were serious as the late afternoon sun stayed high in the sky. She knotted her cardigan round her waist by its arms and the secateurs felt warm in her hands as she pruned the roses right back. They began the bonfire as the sun started to go down and burnt the dead roses, the old wood from the lilac and the lavender clippings that Don had cut. They laid down the grass cuttings as a mulch and then after tea they were on their way again, sweating from their work, sleeves rolled up and hair in their eyes, eager to be back before the black-out but not wanting to leave.

'It won't be long now,' they said as they put on their motor cycle helmets. Tom looked hard at her. 'Get some ideas for design then, bonny lass. Sarah told me it would be a good idea. Then, when it's over, we'll get on.' He kissed her again and pointed to Don. 'That miserable old bugger doesn't want to come in with us.'

Don shook his fist at them both. 'I've got me own business and it'll do very well, thank you, now that I've got Albert doing the right things. He actually smiles at the customers, makes a right nice face an' all he does.'

She heard their laugh well into the night when she lay in bed and watched the stars and smelt the grass clippings and fastened her brothers in her mind as they had been this afternoon because she did not know when she would see them again.

She arrived back at the hospital two days later in the evening, after Pruscilla. The wards were nearly empty and there were crates in the hall. She met Prue on the stairs and she was panting.

'The stairs are really too steep for this rushing about, darling. It's so undignified.' There were shouts from downstairs and the revving of lorries in the drive.

'You're just too fat,' Annie grinned.

'Now don't be cross,' Prue pouted. 'Now come along, back down with me. Matron wants us all assembled.' She pulled her towards the next flight down. The oil paintings which lined the stairs were shrouded in white sheeting and Annie paused to peer at the last picture, lifting the corner of the cover.

There were only dim lights on the stairs and none in the hallway below them. 'Oh, come on, darling,' urged Prue. 'We've got to get down now and strictly no lights allowed so put your torch away and stop poking about looking at pictures that are not yours anyway.'

She was flustered, Annie could see that now. Her forehead was furrowed and her face was flushed.

'So what's the hurry, I thought we had another half an hour?' She put her torch in her pocket and started down the stairs.

'Our transport is arriving then and the old dragon is having a heart attack every five minutes.'

'Matron is very nice,' Annie said quietly.

'To you maybe,' whispered Prue as they approached the hall. There were other nurses there now and orderlies were moving amongst them with lists in their hands which they played their torches over.

Annie stood with Prue over by the corridor. 'All right,' she gave in, 'tell me what's happened.' She leant back against the door jamb and hitched up her gas mask.

'All so terribly trivial, darling.' Prue's eyes would be wide, Annie knew that from the tone of voice. 'I put down her list, that's all, and I can't remember where and before that the corporal in charge of the baggage was heard to say that he was buggered if he'd herd a bunch of camels like this again. When Matron said she'd take down his number if she heard language like that again, some wag said Corp wasn't on the phone but he'd take her on instead. Well, you can imagine, darling.'

Annie was laughing now, so hard that her stomach hurt and Monica, who was standing further down, hissed, 'Shut up, for God's sake, she'll have your head on a platter.'

The train was unlit, unheated and there were no seats left and Annie came to the conclusion as she sat on her kit in the dark corridor and pushed Pruscilla upright that this was no way to fight a war. She wore her tin hat as orders were orders but it was noisy when dropped which it did with every lurch of the train. It was so cold that she could no longer feel her feet and her hands were stuck deep into her greatcoat pockets. The corridor smelt of stale tobacco and dirty bodies. Pruscilla snored but there was no rhythm to it, just a series of disjointed grunts and gurgles.

'Can't you stop that bleedin' din, Sister?' called a man's voice but Annie ignored it. Nothing but a cork would do that or a pinched nose and there was no way she was about to do that and provoke Prue's hysterics. The Thermos was still full and she unscrewed the cap and took a drink as the train rattled over the points. The hot tea was tangy but warming; the steam made her nose run. It was midnight.

The black-out blind banged against the frame and it seemed lighter outside than in and she could see that they were passing through the edge of a town, then the train began to slow. It lurched and Pruscilla flopped forward and they had arrived. It was cold and dark and noise was still forbidden but this was Lime Street Station in Liverpool. Pruscilla had docked here before and recognised the station.

'I want to hear nothing, not even the clink of a hat, not even a snort.' The sergeant-major was very red in the face and Prue blinked.

Searchlights stabbed the sky and an air raid was on. They stayed in the station, listening to the crump, crump of the bombs and the reply of the ack-ack as they pounded the planes.

Annie's head ached with tiredness and the bombs were too far away to be real so there was no fear. But it was still so cold. At last they were able to drag their kitbags over to the transport when the all-clear sounded and she could smell the brine of the sea and feel its stickiness in her hair.

They were still bound to silence as they approached their ship. The gangplank was steep and the non-slip strips were too wide for Annie's stride and the water gurgled beneath them, oily and dirty. Hands gripped her as she reached the top and handed her down to the deck which was vibrating as the engines idled. It was pitch-dark still and she and Prue were passed along to where Monica and two others stood.

'You five Sisters follow me,' said a male voice in scarcely more than a whisper.

Once inside the hatchway, dim lights showed narrow steel-riveted corridors and the tremor beneath their feet was more noticeable and there was a heavy smell of diesel.

They were led along narrow companionways until the sailor stopped, checked his list and opened the door.

'This is your cabin.' He still spoke in a whisper. 'Water twice a day at oh-six hundred hours and eighteen hundred hours. Sea soap is provided for washing. No noise until we're under way.' It was an order and his face told them so.

They moved into the cabin. There were six bunks and one

nurse already in the cabin. Prue sidled up to Annie. 'They look awfully small, darling,' she whispered and they all laughed.

Monica was with them but the rest were strangers. Prue looked tired and frightened and Annie said, 'Have the bottom bunk, lass. It's less far to fall in a rough sea and I'll get you some tea from the flask.' She steered her towards the bunk and patted her arm.

Monica was stowing her kit in the space at the end of the bunks and Annie put hers and Prue's on top. She grinned at the other three Sisters and one with a faint moustache smiled back.

'Would you like some tea?' breathed Annie, remembering the noise regulation.

The other Sister nodded her head. 'I've something which will make it taste a little better,' and she drew out a small hip flask. 'Tea and whisky. Best thing for sea-sickness.'

But it wasn't and they were. They still did not know where they were going but Annie knew it would be nearer Georgie though further from Tom.

CHAPTER 23

Grace stood by the kitchen table, impatient at the time the tea was taking to cool. She wanted to pour it into Tom's morning flask and get to bed before the air-raid siren sounded. It was nearly eleven and in half an hour the bombers would start. The Germans were always on time, had been for months now. Aiming for the docks they were, the papers said, but you could have fooled Wassingham.

After the first week of it, Bob had explained that the Germans were a mechanical people who liked a timetable; his face was serious and his tone that of a teacher and Tom had slapped his back and told him he'd buy him a German watch with a bloody great cuckoo leaping out every hour.

Grace dipped her finger into the tea again. 'Strange how they grabbed you the minute we arrived back up here, isn't it?' she said. 'A disabled agitator one minute, too crippled for the army and an essential worker the next. What a difference a war makes, eh Tom? Two years now and how many more to go, bonny lad?'

Tom grunted and moved the picture frame he was pinning to catch more light from the single bulb which dangled above him. There were a pile of gleaming steel pins on the scrubbed table and a small hammer which lay near them. The room was cheerful in spite of the gloom with scattered patchwork cushions given to them by May and Betsy creating colour, but the heavy smell of size and stove-black from the make-shift black-out curtains permeated the whole house. The furniture was sparse but familiar since it came from Joe and Betsy.

He was glad to be working like this, busy with his art after the shift, but his hands were not as dextrous as they used to be, he had noticed recently, because they were stiff from muscles knotted with manual work and damaged by dust-saturated cuts. His nails were stained black again too as they had been in the old days but he still had the energy, just, to take a painting class once a week at the library, so long as it didn't coincide with his firewatch duty.

He held the last pin in his mouth, scored a small hole in the joint and then tapped it in. He slid his painting of the unfinished air-raid shelter, roofless and stark, into the back and secured it. He felt a sense of continuing exasperation at his situation; painting scenes which depicted the lack of care for the local population when all he really wanted was to be out there fighting the Nazis. But no, it was the pit he was stuck in, with a bit of daubing on the side to make him feel he could still say something about the things that angered him.

'That'll do,' he said to Grace as he arched his back and ran his hands round his neck. 'I'm getting old, lass, creaking and groaning like the pit-props, an old man at 25.' He put a quaver in his voice and pulled her to him, running his hands down her back and over her buttocks. There was not much spare weight on his bonny lass these days but at least rationing had made things fairer and no one starved, like they used to. Everyone was just bloody hungry. Grace bent over and kissed the top of his head, full of the smell of coal again after being clean for four years. She sighed and tested the tea again. It was ready.

'It's a bloody disgrace about that shelter you know,' Tom went on, watching her as she poured the tea into the flask and secured the top. She had nice hands still, had our Gracie, in spite of working in that factory. 'Fancy telling people to go and shelter in the cupboard under the stairs until they find money from somewhere to finish it. We've said we'll do it if they can produce the materials but even that doesn't speed things up. The bloody war will be over before they get round to it or I hope to God it is.' He brushed the pins into his hand and put them back in the old tobacco tin which held them, opening the drawer beneath the table and throwing in the hammer, then the pins. God, he hoped it was over soon but how could it be without help from the US and there was no hope of that at the moment. As it was, it looked as though Hitler could be over here any time and he shuddered, then hoped that Grace hadn't seen.

'Are you glad I dragged you back up here then, hinny, and didn't make you go through the blitz in London?' He was grinning now as he tried to talk away his forebodings. Grace was tipping ash gently on to the fire and she finished before straightening up and tucking a red curl behind her ear.

'Oh aye, lad,' she laughed. 'Much more cosy to be bombed in me own home.' She came over and sat on his lap. It would be time for bed in five minutes, he thought as he stroked her face and laid his head on her shoulder, but they wouldn't go earlier than ten past eleven or they would have more time to think of the bombs that would soon start. They sayed in bed now, didn't rush to the dark tight cupboard. It hadn't saved Ma Gillow's friend or the children who had been crushed just the same. It seemed so pointless somehow to rush like rats into a hole and die anyway; it was too much like the pit.

He remembered Chamberlain's message to the nation at 11.15 a.m. on 3 September as he breathed in Grace's scent and heard the beating of her heart beneath the green jumper that had gone felty in the wash. And how, now a state of war existed, they, like the rest of the population, had headed for home, like animals in a storm. Married they'd been though, the day before, and had stood together in the corridor for the length of the journey because the seats were packed full. It was the children he remembered most, that and the feel of Grace as she had stood close to him and pressed against him as they swung with the train.

To begin with, the bairns had run past them shouting and laughing but had soon subsided into bored lethargy and tearful boredom, sprawled all over their parents and one another, their gas masks sticking into them, making for more tears, more discomfort.

A few hours out of London the guard had come along and insisted on a drill and Tom remembered the smell of the gas mask rubber which was choking, and the misting of the glass which cut down his vision. The train had still been swinging and lurching and the children were crying now except for one red-haired boy who kept his on when others had gratefully dragged the mask from their faces and sucked at the stale train air. The boy had blown out hard and the raspberry was loud enough for the old lady with her luxury gas-mask container in the first-class compartment to tut and wonder how she was to survive the war if she was to rub shoulders with the likes of these. Did she have any evacuees now? Tom wondered, and grinned at the thought. That should knock her delicate sensibilities out of the window.

He had sketched the boy quickly and in pencil while Grace looked over his shoulder. It was good, she had said and then sat down on the suitcase propped against the compartment door. It was splitting with age and she had set her feet apart and hunched herself over her knees.

She had asked whether the Germans would really use gas and he had laughed and said of course they wouldn't, hoping that she would not hear that Mussolini had used it in 1935 against the Abyssinians. So far though, the Germans had not used it, they used bombs instead. He lifted his head from the warmth of her shoulder and checked the wall clock. Fifteen minutes past eleven.

'Come on, lass, up you go. I'll get me boots out and me clothes for the morning.' He laid his pit-clothes over the fender so that the early winter chill would be kept at bay by the small ash-banked fire.

They had called in to see Annie when they had reached Newcastle, then continued on to Wassingham and it seemed as though they had never been away; the slag-carts still churned upwards and there was that smell in the air. But as they walked on to Grace's home, they passed white-painted kerbs and lampposts and heaps of sand which some children had spread on the pavement and turned into a soft shoe shuffle stage. It stank of dogs' pee, he could smell it now, and so did the sandbags which were stacked in front of the library windows and shops as blast protection.

They had gone from Grace's house to Bob's and he had shown them the two up two down he had found for them to rent with a privy out at the back. He looked well, less drawn, and Tom had taken him and Don for a drink while Grace and Maud sorted out the house. She'd stuck her tongue out at him and called that she would tell Annie he was a pig.

It was because there was full employment Bob had gloated as he supped at his beer and the froth stayed on his upper lip until he wiped it away with his handkerchief. There's a munitions factory opening up down the road, he'd gone on, and it'll take our lads and they won't have to care if the pit's open or not. Tom laughed with Don and winced as the lad kicked him under the table. War's done you proud has it, Bob? Don had said, and

Bob had blushed and admitted that, to some extent, Don was right, explaining that the lads would be able to get away from Wassingham now into the services or, if they stayed, they had the chance of better conditions in the factories, not the bloody pits. And of course, Tom thought, as he shut the kitchen door and climbed the stairs, he'd been right.

He boarded up the bedroom windows with the cut-down doors which Bob had unscrewed from his unused bedrooms and was in bed before the nightly raid began but the crump crump and shudder of the house made his mouth run dry as it always did and he soothed Grace who clung to him. The thudding of the ack-ack as it replied did not help his fear. He was glad that Maud was with her parents in Merthyr Terrace while Don was at the supply depot outside Manchester. She wouldn't come to them, felt too much of a gooseberry, she had laughed, and Albert scared her and Tom could understand that. It was better to be where you felt at ease.

'Tell you what, bonny lass,' he breathed into Grace's ear, making her listen. 'We'll take Val's Christmas presents on Sunday shall we, take Maud and clear the garden, now that the old boy can't cope any longer. You tell Maud in the morning.' He pulled her hair slightly and there was a louder nearer explosion and a tremor ran through the bed and the mirror on the dressing-table rattled. 'Listen to me, Grace,' he had to raise his voice to be heard. 'You go and tell her after work tomorrow.' And then she nodded but she was like a rigid board in his arms and he stroked and kissed her but they were too frightened for passion.

He left the house at five in the morning having dozed for what seemed like a few minutes. It was still dark as he joined his Uncle Henry further down the street.

'Everyone all right?' he asked. 'May, Betsy?'

'Aye, lad, and Maud's area's clear an' all but the library got it.'

'God damn it, now where'll I find for me bloody class?' Tom grumbled. The dust was still falling from the bomb damage. It was in their eyes and hair but the fires were mainly under control though the glow was still bright enough to show the smoke rising in a pall from Gladburn Street where the library had been and further over, nearer the slag-heaps on the north side of town.

'That's your problem,' grunted his uncle and they nodded as they passed more miners coming out from doors and alleys to start the shift. Henry was rubbing his eyes, dragging his hands down his face though his eyes were no more red-rimmed than everyone else's, the dust and coal took their toll and the tiredness just came on top of all that. 'Bloody shattered I am. This fire-watch is too much at my age. We'll need some more young 'uns in the pits too, soon. I'm 55 lad.'

Tom gripped his shoulder. 'You're all right, Henry. Good and strong.' But decided he would take more of the face-work. He knew he was a fool to still be in the pits himself but somehow he couldn't make himself take an easy option. It would be bad luck somehow and after all Annie must come back safely.

Their boots were loud on the cobbles as they walked along to the pit-yard. The buildings crowded in on them and the dawn had yet to break though there was a lightening of the sky.

'I hear there's talk of striking,' said his uncle quietly as they waited in the queue for the cage. Men were murmuring all around them. There was the noise of boot against cobble, baittin against bait-tin. A miner spat.

Tom nodded. 'So Bob says.' His muffler was tight up round his throat and his foot was hurting as it always did but it did not swell quite so much these days. He knew he was thinner, his face was drawn and etched with sharp lines that were not there before the pain. A pain which was with him every day, every minute since Olympia.

His uncle was close up to him now, his head near him. 'It'll not do us any good in the country, lad. The press'll have a ruddy field-day and I don't know as I'd blame them, it's wartime, lad, and I don't hold with striking.'

'Aye, I reckon you're right but you can't blame the men. The pay's lousy, the hours are longer and longer along with poorer maintenance and now there's talk of drafting pitmen and their lads back here into the pits, just when the poor buggers thought they'd a chance for some to get away. Why should they be drafted back is what the miners feel, drafted back out of the factories and the war to be killed by coal and for a bloody pittance too? They've still got to support a family, Henry, for God's sake.' His voice was rising and his uncle pushed him along as the queue moved.

'Keep your bloody voice down, lad, or you'll end up being locked up like your pal Mosley and how would you like that?'

Tom pulled at his lip and submitted to the match search before squatting on the floor of the cage. 'Piece-work should be abolished an' all.'

His uncle glared as the men squashed close up to them laughed.

As the cage sank, Tom was quiet. The stench was always the same, the thick dust on the floor of the cage, the dropping, the scream of displaced air and then the crunching of the cockroaches beneath their boots as they wound their way along the main seam, hearing the rats darting away as they approached. They turned off into the tunnel to the face they had been allocated.

There was more than two inches of water today and, as they bent over to squeeze further into the flattening seam, his uncle cursed. 'Picked a right one for us today, haven't they, lad. Might do well to keep your mouth shut, if you ever could, that is.'

The heat was stifling and Tom took the hewing this time with his uncle on the shovel. He lay down stiffly and angled his pick but work was slow and difficult. There were not going to be many trollies pushed down the seam today and it meant his pay would be down again and they'd not enough to cope as it was.

He tugged and tore at a lump which had wedged itself. Thank God, Grace worked in the factory and could pass some over to her da. It was bloody good of Don to have put him in the shop while he was away, it gave him a bit of dignity as well as some wages, and between that and Grace, her parents would survive. He'd write and tell Annie about that, she'd be right pleased.

He groaned as he shifted his weight off his back and his foot and hoped to God he didn't get a chill through lying in the water. It gave that remaining kidney too much to do, said the doctor, but there was a fat lot he could do about it with an overman like his. He heard Henry ease up a pit-prop.

'How many today then, Uncle?' he panted, straining his head round to see.

'Just the two again, lad, for each section.'

Tom swore and went back to work listening to the sounds the props made, listening for a rush of dust, a creak and groan that would mean the coal had finally got him. They needed three props, three bloody props, not two. He turned on his side and heaved at the coal again. There had been two men killed yesterday and that had been less than the same day last week and it would go on if basic safety was ignored.

Thank God, Annie was out of all this and the bombs, the cold and the hunger. She'd written that Singapore was out of this world with just the right temperature and just maybe she'd get to see Georgie. It was pretty close to India wasn't it, he'd asked Grace, and she looked it up in the library and said he was right. Well, at least the bonny lass was in the sun, living like a bloody duchess and looking at the fabrics. Just as long as she was enjoying herself, that was the thing; she'd earned it, every bloody minute.

CHAPTER 24

Durban had been glorious with its surging and plummeting surf. Sun, sea and everything that England had been without for two years but Singapore was incomparably better, Annie thought as she and Prue sat at Robinson's Hotel for coffee as usual on their day off. It was a pattern that had been quickly established in the three weeks they had been here, though it seemed longer because she had become so used to the life of ease and splendour.

It was all so beautiful, so different to Wassingham that it was hard to believe the cold dark hardness of the mining town still existed when life could be as it was here. It was early December now and the sun was still so hot that Christmas seemed an impossibility. She and Prue would have tea at Raffles this afternoon and look for presents until then in the crooked streets which were full of shops and arcades and yellow or blue-white houses splashed with red Chinese lettering. Full of the noise of trading, of birds and fowls that squawked and fluttered in wooden cages, of motor horns and rickshaws and the revving of cars. There was colour everywhere, material which would have made Tom's mouth water and silk which hung in bales in small shops and invited touching.

What on earth would he think of the cathedral which they passed on their way into the centre from the nurses' home? It was like some icing-sugar sculpture. He'd either like it or loathe it and she was pretty sure it would be the latter.

In the narrow streets, washing hung out, not on washing lines but on bamboo poles hoisted across from window to window and fish dried on pavements amongst fowl that scattered as cars thrashed by; flies swarmed over everything. The odour and noise were always present.

Annie smiled as she thought of the first time they had driven out to the suburbs. It was like her first view of Gosforn. A sense of space, of light, only far more so as the palatial white houses of the Europeans blasted back the light. Bougainvillaea, calla lilies and frangipani clustered in the grounds and were repeated in all the parks and their lushness made her want to stop and touch, bury her face in their colour and their warmth.

The early mornings were the best though, she had decided, with the breeze flicking in off an ocean which was even bluer than Prue's eyes. She stood each morning in the hospital grounds listening to the rattle of the palm fronds as they were disturbed by the freshness and again in the evening watching the birds as they settled on the telephone wires and wondered how she could be in amongst this and still have an emptiness, an ache which only Georgie could fill.

She and Prue had only been out into the countryside once, and that was with a couple Prue had known in India, the Andertons, who were now happily settled in Singapore where he, who was moustached, neat and correct, held a post in Government House, and she, Mavis, wore head-hugging hats and presided at receptions. They had climbed into his open car last week and Prue had held firmly on to her hat but Annie had removed hers and let the wind rush through her hair, tumbling it around her face and cooling her.

They had driven past mangrove swamps and coconut groves and she had seen again the coconut shies at the fair where they had slipped the lead coins and heard the lady with the varicosed legs. She had screwed her hands in the car and watched as though from a distance the rubber plantations with their latex smell and the jungle scrub which lay all around.

They had driven past two reservoirs which were as large as lakes and then on past the Causeway before she had pushed her memories back into the box and nodded as Mavis pointed out the villages which were called kampongs. Changi jail was on their route and Annie wondered how anyone could bear to be locked away from all this sun, this life. Was Dippy Denis still in his cold dark prison?

The port was chaotic when they drove through, horn sounding at the Tamil labourers who were everywhere around them, carrying goods into and out of the go downs which loomed high along the docks full of different wares. These warehouses were cheek by jowl with fuel tanks, offices and customs sheds and it had been a relief to relax on the verandah at the Anderton's home that evening drinking pink gin brought by servants and talking of the war in Europe, talking of their good fortune at being where they were, in the peace of Singapore. But that was not what Georgie's letter had said, Annie thought as she sat here in the sun with Prue and moved uneasily in her chair. That's not what he had said at all. Get out, he'd insisted.

Prue interrupted her train of thought.

'Annie, these strawberries are scrumptious, absolute heaven.'

She was licking her spoon and Annie saw strawberries against her white teeth. Her gold charm bracelet clinked as she put the spoon back into the crystal bowl and scooped out some cream. Prue closed her eyes as she swallowed and there were faint freckles across her nose.

Annie grinned. 'Not more strawberries surely, Prue? You'll burst and I am not, definitely not, going to clear up the mess.'

Prue opened her eyes languidly and looked about them at the other tables, then back at Annie. 'Do stop being boring, darling. The fly boys bring them in fresh every day just for us and I should hate them to feel that we did not appreciate their efforts; and who is that gorgeous man over there with Monica?'

Annie didn't need to look; she knew it was Martin Edge who had come over with his battalion four days ago.

'Nice, isn't he?' she grinned. 'And I warn you that I shall remind you of the convoy's zig-zagging and the storms if you eat very many more helpings. You've put all that weight on, you clot, and you were just talking of the new slim you the day before yesterday.'

'That was then. I met the most divine man last night, darling, who said he likes a real armful, so much more womanly.'

Annie grinned as Prue finished the bowl and poured another coffee. She ran the cream over the back of the teaspoon which she held against the inner edge of the cup. It spread thickly over the surface and, when she drank, it left a white moustache on her upper lip until she dabbed at it with her napkin. Prue looked over at Annie, her eyes widely innocent as she set the napkin back beside her coffee cup.

'Talking about self-indulgence, Miss Goody-Twoshoes, I

noticed you tucking into the salmon at Raffles last night and who was that major anyway?'

Touché, Annie thought as she lit another cigarette, drawing the smoke deep into her lungs. She pushed away the silver cigarette-case, seeing the misting left by her finger.

Yes, she thought dryly and lifted her cup to Prue who smiled. Yes, who was the major? Someone she vaguely knew, someone to talk to and dance with. She had not liked the feel of his body as they danced past the Palm Court Orchestra and had missed Georgie and wondered where he was, if he was safe? And if he was safe, would he be so next week, next month? She narrowed her eyes against the sun and looked across as a car narrowly missed a rickshaw while a Chinese child ignored the ruction and offered to passers-by a chicken which flapped hopelessly as he held it upside down by the feet.

Sam Short had brought the letter. He had called in at the QA's mess early this morning, suntanned and in shorts and had given her the white creased envelope which was soft and warm as she took it. Sam explained that Georgie had asked him to deliver the letter as she took it from him, eager and grateful; trying to think where she could take him for a coffee, a drink, but Australians were not allowed in the clubs because they were colonials, not Europeans. She burned with shame because she had not defied the rules and invited him anyway.

He had stood there in his hat with the strap beneath his chin, his eyes wry with amusement. He was off up-country anyway, he had said, making the clubs safe for you people to enjoy and she had put her hand on his arm. We'll meet by the harbour, she replied, have a walk, then you can tell me how he really is, but he had shaken his head and smiled and his eyes had crinkled more on the left than the right where there was a healing scar.

He told that Georgie was fair dinkum and that they had been training together but that she must do what he says in the letter. I'm off to Penang he had said and the Japs are sure to come, Annie. He had stood there, his face in shade from his hat, his webbing and equipment hitched over his shoulder. His voice had grown suddenly urgent. Just do what he says, there's a good girl.

She had watched as he sauntered down the steps then and merged into the bustle of the city and without waiting to reach her room had peeled the flap of the letter back and she could see fingermarks on the envelope and hoped they were Georgie's.

'Penny for them, darling?' Prue was shaking sugar on to another bowlful of strawberries and looking at her at the same time. Annie stubbed out the cigarette and caught Pruscilla's look of distaste.

'I've told you that I'll stop smoking while you are eating as soon as you cut down on this appalling guzzling.'

Prue ignored her and took the letter which Annie handed over.

'See what you think of this,' Annie said.

November 1941

Central Provinces.

My darling love,

I'm writing this quickly and then sending it with Sam. I'm off to Burma. The Japs are getting active and we think they'll go for Rangoon and maybe into India.

But I think they'll also go for Malaya and Java and you too. Get out now. Go sick if you must but get to India. They treat prisoners badly. We've heard about them in China.

Come out my love, bring Prue. The C.O. is working on it too. I'll keep you safe here. I love you. Just come out on the first ship.

I have to go. We're moving out. My love always.

Georgie.

Annie watched as Prue scanned the letter once, then again and finally handed it back. Her hand was on the table, the sun glinted on the gold bracelet.

'Well?' asked Annie.

'Look around you, darling. Does it look as though we're in

342

any danger? Has anyone even hinted that we might not be safe and besides the fleet came in last night, just in case there should be any trouble. There's a difference between us and the Chinese anyway. Europeans would not be treated in the same way, would they, should the impossible happen, which it won't.'

Her plucked eyebrows were raised and there was a faint smile on her lips. Annie looked round at the elegant Europeans who sat as they had done for the last hundred years and would continue, it seemed, to do so for the next one hundred with not a hair out of place. But they were flesh and blood weren't they, they would still bleed, just as the Chinese were doing? She shook her head to clear it of these thoughts, her irritation at Prue's snobbery.

Singapore was taking precautions, she reasoned as she drew out another cigarette. The air-raid sirens went off each Saturday morning and searchlights still danced over the harbour at night but anyway everyone knew that the Japanese could not fly planes with their slant eyes, or so Mavis had said a few nights ago at the dance they had held; she had worn full evening dress and sipped champagne. It had been dry and delicious. Should slanted eyes prohibit flying, she wondered and rather doubted the sense of that sort of reasoning.

'Why has he written it, then?' she mused aloud.

Prue put down her spoon, her bowl empty. She rubbed her hands together. 'That's easy. He can't get you to marry him any other way.'

Annie watched the rickshaw drivers and traders, coins glinting and clicking with each transaction and pencils waving as each chit for goods was signed.

'Thought royalty were the only ones not to soil their hands with filthy ackers,' she said to Prue who answered:

'Let's face it, darling. Here we are almost royalty. Look around, ducky: an awful lot of Indians and not many chiefs.'

Thank God that just this once Annie Manon is out there on top, Annie thought, trying to push Prue's remark about Georgie away. How long was it since she had done any washing for herself or an evening without dancing until the early hours under crystal chandeliers?

'So,' Prue persisted. 'So, why didn't you marry Georgie after all the years of waiting, of missing? Then, when you could have married and stayed together, you didn't.'

Annie collected her cigarette-case and lighter together, putting them into her bag. The lighter smelt of petrol and there was a smudge on the silver.

'Annie, are you scared to commit yourself to anyone? Does it suit you to have him at arms length, there in the background to love and miss but not too close in case he manages to touch something inside you?'

She wouldn't think about what Prue was saying. She talked too much, always she talked too much. She breathed deeply to release the tension in her stomach, in her shoulders.

'Come on, Prue, shift yourself. Let's go and admire the good old *Prince of Wales*, everyone else seems to be.' Prue shook her head.

'You'll have to face it sometime, Annie Manon, whatever it is that comes between the two of you, because he'll ask you again.' Prue groaned as she pulled herself to her feet.

The sun was hot on Annie's feet and the harbour was crowded and she pushed Georgie out of her mind, and Sarah too because the pain of her death had surfaced suddenly.

The *Prince of Wales* looked glamorous against the blue sky, strong and firm and all that was good about the Royal Navy. There was a buzz of well-being at the arrival of the Far East Fleet and the woman on Annie's right was explaining breathlessly to her neighbour, 'Nice to think she's here, even though Singapore is invincible.'

'Will you be at the dance tonight?' Prue asked as she waved her gloved hand in front of her face to ward off the persistent flies.

Annie shook her head, she felt irritated now, off balance and confused. She could not forget his letter and she opened her bag and fingered it. Where was he, she thought again, was he safe and how could she leave when no one else was worried?

The air-raid sirens woke Annie four nights later, on Sunday. She heard the wail through her sleep; Don's watch said it was four in the morning, for God's sake, had the ARP wardens gone mad practising at this time of night? She walked across the cold tiled floor and looked from the window at the street lamps lighting the road below and at the searchlights sweeping the sky. She was tired and walked back towards the bed, then heard the guns thump and the dull drone of aeroplanes. Then there were the crashes and bangs of bombs and her room shook as she clutched at the bed. She threw herself to the floor, her hands pressed to her ears but the vibrations shook the building and she felt and heard the explosions even though she was trying not to. Nothing was stable and she could smell the smoke and feel the rug beneath her where it was damp from her dribble of fear.

Oh God, oh God, my love, you were right, she moaned and she knew she was talking aloud because her lips were opening and shutting against the rug and her breath was puffing back up into her face.

She pulled herself upright, switched on the radio but it was only playing dance music, then she crawled to the wardrobe, pulled on her uniform and staggered into Monica's room where together they watched the flames from the go downs as they burst into the air and the smoke and noise and dust as Singapore exploded into small pieces.

When the all-clear sounded they stumbled across to the wards. Prue was on night duty and her hair was damp from sweat, her face tense from the effort of calming the patients. Matron sent Annie to the Resuscitation Ward and, all day, casualties were brought in and it was as though Tom was here again, smelling of shock. She washed them down as she had done the pitmen, cleared them of dust and black grease, smelling the smoke in their hair and on their clothes along with the shock. They worked for the next thirty-six hours with six hours off in small bursts and at the end they picked their way over the rubble past Robinson's, which had been hit, to Raffles where they were to meet the Andertons to celebrate the entry of America into the war.

They sipped drinks from glasses that were chilled and misty just as always, as though there had been no bombing, no death, no dust, no fear. Servants replenished their drinks and the talk was gentle and not concerned with war. Annie ran her finger up and down the glass and heard but did not listen to Prue's chatter as she watched the big red sun go down and wondered how Americans could help hold the Japs back when they were not here.

She had learnt Georgie's letter by heart now and knew he had been right, knew by the fear stirring in her body, making her hands go cold but she could not leave now, not with the patients coming in every minute, including military casualties dribbling in from up-country. Casualties in khaki with drawn secret faces. And this must be only the beginning.

She eased back her head and rubbed her neck, looking round at the women in smart hats and immaculate make-up. She and Prue should return soon, Matron would need them. She listened for a moment more to talk of the tennis draw and how inconvenient this unpleasantness was and why didn't the boys clear it up at once. So, she thought, talk had veered over to the problem and that was at least a start.

Mavis said, 'The boys are fighting the Japs up-country and they are obviously not trying hard enough, they should have been pushed into the sea by now. They are such small people.'

Annie rose and walked back to the ward, leaving Prue to follow in her own time. She did not belong to those people, did not belong to their irritation over tennis niceties. She belonged here: taking blood pressures, checking drips, soothing Chinese who could speak a little English, Tamils who had burns from the dock fires and never complained when the dressings stuck, Europeans who were stoic. She was busy and glad of it.

The black-out was in force now, she wrote to Georgie, wondering if the letter would get out on any boat and if it did, whether it would find him.

The *Prince of Wales* was sunk and the mess fell quiet at the news. Nurses prepared more bandages and cut tattered clothes from damaged bodies as the bombing continued that night and every night.

She was too tired to feel shock but the fear was still there, fear which made her feel sick and weak because they were hearing the stories which came back with the men. And what about Georgie, was he tattered too like one of these men that she nursed?

Air-raid practices went on when the bombing paused, but were not supported because they clashed with the tennis tournament. Tension together with tiredness drew deep lines around her mouth and hammered pain across her forehead. The stench from bomb-damaged drains hung amongst the dust and made her want to vomit as she gave inoculations against typhoid.

She took Prue to coffee at Robinson's when Matron gave them an hour off, two weeks after the bombing had begun, but Penang had fallen and refugees sat at all the tables so they walked back to the hospital past a team that were digging for bodies, past trenches that were dug in parks, on sports grounds, past crashed aircraft and a school which they could hear rehearsing for the nativity play which was to be held on Christmas Eve at the end of the week.

Sam Short came in by field ambulance, his leg blasted away below the knee and tourniqueted, his liver gone. He died while she held his hand.

'Get out,' he whispered before he died but no nurses were leaving yet, only civilians. She closed his eyes and wished she had taken him to the club while she could.

The rains were sheeting down one day here and one day there and it was humid beyond belief. Prue's roots were showing and Annie had not known she was a bottle blonde. It was better to concentrate on bleach than the queues stretching past the go downs, past the customs houses to the boats which daily took people away to safety but not them. I wish I was going, my love, she called to Georgie as she sponged another body with shaking hands and tried not to listen to the cries and groans from all around.

Hong Kong fell on Christmas Day but the nurses had a turkey and champagne since food was still plentiful. Dancing took place every night in the Centre.

Three nurses were killed when they were caught in a raid down by the docks. The sun was not visible now during the day; it was hidden behind the smoke which hung over the city. Mavis Anderton hosted a garden party on her lawn but it was spoilt by the rumble of guns all around Singapore. Finally trenches were dug at the cricket club but not the golf greens.

The Palm Court Orchestra continued to play and, one night, she and Prue danced at Raffles but not on New Year's Eve for, while the Fancy Dress Ball was held into the early hours, they bathed injured troops who were covered in layers of black grime from the bombed oil dumps they had tried but failed to save over by the Causeway.

The Chinese shopkeepers refused European chits now and would only accept cash and at this the rush for the boats became intense because traders always knew the truth.

The Causeway was blown on the last day of January, Sarah's birthday, but Annie was too tired to do more than nod as she handed a scalpel to the doctor. Neither of them jumped as a

347

plane crashed near the cathedral and made the operating-theatre shake. Her uniform was never clean now, her hands never still. When they were at rest there was still the trembling, still the blood, still the boats, the ships leaving without them. Prue cried all through her three hours off one night and Annie held her and told her it would be all right, she would make sure it was, bonny lass. Her headache was too bad to think, her veins stood out on her hands and Prue felt thinner in her arms.

The humid heat dragged at her feet and each new day the injured increased, uniforms were everywhere. Matron sent Prue, Monica and Annie to the cathedral which was taking the overflow and they went from stretcher to stretcher soothing, calming but unable to do much without facilities. A sip, bonny lad, she would say and pour a little water past split and swollen lips.

'How much longer?' groaned Prue as she staggered to her feet and handed a soiled bandage to Annie and then, in February, she had her answer. Malaya was lost and so was Singapore. On 15 February, the surrender was signed and Annie walked amongst the men and wondered what in God's name would become of her patients now, what would become of the women and what had all this been about anyway?

Two days after Valentine's Day, Raffles Place was crowded with British, Australian and Indian troops, heads hung with weary confusion. It was strange not to hear the sound of gunfire.

In the cathedral, dust lay thick on the pews. The stretcher cases continued to arrive and lay inside and outside the building. Smoke still hung over the city. Small Rising Sun flags had appeared overnight and more were hung even as she looked from windows. Japanese staff cars roared past, their klaxons sounding raw in the square, soldiers in small tanks ground their way past. The flame trees still glittered and the breeze still rattled the palm trees and her fear was still stark. The troops were given until the next day to assemble at Changi prison and Annie cried as she remembered the building they had passed with the Andertons. And where were the Andertons now?

Annie and Prue with Monica and their contingent of nurses picked their way back to the nurses' home, packed up what

348

belongings they could carry and returned to find their wounded moving out.

Later it was dark and cool in the cathedral and Annie stood by the altar, watching the sun as it came in through the window and caught the dust which was leaping in its beam, as it had done when she was last in the shed at Gosforn.

She touched the wooden altar rail and thought for a moment she could smell chrysanthemums and feel the coolness of the convent chapel. Prue was kneeling in the front pew and Monica was down at the font. Three other nurses were sitting quietly behind Prue.

Fear was making her breathing difficult and tiredness was making her head feel apart from her body. Her hands were wet and she wanted to cry, to run and hide, go to Georgie and make him hold her and not let them get her but she could hear their feet outside the big doors coming closer and closer and then they were there, framed in the doorway, their bayonets fixed and their language harsh. Annie made herself move from the rail to Prue who would not look up as the Japanese moved down the aisle towards them, their bayonets catching the sun as they passed each window.

'Come on, bonny lass,' she said as she reached down for Prue's hand. 'It's time for us to go.' Her voice was trembling so much she wondered if Prue could understand.

CHAPTER 25

Tom received the letter from Georgie on Monday, when he came in from the pit.

November 1942

India.

Dear Tom,

I was there when the Japs took Rangoon but got away with my platoon and some stragglers. We walked back through the jungle. Thirty started, ten got back.

It was bloody, Tom. Kraits, the shoelace snake, got some of the men and the cobras too. Then there were the Japs, but worst were the flies and the butterflies which ate their bodies. I can't bear butterflies now, they were like a moving tablecloth on my men. It was so hard, lad.

She didn't get out you know. Where is she, Tom? Is she alive? Have you heard anything? Oh God, she must be alive.

I'm back in the Central Provinces. We'll be going back to retake the Burma Road when we're ready. God help us.

Georgie.

Tom replied that night.

February 1943

Dear Georgie,

She'll be all right, bonny lad. Don't you fret. I know she'll be all right. If anyone comes through, it will be her. If I hear, I'll let you know straight away but you concentrate on keeping your head down and staying alive until she comes back.

We're all well here. The rationing is keeping us fit. Don is still at the depot and Maud is living with her ma and da. I'm still in the pits so nothing changes. I'll write again but look after yourself and get through to the end. She'll need you then.

Tom.

Tom told Grace he meant every word he had written about Annie but sometimes in the dark of the night he would clench his fists and be unable to sleep.

The miners had gone on strike as they had threatened and very soon after that the government had agreed to introduce a ballot system to give pitmen a chance to get out of the mines and fight in the services. Reluctantly a minimum wage was also agreed which would enable the miners to have sufficient money to keep up their strength for six working days each week.

Tom liked the boy who was seconded to their team. He was from Surrey and had been to public school and was called Martin St John. He wrote poetry and hummed to himself on the first day as he helped to push the trolley. None of the boys were pleased that their number had been picked and that they were to spend their war as Bevin Boys and the miners thought they would probably be more trouble than they were worth but it was better than their sons automatically taking the pityard walk.

In the summer, Martin kept his head when Tom's uncle stumbled while shovelling the coal into the trolley and had two fingers shorn off at the root when the trolley was pushed forward on to his hand. He'll do, his uncle had said as he was taken to the surface. Production had been good that day.

Martin had been quieter than usual as he and Tom had walked back through the main seam after they had watched the cage screech up the shaft but had retrieved the short putter's shovel and laboured on with no outward sign of disturbance.

The boy had really wanted to go into the air force, Tom had told Grace that evening as they ate Woolton Pie, which they knew as potato and pastry. His back still stung from the scrubbing Grace had given it because she had not seen the graze down the length of it until it was too late.

Tom was too tired to go to the allotment again that night, like so many other nights. His foot and back hurt so much each day that his face was always white and drawn once the coal-dust had been washed away and there was grey hair at his temples. He was 26.

His days were blurred. He rose at four in the morning on six days a week, freezing in winter and still chilled in summer as he walked down past the same terraced houses each day until the seventh when he limped to the allotment with Bob and pulled some carrots or whatever had been coaxed out of the soil and then called in for a watered beer at the pub. Sometimes he and Grace went to Betsy for lunch, sometimes Bob came to them and would tell them of the *Daily Worker* which had been banned for the reportage of the air raids or that attitudes to trade union negotiations would be different after the war because Russia was in on our side and people no longer feared the Bolshevik menace.

As 1943 changed to 1944, he would struggle home and lie on the bed, too tired to paint, too tired to talk politics with Bob, too tired to notice that Grace was dark beneath the eyes and feeling sick. She was four months pregnant before she told him and that was only because a tip and run raid had scored close to their house and the floor had felt as though it was about to tilt them down into rubble and dust. My baby, she had screamed, and he had wanted the bombs to stop for just a minute to grasp what had just been said.

He had then wanted them to stop forever, more than he had done before or for Grace to stop work at the munitions factory and go to the country or to Val's but she would not leave him or her parents. They need the money, she had said, and anyway the raids are very few now. He wished now that he had taken the money that Annie had wanted to give him before she went, but he hadn't, so that was that.

He would look at Grace. Quiet nights and restful days, was that too much to ask, were the thoughts that spun in his head, and he knew that it was. He would turn on the radio and listen to familiar voices while he waited for the fire to take and the kettle to boil. Listening to the news made him feel that they had come through another day and so had the rest of the world.

He kept chickens in the yard, foregoing his dried egg ration in return for some chicken meal so that she had at least one egg every two days and Val gave them eggs and honey when he took Maud and Grace over to Gosforn having managed to get some petrol. Sometimes Don would meet them there when he could arrange leave from the depot and they would sit in the living-room while Val sat in Sarah's chair pouring tea.

Tom would sit back and smooth down the arm covers, listening to the fire as it crackled. They would talk of victory in Africa, the Russians fighting hard and the need for a second front. They talked of days gone by, of the old cock they had eaten last Christmas and how cross Annie would have been to miss it, but he would never let the silence fall, the faces tense, because she was alive, he would say. And coming back. One day she will be back.

In February 1944, he worked on the pit face with a new mechanical cutter which the government had thought would increase production and it looked as though they were right. It also increased the dust and his eyes became raw much earlier and his throat dry as though it had been rubbed with sandpaper. As he worked, he remembered the fair, the hammer you could whack down and ring a bell. He thought of Annie's mother and the legs near the stall and the voice that had destroyed Annie's smile that evening and for so long after. He remembered her father and how he had done much more than remove her smile. That man had bitten as deeply as the cutter was doing and the jagged sore was still there. Tom knew it was there, because Annie hadn't married Georgie.

This week the team was still on the bad seams and he was still crouched and angled while his uncle and Martin shovelled and pushed the trolley back through the dark damp tunnel which was too meandering to install an automatic conveyor.

The owners had planned the route to avoid Squire Turner's

land and the royalties he demanded for mining beneath the surface of his land. And so it was, bugger the workers, Tom cursed, but think of the profits, you bastards. He attacked the coal, his eyes almost shut as the dust exploded into his face while his uncle worked close to him, still one-handed because the pain lingered in his damaged hand. The noise of the cutter tore at his head and he could no longer listen for falling dust or creaking pit-props and it made him anxious. He knew that the coal was there pressing down above him, each day denser somehow. Martin was thin now and no longer hummed and it wasn't just because the machine cloaked all speech; it was because the noise and the dark choked all thought, all the poetry in his head.

His uncle's sinews gleamed with black sweat in the light from Martin's lamp as he pushed the trolley to the end of the tunnel and returned with another that was empty and the lad shovelled again. Henry's hand seemed easier today, his lips were not drawn so thin. Tom eased his back as he looked at them over his shoulder and stopped the cutter; he could taste the dust between his teeth and he was thirsty.

He pointed to the flasks; his hand was still shaking from the vibrations of the cutter and his ears were ringing. He shook his head to clear it as Henry nodded, but the boy continued shovelling for a while longer since he wanted to get this last load done. Tom sank on his haunches. The tea was refreshingly cold and he spat into the darkness where the slag was heaped against the sides. Coal-dust swirled in the beam from their lamps and his uncle squatted next to him while Martin flopped to the ground.

'D'you hear that Ma Gillow's been killed in the black-out? Run over by an ambulance.'

Tom shook his head. 'Bet she didn't read that in the tea leaves.'

'Bet she didn't read that the Yanks would come either,' moaned Martin gloomily.

Tom and Henry laughed and Tom nudged the boy with his boot. 'Don't you worry, your Penelope will stick by you. One look at the muscles you've developed and she'll throw the nylons back at them.'

Martin grinned wanly and Tom felt pity for the lad. Penelope sounded too nice to leave him in the lurch and he said so.

Martin looked up. 'Anyway, it'll soon be over, won't it, and then we can all go home.' His voice sounded weary. 'Now Italy's given in and there was Alamein in '42, it's got to be over soon.'

'There speaks the sweet bird of youth,' yawned Tom. '1944 and it's all over, is it? We shall see, my brave young poet, but in the meantime let's be getting on with this here.' But they stayed sitting for a while longer, listening to the sounds of the mine, thinking their own thoughts until Tom finally made a move.

'How's Grace?' asked his uncle as they scrambled to their feet.

'Due next month,' said Tom and suddenly felt impatient to be out of the blackness and up with her as she rested after lunch, now that she had finished work in the factory. He loved to crouch by the chair, his hand across her swollen belly feeling the baby kick and then he would stroke her full breasts with their blue veins and want her and she would pull him to her.

'Come on, let's get on with it,' he ground out as he hauled himself back into the narrow space.

His uncle winked at Martin. 'Wants a big load today, aiming to wet the baby's head with champagne.' But the noise of the cutter drowned out Martin's reply and the creak from the pit-props, the warning fall of dust. Henry just felt a blast of air and was knocked off his feet as the trolley shifted beneath the rushing air and coal which roared down and spilled outwards towards his feet. It settled as he lurched back against the side, coughing in the flurry of grit and the smell of raw angry coal.

It was minutes before he could find his breath and move, before he could tear with his hands at the pile of blackness. His Tom was in there and he couldn't hear a bloody thing. He had called, he told the first rescuers but there had been no answer from Tom or the lad, no tapping, no nothing.

His head was ringing from the waves of noise that had come with the fall and his stumps were bleeding on to the ground and he welcomed the throb of pain since it made him think of something other than the two who had been with him just a moment before. His foot kicked Tom's bait-tin and he shoved it back into the slag.

The rescue team were working methodically now, passing the coal back then listening for a tap or a cry but there was still

355

nothing. He moved in to find a space to work but was gently turned away to one side.

'Stay over there then, Henry, we'll get at them quicker this way.' A trolley was shoved passed him, taking the first load back and out of the way.

And then the overman was there, edging along, bowed over, irritated at the lost production. He stood next to Henry, his mouth pursed.

'No point in setting up the siren if there's only two men involved.'

The man at the rear turned, blocking Henry's fist as he swung.

'No, don't waste your bleeding siren, any more than you waste your bleeding pit-props. Not enough props, not enough rest and you expect more bloody coal.' The man spat at the ground. 'This is the second accident today.' His headlamp caught the overman in its beam, his face was too black to distinguish any features. 'Aye, save your bloody siren, man. You should be sick of yourself and them out there. How many deaths, how many legs, hands, feet do you want?'

'Leave it out, man,' called the leader, his voice strained from wrenching and heaving his pick. The miner stared and Henry moved in closer until the overman backed away. Then they both ignored him as the struggle continued well into the night.

Grace knew it had happened when Tom was not home and the bath water was getting cold by the kitchen fire. She pulled her coat around her and would have run to Betsy's but she could only walk with her hands holding her laden body.

Betsy was at the kitchen window and saw Grace come in past Beauty's stable and when she did not stop to hand in a quartered apple she felt her mouth go dry and she turned to Joe. 'It's my bairn Joe, it's my Tom.'

He put her coat around her and took each of the women by the arm, making them walk at a gentle pace, for it had snowed during the day and was slippery.

It was so quiet, thought Betsy, with the snow. There was no sound of striking boots, no wind to buffet them as they passed the alleys. It was a clear night and the stars and the moon were sharp and she felt as though she could reach out and draw them to her.

As they walked down the hill, she could see the men clustered round the pit-head. More women were coming out of their houses now, their shawls drawn round their heads and no words were spoken as they slipped in the gates to the head. There were no lights because of the black-out but the moon was so bright and the snow so fresh it did not matter. Joe forced his way through to the Manager's Office and shouted above the clamour of women's voices as they called to find out who it was that was trapped.

'Tom Ryan and Martin St John,' Betsy heard and held on to Grace as she moved to run to the cage. She was moaning and pulling from Betsy, her face drawn apart with anguish and Betsy saw May and together they held her back and Bet stroked her hair as Grace said, again and again, 'He should never have been a pitman, he should have been painting. He should have been painting.' And she was screaming now, her mouth stretched wide as though it would tear across her face. Betsy held her close, her arms tight around the girl.

'There now, hinny, he'll be all right. The lad'll be all right.' She looked up at the sky and couldn't see the stars and moon because of the blur in her eyes and hadn't realised until then that her own pain had turned into tears.

They waited by the office. Grace would not go in but stood shivering in the cold and Betsy chafed first her hands, then her arms and kept it up until Grace jacked over and her labour began. Bob was here by now, standing quietly with Joe, his face calm but his eyes watching every movement of the cage, every change of rescue team.

An ambulance came for Grace and Betsy went with her but she wanted to stay to wait for her son.

It was late that night when the team reached them. The air was fetid behind the coal wall and Tom was half buried. He had been unable to call because of the weight across his chest and had lain there in the pitch-dark, his fear catching him and the cold seeping into every part of him. I hate you, I hate you he had sworn with every breath at the coal which hung above him. It creaked and groaned and tormented him with its hanging weight. He couldn't see or hear Martin or Henry but they would be on the other side, clawing at the fall as the rescuers were.

As the pain in his foot increased and the cold made his kidney grip and send him into fever he looked at the girl who came running across the beck towards him, her hair kinked by overnight plaits, as he sat in the water on a summer's day. Annie, Annie, his mind called and she laughed and said, 'Hang on, bonny lad, I'll come for you. Just hang on, Tom,' and so he did.

It was late that night when they reached him. Martin was dead and looked as Davy had done, with blood from his nose and ears and mouth. He was never going home again.

Tom went to the hospital and was washed and his leg was set. His ribs were bruised but not broken. He thought she was Annie until his fever subsided and the nurse was blonde with blue eyes and then he wept.

Grace had a baby one hour after Tom was sent into surgery and she called him Robert.

Bob sat with Tom while he lay in traction the next day and plumped his pillows and poured him lemon barley-water.

'This is getting to be a habit, lad.'

Tom turned and looked at him. 'Poor little bugger, poor Penelope.' He could say no more for minutes, then, 'Thank God, Grace is fine. He's a bonny lad, is our wee Bobby then?'

Bob nodded, his face breaking into a smile, his eyes shadowed and dark through lack of sleep. There had been air raids the night before and plaster from the ceiling lay in the corner. He moved over and picked it up, throwing it into the bin before he sat down again.

'You'll take the checker job I got you, lad.' It was not a question but a statement and Tom nodded. He'd been offered the surface job in '42 but he had not taken it because he had to trade off for Annie's survival.

'Aye, Bob, I'll take that now. She'll be coming back, will our Annie. I know she will.'

CHAPTER 26

So far during this roll-call, there had been no beatings. The numbers though still did not tally with this morning but then they could not, could they? Annie's hands hung open by her side, still raw from digging three shallow graves which would receive rigid bodies but no coffins. The gods had not been smiling, had they, for there were no boxes of adequate length yet again.

Sweat dripped slowly from her bowed head on to the dusty earth, enlarging the already darkened patch and in the submissive silence her hair hung limp, her neck was raw and she felt and saw her feet swell and crack in the pounding heat. Feet really should have shoes, she thought. Shoes as clean as Sister Maria had always ordered for chapel. But not too shiny, Tom had laughed. Yes, she heard his laugh deep inside her head and she grinned in spite of sun-tightened lips. You'll never improve if you don't obey rules, she had been ordered to chant after one service, head bowed over dull shoes, breath visible in the autumnal cold of the conservatory.

She eased her neck as much as she dared. Her hands were throbbing now and one foot was hidden by the collapsed body of Prue. How strange, she thought, I hadn't noticed. She felt no pity, just relief for its shelter since Prue was no great weight any more. Cold, she pondered, daytime cold was quite beyond imagination and as for rebellion, that seemed merely a way of sapping energy already drained and wrung out like the sparse rice around which their lives revolved.

Would you be proud of me now, Sister Maria? Would you write home to Sarah that I was a credit to myself, the school and my guardian as you did at the end of my first year? Don't you worry though, I shall revive my friend as I did yesterday and she for me the day before but I can't promise for tomorrow

359

because she is a little under the weather, dear Sister Maria and your God seems to be busy elsewhere. Perhaps you could write on his report: Could do better if he tried?

She listened to the count of the Japanese guard begin again. She did not dare to flick at the flies that were crawling over her lips and eyes for she would be beaten if she was seen.

'Ichi, ni, san, yong.'

One, two, three, four, she echoed in her head. Look at me now, Sarah. I'm learning a new language, experiencing new things, or isn't this quite what you meant? God all bloody mighty, how much longer would this go on, the stupid fool has been told by the doctor that three died before lunch so, unless there's been a few immaculate conceptions since then, how could the numbers bloody well tally?

They always did this before a move, dragged them out into the compound three times a day instead of the morning and evening delight. Was it their way of saying sweet farewell she wondered? Along her row, a child cried out and was quickly muffled. She felt the tension that the noise created ease as the guard continued his walk, his boots clumping and throwing dust into the cracks which meandered in the baked ground. At her da's allotment, ants had wriggled in and out of the summer-dried cracks that she had thought led to Australia; deep down and out of the other end. She must tell the doctor about that. How would she like her home town to be at the end of a Wassingham crack?

She lifted her head slightly to ease the stiffness. He was in the row behind now and the commandant still stood rigid on his platform, pale lavender gloves immaculate, eyes straight ahead as though he found them too distasteful to set eyes upon. Likewise, you bugger, Annie thought. The guard was returning now to the front and then it was over. They were dismissed.

She and Monica grasped Prue beneath the armpits and dragged her back to their hut, her heels bumping and kicking up clouds. Annie tightened her grip because Prue was slippery with sweat. They propped her up on the verandah against the wall of the hut. Monica was on duty at the hospital hut and wiped her arm across her face, pulled down the hat she had made from a pair of old shorts.

'All right then, Annie, I'll be off.' Annie nodded and reached for the old tin can which held the water that she and Prue had earlier strained through muslin before the heat of the day had really begun to bite. There were always a few worms left wriggling in spite of the filtering and she dipped her fingers into the brackish water and scooped out the two that she could see, squeezing them between her thumb and finger before grinding them beneath her clompers. Her skin crawled; she hated them.

'Here, hinny, take this.' She held Pruscilla against her and trickled some water into her mouth and over her breasts to take the heat out. She poured some on to her own hand and dabbed at Prue's forehead, then waved the fan she had made from *atap*. She had split the bamboo and folded palm leaves round it, then fastened this together with pieces of *rotan*. It was a small copy of the tiles they had made to roof their huts when they arrived at their first camp after the march from Singapore. Nearly three years ago now, she mused, as she rubbed Prue's hands then resumed her fanning, which made a welcome breeze. Dr Jones had asked her to make more for the hospital hut and it had kept her busy during the first long weeks of their internment when they did not know whether they were to be killed like the people they had seen as they passed a village. Weaving the *rotan*, pushing it down and threading back again, helped her not to wonder about death, about where they were, not wonder how long the war would take to end and who would win when that happened and if Georgie was still alive.

They had been marched for two weeks after leaving Singapore. At first they'd been able to buy food from the natives in the kampongs but soon their money had run out and they lived on rice that the Japanese dug out of sacks and handed them, glutinous and stinking. They had stumbled and dragged one another along and been kicked when they fell and when they cried; killed when they would not bow their heads. Two elderly women had died like that, not shot but bayonetted. The children had been made to watch and had become quiet and Annie had sold Don's watch to the headman of a village for four chickens and that night they had cooked them and the children had eaten a piece each and had walked better the next day.

Natives had stoned them at one village, stoned the memsahibs and Mavis Anderton had cried then and said that nothing would ever be the same again.

The hardship had not been as difficult for her as for most of the others. She had thought of Albert and Wassingham and

361

told herself that she had always liked the heat and she should be grateful for that at least. It was different for Prue.

Annie shifted Prue's weight on her shoulder. 'Come on lass,' she murmured. 'Three years in the camps and you've still got a bunka wallah fanning you so open those eyes and throw me a rupee.'

She eased her back. There was no one in the hut with its moist panting heat; they were outside as she was, sitting in the shade or hoeing the vegetable patch; teaching the surviving children over in the hut by the commandant's office. Annie stroked Prue's hair.

'Come on, my wee lass,' she whispered. 'Don't give up now, don't leave me here on my own.' Louder she said, 'One of the Dutch has some peroxide, we need most of it for the hospital but I've earned enough with the washing I did for Van Eydon to dye that streak in front. Give old bandy legs a thrill, eh, make him faint on parade for a change.'

She felt a stir from the girl and smiled as Prue slowly straightened.

'That, darling, is quite the best idea you've had in a long time.' It was faint but it was good.

'What a vain bitch you are,' Annie laughed. 'I'll tell you one thing. We must write to the girls in Oxford, when this is all over, and tell them they've lost their bet. There is a new slimline you with a fetching streak in your fringe as well.'

Prue pushed herself from Annie and sat up against the wall. Her eyes were dull and heavy-lidded and she had a sore at the corner of her mouth. 'This will never be over, it's nearly three years now and we won't be alive much longer. It's too hard and not worth the effort.' Her head sagged on to her chest and Annie scrambled to her knees. A pebble cut into her leg, then scraped her ulcer as she shoved it to one side. The pain made her feel sick.

She took Prue's chin in her hand but she would not lift her head, so she took her hair and gently pulled until she could see her face, then shook her until she opened her eyes.

'We'll survive and it will be over. Lorna told us that "D" Day happened in June, you remember? They'll come for us, you see. Just hang on, Prue. We must hang on. There's India waiting for you and your da. Think of your da. How would he feel if you left

362

him alone?' Prue's eyes were closing again and Annie took her chin in her hands, smoothed back the hair from her face.

'What about me if you let go? Who's going to drive me mad, keep me going? What would Georgie say if you let me die, because you weren't here any more?'

Prue's eyes were open again now, but her mouth was slack with weariness. She was worn out with dysentery and malnutrition like them all but there was no way this girl was going to die. She was too young and it would be a waste, as Sarah would have said. And Annie would miss her too much.

'We'll survive,' she said through gritted teeth. 'If it bloody well kills me, we'll survive.' And suddenly Prue's eyes were not dull any more but alive with laughter, and Annie grinned, her body limp with relief. She rose, then dusted off her knees and entered the dark heat of the hut to fetch the scissors.

She cut Prue's hair as she had been asking all week and told her she looked like Veronica Lake but piebald. Monica called then from the hospital hut next to them and Annie patted Prue's shoulder, feeling her bones through her flesh.

'Tea-break over.' She picked up the tin can and checked that some water remained. 'Take a bit. It's clear of worms. Just stay in the shade and I'll do your shift.'

They had built the hospital hut large enough to take twenty patients and it was always full. She went from bed to bed with the doctor, checking pulses and bathing foreheads, easing discomfort if possible.

At five she had supper, the last meal before the long night. The rice grain had been spread and sorted all through the day, she had seen the team busy over by the kitchen hut. There were a few vegetable scraps today which was good but nonetheless her throat closed as it did now against the meal which had not varied since they had been interned. She pushed rice deep into her mouth with her fingers, forcing herself to swallow.

Monica was sitting next to her. 'Prue all right now?'

Annie nodded. 'I saw her come across for first sitting earlier so she's eating anyway.'

It was dusk outside. It had come quickly as it always did and the evening felt cooler after the heat of the day but still sticky and Annie walked back to their hut while Monica went over to the Dutch to cut hair for cigarettes.

Prue was waiting on the verandah, propped against a

363

doorpost, her eyes half-closed, her mosquito-net pulled about her. She smiled as Annie sat down next to her and took the blanket that she passed, wearing it as the pit women wore their shawls only this was for protection against mosquitoes, not the cold. There were groups of women all along the verandah talking in low voices, and in the huts. She took a piece of bible paper from her pocket and rolled it round the shredded leaves they had dried in the sun during the day. Pruscilla hugged her knees.

'Feeling better?' Annie asked as she put the cigarette in her mouth and lit it. She had packed the leaves tightly so that they would burn slowly. Prue nodded.

'I don't fancy the idea of the move tomorrow,' she said.

Annie drew in the smoke. 'I'm 30 tomorrow and don't feel like that kind of a party either. Don't worry though, you'll be feeling better by then.' She swatted at a mosquito that buzzed close to her. It was never silent here; there was always the noise of the jungle, the murmur of insects. She had seen the flash of colour as butterflies wove in and out of the undergrowth around the camp and she had thought how Georgie would love it. Then there were the moans and restless turning of the patients which they could hear easily from here and the children who cried out in the dark, especially those who no longer had a mother living. One hundred human beings here now she reckoned, minus three of course. No wonder there was always noise.

Prue reached in under her net and held out her hand to Annie. 'If we hadn't been on the move tomorrow, I would have given you this in the morning. But since you're 21 again I thought I'd push the boat out for you.'

There was a chilli in her hand. 'More precious than bloody gold,' breathed Annie. 'All those vitamins.' She fingered its shiny smoothness and leant back against the hut.

'Thanks, bonny lass. The best present I've ever had. We'll have a party when we arrive. Chilli con carne but without the con carne.' She paused. 'Do you remember the strawberries and salmon, Prue, and how we thought it would last until the end of time? We were wrong and Georgie was right.'

'I know and I said some things I should never have said to you then, about you and Georgie. I've always wanted to say I was sorry.' Prue's face was in shadow. They were talking quietly as everyone was doing in these moments before they crawled on to their beds.

Annie drew on the last of her cigarette, feeling the heat near her fingertips. 'I don't remember you saying anything,' she replied, but she did, every word and suddenly she could not wait to be on her pallet and able to think of him. Of the coldness of the beach as they had lain together the first time, of the feel of his skin, the scars that ridged down his back, of his arms as they held her and of later, when they met again and loved again. This is what she thought of each night, what she saved up through the day using it as a prize which beckoned her on through every hour. Georgie kept her sane, kept her alive. That was how she thought of Georgie and all the questions were kept in that little black box in her mind where dark things belonged.

On the third day of the march, it rained and Annie's clompers stuck in the mud with each dragging step, wrenching her toes and rubbing further raw patches. It swept over struggling bodies as they toiled along the tracks which seemed to lead nowhere. It was still hot, in spite of the rain, and the humidity sucked away their strength. Four died on that day, and a child. The guards threw the bodies into the swamp and would not allow time for burial.

Annie watched Monica's back and counted to fifty and then again and again. They kept in step because it helped them to keep going and made the stretcher they carried less bumpy for the patient who was bloated with beri beri and should not last the night, or so the doctor thought.

The camp was reached on the seventh day at noon and the woman only died when they laid her down inside the wire. Annie's hands were bleeding and her shoulders felt as though hot wires were strung from shoulder to shoulder.

The doctor organised the burials and explained that the smell which was strong was latex and that this was a work-camp. The rubber plantation was all around.

'There'll be more work for us, more injuries to the women Sisters,' the doctor said, her face drawn and looking older than her 40 years. Her auburn hair was now almost completely white though she had once been a beautiful woman. 'Now come on over, we're to be addressed by the commandant.'

He spoke through an interpreter while the rain beat down

and it dripped down Annie's bowed neck and face and off the end of her nose.

'Nippon number one,' he said. 'And the war finish in one hundred years. You work well, you be treated well. Remember that.'

They stood up straight as he picked his way through the mud to his car and roared away, klaxon sounding.

'Thank you and goodnight,' murmured Prue as she walked painfully with Annie over to the hospital hut. Their legs were trembling and so were their arms. The bamboo slats laid down for mattresses glittered with bugs which scattered and scuttled across and down the cracks where each cane met the other, so when the rain had ceased they lit fires with a lighter made of plaited cotton dipped in coconut oil and a flint. Annie felt the heat as they passed the slats quickly through but they knew that still some would survive and that the night for the patients would be one of torment as the bugs bit and the smell of bad burnt almonds rose as they tossed and crushed, and not just for the patients of course.

There was more rain again the next day and it poured through the *atap* tiles which were too few to create a proper roof on the bamboo huts. They had to move the patients so that rain dripped only on their bodies not their faces. Then they heard shouting in the compound and a woman's screams, loud and long and despairing. Annie felt cold rush through her body.

Guards burst through into their huts then, their boots clumping and kicking at the platforms, tipping patients on to the floor, emptying out the doctor's bag where they kept what little medicine they had, smashing bottles with their rifle butts. Her mouth went dry. She should stop this but she was too afraid. The guards came towards them, their bayonets fixed, their faces bulging with rage, words spitting from their mouths.

They were pushed, patients and nurses, out of the doorway. Prue stumbled and Annie caught her and held her upright as they were slapped down the steps. She turned and helped two patients and Prue took another across the compound to where the other prisoners were waiting in silence in three long rows. They were not to bow their head, the interpreter said. They were to watch what happened to those who disobeyed.

Lorna Briggs's radio had been found. She was 24, still with her Scots accent and covered in freckles from the heat of

Malaya. Now she was beheaded quite silently in the centre of the compound and the blood that shot two yards was washed away in the deluge before it had settled.

And Annie drew in her head beige and pink flowers, any sort of flowers that might do for wallpaper, for curtains, as she had done before in the camps when her friends had been swatted and destroyed and she had been unable to bear it. Why not have matching lampshades and crockery? While the rain sheeted down and they all stood there she closed her mind to the pain, the body and the blood, pushing it into that black box at the back of her head.

Later she rolled her cigarette on the verandah with Prue and they listened to the cicada and she thought of Sarah's house, her house now and decided she would start with the bedroom. Tom could help. They would design that first, see how it worked before they went into production. Yes, they would do that and now she must think of a design, a design that would keep today out of her thoughts tonight. She drew on the cigarette and lit Prue's from the stub.

Not lush flowers but small gentle pink and beige with an indefinite outline for wallpaper and larger flowers for the bedspread and the curtains. Slowly she cut, pasted and papered the bedroom up to the picture rail and brought soft beige emulsion across the ceiling and down to meet the paper. The lighting was a problem and she turned to Prue.

'Right,' she challenged. 'I've decided on the wallpaper and curtains, the bedspread too, but what about lighting?'

Prue flicked away her cigarette stub into the compound and it was doused by the rain before it hit the ground.

'Is this your business idea you're on about?' she asked, smiling slightly.

And Annie nodded. It always worked and made them turn from the present when it became too cruel.

'Yes, but first I've decided to do the house and I'm stuck on the light fitting.' Their voices weren't quite right yet but by the end of the long night they were sounding normal and they had not had to bother with the agony of sleep.

It took weeks of arguing through their off-duty hours while they discarded Prue's chandelier and Annie's ruche material but finally Annie decided on a glass bowl with bamboo etched on as a centre light with duplicated bedside lamps.

The monsoons were over and it was not quite so humid though the latex still permeated every corner. 'How can you want anything that reminds you of this place? You're inhuman,' Prue flung at her as they scooped Mrs Glanville's ulcer. 'Bamboos, how can you choose bamboos?'

'Come on, Prue,' retorted Annie as she dropped the final swab into the tin that Prue was holding. 'Just because we're in the wrong place at the wrong time doesn't mean that ugliness is everywhere; the flame trees still flame and the sun still sets.'

'It does that,' said Mrs Glanville. 'Right over good old Blighty.'

They both stopped glaring at one another and turned to the emaciated woman who lay beneath an old torn sheet. Annie ran her hands down her torn, dirty uniform and looked at Prue's which was the same.

She laughed then. 'None of that talk, Mrs Glanville, or I'll have to talk with the doctor,' she scolded, 'and then there'll be no more grapes at visiting time.' She took the woman's pulse and touched her cheek and was glad that she also smiled. They moved on to the next patient.

'God, my legs,' Prue groaned. Their periods had stopped long ago along with most of the women and their legs had swollen and permanently throbbed but whether it was as a result of this or just the diet and the work no one really knew.

Not exactly the place for research the doctor had said as they had talked it over in the early days of their captivity. She had worked in a children's hospital in Sydney and had come to Singapore in 1939.

Annie stood with Prue at the side of the beri-beri case who was dropsical and exhausted.

'The doctor has asked Cricket Chops for some Vitamin B again but he made her wait two hours in the sun, then sent her back speedo to look after the sick she was neglecting. Without the vitamins of course. No red cross parcels again, he said.' Annie was angry as they moved away to sit at the end of the hut until they made another round in half an hour.

'Did you do Van Weidens's washing?' Annie asked.

'Only half before roll-call. Can you finish when you get off?'

Annie nodded. 'It might buy us a banana from the guard, but don't for God's sake try with the big one. He belted Monica last week and took her money anyway.'

Prue raised her eyebrows. 'Sounds pretty par for the course. Anyway, Annie, you really can't have that glass bowl. It's unpatriotic.' She was looking down the hut towards the other door which corresponded with the one behind them. There was sometimes a slight draught but not today.

Annie picked up the fan from the desk and rose.

'Well, I'm going to anyway. I like the lines of the bamboo. Tom would too.'

She stood waiting for Prue to join her in fanning the patients and she did pull herself to her feet but would not look at Annie as she started alone for the first bed.

'Then you'll have to sort out your own damn sitting-room, because that's next on your list isn't it, darling. I want no part of it.' Her voice was full of bitterness.

Annie turned her back on her friend and tried to decide on colours for Sarah's room as her stomach tightened. These rows were breaking out all over the camp as people became as taut as over-stretched elastic about to snap. She soothed Mrs Glanville then moved to the next bed, fanning the woman who lay unconscious on the pallet. Annie wondered if the sitting-room was always empty now or whether the boys were there from time to time to see Val and had anyone heard from Georgie? She knew from the radio – she would not think of Lorna, just the radio – that Rangoon had fallen long ago but that did not mean he was dead. She must not think of him being dead. That would make it impossible to live. So she thought instead of Tom reading letters from Georgie, sitting by the fire with Maud and Grace and Don, eating hot buttered toast while Val poured tea. Were the girls pregnant yet, she wondered? Was Tom safe in the pits and Don in his supply depot? But she would not think of these questions, only of scenes; of people sitting as they had always done; of Georgie watching the sun setting over the lakes and the ducks against the sky.

A patient called and she moved towards the bed. Her hair hung limp and irritated her neck; she'd have to cut it again although Georgie liked it long. She rubbed the back of her hand across her forehead.

'Nurse, go and wash that hand. Septicaemia we definitely do not want.' The doctor was watching her from the end of the hut, then stooped again to her patient.

Annie stood still, her legs trembling as she saw again the

varicosed veins at the fair, so vividly that she was startled. She washed at the basin and wondered whether plain white paper would suit the sitting-room.

At lunch Prue sat on the Dutch table and did not look up as Annie came in, so she sat with Mavis Anderton who smiled. Her face was drawn and her teeth had rotted into black stumps; her hair was quite white and cut very short.

'Had a row, my dear?'

Annie murmured. 'It's the heat, it gets us all down.' She felt so tired today, even more so than she had done yesterday but not inside her head, not where she planned the sitting-room and, when that was finished, there was the kitchen and then the greenhouse to plant out.

'Wallpaper can be so dull, can't it?' she said as she swallowed the last of her rice. A piece fell on to the *atap* table and was lost between the weave. The women either side of her stopped eating. Mavis shoved her fingers in her mouth and sucked hungrily at the rice water while her eyebrows lifted. Monica looked round at the walls of the hut.

'Yes, I have to agree, palm and bamboo do become a trifle tedious. Let in the the draught too.' Mavis waved her hands to the walls. 'Should we complain to the management, do you think?' The whole table was laughing now and Annie glanced at Prue but she had turned her back to them and was busy eating.

'What are you up to now, Annie?' someone called from another table. More rice was pushed into open mouths again.

'Just thinking of doing up my house when I get back.' And that sounded good.

'You'll use your own firm, will you, the one you keep talking about?' Mavis was wiping her mouth with the back of her hand.

'I thought so, my brother and I together.' The sound of running feet broke into the conversation.

Camp leader stood panting in the doorway, holding on to the frame. 'Roll-call, *tenko*, quickly now everyone.' Her hair was falling over her face and she flicked it aside with an impatient hand. The women pushed the remains of the rice into their mouths as they ran towards the door knocking over stools in their haste. Mavis was in front of Annie and gripped the leader's arm. 'Not another Lorna, is it?'

'No,' she gasped, still trying to catch her breath. 'They've decided on three a day that's all, but they're creating merry hell anyway.' Then she ran back to the compound past Annie who had begun to run to the hospital. There would be a beating if they were late but she was on duty and needed for the stretcher-cases. She pushed through the running women and struggled up the steps. She could not run for more than a few paces now, she was just too tired and the heat was beating on her head. Oh God, she'd left her hat in the dining-hut.

The doctor was just leaving. 'It's all right, Sister, stretcher-cases can remain inside today. For God's sake, hurry. He's in a rage, just look at him stamping.' The doctor took her arm and they stumbled down the steps and ran again for parade. The others were already lined up and bowing and Dr Jones's hand tightened on her arm and Annie felt her bowels loosen with fear.

They reached the lines and bowed and barely breathed as feet slopped along in boots which seemed too large always and had to be held on with binding. It was frayed Annie saw and the boots were dirty and scuffed up small clouds of dust as they approached and stopped. The blow knocked her across the doctor on to the ground and the sand was gritty in her mouth, blood trickled from the corner; she lay motionless.

'You come speedo, you bad woman.' The boot kicked and hands dragged her upright and Annie felt the stickiness of his spit as words were hurled. 'You stand here all day. Look at sun, all day.'

Her face was rigid with animal fear, she felt urine escape and stain her shorts. The bamboo caught her across her midriff cutting into the flesh where her uniform was torn. She was silent. It struck across her hands and she screamed and though her eyes were open she could see no faces and then they filed away as the pain covered her.

'Ichi, ni, san, yong,' kept leaping and snarling in amongst the pain which coiled tight now around her broken finger. The guard smelt and beige roses merged into glaring white suns which wrung the sweat from her body. Her tongue grew large in her mouth, her lips cracked and burst and her throat was too swollen to swallow.

'Look at sun.' The guard kicked and turned her body, but her eyes stayed shut and he could not force them open. She fell and large boots kicked her up. She partially opened her eyes and fixed them on the tear in his trousers, then the verandah in the distance and then at Prue standing on the steps and she did not fall again.

'Chin up, darling.'

Not bloody likely, sang her mind, and dehydration wrung her miles away and she heard the wind on the dunes and felt the sharp sting of the sand and the waves as they rushed and swirled and she felt his hands and drank his tears. Look at the boots, she thought, look at the huts. What can I put on the white curtains? And finally dusk came and Prue and Monica carried her to her bed, away from the mumbles of the hospital. They pushed her in from the end of the pallet since there was no space between the platforms. Prue slowly poured a little tepid water into her half-open mouth and Monica held a soaking cloth to her head and the doctor strapped her hand.

'That'll teach you to be late, you silly clot,' Prue said and pressed her hand to Annie's cheek. 'For God's sake, I'll get you there on time if I have to drag you tomorrow.'

Annie spoke and Prue leant close.

'Glass bowl with bamboo, OK.'

During the next five months Annie finished all the bedrooms and the sitting-room and her finger was beginning not to hurt and her eyes to see clearly again. One Monday in June, the guards issued postcards and Prue had the only pencil in the hut. It was short and an HB which smudged in their sweat-drenched hands. They filled in the blanks. 'I am quite . . . . ., what should we put?' asked Annie.

'Quite well, if you value your other hand,' responded Prue. So she did. Flies were crawling over her face and the corners of her mouth. She was too tired to move them, only to have them resettle in the next breath.

'I'm sending mine to Daddy. What about you Annie?'

Annie had been looking at the work-party breaking up dried lumps of soil with emaciated fingers, shorts stained with dysentery. It seemed a betrayal to name a survivor for surely, if she pointed a finger, God would find them and they would be killed. Georgie or Tom or Don, who should she send it to?

She watched as the working women fingered the small segments to dust and moved, crouching, along the line to bang another large piece on to rock-hard ground, then again and again. Vegetables were to be growing for the 1945 September inspection, so they would be showing if they wanted to live. It was her turn tomorrow when she had finished her duty.

'I'll send it to Georgie,' she challenged. 'He'll think I've turned senile looking at this writing though.' Her hands had shaken since the beating. They were improving but not much.

Doctor Jones came out on to the verandah and looked down at them. Her face was set and she held her finger to her lips.

'Number three bed has diphtheria,' she whispered, and Annie broke out in a rush of sweat as she scrambled to her feet, pulling Prue.

Doctor Jones stood with her hand in the pockets of her linen coat. 'It could go round the camp like wildfire. Absolute rest for her and isolation; my room at the end.' She walked out into the heat of the square. 'I'm going to see the commandant. They don't like epidemics in case they catch it. Perhaps we'll get some disinfectant from the old devil.'

She turned. 'Write her postcard for her Annie please and we'll steam her pallet when I get back. For now, strain her water through the last of the disinfectant. The two beri-beri cases are in the last stages. Both of you pretend to write their cards please.'

The disinfectant came while they were dragging the large oilcan from the cookhouse to the bricks which the commandant had given them for the sterilization of the bedding. Their legs shook but the can had to be back for lunch and they could not bear the thought of the mid-day sun as they worked. They worked up the fire inside the bricks and boiled up the can; the steam began to rise and they stood either side on old buckets and held the pallet over the top. The steam billowed out at their faces and their hands and Annie's arms shook and her hand ached.

'Frightfully good for the pores, darling,' breathed Prue. Finally it was done. They damped the fire with earth and tipped the water out of the can before stumbling back to the cookhouse balancing the pallet on the top of the can.

As they placed it down there was a shudder and Annie staggered slightly, grabbing at the verandah for support but that was shaking also. There was another shudder and a distant rumble and Annie remembered the tiled floor in the nurses' home and the crash of falling bombs, searchlights which stabbed the sky and knew that it was here again.

'Air raid, Prue. It's a damned air raid.' The doctor was calling them back to the hut and they ran with the pallet, past guards whose neckcloths flapped as they rushed across to the prisoners and herded them inside, standing guard outside the closed doors.

The hospital door was also slammed shut and in the dark they each went from bed to bed soothing until Doctor Jones sent Prue into the diphtheria case and Monica to the two with beri-beri.

'It's the allied planes,' Annie soothed as she passed between patients. 'Yes, it must be getting near the end.'

Near the bloody end, she sang to herself. Can it really be near the end? Was there still a world out there beyond the wire and, if so, would their guards let them live to see it?

The guards pinned up black-outs and the beatings became more savage and Annie's finger was broken again. Prue had a bad sore throat and couldn't eat her rice. It was diphtheria.

Annie nursed her in the doctor's room, swabbing and sponging, straining the water until she could smell nothing but disinfectant, but still the disease ravished what little was left of Prue's body. For weeks the bombs came but never hit the camp. The ground shuddered, not every day or night but enough to make the guards more cruel and the women more frightened, for now they all asked the question; would they be allowed to live if Japan was defeated? Long into the night Annie sat and held Prue's hand and somehow she lived but lost her mind and sat winding her hair round and round her middle finger and smiling and doing as she was asked but only for Annie.

Annie cut her hair and streaked the fringe and took her to *tenko* and made her bow when she should and stand when she should so she was not beaten. She made her eat her rice but Prue whimpered unless the rabbit was made to find its hole.

'She could pick up, Annie,' the doctor told her as they wound the bandages in the evenings. The smell of the coconut oil lamp was not unpleasant. It was the same as it had been for three and a half years and perhaps it kept the mosquitoes away.

'It's not exactly a world anyone in their right mind would rush back to, is it?' Annie replied. 'So perhaps she is the only sane person here.' She put her hands on the table; they were trembling badly again. 'Do you think the Allies will ever come and, if they do, will we be alive to see them?'

Doctor Jones patted her hand. 'I don't know. Sometimes I dare to hope that we'll survive but at others . . . ' She shrugged. 'I just don't understand these people.'

'At least they've broken the sahibs' rule, haven't they? They've pricked the bubble now. We've been coolies too and we bleed like the Malays do. We've spoilt it for the ladies who danced at Raffles, spoilt their image haven't we?'

'Perhaps not before time?' the doctor murmured and Annie was surprised.

'I worked in Liverpool in the thirties, before I went back to Sydney. Those bloated little bellies were not so very different to these in the camp.'

They sat in silence for a while. Moths flew at the flame and one was caught.

'Will you go back to England or Australia?' Annie asked.

'I'm not sure yet. What about you?'

'I have a house and I'm going to decorate it but I want the sea as well. I want to walk by the sea again where the wind can clean me and my eyes can stretch forever. I want to run my business and to live with Georgie.' She said it quietly, rolling the bandages again, feeling the creases and smoothing them out.

'In that order?' the doctor asked.

Annie could not answer.

CHAPTER 27

Bob and Tom sank yet another beer. It was still watered down but it tasted like ambrosia and, bugger me, thought Tom, if I don't feel like a bloody God. VE day had been grand with lights blazing from windows out into the streets for the first time in years but this was even better.

'July 5th and Labour's in.' Tom drummed his fingers on the table. 'Hitler would turn in his bunker if he knew, eh Bob. Socialism in England when he wanted to kill 'em all. Bye, makes you feel grand doesn't it, man?'

Bob chuckled. 'Aye lad, it does, that it does. No depression after this war and if there is, no one will starve anyway.' The pub was full of men, sun streamed in through windows and there were banners on all the sills.

'Have another drink, Bob.' Tom wiped his mouth with his hand. 'A toast to Clem Attlee, eh, and how about one for Wainwright, wherever he may be.'

Bob laughed 'We've had enough, Tom. Let's get back to see Bobby before Grace takes him to bed.'

Tom sprang to his feet, his face breaking into a grin. He shoved his change into his pocket. 'It's all been worth it then, Bob. War's over and Labour's in and Don's bloody livid.' He showed Bob Don's postcard. He would be demobbed by August.

The pub had filled since they came in and they pushed their way through the groups of excited miners, slapping backs and grinning, until they reached the door. The sun was still hot and the light creased their eyes until they adjusted to the glare. The streets they walked down were humming with activity. Women hung around their front doors, aprons on and sleeves rolled up, some with bairns on their hips. Men laughed over cigarettes,

376

dark from the pit still, unwilling to go home until the victory was talked into manageable size.

Tom and Bob turned into the back alley and then through the yard gate. The kitchen door was open with Bobby sitting on the step. Grace turned from the wall; Mrs Fenney was leaning over and they were laughing.

'Now you're here, Tom Ryan, you can wind down this line for me,' ordered Grace and collected together the last of the washing. 'Staying for a bite are you, Bob?'

As she carried the basket into the house, Tom slipped up behind her and kissed her neck. Mrs Fenney laughed and Grace squealed.

'Tom, I can smell beer on you. You can just behave yourself.'

But by now Bobby was pulling at his trousers and laughing. He weighed nothing at all as Tom swung him into the air, then back close into his arms. He blew gently down his neck and nuzzled his son, who had skin which was almost too soft to feel.

Working as a checker gave him more time for the lad and it pleased him. The committee work at the pit consumed one evening a week and was as interesting as Bob had promised it would be and still gave him time for his painting class with the lads.

'Come on Bob, get sat down.' He steered him into his usual chair to the left of the fire which was a dull glow on this hot day. The irons were already heating on the hot plate. He slapped his cap on the table and, still carrying Bobby, sat down and stroked his brown hair as they gathered their thoughts in silence. The beer had made his body loose and he kissed his son's head. The clock was ticking on the mantelpiece.

'It was the bombers really, wasn't it?' Tom said eventually. 'That's what won the election. It dragged lice and smelly kids into posh homes all over the country. Bye, I bet some noses had a shock. The old 'uns too, bombed out and nowhere to go. Made a few people think, I reckon. Think about how the posh lived, how the poor lived.'

'The press certainly splashed it all over the papers,' agreed Bob.

'Free milk, free school dinners, they'll be keeping those on, I reckon, and Davy should have been here since I dare say they'll be extending that Family Allowance the evacuees had.'

'Archie will be the one turning in his grave if you're not

careful, Tom. Can't you hear him saying, "Lunch, if you don't mind, Thomas."'

They both chuckled now but their eyes were thoughtful at a picture of a man defeated by a life that would not be allowed to happen now.

'Tough on Winnie, though. Must feel like a kick in the teeth,' mused Tom, watching as Grace brought the washing in and then wiped a flannel over Bobby's face, which was sticky with toffee Betsy had made. He was asleep now on Tom's lap and Tom kissed Grace's arm below the elbow as she reached across.

'Nationalisation must feel that way to him anyway. Poor old soldier and now it'll come, thick and fast.' Bob patted his lip with his forefinger.

Grace nodded. 'It doesn't seem fair somehow.' She was folding the clothes into a neat pile, ready for ironing, then smiled at them. 'Come on, you two, get up the allotment, the pair of you, while I do a spot of ironing and then put the bairn to bed and fix a bit to eat. You can sort out the world up there. The birds will appreciate a few crumbs of wisdom.'

Bob and Tom raised their eyebrows at one another.

'We've had a better audience than this when we've been canvassing. Cheered I was, on the waste land,' puffed Tom.

'Out!' Grace laughed.

So they linked arms, bowed and ducked the cloth that Grace aimed towards them. Tom curtailed his limping stride to fit in with Bob's frail step as they walked up the hill. They did not hurry but nodded to Sam Walker, as they passed, before continuing in a contented silence until they reached the allotment bench, which Tom had angled in between the shed and the wall so that Bob could have a windless patch when he joined Tom here on Sundays.

The bench was warm from the sun and they leaned back against the wall. Bob filled his pipe, still with tea leaves. He had said he'd only use tobacco again when nationalisation had taken place and Tom was right glad that it looked as though it was on the way; the smell was dreadful. There were still a few hearted lettuces but the cabbages were young yet and the beans were beginning to hang heavy on the poles.

'I suppose the government will have to buy the owners out?' Bob nodded. 'Yes, they'll be offered compensation. It'll be better than the way you once proposed. A revolution with a temporary dictatorship?' He looked at Tom sideways.

'Aye, and you could say the war had one and look at what was achieved.' But he put his hands up as Bob started to argue. 'I know, I know, I was only mithering. Wish to God the buggers would put some of their compensation into newer industries up here though, Bob. That's always going to be the trouble in coal you know. Heavy industry is vulnerable. Even if mining is nationalised it will always be vulnerable. It's a declining industry.'

'I know, lad, but one thing the men'll have to do is to have a national union, not the various groups making up the Federation.'

Tom nodded. 'That'll be more work for you, Bob. Can you handle it? The campaign took it out of you.'

He looked with concern at Bob who had door-knocked and spoken on street corners alongside Tom and that had tired him enough, damn it. The man couldn't be far off 60.

'I'll do a bit, lad, but what about you? Could be a great opening for you. You'd make a grand union man.'

The sun had dipped almost out of sight behind the slag but it was still light and the honeysuckle which climbed the wall to their right made the air heavy with its fragrance. A sparrow was busy where the chicken meal was kept. Tom stopped and threw a pebble towards it. As it flew off in a flurry of fear, he said, 'No Bob. It's time I was off out of it now. Me foot hurts, me mind goes round in circles. I want to get on with our own ideas now.'

Bob stopped sucking on his pipe and turned to look at Tom.

'Your Annie's not been found yet, Tom. They've opened a few camps, found such dreadful things. You must not be so sure of the future.'

Grace had spoken to him, asked him to make Tom consider that Annie was probably dead, try to get him to think of life without her. He patted Tom's knee. 'You must think in terms of yourself, not ourselves, lad.'

Tom shook his head. 'Don't you fret, Bob. She'll be back. There's a lot for us to do. Houses will be rebuilt, they'll need decorating and it will give a great deal of work, half of it to women. She knows that. She'll be back, I tell you.' It was now the half-light of a summer's evening and the birds were still swooping over the allotment and, in the honeysuckle, a finch was fluttering.

'Georgie's going when Japan is finished and he won't stop until he finds her. I can't live without her. I couldn't work at the business unless she's with me.'

Bob felt a cold shaft cut down through his body.

Tom tapped his arm. 'Let's get back, shall we? Grace will mither us for letting the food get cold.' He took Bob's arm as they walked out of the allotment, past the alley that led to Betsy, on down the darkening streets which could now be lit with street lamps.

He saw again the girl standing by the school, saw her run towards him with her shoelace undone; felt again the coal squeeze his breath and kill Martin, heard her voice.

A dog barked and children ran out of one street and on to the pavement behind them, laughing and kicking at a ball. She'd come back, he nodded to himself. Annie would always come back.

Bob rubbed the back of his left hand. There were age spots on the translucent skin now and his knuckles ached much of the time. He felt immensely weary. What would happen if Annie did not come home again?

CHAPTER 28

It was morning and Annie woke and undid the rope which tied Prue to her wrist for the night, since she had been found wandering in the compound one night and was lucky not to have been shot. Annie sat her up and washed her hands and face. The sore at the corner of her mouth was larger now.

'Come on, lass, it'll be roll-call in a moment and then it's time for the rabbit again.'

She took her hand and Monica stood with Prue while Annie straightened their pallets and put Prue's net under the blanket to hide it from the guards. They turned as the leader came into the hut.

'They've gone,' she said, her voice full and tears running down her face. 'The gates are open and they've gone. It's over. It must be over.'

Annie caught at Prue's hand and pulled her to the doorway then out on to the verandah. It seemed so quiet. Women were walking slowly out of their huts and into the compound, their clompers causing dust to rise. There was no cheering. The gates hung open and the guard-towers were empty. The plantation began just outside the wire and women were at the gate but not going through.

She took Prue down the steps slowly at first and then faster, edging sideways through the others, easing her way to the front. There it was, the open gate and the dark tumbling trees beyond.

They were free, at last they were free but the air was still that of a prison, the wire still stretched around the camp and they must pass beyond it and so she walked with Prue out into freedom. She held her hand and slowly they passed from the baked earth to the undergrowth of the rubber trees. Others now followed, taking different paths. She felt tired as she stepped over a fallen tree; she was free but she still felt tired. How strange.

'Mind the undergrowth,' she warned Prue. It had tangled and woven itself up and over the trunks of once-tapped trees and the musky smell overrode the latex. She stood still and lifted her head high and watched the branches link overhead like a steeple and for a moment she was back in the lane leading to the beck, back listening to Beauty's hooves and watching Georgie as he showed the bee to Tom. But here there was really only the chatter of the monkeys, the crackle of other feet now, on other paths. Voices which had at first whispered were now shouting because there was no one any more to crash a rifle butt into your head.

'Come on, hinny,' she said gently and Prue smiled and stumbled alongside her. Annie could no longer find some of the graves which were now hidden completely beneath the fast-reclaiming jungle. Prue's hand lay in hers and, when Annie finally stopped, she did also.

'I want to be able to tell Mr Anderton where Mavis was buried, but I can't find the place.' Her stomach was tightening again. Prue's face screwed up into tears because Annie was sad.

'Don't cry,' said Annie gently and so she stopped.

The jungle had come down into the plantation. There were creepers as thick as ropes hanging from the trees and green moss everywhere. Annie ran her finger down a rubber tree and looked at the green lichen on her finger and then at the smear on the bark which would be overgrown by tomorrow.

'We'll go home now,' she told Prue who obediently followed her back to the cookhouse where they were queueing for rice.

The doctor was counting packets in the hospital when they had finished. 'We've broken into the store. Camp leader brought these over, marmite tonight for everyone please, Sister. Monica is already giving some to the beri-beri cases. One way of getting Vitamin B into them anyway. The fluid will pour out of the dropsy cases.' Her voice broke. 'The Red Cross parcels were here all the time. We could have saved so many.'

Annie felt her own eyes blur. 'Shall I tell everyone to eat only a little, they'll be ill if they dig into the parcels straight away, won't they?' The doctor nodded.

There were boxes stacked in the middle of the compound as they stepped out into the sun. 'What are those?' Annie asked.

'Our postcards,' replied the doctor. 'They were never sent.'

The allied trucks arrived seven days later. It was strange to hear English spoken by male voices, to hear rounded vowels which rolled off the tongue rather than harsh words that spat at you from the conqueror. It was strange to see khaki and if they weren't all so ill and tired they would have minded being dressed only in bras and shorts or torn dresses held together by the merest of threads.

There was nowhere for them to go, they were told, so would they mind awfully staying here until repatriation could be arranged. They did in fact mind awfully, but there was no strength left in anyone to complain. Clothing and food were trucked in and the sick taken to hospital.

The doctor insisted that Prue should go, though she screamed and cried when she was taken from Annie, who kissed her and said it wouldn't be for long. She must go home now, to her da.

Annie lay that night beneath Prue's mosquito net which was so much cooler after the blanket that she had used for the last three years. The real cigarette tasted wonderful and kept the mosquitoes away better than the leaf tobacco. She could not hear them buzzing all around now but her head was swimming with the pungent inhalation. Her wrist felt strange without its tether and she felt frightened now that she was quite alone.

With no duties, they all had little to do and Annie's mind was full of thoughts and dreams and shadows that darkened with each day, leaping from the black box and then disappearing before she could keep them long enough to examine.

Early in September, the heat of the day was rising and her sweat dripped on to the verandah floor. Monica was bartering for bananas from a native down by the gate. More jeeps were driving into the compound, racing up to the Union Jack which now flew where the Rising Sun had done. Georgie climbed out of one and the doctor spoke to him, touched his arm and pointed. He was tanned in his shorts but dust lay on him in a light layer and only her eyes moved as she watched him walk towards her through the heat. She felt the verandah sag as he climbed each step but she sat quite still; so tired, so very tired. He sat beside her and took her hand. It was the same hand that it had always been. After this time, it was still quite the same.

'You never change, do you, bonny lass?' He held her head

between his hands and his eyes were as brown as they had ever been, though lines dug deep. His eyelashes were as thick as hedgerows, if hedgerows still existed. His smile was still one-sided.

'Yes, I do,' she replied. 'I do change, my love.' It took time to form the words, her mouth felt stiff these days and her voice sounded as though it came from someone else.

'Not to me, my bonny lass,' and he kissed her tired thin old face and rested his head on hers so that she should not see how his eyes had filled and his mouth trembled.

Annie sat just as she had been but rested her head in his hands and breathed him in and wanted to sit like this until she died and the dreams that were so dark went away.

She didn't look back at the camp as she left. It was her home and she was leaving her friends but this had happened before, hadn't it, long ago, and Georgie had said that she would see them again anyway, so she would, wouldn't she?

In the Raffles Hotel she lowered herself into a full bath; her legs lifted and floated, her arms did the same and her body sank into the warmth while the water blackened. She rinsed herself again and again but still she felt unclean. In the mirror the face that was reflected was an old skull with yellow skin and eyes that were sunk too deep, and there was no life in them.

She lay that night with Georgie on a bed too soft for sleep but she did not want to sleep for then the darkness came and the black box bulged and struggled to open. She lay beneath the net and he held her hand but on the other wrist she could still feel the tether and hear the noise of the hospital hut and smell bad burnt almonds. He took her in his arms and held her close and her love for him was in every part of her body but she was dead to his touch because passion was a luxury and she had no strength for luxuries. No strength to do more than see and feel him from a distance. She heard his voice, felt his touch, watched his lips as he talked softly to her, but he could not come inside her head and help her with the black box and that was what she must concentrate on, all the time, keeping the black box closed.

The next day, the jeep took them to the blackened airfield past platoons of Japanese soldiers who guarded buildings, directed natives, dug at bombed buildings.

'We haven't enough soldiers, my love, so we are using the

Japs for now to keep things ticking over.' She nodded and looked straight ahead. She would not look at these men who had kept their marmite from them and stolen Lorna's head.

Bombay burst in on her as she stepped out of the aeroplane, the heat surged against her face and the smell of the continent was all around. Diphtheria did not creep up gently on her but suddenly with violence, that first day in India. It closed her throat and hurled darts of pain to every nerve-end and here, in this strange clean white hospital, dry fingers held her and gave her injections of something called penicillin. Soft hands bathed her and there were no insects, no moans from other huts, no guttural screams from booted guards, no lover. Just a fan that purred.

She ran her fingers softly round and over the raised embroidered laundry mark. The fan moved round, her arm was brown against the turned-down crisp sheet and only her eyes played with the branched shadows which flickered and rushed silently across the pristine white tiles, and she wondered what tree it was that so silently teased the everlasting sun and denied its passage to her room.

Four weeks it had been, the nurse had said. Four weeks of gentle hands, four weeks with no need to speak, with sips taken from cool glasses and a head which was held up by another's efforts. Four weeks of protection and now there was a world out there forcing its way in. Along the corridor she could feel it march, hear the ringing of its heels and then feel finally the click and rush of sound. Holding the door open, Georgie smiled. How brown he is, all brown, she thought. His uniform was khaki, his belt was brown but no, she was wrong. His shoes were coal-black, his buttons were icy yellow. So, she smiled, he's not just brown, nobody's just anything. But what does it matter anyway.

'You're coming home, my love,' he said, his mouth buried in the palm of her hand.

'Yes,' she replied. 'I want to go home.' She touched the bleached streaks of his hair. I'm coming, Tom, she called silently. I'm coming at last.

'Next week, the doctors say, and I have arranged the ceremony here and we will spend two weeks in Kashmir. Do you remember me telling you about it and how you'd love it? The waters go on forever, Annie, but never seem to flow. The mountains lie and wait and when you are there you will wait with them and recover.'

She stroked his face and it was rough. 'I'd like that and then I must go home.'

He kissed each finger. 'Yes, I've found a nice bungalow. It's all ready and Prue is back on station with her father. She's so well, Annie, and young Sanders seems to have taken quite a shine to her. He's a good sort and she's blooming again. A bit quiet perhaps. A bit strange but well. She's coming to the wedding, blonde hair and all.' He laughed, his face was close to hers. He held her hand tightly to his chest. 'I'm so happy that at last we're to be together. Each day has been an agony, not knowing if you were alive or hurt. I shall never let you go again, my darling Annie. I shall look after you from now on and nothing will hurt you ever again.' He laid his head against hers and she felt his breath and wondered why he could not hear her screaming. Why no one could hear her screaming.

She wanted to go home, to have space around her to breathe. Could no one hear her screaming?

Kashmir was high above the plain of India, nearer to the sky than she had ever been. The houseboat nestled quietly and gently in its berth. Georgie wore a white shirt, the sleeves of which he rolled up above his elbows and she watched his sinews, his strong familiar arms and clung to him as he carried her over the threshold.

'Kiss me, darling,' she pleaded desperately and he did, his lips soft at first and then hard and urgent and he carried her to the bedroom, past the bearer who stood to one side. He laid her on the bed and she watched as he dragged his clothes from his body and, gently then, removed hers. He kissed her and stroked her, licked her breasts which were fuller now. Kissed her thighs and she ran her hands down his back, his stomach until she held him in her hands, large and hot and he groaned and entered her and she cried out to him, 'Deeper my love,' but he was still not far enough into her. He could not push back the heat of the compound, cast off the tether from her wrist or the blood that shot two yards from Lorna's body. She wept as he came inside her and he held her and tears were on his cheeks too as he cradled her in his arms and kissed her hair as they lay together.

'You've made me so happy, my darling,' he whispered and she smiled and looked at the curtains which hung round the walls of the bedroom. Yes, she still had the dining-room to sort out. Still the wallpaper in there.

That evening, they sat out on the verandah and the bearer brought them gin. The glass was heavy and cool. Georgie's wicker chair creaked as he reached forward to take her hand. He turned the plain gold ring which he had placed on her right hand. He reached over and touched her broken finger gently with his. His wrist was strong and she wondered if he would like to take the tether for a while but did not want to trouble him.

That night, she did not want to close her eyes, so lay there planning a pale green cool dining-room but her lids were heavy and soon there were shapes which squeezed out of the box because she couldn't keep the lid down. She pushed and pushed and cried for Georgie but he was on the outside of her head and could not hear. They were tumbling out now, secrets which slithered out and over the floor of her mind. She pushed them back: Lorna, varicose legs, broken fingers, Albert's hands which lunged at her, panting men on a playing-field, a hose-pipe which writhed out gas and her da, mostly her da, his face yellow, his mouth gaping. She pushed them back, her screams so loud that it made her head ache. Slowly, steadily, she pushed them back with her hands inside her head but now her hands were slimy.

The bungalow was square, its edges cut through the parched bleached air. White stones marked the pathway.

'Welcome, memsahib,' bowed the bearer, bearded and dark.

'Thank you,' she replied and entered Georgie's home wiping her hands down her skirt.

Prue was on the station, rounded now, with a bloom to her cheeks.

The days were long, movements were slow and the plains seldom varied. The heat rolled across the earth and Georgie was often late because he was in bomb disposal again and busy with the troubles.

The bungalow was painted plain white and the floors were tiled black and white and her feet left damp impressions as she walked.

'What would the memsahibs say, darling?' Prue asked as

they sat one morning in floral-covered chairs with cane tables scattered between each one. 'One really does not bare the feet in front of the servants,' she mimicked.

'Well this one does,' Annie rejoined. Her voice was quieter these days and each morning she woke unrefreshed, but Prue was the golden girl again though she would never be without the extra lines. She was better for them, Annie decided. They sat opposite one another. Fans disturbed the air and made the heat bearable.

Prue tapped her half-full glass of lime juice. 'You will come to the club for tiffin, darling, won't you?'

'Must I?' asked Annie, her legs curled up beneath her. She wiped her hands down her skirt and then rose.

Prue said, 'Yes, you must, and where are you off to now?'

'To wash my hands.' They were slimy again.

The water was not cool. Prue called from the sitting-room.

'You must come, Annie. It will do you good. Your mind is obviously on Georgie and there's no need. They're not using too many explosives in this area. The troubles are further from the border. Come on.' There was a smile in her voice. 'They are dying to have a proper look at you.'

Annie dried her hands and walked back. She liked the cool of the tiles.

'That's not much of an incentive.' She felt better when she was with Prue somehow. The tether had slipped from her wrist now that Prue was well but she wouldn't think of the rest because they would be here again tonight as always.

'Very well.' Prue sat forward, her finger pointing. 'I suggest a trade. You want to ride? I shall take you. You will come to the mess – and before you object – I have some jodhpurs but wear your topee. It's cracking down outside.'

The plain shimmered in the distance, the scrub clung in parts to the wide-cracked surface and the pony shambled beside Prue's. The palace on the hilltop brooded as they passed. Their escort stayed behind them at a suitable distance, the stirrup leather pinched her inside leg and the sound of their shifting harness was all that disturbed their progress. Annie wondered if Tom still had Beauty. She had written to him but had not heard back yet and would not try and picture him because the missing was too much.

'The maharajah hardly ever comes now,' said Prue, lifting her crop to the palace. 'He lives in Bombay and sends his sons to school in England.'

'Crazy, isn't it,' mused Annie. 'While the British sent their daughters to live in India to find a husband. How is Lt. Sanders by the way? You haven't mentioned him yet today, or perhaps only a hundred times!' She smiled as Prue blushed.

'Just maybe, Annie, maybe this is it. I do love him and I think he loves me. I'm so glad you've decided to stay here with Georgie. We can all be together now.'

Annie rubbed her hands together then down her trousers. She couldn't get them clean, couldn't breathe; everyone was too close. She urged her pony forward, taking in gulps of air.

'Though how long any of us will be here is a moot point,' Prue continued, keeping up with her. 'Georgie was telling Daddy that in a couple of years he'll take you back to start the business because he doesn't give the English any longer than that anyway.'

Annie nodded.

'Is that what you want? We must settle close to one another Annie, when we do all go back.'

They were moving along the edge of a gully now and the earth scudded down into it. Annie nodded again. It would be nice to have Prue close and yes, she wanted to go back but two years had a great many long days inside it.

'We should all have left before the troubles became so bad. All such an undignified scramble, darling. So much tension everywhere, you can feel it even before the shouts and riots break out. Suddenly India isn't home any more.'

Annie dragged herself back.

'You must be the only insider who thinks so.' She wound the reins round her hand. It had healed quite well.

Prue shrugged as her pony pawed the ground and they began to move again. 'They must know, deep down, but if they admit it to themselves, let alone anyone else, it is too real. But there'll be a few more years anyway though it won't be the same as it was. I so longed for it in that dump as well. Shall we ride back now, nearly time for tiffin remember?'

Annie pushed the thought of home aside, the thought of cool sea-breezes and followed Prue back down the wadi. The palace seemed very empty and vast. What will happen to you, she wondered, when we've gone and the country is free?

The party sitting around the table was languid in the mahogany-darkened room. Conversation was desultory, tea-cups rattled softly and always there was the hum of the fans. The brightness seen through draped windows and shaded verandahs seemed distant.

Annie shook her head at the cake. There was dark panelling on each wall and oil paintings with heavy gilt frames.

'Surely not slimming, my dear?' Tea was laid on a walnut table.

'No, it's still rather too rich for me, thank you.'

'Not for me either, thank you, Mrs Bearing.' Prue waved the plate away.

'Slimming too?'

Annie glanced at Prue.

'We're not slimming, Mrs Bearing.' Prue raised her voice and spoke slowly, each word clearer than the last. 'We can't digest rich food yet. We've only been back in India about two months.'

The woman shifted her gaze to the spot between the two. She had white hair and spectacles and wore a blouse that was ruffled at the neck. Her lips were thin.

'Quite so, my dear. Did you have a pleasant ride?'

'Lt. Sanders was asking after you, Prue dear. He has just come in from up-country. He's a good boy and has rather a soft spot for you, I think.' An elderly woman was speaking, her skin was sallow and lined, her grey hair short and crinkle-permed. She had a nice face, Annie decided. The bearer stood in the corner, ready to renew the teapot. 'And it's so nice to see you looking so well,' the woman continued.

'Yes, yes, indeed,' Mrs Bearing called across the table. 'One heard such frightful stories. Such bad form, don't you know, women in coolie hats and rags. I mean, how can one be expected to keep the Empire intact with that sort of thing being allowed to happen? Can't have been our sort. Others brought in for the duration most likely.'

The elderly woman laid her hand on Annie's arm. A sapphire stone was set in plain gold and her skin hung loose beneath her arm.

'More tea, my dear.'

Annie shook her head. She must strip the dining-room wallpaper; she must pull large sodden strips and drop them into piles until her feet were covered. Then it would be green stripes, pale green and cream stripes. It would be so cool.

'I think, Prue, I shall have to make the curtains, they don't seem to match material to wallpaper, do they?' She rubbed her hands on her napkin, again and again.

Prue sat quite still in the silence that drifted outwards across the table; faces looked blank, then embarrassed. Mrs Bearing fingered her pearls.

'Do have some more tea, Mrs Cantor,' she offered the elderly woman who kept her hand on Annie's arm. She smoothed her collar as she asked the other women too.

Prue leaned forward, making room for her cup and taking Annie's from her. 'I think it is time we left.' She spoke carefully and equally carefully, she said, 'Thank you so much for an enlightening afternoon, Mrs Bearing, but now we have letters to write, to our coolie friends.'

She rose, touching Annie's arm. 'Yes, I rather think you will have to match them up yourself or perhaps it would be easier just to paint.' She led Annie from the table.

Mrs Cantor also rose, taking Annie's other arm. Annie liked the older woman's eyes, they were deep and they smiled.

'Come on, Annie, let's go home,' Prue said gently.

'Yes, I'd like that,' and the brightness of the window seemed further away than ever and the darkness of the heavy mess furniture with its cold silver loomed larger than ever.

'Make her rest, Pruscilla, and do not overdo it yourself.' Mrs Cantor spoke softly and watched as they walked out into the heat. It was pre-monsoon and their lungs expanded with effort.

'When is Georgie coming home?'

Annie wondered why Prue was so careful, her voice so tightly pitched.

'Perhaps not until tomorrow but probably tonight.' She stopped. A thought had flickered past her eyes and gone but here it was again.

'Why does he do this, Prue? Does he want to die? Every time be probes for the fuse he must think, this time may be the time. It's a bit like suicide, another suicide. Such a lot of suicides.' She walked on. The bungalow was not far now. It would be cool there. She could wash her hands, tear off these clothes, lie on the bed. She ran her fingers round her collar, rolled up her sleeves. They stood on the verandah.

Prue said, 'Father says the best at the job are those who want to live most. Georgie's the best.'

'But he shouldn't be doing it, not now the war is over.' The verandah rail was smooth and painted white but she could see a knot slightly raised. 'There is no need for anyone else to die.'

'He won't die, Annie.' Prue frowned. 'You're very tired, I'll come and see you later.'

'It's the bedside lamp that is the problem. Shall I match it to the light or to the paper?' Annie shook her head. Everything flashed through too quickly for her to hold all her thoughts. She watched Prue leave but she turned at the bottom of the step.

'I'll hang on for a bit I think, Annie.'

But Annie shook her head. 'Don't be silly Prue, I'm fine. Just want a bit of peace, that's all, just a bit of peace.' She waved. The square shimmered and the lines of quarters broke down into heat-fragmented images. It seemed the same, day after day, week after week. She fanned herself and held the rail. Oh for a cold sea-breeze. She smiled at Kassim as she entered the bungalow.

'I'm lying down for a while. Please don't disturb me unless it's an emergency.'

Beneath the mosquito net, she heard the monsoon begin and saw it suck the light from the day. She lay in a cotton nightdress but still the sweat ran from her body in the stifling heat. The rains plunged, water ran off ground too hard-baked to absorb its ferocity. It seemed hotter still and the noise drummed, punctuated by a shutter that banged, and Annie watched the black box. Even with her eyes wide open, she saw it. It was bulging and, unless the lid was opened, it was going to explode in little pieces all over the room, all over her brain and then she would never gather all the pieces together and back into the box and they would creep and slither around her forever and so she lifted the catch and let the secrets out. The moans came first and then Lorna and Albert's hand which grabbed for her and the vicar who could not say God. They were crawling across the floor and she could not catch them all. They were nearer now, the boots which kicked at her hands were stamping up dust and varicose legs were dancing round and the moans were mixed with music from the fair and then Da came out and across the room towards her and Georgie wasn't here to help. He was out there trying to die like her da and she had always known that the man she loved would leave her if she let him close to her. He would die like her mother, like Sarah, like her da.

There was pain in her head now. It was bursting as it beat in time with the noise of the rain, the fair, the shutters, the screams and she took pills for the pain. They were sour and the water was warm. Her hair rubbed her neck; the pillow was too full. She pushed it to the bed edge and over it fell and was forgotten. The rain still drummed and the music went round and Albert's hands were nearly at her and the pipe which wriggled with gas was closer still. More pills but they were sour again and the pain was still with her. The fan was drumming now in time with the rain. And still there was the throbbing in her head and the blood from Lorna's head began to lap closer even than the gas-filled hose and then there was her da coming closer with his mouth wide open. The pills were not sour the next time and the noise was fading at last and the pain was easing. The black box was empty and everybody was leaving now in a spiral through the top of her head.

Her body was quiet, there was just her mouth that breathed and even that was slipping. She smiled at the peace. There was no heat, no noise and now the deep darkness was near. The peace.

Prue shook her hair as she arrived. It was wet and the water dripped off her mackintosh. The house was quiet.

'Thank you, Kassim. Is Memsahib awake?'

'She still sleeping. No want to be disturbed.' He took her coat and watched as she walked to the bedroom door. There was no answer to her knock. She turned the handle and entered. The shutters banged, they were unlatched and there was no light.

'Annie, are you awake?' she called but only the shutters crashed.

'Come on, darling, Georgie's with Father, then he's coming straight over.' She felt for the light, it was dim yellow and she saw the pillow half under the bed. Annie's hand was hanging not far above it, her arm half-hidden by the mosquito net. Prue's scalp tightened. She walked quietly across and pulled back the net.

She was too pale, too sound asleep.

'Wake up, Annie, let's clear this place up a bit.'

Her wrist was still warm but the pulse was faint. The brown bottle lay on the bed; it was only half full. Pruscilla pressed her lips together, her pulse was hurting in her throat. She heard steps on the verandah and the door opening.

'Shut it quickly, George. Do not let Kassim in. No one must know.' Her voice was low but steady and she did not look at him but at Annie.

He stood in the doorway. Pruscilla gestured sharply and he shut it behind him.

'What's wrong with Annie?' His voice was loud.

'Come over here and for God's sake keep your voice down. Let's get her up. She must walk, walk it off.'

He threw his hat to the corner of the room and caught Prue's arm. His face was suddenly anxious.

'Is she drunk?'

'Don't be so bloody ridiculous. She's taken an overdose.'

His arms felt slow at first but he reached her at last, his Annie, his love. Her shoulders were so fragile, her head lolled back. He looked at Prue.

'Will she live?' It was a desperate question, a whisper.

'If she doesn't sleep.'

'I'll get her to the hospital.' He was on his feet striding to the door.

'No time for that my lad and do you want the whole station to know? Do you want her to face criminal charges if she lives?'

'Can we do it, just the two of us?' He had turned helplessly to face her.

'I rather think we should, it will be much kinder.' She moved to the other side, regretting already the sharpness of her tone. They heaved Annie upright, the net caught on her hair and Prue pulled it away.

'Come on darling. Let's get those legs moving. Come on now.' Her voice was urgent. Nothing happened.

'Drag her, come on, drag her,' she hissed. The shutters still crashed against the frame, the rain was heavier.

'It's no good,' Georgie groaned. 'We're not getting through.'

'Hold her,' Prue snapped. She slapped Annie's face again and again, harder each time and still the shutter banged.

'Sahib, do you need me?' called Kassim.

394

'Go to your quarters!' roared Georgie, sweat rolling down his face, his hair wet with it.

'Shout at her, Georgie, shout ichi, ni, san, yong,' and he did.

'Speedo, speedo,' urged Prue roughly and again and again they shouted and dragged and her feet began to move and soon she started to retch and dawn made the lamp redundant. She was sitting in a chair with Georgie at her feet, his head buried in her lap, his shoulder shaking as he wept his pain.

'I'm going now,' Prue said, her voice soft and weary. 'Tell him, Annie, you must tell him you want to go home. How can he help if he doesn't know?' She touched his shoulder and wondered if either had heard her.

It was later, much later that Georgie opened his eyes. Her hand was on his head. He stirred and his movement lifted Annie's heavy lids. He rose and took her in his arms, carried her to the window.

'The rains are lighter now, my love,' he said softly and she nodded.

'I want to go home, Georgie. I must go away from the heat, back to my house, back to walls that are solid, pictures I know. I want to breathe again. I want space to breathe, that's all.'

'Aren't I enough for you, Annie?'

Her mouth was dry and she touched his hands which had pulled clover and held it to her lips, stroked his arms which she had bathed when they were stung. Touched his mouth which had smiled when she turned somersaults on the bar and she smelt again the leeks wilting in the heat on that summer day.

'You are too much for me.' And she did not know what she meant. 'I'm in small pieces and I want to go home.'

His eyes were reddened and pain was drawn into every corner of his face and she knew that all she wanted now was to be away from anyone who had ever pulled at her. And as he had done before, so long ago in Albert's kitchen, Georgie made it easy for her.

CHAPTER 29

The gangplank was gone, the sprawl of India was retreating; the smell was of the sea and for six weeks she sat or walked the deck, breathing easily now for the first time since she left the camp. Her hair was thick with salt and her skin was white-smudged with it too.

It was winter as they docked, and crisp. The bare-branched trees and darkened green fields first filled the train windows as she travelled towards the North and then fell away in the face of ploughed fields lying fallow.

The train embankments were blackened from sparks and stubble fires. Small fields and small horizons, Annie thought. The seats were the same; they still prickled. The pictures behind glass above the seats were faded as they had always been.

As she walked up the path to the Gosforn house, the privet leaf snapped as she bent it between thumb and forefinger, and then there was Val. She came down the path, her arms outstretched and Annie stood quite still as she laid her head on that familiar shoulder. She did not weep but stood silent as Val rocked her, then walked to the door and into the sitting-room. It was so very much the same and she put her case down and held on to Val's arm.

'I'm so glad I'm home.' The fire was in the grate, red and crackling but Sarah was not there.

'Let me take your coat, my dear,' said Val and kissed her cheek as Annie handed over the Harrods mackintosh that Prue had given her to brave the English winter. Her hands were cold and her cheeks too but it was a good feeling.

She woke the next morning and there was no sweat-drenched sheet, just a slow awakening. The black box had stayed shut when she had pushed the lid down. Was it over? Was the darkness over now that she was alone and at Gosforn? But she knew it wasn't; it was just waiting.

She lay with her hands beneath her head and looked up at Val's knock. The blue cup on the breakfast tray was the same as she remembered. She traced its scalloped lines with her thumb and sipped slowly. Val turned on the electric fire and drew back the curtains.

'Misty again,' she said and walked across to smooth the sheet down. 'Why don't you stay in bed today? You look so pale.' She had her hair drawn back in a bun and it was very white now, but she was still rounded, still as soft.

'Val, I love you. I'm as brown or yellow as a bunka wallah. No one could possibly call me pale.'

'Well, I do and Sarah would too, if she could see you now.' She folded her arms across her bosom. 'You are pale.'

Annie shook her head and leant back on the pillows. 'We've a great deal to do, Val. I want to start on the house, get the business going. You don't mind, do you, if I change things here?' She was restless and fingered the sheet. She wanted to be busy, not to have to think. 'It's not that I want to forget Sarah, I'll never do that. It's just something that I'd like to do.'

Val smiled and walked to the fire, flicking on the second bar.

'Do what you think best, lass. It would look good with a bit of paint.'

'Paper mostly.' Annie said firmly.

Val was standing by the window, rubbing at the condensation.

'Has it changed you very much; this dreadful business, I mean?'

Annie picked up her toast. 'I don't know, Val. I don't know about anything very much, any more.' The marmalade was tart, the toast crisp and the butter hard. That was enough to be getting on with and she would feed the hens soon.

Tom read the letter which arrived in the morning as he was cleaning his boots. It was his day off from the pit.

October

India.

Dear Tom,
  It will be early December when you receive this. Annie will be in England now. Look after her for me. She thinks I don't understand but I do now. I love her you see, I always have and I always will. I want to come to her but won't unless she decides she wants me. Her da comes between us, Tom. Makes her scared of loving me. Help me, Tom. Help her.
                    Georgie.

Tom put on his boots half cleaned and threw the letter on the table. Grace looked across from the sink, her sleeves rolled up, her hands red from washing.

'We'll not be going to Betsy's for lunch,' he told her as he took down his crash helmet and goggles. 'Read the letter, bonny lass, then go and tell me mam we'll be there this evening, Don too and that I'll be bringing Annie round in the afternoon. I want to show her a few things.' Bobby was playing by the table with bricks Bob had made and Tom had painted. He looked up at Tom and laughed as a pile fell over. Grace put the letter down again.

'Be careful, Tom. You can't go interfering in people's lives.'

He turned as he went out of the door, his face firm and set. 'It's about time someone did,' he said.

Annie stood by the wire. This new cock was as arrogant as the last had been. It strutted backwards and forwards just as the camp commandant had done. The wire dug into her hands and she made herself loosen her grip, rubbing at the deep red grooves it had made on her fingers. She didn't hear Tom until he was almost by her side and then she turned and his face was grimy where the goggles had been.

It felt so good, so very good to have his arms round her, his blue eyes smiling down into hers. He was grey at the temples and he had far more lines than when she had last seen him. His leather coat was cold against her cheek and she felt a calmness, a coming home. The hens were clustering at the gate and the cock was preening and flapping.

'I was just going to feed the hens.' She stood back and smiled at him. 'You have always been such a bonny lad, Tom.' She felt her voice begin to break so stooped and picked up the bowl, passing it to him.

He laughed. 'I knew I shouldn't have come.' He held open the run gate and stood with her and they threw corn from the bowl. He saw that she used her right hand, that her left had a finger which was crooked and misshapen.

'So someone didn't like your Ruby Red then, eh bonny lass? You and me is gimpy together.' He tapped her hand gently and she smiled. The hens were pecking at the ground which was bare of grass now and hummocked like a bomb-blasted moor which had been rounded in the wind.

'Is Don home yet?' she asked.

'Aye, we'll be seeing him later.'

Tom lifted his head and tilted back his cap. He looked steadily at her but she turned from him, throwing the last of the corn to the furthest corner of the run.

'Let's go to the shed,' he said softly and she nodded. They walked together past the laurel, its waxed leaves moving in the wind. She looked at her watch, it was nearly midday. The rice would be . . . She stopped herself and shook her head. Tom opened the door. Creosote still stained the wood but the smell was only there if you brushed close. The bike was rusted and the rubber grips had perished right through and lay on the floor. She moved to the window and rubbed at the glass and her finger came away grey. She looked out over the Thoms' garden up into the sky.

'So, my bonny lass, you came back. I always knew you would.' Tom was squatting near the pile of sacks and dust rose in clouds as he picked at the frayed edges.

She nodded. 'I wanted to come home. We have lots to do, Tom. I thought we could start on the house first. Try out some ideas, then go into production.' Her breath was misting the glass and she rubbed at it but the moisture smeared so she pulled her sleeve over her hand and wiped it dry.

Tom said nothing. Just sat on his haunches picking at the hessian and the smell was acrid.

She turned and his eyes were still looking at her steadily and this time she knew she had to answer the question he was asking her.

'I had to come home without him. I needed to think, to get things sorted out.'

Tom still looked at her. 'Get your coat on, lass,' he said. His face was calm but firm. 'We've some places to visit, you and me. It's time we nailed this shadow, time you faced things once and for all. You can't go on hiding.'

Annie stood rigid, gripping the cold steel handlebars of the bike. She squeezed the brake and it hurt her finger. She squeezed it again. She wanted the pain. It stopped her sinking beneath the fear which crept through her and lodged in her chest. Her stomach was tight and her shoulders rigid. She wouldn't go. There was no way she would go back, even with Tom.

'I'm not coming with you, I have too much to do here. The walls to strip.' She thought of the cool green stripes for the dining-room but suddenly he was up off his haunches and standing before her. 'Get your mac, hinny, you're coming with me. We'll take the Morris. You might as well come back as you left.' He did not touch her, just looked and his eyes were dark and they saw right through her to the box and she knew there was no hiding from him.

The Morris breasted the hill and Tom drove it down towards Wassingham and there were the slag-heaps, bigger now but still with carts churning up the slopes showering dust on to the mountain which was growing each year. He drove her down into the streets which pressed together and shut out the pale December sun. There were no daffodils on window-sills to relieve the black-coated red brick and the windows were blank without the lights of evening shining out on the cobbled streets.

Down through the town, past Mainline Terrace and the bombed-out Garrods used goods shop. She and Tom had not spoken since they had left Gosforn. She did not want to. She was busy wallpapering the hall, but now as they rattled over the cobbles she could not hold the striped paper in her head. Could not hold the walnut table and the gong tightly to her. Women were walking with shawls over their heads, children were playing football in the street and Tom stopped near the school, close to Wassingham Terrace, Sophie's old street.

He switched off the engine and it jumped before falling silent. They sat and she rubbed her hands together. They were slimy and she ran them down her mac until Tom leant over and took them in his.

'Don't do that, bonny lass. You'll wear out that posh mac of yours.'

She focussed on him then, on his warm hands as they held hers, on his eyes as they creased in his gentle smile, on her mac which Prue had given her. 'I'm so very tired, you see, Tom.' Her lids were heavy, she wanted to sleep, not to climb out in this place.

'I know you are but this has to be done, my little lass. Out you get now. I'll come with you.'

He took her to where she had first seen her father. She turned and looked down the street, bunching herself deeper into her mac, leaning back against the railings and their chill sank into her back as it had done that day all those years ago. It had been misty then and Don and a small man in a brown coat had come down the road, out of the mist. She saw them again, the boy and the man with his thin face and his hazel eyes; drawn and tired he had been, so tired. She held the railing behind her and it was so cold it hurt, but not as much as it had done on that cold winter day. There was no wind to chap licked lips today. She looked at Tom, her bonny wee bairn, but he was a man now, standing taller than her and holding her arm as the day turned dark and she saw the man and boy coming closer and closer through the mist.

'It's a fine day today, Annie,' Tom murmured, and she saw the boy and the man stop and slowly go back into the mist which lifted as shadows of lampposts took their place and lay long across the cobbles and were crossed by the colours of the women who passed by them. She saw that two children were sitting on the kerb playing marbles; she heard the click as two collided. Tom looked at her and she nodded though she knew he had not yet finished.

The Morris started on the second try and Tom's boots seemed too large on the pedals; she saw that one was shiny and one was dull.

'Is this the new way of wearing boots these days, bonny lad?'

she asked, her voice strained, but he laughed as he steered the car away from the school and that misty day.

They stopped outside the front door. There were no railings now.

'Gone for the war effort.' Tom explained.

So Don and she would never know now whether they were sharp enough to pass right through someone. She sat still, wiping her hands, feeling the seat at her back hard along the seams where the leather was pulled into panels. Tom was out now and coming round to her door but she would not leave the car and go into her da's house. No, that was too much of him to expect. He opened the door and the cold struck. She shook her head and he leaned in.

'Come with me, we're not going in yet, Annie. I have something else to show you.' He smiled and his face was so dear that she pushed herself from the seat and held out her hand to him. He did not take it though, but took instead her arm since her distorted finger broke his heart almost as much as her eyes set so deep in her strained thin face.

They walked down the back alleys and although there was no frost it was almost the same as before but they were not carrying trays which stretched their arms and froze their hands. The smell of coal was in the air and decrepit back-gates hung in frames at the back of yards. Down they went, on through the lane which led out to the field, but it seemed so small now and there were only boys playing football in bright red shirts and they aimed at proper goals. She stood silent.

'I ran away when we brought the bread and cheese. Do you remember, little Annie?' Tom stood next to her and looked across the field to the slag beyond. His cap was pulled down and his scarf was tied in a knot at his neck.

'I found it hard to forgive meself for leaving you here. It was something I kept feeling I had to wipe away, but I couldn't. I just had to grow into it somehow.'

He put his arm through hers and she gripped his hand. How strange, there were no large men walking towards them with dragons' breath, not any longer. There were just boys and white marked lines. No dog pulling at the coat which marked the goal, no Da standing before her, just green grass and so much more sky than she remembered. More light.

'You have always been so brave, my bonny lass, and I cannot

go on without you.' Tom said. 'Your da is dead. He's found some peace. You must too, Annie Manon.'

She tried to pull away now, tried to push the picture to the back of her mind, into the box, but Tom was hanging on, making it all come back, making her see her da.

'You must have wanted peace, Annie.' He had swung her round to face him now. There were the shouts of boys in the background. 'You must know how he felt. For God's sake, Annie, you must understand the man.' He held her chin so that she must look at him.

But she shook her head free. She wouldn't listen to him. She would carry on stripping the paper, pulling it down strip by strip, piece by piece. She would not let him into her head, would not let him pull out her box, lift the lid, take her secrets out and make her see them. She wouldn't see the field, only the hallway that needed stripping, but he kept on pulling her back to the black box. He kept on, his voice was pulling the box closer, pushing aside the hall at Gosforn until she could stand no more and screamed until the sound filled her head and she could not hear him any longer but his mouth was opening again and this time she tore from him and his words and ran from the field as he had once done, down the lanes, the alleys but he was still behind her but she couldn't hear his words, thank God she couldn't hear his words, but there was his voice as he called:

'Annie, wait.'

But she couldn't, not for what he had to say. She could hear his feet, his uneven tread closer now. She ran and ran, her breath hard in her chest, in through the gate past the stable and then Tom reached the yard gate, gasping and clinging to the upright, watching as she checked at the door.

The door was ajar and she stood there, her head on the wall, her breath quick and heavy in her chest. She rolled her head against the brick and felt him come to her. She was home but she could not go in.

'Beauty's here,' Tom panted, and led her over to the stable and Beauty was so small. Her mane was still coarse and she wound it round her fingers and couldn't see clearly because her eyes were full and the tears might fall and she was not going to cry over him, over her da. He had left her. He had killed himself and left her and it hurt too much to love and then be left. She could not bear it again, ever again, even with Georgie, and she hated her da for making her as she was.

'I hate him,' she shouted, turning to Tom. 'I hate him. He left me and I hate him for it.'

Tom watched her lips draw back. Her skin was almost transparent, her cheekbones seemed to be breaking through.

'You don't. You loved him and he hurt you. You must understand how he could do it. You of all people should understand now.' He was shouting too. 'After all you've been through, you should understand.'

He was holding her shoulders, shaking her and her hair fell down and across her eyes. She brushed it aside. Anger was forcing its way up through her stomach which tightened against it but still it came, up and through and into her chest and then her head and there was the box again.

'He filled himself up with gas, didn't he? And yes, I understand the need for peace, but how am I to have any from him? He's dead, he can't hear me when I ask him to leave me alone.'

Tom was still holding her. His lips were as stiff as hers were, his throat felt as though it was swelling.

'You must just tell him, Annie. It's up to you,' he cried. 'Tell him and then yourself. If you don't, there is nothing for you but to run away for ever, for the rest of your life. Free but alone.'

'We've always been together, you and me. Why can't it go on like that?' She was holding his arm now, her lips were still drawn back as she shouted and her eyes were so dark that they were hazel no longer.

'That is not enough for you. I don't ask anything of you and ours is not that sort of love. You need Georgie, you bloody fool. You need the man you've always loved. You must let yourself love, Annie, if you are going to be any sort of a person, have a life which means anything. Don't let your da spoil that.'

His voice was filling the yard, her head. He would not let her think of green stripes, of lamps that must match. His voice was bringing the box closer and closer to the front of her mind. Her da would come soon.

'Come in with me.' He was still shouting and she pulled back.

'No, I can't face that.' She held on to the stable door. She would rather be alone, free and alone. She had already decided.

404

He turned and wrenched her hand away. It was her broken finger but he didn't care. 'Get in here with me.'

He pulled her now, took her hand and put his arm round her and forced her to the door which now opened fully.

'There'll be no need for that,' Betsy said, and came to Annie and took her and held her against clothes that smelt of freshness and arms that were soft. Annie tried to find air to breathe as she walked into her father's house with the wife whom he had despised.

On through a kitchen which was no longer bleak and bare but full of light and colour with Tom's old cut-down chair still by the fire. Patchwork cushions lay everywhere. On through they went, she and Betsy, up to the hallway and past the clock which had chimed so loudly that first day. She did not want to go further but Betsy would not stop. On up the stairs which were gently lit until they came to the room. The door was shut and the box in her head was opening now. The lid was coming up and he would be here soon, in her head. She would see him coming out with his gaping yellow face if she went into the room which he had filled with gas rather than live with her.

Betsy opened the door and Annie would not look but then she did. The study was gone; the dark table, the prints so faded that there was no picture; all were gone. His chair where he had lolled, yellow and dead was gone.

Tom slipped past them into the room holding out his hand to her. 'Come into our studio, Annie.' He would not come and fetch her this time and she had to walk in by herself. And she could not.

Tom watched her, then turned to the easel. 'This is Bobby,' he said. 'I'm doing it for Gracie.' The smell of linseed oil was strong and from the window he could see the washing hanging out in the yards. He moved on then. 'Here are the designs I've done for the first batch of wallpaper. I thought we could work from here to begin with.'

He was over by the table that stood against the wall, flicking through the paper. It was cool because the room was unheated. His hands felt cold and his foot hurt. His ears strained to catch the sound of her entry and he did not know what more he could do if she did not come in. How else could he bring her back to them?

But then, at last, there she was, next to him and she reached across and took the top design.

'It's good, bonny lad,' she said and there was a shaking in her voice.

He leant over and did not take the paper but held her hand so that it was steady enough for them to look together. 'Aye, better up the right way though, lass.' They laughed and it was a gentle sound and Betsy walked back down the stairs. She had a meal to cook for them all this evening.

They stayed in the studio, for that is what it is now, Annie thought, and felt the shadows lift and her stomach was no longer tight and the black box was growing fainter. Her da was not in this room, he was dead and gone. She said it twice and finally believed it.

Slowly, haltingly, they talked about fear, about pain and anger and it was like a river which washed through them both carrying away the debris of years and, as the light waned, it was time for the planning of their future, their dream which they had held for so long. They talked until the sun moved lower in the sky and the shadows were longer, casting themselves across the yard and then she knew it was time for the place she had still to visit, the peace that she still had to make.

There was no barbed wire along the miles of beach and Tom walked with her along the track that she and Georgie had once cycled down, beating against the wind. It still roared and blustered and she gripped Tom's arm and he held his cap on with his other hand. When the sand met the foreshore she left him and lifted her head into the North-East bite, letting it whip past and round her.

Down through the sand she walked, pulling free as it clutched at her shoes and ran in over the sides. She removed them and felt the sand beneath her feet, felt it run over her as she dug in and took another stride. It was white as far as the eye could see as it had never been in those days of her childhood.

It was cool, so cool and the sky was full of battling clouds and the sea full of buffeting waves which arched, hung, then crashed frothing before sliding back into oblivion with just a few surf remnants fast bursting on the sand. The wind tore at her hair and the gulls screeched but, beyond them, all she could still hear was the crashing sucking waves. She was home now and there was no anger left in her at da and there was no need for the box ever again. He could stay inside her with the good memories, with Beauty and Peter Pan. He had only wanted peace and she could admit that she knew all about that now. She had tasted the sour pills and the noise and shapes of horrors she could not escape until now. He was not to blame any more.

She sat down near the sea where the sand was not yet wet from the incoming tide. The years had passed quickly but now she allowed herself time to remember every moment tracing her way back from that misty evening to the salt wind of today.

At length she saw that the sky was darkening and the wind began tearing at her body, plucking at her hair and snatching it across her face, stinging her with sand. Her back was stiff and her hands were numb with the lost minutes, or was it hours, that had passed.

The wind lifted her hair again. You're lucky, she thought. That's all you carry isn't it, sand and the scent of brine. We have to carry everything that touches us and sometimes it is too heavy. She picked up a pebble and threw it hard across the waves but it was caught by a crest and dragged under, and now she was shouting to the wind: 'I'm glad, at last I'm glad that I have something more to carry than grains of sand and the smell of salt.'

She looked round at the hollow curves of the dunes which lay behind her. Memories can be good, Georgie had said and he was right. The wind tugged at her cuffs as she lifted her hands to her hair which was tangled and sticky. She tucked away the flaying strands.

He had stroked her body, but left her whole. He had let her go with Sarah, let her return to England. It was all so simple really but she had not allowed herself to see it; all these years it had been hidden behind dark shadows. She could trust him. For God's sake, she could trust him and love him safely.

She wanted to hurry now and the wind was behind her as she turned and ran back through the sand. It helped her now, pushing back towards Tom. She ran and her breath was struggling in her chest and her legs were thrusting into the dunes and then Tom was there, helping her, pulling her along. The time for peace was over, there was so much to do, but first she needed Georgie.

The Post Office was closed when they reached it but that didn't matter; she would break the door down if she had to.

Tom watched as she beat on the door. It was almost dark and lights shone out into the street from the surrounding houses. He was smiling and seeing again the lass who shared out pies. The lights came on in the shop and Mrs Norris opened the door.

'We're closed,' she said.

Annie looked at her. 'I've just come home from the war. I've watched my friend have her head cut off. My husband is still in India defusing bombs. I need to send him a telegram. Are you still shut?' Her voice was fierce. Annie Manon was back, Tom knew that now.

The woman sighed and stood aside, tugging at her grey cardigan which was done up on the wrong buttons so that one side hung below the other. 'Get yourself in then. I'll find you a form and then a cup of tea. I know you now, Annie Manon. So like your da you are.' Her smile was kind now. She shuffled back behind the counter and Annie grinned at Tom.

'Aye, maybe I am, but I'm Annie Armstrong now.'

Mrs Norris was reaching down into the cupboard behind the counter.

'I know I have some somewhere,' she mumbled.

Annie looked round, tapping her foot, wondering why everything was so slow. She was in a hurry, didn't anyone understand? She looked at the brown wrapping-paper that stood in rolls in the wooden bin to one side of the shop, at the birthday cards that were stacked in the rack to the left of the door, at Tom who was still grinning.

'Hold your bleeding horses, Annie,' he whispered. 'He'll wait until she finds the form, don't you fret. Then we can begin again, all of us.' As she stood there she heard the clink of lead coins, the boy who took her hand, smelt the sun-sweated leeks, saw the red flowers of the setting beans.

In the heat of the midday sun, Georgie opened the telegram which Prue had brought him. His hands were shaking so much that he could barely read the words.

The wallpaper business is safer than bombs Stop I love you darling Stop You never did teach me how to swing from the bar Stop Come home my love and show me Stop Annie

Pruc held him as he cried and she smiled. He would be in England soon and not long after she would too with Dick Sanders.

It was time the British went home.

The Future is Ours

For Mum and Dad

I would like to thank
Sheila Doering of the United States,
Helen and Danny Buckley of Dorset,
Jackie Gaines, Marian Farrow,
Miss E. M. Glass of Somerset and
of course Sue Bramble and her library team
for their invaluable help with
the research for this book.

CHAPTER 1

Rosie gripped the ship's rail, feeling the throb of the engines, feeling the surge of the ship through the sea, seeing Frank and Nancy standing so far away on the quay, so far away and so small. The wind was harsh and hot but it didn't matter. It was 1946 and she was leaving America. That's what mattered. She was leaving to return to a family and a country she had almost forgotten after six years as an evacuee and it was unbearable.

The wind carried spray into her face but still she stood there; there was nothing else she could do. Just stand and watch the two people she had grown to love become smaller. Just stand and wonder whether she would ever see them again, whether she would ever see the bedroom where she had read Grandpa's letter three weeks ago and heard the jazz sweeping out from the gramophone, as always, across the sloping Pennsylvanian lawn.

No breeze had ruffled the maples, the sycamores or the chestnuts that day as she stood at the window. There were skis in the corner of the room, Cougar pennants on the wall. She had wanted to be a cheerleader but that wouldn't happen now. The letter had said it was time she came home – there was a job waiting for her at Woolworths – it was only fair on Norah – the war was over and the two sisters should be together again.

From the ship, Rosie had to strain to see the two small figures. How could they be so small? Frank was big, with arms that had held her when she had finished reading the letter out to them in the kitchen. Nancy was large too, and had put her arms around them both and said, 'We'll write to your grandfather in London, Rosie. We'll ask him to let you stay and complete your education, and become the journalist you want to be. We'll tell him how much we have grown to love you.'

'Woolworths, goddamn it,' Nancy had said while 'Rinso

417

White, Rinso Blue' filtered out from the wireless. 'Woolworths for Christ's sake.' They had all had tears in their eyes which Frank blamed on the onions sliced up on the side for the evening's barbecue. 'Goddamn onions,' he said and then stamped into his study, his pipe clenched between his teeth, and Nancy had laughed gently.

'This'll be the third he's broken this year if he's not careful,' she said, 'and the Sub-Editor will just love that. They've got a bet on that this year it'll be three within six months.'

But Rosie hadn't laughed. She had stood with Nancy's arms around her, wanting to cling to this plump, grey-haired, blue-eyed woman who had become her mother, who had watched her grow from a ten-year-old English girl into a sixteen-year-old American. But she didn't, because Nancy wasn't her mother, was she? She had no mother. She had a grandfather whom she knew she had once loved, and a sister whom she had never known whether she loved or even liked, a sister who had never written.

The wind on the ship was steady, no longer snatching at her cotton jacket, just streaming past her, through her, and now she looked out to the yawning emptiness of the sea and the sky, beyond which lay England. But she wouldn't think of that, or of Manhattan which was fading behind her. She would think instead of the lake, where they had gone the day after Frank had written the letter.

They went upstate each summer but this time it was different. This time they were waiting.

They had driven down through small towns which smelt of diesel as they passed the petrol stations. Her tanned legs had stuck to the seat in the heat. She could still feel the stubbled kiss from Uncle Bob who had wrapped his arms around her before she climbed into the car. His new jazz band had played at the barbecue the evening before.

He had hugged her and said, 'If you go back, Rosie, don't forget that it's the half valving that sets jazz apart, gives it the variation in pitch, oh hell, which sets it above other music. You remember us, you remember jazz, you remember that we love you. You hear me now. And you scout out for bands to send me. I want one with a middle tone, hear me? I love you, hear me? I'm glad you came. You made me glad we fought with Europe.'

She heard him. She had heard him on a dark evening five years ago too when he had been an isolationist shouting at Frank in the living-room that there was no way the States should be drawn into a war. There was no way they should supply the Britishers. For Christ's sake they wouldn't even pay their debts. She had stood then, gripping the banister, shouting at him, 'You silly old bugger. Over there the 'ouses are being bloody bombed. Me grandma's been killed and there ain't no kids in London any more. Even me best friend Jack's 'ad to go to bloody Somerset and you carry on about bleedin' money.'

The banister had been hard, but warm, unlike the ship's rail she was still clutching.

Bob had called up, 'Why did you run away then?'

And now she heard her voice as it had been then; so young, so different.

'I didn't. I was bloody sent. No one asked me. I was just sent.'

Rosie said those words again now, into the wind which stretched them out then scattered them. 'No one asked me.' And her voice was now an American drawl and there was the same anger in it that there had been then. 'No one asked me, did they, Grandpa?'

They had stopped to eat at a roadside diner surrounded by walnut and ash trees and the earth had oozed out the last of its heat as they drove the last leg towards their wooden lake house. Rosie had stood in the hall. It had smelt the same, dry and warm, filled with the scent of pine. Frank's rods were there, the old clock. But this time there was the dark sense of waiting.

She barely slept and rose with the dawn, not allowing herself to look out at the lake. She never did. She liked to feel the cool of the polished floors as she walked silently, barefoot, through the house, and then across the grass, and then the mulch of the woods before she saw the water. It was a ritual. It would keep her safe. But it hadn't this time, had it?

Still beneath the trees she had heard the lake, rippling in across the stones and on up to the sand which might still be

419

cool. Then she was out into the light and at last the lake was there, glinting, easing in across the shore. And yes, the sand was still cool and loose and fine-grained. There had been no storms recently then. No storms to force the water into three-foot waves, to smash down beyond the pebbles, soaking the sand.

Rosie looked out on to the grey sea now. The prow of the ship was slicing through the waves, her hair was thick with salt and still she could see the skyline of Manhattan and she knew that Frank and Nancy would remain there, waiting until she disappeared.

And so too they had waited at the lake, day after day, swimming, sitting, beating time to jazz; Erroll Garner, Billie Holiday, Bix Beiderbecke, always Bix, and Grandpa's reply to Frank's letter had not come.

On Nancy's birthday, towards the end of June, they had driven to the Club, taking their costumes, swimming in the pool. She hailed her friend Sandra who was up here from town too. They sat on white wrought-iron chairs which dug into the grass at the edge of the terrace overlooking the pool. They slid ice-crowded glasses to the table's edge to break the vacuum the condensation had produced. They sipped their Cokes, slowly. Behind them was the lawn which stretched back to the Clubhouse.

Frank passed them bourbon-soaked cherries from his and Nancy's cocktails and the talk was of the latest jazz band Uncle Bob was promoting, or the parched grass back home behind the rhododendrons where the hose did not reach; anything but England. Anything but Grandpa. Anything but the waiting.

And then Joe came towards them from the Clubhouse – Joe who had been here last year, who had been a Senior at their school, who was now at College. Joe who she had thought was beautiful since she had arrived in Pennsylvania, who was even more beautiful now that she might be leaving. But no, she wouldn't think of that. If she didn't think of it, it might not happen.

He was nodding at the girls, holding his hand out to Frank.

'Hi, Mr Wallen.' His voice was deeper than last year. He was taller, more blond. The hairs on his arms were bleached by the sun. Sandra nudged her and grinned. Joe didn't look, not then. But then he hadn't looked last year either. He did after dinner, though, when he smiled, his teeth white against his tan, his watch gold against his skin, and he asked her to the Subscription Dance which was being organised to raise funds for a new tennis court.

That night she had dreamed that she was on a ship, like this ship, being pulled in half by Grandpa and Norah at the prow and Frank, Nancy and Joe aft.

But she'd gone to the dance, goddamn it, she thought as she pulled her jacket round her throat and let the wind tear more strongly at her clothes. Yes, I went to the dance.

She shut her eyes because the wind was dragging tears across her cheeks. That was all. Only the wind.

She had gone to the dance because the letter had not yet come, and therefore there was still time. And now she laughed, but it was not a proper laugh as she thought of Joe's arms around her, the taste of vermouth and lemonade, the talk of College, of majoring in Politics, of his wish to enter journalism, his hopes that he might work on Frank Wallen's newspaper.

She had listened to his ambitions, which were also hers, and pushed away the thought of England. Later she watched the lake as they drove back to the house in his Buick, and then smelt his skin as he leaned down, his lips touching hers, but then his tongue pushed into her mouth and she drew back, uncertain. She had never kissed like this before.

Her feet crunched on the gravel as she walked towards the porch. 'I'll see you, Rosie,' he called as he drove away, his wheels spinning.

'Sure,' she said and had hoped that she would, in spite of drawing back, because he made her heart beat faster and her lips feel full, her skin feel as though it needed to be touched, and if she felt like this, she thought, it couldn't all end. Could it? Grandpa? Could it?

She did see him again, within two days, because Sandra had rung and asked her to a barbecue on the beach, where Joe would also be. She had answered the phone then grinned at Nancy as, later, they both strolled down to the lake and Nancy sat while Rosie swam in the cool clear water out to the raft. She lay on the wet wood, then dived into the water again, swimming back to shore, to the beach house.

She had rolled down her costume, running her hands down her body, brushing at the wet sand which had caught between her breasts and along the top of her cold buttocks, and between her thighs. Should she let his tongue search her mouth? What did she do with her own? What did other girls do?

She returned to Nancy, and sat against her chair, taking handfuls of sand and letting it run through her fingers on to the ground.

'So why don't you ask that Joe over for a swim?' Nancy had said, handing her a salad roll.

The tomato was warm and the lettuce limp. It was the taste of summer by the lake for her.

'I don't know really, Nancy. I guess I just don't want to somehow.' She had bent her head down, resting it on her knees.

'You know, when you've just come out of the water and your hair's wet it's just the same as when I used to wash it back in 1940 when you first came,' Nancy said, her voice lazy. 'I remember my first date. I didn't want him to see my body, even in a costume. Too kind of personal if you know what I mean?'

Yes, she'd known what Nancy meant and now she remembered the feel of Nancy's hand stroking her head, her voice as she said, 'You've really grown, Rosie, and I guess Joe has too. I remember it was difficult to know what to do with a new date at your age. Sometimes things that you've read in books become real and you don't know what you think about it.'

Rosie remembered now how the lake had lapped at the shore while Nancy continued.

'I guess my mom was right, Rosie, when she said that you do what seems right at the time but don't let yourself get hustled, if you know what I mean, my dear. Letting a boy go too far is wrong at your age. Kissing is enough, I think.'

And Rosie remembered saying, 'But Grandpa is hustling us. Can't we just say I'm going to stay here?' She had gripped Nancy's hand, looking up at the woman who had come to her in the night when she had been ill, the woman who had smiled from the front row when she collected her literature prize. The woman who now said that Grandpa had the right to make the decision for them all. Rosie was sixteen, not twenty-one. It was only right, but Nancy had turned away as she said this.

At the barbecue they had all jitterbugged in the humid heat which was heavy with the smell of hamburgers and onions. Joe was good, very good, but so was she and they picked up the rhythm and didn't talk, didn't laugh, just danced as a breeze at last began to ease in from the lake. Dave, Sandra's date, tapped Joe on the shoulder and they swapped partners and danced again, but though the rhythm was the same it wasn't Joe's hand which caught her and turned her and threw her up and then to one side, and so it was good to be called to eat, over by the glowing barbecue.

She didn't eat the onions but sat with Sandra on blankets out where the woods met the sand and they laughed while the boys fetched root beer which Sandra's mother had brought from the ice-box. The parents smoked cigarettes which glowed in the dark and Rosie watched the lanterns blowing near the barbecue. Frank and Nancy hung up lanterns in their garden when they had a barbecue and people danced and ate. Did Grandpa? Of course not. But it hurt too much to think of that, so she watched as the moths beat against the lights.

'Don't they know it's hopeless?' she murmured.

'D'you remember that darn great Polyphemus the old coach stopped the game for in ninth grade?' Joe called across to Dave. 'He stopped play and we watched it crawl out all wet. We had to wait until it dried and the wings got as tough as Flying Fortress wings. Jeez, those moths are more like birds. Six inches from wing-tip to wing-tip. We swatted it.'

The breeze had become a wind as the music played again and Joe pushed his fingers between hers, pulling her up, dancing so close. Her head had lain against his shoulder. The humidity remained and they were drenched with sweat and Rosie had thought of the wings beating about her face. She hated moths. She always had done and she remembered Grandpa swatting at a hard-bodied one which had banged into the kitchen light but it was Jack who had come in, cupped it in his hands, taken it into the yard, set it free. Grandpa, let me stay.

She shivered and Joe held her, looking into her face, but it wasn't the moth, it was the thought of England. Joe kissed her and she felt his lips on her forehead, in her hair, his breath on her skin, and it was what she had wanted all evening.

The music was slow and she felt his chest against hers, his hips, his legs. She wasn't going to think about moths any more, about anything any more. Not about school, not about ninth grade – only kids were in ninth grade. She was sixteen, Joe was eighteen. They were no longer kids.

Her breath made a wet patch on his shirt and she concentrated on this, not on the mailbox which would one day soon hold the letter.

Then they were dancing in the darkness beyond the lanterns, and all she could smell was him, all she could feel was him, as he moved his hand all over her back and kissed her, again and again, and her mouth opened under his, but this time his tongue didn't flick into hers.

The hand which led her off to the shelter of the wood was soft and sure and kind. The ground was dry, his kisses were on her face, her neck, and hers were on his, but then he unbuttoned her dress, slipping his hand across her shoulders, her neck. Her breathing felt strange.

She put her hands either side of his head, holding his face so that she could kiss his mouth, see his eyes which looked at her, then through her, heavy-lidded. At his lips which were as full as hers felt. Now she let his hands stroke her breasts and she knew the adults would not approve and she thought they could go to hell.

She closed her eyes as he pushed her dress back off her shoulders and it was now that he kissed her breast with his open mouth, with his tongue. She felt it, soft and warm, and allowed him to do all this because the adults were making decisions, had always made decisions, and this was hers. And they wouldn't like it.

But then she opened her eyes. The wind was howling now and she saw his head down against her skin, her body felt his hands along her thighs and his mouth was no longer soft and neither were the sounds which came from him. She was frightened, wanted Nancy. Everything was so quick. After six years everything was rushing, too fast, too goddamn fast, even this, and she didn't know how to stop Joe, how to stop anything, anything at all.

424

But then the rain came and Joe lifted his head, pulled back her dress, took her hand, helping her from the ground, laughing, running, and that night the waves on the lake were three feet high as they drove along the surface of the water. Tomorrow the sand would be solid and wet as she walked on it and she knew now it would be all right because the rain had fallen tonight when she needed it. So that meant everything would be fine, wouldn't it? And she and Joe would have the time they needed to take everything so much more slowly.

But she did not walk on the sand the next day and everything was not all right, because there was a letter from England in the mailbox. Norah insisted that she came home and Grandpa agreed. The waiting was over. There was only grief and anger to take its place.

Rosie lifted her hands now, leaning against the rail, standing on her toes, looking back, and, yes, Manhattan was still visible, she hadn't quite left, not yet.

She hadn't said goodbye to Joe, or to Sandra. Frank had driven them back to the house on the last day of June and there had been an ache inside her which seemed to reach into the air, taking the colour from the maples, the sky, the whole world. The ache hadn't left her still. She wondered if it ever would.

She had packed her trunk, listening to Louis Armstrong, ignoring the visitor from the Children's Aid Society who called to speak to Frank and Nancy. She folded her clothes neatly but left her baseball bat, skis, her pennants on the shelves and on the walls, because there would be no place for them in London.

She looked out at the baseball target set up by Frank on the back of the garage, then took the ball from the shelf, feeling its stitches, its leather-covered hardness, the slap as she whacked it into her other hand. The mitt was there on the shelf. She put the ball with it. It was all over and the tears would not stop running down her face.

They took a cab from the house the next day and she waved at Mary, the domestic help, who cried, but Rosie did not, she seemed too empty, too grey, too tired. But she had cried all night. Had Frank and Nancy?

They talked on the train to New York but the words were dry and flickered from her mind and it was as though everything were happening two feet above the ground and there were no shadows.

At Grand Central Frank showed her the bulbous clock above the information desk.

'This is a good meeting place,' he said, taking his pipe from his mouth. 'You just remember that when you come back.'

For a moment she had seen the colours and shapes of Grand Central Station and then it slipped back to the flatness and to the noise which whirled around her, sweeping in and out of her head but never staying, and she turned away but Frank pulled her back, put his arm around her. His brown eyes close to her brown eyes.

'You've got to fight a good corner. Make something positive out of the next three days before you get on that boat. We want you to soak it in, remember it. Remember America. That's why we're filling in the time here, not back home. The future is yours, Rosie. You must make something positive out of the rest of your life. Have we got a deal?'

Rosie looked at Nancy and then back to Frank and wanted to shout, But there's this pain, deep inside and it's because I'm leaving you, the lake, Sandra, America; and Joe. And I'm angry with Grandpa and Norah and you, for letting this happen. And I'm frightened because I'm going to a place which used to be home but which isn't any more.

Nancy touched her face as the people parted around them. 'None of this is the end of the world, you know. We can write. You'll come and stay, or we'll come over.' Her voice was heavy with sadness, her eyes shadowed as Frank's were, and Rosie knew that these two people were hurting too. That they loved her, that they didn't want her to go, any more than she wanted to leave.

They walked on through the pillared hall and the noise was greater. People clustered at the ticket booths. Were they going home? Were they laughing and smiling because they were going to people they knew and loved?

Frank had gripped her then, as Rosie now gripped the rail again, her hands down from her face, Manhattan all but gone, though not quite.

He had gripped her, pulling her back to him. His hands had

been the same as they had always been, short-nailed, strong. Would they be old when she saw him again?

He had said, 'Nearly sixty cleaners come in the early hours, just so you can put your toots down on the great big shine. Now isn't that something?'

She had nodded, but it was nothing in amongst the pain. She had leaned her head back at Nancy's command and looked at the picture of the zodiac on the towering ceiling.

'There's something wrong with it, so people say. Maybe Orion is back to front or something. But it looks pretty good to me.' But it was nothing.

They called in to the Oyster Bar, then passed the movie house and stood and looked at the bronze doors behind which the trains waited at their platforms. There would be one taking Nancy and Frank back to Pennsylvania on the fourth, but not her. No, she would take a ship and a train and then a cab, each one taking her further from them, from Joe, from them all.

'These trains leave at one minute past the scheduled time. Always one minute past. Remember that when you come back,' Nancy said.

They took a cab to the Plaza Hotel but Rosie turned before they left the station and saw 89 East 42nd Street in gold lettering above the main doorway. Did Euston have its address written up? She couldn't remember. She didn't care.

She still didn't care, standing here, surging away from America, remembering the avenues they had driven along and across, the streets they had turned down which were plunged into darkness by the shadows of the skyscrapers. They had driven beneath bridges, slicing in and out of the shadows of the girders.

'In winter the tops of these skyscrapers are sometimes in the clouds,' Frank had said, his hand clasped over the bowl of his pipe because Nancy would not tolerate that goddamn smell in the car.

The buildings reared up, jagged against the blue of the sky. They were complete, untouched. But the place she was going to wasn't. The bombs had made sure of that.

In the Plaza lobby there were plants with rich green waxy leaves. They looked so cool in the heat, like the lake. She touched one. It was plastic and warm.

Her bedroom was silent, empty. She had no energy to draw the drapes across the full-length window, she just let her clothes drop to the floor in the bathroom and stood beneath the cold water, wanting the sharpness, the intake of breath, the soothing of the pain which could not be soothed.

They walked in Central Park. There were tennis courts.

'Will the Lake Club raise the money for another one?' she asked and Frank nodded.

'They usually do.'

Would Joe take someone else to the next Subscription Dance? Would he kiss her breasts too? If she had stayed, would they have been able to take it all more slowly? Would she have been able to ask him to kiss her gently, to hold her in his arms, not press his lips against her nipples, not yet. Not until she was less of a child. Not until they really knew one another.

Would Frank and Nancy still sit around the pool, would the glasses still stick to the table? Would the world go on?

Frank had stopped and was pointing his pipe towards the grey rocks, the drying grass.

'This was covered with squatters' shacks in the Depression but wars are good for us. We make money, we save money. Now we need something to spend it on, so we'll have a boom. Poor old Europe won't. It's been drained white. It'll be tight back home, Rosie.'

But London wasn't home, and neither was Pennsylvania any more. She was in no man's land. Didn't anybody see that but her?

That night when midnight had been and gone she stood at the window of her room, a strange room in a strange city. She listened to the garbage trucks wheezing and clanking, the air-conditioning humming, the police sirens wailing, and knew that she had felt this lonely before. She recognised the panic which surged and tore into her, gripping her hands into fists, squeezing the breath from her throat. She recognised the pain which tumbled along with it.

It was the pain Grandpa had tried to hug and kiss away so long ago on the wharf at Liverpool but he had not been able to touch the rawness inside her because he was the one saying she couldn't stay.

He was the one saying those words again.

Rosie held the drape tightly, screwing it up, holding it to her mouth, leaning her head against the glass. All around her was the humming, the wailing, the clanking, and now there were tears too. Tears which turned to sobs and the drape was creased and damp when she turned to her bed, but even then there was no peace because the waves of the lake lapped and rippled and its glare hurt her eyes as she dipped in and out of sleep. In and out. In and out, until she woke, sweat-drenched, the sheets twisted about her limbs.

But it was still night, and the water was cold from the shower as she let it run over her face, her body. She was almost a woman now and had been a child when Grandpa had held her with the cold September wind whirling around them on that Liverpool dock.

'My little Rosie,' he had said. 'My darling little Rosie. It won't be long, my love. I promise you that. It really won't be long but I want you safe.' And he had cried. Tears had smeared – not trickled – just smeared all over his face which had been old even then.

Rosie turned the shower on harder. 'It's been too long, Grandpa. It's been such a very long time and I don't remember you any more. I don't belong any more. You are tearing me away from my home again and I think I hate you.'

In the morning they watched the riders exercising their horses in Central Park, then took a steamer which smelt of diesel. They looked at Staten Island, Ellis Island, the ancient ferries which plied to and fro, one with funnels, and it had meant nothing because she was leaving.

They took a cab up to Fifth Avenue, driving past the steam that drifted from manhole covers and came from the cracks in the hot water system carried in underground piping.

They shopped in stores for a crêpe de Chine nightdress for Norah which Nancy chose and Rosie knew should have been flannelette, but then, Norah might have changed. But what did it matter?

She looked up. Behind her, captured by the mirror tilted on the counter, was a red-haired girl, and for a moment she thought it was Sandra. But of course it wasn't.

They moved on to the candy department and bought maple candies, butterscotch and toffee because, Nancy said, the neighbours would like sweets especially now that the rationing was so intense.

She bought gum and fruit-flavoured envelopes. And stockings for herself, for Norah, for Jack's mum – and Camel cigarettes, too, because Maisie was a twenty a day girl. She bought a toy car for Lee, Jack's new brother, but she didn't mind whether it was a Buick or a Cadillac. None of it mattered. She bought a sweater for Grandpa and another for Jack, another for Jack's dad, Ollie.

For lunch they put nickels in a slot in a diner and she saw a boy who she thought was Joe. But of course it wasn't and by this time tomorrow she would be drawing away from Manhattan, hearing the gulls, losing Frank and Nancy, losing them all.

Now Rosie, standing by the rail, looked up at the sky. She hadn't noticed the gulls before.

They hadn't been able to eat their meal and had taken a bus to the Rockefeller Center and Rosie had watched the coins clink through the driver's change machine, like the hours and minutes of these last few days. They had stood on the sidewalks as Nancy told them of the cleaner employed full-time to keep the Center floor clear of gum and she had thought of her Grandma who had worked as a cleaner at the bank. It was there that she had died when the bomb had fallen just before Rosie left for America.

That evening they went to Chinatown and she bought a jar of spice from a shop which had varnished ducks hanging in the open shop-front. An old woman passed with shoes that slopped as she walked.

They sat and drank cold tea at an outdoor café and Rosie bought a book of Chinese art from an old street vendor. Maybe Jack would like that. And still the minutes clicked away.

The cloud layer had not dispersed with the coming of night and reflected the Manhattan lights. The London skies had been aglow on the nights before she left. Not with light but with flames.

It was nine o'clock now. It would soon be the fourth. They flagged down a cab and drank Manhattans in a restaurant which spilled seats out on to the pavement.

They sat and watched the women in hats, the men in smart

grey suits, the boys in shirtsleeves, the girls in cotton dresses. Each girl looked like Sandra, each boy like Joe. She picked out the ice-cube from her drink. It numbed her tongue, but not her pain.

'I'm saving the best for tomorrow,' Frank said, taking her hand in his. 'It's somewhere you'll never forget, somewhere that'll warm you on the long trip home, on the nights when maybe you can't sleep.'

Nancy touched her shoulder and smiled.

Frank continued. 'It's a place I always think of when times are tough. It's the street where Bob and I used to visit to soak in jazz. Real original jazz.'

Rosie looked at him and saw that his eyes had lost the shadow of pain which he had carried over these last days.

She stood at the window again that night listening to the lorries, the garbage truck, the sirens. She showered, she cried and drifted in and out of sleep and there was Joe, his wristwatch glinting, his hand on her skin, his mouth too. There was Grandma, lying beneath the rubble. Jack reaching out to her. Then Frank and Nancy holding her, sure and strong, then Grandpa calling her from their arms but she couldn't see his face.

They didn't talk over breakfast. The pecan waffle looked good, the celebrations in the street outside were loud for the fourth of July but it didn't matter. Nothing mattered.

It was hot again, so hot. They took a cab to Frank's favourite place. She stretched out her arm along the window, loosening her fingers, breathing slowly, keeping the panic in, mixing it up with the pain. They passed in and out of shadows and the noise of the streets was loud. Life was all around them but not in her. Not with her.

Frank was clenching his unlit pipe between his teeth, his fingers tapping on the armrest of the door.

'Charlie Parker and Dizzy Gillespie played in clubs next door to one another down fifty-second Street, this goddamn great street. I heard them. Billie Holiday sang too. Dixieland and New Orleans just roared out across the street all day and into the night.' He was stabbing the air with his pipe now. 'There was nothing to pay, just the price of a beer and the love of the music. It's stayed with me. It'll stay with you, keep you warm.

431

It's special for me, and for Nancy, and Bob. Now it'll be special for you.'

The cab slowed, turned into the street and Rosie watched as Frank leaned forward, his face eager, and then she saw the bleakness begin in his eyes and his mouth set into a tense line. She had looked then, out of the window, at the clubs which would warm her, remind her, and she saw what Frank had seen.

She saw the smoky brownstone buildings which were still there, but without the clubs. There was just paper which scudded about the street and paint which was peeling off doors and window glass which was cracked or gone. Dented cars lined the street, a trash can rolled on the sidewalk.

They drove down slowly and where there had once been jazz sweeping out of the windows were groups of men lounging, staring. There were more standing in dingy doorways, buying drugs, selling drugs, taking drugs, and Rosie held Frank's hand and told him that it was jazz sweeping across the sloping lawn that she would remember. It was Uncle Bob's groups, the barbecues, the baseball target, the maple syrup on pancakes at breakfast – those were the things that would warm her.

'This is nothing. This doesn't matter.' But then she could speak no more and her pain was gone as she saw his in the tears which were smeared across his face, as Grandpa's had been. Frank looked old too.

And now, standing on her toes again at the rail, she could no longer see Manhattan. They were gone and she finally turned from the wind and wept. It was over. All over.

Frank and Nancy stood hand in hand now that the ship had quite gone and Frank didn't look at Nancy as he said, 'When I saw those clubs had gone and everything had changed I felt my heart break. It looked like us with her gone.'

Nancy put her arms around him, holding him.

'It's over,' he said. 'Those six years are gone and I love that girl more than I ever thought I could love anyone, other than you.'

Nancy said into his jacket, 'We knew she had to go back. We chose to forget. That wasn't fair on her. We let her down, but maybe we could go visit in a few months, make sure she's OK?'

They were both crying and the sun was too hot.

Frank said as he looked back to the ocean again, 'No, she must settle back with her family and only come when it's right for her. She's had a safe war and it's over now. We all just have to get on with the rest of our lives.'

Neither could speak any more and they caught a cab, and then a train and then drove back to the lake, but Frank did no more fishing that summer. He and Nancy just sat and listened to the waves on the shore.

CHAPTER 2

For the first three days of the voyage to England, Rosie lay on her bunk, not eating, not sleeping, just pushing the sheet into her mouth to smother her tears. The other three girls thought she was seasick.

On the fourth day she dressed, showered and walked the deck, feeling the rise and fall of the ship. There were loungers lined up near the rail, quoits to play, music in the evening, and space. She leaned against the rail, the sun was hot, the wind fierce. It tore at her hair. She was going back to England because she had been told to and that was that.

But there was all this anger and pain which seemed trapped inside her body, inside her mind, and she wished it would break free and be swept into nothing by the wind. Hadn't Grandpa realised that she'd grow to love her new life? Didn't he know how she would feel being dragged away again? But then he didn't know her any more. She didn't know him.

She walked on, holding the hair back from her face, watching as a child threw a bean bag to his mother, and then to the father. Some others were playing French cricket. There was room for that on the upper deck.

On the trip six years ago there had been no room, no parents. Just children with labels pinned to their lapels, wearing plimsolls, gumboots, their faces grown wary and tired. There were destroyers and other ships ploughing through the grey waters, not the space about the ship that there was now.

One morning Rosie had come with the others to the rails to wave but the destroyers were gone and each ship had to make its own way. It was that dull grey expanse of sea that Rosie remembered because that was when she realised that she and all the other children really had left their homes. They had to

434

make their own way too. There had been a bleakness in her then, deeper than tears, and anger too.

But that night some of the boys had rolled marbles across the dance floor and the children's escorts had fallen, in mid foxtrot, on to great fat bums. Rosie and the boy who reminded her of Jack had laughed, along with so many others. The escorts hadn't laughed, they had gripped the children's collars and with red angry faces had told them of the dangers of a cracked coccyx. One lad had said that he didn't know you could break your flaming arse on a marble and they had laughed again.

Rosie stopped now, near the stern, watching the flag streaming out and the wake frothing and boiling. Yes, they had laughed a lot, and cried with despair and anger, but in the end it had been all right, hadn't it? She looked down at her shoes – open-toed, leather – and the tanned foot, and remembered the plimsolls, the child that she had been.

Yes, that had turned out all right, and so would this. Wouldn't it? But the child was almost a woman, and the pain seemed deeper, more sharply etched, and she wondered who would be there to meet her when the ship docked.

There was no one to meet her at Liverpool. She took a cab to Lime Street. The streets were so small, the sky so grey, the rain so heavy and no one had come to meet her.

There were no gold letters above this station, no drawling men in short-sleeved shirts, no women in slacks and dark glasses. No one who called her honey and showed her a bulbous clock under which they would meet when she came back. No one to meet her here at all. She wouldn't cry, not here, in this strange land. Later she would though – in Grandpa's house in Middle Street, but only when it was dark and everyone else asleep.

She bought tea from a trolley and handed over a sixpence.

'That's swell,' she said, picking up her case, shrugging so that her bag wouldn't slip from her shoulder, moving to one side to let the man with the cap buy his.

'Yank, eh?' said the woman, passing the man his cup without looking. Her headscarf was knotted at the front and her hair hung down her forehead. She looked tired and thin.

Rosie sipped the thick stewed tea and looked at the woman,

435

the man, all these people who spoke in a thick scouse that she could barely understand.

'I don't know,' she replied, putting the cup back down on the trolley and moving towards her platform, tears stinging the back of her throat. I don't know goddamn anything. I only know I'm hurting. I only know I shouldn't be here. And nobody has come to meet me.

The train shuddered out along the tracks, through suburbs which were torn and jagged, splashed with purple from the rosebay willowherb. There were great gaps in the streets and bomb-damaged houses with rooms hanging open to the air, their damp and peeling wallpaper still clinging to the plaster. She had seen photographs in the newspapers but nothing had prepared her for this.

The train was taking her further from the sloping lawns, making her see what she had escaped. But that wasn't her fault, was it? Grandpa had made her come back and he hadn't even come to meet her, and neither had Jack.

She wiped the train window clear of condensation, felt the wet on her skin as she made herself count the telegraph poles, made herself smell the train, taste the tea thick on her tongue and teeth, watch the rain, because all this was England. The raindrops jerked down the pane as the train rattled slowly over the points.

Poor little country. Poor goddamn little country – and she saw tired brownstone buildings where no jazz played.

Guilt came then and it was shocking in its forgotten strength. It was the same guilt which had come on heavy heat-laden nights when she was safe and thousands of miles away from the bombs, the rationing, the grind. But the feeling had faded with the years and she had forgotten it until today. And now there was so much pain, so much anger, so much guilt that she thought her head would burst, but then this too faded. All of it faded. Nothing stayed. She was too tired. Right now she was too tired but it would all come again, along with the panic. She knew. It had been the same six years ago.

She wiped at the window again then sat with her hands clenched. She watched as the man opposite took out a packet of Woodbines, and struck a match. The smell of sulphur filled the carriage before being swept away in a rush of noise and wind as he hauled on the window strap, flicked out the match, then snapped it up again.

She watched as he drew deeply and read his paper again. She watched as the woman opposite took out sandwiches wrapped in greaseproof paper. The tomato was warm and had stained the bread. The child in the corner was kicking his leg against the opposite seat. He had soft brown eyes like Jack's. She looked away quickly.

Why hadn't Jack met her? She pressed her hands together tightly in her lap. Why? He had written all through the years and had said he would come. Frank had cabled Grandpa telling him the time and date. Why hadn't one of them come?

She looked at the boy in the corner again and then out at the fields, so green, so lush, even in the greyness, even in the rain. She had forgotten how green it was, how small the fields were. They passed old houses made of deep red Cheshire stone, and copses. She'd forgotten there were copses.

Yes, why hadn't either of them come? She had known Norah would not. 'Norah's walking around like a flaming great purple bloodhound,' Jack had written in his first letter to her. 'She'll not forgive you for going, leaving her here with iodine and impetigo. It'll be your fault that the programme was scrapped before she could come too. Just shrug her off.'

Rosie had, she'd forgotten about the older girl who had increasingly pushed, shoved and scowled her way through life the older she became, but now they would be meeting again. Would it be any better?

The man opposite stubbed out his cigarette on the floor, grinding his heel down, squashing it, mixing it with the dirt from the floor.

Rosie remembered salvaging dog-ends with Jack before the war then rolling them into new fags and selling them for two-pence a pack. She and Jack had done that together and his mum had laughed but Grandma had never known. She would not have laughed and now so much of the past was coming back. Grandma would have told Grandpa he was a fool not to tan 'that girl's backside'. He had always loved Rosie so much, but he hadn't come to meet her, had he? He had just issued the order.

Rosie hadn't cried when Grandma died beneath the rubble

of the bank. Norah had cried while the funeral guests were there and then she had gone up and sorted through Grandma's mothballed clothes trying on the coat with the fox fur and the paws and the head with eyes which followed you around. It hadn't suited her purple face, Rosie thought.

Norah had kept that and the cardigans and given the jumpers to Rosie to cut the arms off and sew into blankets. They had smelt of sweat until Rosie had washed them. Norah had sold the rest to the rag and bone man and kept the money.

Rosie shifted in her seat. Surely she had changed? They were grown up now, things were different. The seat prickled and the view of Arundel Castle on the wall above the man's head was faded.

Jack had unscrewed the one of Weymouth on the evacuee train carrying their school down to Somerset when war first began. He had sold it to the owner of the village pub to get them enough money to travel back at Christmas when the bombers still hadn't come.

His mum had sent him again though, after Rosie had gone and the bombs were falling night after night and after old Meiner's house down the road was crushed. Rosie had liked Mr Meiner. Jack had fiddled them both a job lighting fires at his house on the Sabbath by saying they were older than they were. 'Meiner left Germany but the buggers killed him anyway,' Jack had written and his mum and dad had sent him back to Somerset then. But it was to a different area. Norah had gone too.

Rosie watched the woman next to her peeling off the crust of her last sandwich, eating it piece by piece, licking her finger and stabbing up the crumbs. Then she folded up the paper and put it away again in her bag.

Rationing was still on in England. They had debts to repay, the country to rebuild, and Rosie couldn't take out her great slab of cheese, or the fruit, and the biscuits prepared on the ship. Instead she put her hand into her bag and pulled out a bread roll she had saved from breakfast.

They were passing through towns now and these were damaged too. They pulled into stations; doors slammed, whistles blew, and there was never the long mournful hoot of the American trains.

The man smoked another cigarette and this time the sulphur filled the carriage, and Rosie remembered the oast-houses and the hops, and smiled. Then there were the candles which the fumigation man lit when she and Norah had scarlet fever. How ill they had been, how the bed bugs had bitten, how they had tossed, turned, sweated, ached.

Rosie threw the little boy a sweet and his mother smiled.

'How old is he?'

'Seven.'

Their father and mother had died in the year of Rosie's seventh birthday. She knew she was that age because her grandpa had said Martha, his daughter, her mother, 'had seven years of sunshine with you, my little Rosie'.

Grandpa had bought the house then, because the landlord wouldn't improve it. How he had managed she didn't know. He wouldn't tell, he had only muttered that his daughter hadn't worked herself to death in that laundry and he hadn't worked two shifts twice a week to see it all slip through his hands. So he had bought it off the landlord and together he and Ollie, Jack's dad, had chipped at the plaster, stripping it down, disinfecting the bricks, replastering, reflooring both houses, because Ollie had bought his too.

Since then there had been no cockroaches to scuttle from beneath the wallpaper and no bed bugs. No tins of paraffin at the foot of each bed leg. Rosie scratched herself as the train gushed into the blackness of a tunnel.

There had been no more bed stripping, mattress scrubbing, but there had been . . . what was it? Oh yes, roses. Roses whose fragrance filled the yard. She had forgotten those until this moment.

The train slapped out into the light and Rosie put up her hand to shield her eyes. The rain had stopped. It was four p.m. and they would be in London in an hour.

She leaned her head back, letting it roll with the train, watching the man opposite tap his knee with his newspaper. The child was asleep, his head against his mother's arm, and she missed Nancy and felt the pain again, raw, savage, and the sky seemed darker.

There was no one to meet her at Euston either and she gripped her case more tightly as she queued for a cab. 'Putney, please,' she told the driver, leaning forward, easing her case into the taxi. The trunk was tipped on end by the porters and juggled upright in the front. She tipped them half a crown.

'Bloody Yanks,' she heard a man say behind her, and his voice burst through her pain.

She turned as she got into the cab. 'Bloody Britishers,' she said. But she wished she hadn't as they drove through a ruined London. The skyline was different and there was uncleared wasteland where there had once been streets.

She pulled herself forward, looking out. It was drizzling now. It would be hot at home in Pennsylvania. But no, that wasn't home. This was home. She pushed the strap of her bag from her aching shoulder, remembering the same ache from her journey to Liverpool so long ago. But then it had been her gas mask which was heavy, filled with sandwiches and fruitcake.

A man with a long nose and dark suit had taken the gas mask away from her. He had given it to Grandpa to take home because she wouldn't be needing it where she was going. Had Grandpa given it back to the Town Hall?

They were getting closer now. The streets were clustering. The lampposts had cracked bulbs. There was rope on one of them. So children still swung on them as she and Jack had done. Why hadn't he or Grandpa come?

She sat back, pressing herself deep into the leather seat. She didn't want to go on. She didn't want to reach Middle Street, leave the cab, see Norah, see Grandpa. She wanted to go home.

But they were there now, turning into Middle Street, and the taxi slowed.

'Which one, miss?'

She didn't know. It was all so small, so narrow, and the far end had gone; flattened into piles of bricks, tiles, rosebay willowherb. Grass spurted out of the hard-packed earth and there was a surge of sadness within her for the people who had once lived and laughed here where children were now scrambling, shooting guns made out of wood, cowboys shooting Indians.

'Your grandpa's been watching too many bloody Hopalong Cassidy films at the flicks,' Jack had said when she had told him she was leaving for America.

'Will you write?' she had asked, sitting on the kerb rolling marbles, trying to get his tenner, and he had, though he hadn't come to meet her. But she mustn't keep saying this, she must try and remember which house had been her home. She must try and stop the panic.

'Which one, miss?' the cabbie asked again, almost coming to a halt, and then she saw it. Number 15, with a front door which had once been bright red and was now dark, dirty, almost colourless. It was only now, with the taxi halted and the meter still clicking over, that she remembered the colour it should have been. It was all so small.

The panic was gone. There was nothing in its place, just an emptiness.

She couldn't leave the cab. She couldn't move. She fumbled in her bag, looking for money. But it wasn't money she was looking for, it was just time, and then Norah came out, standing by the open dirty door, leaning back against the wall, staring at her, her face just the same but her hair frizzed up into a perm, tight like her face. She looked more than her eighteen years and Rosie felt a rush of pity for the sister who had been left behind.

She pulled on the handle, pushed open the door and walked towards her.

'Hi, Norah,' she said, leaning forward, but Norah stiffened and so Rosie pulled back without kissing her cheek and the emptiness was filled again.

'You're back then,' Norah said, and her voice was the same too. Sharp and hard. 'Grandpa's asleep, don't disturb him.'

Rosie could hear the children playing on the rubble at the end, where Mr Sims and Mr Elton had lived, Mr Meiner too. She looked down there, not at Norah. She had come back as she had been told to, and Grandpa was asleep, Jack was nowhere and Norah had not changed. So this was it, was it? This was goddamn it. But she wouldn't cry. Not yet. She had no right to in this ruined street.

'Mr Sims died then, did he?' she asked. 'It seems kind of sad. He used to give us toffee, do you remember?' It was better to talk, to drawl out the words slowly and make sure her voice did not shake. It was better to do that than stand here making no attempt to reach out and touch this girl she had not seen for over six years.

Norah moved back into the house. 'That trunk will have to go into the yard. There's no room in the house,' was all she said.

Rosie knew there was no room. The small hall ran into the only downstairs room and upstairs there was just a bedroom and a large boxroom which she and Norah had shared, head to toe. Would that be the case again?

'Hey, miss, how're we going to get this lot in?'

The cabbie was out now, heaving at the trunk, and Rosie called after Norah, but there was no answer and so she dumped her bags on the sidewalk and tried to help him edge it out and lower it to the road, but it was too heavy for the two of them.

'I'll see if those kids will help,' she said, running on down the road, calling to them, wishing that she was running back to Liverpool, back to Frank and Nancy. But then she heard her name, and then again, and footsteps sounded behind her, closer, catching her. Then a hand caught her arm, slowing her, stopping her, and it was Jack. At last it was Jack, turning her to him, gripping her shoulders, shouting, 'Where the hell have you come from?'

'I'm back from the cowboys, didn't you know?' she whispered. 'Didn't you know? Why didn't you meet me?' His eyes were brown as they had always been, his smile the same.

He picked her up now, swung her round.

'Where are your plaits? I've always thought of you with your plaits. Where are you going to bung your rubber bands now?'

It was so good to feel his arms, hear his voice, see the hair which still fell across his forehead, because he was her friend. He had always been her friend. She laughed and cried and held him close and he put his arms round her.

'God, I've missed you,' he said and it was almost more than she could bear.

He pulled her back towards the cab. 'I didn't know you were coming back.' He squeezed her hand then dropped it as they reached the cab.

'But Frank cabled Norah to tell you.'

'Then it's your own bloody fault I never got the message. You should have known better.' He was heaving at one end of the trunk and they had it up, and he and the driver went down the alley between the houses, through the alley at the back where the gutter was damp from the drizzle which had now stopped.

Jack was so tall, his shoulders were wide and his body was thick. He looked more than sixteen. He sounded more. His voice was deep like Joe's but there wasn't the tan, there wasn't the soft quality of the clothes, of her clothes. He was like England, worn and tired. Norah was right. It hadn't been fair that she had missed all this. She turned and looked at the crumpled skyline of the houses backing on to the alley.

They were at the back gate and she didn't want to go in, she held it for them because the yard was home and she couldn't go in, not yet, because Grandpa was in there, and he hadn't come to meet her, he hadn't even stayed awake. He had just dragged her home and she thought she hated him even though he had once loved her so much and she had loved him.

They walked back to the taxi. She paid the fare, tipped half a crown and didn't care what Jack thought, even if it was 'bloody Yank'. He said nothing, though, and she watched the taxi drive away, leaving her here. Her journey was over. She turned to Jack, to his warmth and his smile, and looked at the hands which had written her letters when others hadn't.

'So where *are* you going to put your rubber bands then?' He was leaning back against the wall, putting his hands in his pockets, sloping one leg over the other.

'Round my little finger, I guess,' Rosie said, leaning back on the lamppost which threw light into Grandpa's bedroom.

'Will Woolworths like that, I ask myself?'

'Woolworths will have to get stuffed if they don't,' Rosie answered, looking up into the sky where a weak sun was filtering through.

The sun would throw sloping shadows across the lawn tomorrow. It would glitter on the lake. Nancy would wear goggles to sunbathe. Frank would fish.

'Are you glad you're back?' Jack asked.

'Now you're here,' Rosie said, and flushed because the boy she had known was gone and this half-stranger was in his place. 'Can I come and see your mum?'

She said this because he had blushed too and she felt awkward and wanted to include his family in her feelings, in

443

her words. She loved his mum anyway. She was full-breasted like Nancy, and kind too.

Jack took out his cigarettes, ducking his head down to catch the flame of the match. Something was different between them. Had there been too many years? Too many miles? Had they grown too far apart to be friends? But that could never happen, not for her anyway. This was the boy who had swung her at the rec, who had beaten her at flicksies, helped her tie string to all the knockers in the street, then pulled them with her, heard the knocks. This was the boy who had run whooping through the streets with her when their neighbours had come to their doors, shouting and swearing at them. Who had written.

'Make it tomorrow,' Jack said, pushing himself up from the wall. 'Come and see me on the stall first, down Malvern Lane. We'll talk, catch up. Things aren't the same in there.' He nodded to his house, his face angry, and then he smiled. 'Get in there and see your grandpa. He's been waiting. He's missed you.'

He sauntered off, nodding at her, not going into his house but on down the street. Then he stopped and called back, 'Got any gum, chum?'

'Sure, a goddamn trunkful,' she called back.

He walked on. Then turned again. 'Glad you're back, Rosie. I would've met you. We've only grown, we ain't changed, you know. Not really. Tomorrow then.'

The hallway was dark and so small and there was no sound in the house. No Bix Beiderbecke, no Erroll Garner, no New Orleans with the banjo cutting through the jumble of sounds, keeping the rhythm going. Rosie stood still, her hands on the wallpaper. It was the same; she could feel the pattern running on down beneath her fingers. She had done this when she left. She remembered now.

She thought of the houses she had passed on the train, with their rooms hanging open to the world, wallpaper torn and flapping. That could have been this house. Her grandpa could have been one of those who died, and she pushed open the door into the room where they cooked and washed and lived because she couldn't bear the thought of that and knew now that she still loved him.

444

There he was, sitting at the table with the brown chipped teapot in front of him. It was the one Grandma had bought. So that hadn't changed. But, dear God, he had. He turned as she entered.

'Rosie, you're here. I didn't know when you were coming, if you were coming. I couldn't rest. I've waited all week for you.'

Somehow she smiled, put down her bags, her jacket and walked towards him, her hands held out. He stood and pulled her to him, holding her close. Her arms were round this man who had once been strong and firm, who had held her with nailmaker's arms and told her he loved her. He was thin, and so small, so old with an old man's smell and he had always been so clean.

She looked past him to Norah. You bitch, she thought, you've just lied to me, you lied to him, kept my cable from him. You black-hearted bitch.

'I'm sorry, my Rosie.' His voice was cracked, stumbling, and his words were loose, clumsy, as he whispered, 'I'm sorry for bringing you back. Norah wanted you here and I promised your grandma you'd come home. I thought you'd want to. Norah said you'd think we didn't want you back, if we let you stay. Sometimes I can't think straight, like I used to.'

She held him, remembering how much she had loved him, knowing how much she still did.

Norah was washing dishes in soda, her head up, listening for the words Rosie knew Grandpa did not want her to hear.

'I love you, Rosie. I couldn't have you thinking we didn't want you back,' he repeated.

'I know, I know,' she soothed because the man was now the child and that hurt more than all the pain so far. 'I love you too.'

Rosie moved back, holding his hand, guiding him on to the chair again, pulling another round to sit at the table with him. He wouldn't release her hand. His joints were loose, his face long, his jaw slack and he had no bottom teeth.

'I've sure missed you, Grandpa. Every day. I guess I couldn't wait to get home, to you.' A lie, but what did it matter.

Norah banged down a cup she was washing on the draining board. 'Took your time, then. Planning to stay for more school. That wasn't fair. I told him so.'

You talk too goddamn much, Rosie wanted to say, but she didn't because Grandpa didn't move, didn't say anything, just dropped his head and Rosie rubbed the back of his big veined hands, touching the swollen knuckles with her fingers.

'Woolworths not good enough for you, then? It suits me.' Norah was wiping the cup with a teatowel.

Rosie sat back. 'Woolworths will be fine. Just fine. I can't think of anything I would rather do, Norah.' But she wanted to say, You still got that dandy fox fur? You must think you're the tops waltzing in wearing that, but she didn't because Norah had been left behind and no matter what she'd said or done since, it wasn't fair. And that was that.

Norah turned back, tucking the edge of the towel into the cutlery drawer beneath the drainer.

'You'd better get down to the Food Office tomorrow to get your ration book. You're eating our points.' She gestured to the pan on the old gas oven. 'Put that on the table.'

Rosie wanted to tip the pan upside-down on that prissy perm but instead she smiled at Grandpa, who brought out a handkerchief with a trembling hand and raised it to his mouth, wiping the corners, putting it away again carefully. So careful, so slow; like his writing had looked, but she hadn't noticed.

Too many years had passed and Rosie saw the old brown-stones as she fetched the pan full of mashed potatoes. She looked for a bowl.

'Put it on the table in the pan. Or have you forgotten how we live?'

Rosie flushed. There was nothing she could say because she had.

'I've got tins of ham in the trunk. Shall I go get them?' She moved towards the door.

'No, the Spam's cut. We'll save the ham for something special.'

So there we are, Rosie thought as she sat down. I'm home. I sure am home. But she wouldn't cry, not here, and she reached again for Grandpa's hand. Now she was here she remembered the room and it hadn't changed. Along one wall were all Grandpa's books. He'd read each one and had wanted her and Jack to do the same, but she'd run out of time, and so had Jack. Norah had refused to read them.

She looked round as she cut the pink Spam, eating it with mashed potatoes but no salad. The dresser was the same, the bread board, the bread knife with the burned handle, the worn lino, and there were no cockroaches, maybe no bed bugs. There was a bed in the room though, the folding one that her mother had slept on whilst her father used the chair.

She turned to Norah. 'Is that my bed?'

Norah pointed her knife at Grandpa. 'No, it's his. He has accidents. It's not worth soiling a proper bed and he can reach the privy quicker.'

Grandpa continued to chew but flicked a glance at Rosie, then reached for his handkerchief and wiped his lips, again.

Rosie talked then about the trip over, the train, the damage, the bombs. She talked of anything and everything because she couldn't bear to see the shame in Grandpa's eyes, to hear that voice slashing and wounding as it had always done. The war had changed nothing in Norah.

Norah ate on, chewing, drinking her water, not listening. Rosie knew she wasn't listening but at least she wasn't speaking.

Grandpa rose and walked to the back door, out to the privy. 'Won't be a moment,' he said.

Norah continued to eat. Rosie talked then of New York's rundown East Side, the 'lung blocks', those tenements which gave their people TB.

'Like Mum and Dad,' she said. 'If we hadn't had Grandma and Grandpa, what would we have done? He was just great to us.'

'They wouldn't have been working in the laundry anyway if he'd stayed in Bromsgrove.' Norah pointed her knife at the yard. 'What was wrong with being a nailer? He goes on about it enough. Grandma didn't want to come down. She told me.'

Rosie said, 'Grandma was always complaining. You couldn't take anything she said seriously and you've got awful like her. You've got a tongue like a . . .' but Grandpa came back and so she hurried on and spoke of the hop-picking they'd done in the years before the war. The sun, the smell, the fun.

'Couldn't go to Kent like the rest though, could we? Had to be up in Malvern because that's where the Midlanders used to go.' Norah didn't look up as she spoke, just hooked a piece of mash at the corner of her mouth with her tongue. 'Why couldn't we be the same as everyone else? That's what I want to know.'

Rosie cut in. 'So, how was Somerset then, Norah? Did you settle in?' She wanted to draw that sour tongue away from the old man who had sent her away and then brought her back, but only because he thought it best for her. She knew that now. She had always known it really, but the anger was still there, inside her, mingled with the pain.

'Not as good as America. Country life is hard. I skivvied, worked my fingers to the bone.'

Rosie looked at her. 'Got enough flesh on you now then, Norah, you could slip on a marble any day and not break that goddamn backside.'

No one was eating now. Norah sat back, her eyes dark with rage, her mouth closed into a thin line. Then she finished her potatoes, stabbing them with the fork. Rosie took the plates, washed them in the kettle water. It was nearly dark now and the cracked clock above Grandpa's bed said nine o'clock.

'I've got presents in the trunk,' Rosie said, turning, leaning back on the sink. 'A great nightdress and stockings for you, Norah, a sweater for you, Grandpa.' Her voice was conciliatory. She must try again if they were to live together. She must keep telling herself that, because Norah had suffered, while she hadn't.

Norah was reading a magazine at the table but she looked up now.

'You're sleeping in the boxroom. I've got the front bedroom.'

Of course you've got the goddamn front room, Rosie thought, and I bet that goddamn fox fur is hanging on the back of the door, his goddamn eyes glinting, but she said nothing.

She pushed open the door into the yard and took Grandpa's arm, feeling him lean on her as she helped him to the bench under the kitchen window. The air was full of the fragrance of his roses.

She put the newspaper on the bench which was still damp and then they sat, neither speaking, for what was there to say? So much, too little.

'Of course he wouldn't dig up his precious yard to put in a

shelter. It would have disturbed the roses,' Norah called through the door.

Rosie put her hand on Grandpa's. 'Quite right too,' she said quietly.

'Wouldn't go down to the shelter in Albany Street either. He wouldn't sleep with strange people. Got to be different.'

'I like my privacy,' Grandpa said loudly now.

'I guess we all do,' Rosie nodded, patting his hand, glad that he was answering Norah, jerking his head up, sticking his chin out. Glad too that she need not sleep in the same bed with that girl ever again.

She leaned forward, smelling the dark red cottage rose which was growing well in the raised bed which Grandpa had built years ago. There was a trailing pink clambering up the privy.

Rosie walked round the plants now, looking closely. There was no greenfly. She drew near the shed which still smelt of creosote but only faintly.

'I guess we need to do this again,' she called to her grandfather.

'If you can find any, go on and do it. Don't forget we're rationed even if you haven't been,' Norah shouted. Rosie didn't bother to tell her that America had in fact been rationed. She knew it couldn't compare with British measures.

In the shed the trunk was laid down flat and behind it was an old upended pram turned into a cart. Rosie edged past the trunk. She had forgotten all about the cart. Ollie and Grandpa had made it and she and Jack had raced it against First Street. Norah wouldn't race with them. She might get hurt, she might get dirty. Rosie leaned down and smelt the old leather, spun the wheels.

'I told him to get rid of it but he wouldn't.' Norah was there behind her now. She was waiting for her present. Well, she'd have to wait a little longer.

Later, when it was quite dark and the curtain had been drawn round Grandpa's bed, Rosie called good night.

'I couldn't let the pram go,' he replied softly. 'It reminded me of you, see.'

Rosie did see and she called, 'I love you, Grandpa. I've missed you so much.' And to begin with she had.

That night Rosie didn't shut the door of her bedroom. She

449

hadn't shut the door on her first night at Nancy and Frank's either. She had felt too lonely, too homesick and had cried silently. She cried now, silently too, thinking of Frank and Nancy, of Sandra, of Joe, of the lake. Crying more as she thought of this house where she'd been born and which wasn't home any more, of this country which was strange to her, of the anger, the pain, the confusion which swept over her in waves. And the despair.

She clenched the woollen knitted blanket she had made before she left and sleep would not come as she tried to cling to Frank's words. 'The future is yours. Make something positive out of the rest of your life.'

Downstairs, Albert lay back on his bed. He could see the table, the cooker, the sink in the dull moonlight. She was back, his Rosie was back. She had looked like her mother when she came in, her hair short, her plaits gone, but the same love in her face that Martha had always had for him.

He coughed, his chest was bad. He was old. The rubber square beneath his sheet made him sweat and it smelt, but then, he smelt too. He turned from the room, lying with his face to the wall. Perhaps he shouldn't have brought her back.

He turned again, back into the room. It was hot now and he was tired but he didn't want to sleep. He sometimes had accidents when he slept.

Perhaps it had been too long, he thought, for he had seen that behind the love there was despair. But he had to believe he had done the right thing as he had had to when he waved her off from Liverpool. It had broken his heart to see the ship becoming smaller and then the loneliness of the war had broken him somehow.

He struggled now, pushing himself up, looking at his books. Maybe Norah had been wrong to think that Rosie would feel deserted if they left her there. And there again she was right, it wouldn't have been fair if one sister had advantages denied to the other. It was all so confusing. He just didn't know. Norah was wrong too, about Nellie not wanting to come to London.

Nailing was dying in Bromsgrove, there was nothing to be made from it any more. His wife had wanted to come south and he remembered with bitterness her face that day when she had insisted they move. But then he pushed the memory from him and thought instead of the land of his roots and Herefordshire too; the sweeping hills, the lush green of the fields, the hops strung so high – and he smiled at the comfort the memory brought.

Yes, there had been despair behind Rosie's love, and he knew it was because she'd left a land and people she'd grown to care for and there was an ache in his chest at her pain. He eased himself back down, pulling the sheet up round his shoulders. He understood that and he would try and take her back to those hills where the scent of the past would ease the present, perhaps for them all, even Maisie and Ollie.

CHAPTER 3

The night had been long, and as Rosie washed in the sink she longed for her own shower and scented soap back in Lower Falls, but there was only the tin bath which hung on the yard wall. Tonight, she thought, she would drag it in when Grandpa was asleep and Norah in bed. Tonight and every night, not just once a week like before she went away.

Grandpa was sitting at the table. Rosie had washed through his drenched sheets and his pyjamas and they were hung on the line, along with his rubber square. She had hoisted them high with the pole but not too high, because he had said that he did not like the neighbours to know.

'Even Jack's mum and dad?' she had asked gently as he dipped his bread in some warm milk after he had sponged himself down standing on newspaper behind the curtain.

'Even Ollie and Maisie,' he had said.

She carried her tea out into the yard, standing by the shed in the spot the sun reached at this hour of the morning. She listened to the sounds of the street, the dogs, the children, the whistling bike-riders, the rag and bone cry. She looked up at Jack's house. The windows were blank and there was no sound. Before she left there had always been laughter and music and shouting.

Her grandfather walked out now and sat on the bench, his back against the wall. He had a walking stick which he propped between his knees. When she was young he would bring peas home on a Saturday wrapped in newspaper and on Sunday they would shell them, sitting on the back step, eating some, putting the rest into Grandma's pan.

Jack would come in and pinch five, always five, throwing them up and catching them in his mouth. Then Maisie would shout across the wall that there was bread and hot dripping

452

from around the piece of scrag-end. She, Jack, and sometimes Norah would go while Ollie and Grandpa went to the pub on the corner for a pint.

The pub had gone too, she realised now. She had forgotten that it had existed, down next to Mr Meiner. She fingered the peach rose, The Reverend Ashe, which grew up against the shed. It had taken a fancy to the creosote, Grandpa had laughed in the year before the war. She had made perfume with its petals. The water had gone brown but there had been a weak scent.

She had given a bottle to Grandma, Norah and Maisie. Maisie had laughed and dabbed some on behind her ears, heavy with earrings, throwing back her head, patting her hair, telling them it made her feel like a ruddy duchess. Ollie roared and slapped her on the backside. Grandma and Norah had thrown theirs down the sink.

As Norah grew older she had always copied Grandma, though Rosie could remember that when they were small sometimes they had laughed together. But as Grandma grew more bitter, more angry, Norah copied her. They froze Rosie out. They formed a team. A team 'who knew better', who were older, wiser. Just more crabby, Jack had always said.

Rosie drank her tea, which was too cold now, then threw the dregs around the roots.

'You remembered then, Rosie,' Grandpa called.

Rosie smiled. 'Yes, I've never forgotten.' But she had until this moment. She had forgotten that the tea leaves nourished the roots.

She moved into the shadow, sitting with him, tucking her hand in his arm. It was thin and his armbands sagged above the elbows. His cuffs were drooping on his wrists. 'I'll sew a tuck in those sleeves for you, shall I?'

She smiled as he nodded and patted her hand. His joints were swollen, his skin was dry and thin, stretched too tight. They sat in silence now and still there was no movement from Jack's house. At home there would be the smell of waffles cooking and the sound of jazz playing, and she had to talk to muffle the memory.

'Do you remember the peas, Grandpa?' Rosie asked as she watched a bee weave in and out of the rose bushes.

453

He chuckled. 'They were good times.'

Rosie nodded, looking up into the sky, which was pale blue with small white clouds that seemed to fit the size of England. Yes, perhaps they were but she had seen another world and she couldn't leave it behind yet. Would she ever be able to? She looked at Jack's house again.

'What's wrong next door? Jack seemed strange. He told me not to go in. There was something in his eyes.'

Grandpa leaned forward, poking the ground with his stick, rubbing it backwards and forwards across the cracks in the concrete. 'You'll have to ask Jack. People have a right to their privacy. He'll tell you what he wants you to know, if there is anything. It's maybe just the war.'

He brought out his handkerchief and wiped the corners of his mouth. 'It's maybe just the war, Rosie. It changes so much.'

'Yes, Grandpa. But you haven't changed and neither have I.' Did he know she was lying?

Rosie left him in the yard then because she was thinking too clearly of Frank and Nancy, of Sandra and Joe, and there was no place for them here where there was no shower, just a tin bath. Where her grandpa's skin was tight and old, where there was no laughter from Maisie.

She was glad she had to sort out ration cards, jobs, shopping. That would do for now. Later, when the sun was past its height she would talk to Jack. Later still she would write to Frank to refuse his offer of money to finance further education. All that was over. They were no longer responsible for her. She was back in her old world. She looked at the list Norah had written, this was her reality now.

Rosie spent an hour at the Food Office waiting for a ration card, then joined a queue forming outside a small shop and waited for half an hour shuffling forward slowly while the sun beat down. Norah had said, join any queue you see, there'll be something at the end of it, but today it was dog food and they didn't have a dog. She bought a pound anyway and gave it to the woman at the end of the queue with two crying children. She knew Jack would have sold it to a man without a dog for twice as much and she smiled at the thought.

She registered with Norah's grocer round the corner whom

she had known as a child, collecting tea and cheese at the same time. The shop seemed so dark, so small. The goods on the shelves were dull, meagre. He nodded to her. 'Back then. Norah told us you'd had it easy.'

'I guess I did,' she replied and watched his tight withdrawn face, wanting to apologise, wanting to take the years back, stay here, be one of them again. But at the same time, wanting to shout her anger at him.

'Next please,' he called, hurrying her, looking past her.

'I'd like some Players, please,' she said, resisting the push from behind.

'Only available to our regulars.' He was reaching forward for the next customer's ration card.

'They're for Grandpa,' Rosie insisted, not moving over. She had just enough for a packet and then her money from Frank was gone.

The man sighed. His brows met across the bridge of his nose and his eyes were tired. He bent below the counter and passed her one pack.

'Thanks.' She paid and walked past the queue which was jostling behind her.

'These Americans think they can come here and throw their money about. Isn't right, it isn't,' one old lady said to the woman next to her. Rosie didn't look at them, she didn't look anywhere but in front, thinking of the lake, of the sloping lawns and the soaring music. I didn't choose to go, she wanted to scream at their shadowed faces and resentful backs.

She walked back down the street towards the Woolworths in Albany Street. She wouldn't cry, she mustn't. Whatever she did, she mustn't let these Britishers see her pain, or even her anger because she had no right to that. They had stayed and endured. She had fled.

Outside Woolworths she stopped, looking in through the glass doors, seeing the lights, the long alleys of counters. She and Jack had pinched a 6d car from here when they were eight. She'd longed to work in amongst it all. But that was then.

At eleven she stood in an office before a white-haired supervisor, her hair permed like Norah's.

'So, you're Norah's sister. Good worker, that girl.'

The woman had run her lipstick outside her top lip to

455

thicken it. Her breath smelt of tea as she moved behind Rosie to take out a file from the cabinet and then returned to her seat.

'Sit down then.' There was a cup half full on the desk with a cigarette stub floating in it.

'Thanks,' Rosie said, smoothing her skirt, not looking into the cup.

The woman brushed at the corners of her mouth with her little finger. There was a brass ring with a bright red glass stone on her wedding finger. 'Well, you'll have to do something about your voice, if you know what I mean.'

Rosie looked at her. 'No, I guess I don't.'

'Well, listen to that. You sound like a Yank. I don't know what our customers would think, I really don't. This is Albany Street, not Hollywood.' The woman frowned. 'But Norah did put in a good word for you. You've got that old man at home to support, haven't you? Need all the help you can get, I should think.'

'My grandfather, you mean. He has his own money. He doesn't need ours. Norah and I have to work to keep ourselves, not him. It's his house, you know. He gives us a home.' She was tired now, so goddamn tired of it all, so sick of Norah. 'He's a real nice man. Kind of quiet but nice.'

She looked out across the store with its counters glistening with goods. Norah was on jewellery, leaning back talking to the girl at the other end. She was smiling, her mouth a slash of red.

'Oh well, we need someone on records anyway though the stock is very limited these days. Maybe the voice will fit in there. All American anyway, aren't they, these singers?' The woman's voice was slower, kinder. When she smiled the lines cut deep. 'My dad was a nice man too.'

Rosie looked at her closely now and felt her face begin to relax.

'We had a lot of Americans here in the war. They'd come and talk. My friend married one. She's in California now.' The woman was pulling her overalls across her breast. 'Yes, proper little meeting-place in here. It's very dull now. England is very dull. I expect you've found that.'

Rosie looked out again, across the aisles. 'I only got in yesterday and I guess it's real good to be here.' If she said it often enough it might help it to be the truth.

'Oh well, that's nice.' The woman was moving towards the door. 'Perhaps we can move you into the snack bar when we get one. You seem like a good girl. Start tomorrow, why don't you.'

Rosie walked out of the office into the hub of the store. The Andrews Sisters were singing 'The Three Caballeros' and she wondered how Albany Street would take to Bix Beiderbecke. She walked past Norah and smiled – after all they were not children feuding any longer. Norah had been unfairly treated and Rosie must damp down the anger.

'I'm on records,' she said.

'Well, don't be late. Grandpa needs his lunch. There's a nice bit of Spam in the meat-safe.' Norah turned away, then back again.

'I suppose you're meeting that Jack. Well, not until you've done the chores, you're not.'

'One day, you'll find yourself being pleasant and it will be as much of a goddamn shock to yourself as it will be to the rest of the world.' Rosie walked away, leaving Norah to close her open mouth, and all the way home she was glad she had let the anger out. It helped her to lift her head, but from now on she must rein back in.

She opened a tin of American ham for Grandpa instead.

'This is our celebration,' she told him. There was no ice-box so Rosie drank lukewarm milk, then sank the bottle into the pail of water again. She stood a bowl in water and left half the ham in it for Norah's meal that evening. It was only fair.

She and Grandpa ate tinned peaches which slipped on the spoon and were easy to eat. Juice trickled down both their chins and they laughed as they had done before she left.

It was only when he was asleep and the floor was washed, the dishes too, when the cooker was cleaned and her arms were black from the grime, when the beds were made, that she left, wondering how Norah could sleep with those fox's eyes glinting on the back of the door. But what did it matter? She was going to see Jack, but then she heard her grandfather calling. She turned. He was in the doorway, waving to her, leaning on his stick with the other hand.

'You forgot your matchbox.'

For a moment Rosie paused and then she remembered the ladybirds which she used to catch in a matchbox she always

457

carried when she went out. She called, 'No I didn't, I've got one in my pocket. Don't worry, we'll keep the roses clear of greenfly.'

He smiled and waved again and turned back into the house. Rosie stopped at a tobacconist, bought a matchbox and tipped the matches out into the bin. He mustn't know that she had forgotten.

Malvern Lane was too narrow to receive much sun and Rosie watched as Jack moved backwards and forwards in front of his stall, holding a flowered teapot high above his head, laughing with one woman, nodding to another who picked up a saucer and turned it over in her hands. She dropped money into his left hand and pushed the saucer deep into her shopping bag.

'Come on then, ladies. Don't let the rationing get to you. Look, it's a lovely day up there above the clouds, let's have a smile, shall we?' He was laughing now and the crowd laughed with him, Rosie too, but he hadn't seen her yet and she was glad. She wanted to stand here, listening, watching, trying to ease into London just for a moment. Trying to push away the thought of the intersections, the streetcars, the ice-cream parlors.

'Just look at this.' Jack pointed to the teapot which he still held high. 'When did you last see a splash of colour like this then, eh? Can't buy it now, can you? Certainly not. Only white can be made the chiefs have said.' He looked round at them all. 'Well, that's as may be, but today is your lucky day. Here – ' Jack turned and gestured to the back of the stall – 'I have just a few little treasures so who's going to give me five bob for this then?'

It went on like that for half an hour and by that time all the coloured china had gone, as Rosie knew it would, and as the crowds thinned he saw her and called across.

'Did you remember your matchbox, then?'

The woman in front of Rosie turned. Her cheeks were red and her smile broad. 'He's a one, that lad. Could charm the bleeding birds out of the trees.'

Rosie laughed and held up the box. She didn't want to speak, to drawl. She didn't know if the woman would stop smiling.

'Be with you in half an hour. The gang's coming,' Jack called

458

again, then he laughed as a woman came and slapped his arm, giving him money for two plates and telling him she'd take another if he threw in a kiss with it. He looked at Rosie again and pointed to his watch. It wasn't gold, his skin wasn't tanned. Was Joe playing tennis now? Was Sandra?

She wandered off, down the lane, moving out round a heap of yellowed cabbage leaves whose smell followed her on down past the potatoes, the lettuce, and drowned the scent of the pinks tied in small bunches and left to stand in a tin jug.

There was a tea stall and she bought a cup, sipping it, hearing the past all around her, the noises, the voices, breathing in the smells which had faded and vanished with the years. But they were here again, all here.

So, the gang was coming too. She didn't remember them, not their names or their faces. It was only Jack she had pictured over the years and the miles. Would Joe and Sandra forget her too?

When she returned Jack was waiting, his old leather money apron now tied around the waist of his father, Ollie, who had run the stall for as long as Rosie could remember. She started to walk towards Ollie but Jack caught at her arm.

'Leave it for now.'

They walked to the rec where they had scuffed the ground with worn plimsolls on hot days as they pumped themselves higher and higher on swings already raised by being thrown over the bar. They didn't talk as they walked through the streets, and Jack had to lead the way because she had forgotten. He sauntered, hands in pockets, his two-tone shoes worn, his hair hanging down over his forehead.

She remembered her shoes, and the sweater she had worn back to front as all Lower Falls girls did, but they were in her room, on the shelf below the Cougar pennant and she mustn't think of that.

They crossed wasteground which had once been three houses. The rec was across the road from Oundle Street where there were houses with black-tarred casement sheets instead of glass. They were all deserted and two were ripped apart; just as she felt.

She remembered the park with railings but they were gone and now Jack told her how his mum had written to say that they had been taken away by men with oxyacetylene cutters to build Spitfires.

'How's your mum?' she asked. 'It was so quiet today.'

His eyes were dark as he turned, then looked past her. 'Race you to the swings.'

He ran, catching her arm, running with her across worn asphalt where weeds were breaking through, running faster than her, goddamn it, and so now she spurted but he was still ahead and the breath was leaping in her throat as the swings drew nearer. But he was first, throwing himself on to one, pushing back with his feet, lifting them high and then surging forward, up into the air.

She sat on hers and looked at the sign that said, '12 YEARS AND UNDER ONLY.'

'Hey, we'll be done.'

She heard his laugh. 'Come on, Yank. We've just been through a war. No one's going to stop me swinging if I want to.'

She pushed off now, feeling the air slicing through her, half pain, half pleasure. The links were rusty and stained her hands and then there was only the squealing of the chain and their laughter. She leaned back, the sky was blue. It was the same sky over America. Maybe it wasn't so far after all, but she knew that it was.

Afterwards they talked, still sitting on the swings, Jack's legs gently moving his, his shoulders leaning hard into the chain, his hands between his knees.

He told her then that Ollie was drinking, snarling. Sleeping a little. Working a little. That Maisie seldom laughed now.

'But they were so different. Was it the war? What about Lee? Hasn't he helped?'

There were two small children standing by the swings now and Jack winked at them, standing, nodding to them.

'It's all yours,' he called and they ran past him and Rosie, who stood too and watched as they scrambled on to the swings.

'Give us push, mister,' the boy with red hair said.

Jack did and Rosie watched as his broad hands pushed and caught, pushed and caught the swing.

'I'm OK now,' the boy said and they walked over to the bench. The dark green paint was flaking. Rosie brushed the seat with her hand, rubbing the paint off as she sat.

'Didn't Lee help?' Rosie insisted, watching the two children, hearing their yells clearly across the intervening space. She didn't want to hear of Ollie snarling, of Maisie silent. She wanted to hear of laughter, of bread and dripping, of earrings jangling.

Jack shrugged. He reached down, pulling at a dandelion which had lifted the asphalt. 'He seems to have made it worse and he's a lovely kid. It can't have been the war either. Dad didn't get called up. It's his chest you see, collapsed lung. He built the new airfields, that sort of thing. Did a bit of dealing.' He smiled slightly but his eyes were so angry.

Rosie smiled, looking away. 'I just bet he did.'

'I wasn't there, you see. The kids that came back after the first evacuation went away again with the Blitz, like you did.' He flicked the shredded dandelion at her. 'She was good to me though, Mum was. She came down visiting, you know. All the time. It was good fun.'

'Was your dad jealous of that?'

'No, I don't think so. He didn't change until later. When he came to see me first he was fine. Took back a few hams, sold them well. Even did a bit of dealing with the GIs who were camped in the village.' He paused and looked up at the sky, and his voice became angry. 'But then, all of a sudden like, he stopped coming. Didn't see Mum much come to that after D-Day. Busy, I expect, and then there was Lee. He's got red hair too.' Jack flicked a piece of grass off his trousers, nodding towards the boy he had pushed on the swing. 'I don't know what's wrong. It's just wrong. I wanted to tell you before you came. I didn't want you upset.'

His face was red now and he didn't look at her. She wanted to reach across and hold him as he had once held her when she cut her knee and needed stitches. But they were children then. They were grown now and there was a difference somehow.

He looked at her now and the anger had gone, there was just tiredness, like hers. 'Come anyway. They want to see you but it's funny, me dad doesn't like Yanks.'

Rosie looked at her hands. 'He's not the only one.'

'Oh, I reckon it's this rationing, you know. Makes people crabby.'

There were voices behind them now, calling, shouting, and a

football bounced behind them and over them and Jack looked at Rosie. 'Remember the gang? I thought it would help you settle back in.'

She did remember when they were all around, touching her clothes, laughing at her tan, at her voice, asking about Lower Falls and New York and the skiing. Telling her about Somerset, where they had all been evacuated. She looked away, wishing she had been with them, wishing that she belonged as she had once done.

It was Sam, the old second-in-command, his hair in a crew cut, who showed her that for him at least she no longer did.

'So you came back. Slumming, eh?' he said, not looking away when Jack told him to shut his mouth. His pale eyes held hers as he bounced the ball, then threw it to Ted, then Jack. Then bounced it again.

Her eyes were blurred but it was tiredness, she mustn't think it was tears. She remembered Sam all too clearly now. He had tied her to a lamppost when they were nine and fired arrows at a potato he stuck on her head. She hadn't cried then and she wouldn't now.

There were laughs and jokes, and always the ball was on the move. She watched, listened, smiled, waited and then Sam threw the ball to her, hard. She had known that he would and batted it straight back at him with a clenched fist as Frank had taught her. He caught it and threw it again, talking to Ted as he did so, but looking at her all the time.

She threw the ball to Jack. He looked at Sam, then back at her. There was a question in his eyes and she knew he had brought them together deliberately, to face up and get it over with. She shook her head. She was angry now and she would deal with this herself. This was her rec too, her gang, and nobody was going to take it away from her. They'd taken enough already.

She hurled the ball hard at Sam, and nothing more was said as they caught and threw, caught and threw, just the two of them. Her arm was tired and she was hot, but it didn't matter. Frank had trained her well.

It was Ted who broke the silence. 'So, how's po-face taken to you coming back?' he asked.

Rosie kept her eye on the ball, waiting for it to come again, feeling the stinging in her hands, seeing the two small boys running over from the swings, leaving a space beside her for them to join in. Waiting, too, for Sam. The ball came. She hurled it back. He caught it; she heard the slap of skin against leather. She needed her leather mitt.

'You can't blame Norah, she had a lousy time, like the rest of you,' she panted.

She caught the ball again, then batted it back but Jack intercepted and passed it on to the small red-haired boy. Rosie felt the throbbing in her hands, but she wouldn't look at them. She looked instead at Sam. What would he do now?

'No way that old bag had a bad time. Come on, let's sit down,' Dave called.

Sparrows were sitting in the clubbed trees around the rec, singing and flying. Jack walked to the bench and the others followed. Sam took Woodbines from his pocket, shaking his head, looking at Rosie, his eyes still cold. His hands were red, like hers. Did they throb like hers too?

'Your Norah should have gone too. Bloody unfair, I call it.'

Jack looked up at Sam, then at Rosie and she shook her head again.

Ted said, 'That's a load of rubbish. She was billeted with the doctor over in the next village. Had a life of old Reilly, never even had to flick a bleeding duster.'

They were sitting and leaning on the bench now, cigarette smoke drifting up into the air, watching the two small boys kicking the ball from one to another, hearing the thuds. Rosie said nothing, not yet.

Sam flicked his ash on to the ground, rubbing it in with his shoe. 'I bet Rosie never had to flick a duster either. Bet she never had to queue for food. Bet she stuffed herself with ice-cream, steak, got taken out by flash American boys, the brothers of those GIs who swanked over here.' Sam laughed but it was a hard sound. 'Well, go on. Did you?'

Rosie flushed, looking across at the two boys, then back at Sam again. 'What's wrong, bud, did a GI steal your girl?'

Ted laughed, clapped Sam on the shoulder. 'She got you there.' They were all laughing now, Jack too, but his eyes were still watchful. Sam did not laugh.

He stubbed out his cigarette carefully on the sole of his shoe

463

and put it back in his cigarette packet. Rosie watched. She had forgotten people did that. She had forgotten that they needed to and she wanted to say she was sorry, but no, she had to fight Sam. That's all there was to it, or there was no place for her here, with them.

'No,' Sam said, 'nobody stole my girl. I just don't like freeloaders who come back home and lord it about in their new clothes, expecting everyone to bow and scrape because they're back. This is the real world here.'

They were all standing now and Rosie looked at all their faces. They were uncertain, all except Jack, who was looking at her, waiting to see if she could make it on her own. It was only if she couldn't that he would come in. He had always been like that. He had always been there behind her.

Sam turned to her. 'You've had it on a plate. No rationing, no bombs, just bloody everything you want. So just don't come back here, Rosie Norton, and drawl all over the rest of us.'

There was silence. Jack was still watching her. 'There *was* rationing,' she said but that was all because they were never really short of anything, and there was no danger for her.

'Oh yeah, when did you last have a banana?' Sam said, his eyes narrow. Jack's were, too, but they were looking at Sam.

Rosie couldn't answer because Frank had exchanged a piece of pork for a hand of bananas last year and the year before. She looked at them all, at their pale skins, their tired faces, and said, 'You're right. I had it cushy, I have a drawl. I had bananas last year and I'm sorry. It's not fair. Do you think I don't know that? But I'm back. I haven't changed.'

There was silence as they stood around her. Sam's lips were still thin. Jack's eyes were steady. The others were nodding, smiling, all uncertainty gone.

Sam still didn't smile though. He said, 'OK, you say you haven't changed.' He looked at Jack. 'You tell her about tonight, then bring her along. We'll see if she's changed. We'll see if she's got too good for us all.'

Jack's face set, he took Sam by the arm, moving him along towards the pavement. Ted followed. Dave and Paul too. Rosie didn't. She watched them, then the delivery boy cycling past. He rode 'no hands' and sat with his arms folded, whistling. She looked back at the gang. What was happening tonight? Whatever it was, she'd do it.

Ted turned towards her, then nodded to Jack, so did the others. Sam just stared and then called to her, 'Be there.'

The delivery boy had reached the corner. Rosie called back, 'Bank on it, Sam.' But what was it?

As they walked back without Sam and the others, Jack told her about the bomb which had killed Sam's mother, the GI jeep that had killed his sister. But he wouldn't tell her about tonight. 'Not yet,' he said. 'I didn't want you involved. I have to explain some things first.'

They passed the black-tarred replacement windows in a damaged house and he told her how in this time of shortages he, Ollie, Sam and the gang had bought demob suits off the men coming home and resold them at a profit, and that didn't hurt anybody because the soldiers didn't want them anyway.

He told her about the drivers who would deliver twenty-one pigs to the wholesalers and be given a receipt for twenty. How the odd one would be sold, piece by piece. For a lot of money. It was big business. Nasty business.

'But what about tonight?'

He told her about the police swoop on marketeers in March designed to end the racketeering. About the major roadblocks around London and other cities. About the lorries and vans the police searched for eggs, meat, poultry. He told her about the market stalls being raided. He told her that the police were still stopping and searching anyone who seemed suspicious. That it was a dangerous time to be out and about if it looked as though you were up to anything shady.

'But what about tonight?'

He asked her if she remembered Jones who had owned their houses. Jones was getting very flash, he said, because he took people's money for black-market produce like that extra piece of pork – and only sometimes delivered the goods. He also pinched produce from the local allotments, but they could find no proof. Last of all, he had taken two cheeses from a farm where the neighbourhood owned two cows and had a cheese club.

'Sure I remember him, now what about tonight?' She

grabbed him now, turning him to her, laughing, and it was the first time she had done that for so long.

'Tonight we are not banging door knockers, we are not cutting up sleepers for fuel and selling it, we are not making cigarettes out of dog-ends. Tonight we are breaking into a warehouse owned by Jones and taking two of his cheeses. You, me, Sam and Ted. All the gang. We're taking back what's ours. Are you coming?'

He was still facing her, his eyes serious, though his mouth was smiling. She thought of the lake, but all that was slipping away from her. Just for now, it was more distant.

She thought of Grandpa, the police action Jack had just explained. 'We could get caught?' He voice was serious.

'Yes.' He didn't hesitate. 'Yes, we could. It might be big trouble.'

'Does this cheese really belong to the street or is it all for money?'

'No. The cheese is ours. We're sick of getting taken for a ride, and being pushed around.'

She smiled, walking on now, hearing him catch her up.

'When do we start?' she said because she knew all about being pushed around.

It was dark when she left the house. She had bathed in the tin bath as she said she would and felt better. She wore a loose dress, it was so hot.

They met outside Jack's and walked quietly, neither speaking until they reached the end of Middle Street, then cut across to Vernon Terrace, up the alley, down to Futcher's Walk, picking up the others, picking up Sam. Nothing was said as they approached the wall which ran round the warehouse.

There were dogs but Jack knew them and called to them quietly. Then he was bunked up and over by Sam who shot Ted up too. Sam went next, the others after. She was to be look-out. Sam would wait the other side of the wall to relay any warning.

A cyclist approached and Rosie walked slowly on, then back again when he had overtaken. She listened and looked and wished they would goddamn hurry. She thought of Grandpa asleep, of Norah too. She thought of Joe and Sandra, Frank and

Nancy, but still she looked and listened for over half an hour and again wished they'd hurry because she was out here on her own.

There were sounds now, the soft bark of a dog, voices, and Jack called, 'All clear?'

It was, and so he threw one cheese, then the other, then scrabbled over himself. It had all been so easy. She had proved herself to Sam, to them all.

But then they saw the police, walking towards them, dipping in and out of the lamplight, and Jack grabbed her, told her to run, told the others to stay – for Christ's sake stay behind the wall.

She felt her fear and his. She thought of Grandpa, and then of Sam, and now the fear was gone. She turned to Jack.

'No, put your arm round me, kiss me.'

He looked at her, then at the police. He ducked his head and kissed her with soft lips and she hugged him, turning her back, pushing the cheeses up inside her dress, and then they walked towards the police. Everything was quiet, all they could hear were the footsteps walking in time towards them. She didn't know if they had seen. She didn't know if a hand would grip her shoulder and her Grandpa would know what she had been doing.

She held her stomach, walking with legs slightly apart, feeling Jack's arm around her. It too was tense, trembling, and then she started to cry, asking him why they couldn't marry, especially with the baby due so soon. She clutched the cheeses to her.

They were level with the police now and Rosie turned her face into his shoulder. It was warm, as Joe's had been.

'Just don't leave me, that's all. If you won't marry, don't leave me.'

The police looked away, embarrassed, and Jack held her closer, his breath warm in her hair, and his arm was relaxed, warm now because they hadn't been stopped yet, and maybe they wouldn't be. He held her close and said that he would stay for ever, but she must eat more calcium, more cheese. Then they were well past the police and near the corner.

'Oh Jack,' she said, 'I know the baby will look just like you.' And now they were round the corner and running, laughing.

That night she lay in bed, hearing Jack's voice, feeling his lips on hers. Sam had bought her a ginger beer. Ted had said it would be bad for the baby. She had laughed with them. The anger in them had eased because they had taken what was theirs and she knew she could do that too. She could take back the future which had seemed to be hers until last month. She would have her journalism, somehow, and she would start tomorrow.

Welcome back, Jack had said when she told him.

CHAPTER 4

The next day Rosie enrolled at evening secretarial classes which would begin in late September. Frank had joined his paper as a cub reporter after teaching himself shorthand and typing. If college hadn't been necessary for him, it wouldn't be for her.

September was too long to wait, though, so she brought home a shorthand book from the library because she was working towards her future now, this very day. It was the only way she would survive the loss, the separation from that other world, those other people she still loved, still grieved for even though she had Grandpa, the gang, and Jack.

July turned to August which was heavy with heat and with rain too, but by then Rosie had learned the rudiments of shorthand on her own late at night in her room, though she still had no speed. But it would come. Goddamn it, it would come. She would make sure it did.

The weather didn't matter during the day either because she had coaxed Mrs Eaves into letting her play Bix Beiderbecke through the speakers so that his mellifluous cornet-playing filled the store. But only once a day, Mrs Eaves, the supervisor, had said, jangling the keys on the belt of her overalls, leaning across the mahogany counter, because the public prefer the Andrews Sisters, Glenn Miller – the romantic, the slick.

So too did Norah, but Rosie didn't care so much about that now that she knew. Norah had not had such a bad war. She had pranced around, showing off, drinking tea with a cocked little finger, putting the milk in last.

'So why lie?' Rosie had asked Jack.

He had shrugged and so she had asked Norah that same day, leaning on the rectangular counter, talking quietly so that the other assistants could not hear.

Norah had flared with anger. 'I'm not lying,' she said, 'not really. You had a much better time. It should have been me. I'm older.'

Perhaps, Rosie thought now as she ticked records off against the stocklist, Norah was still trying to adjust, to come to terms with leaving Somerset. Perhaps she yearned for the people who had been her family for that time. If so, she understood and so she played the Andrews Sisters and smiled at Norah, who didn't smile back.

Rosie turned as a customer, a woman in a felt hat, asked for 'Chattanooga Choo Choo'.

'It's sure nice. I really like Glenn Miller,' Rosie said as she wrapped it. Grandpa did too. He had heard it on the wireless and tapped his foot as he read *Silas Marner*. Rosie had laughed and told him that she would try to buy a gramophone and he could bop to Duke Ellington. He had stopped having accidents now. There had been no soiled sheets, no embarrassed lowering of the eyes, and he even wanted to hear of her evenings at the Palais with the gang.

She told him how she and Jack jitterbugged around the floor, feet moving fast, swirling in and then out, up and over his hip, his shoulder, while the MC shook his head, tapped them on the shoulders and pointed to the sign on the wall: ABSOLUTELY NO JITTERBUGGING ALLOWED.

They didn't stop. No one stopped. They all danced. The war was over. They had all fought it, Rosie too, Jack said. They all bore the scars. He could see hers, he had told her, in her eyes, and they were still fresh, but they would go. One day they would go. And we're alive so we'll jitterbug like the others and no one will tell us we can't. So they jitterbugged and it kept the shadows and the pain away.

But there were nights when Ollie lurched home drunk and there was shouting and banging to be heard through the walls. On these nights Jack didn't come dancing, he stayed behind to stand between Maisie, Lee and Ollie. It wasn't the same without him. Dancing with Sam and Ted, Dave and Paul didn't stop her wanting Frank and Nancy. It didn't stop her wanting Maisie and Ollie as they had been before the war. It didn't stop her wanting a much earlier time when there had been no pain or anger in Jack's eyes. And it made her think of Joe.

Rosie tipped the Beiderbecke record back into its sleeve. Her legs ached. There was no air in the shop and the heat was thick about her. She longed for a draught or the cool of the evening. She pulled her burgundy overall away from her back and then stood still. Nancy had said it was the best way of cooling down. It did no good to fret. Maisie had said that too last night when at last she had come round and Rosie stood still now, thinking of Maisie's plump arms, so like Nancy's.

For a moment it had been like Pennsylvania again but then Nancy had never smelt of lavender. Maisie did, always had done, Rosie realised as she was pulled against that warm, plump woman who had pushed open the yard gate as she and Grandpa were hugging mugs of tea between their hands and breathing in the roses.

What were they talking about? Rosie served another customer, smiling, giving change, settling back against the counter. She couldn't remember, but she smiled again at the thought of the pushchair coming through the gate, the child wide-eyed and unsure. Then Maisie, her red hair brown at the roots, her earrings jangling and her face bright with a smile.

Rosie had stood her mug in the earth of a rose bush and run to Maisie, flinging her arms round her, smelling the older woman's lavender scent. She had looked at Maisie, taking in the circles beneath her eyes and the lines from her nose to her mouth. But the smile was the same and the voice too.

'You took your time coming home. We've missed you,' Maisie said, pulling her close again. 'We've really missed you.' Rosie hadn't spoken. She knew she would have cried, for these arms were Nancy's too and she could hardly bear the pain.

She squeezed Maisie, then turned, her head lowered, to Lee. He was squirming round, his eyes watching her; his smile was Jack's but his skin was pale, freckled. Not like any of the others.

He reached up his hand and gripped her finger and she said how cute he was, and lifted him from the pushchair, taking him to Grandpa, sitting with him on her knee. Maisie poured tea from the pot for herself, fetched Rosie's from the rosebed, dusted the earth off the bottom with her hand, and called Rosie the same mucky devil she'd always been. They laughed together, as they used to do, and then just looked at one another.

'You look tired,' Rosie said, rubbing her cheek against Lee's head. He pulled away and looked at her, his smile there, his eyes watching hers.

'Don't fret at what you hear,' Maisie said, her face drawn. 'It sounds worse than it is.'

Would she come again tonight? Rosie wondered. She'd said she would.

Maisie did come, with Lee again, while Rosie washed clothes in the sink. 'Sit with Grandpa,' she called through to the yard. 'I'll bring the tea out in a minute.'

Norah slammed through from the hall. 'I'm going out, especially now that kid's here. There's no bloody peace.'

'Why don't you stay?' Rosie said as she wrung out the blouse and dress. 'We should try to get on.'

She had decided to be pleasant again, to try and build some sort of a bridge between them this summer because they needed one another. Couldn't Norah see that? Families were important, but then it seemed that Norah preferred her friends.

Norah pulled her cardigan over her shoulders and checked her make-up in the mirror, tucking the lipstick she had melted down last night into her bag.

'I've got better things to do,' she said. 'We're going dancing. Not at the crummy Palais but up West.'

Rosie smiled, wanting to wring her neck instead of the blouse. She shook her hands over the sink, dried them, then picked up the tea tray. Norah's dress didn't fit. It was too tight over the hips.

'Have a good time,' was all Rosie said.

Lee put out his arms to Rosie as she sat down between Maisie and Grandpa.

'Go on, pick him up then,' Maisie said. 'He gets nothing but spoiling from Jack too.'

She was smiling as she pulled out the Camel cigarettes from her bag. 'Thanks for these, Rosie. I should have been in sooner to say thanks – and to say hello. Here you are, Albert.' She leaned past Rosie, handing him one. 'Got your own matches, have you?'

He nodded.

Rosie let Lee walk up her legs and body, holding on to his hands while he arched away, and then she put him down, watching his unsteady walk. He reached into the raised beds, picking up soil, looking at it, dropping it.

Grandpa laughed. 'It's good to have you here, Maisie. A bit like old times. Can't believe this little nipper is one and a half. Seems only yesterday it was Jack and Rosie digging up me roses.'

They flicked their ash into their hands and Rosie leaned back, her face to the sun, watching the smoke spiralling, disappearing. She didn't like the smell and moved to the upturned pail, hugging her knees, laughing as Lee tottered towards her.

'Yes,' Maisie said. 'Just like old times.'

There was silence except for the grunts from Lee.

'Can you put back the clock then, Albert?' Maisie said.

'Yes, can you, Grandpa?' Rosie echoed.

That night Rosie replied to the letters she had received from the previous week. She was glad the lake was so warm, and the swimming good, that the Club tennis court was already being built. But, she wanted to say, how can it all continue as though I've never existed? How can all these things go on when I hurt so much inside?

How many Subscription Dances had gone into the court? she wondered. How many girls had danced with Joe? Had Frank leaned back in his chair and said, 'You make sure you don't drink when you drive that girl.' Of course he hadn't. He only said that about her. But not any more.

She told them of the evening classes to begin at the end of September with Miss Paul over the piano shop – short-hand, typing, book-keeping. She told them of the rationing, of the cheeses; of the roses which were still free of greenfly. She did not tell them about Woolworths, nor about Norah or Maisie. She cried all night and she thought her sobs were silent but they weren't. Grandpa heard them and it was more than he could bear.

The next day, which was a Sunday, he held her hand and said that they would go to Herefordshire again this year. They would go hop-picking as they used to, before the war, before things changed. All of them, Maisie, Ollie, Jack and Lee, just like they used to, and perhaps there she would learn to laugh again deep down inside, and the others would too, and they would cast the war from their lives.

They did go, even Ollie. Even Norah. They took a train on 1 September and then a bus along the roads which wound round and along the rolling green hills because here no one had sliced through nature, but had fitted in with it. Or so Grandpa had always told them when he brought them here each year before the war. Rosie remembered the American street grids, slicing up the towns, and the long straight roads of Pennsylvania, thinking of Frank and Nancy returning to Lower Falls without her now that it was September.

She pushed that from her. She looked out at the fields. There were cider apple orchards. There was space, sky, air. It was green in the distance, not grey and cramped, and slowly she began to remember what had once been, so long ago.

Close by, the barley had been harvested and the ground re-ploughed and that was still the same. Though not each field, not yet, and now those that were left unploughed must wait until the hops were in because for those few short weeks of the harvest all else was put to one side. Would her pain be put to one side too, and everyone else's?

Jones's farm with its large spacious pigsties was the same too. Swept, scrubbed, white-washed, for this was where they always slept. Jack laughed as they stuffed straw into the palliasses, chasing Lee with a handful, pushing some down Maisie's back, then Rosie's. Maisie crept up behind him and they pushed him on to the heaped pile, sitting on him, stuffing straw up his trousers and down his shirt until he begged for mercy, and even then they stopped only when he had gone down on his knees.

Grandpa, Ollie and Jack slept in the end partition. Rosie, Norah, Maisie and Lee were in the next. The rest of the sties were taken by Black Country people and a few from Bromsgrove, and this was why Grandpa came here, and not to Kent. It was here that he heard his Bromsgrove dialect, his roots. Where were hers? Rosie thought.

'Just you wait, he'll be calling us "me dooks" before the day is out,' Maisie said as she gave Lee a biscuit to chew. As they ate supper heated over the primus in the end building he did and they all laughed, even Norah, even Ollie, even Rosie, and it was from deep inside.

Jack and Rosie walked down the lane to the road, watching for the caravans that they knew would come bringing gypsies on from the plum-picking at Evesham, the cherries at Shropshire and the peas at Worcester. The gate was warm from the sun, deep cracked, chipped with the initials they had carved in 1938. Jack covered it over.

'Your Grandpa would catch us with his stick,' he laughed.

Rosie nodded, looking down the lane, hearing the caravans, the barking of the long dogs and lurchers, the ponies which plodded, the brasses which jingled. She felt the wind in her hair and was happy because for the four weeks they were here, this place belonged to her, just as much or as little as it belonged to the others.

The gypsies came now, the women walking at the pony's head, one smoking a clay pipe. The men sat, the reins in their hands. The children sat too, looking ahead, not at Rosie or Jack.

'Never changes, does it?' Jack murmured, watching as they rolled past.

They walked then, up to the hop-fields, neither speaking, taking the path which ran along the top of the kale field. She remembered where to go, she realised. Somehow she knew where to go.

She walked ahead now, confident, hearing Jack close behind. On round the kale which looked like small trees, then further to the ragwort-spotted meadows. At the bottom of these, past clumps of purple-crested thistles, lay the stream. They used to picnic there at the end of the day. She turned.

'Do you remember . . . ?' she began, but stopped for Jack was nodding.

'Yes, I remember. Tinned salmon sandwiches.' He was smiling and there were no shadows in his eyes today. Rosie hoped that there would be none as the four weeks went by. Would Ollie and Maisie be able to go back in time, enough for a fresh start? Would she?

In the distance rooks clawed up into the sky from the copse planted on Trafalgar Day. She turned further up the hill and they were on to the worn top path and into the hop-fields where the bines swung fifteen feet above them in the wind and Rosie stood still, looking about her, remembering.

Her mother had come every year before she died. They had picked all September and her mother had said it made her feel safe, standing here, as Rosie was doing now. Safe from the world. She had died though, her father too. They hadn't been safe. Was there such a thing as safety? Everything changed. It always changed.

'It's like being under the sea,' Jack said, standing close to her, looking up.

It seemed so quiet, no dogs barking, no cyclists whistling, no children playing. She loved this first evening before the picking began and the hops were stripped.

'I love this first evening,' Jack said.

When they returned to the sties the Welsh had arrived and were in the barn, singing, shouting, laughing. One child was crying but Lee was sound asleep and Maisie too. Norah lay on the straw mattress. It always itched the first night, Rosie thought as she settled on hers, but she could see the sky through the window, the clouds scudding over the moon, and then she slept and dreamed of nothing.

In the morning she was up early, walking along the lane again. The mist lay still over the land and there were blackberries on the bushes as she passed. She picked two and they stained her fingers. They were sweet and cool.

The oasts were shrouded by the mist, the farm buildings too. A cockerel crowed. She was at the kale now and there was dew on the leaves. She reached down, rolling the drops off into her hand. There were ferns at the edge of the field and everywhere the earth was red and smelt of a long warm summer.

There were partridges flying up before her, and a lurcher dog over from the caravans was leaping and bounding in the kale, making more birds rise. There was smoke from the gypsy caravans and washing strung across the bushes. The hedges nearby were stripped of branches for their fires. Rosie turned now, back to the farm, to the white-washed, partitioned sties, because the sun was breaking through, the mist was rising and soon the picking would begin.

As they left for the hop-fields, the sun was casting sharp shadows from the two oasts and the distant Welsh hills were

476

black. Rosie tightened the hessian sacking around her waist and took Maisie's bag from her, passing it on to Jack when he nodded. It left both Maisie's hands free for the pushchair.

'That's better,' said Maisie, pushing the chair and laughing.

The hop strands had been strung in the spring by men on stilts and now the pickers pulled at the bines, flip-flipping the hops into the wattle bins. The Welsh were ahead of them, the Black Country people with them, and Grandpa was laughing and talking, his voice soft, almost young again. The gypsies were further back, the children silent as they worked. One had a ferret and carried dock leaves in his pocket as a cure for its bites. Rosie looked at Jack and they laughed.

The hop-leaves hung down from the strings, deep etched by the sun filtering through. The sprays of hops were a delicate green, the pollen-like powder was yellow on her fingers. It made the beer bitter.

Her fingers grew sore but soon she was picking without looking, flipping the hops into the bins, smelling them on her hands as she pinned back her hair. Norah wore grips in hers.

'Sensible,' Maisie whispered, 'but not going to set anyone's heart on fire.'

They worked until lunch, then sat in the shade eating sandwiches, drinking water that was warm from the heat of the day. Grandpa went back to the sty to lie down but he returned at four looking rested and happy. Rosie lost count of the hours, measuring time by the level of hops in the bin, watching the pale green piles rise. The hoverflies were all around, humming, buzzing. Butterflies too. There were moths at night, she remembered now.

The busheller came round again and again, dipping his bushel basket into the bin, counting aloud each time as he filled it. He tipped the hops out into one of the big sacks, giving them a card with the number written on, and Ollie initialled it each time. They heard him counting as he went down the next aisle and the next.

So it went on from day to day and the sun never faltered and in the evening they sat around the fire and never raised their voices, even Ollie, even Norah.

Rosie told them of the moth as big as a wren and shrank back as smaller ones came, attracted by the kerosene lamps. She watched as Jack gently brushed them away. Joe would have crushed them.

On Sunday this hop-farm did no picking and there was a stillness in the hop-yard, but the kiln was still in use, drying off the hops picked late yesterday afternoon. She and Jack walked into the oast-house and below the hop-floor was row upon row of long white sacks waiting for collection by the brewers who would come when all the hops were in.

'Tidy little sum,' Rosie said, breathing in the scent of the sulphur, the sweetness of the baking hops.

'Yes, I'd like to live here amongst these hills,' Jack said, fingering a sack. 'I like the country.'

'What about Somerset?'

'Yes, I like that too, but this is more like home, somehow, if you know what I mean.'

She did know what he meant. The lake was fading from her dreams, the baseball target too.

They packed a picnic and went to the stream where the cattle came down to drink. They laid blankets on the dry warm grass and lay back, listening while Maisie and Ollie laughed together and Grandpa took Lee down to the water and Jack told Rosie about Somerset.

He told her about the cart he had driven through a stream like this to soak and tighten the wheels. About Elsie, the farmer's wife, who wore cord trousers, and Tim the farmer, who gave him books to read because they only had a morning of lessons in the school below the big hill where the locals had quarried for hamstone before the war.

The quarry was fenced off in the war, Jack said, used for 'something 'ush 'ush' the old men had said. He told her about the cows he had to milk, the udders he had to wash, the apples he had to pick. How he had stayed down there to work on the farm when he was fourteen, rather than come back to the V1 and V2 raids, but really because he didn't want to leave the country.

He told her about the hams that had hung from the ceiling, the blackberries he and the other lads picked down by the fields which were joined to the next village by a long path.

He told her how Maisie had come down and how they had laughed with the farmer and his wife over thick fat bacon and pints of cider. How Ollie had come too, released from his job building airforce huts for a weekend. How they had herded in the cows for milking. How he had shown his dad the pigs he was rearing, how Ollie had kissed him when he left, and Maisie too. They had been happy then.

He told her about the Blitz and how he had worried, though he had never written about this in his letters to her. How he had thought of his mum and dad beneath rubble, burned, suffocated, but they had never been hurt, not so you could see anyway, he said.

He rolled over then, pulled at a shoot of grass, chewed the end, spat it out. He told her of the GIs who had come and pitched their tents opposite one of the village pubs and further up too, opposite the blackberry bushes. How they had danced each week at the social club, how they had made friends. And he told her of big Ed who reminded him of his mother because of his laugh and his hair.

'He gave me candy,' he said to Rosie, lying on his back now, his arm over his eyes. 'He sort of adopted me. He was good, and kind, and clumsy. He'd meet me on the green. I'd lend him me bike to go to the village across the main road for the bigger dances. That was where Norah lived.'

'Do you miss him?'

'Yes I do. We laughed a lot. Those GIs were good to us kids. Really good, they took us under their wings a bit, one to one. They were warm and friendly, not like us. D'you know what I mean?'

Yes, she thought. She did know, because that is what her American family were like. Then Rosie told him about Frank and Nancy because they, too, had taken *her* under their wing. She had not seen her real family for six years and so they had become unreal, too distant, too different. She told him about her pain, but he already knew, he said. She told him about the lake, and about Sandra. But she did not tell him about Joe.

She told him how she would not pledge allegiance to the flag as she was supposed to each morning before the start of school. She told him about the barbecues, and about Uncle Bob – of the jazz and the long shadows across the sloping lawn.

Then Grandpa called from the stream and she took Lee,

479

dipping him in and out of the water because Ollie and Maisie were talking to one another at last.

Jack felt the sun on his face and he thought of his own pain. He remembered how Maisie had come again and again to Somerset, how she had laughed when she met Ed, how she had popped out when Jack was asleep and he was glad that she did because the war was long and dirty for her in London.

He looked across at Rosie, at her legs, which were tanned as his were not. Tanned and strong, she lifted her skirts higher as the water rippled around her. She was pretty, not really changed. She reminded him of Ed, the way she spoke, and it warmed him. He had trusted Ed, liked him.

He looked across at his father. He loved him, too, he knew he did, but he didn't know this dark, fierce man that Ollie had become. He didn't know this father who wouldn't throw Lee up in the air, or blow on his stomach to make him laugh as he had made Jack laugh. No, he didn't know him at all and he didn't like him. Jack sank back on the blanket. His father had taken the laugh from his mother's face and didn't love their baby. Is that what the war did to you?

Rosie was calling him now and he pushed himself to his feet.

'Go on, son,' called his dad. 'I bet she splashes you.'

Jack laughed then because his dad looked like he used to and sounded like he used to and he hoped it would last so that the anger, confusion and pain which swept through him and frightened him would go.

The sun kept shining and the hops were brought in and neither Jack nor Rosie wanted the weeks to end. They walked to the shop pushing Lee and bought him liquorice shoelaces. They all sat outside the pub with the Welsh and the Black Country people and watched the gypsies running their ponies up and down. They drank ginger beer and cider while one old gypsy bought a pony 'With All Faults'.

They paid the sixpence deposit on the glasses just to sit outside in the last of the sun, and talked again of Somerset and America and watched as Ollie and Maisie sang 'Roll Out the Barrel' after three glasses of beer and Grandpa asked, 'Will you have another drink, me dooks?'

They sat round the fire on the third Sunday night and

listened as Grandpa told them, as he always used to, how the nailers would put their babies on the bellows to rock them to sleep. How he had been bellow-rocked by his parents, and had then pumped the bellows when he was a bit older than Lee, standing on a box. How he had learned to have the irons in the fire ready for his father as he finished one batch of nails, so that a few seconds could be saved on each nail and a few more pennies earned from the middleman.

He told them how some children had stood in the roof with their backs against a beam and pumped the bellows with their feet. He looked at his hands as Jack put more wood on the fire and told how he had grown tall enough to work at the nail bench. How he had made his first good nail. How he was given a penny dated for that year.

He told them how one boy had not wanted to work. How he had been nailed by the ear to the doorpost and left until he promised he would work.

Rosie held his hands but Norah just looked bored.

That night Rosie wrote to Frank and Nancy, telling them that she was living in a pigsty, and about the smell of hops on her hands, and the feel of the water about her legs in the stream, telling them that she was happy. And she was. She still missed them, but she was happy. She had been taken back to her childhood, reminded of so much, and, yes, now she had found her English family again.

As the last week drew to a close, all the pickers dragged down the longest bines from the end of the rows and Rosie picked up the hop-dog caterpillars which fell out and carefully laid them to one side.

'They'll turn into moths, you know,' Jack teased.

'I know but I guess I can handle it.'

They carted the bines to the oast-houses, the largest of which had been scrubbed and swept that afternoon. Jack and the rest of the boys stood on ladders and draped the bines, because tonight there would be a dance. There was always a dance.

Everyone came, and the band played jazz for half an hour and Jack told Rosie how much he liked it too, but his favourite was Duke Ellington, not Bix Beiderbecke, and then the band played swing and jive and they danced in the heat, their bodies touching and then away again. And always there was the smell of the hops. Norah danced with a Welsh boy. Their bodies did not touch but she smiled, and that was good.

Rosie went outside, sat with Grandpa and drank cider while he had a beer. Maisie and Ollie drank too, and laughed and then Maisie pulled out her cigarettes and Grandpa took one, and Ollie too. Then he stopped, his hand too tight on her arm. His face was hard and Rosie looked at Maisie, at the tension on her face. Now Jack was there, leaning over, trying to take his father's hand from his mother's arm.

'Where did you get those bloody Yank fags?' Ollie shouted and those about them looked. Lee was in his chair and he was crying now.

Maisie winced at the tightening grip. People closed in and now the band were playing 'I'm Dreaming of a White Christmas'. In goddamn September, Rosie thought, even as she moved closer to Maisie, pulling at Ollie's arm, wanting them all to be safe again, as they had been just a moment ago.

'I gave them to her,' Rosie said. 'I brought them back from America, don't you remember?'

It was over then, over as though it had never been, and Jack took her back into the dance and the heat. The music was slow as Jack took her in his arms.

It was too hot but it didn't matter, he was with her, touching her, and she almost felt safe again but she could still see Ollie's anger and Maisie's fear. She didn't tell Jack that she had given Maisie Camels, not Lucky Strikes.

Jack was leading her out now, into the dark cool air, away from the music and the people, and they stood down at the gate again, feeling their carved initials with their fingers, seeing the wild hops winding round the hedge and the telegraph pole, seeing the lights from the farm, hearing the owl in the distance, the music from the oast-house. It was now that he kissed her, with soft, gentle lips, and it was as though she had known this feeling of warmth and safety all her life because his tongue did not intrude into her mouth, nor his hands move to her breast, and his skin had the smell of the boy she had grown up with.

She kissed him back, holding his head in her hands, wondering at the children they had once been, and the people they had become, and it seemed that their friendship had become something stronger. Something good. Yes, she was home at last, safe at last, and the cigarettes meant nothing.

CHAPTER 5

On their return Mrs Eaves had assigned them to different counters. Rosie didn't mind. She stacked the notebooks, laid out the pencils, the few sharpeners clutched inside the tiny globes. She looked at America. So large. And at Britain. So small. And as Glenn Miller played 'The Boogie Woogie Bugle Boy of Company B' she thought of Nancy and Frank, of Sandra and Joe, and it didn't hurt so much, because she had spent September in the soft warm hills with Jack and was at her evening classes twice a week.

Norah minded though. She had been put on haberdashery and measured out quarter-inch baby ribbon, cord, and tape and added up on a pad, her face set, her voice sharp.

At home she sat nearest to the fire, her stockings rolled down round her ankles, her slippers trodden down beneath her heels, and would not talk of hop-picking, or the sun which had turned their skin brown, or the stream which had lapped at their legs, because if they hadn't been there she would still be on jewellery.

Rosie and Grandpa talked though, long into the night, and his skin was tanned too, his eyes bright again. They talked of the bines which floated like seaweed in the evening breeze, of the gypsies who danced on that last night as though they were part of the earth and sky. They talked of Maisie and Ollie whom they often heard laughing in the yard now, of Lee who was tossed into the air, Ollie's hands strong around his waist. They talked and they laughed but Grandpa did not discuss Jack, he just took her hand one night, and said, 'I'm glad you've found your friend again. Sixteen is difficult, it's half child, half adult. You need someone you can trust.'

Rosie told Jack as they walked to the Palais, Sam and Ted behind them, and Jack nodded. 'Yes, that's it. It's the trust.'

Jack came dancing with them every night now, because Ollie wasn't drinking and shouting and sleeping. He was working on the stall, selling nylons out of a suitcase, his finger to his nose if he was asked what else.

On Mondays, Wednesdays and Fridays the gang went dancing, slipping 1/6d on to the pay desk, making for a table at the edge of the floor. Sam and Ted looked at the girls who clustered down one side, deciding, choosing. Then they danced beneath a great glass revolving chandelier while the band played swing and jive, but never jazz. They coasted around the MC who stood in the middle of the dance floor, checking that no one kissed, that they all danced in the same direction, that they did not jitterbug.

Few kissed. All went in the right direction. All of them jitterbugged and her hand didn't sweat in Jack's and she could smell his skin as he swung her close, and then away.

They drank warm ginger beer mixed with cider and it brought back the buzz of the hoverflies in amongst the bines, the smell of the hops on her hands, the sun which washed her past back into her bones.

They walked home, dropping Sam and Ted, standing in the alley at the bottom of their yards. They stood looking at the light thrown out across the roses, looking at the shed rotting in the left-hand corner, looking at one another.

He would kiss her, gently, lightly, squeeze her hand and then leave her, walking in through his gate, she through hers. She would hear his steps in time with hers, and it was only with the closing of the door that the sound of him left her, but the knowledge of his presence in the bedroom next to her wall kept him close.

Tuesdays and Thursdays she went to Miss Paul's above the piano shop and typed to Chopin, chasing the notes, rubbing out the errors, blowing the rubber dust from the keys, cursing inside her head because Jack was watching Jane Russell at the Odeon whilst she was here.

But each week she was faster and her shorthand was better, and she wrote to Frank and Nancy that next spring she would find a job in Fleet Street. Just you wait and see, she wrote, and she knew that her letter was strong and positive, and that they would be glad.

By the middle of October she was moved back to records and played Duke Ellington for Jack and he touched her face when he walked in and heard. He stood still, listening to the piano as it beat its rhythm.

Norah was on spectacles and would stand waiting while customers read the printed card with the letters that diminished in size. Her nails clicked on the metal frames that she held in her hand while she waited, her face long as she fitted them around strange ears.

Rosie played 'I'll Be Seeing You', and smiled across as Norah scowled, but then regretted that she had done it, because the bridge between them had not yet been rebuilt.

October became November, and though there was still grief in the quiet hours of the night, she no longer kept her bedroom door open. There was hope, there was fun, there was Jack.

They danced and they kissed but still lightly, gently, and his hands didn't slide beneath her blouse nor his tongue probe her mouth and she was glad. She didn't tell him about Joe though, even when he told her of the girlfriend he had had in Somerset, the one he had kissed in the apple orchard. She said instead that it was only another five months until her exams and that she must work until midnight again.

She said this too when she wrote to Frank and Nancy but she also told them of the rationing, and the wind which grew ever more cold. She told them how Maisie called over the fence every Sunday and passed bread and hot dripping and how she and Grandpa ate it on the bench, wrapped in scarves and coats.

She told them how she, Jack and Ollie had helped Mrs Eaves's sister move into an old Army barracks north of London along with two hundred other squatters. They had pushed an old barrow with some furniture down the road from the flat she shared with her son and his wife and three children – a flat which had only one bedroom.

She told them how the people were taking over these empty buildings because there was nowhere else for them to live. How the Local Authorities were accepting them and connecting water and electricity, for what else could they do? There were no houses available. She told them that these were the things that she would write about when she started her proper job in the summer.

Frank wrote back asking why Mrs Eaves's sister hadn't moved into one of the prefabs they had been hearing about. If she didn't know, she should find out, get the complete picture, start thinking like a journalist.

Rosie asked Grandpa as they sat in front of the coal fire while the rain teemed down as it had done for the last seven days. Jack had collected some wood from a flooded bomb site and this was stacked on its end to one side. There was a smell of wet dust from it which crept through the whole house, but it would make the coal last longer.

'There aren't enough. They're having lotteries in some Local Authorities, though why anyone would queue to live in one of those I don't know,' said Grandpa, flicking the ash of a Woodbine into the fire. He coughed. The damp November air was making his chest thick again and his tan was fading, but he had had no accidents for months.

'Well, I can,' ground out Norah. 'A nice clean bungalow with a neat garden, a nice sort of neighbour. A nice new town away from London's mess. I'd want it.'

Rosie looked round the room, at the books either side of the fireplace, the American oilcloth on the table, bought from Woolworths. She thought of the house by the lake, the house in Lower Falls, and knew now that all three were home. At last all three were home.

As Christmas drew near she sewed cotton sheeting into two small pillowcases and filled them with hops, sending one to Frank and Nancy, hiding one for Grandpa. She bought a Duke Ellington record for Jack and Evening in Paris perfume for Maisie, Californian Poppy for Norah (because Norah needed all the sweetness she could get, she told Jack).

She bought Ollie paint brushes because he was always talking of doing up the house, but there were so few materials available. She bought Nancy a Union Jack brooch which was left over from the war. It was luminous 'so Frank will be able to track you down wherever you are', she wrote as she put their card in with the parcel.

She told them that her typing was still improving, the Palais was still fun. She did not tell them how Jack kissed her good night or that, as she crossed off the days to Christmas, her grief was deep and dark again because she remembered Lower Falls and the times they had spent together.

Instead she sat by the fire with Grandpa on 20 December until ten p.m. colouring, cutting and sticking paper chains together as they had always done.

'I've missed this,' he said, his hands folding the strips slowly, holding the ends between thumb and finger while they stuck together. 'I've missed our Christmases.'

'So have I, Grandpa,' she said. But she was not thinking of paper chains. She was thinking of the thick snow where here there was rain. Thick snow which had turned the world into a Christmas card as they had travelled by tram on her first American Christmas to the main shopping centres which were decorated with lights, and with streamers and garlands, snowmen and Father Christmas. The air had rung out with carols and there had been a Father Christmas on each floor, wilting in the central heating.

That night she didn't sleep at all. The next day when she walked home from work, there were no lighted trees in the windows, no people on skis and horse-drawn sleighs, no sparkling snow. There was nothing of the excitement she had known in Lower Falls for Lee, who was looking out into the street, his face pressed against the window. It wouldn't goddamn do.

At home there was a small piece of fatty bacon to boil along with carrots and potatoes. She did this but didn't talk. She poured Grandpa's tea, smiled at Norah and then went in to Maisie, wrapping Lee up warmly, taking the pushchair, going to the market, talking to Jack who nodded and asked Ollie to mind the stall.

They went by bus up West, and walked down the streets where there were some decorations, but not many and no Christmas lights. They saw the tree in Trafalgar Square, a gift from the Norwegians, then went into an Oxford Street store, up in the lift, Lee looking, laughing, touching, until they reached the grotto.

They queued, Jack's arm about her waist, holding the folded pushchair with his free hand. She held Lee, kissing his face. His skin was soft and warmer now than it had been in the street. He pulled her hair and she laughed.

487

'You should have kept your plaits,' Jack said. 'He could have swung on those.'

He leaned the pushchair against his leg, and took Lee from her, holding him up, turning him round in the air, laughing as he laughed, dropping him down against his chest, blowing on his neck.

'I love him,' he said, looking at Rosie.

She nodded. 'Silent Night' was playing on the gramophone. The record was scratched but it didn't matter. She wanted Lee to see and feel the magic as she had done because it would help her own grief this Christmas; her first away from Frank and Nancy.

She told Jack of the sleighs, the Christmas tree they had put up in the front garden, the garlands that hung on every wall and from every ceiling. She told him of the trams which had flattened the nickels she and Sandra had laid on the tracks when they were eleven. Jack blew again on Lee's neck, then bent and kissed her cheek.

Lee cried when Father Christmas took him on his knee in the dimly lit grotto, but Jack dropped down beside him and the crying stopped. The present was wrapped in red paper and Lee tore at it as they left. It was a wooden car. Blue and red, with wheels which spun.

Rosie remembered the bald tyres which Frank had heaped into the boot of the car during the war in case the worn ones he was using punctured. There were no new ones available.

There were plenty now, though, and new cars too, but here, in England, new cars were to be sold abroad to help the national debt and people patched up their old ones and made do. In America they were pitching into a boom, Frank said. Over here they were trying to pay for the war which had bled them dry.

'I don't mind queuing. I don't mind being rationed, or being cold,' Rosie said as they walked back down Oxford Street. 'It's time I had my share of that. But I wanted Lee to see another world, just for tonight.'

That night she slept, at least for a while.

On 23 December Jack called as she was settling Grandpa by the fire, his newspaper on his lap, his Woolworths glasses catching the light from the flames. The coal was wet, hissing and smoking. As Jack came in she put a sheet of newspaper to the fireplace.

'Leave the door open for a moment, Jack. Let's get a bit of a draught.' She held the paper with her fingertips as the fire roared suddenly, blazing red, browning the paper, which she snatched away, the heat hurting her face.

'That's great.'

She dug into the coals with the poker.

'There you are, Grandpa, that's a bit better.' She turned to Jack. 'Are we going up the Palais?'

She was reaching for her gloves, catching the coat which Jack tossed to her from the back of the chair.

Jack looked at Grandpa and winked. 'What d'you think, Grandpa? Shall we go up the Palais? D'you reckon this girl could take a change?'

Grandpa looked at Rosie. He rubbed his hands together, then picked up the paper. 'I expect she can. It sounded a good idea when Maisie told me.' He looked over the top at Rosie. 'Just put the guard up, there's a good girl, and don't hurry back.'

Rosie looked from one to the other. The guard was warm, she pushed it up against the fireplace, pulling the hearth rug well back.

'What are you two goons talking about? What's wrong with the Palais? It's the special Christmas night.'

She was pulling her coat on now. The buckle was cold as she threaded the belt through. Jack pulled up her collar.

'Keep that up, it's cold enough to freeze the balls off that monkey in Elm Street.' He pushed her towards the front door. 'Bye, Grandpa,' he called. 'Be good. And if you can't be good be careful.'

Rosie heard Grandpa laugh and said, 'If I'd said that he'd have lathered me.'

Jack marched through the yard, past the hard-pruned roses, out down the alley to the Tube station where people were rushing, their faces pinched. Rosie was tired, cold. Presents had arrived from Frank and Nancy for them all this morning. She had asked Norah what she had sent to the doctor and his wife in Somerset. What had they sent her?

Nothing, Norah had replied. They have their own children. There was nothing in it for me. Everything will go to the kids. All they offered was college, like yours did. I don't want that, too much hard work. Why keep in touch?

Rosie told Jack now what her sister had said.

'I don't know why she can't love or why she's so bitter,' she added.

Jack shrugged. 'She always has been. When will you realise that? Nothing will change her. It's in her bones. She's just getting more like your grandma every day. Nothing is ever enough. Nothing is ever right, but I think she misses your grandma too. It was always the two of them against you and your grandpa.' He shrugged. 'It's made her more spiteful. Maybe she'll change when she gets a boyfriend, someone of her own.'

The Tube train lurched and swayed through the tunnels and Jack held her hand. He never wore gloves.

'I'm hot,' she said, removing her own, because she wanted to feel his skin against hers.

'Nearly there,' Jack said, standing up as the train stopped in Bond Street station.

'Nearly where?' she asked as she was pulled along behind him, still holding his hand but jostled now by the crowds surging up from the train into the evening air.

'Nearly reached your Christmas treat,' Jack said, turning and grinning at her as they reached the pavement, slowing until she was up with him. 'You've been looking as though you've been hurting, deep inside. Can't have that, can we?'

He wasn't looking at her as he said this. His cheeks had flushed. 'Thought this might help. You gave Lee a treat. This is yours.'

They were south of Oxford Street now, in Soho. They were strolling along with many others and Jack told her that Soho had been the hunting cry of the Duke of Monmouth and that he had built a rather 'super' house on one side of Soho Square.

Rosie laughed. 'This is my treat, is it? A guided tour of Soho?' She dug him in the ribs.

'That's right, but there's more, my dear girl. Just you wait and see.'

They were walking past an accordionist who held his cap

between his teeth. There were two sixpences in it. Jack gave him another and then they turned into a pub, past two tarts who stood either side of the door.

'Not tonight, ladies,' Jack said.

'Too young anyway, ducks,' the blonde with black roots called back. Rosie flushed but Jack laughed.

Inside it was dimly lit but warm . . . There were sailors at the far end, sitting with civilians, all men.

Jack ordered a beer and a ginger beer for Rosie. Rosie stood back in case they were thrown out because they were too young. Jack was grinning, chatting, and he was served with a beer after all. Charm the bloody birds out of the trees, Rosie echoed the woman in the market.

She moved towards the end where the sailors sat, and Jack pulled her back as he sipped the froth and edged her towards a table nearer the other end.

'That's a pick-up,' he said, nodding towards the sailors.

Rosie looked again. 'But they're all men.'

Jack smiled and leaned his head back against the dark wood panelling.

Rosie looked at her own drink. 'I haven't seen this in the States,' was all she said.

'Or this.' Jack nudged her, pointing to the onion seller who wore his strings of onions over his shoulder. One woman sneaked up behind and cut a single one off, disappearing into the crowd. No one said anything.

Rosie remembered the cherries she had put over her ears in Frank's back garden. Rich red shiny earrings and they would be having Christmas over there without her.

They finished their drinks and moved out past the tarts again.

'A little older but not enough,' the blonde said again, rubbing her shoe up the back of her leg. 'It's a bit bloody cold.'

'You're right there,' Jack said, steering Rosie past them, strolling with her along the street. The restaurants were busy, holly hung from the ceilings and the white-bibbed waiters looked like the dippers which flew in bursts around the hop-yards. Rosie felt the tears gather in her throat because it was dark and cold and she was a long way from Lower Falls, a long way from Herefordshire.

It was further on that she heard the cornet, wailing up from the basement of a house just ahead of them, and then another and another and it was like the brownstones, though here, this time, the buildings weren't empty and dead. Here, close to her home, there was jazz.

She said nothing, just clutched at Jack's arm as they stood on the pavement, hearing Dixieland, New Orleans, hearing the drums. It was 'Take Your Tomorrow'. Pure Bix, pure gold breathing life into the streets, and into her mind. She looked at Jack, his head bent towards her, watching her face carefully.

'Does it make it better, little Rosie?' he asked, his voice quiet.

She reached up and kissed his cheek because she couldn't speak. He drew her towards him and this time their kiss was not soft and gentle, but filled with an excitement which left them both breathless, both awkward, until Jack turned towards the steps leading down to the door.

'You coming then?'

Inside it was dim and smoky. Rosie sat at a table near an opening which led to a counter where Jack bought coffee and rolls. Rosie watched as he put sugar in using the spoon which was chained to the counter. She wanted to hold the kiss in her mind but the music was surging and as Jack joined her she sat back and listened, feeling the heat of summer, hearing the jazz across the lawn. Seeing the faded, empty New York brownstones. But here, in England, they were not empty, and she was sitting with Jack, breathing in the rhythm once again.

All evening they sat as the trumpet played that deliberately impure tone which distinguishes jazz from straight playing.

'He's using his lips,' Jack said quietly.

'No he's not, he's half-valving.' But then she saw that he wasn't. 'OK,' she said. 'You win.'

'I like the banjo, it's cleaner than the guitar.'

'No, it's not. Charlie Christian showed us that.' Rosie pointed towards the guitar player. 'See, that guy's using his fingertips to strike the strings as well as stop them. How about that for a clean note.'

'How about that for a know-it-all.' Jack was leaning towards her and they laughed together quietly while the music played and all pain ebbed away. They kissed, lightly, but they were older tonight, closer tonight.

492

They listened to the trumpet's break, tapping the table with their hands as the player improvised and the others in the band fell silent. He was good, a young man with long hair, and then the rest came in. Jack picked at the wax which had clumped around the candle which stood in a jam jar. 'Duke Ellington is right not to like improvisation. He plans everything, you know.'

Rosie looked at the candle. They had used candles to burn the bed bugs from creases in the mattresses when they were young. They had used candles for the Christmas table in Lower Falls but it didn't hurt to think of that here. She picked at some wax herself. It was slightly warm. She rolled it into a ball. Looked at the band again. Did they play to a written arrangement or to one made familiar by use?

'Their improvisation works though,' she said as the band broke for a coffee.

'Yes, you're right, but it can turn into a right mess. Like your shorthand when I read to you too fast.'

Rosie sipped her coffee. It was cold but it didn't matter. 'What about you?' she said. 'What about your plans. Will it always be the stall? Once you were going to be an artist.'

Jack sat back, tipping the chair, resting it against the wall. 'Don't know. Me art's not good enough. Not much point sorting anything out. Not yet anyway.' He turned round to look at the band. The trumpet player was standing near them, talking to a girl with long black hair.

Rosie drank the last of her coffee. It was bitter at the bottom.

'Why not? What's stopping you?'

Jack turned and smiled. 'Look, you had a good schooling. We had very little. Just mornings and then it was bloody chaos. All the evacuees in the one large school hall.' He leaned forward taking her hand. 'It's not that though. Got to do me National Service, haven't I? Not worth starting anything until then.'

She had forgotten about that. Forgotten that he would be going away for eighteen months. It was too long. She couldn't bear to be without him. She squeezed the wax, looking at that, not at him. 'When?'

'Not until I'm eighteen. There's loads of time. Bit more than a year when you work it out.'

The band were playing again and she looked at him as he sat four-square on his chair again, his hands slapping on his thighs in time to the beat, and then he turned to her.

'I'll fix something up afterwards, like everyone does.'

They didn't leave the club until eleven p.m. and then travelled home, talking and laughing because tonight had been filled with music, with talk, with gently held hands. The kiss he gave her at the back yard gate was soft again but as he held her there was excitement too.

She slept that night with scarcely any dreams, only one about a silent brownstone house that turned into a noisy jazz-filled Soho basement. She woke in the morning and scratched the frost from the window. The cold didn't matter because they were young and the war was over. Their lives were just beginning and they had a year before he had to go and that was a long time. Besides it was Christmas Eve.

Maisie cooked the turkey in her kitchen on Christmas morning and Rosie helped Jack to carry the table from Grandpa's house and they all ate together, pulling home-made crackers, drinking beer that Ollie had 'found'. They ate tinned peaches and tinned ham for tea and Grandpa raised his cup of tea.

'To Frank and Nancy, God bless them.'

Yes, God bless them, Rosie thought, thinking of the stockings which had hung at the mantelpiece last year, the turkey, the Christmas lights, the smell of spruce throughout the house. The wine, the liqueurs, the guests, the warmth, the skiing in the afternoon, and the ache wasn't as sharp, and she knew it was because of the jazz, and Jack.

She fingered the light woollen scarf which Nancy had sent. It was warm draped around her shoulders and she barely felt the draught coming from the ill-fitting windows and the gaps in the doors. All the houses were the same after the blast of the bombs which had rocked and cracked the buildings.

She looked across the table which she had helped Maisie to set for tea and smiled at Jack. His bed was down here now, moved from the boxroom to make room for Lee. Rosie wished he hadn't moved, she wished she could still hear him shut the door, sink into bed, cough. Lee climbed on to her knee now and she hugged him, rubbing her face into his neck, making him laugh, making herself laugh.

'That's a nice scent,' she said as Maisie leaned over her shoulder to put a toast soldier into Lee's mouth. 'What is it?'

'You should know, you gave it to me,' Maisie said, turning from the table quickly, moving towards the sink. Ollie stopped eating his Christmas cake, looked at Rosie and then his wife. He dropped his knife and the noise was sharp in the sudden silence. Maisie's back was still and Ollie's face was dark again as it had been before the hops were picked.

Rosie looked at Jack. His face was tense, his eyes wary, pained.

She turned to Maisie and laughed. 'I'd forgotten. It's Evening in Paris. It's nice, isn't it? I've got some myself at home.' She poured another cup of tea for Ollie. 'Drink up, Ollie, that cake of Nancy's is pretty dry.'

He looked from her to Maisie, his eyes guarded, his thoughts elsewhere.

'Don't make those bloody crumbs,' he said to Lee.

Rosie looked at Norah. 'Did you like your Californian Poppy? Maybe I should have bought you the French one too.' Norah wasn't listening, she was reading the book of women's love stories which Maisie had given her.

Ollie was relaxing again now with his cake and tea and Maisie brought Lee another toast finger, smiling at him, at Jack, at Ollie, at Rosie. But Rosie looked into the fire instead because she knew the perfume was not Evening in Paris. But she saw that her words had taken the anxiety from Jack's face.

CHAPTER 6

January 1947 brought bitter cold and a letter from Nancy.

Lower Falls
January 1st

My dearest Rosie,

We were so very pleased with your presents and the good wishes from your Grandpop. Please give ours to your family for a happy and safe New Year.

I say safe because Frank is getting real uptight. He's been seeing bogeymen in the woodpile ever since Churchill's Iron Curtain speech at Fulton, Missouri. He sees East Europe falling under the Communists and Truman's Government getting real upset about it. Thinks they'll have bad dreams about the Reds sweeping over here too.

Already that goddamn busybody, Gallagher, in Local Administration, is getting busy sharpening his knife, asking questions about Art, our friend in planning. Do you remember him? Had some kind of a soft spot for those revolutionaries in Russia in the thirties. He's got a wife and kids now. Doesn't think of politics any more but this LA is really sniffing. Does he think that there are Reds under every bed or something crazy like that? Even came round to the newspaper offices asking how long Frank had known him.

But, let's not go on about that now. I guess Christmas without you has made me mope. I can't tell you how we miss you. We took a ride into town. It wasn't the same.

We're off skiing for a week at the end of January but that won't be the same either, without you. Sandra is busy, having a good time as always. Talking without drawing breath. We see Joe from time to time. He'd like a job on the paper. Maybe he will, but we'd rather it was you.

How are things with you, Rosie?

All our love,
Nancy

Rosie read the letter standing in a queue during her lunch-hour hoping that at the end of it there would be some sort of meat. But there wasn't and she walked back to Woolworths, her feet cold in her Wellingtons even through the thick socks she had knitted from a pulled out jumper.

It hadn't mattered until she read the letter, saw the round handwriting, remembered the feeling of Nancy's arms, the smell of Frank's pipe. Perhaps it would be better if they didn't write, didn't stir up memories, but then she shook her head. No, her feet would still freeze and she wanted to feel Nancy reaching out to her.

She shook her head at Norah and Mrs Eaves as she went in.

'The soldiers couldn't get through with it. They're slower than the lorry drivers. Maybe tomorrow.' She shrugged and pushed her numb feet into her shoes before taking her place behind the counter, feeling the letter in her pocket.

She wrote back to Nancy that night telling her that the road haulage workers were on strike, the meat was rotting in the warehouses, the soldiers were slowly getting it through. She told her how they thought they'd bought some from a guy called Jones at the pub who had meat which would otherwise rot, but he took their money and ran. We never seem to learn, she wrote.

She told Nancy how the greengrocer was rationing potatoes to two pounds a head a week. But there *was* corned beef – 'So we party every night, Nancy. You'd love it.'

She switched out the light and lay back in her bed. Did her letter sound angry or just plain tired? She felt both as she lay here listening to Grandpa moving about beneath her. She sat up, read the leader column of *The Times*, and analysed a report which Frank had enclosed for her as practice. Wrote it up. Transcribed her shorthand because there was no time to waste. It was 1947. She was moving forward. She had to keep telling herself that.

She had said it as she heaped the fire with ash before she came upstairs, banking it up, hoping it would stay in until the morning. They were wrapping coal in soaked newspaper to make it last longer and Jack's wood from the bomb site helped.

She lay down and pulled the blankets up round her ears not thinking of the food in the American shops, not thinking of the

497

skiing slopes. Beating back the anger at the ease of the world which she had left behind.

Maisie hadn't been any luckier with her meat queue either. Lee had been so cold after two hours she had come home and Rosie had rubbed his hands between hers to warm them up. She listened to his crying and coughing through the wall.

He was ill, his temperature was high. She put on the light again and added to her letter, telling Nancy that on New Year's Day flags had been raised at all Britain's collieries as they were nationalised. It hadn't meant more coal though, not yet. A fuel crisis was threatening.

Here Rosie put down her pen. Lee was still crying and now she could hear Jack's voice, soft and gentle, and Maisie's too. She listened, wanting to speak through the wall to Lee, to reach out to him, but she didn't, she just waited until there was no more sound and then she wrote again, wondering how long it would be before the new National Health Service took effect. She did not mention the Local Administrator or Eastern Europe and the Iron Curtain. It was too far away, too trivial against Lee's cough and the bitter cold.

The next day Jack came round. It was Sunday and Lee was a bit better, he told her, his muffler up round his mouth, his dad's old coat worn at the cuffs, the belt missing. Rosie nodded, heaping Grandpa's sheet from the sink into a bowl, drying her hands, pulling down her sleeves, throwing her coat around her. The accidents had begun again, but Jack was here and nothing else mattered.

Jack carried the sheet into the yard and they each took an end, twisting it, hearing the water pouring on to the yard, seeing it begin to freeze even as it hit the concrete. Again they twisted. The water splashed on his coat.

'Why are you wearing that thing?' Rosie asked. 'It's so darn big.'

Jack just shrugged and grinned. 'Makes me look older. Maybe those tarts up West would take me on now.'

Rosie looked at his face, then flicked a corner of the sheet, splashing him. 'There'd have to be a pretty thick fog, and a Derby win to make it worth their while.'

She carried the sheet in and Jack hung it over the airer which hung from the ceiling above the fire while Rosie lifted out the other sheet from the sink. They did the same a second time and Jack asked how Nancy was, and Frank. As the cold sliced into her wet hands she would not let herself think of the skis which would be propped up in her old bedroom. She would not let herself think of the central heating, the washing machine, the hamburgers oozing out of toasted buns. Nor would she think of the Local Administrator, or Art, or Frank, because as dawn had come she had realised it wasn't trivial, or Frank would have written himself. Nor would she think of the big coat that Jack was wearing because she thought she knew what it meant.

She made mugs of tea with twice-used leaves and they cupped them in their hands, Grandpa too, his eyes not meeting theirs because he was ashamed. Jack pulled a newspaper out of his pocket.

'Ollie sent it round. He's stuck on the crossword. Wants you to finish it, if you've got the time.'

Rosie smiled as Grandpa took it, concentrating on this, not that land across the sea.

'Number five down. Can't get that at all. None of us can.'

Grandpa took the stub of pencil from Jack, read the clues, knew the word and they all smiled as his eyes met theirs.

'Hypothermia, that's what it is,' he said.

Rosie looked at Jack. He had known all along, she could tell from his eyes.

'Where are we going?' she asked, blowing on the pale tea, feeling the steam damp on her face. The room was damp from the sheets too.

Jack drank his tea, wiping his mouth with the back of his hand. 'Nowhere today, Rosie. I'm a bit busy.' He reached forward, giving her his mug. 'Thanks for the tea.'

She had known he would say that. Ever since Jones had taken the money and not brought back the meat, she'd been waiting for this because she had seen the anger in his eyes, and knew it was reflected in hers. And today he was wearing that coat which would cover any amount of meat.

'I'll come.' Rosie was up again but Jack was at the door now.

'No, you won't come. Stay here. I've just got a bit of work to do.'

He didn't turn back as he moved quickly through the yard, stepping over the ice from the sheets, slamming the gate behind him. But then he heard the latch lift and she was there, shaking in the cold, her coat slung over her shoulders. There was a freezing fog coming down now, its droplets were on her hair.

'Rosie, get the hell back in the house. Do as I ask, just for bloody once.' His voice was angry but she looked so small, so cold, and so he came to her, taking her in his arms. 'Go on now, get back in. It's nothing. Nothing, just a job.'

'Like the cheeses?' Her voice was indistinct, muffled by his coat.

He laughed. 'Yes, a bit like the cheeses.'

She stood back from him now. 'Well, I'm coming. He owes my grandpa too. And we should do this together.'

Jack looked at her. 'You're crazy. You won't give up. I'm getting it for all of us. Let me and Dad do it. You don't have to be involved. Just go back in and wait.'

But Rosie was walking into his yard now. Didn't he know that waiting was too hard?

Ollie drove out of London, grinding the gears of his friend's car but using kosher petrol. 'Don't want to be stopped before we start, do we?' he said as he wiped the windscreen again, scraping his frozen breath from the screen, passing Jack the rag. 'Here, you keep at it. Make sure I can see my way. And you keep quiet in the back, Rosie. You shouldn't be here anyway.'

Jack looked out through the small patch he had cleared for himself, scrubbing the windscreen in front of Ollie. The fog was freezing on the screen, the wipers were scraping some of it away. His dad was peering down at the map then out again at the road signs. Fog was seeping thickly around them now.

'Don't matter. It could help,' his father murmured, pointing to a turning on the pencil-drawn map. His nails were thick with dirt from the tyre they'd had to change ten miles back. They turned at the next crossroads. There were factories either side, flat-roofed. Two in ruins, burnt out by incendiaries. There was another old three-storey building with blackened bricks. The edges were indistinct, the fog was thicker now.

'Bert said it's along at the end. Might be guards though. Do you want to go through with it?' Ollie was looking at Jack now.

No, I don't want to go through with it. I'm frightened. I

500

want to go home. I want me mum, I want to turn round and take Rosie back with me. I don't want the bloody meat. But all he said was, 'Course. Why not? That old bugger should have let us have it. He took our money.'

He wiped at the windscreen again. Lee needed it. He needed some good red meat inside him. He was pale, his cough was bad. It was crazy to let the meat stay in there – and besides Rosie was here. She had made him bring her. She wouldn't give up. It warmed him, made him smile, gave him courage.

They were close now and it was quiet as Ollie turned off the engine and drifted into the side of the road. Had old Jones posted guards? Jack wondered. He must have known that if he cheated them they'd come after him. He knew Ollie too well, didn't he?

'He did the same with the Wind and Flute regulars. Took their money, said they could come and transport their own meat, then said the meat had gone off. They'd paid their money, it was their loss, the old devil said.'

Ollie was tapping the dashboard, peering through the fog. Jack wound down his window. He could hear nothing but church bells. He looked at his watch.

'What time are the others supposed to be here?'

'By now,' Ollie said. His voice was short. His eyes darting to the mirror and then to the front again.

'What if the meat has gone off?' Jack asked.

'Then we've done all this for nothing but at least we've tried. You see, he stamps on us, that bugger, always has. Runs the Pawn, runs the betting shop, thinks he runs us. Someone pinched two of his cheeses, you know. Upset him for weeks that did.'

Jack nodded, remembering Rosie walking beside him with a swollen stomach and now, as he leaned his head out of the car, he grinned, banging lightly with his hand on the side of the van, hearing her knock back.

She was his past and his present. She was everything and she was tired and hungry because Grandpa had all that she could spare. Rosie had never told him that, but she didn't need to, he had seen it for himself.

Ollie pressed his mouth to the grille between the cabin and the back.

'We can't wait any longer. You come through to the cabin,' he called softly to Rosie. 'Keep a look-out for the cops, for anyone. If you see them, come and get us, don't hoot the horn.'

Jack followed Ollie from the van, walking on the grass to deaden the sound of his footsteps. They could see the fence ahead. There was barbed wire on the top. Ollie gestured and Jack crept round to one side, Ollie to the other. There was a gap, but it was too small for Ollie so it was Jack who went through alone, carrying cutters for the padlock, carrying his fear.

The fog was thicker now, he could taste the sulphur in his mouth. It stung his eyes and was thick in his throat. His feet were frozen in his plimsolls but they were quieter, like the GIs' rubber-soled shoes had been, like Ed's had been in the Somerset village. Had they worn them in the Ardennes? Had Ed been frightened? Had he shown it? He'd always said there was nothing wrong with fear. It kept you alive. Why had he never written? Why do I think of him so much? Why do I lie awake at night and think of him?

He stopped, gripped the cutters. Keep your mind on the job, you bloody fool. He listened again. Had there been a noise? He waited. No, nothing. Fear kept you alive, Ed said. He repeated it to himself. There was nothing wrong with it. The door was ahead, the padlock dripping in the fog.

He eased the cutters round the chain, bending his elbows, putting his weight behind it but it was no good. He tried again and they slipped and fell. He froze, his breath loud. He couldn't hear. He breathed through his mouth. That was better. There was nothing. No one.

He stooped and picked up the cutters, tried again, and this time fear had put strength into his arms and he ground the cutters through, catching the chain before it fell, laying it gently on the ground. Ed was right, it helped. He took the sack from beneath his coat, opened the door, and crept on, into the cold store. Looking. Listening. Breathing. Christ, why was he so loud? He could see his breath. He had seen Rosie's in the yard. Shut up, concentrate. Listen. Look. Breathe.

There were carcasses hanging on hooks, others cut into joints. He took only what they had paid for. There was no rancid smell. This meat was good. He turned, easing his way back out, shutting the door, running now, back to the fence, but where was the gap? He edged along. The fog was thicker now. He couldn't see. The meat was heavy in the large pockets inside the coat. His hands were numb, his feet too.

'Dad,' he whispered. 'Dad.' But there was no answer, there was just a noise behind him, an arm round his throat, a fist hard into the side of his head and pain which for a moment crushed him but he didn't drop the cutters because he knew they could be traced back to Ollie.

There was another punch and he felt his lip burst. He spun round, out of the grip because he didn't want to be locked up, he didn't want to be kept from Rosie, from Lee, from his mum, from Dad.

No, he didn't want to be kept from his dad and he swung his fist at the large dark man whose face he couldn't see in the fog. He felt the shock of contact up into his shoulder, saw him fall, begin to rise. He swung at him again. Rosie needed her meat. Lee needed his.

'Dad,' he shouted. 'Dad.'

But his father was already there, the fence planks that he had torn away thrown across the yard.

'Get out now, son.' Ollie was struggling with the guard, his breath coming in grunts, warding off the blows, parrying, grabbing an arm, twisting it up behind the guard's back now, bringing him to a standstill.

'Quick. I'll cover you. Get to the van. If I don't come, drive off. There might be more than one.' He was tying the guard's arms together.

Jack ran off through the gap, the meat heavy in the coat, but then he stopped and waited by the fence. His dad had come for him. His father was putting the guard into a hut.

'Out of the cold,' he told him as he ran back. Together they went to the van, pushing the meat beneath sacks, keeping Rosie in the cabin. Together they drove until they found a phone box. Then Ollie rang the police, telling them that there was a guard tied up in a shed in Jones's warehouse, nothing more. They drove back, neither speaking, scared the police might see them, might stop them, but they didn't.

They threw the sack into the back yard, then drove the van back to Bert. They were stopped and searched but Rosie had wiped the blood from Jack's face with her handkerchief moistened from the yard rainbutt and there was nothing to be seen but the sweat on the palms of their hands, the fear in their eyes.

That night those who had paid Jones received their meat and Jack held Rosie and told her that he hated the cold, he hated to feel such fear, but Ollie had been like he was before the war – strong and reliable – and it had been worth it for that. She kissed his bruised cheek, his swollen lips and remembered that she had never been able to see him hurt, even when they were children.

That night she wrote again to Nancy, asking about the Americans' fear about Russia. Asking about Frank and the Local Administrator because she couldn't bear to think of Frank being hurt either.

As January turned to February the cold was like nothing anyone could remember. The snow heaped itself in drifts over the roses and up against the windows. They dug paths through to the road and walked in the gutter. They slipped and fell but went on and heard in the grocer's queue that Mr Philips's son, a conscript, had been killed in Palestine.

Nancy wrote that it was suspected that the Polish elections had been rigged to allow in the Communists and that the United States Government feared that the Soviets had atomic secrets. Would they too build a bomb? Would the Government feel forced to stand out against the Communists?

Rosie didn't want to read this. She wanted to read words of love that she could hug to herself at night, keeping out the darkness of the winter, the worry that the world was going crazy again. That there might be war. Is that what they were saying? Hadn't they all gone through enough in the last one? Weren't they still going through it?

Wasn't it enough that there was snow *and* that there was a fuel shortage? That there was no power during the morning and afternoon at home, so Grandpa had to go to Maisie's to huddle round one fire, and one set of candles? For Christ's sake, wasn't that enough?

She was standing in her room, tearing up the letter, talking aloud, going mad. Is that it? Am I going mad? She took down her books and her pencil and transcribed long into the night because none of this mattered. She must keep saying that. All she had to do was get through to the summer, because then her career would begin.

In March the snow turned to floods and drowned sheep that would have been part of the meat ration. Violence continued in India, terrorist attacks continued in Palestine, and President Truman told Congress that America must be prepared to intervene throughout the world to oppose Communism.

There was another letter from Nancy.

Lower Falls

My dear Rosie,

The snow sounded like fun. Are you getting in any skiing? How is the rationing? That doesn't sound fun.

Here it's pretty mopey. The Local Administrator has interviewed Frank again. His friend Art lost his job. He was once a Communist. He'll never work again unless Frank can take him on. He's looking at it. The LA asked Frank if he is, or ever has been, a Communist. Of course he threw the goddamn man out.

It'll all settle. A few people are getting a bit uptight but it'll pass. Your exams are soon. Keep working but have fun too.

Sandra says she'll write but you know her. Too much partying, too much talking. She means well though. Mary sends her love. Wonders if you're missing her hamburgers.

Will write again soon.

Nancy

That night Rosie danced with Jack at the Palais, she swung, danced, smiled and clung to him. That night she couldn't sleep. Hamburgers – what the hell were they? All she knew about were the sheets from Grandpa's bed to be washed in the morning, the coal to wrap in newspaper, records all morning, queuing all lunchtime, like the rest of this country.

March turned to April and the blossom came, filling the parks with colour, the daffodils too and hyacinths which scented the paths. While Rosie queued she read her shorthand book, testing, thinking, transcribing in her head. She had no time to dance in the evenings because she was practising on an old typewriter of Maisie's.

505

'It's the exam in two months. It's so important,' she told Jack, and he understood and read to her from a book. She took it down in shorthand, typed it up while he timed her, sitting at the kitchen table, his feet up on another chair, chatting with Grandpa. Norah wouldn't help.

In June she took her exams and they danced that night and kissed in the yard because she dared to believe she had done well. Ollie brought round bottles of beer and Grandpa had some too, and Norah. Jack winked at Rosie.

In July, the results came through and that night they celebrated again and then danced at the Palais until midnight because there was no more shorthand, no more typing to be learned.

'We've done it,' she told Jack, kissing him on the mouth, tasting the beer on his lips, knowing that he could taste it on hers. 'We've goddamn done it.'

Tomorrow she would walk up and down Fleet Street and find a cub reporter's job and she ignored Norah's scowl as they danced in through the yard, because now she was really on her way and Jack had said that he was proud of her, and so too had Grandpa.

CHAPTER 7

The newspapers would not take a girl of seventeen. They wouldn't take her if she was older either. She was not sufficiently well educated. She was a girl. There were too many men back from the war. They wouldn't even take her as a messenger. It wasn't suitable work for a girl.

She thought of the baseball she had thrown, the bike she had ridden, chasing down other kids on the block, down the street, in and out of cars, trams, hunting for Indians when she was the cowboy. The nickels she had pushed on to the tram lines for the trams to flatten. That wasn't suitable play for a girl either. This was the end. Somehow it brought everything to an end.

She didn't go back to Woolworths for two days because she couldn't stop the tears. She lay on her bed, the curtain drawn across the small window, but there was no light anywhere, anyway, any more. Everything had gone, nothing was worth getting up for, going on for. It was not only that her plans had failed but her protection had been stripped away and now she faced again the pain of her separation from the two adults she had loved with all her heart and it was all too much.

Jack came. He sat on her bed, held her hand but she couldn't feel him, she couldn't hear him as he told her she must not give up. She must get angry again, he said. She must fight. Remember the cheese, and the meat. Remember the rec, the hop-yards where it had been warm, where things had changed for them all.

'Don't let yourself lose, Rosie, not now, not ever. Don't let yourself despair. You'll see Frank and Nancy again.'

She turned from him. She was too tired, couldn't he see that? And she hurt too much. She wanted Nancy's arms to make it better. To take the ache away and to wipe out the hours of work which had all been for nothing. It had all been taken from her, as she had been taken from America. She felt dead and to tell him would be to hurt him. How could she do that?

Maisie came too, and Grandpa sat with her, but how could she tell any of them about the emptiness, the pain? How could she hurt them like that?

On the third day she returned to work because there was nothing else to do. She must live every day, Frank and Nancy had said. What would they say now, when she had failed to use all that they had given her? How could she hurt them like that?

Mrs Eaves gave her Erroll Garner, Louis Armstrong, Duke Ellington, Charlie Parker to play because Jack had been in to explain her absence. She took her by the arm, and led her to the office.

They sat and drank Camp coffee while Mrs Eaves talked of the Americans she had known, the GI, Stan, she had loved, although she was married.

'My husband came home in the winter of forty-five. Desert Rat he was. I was white haired by then and he thought it was the Blitz that had done it. It wasn't though. Stan had been killed in the Ardennes. It broke my heart and turned me white nearly overnight.' Mrs Eaves was holding Rosie's hand tightly.

'It's all right,' Rosie said. 'Don't talk. Don't say any more. Don't hurt yourself like this.'

Mrs Eaves swallowed but then continued. 'War breaks hearts. It breaks lives too. There's so much love that can never be spoken about; so much pain. There's so much death. So much injury which takes away futures. Really takes them away, Rosie.'

Mrs Eaves leaned back and lit a cigarette with trembling hands, letting the match drop into the ashtray. They both watched the flame die.

'Life's not a bowl of bloody cherries you know, Rosie.' Mrs Eaves's voice was tired, quiet. 'You're growing up. Frank and Nancy aren't here. Your Grandpa's old. You're on your own, my dear. Everyone is.' She flicked her ash into the ashtray, picking a shred of tobacco from her lip.

'But . . .'

'No buts. You can either sit down and give up or get out there, find a job as a secretary on a magazine, a paper. Get into it that way. Then maybe go back to America if you want to.

You're lucky, you have people who love you. You have a life and a future. So many haven't any more.' Mrs Eaves was crying now and Rosie held her and wept too and then she went back to her counter and played Bix, smelling the hamburgers cooking on the barbecue, feeling sand beneath her feet, seeing the hops on the bines. She thought of the cheeses she had clutched to her, Jack's bruised face in the van, Frank's struggle with the LA and she knew she'd have to go on. She wouldn't let herself lose, not now, not ever and this is what she told Jack, when he came in, but although his smile touched her pain, it didn't make it go away.

When she returned that evening, Grandpa was ill; he had the same cold as Lee had struggled with. She sat by his bed all night and every night for ten days and though he was better he was not the same, and she knew that she couldn't go on with her plans. Not yet.

He needed her at lunchtime and when she finished work and during her tea breaks, and she was there because she loved him, not because Norah shouted at her, 'You've got to. It's only fair.'

She was young, only seventeen, she told herself as she brushed her hair, tucking it behind her ears. There was plenty of time. She would wait, but waiting was so hard.

The next day she made Norah queue at lunchtime while she came home and sat with Grandpa because Norah had shouted at him this morning.

When Norah complained she said, 'You're not fit to be near him. You're cruel, you always were and you still are. But you'll do the goddamn shopping. It's only fair.' She no longer felt guilty where Norah was concerned. The feeling had faded when Rosie had begun to look after Grandpa day and night, out of love but out of duty too. She and Norah were equal now and there was no room in her life for guilt any more – or almost no room. Besides, there was too much pain in the darkness of the night and she wondered how many tears a person could cry.

It was on Friday that they went to the jazz club again, and Jack told her he had won twenty pounds when Pearl Diver won the Derby and that the bookmaker had been Mr Jones. She laughed but stopped when he said she must have the money to go towards a ticket to America, to see Frank and Nancy. To go back for ever, if that is what would take the shadows from her eyes. Maisie had said she would look after Albert, and Jack would too.

The smoke was all around them in the club. A man in the corner was rolling a reefer, his girlfriend was smoking hers. The smell was sweet.

'Go on, you use it,' Jack said, pushing it across to her. 'It's your birthday present. A bit late, I know.' He was drinking his beer, not looking at her, and Rosie thought of the sweater she had knitted him for his birthday, out of two of Grandpa's old ones, and here he was, offering a way of life back to her.

He looked tired too, and she felt like a spoilt child who had kicked and screamed because she had been hurt, ignoring him. Thinking he couldn't see what she was feeling.

She pushed the money back. It was held together by a rubber band. 'I couldn't leave you,' she said. 'I couldn't leave any of you. And anyway,' she said, leaning back and drawing circles in the beer which had spilled on the table, 'now my plaits have gone, where would I put the rubber band?'

He laughed, very loud, and the boy rolling his reefer looked across at them, nodding his head at his girlfriend, licking the cigarette paper, lighting it, breathing it deep into his lungs.

Rosie drank some of Jack's beer and knew now that she loved him, more than anyone else, and the pain receded and she slept each night and woke to sunlit days.

Since Rosie would not use the money, Jack took them to Butlins in August instead, after a summer of austerity with rations reduced yet again. Mr Attlee said, 'I cannot say when we shall emerge into easier times,' and Rosie nodded as she read these words. She was already emerging.

Grandpa was pleased because Marshall Aid appeared to be a possibility.

'I knew humanity would prevail,' he said.

But Frank had written to tell her that in the spring President Truman had embarked on an American crusade against Communism. He wanted the West strong enough to buffer the US and Rosie wondered if this was the only reason they were receiving aid. She didn't tell Grandpa that. She didn't tell him either that Frank had been visited again by the Local Administrator because Nancy seemed to think it was just a nuisance not a problem. And maybe she was right.

Only Norah, Rosie, Ollie and Jack went to Butlins. Not Grandpa, he was still weak but feeling much better, and not Maisie, who stayed behind with Lee to look after the old man. She wanted to, she had insisted when Rosie went round. Lee's too young. You all go and enjoy yourselves. And I don't mind about the sheets either.

They travelled by charabanc past verges sown with barley which were now being harvested. They saw a man scything an entry for a reaper-binder into a field of wheat. They stopped and watched him rake up the wheat he had cut. It was too precious to waste.

As the charabanc engine started again they began to sing on the back seat, Jack and Ollie drinking beer, and soon the whole coach was joining in, even Norah. The camp had rows of flat-roofed chalets, a swimming-pool, a gym, a dining-room, and over on the edge where the hedge leaned over from too many years in the path of the wind, there was a fun-fair.

She and Norah shared a chalet and Norah walked around touching the wardrobe, the dressing-table, the basin.

'This is what a prefab must be like,' she said. 'Nice and clean, fresh and new. That's what I want. My own new prefab. You can win competitions for the best gardens, you know.'

Rosie sat on the bed and nodded. Norah had never gardened in her life. She looked around. She preferred Grandpa's house with his books, the fireplace, bricks which had been there for years. Bricks which had housed him, and her.

Jack and Ollie had a chalet in the next row.

In the morning the tannoy woke them, shouting 'WAKEY WAKEY', but she didn't mind because she had no sheets to wash and wring. They straggled with the other campers past rose beds clear of greenfly into the dining-room, to eat beans and bacon, and Ollie wondered whether the roses had been there when the services took over the camps in the war. Rosie felt in her pocket for her matchbox. It was there. Why had she brought it? Would Maisie remember to catch the ladybirds for Grandpa?

She drank her tea and smiled at Jack. They were here together for a week and it was as though the years had fallen from her and she needed nothing else. Just him. They ran to the pool when breakfast was finished. She stood in her swimsuit on the edge of the pool, the tiles cold beneath her feet. She felt Jack's eyes on her. She flushed and dived into the cold water. Jack's body was strong and as pale as hers was now. Her lakeside tan was gone.

She hauled herself up on the edge, then stood and dived again, hearing the water gushing past, kicking out, reaching the other side. It was as good as the lake and it was fun. She hauled herself out, dived a third time, heard the water again. Yes, it was just as good. She surfaced, wiped back her hair and smiled at Jack.

Now the Redcoats were blowing whistles, and they were formed into teams for racing. Jack's team won. Again and again they plunged into the water, throwing balls, racing when the whistles blew, then filing into the dining-room again for lunch.

At three Rosie went with Norah to keep fit in the gym, throwing her arms up and down, feeling the sweat on her face. Again and again until she was too tired to think of Frank and the LA, Grandpa, even the journalism, but not too tired to think of Jack.

That evening they danced in the ballroom. She and Jack did not jitterbug but held one another close while the lights caught the chandelier and the MC called out numbers, giving prizes to those who won.

Jack smelt of chlorine, and his hands were cold and dry against her skin. She wore nylons he had bought for her, for Norah too. He pulled her closer and she felt him down the length of her body and they danced as though they could never be apart.

'I love you, Rosie,' he murmured, his breath warm in her hair.

'I love you too,' she said and she did. She always had, she always would.

The band struck up now, loud and fast into the Hokey Cokey, and they both laughed as they formed a circle, Rosie holding Ollie's hand, Jack holding Norah's, and it was like the ship's dance as they sailed away from Liverpool. But tonight she was home, her pain had been faced and this was better than the Lake Club had ever been, better than the barbecue with Joe.

That night she dreamed of Gallagher in Lower Falls. The next day she wrote to Frank and Nancy, asking them if there was any danger that Frank would have to give up the paper because of this LA. It was his life.

She wanted to know what they were facing because she could think of them without pain now. She licked the envelope as the tannoy called 'WAKEY WAKEY'. Breakfast was an egg, a soft-boiled egg, and she dipped her soldier into it, remembering the egg cosies her mother had knitted, asking Norah if she did too. She nodded and smiled.

They swam again, watched by other campers in deckchairs, some with knotted handkerchiefs on their heads, and Jack put Ollie's name down for the Knobbly Knees Competition in the afternoon.

At twelve-thirty they rushed to queue for lunch because the food was put on the tables exactly on time and yesterday it had been cold but that hadn't mattered to Rosie, because she hadn't had to buy it, or cook it, or wash up afterwards. Rosie wrote a postcard to Grandpa and Jack sent him one of a fat lady and a thin man doing something with a banana and Rosie was glad Grandpa needed new glasses.

Ollie didn't win the Knobbly Knees Competition, a sandy-haired young man with a moustache did. He was on holiday with his mother. Jack gave him a wolf whistle and Rosie gave Jack a slap.

They swam again though it was cloudy and cool but she liked to feel the water around her.

'Do you remember the stream at the bottom of the hop-yards?' Jack called over from the other side.

Oh yes, she remembered it. The pebbles beneath her feet, the water lapping around her calves, Jack lying on the grass, his hair hanging over his forehead, his sleeves rolled. Oh yes, she remembered it.

She put make-up on that evening, wearing lipstick for the first time. It felt sticky and tasted of peppermint. She wiped it off again. They went to the Tyrolean beer garden before dinner, singing along to an accordion player. Jack bought Ollie a beer while Ollie went to phone the local pub back in London, where Maisie had said she would be.

He was angry when he came back, throwing his jacket on the back of the chair, furious that she hadn't been in the bar.

'You said you'd ring Monday and Friday, didn't you? Maybe she got muddled. Or maybe Grandpa's cough's not so good?'

'Maisie said she'd ring us here if he wasn't, didn't she?' Norah said, looking over Jack's shoulder at the sandy-haired young man, primping her hair, pulling out her mirror and checking her lipstick, which had smeared on to her teeth.

Rosie looked at Jack, then at Ollie who was sipping his beer, his eyes dark again, his foot tapping beneath the table, on to the tiles, clicking, clicking.

'No, only if he was very bad. She'll be there on Friday night.' She wanted to slap Norah because Jack's eyes were darkening now and she remembered the months following her return, the shouting, the pain and anger in the boy she loved.

The accordion player was near them now, playing 'Roll Out the Barrel', and Jack bought another drink and they talked of how they used to collect tat for the rag and bone man and keep it in the old barrel at the bottom of Ollie's yard, but the laughter in Jack's voice was forced.

'You remember, don't you, Dad?'

Rosie watched as Ollie looked up from his beer, wiping the froth from his upper lip.

'You remember the tat, don't you?' Jack repeated and Rosie watched the accordion squeezing in and out, the fingers pressing the buttons and keys. Where the hell was Maisie?

'Yes, I remember.' And now at last Ollie was smiling. 'What about you two finding those dog-ends and selling them? Bloody cheek, that's what it was.' He was laughing now.

Rosie remembered the saliva-limp ends which Jack had made her tear off and which made her feel sick. She remembered the man on the train on her way back from Liverpool, stamping out his cigarette end. She remembered the Lucky Strikes Maisie had been smoking in the hop-yards. She looked at her hands.

Ollie had stopped laughing and was just staring into his beer. Rosie spoke again because she wasn't going to let Ollie and Maisie ruin Jack's holiday. They'd already hurt him enough.

'We sold them for twopence. Pinched your cigarette paper too.' She paused as he looked up. 'I bet Jack never told you that.'

Now Ollie laughed again and Rosie looked at Jack, who smiled, but his face was still tighter than it had been. She took his hand and as they hurried to dinner with the rest of the campers she said, 'It'll be all right. She got the time wrong. We're together. We're safe together. Forget about everything. Now come on, catch me.'

She dodged ahead of Norah, weaving in and out of the people streaming to the dining-room, doubling back round the rose bed and then up to Norah again. He hadn't caught her, though it had been close and he was really laughing now.

After dinner they sat in the ballroom and shook hands to left and then right as the compère directed. The young man with knobbly knees was on their right, sitting with his mother. Norah shook his hand, and Rosie watched as she smiled, her head tilted, her mouth pursed.

'Good evening,' Norah said.

His reply was lost in the chorus of 'Hi-di-hi' from the campers to the compère. What would the Lakeside Club think of all this? Rosie thought, laughing, happy, free. Frank and Nancy would love it.

The band played Glenn Miller numbers most of the night and Rosie tapped her foot to 'Little Brown Jug'. At the Ladies' Excuse Me she watched Norah, who stayed in her seat, her neck rigid, her eyes lowered. The young man had not yet asked her to dance.

Rosie nudged her sister, who ignored her but turned to Ollie and said, 'I think I'd like to try one of your cigarettes please, Ollie.' Her mouth was rounded, her vowels careful.

Ollie turned, his hands red from clapping to the music, his forehead sweating in the heat.

'Eh, what's that?' he said.

Rosie stood, walked round the table and tapped Knobbly Knees on the shoulder, drawing him to his feet. Norah's neck became even more rigid.

'Well, hi there.' Rosie's voice was more of a drawl than it had ever been. 'Sure is a great little dance hall.'

She was leading him on to the floor now. His hands were sweaty, his nose was too and the pores of his skin were big. His glasses were steel-rimmed and glinted beneath the chandelier. She stood with him, her hand on his shoulder, waiting for the beat, feeling Norah's eyes drilling through her, to him.

'Say,' she said, 'I guess this dance is way beyond me. You come on over and we'll get Norah to show me how it's done.'

She pulled him behind her. He still hadn't spoken.

'Say, what's your name?'

'Harold Evans.' His voice was high-pitched.

They were almost at the table now and Norah turned from them. Jack was looking down at his drink.

'So, Norah,' Rosie said. 'This is Harold Evans. We can't seem to get the hang of this dance. How about helping us out?' Rosie pulled at her arm, hauling her up.

'Harold Evans, this is Norah Norton. Naughty Norah for short. That's Jack and Ollie Parker. Now off you go, before you miss the music.'

Rosie stepped round them, walking off to the bar to buy a cool drink, not watching to see if they danced. She had done her bit. It was up to them.

Jack was still laughing when she got back, his head down, his shoulders shaking.

'I didn't recognise him with his trousers on,' he said. 'And where do you get the brass nerve?'

Rosie sipped her drink, winking at Ollie. 'I just pretended I was Nancy. I didn't want Norah's long face all week anyway and it would be nice for her to have someone. I have.' She touched his hand.

The dancers wouldn't leave the floor that night, even when midnight had been and gone, so the Redcoats formed a crocodile and danced them out in a conga and had to do that each evening from then on.

The next day Norah met Harold and sat on the deckchairs around the pool, watching as others swam. His mother sat with them, knitting, but Norah looked happy.

'He's a clerk in a bank,' she had told Rosie the previous

night. 'An office worker, not just someone selling things off a stall.'

'I expect he likes prefabs too,' Rosie had said, not showing her anger.

Rosie went to the gymnasium on her own, Norah was too busy sitting round the pool. She met Jack and Ollie and they walked to the fairground and shot at pitted yellow ducks which flapped up and down on a revolving belt. Jack and she pulled ropes in swinging boats and the wind rushed through her hair and Jack whistled as her skirt blew up. Ollie laughed and went to watch the Beauty Competition.

Jack and she sat on the ghost train. She screamed when the cobwebs dangled in her face and she remembered the Polyphemus moth and screamed again, glad that it was Jack's arm around her, not Joe's. Glad that it was his lips which touched hers, clung to hers, and his hand that now stroked her breast, but gently on top of her blouse.

They looked ahead as the train burst through the rubber doors, out into the daylight, past laughing campers, past a Redcoat who called 'Hi-di-hi'.

'Hi-di-ho,' Rosie yelled back and Jack too and they looked at one another as they walked away, their hands touching. His closed round hers and squeezed and now they smiled. 'I love you,' they said together.

They stopped again at the yellow ducks. Jack shot three down out of four. He tried again and shot down all four.

The Redcoat behind the counter handed him a pink teddy bear.

'When your turn comes, you should do well on the ranges. I was bloody hopeless.' He was fair-haired and hazel-eyed. Jack handed the teddy to Rosie.

'What was it like?'

'Not so bad if you like being kicked around a square, having no sleep, and peeling spuds until your arms drop off.' The Redcoat picked up his cigarettes from the counter, flicked one out to Jack who shook his head. 'Just put one out.'

The man laughed. 'You'll be smoking sixty a day before you're through your first week.'

Rosie knew what he meant and she gripped Jack's arm. She

had forgotten about National Service. She had forgotten that Jack would go.

'It's not dangerous though, is it?' she asked.

Jack jogged her arm. 'Come on, don't be daft. We've got loads of time anyway.'

Rosie didn't move. 'But it isn't, is it?' Because they were talking about Jack and this was important.

'No, you have to volunteer to go to the hot spots. Most of the time.' He nodded and winked at Jack. 'Go on, have a free go.'

Jack picked up the air gun. 'You sure?'

'Well, can't nick any money with these jackets coming down over me trouser pockets so you have the perk instead. Even have to keep me fags on the counter so I don't need to reach in me pockets.' He shrugged. 'Go on. Won't hurt anyone.'

Rosie paid anyway and gave Norah the second teddy.

The weather held up all week and Rosie wouldn't think of him leaving her. It was so far away. Conscription might be stopped by then. By Friday her tan was deeper and his lips were on hers and nothing else mattered.

That night Harold sat with them and told them about his brass-rubbing weekends. He told them how he travelled round churches and was always losing his cycle clips. Norah laughed, her finger dabbing at the corner of her mouth.

'Yes, fascinating hobby. I used to do some in Somerset.'

Jack spilt his beer and Norah frowned at him.

'We have some very old churches near us in Middle Street, you know,' Norah continued. 'I should think you might find some rather nice things to rub.'

Ollie coughed, then stood up. 'Must go,' he said hurriedly, 'need to phone.'

Rosie said, 'Why don't you come over, Harold? You live near Putney, don't you? Could be a change of scene for you.' She was shaking Jack's leg. 'That would be nice, Jack, wouldn't it?' It would be lovely, she replied to herself. It would be 'real swell' to have Norah happy and away.

They rushed to dinner as usual and Jack said that Norah had never been near a brass in her life, let alone rubbed it.

Ollie didn't come for his meal. They found him in the Tyrolean Bar when they had kicked their legs out in the last conga, singing, whistling out of the dance hall with streamers draped round their necks, and hats lopsided on their heads.

He was drunk. Maisie had not been in the local as they had arranged and his anger was frightening.

CHAPTER 8

When the charabanc dropped them Maisie came to the front door and pushed aside Ollie's hands which were shaking from the beer of the night before. She pushed aside his muttered oaths and questions and took hold of Rosie who had been bracing herself for the row that would come, wanting to shield Jack from the tensions of these two.

Rosie watched Maisie's lips, heard her words, then dropped her bag, turned and began to run, up the road, past the grocer's down First Street, then Wellington Avenue, past the glue factory and through the smell which always hung so thickly in the air.

'Grandpa's very ill,' Maisie had said. 'He wouldn't get the doctor. It was too expensive. He made me get medicine from the chemist but it wasn't enough. The doctor came in the end. I fetched him. It's his chest and his heart. He's in St Matthew's. He's never going to come home, Rosie, but he wouldn't let me bring you back. He wanted you and Jack to have that time together.'

He's never going to come home, come home, come home. Her feet were beating it out now and the breath was harsh in her throat. He must come home. He's Grandpa. He mustn't leave me. She was dodging round people, leaving them staring. One man pulled at her arm. She shook him off.

'It's me grandpa. He must come home,' she shouted at him. 'He mustn't leave me.'

Then Jack was with her, running alongside.

'It's all right. It'll be all right,' he said, his voice coming in bursts as he ran, but how could anything be all right now? she wanted to scream at him. I left him alone and now he's dying. But there was no breath left and at last she had to slow down and walk, bent over, the stitch digging into her side, her mouth dry, her shoes scuffed and dirty from the street dust. Then she was off again as it eased, Jack alongside. Norah hadn't come and she was glad.

There were long tiled corridors in the hospital with green ceilings and notice boards on chains, like the swings in the park.

'But they're not rusty,' she said, walking quickly, her shoes clipping along the floor, hearing the squeak of the swings, remembering the smell of rust, the scent of summer.

Jack pulled her back. 'Slow down, calm down.' But she pulled away. Grandpa was in here, alone. Didn't he understand? She had left him and now he was in here, alone.

They found his ward but the Sister stopped Rosie at the doors, her cap starched and upright, her face thin.

'Visiting hours are between three and four or six and seven,' she said. She held a clipboard in one hand and her watch was upside down. Why was that? So that she could see it of course. There was another sign hanging outside the ward. WARD 10. Would that squeak?

'It's my grandpa. He's been brought in and I've just arrived. I have to see him.' Rosie was calm now, her voice strong. She could see him down at the end, pale against the white pillow, the white sheets. He was her grandpa but somehow he wasn't. His eyes were sunken, his chin had dropped and his mouth hung open. She looked again at the Sister. 'I must see him and then I must talk to you.'

The Sister looked at her, then down at the clipboard, tracing a pencil along a list of names and words and numbers. Rosie didn't move, just waited. She would wait all afternoon, all evening, all night. She was used to waiting. Didn't they know? All her life she had waited.

A staff nurse eased past carrying a covered bedpan. An old man sitting next to his bed in a checked wool dressing-gown was picking at the air with clumsy fingers, again and again.

She looked back at the Sister whose navy uniform drew the colour from her tired face. The woman looked up at her, smiling slightly.

'Well, Doctor has finished his rounds. Perhaps it would do Mr Norton good. But just this once, mind. And I shall be in my office just behind you, to the left.' She pointed over Rosie's shoulder and Rosie felt Jack turn, then saw him nod.

'Thank you, Sister,' she said and walked down the ward, alone.

She talked gently, quietly to Grandpa who smiled at her but did not speak. She told him that he was looking well, that he would soon be home. But he wasn't and she knew he wouldn't. She held his hand which was so much thinner. How could people become so thin so quickly?

She talked of swimming in the pool on holiday, telling him how it had been boarded up when the Navy had taken it over.

'It would have been more good to them as it was,' she said. 'They could have practised their battles.'

She told him about Norah's clerk, of the Knobbly Knees, of the fun-fair and all the time she held his hand and wanted to say, 'I love you, Grandpa, and I can't imagine life without you. I've just found you again and I can't bear it if you die.'

But part of her remembered the words Norah had shouted down the pavement after her. 'You'll be pleased. Now you can get on with your bloody job.' Was that true? She looked down at his hand in hers. No. She would rather there was never a job for her if he could come home again.

She kissed his hand, held it to her cheek and couldn't say how much she loved him because she would cry and then he would know how very ill he was. So she listened as he tried to talk of the roses but, halfway through, the words died behind lips which were too clumsy to be his.

'I'll look after them, don't worry. There are no greenfly,' she murmured, watching his face.

'There are no roses here,' he murmured, nodding at the dark and grimy yard outside his window.

She touched his hand. 'Just rest,' she said.

Though his eyes were sunken, they were the same. They were dark and kind and the eyes of the young man he had once been. The lids, though, were heavy and closing and she reached forward and stroked his cheek. He hadn't been shaved properly. There was stubble beneath his chin and it was this that made her weep as she walked home with Jack because Grandpa had always shaved each day.

Norah was sitting in the kitchen eating Spam and boiled potatoes. There were some left in the pan. They were overcooked and in pieces. Rosie drained off the cold, thickened water, tipped the potatoes on to a plate, cut a slice of Spam, then a tomato.

'It's his heart and his chest,' she said as she sat down. 'The Sister says that he might die tomorrow or in three months' time, or in six months' time.'

Norah took a drink of water. 'As long as we're not expected to have him home.'

Rosie looked down at her plate. 'No, he's too ill. But he misses his roses.' She was tired and the tears were too close to tell Norah that she had a voice like a goddamn saw and the soul of a witch.

As she lay in bed that night she thought of the bleak yard, the soot-stained walls, the emptiness of it all.

At lunchtime Mrs Eaves said she could leave half an hour early because Rosie told her she must sort some things out for Grandpa. She walked home and put two of the smaller roses which grew in pots into the wheelbarrow. They were not strongly scented but their colour was rich. She pushed them through the streets in her Woolworths uniform. The same streets that she had run along yesterday.

Her arms were taut, her shoulders ached and people stared at her again, but it didn't matter. None of this mattered. Didn't they know what had happened to her grandpa?

She passed the back of the terrace which fronted on to the rec and turned left down the alley, coming out opposite the slide. She pushed the barrow across the road along to the swings and the footworn grassless earth. She pushed a swing. It squeaked. She looked back at the houses, ripped apart, unrepaired. There was more wallpaper than ever flapping on the end wall.

The park in Lower Falls had been grassed. Picnic tables and ice-cream vans had spotted the ground. She preferred this one. She looked down. The rust from the chains had stained her hand again. She moved behind the swing and pushed the seat, sending it soaring, hearing their laughter from the long lost years.

She pushed the barrow in through the hospital gates and past an ambulance which was parked with its back doors open. She edged round to the left-hand side, walking beside the main building, checking where she was in relation to the annexe which housed Grandpa's ward.

She walked alongside the soot-blackened walls until she saw the peaked roof of Ward 10. She pushed open two gates which were set into the wall. There were dustbins in one yard and old trolleys in another. She moved on. There was no one else walking, or standing, or watching. There was just the distant smell of cooking; the distant clink of plates, pans, cups.

Rosie stopped. Her hands were blistered. There was a lower wall now and she looked back at the building, shading her eyes against the sun. Then back at the wall. This had to be where the yard was but there was no gate.

She clutched the handles, pushing the wheelbarrow on again, welcoming the pain in her hands because it deflected her grief. She wheeled the roses round to the other side. Here was a small brown gate with a rusted latch which she lifted and then brushed back her hair. She could smell the swings on her hands.

She eased open the gate, looking towards the ward. There was no face looking out but she could see Grandpa eating in bed with a bib on. She lifted first one, then the other rose, putting them where he could see, checking for greenfly though she knew there was none.

She pushed the wheelbarrow home and bathed her hands. The blisters were bleeding. She bound them and then she climbed the stairs, taking a chair from Norah's room and heaving herself up into the loft, searching through old boxes. At last she found his nailer's penny. Grandpa had looked diminished in other people's pyjamas, in a ward which was not his home and she wanted him to remember who he was. She wanted to remember who he was.

That evening she took it in to him and he held it, holding her hand tightly too.

'They call me Bert here, but my name's Albert.'

'I'll tell them, Grandpa.'

'I tell them all the time, but it doesn't make any difference.'

'I'll tell them now,' Rosie said, leaving him, feeling his hand about hers as she found the Sister and told her, and then found the Matron and told her also.

Grandpa was asleep when she returned but he still held the penny. She kissed him and started to leave but as she reached the end of the bed he opened his eyes.

'There are roses in the yard. They'll have a gentle scent.' He was smiling at her, his eyes full of love.

She came the next day and he gave her the penny to put away safely.

'They called me Albert today,' he said.

'Of course they did. They know that's what you like.'

It was hot in the ward and the water in the jug was warm but he didn't mind and sipped as Rosie held the glass and then he told her how hot it had been around the nail furnaces, how thirsty they had all become. Rosie stroked his arm and listened as he told her how he had made Flemish tacks, so small that a thousand weighed only five ounces, but he had made hobs, and brush nails, and clinkers too.

He sat up, and she straightened his pillows and he told her how the fire and the chimney were in the middle of the shop, how he used to watch the different colours in the flames when he was a child, how he had woven stories in his mind then, but once he was a nailer he didn't have the time.

He told her how he would take one of the three iron rods from the fire, turn it with one hand and hammer out the tang, or point, to make the iron harder. He told her of the special coke that was bought from the gas works. It had already been used but was good enough for them once it had been broken up.

Rosie asked him about the boy who had been nailed to the doorpost by his ear, the one he had taken down. Grandpa stopped smiling then and asked for more water. It was still warm and Rosie held the glass to his lips and now he was crying.

She stood up, putting her arm around him, feeling like the parent he had been, listening as he said, 'He repaid me, you see.'

He wouldn't talk any more about nailing and she left that night wondering if his heart had broken each time she had cried throughout the years, as hers had just done. And wondering why it was that the tears had come.

As August turned to September and September to October, Rosie and he talked of other things, other people, but never of the nailers. He told her of the books he would like to have written and how he had read them instead.

She told him of Norah's clerk who had ridden over on his

bicycle. How Norah had taken him brass-rubbing at St Cuthbert's, how she had come back with sore knees and a mouth like a sparrow's bum which had flashed into a smile the moment he looked at her. They were going again next week, and the next and the next.

'With a bit of luck and a following wind,' Rosie said, and Grandpa laughed.

She told him of the letters she had received from Frank and Nancy. They had asked her to write a feature for their paper because, Nancy said, it would cheer Frank up to think of her working at something like that.

'Why does he need cheering up?' Grandpa asked as the leaves swirled into the yard, over the wall, snatching at the roses, scudding into corners.

'Things are a bit difficult on the paper right now. You know how work gets, Grandpa. There are ups and downs.'

But it was more than that, she knew, as she slipped into the yard and pruned the roses before she left that night, putting the old blooms into the canvas bag she had brought. Frank had spoken up for the Anti-Nazi League during the war and the Local Administrator had discovered this. Frank had been questioned by two other guys now, Nancy had told her, adding that Commie-hunting was getting to be quite a sport.

Rosie put away her secateurs and waved to the nurses who were watching from the window. They hadn't minded about the roses. They had been pleased.

That night and for the rest of the week she worked on an article about Austerity Britain, telling America of the fuel cuts the Midlands would have to suffer, losing power for one day a week; of the imports which still had to be kept at a minimum; how Britain had to export or die; how in 1946 even the new cricket balls for the Test Match had had to be rationed.

She sent this off with a letter to Frank and Nancy telling them that Grandpa was a little stronger but really no better and that she needed to be able to delay her lunch-hour and visit at three, which Mrs Eaves allowed. Maybe another employer wouldn't and so her career would have to wait for just a while longer.

In October she read that the film star Ronald Reagan had appeared before a Congressional committee investigating

Communism in the USA. She read how he had opposed a Hollywood witch-hunt against Communists or anything which might compromise the democratic principles of America. She read that already there was evidence against seventy-nine Hollywood subversives but Nancy wrote and told her that none of these had been named and hysteria was the order of the day.

'Where the goddamn hell is it all going to end?' Rosie asked Jack as they walked to the hospital in the afternoon on 1 November. He shook his head.

Frank wasn't too well, it was the strain of being questioned about activities which were deemed patriotic during the war years. But now the enemy was different and she felt the anger rising again as the wind whipped through her coat.

She kicked the leaves, angry and confused that the world had broken into enemy camps again, before anyone had yet recovered from the last war, and even in America, the land which had always seemed so free, so happy, there were victims.

Nancy had also written to say that the feature was not what they had wanted. They could read that in any paper. 'What we want from you, my girl, is something from the point of view of the people and don't leave the new career in the air for too long.'

Rosie and Jack leaned against a lamppost, watching as children swung from a rope tied on the next one, playing chicken with the bikes which raced past in the gloom, listening to the curses of the riders who shook their fists and told the kids that they should be at home in bed.

'I'll try again,' she said to Jack.

That evening Grandpa talked of Bromsgrove again. He sat high up against his pillows, his eyes looking into hers as he told her of the foggers. His breathing was too loud tonight and the Sister had said he was not so well again. He was speaking quickly, as though there was no time, and Rosie felt the fear tighten within her.

He told her how foggers were middlemen who employed nailers and sold their products to the nailmasters. How the nailmaster liked them because the fogger could provide him with whatever he wanted at short notice. This meant that the nailmaster did not have to carry large stocks. It also meant that he did not have to supervise the nailers.

'The fogger did that, you see,' Grandpa panted.

Rosie gave him more water. 'Not now, Grandpa. There's no hurry.'

'But I want you to understand, little Rosie. Can't you see that?' He paused, coughed and she held a handkerchief to his mouth. 'Can't you see that?' he repeated when he could talk.

Rosie nodded. 'Yes, Grandpa.' But she couldn't.

'Those foggies could play tricks, you see. They could say them nails weren't a proper job. Give you less for them but charge nailmaster the same. They could bore a hole in the weight. Weigh up your nails light, so you gave him too many. They were smart. They made money. They were hard.'

Rosie patted his hand. 'Sshh now.'

There were screens round the bed next to Grandpa's and a doctor had gone in.

'But I want you to see how he made his money.'

Rosie looked at him. 'Who made his money, Grandpa?'

'Barney, the boy with the nail through his ear. Your grandma loved him, you see. That's why we came to London. He moved down here.' He was panting, leaning forward. His shoulders were so thin beneath his jacket. 'He moved with the money he'd made. That was when she wanted to come down here. It wasn't me at all. But he was married when we got here.'

Now Rosie couldn't see the screens, she could only see Grandpa's face as he picked hops in his beloved hills, his body easy, his eyes at peace. And then she thought of Grandma, whose eyes had seemed devoid of warmth. Could a woman like that ever have felt passion, love?

Grandpa was coughing again and it was longer before he could catch his breath this time and while he did she smiled and said, 'Oh no, Grandma loved you. You know she did.'

Grandpa lay back, his eyes closed. 'Maybe you're right.'

'Anyway, Grandpa, she was married when she met this Barney, wasn't she?'

'She met him the week after we'd wed. After she'd come over from Dudley, and somehow the light went out of her face, if you know what I mean.'

Rosie could say nothing because suddenly she saw Maisie and knew exactly what Grandpa meant.

His hand was clasping hers now. 'You must marry someone

you love, someone who loves you, Rosie. You wait for that person and don't you settle for anything less. Do you hear me, Rosie?'

The screens were being moved back now and the visiting bell was ringing.

'Do you hear me, Rosie?' His grip was firmer than it had been since he had come in here.

'I hear you, Grandpa, and I promise. But she loved you, you know.'

She kissed him, smoothing the sheeting around him, brushing his hair to the side with her fingers, smiling into his eyes.

He watched her walk up the middle of the ward, waited for her to turn and wave. She always waved, she always smiled and thought he couldn't see her tears. But he saw them, all right. He had seen them when he had taken her to Liverpool. He had seen them as she had walked up the gangplank and he had felt her gas mask in his hand and had wanted to run after her, push everyone else away and take her back with him.

But she had needed to be safe. That was what had been most important, that the children were safe. He lay back on the pillows, looking out into the yard, at the pruned rose trees. He remembered the children waving from the portholes, singing 'Roll Out the Barrel' as the tugs eased the ship out into the fairway.

He had still heard them singing as the ship moved away. He hadn't heard for four weeks whether she was safe and then each day, each week, each year had been empty without her. He loved her, like the air he breathed, like he'd loved Martha, like he'd loved Nellie, and Norah. He'd been down to Somerset to see Norah every three months but she'd been ashamed of him and had no more love for him than she'd ever had. She was her grandmother's child and had learned all her bitterness at that woman's knee and now there was no love left in him for Rosie's sister, none at all.

On 20 November Ollie said he would visit Grandpa while Rosie slept out overnight along the Mall with thousands of others to cheer as the King and Princess Elizabeth drove to Westminster Abbey.

Jack arrived at midnight and they lay side by side on old

blankets and newspapers and it was good to hear him breathing so close and to drink steaming tea together from thermos flasks as dawn came.

She wrote it all down, the bitter cold, the woman who sang 'Knees Up Mother Brown' at dawn and toasted the Royal couple with stout. She toasted Jack and Rosie too.

'Because, God bless us,' she said, 'I like to see some love in this bloody awful world.'

Jack's kiss had tasted of tea, his lips had been soft, and now, as she peered over the heads of the crowd and snatched a view of the Irish State Coach escorted by the Household Cavalry in their scarlet uniforms and riding black horses, she could still feel his body alongside hers.

She wrote of the tulle veil which hung from a circlet of diamonds and the coupons which had been needed. She wrote of Lieutenant Philip Mountbatten who had been born in Corfu, the son of a Greek Prince, and would now be known as Prince Philip, Duke of Edinburgh.

Rosie wrote of the cheers from the crowd after the service as Princess Elizabeth and the Duke of Edinburgh travelled to their wedding breakfast at Buckingham Palace, cutting the five-hundred-pound wedding cake with Prince Louis of Battenberg's sword.

She knew this because she and Jack had moved along to the Palace and she had listened to the reporter in front of her. Jack had laughed and said she'd go far with ears that could flap that well. Rosie turned to laugh with him and as she turned she thought she saw Maisie at the back of the crowd. The light was back in her face and she was looking up at a big man with red hair who stooped and kissed her mouth.

Rosie typed up the story that night and sent it to Frank, then visited Grandpa and wouldn't let herself think of Maisie, or Grandma and the fogger. She wondered whether to tell Jack but she couldn't bear to see the pain in his eyes return and besides, she might have been mistaken. Yes, that was it. It was a mistake. It wasn't Maisie, the crowds had parted and then closed, it could have been anyone.

At the end of November Frank wrote and said he loved the

piece and it would be used. He also said that the Russians had tested an A bomb which was putting some members of the town into a total sweat. But do they seriously think anyone would use those bombs? he wrote. Rosie didn't know because the world seemed crazy enough to do anything and she held Jack tighter that night as they walked back from visiting Grandpa because he would have to register for National Service in April.

A letter from Nancy arrived at the beginning of December, when there had been a flurry of sleet which had frizzed Norah's perm.

Lower Falls
November 26th, 1947

Dearest Rosie,

We think of your grandpop every day and wonder how things are. You know we send our love to you all and only wish we could be there to help.

Great things are happening in Lower Falls. Our Local Administrator is becoming positively peacockish with importance and self-righteousness. A deadly combination. The big boys of the film industry have blacked ten Hollywood writers and producers who were cited for contempt of Congress after allegations that they were Commie sympathizers.

They have said that none of these will be re-employed until 'he is acquitted or has purged himself of contempt and declares under oath he is not a Communist.' Many liberals feel that in America we should not have to declare anything at all. This should be a free country.

I guess I lie awake at nights now because all that work Frank did in the war to encourage people to support the Britishers against the Nazis is beginning to look as though it is going to cause him pain. It somehow makes him an automatic Red. He is very tired, very strained. But I can't believe that any of this can go on for long. Sanity will prevail, as my old mom used to say. I have to go. The old boy has bitten through another pipe. We will write soon.

Nancy

The next evening Jack and Rosie went to Soho, to walk down the street and hear the music pitching and soaring because she had dreamed all night that the jazz had become silent and the buildings were derelict brownstones.

They stopped to listen to banjos, pumping tubas, four-square rhythms. They leaned against railings and drank in the Chicago-style jazz which was drifting up from a basement window, closing their eyes at the solos with their riff backing, squeezed between snatches of the theme.

Later, back in Middle Street, they kissed in the yard and Jack stroked her breasts and kissed her neck, her shoulder, the soft rising flesh, and Rosie didn't feel the cold which had earlier chilled her. Then they held one another close, so close, because they were both new to such passion, such longing and wanted more, much more.

On 20 December Rosie took paper and glue to the hospital and together she and Grandpa cut and stuck paper chains. They gave some to the ward and some she took home, and could not forget those swollen hands which could barely hold the paper together as it stuck.

The next night they just sat and there was snow in the yard, settling on the rose bushes, and Rosie said that in no time at all the spring would be here.

'Not for me, my little Rosie,' Grandpa said as a nurse walked past with the old man who still picked at the air. 'Not for me.'

But Rosie wouldn't listen because she couldn't imagine a time when he wasn't there and so she talked of the jazz which had played in Soho and Lee who wanted a cart for Christmas. She talked of the pram in the shed which she and Jack had raced on and Grandpa just sat and smiled and listened until she fell silent, watching the clock, wanting to go, but not wanting to ever leave.

'It's because of Barney and your grandma that we got the house. I want you to know because you'll need to understand this when I'm gone.'

He shook his head as she interrupted. 'No, Grandpa. It's Christmas . . .'

'Rosie, listen to me.' It was the voice he had used when he was younger and firmer, and she knew she must listen, and so she did, holding a handkerchief to his mouth as he coughed, again and again before he could begin.

'You know that man Jones. The one who owns the warehouse. He owned our houses too. He was going to sell. To kick us out. Ollie and me and all the families.' Grandpa coughed again and Rosie poured a drink, holding the glass for him, then wiping his chin. There was still stubble and his hair was too long.

'We needed to buy the house and your grandma told me to go to Barney. To borrow enough and for Ollie too. I had to go with me cap in me hand. I can remember twisting the brim so much that I couldn't wear it again. The words sort of stuck in me throat but he lent us the money and that was what was important. Nothing else. Nothing else at all.' He was coughing again and Rosie didn't want to listen. She didn't want to see the tears smearing over his cheeks. This was her grandpa, and she didn't want to see him like this but she had to.

'Your grandma always said it was her house. Barney did it for her. She was right. I tried to think it was because I took him off the doorpost but it wasn't. He told me so. He said he'd had her on the foggers' floor. That she'd loved him, followed him to London. But he didn't love her. So he owed her something. He laughed, you know.'

Rosie wiped his face. 'Don't, Grandpa, please don't. It was probably just words, to hurt you. He was jealous that you'd got Grandma. That's all.'

'But you've got to understand that it was your grandma's house really. And you mustn't blame me. I've made sure you're all right.' He was gripping her hand now. 'Promise you understand. Go on, promise.'

'Sshh. It's all right. I promise.' But she didn't know what she was promising and before she left she said, 'But why did you go to him? Why not just find somewhere else to live?'

He was lying back now, his jaw slack, breathing through his mouth, his eyes following the movements of the nurse behind Rosie. He said nothing for a moment and then lifted his head, wiping his mouth with a clumsy hand.

'Your mum and dad were dead. How long would we live? I had to work hard and pay it off so you always had somewhere to live. It was for you children. It didn't work out quite like I wanted, but you'll be all right. I promise.'

Grandpa didn't die that night, or the next, but on Boxing Day, after Rosie had kissed him, and held him, then left. There had been the peace of Herefordshire on his face all evening and so she was not surprised, but that did not make it any easier.

CHAPTER 9

Rosie stood in the churchyard, hearing the vicar but not watching him, hearing Maisie's sobs, but not watching her, or Norah, Ollie, Jack. Instead she looked above the heads of all of them to the trees which lined the cemetery. There were no leaves, there was no sun. There was no Grandpa any more but she still could not believe that.

She picked up the handful of earth and dropped it on the coffin but it meant nothing. The vicar's words meant nothing. He was gone. That was all. He was gone.

At the solicitor's office she sat with Norah on raffia-seated chairs. A strand was broken and dug into her leg. It meant nothing.

In his will Grandpa left the house to Norah, in pursuance of his wife's wishes, the solicitor intoned. With Rosemary to have residence for so long as she required. The nailer's penny and his books were to come to Rosie, along with the letter which was now handed to her. It all meant nothing. Because he had gone.

Rosie walked with Norah towards Maisie's for sandwiches and tea and to accept the condolences of the neighbours. She listened to her sister, saw her smile, felt the letter in her pocket which she would read alone, because Grandpa had said that people needed their privacy.

They walked past the torn houses but she didn't feel torn, she felt nothing. When they reached Maisie's she smiled at Ollie and the people who kissed her with sweet tea on their breath and kindness in their faces. She drank sweet tea herself. She didn't take sugar. Had Maisie forgotten? But what did it matter? She didn't eat though. Even with the tea her mouth was so dry, her eyes were dry, her heart was dry.

She put down her cup, carefully, still smiling, still nodding, still thanking Grandpa's friends for their kindness as she walked out through the yard, past Jack, who didn't stop her because he knew she had to be alone. But there was love in his face and grief too.

Grandpa's yard was empty. The rose trees were stunted from her autumn pruning. She touched The Reverend Ashe, running her fingers along its thorns, remembering its summer scent mingling with the creosote of the shed, seeing the roses which she had left in the hospital yard to bloom for someone else.

She went up to her room, taking her jacket and her dresses back into the kitchen, fetching Grandma's green wicker sewing box from beneath the bottom of his bookshelves. She measured and cut the black tape she had bought from Norah's counter and then sewed, stitch by stitch, a black armband on the left sleeve of the jacket. And then there were the dresses.

The needle went in and out, in and out. The scissors cut the thread cleanly. One done. The needle went in and out again and again. The fire was burning low. She had wrapped the coal in damp newspaper last night. She had heaped the fire with ash before she climbed the stairs. She had riddled it this morning, holding up newspaper to draw the heat, but Grandpa would never sit here again.

Middle Street

Dear little Rosie,

Please try and understand. Your grandmother felt that Norah should have gone to America too. She felt it was unfair that it was just you. She felt the house was hers and when the bomb fell and she was dying she made me promise that Norah would have it in my will. She knew then that the impetigo would keep her from America.

I couldn't cry for her. Not after that. But I promised, you see. You must stay in the house for as long as you need to. That was the best I could do. I find it hard to forgive myself. I leave you my penny and my books. I loved them but not as much as I love you.

Grandpa

Rosie put the letter back in her pocket. She felt nothing. She picked up the needle again, in and out, in and out.

536

There were footsteps in the yard. They were not Jack's or Norah's but Maisie's and her arms were plump and warm as they hugged her, but Maisie's face was without light, and as Rosie let the last of the dresses fall from her hands she thought of the big red-haired man but it was all too distant. And what did any of it matter?

'I wasn't there with him, you see, when he died. And I left him for too many years. He was so alone and I even left him to die alone,' Rosie said.

Maisie's arms were no help. They didn't reach inside her. But there was a lavender smell in the crook of her neck and Rosie rested on her shoulder for a moment and wondered how you could take away the years and return to where the sun smiled and you shelled peas on the back step.

'Come to me next door whenever you need help or you want to talk.' Maisie stood up and Rosie didn't watch her but looked instead at the flames of the fire as Grandpa had watched the flames up in Bromsgrove.

'I know things are bad again but come. Don't be put off by the rows. We love you. All of us. Jack especially. And we all loved Albert. It won't be the same.' Now Maisie was crying and Rosie turned from the flames which were easing round the lumps of coal. Maisie's eyes were red and her skin was blotched and Rosie stretched out her hand.

'No, it won't be the same. But nothing's been the same for so long.' And she wanted to say, why are you quarrelling again? Who is that man? Did he exist or did I imagine it? But she wasn't imagining the pain in Jack's eyes.

She said nothing though, just watched Maisie walk away through the smog that was creeping into the yard, edging her hair and clothes with droplets.

She looked around the room, at Grandpa's books, at his ashtray bought in Malvern. At the slippers which still held the shape of his feet. At the table covered in oilcloth. At the back step where they had shelled peas. No, nothing was the same.

All this was Norah's and she couldn't believe this had happened. That she no longer belonged in the house she had been brought back to. She couldn't believe that Grandma could do this to her. That Grandpa hadn't fought her. But she shouldn't feel angry because Grandpa had told her why and she should understand. She should goddamn understand.

But there was a noise now from the yard and then another, sharp and loud. She saw through the window that the shed door was open and that Norah was pulling and heaving at something, her coat rising at the back and her petticoat hanging down beneath her frock.

It was the pram she was pulling out, dragging it to the alley, chucking it at the children waiting outside playing flicksies in spite of the fog.

'Have that, and good riddance,' she said and Rosie watched as she went back into the shed. It was Norah's house now. Rosie couldn't stop her, and she would stamp down on the rage which was making her head burst.

But then Norah came out with the saw which was rusted and hadn't been used for years. She took hold of the thick trunk of the peach trailing rose, The Reverend Ashe, which had held the warmth of the summer. She took hold, leaning down, her breath thicker than the smog, and now Rosie moved.

She wrenched open the door, calling, 'Leave that alone, you greedy bitch.' She didn't recognise her own voice as she tore through the yard, pushing Norah backwards, snatching at the saw, feeling the raw cut it made on the palm of her hand.

'Get away from his roses.'

She held it to one side as Norah grabbed at it, hitting and slapping Rosie, pulling at her arm, shoving her, shaking her, but she couldn't reach the saw. Rosie was on her knees now, forced back by Norah, who shrieked and gripped her hair, pulling it hard, forcing Rosie backwards, her eyes pulled into slits, pain searing through her.

Norah's face was close to hers now. She was bending over and Rosie felt the spittle which sprayed from her mouth.

'This is my house now, Miss bloody Hoity Toity. If I want those roses down, I'll take them down.'

Now Rosie twisted free, slapping Norah hard across the face and then again, hearing the saw crash to the ground. 'You leave them! You leave them or I'll tell that apology for a man you've got that you've never rubbed a brass in your life. That you sulked all through your time in Somerset because you didn't get a GI button.'

Norah came at her again, her hands like claws, fury, rage, hatred in her face, and Rosie held her wrists, keeping her away, forced back now on to the rose, the thorns digging into her scalp, her back and hands as Norah pushed back, harder.

Then Norah stopped, pulled away, stood there panting. 'This is my house. His roses can stay. You can't.'

Rosie eased forward, the thorns dragged at her hair, at her cardigan, snagging, pulling.

'His roses will stay and so will I. Go and look at the will again.'

Norah wiped her nose with the back of her hand.

'Then you'll be in the way. Harold will marry me now I have the house. Why don't you just get back to where you belong? Nobody wants you over here now that he's dead. Grandma never wanted you, only me. Now they're both dead. You haven't got him to stand by you.'

Norah turned, pulling her coat straight, walking into the kitchen, slamming the door. The light came on and Rosie cried in the yard that was empty and cold.

The fog was catching in her throat and her tears were warm. She'd never noticed that tears were so warm. She leaned against the shed and then Jack came and held her, saying nothing, just holding her until she walked to the bench where she used to sit with Grandpa.

'Will you go back to Frank and Nancy?' Jack asked, still holding the saw that he had taken from her. 'There's nothing to keep you here. Not now. It's the sensible thing to do.'

He propped the saw against the shed, squatting, taking a packet of Woodbines from his pocket. Rosie saw the match flare, smelt the sulphur. Saw the oast-houses, saw Frank striking a match against the kitchen tiles. Heard Nancy say, 'Get that goddamn thing out of here.'

'You must do what makes you happy, Rosie,' Jack said, smoke pouring from his mouth. His face was pinched, pale, alone. He didn't go to the Palais any more because the rows were so much worse, and Rosie held out her hands to him, watching as he pushed himself upright.

'You're here. That's what makes me happy,' was all she said because he was alone and she loved him and she couldn't leave him, not as she'd left Grandpa.

The next day she applied and was accepted for a job as a typist at a magazine and handed in her notice at Woolworths. The day after that she took the train to Herefordshire and watched the winter claw deep into the earth and into her body where there should have been pain, but there was nothing again.

She took a bus from the station to the village, driving along mist-draped roads which curled around the base of the hills, then up between them, weaving and turning. There were oasthouses drained of colour, their cowled vanes motionless. Sulphur would not sting anyone's eyes today.

The bus passed a broken wagon with its shafts upended at the entrance to a field. Cobwebs were moisture-laden in the hedgerows. No birds sang as she stepped from the bus and walked up the lane to the farm along the frost-hard track. The blackberry leaves were dark, torn, furled. Her fingers had been purple last year from the juice. Norah's face had been purple all those years ago.

She walked past the yard where manure steamed through the mist. A dog barked. She didn't stop until she reached the pigsties, the sties where Grandpa and she had slept. Where they had all slept and laughed and talked.

The cold was deep in her now, her hair was heavy and damp. She dug her hands deep into her pockets and turned towards the path to the hop-yards. The dog still barked but there were no other sounds.

The grass had overgrown the path and its wetness soaked her shoes, but it did not matter. The sloping yards were empty of bines, as she knew they would be. There was no sea of green, no Roman Candles of green sprays. She took her hands from her pockets, lifted them to her face and remembered the hop smell of sticky hands, the yellow powder under nails, Grandpa's last season.

She cried, standing in the long wet grass with snow spattered on the distant Welsh hills and his 'me dooks' echoing again and again. It was here, standing in the hop-yards, that she said goodbye and at last believed that he had gone.

She waited for the bus at the end of the track, next to the telegraph pole where no bines wound today. But in the spring they would grow again, twining up clockwise, always clockwise, two feet in a week, and the pickers would come. She could hear the bus now, lurching up the lane, and turned again to the hop-yards.

One day she would come again because this is where the sun had always shone. One day she would come back, with Jack. And in the meantime she would stay at 15 Middle Street, to be near him, to make something positive out of her life.

The office was pleasant to work in. She watered the flowers, typed all day, listened, watched, learned and asked how she could move into Features. The Editor laughed.

'Give it time,' she said. 'At least now we know you're keen.'

She wondered if Frank had liked her feature on the jazz clubs. She had heard nothing from him or Nancy.

She and Jack no longer went to the Palais for Jack had seen Ollie hit Maisie after the funeral and now he didn't like to leave them alone. So they spent their evenings walking up and down the alley behind the houses and listening for the sounds of angry voices.

In February Frank sent her twenty dollars for the feature, which had drawn letters from his readers. More, please, he said, when you have time. He didn't talk of the Local Administrator, just of Grandpa and how sad they were for her and would she be coming back to Lower Falls?

That night she sat in her boxroom and wrote, telling them that she would come back but only when Jack had gone for his National Service because she couldn't leave him. She didn't tell them she loved him and that he was her reason to breathe, to live. But he was.

Each night they would just be together. Sometimes they talked, sometimes they kissed, but it was enough that their hands were joined and that their voices mingled, that their lips touched and then drew away because they were both frightened of too much passion.

In March Frank wrote of his distress at the news that the Communists had staged a coup in Czechoslovakia, and journalists who had attempted to get through to the President's Palace had been turned back by police and militia wearing armbands and carrying guns. Coming only nine years after the Nazi takeover it chilled the blood.

Nancy also wrote and said that the Local Administrator had written a letter to the newspaper calling on all good Americans to be extra vigilant as the Communist Menace crept forward yet again. Frank had not published it, of course. 'And come when you can,' she wrote. 'We love you. We grieve for you. This Jack must be important to you. I'm glad. Keep going with the writing.'

On 23 March Harold and Norah were married in St Cuthbert's. Rosie wore a new hat and so did Maisie. There was to be a small reception at a local hotel which Rosie had paid for because Norah had cried and said that Harold's mother would expect one.

Rosie had nodded and given her the money as her wedding present as Grandpa would have done, and besides, it would stop her goddamn crying. Maisie made the cake, though she had wanted to use hemlock as the flavouring, she told Rosie as Norah came down the aisle while an elderly man played the wedding march. He had a drip on the end of his nose.

Norah looked almost beautiful but Jack said that was because the veil was thick and hiding her face. Rosie nudged him and then held his mother's hand because Maisie had begun to cry. Her tears were silent but Ollie saw and looked away. Rosie watched his hands tense, but then Lee wanted Jack to lift him so that he could see Harold put the ring on Norah's finger. They kissed.

It was the first time Rosie could remember Norah kissing anyone, even Harold. Usually they cycled to their latest rubbing or sat either side of the fire, neither speaking, while she sat at the table, working up a Feature, practising, always practising.

At the reception Ollie toasted them, his voice thick from the beer he had already drunk, while Maisie held Lee and kissed his neck and Rosie saw that there was no light in her face, and that her eyes were bleak and red.

Norah didn't thank Rosie for the reception, she just simpered to Harold's mother, who was cold and distant because her son was leaving her alone in her small flat for something bigger and better.

Rosie squeezed Jack's hand and moved through the people who were crowding around Maisie's cake. They were mainly

542

Harold's friends. Sam and Ted had already joined up. Dave and Paul too, and Norah didn't seem to have many. But Mrs Eaves was there and Rosie touched her arm.

'I'm so glad you could come,' Rosie said, leaning forward and kissing her powdered cheek.

Mrs Eaves smiled. 'I've missed you, young Rosie. Is it going well? The job, I mean.'

Rosie nodded. 'But I miss you and the girls.' It was true. She did.

'And will you stay over here, now your grandpa's gone?'

Rosie looked at Harold who was pushing cake into his mouth. There were crumbs on his chin and his glasses were crooked.

'Yes, I'll stay but when Jack goes I'd like to visit back there.' She wanted to go, but more than that, much more than that, she didn't want Jack to leave. She couldn't imagine life without him, not for eighteen months. But at least he would be safe. There wasn't a hot war now, only a cold one, and you had to volunteer for the dangerous postings.

She had another drink. She mustn't think of April, of losing him too. She moved from Mrs Eaves, back to Jack and the warmth of his arm as he held her closely to him.

In April Jack heard that he had to report to the Ministry of Labour and National Service. He woke up Rosie, throwing stones at her window because Norah and Harold would play hell if he woke them by banging on the door. It was still cold and Rosie, wrapped in her cardigan, stood at the back door and laughed while he held her, kissed her, because she thought he was just impatient to see her but then he told her the news.

She felt cold inside at the thought of the months without him. Haven't we all been through enough, all we children of the war? Haven't we spent enough time away from the people we love? What did their Lordships want – our souls too?

'Don't go,' she said. 'You can't go.'

She was holding his sleeve, tightening her grip, pulling at him.

His face was still pinched and pale as he kissed her, held her, and the lines from his nose to his mouth were deep but his smile was the same.

'Don't worry, my little Rosie. Trust me. I've got to go and

see someone I know to try and sort something out before I report. I'll come back later. Don't worry.'

But she did worry. She forgot to water the plants at work. She made mistakes. She couldn't eat and wasn't interested in the letter which had come this morning from Frank. Frank was worried about the turn events were taking in Europe with the Berlin Blockade and the possible murder of the Czech Foreign Minister, and, worst of all from an American point of view, Truman's guarantee that US troops would step in in case of Soviet aggression in Europe. What did she care what was happening out there in this crazy world when Jack might be leaving her?

But then all afternoon she did care because was Frank saying there might be another war? She was tired. The world was mad and Jack was leaving as Grandpa had done.

He was waiting for her in the garden on her return. He had been taken on as an apprentice by old Jones. A phoney apprenticeship but at least his National Service would be deferred and he could stay home and look after Maisie and Lee.

'And you, Rosie,' he said, his breath warm in her hair.

Rosie held him, breathing in the smell of his skin.

'But Jones, you hate him. He'll squeeze you dry, rub your nose in it.'

'I know, but it's worth it to make sure Mum and Lee are all right. Dad hit Mum again last night. I don't understand him any more.'

That night Rosie dreamed of Grandpa twisting his cap in front of Barney.

In June Ollie put money on My Love to win the Derby. It won and he gave money to Maisie for a new dress but still there was no light in her face and the quarrels continued.

Harold and Norah seldom took their cycles out now, because Norah didn't want to. They didn't quarrel though, they sat either side of the fireplace while she knitted and he watched Rosie and sucked his teeth just because she was there. But Rosie just looked back, because there was nowhere else she was goddamn going, not yet.

On the day that the Berlin airlift began and the Dakotas shuttled in the food that would break the Russian blockade, Jack had to attend for his medical, which he passed but he wasn't required to report. He was an apprentice, wasn't he, he told Rosie when he met her from work.

They picked Lee up and went straight to the rec to push him on the swing. The wallpaper was still hanging off the damaged houses but there was more and more grass pushing through the caked earth over by the slide.

'The bines will be growing,' Jack said, his voice lurching as he pushed. 'One day we'll go back.'

Rosie watched his hands on the back of Lee's seat, the muscles in his arms, his shoulders. His skin was tanned now and she wanted to reach forward and kiss him.

She remembered their most recent trip to Soho. They had listened to jazz and he had said that Duke Ellington was always changing, that was why he liked him. She had said that she was tired of change. That was why she liked New Orleans, Dixieland. Bix Beiderbecke. He was dead. He couldn't change.

She did move now, putting her arms around Jack as he swung Lee, wanting him close. Because soon he might go. How long could he get away with all this?

In August, the Olympic Games were held in London but without Germany, the Soviet Union and Japan. Frank and Nancy had written to her asking for a feature on it from her point of view. They sent money for her travel expenses to Henley for the rowing, to Bisley for the shooting and to Cowes for the yachting. She arranged for some time off work and they said that she should show them her work and they would consider it for publication.

Norah was jealous and angry and told her as she slopped potato out of the pan on to her own plate that she should go back to America with her superior ideas and leave them in peace.

At Cowes she loved the feel of the wind in her hair and as she leaned on the rail of the ferry leaving Portsmouth she thought how Grandpa would have enjoyed this. She had Lee with her to give Maisie and Ollie a bit of peace.

They stayed the night at a small cottage where they ate scones and homemade jam. The landlady's son was in the Army, a National Serviceman who was fighting the Malayan Communists. His friend had been killed next to him, three weeks ago, in the jungle, Mrs Mallory said, but so far her son was fine.

The tablecloth was crisp and white and Lee picked up the crumbs he had made. His hands were like Jack's and Rosie held them and kissed them, wanting to catch the ferry back to Jack. Not for the first time she was grateful to the man whose cheeses they had stolen.

Lee pulled away, and reached for another scone, so she stroked his hair instead and looked at the horse brasses on the wall, the black beams across the ceiling and thought that one day she and Jack would have a home like this, but within scent of the hops.

The next day they watched the yachts and the crowds and Rosie described the gulls which wheeled and dived on to a bald man's head. She wrote of the blazers, and the women in sleek dresses who burst into cheers as Britain won a gold medal, of the ice-cream which tasted almost as good as maple walnut, of the trees around Osborne which were almost as tall as the white oaks. She wrote of all this but thought of Frank disappearing out round the point to fish. One day she would see them again because Frank was still stressed, but there was no time now. Each moment must be for Jack.

She took Lee to Wembley too and wrote of the thirty-year-old Dutch housewife who was cheered on by the British women because, though she was world record holder in both the high and long jump, she competed in neither and won four track events instead.

She wrote of how the cinder track seemed to beat back the heat and the disappointment when Britain failed to win an athletics gold. She lifted Lee on her shoulders to watch the Czechoslovakian Emil Zatopek win the 10,000 metres and thought of Frank and his love for that small country as the crowd rose to cheer the runner. Tears were pouring down her own face and Lee laughed, bent over, digging his heels into her arms, and wiped them for her with his sleeve.

She bought him a drink and a sandwich from a stall, and they sat on some steps, Lee tucked in next to her in her shade, laughing as he pushed some bread into her mouth. The egg was warm. The sun was hot on her neck. She put her arm round him and held him to her.

'I love you,' she said, rubbing her face on his hair.

'Love you, and Jack,' Lee said. 'Still will when I go to school next year.'

'And we'll still love you, even though you'll be really big.' Rosie unwrapped some biscuits she had made and poured him some milk from the flask. The ration had gone up to three and a half pints.

Lee turned his face away.

'Go on, it's good for you.' Rosie held the mug for him, hearing the crowds cheering in the background. He wouldn't drink it.

'Why should you?' Rosie murmured as she poured it back into the flask. 'There's too much you have to do because someone tells you to.' She thought of Jack and the landlady's son in the Malayan jungles. He must have volunteered. How crazy.

She watched Lee eat his biscuit and then took him by the hand because she wanted to watch the Americans running in the relay. It reminded her of Lower Falls School somehow, the heat, the ice-creams, the fun. They pushed their way up, squeezing on to seats, looking down at the track. Maybe there should be majorettes. She saw her old room, the Cougar pennant, the programmes.

It was hot and she pulled Lee's hat from her pocket, and made him wear it although he wriggled. She sat him on her knee, holding his legs, knowing her dress would crease but not caring because he was Lee and she and Jack loved him.

The crowd were noisy, the relay hadn't begun. People were still going up and down the stairs, seeking seats. Rosie wiped her forehead. It was so goddamn hot. She shielded her eyes. The race must begin soon. The athletes were limbering up, shaking their arms and legs. She could almost hear the cinders crunch.

But then she saw Maisie walking down the steps between the seats twenty feet away. She watched her turn, and stretch out her hand towards a big red-haired man and her face was full of life and full of love and Rosie could not breathe, but held Lee tightly. It was a mistake. She looked away, then back again, and knew it was no mistake. The man was the same one who had been at the Royal wedding, and there was still the same love on both their faces.

Rosie didn't watch the race, only those two people who walked on and disappeared, and then she took Lee down the steps too, pulling his hat even further on to his head because his hair was the same red as that man who had looked with love at Maisie.

That evening she heard Maisie carrying washing into the yard and left the roses she had been dead-heading, throwing the faded blooms into the compost in the corner, opening the yard gate, shooing away the children that played in the alley, entering Jack's yard.

'I saw you today,' she said, not looking at Maisie but helping to peg up the sheets, smelling their freshness, hearing the dogs and children further down the alley, knowing that Lee would be out there soon kicking a football with his friends.

'I saw you, Maisie, and you've got to decide. You can't go on like this. It's not fair on Jack. Or on Ollie. You're tearing them apart and yourself.'

She still didn't look but heard Maisie throw her pegs back into the old cocoa tin and lean against the back wall, her face to the sun.

'I can't decide, you see, Rosie. That's just it. I'm torn between two worlds. But don't tell them. Please.' Maisie moved now and took her arm. 'Please. I'll sort it out. I'll make it all right. Just don't tell anyone. Albert always said you had a right to privacy.'

Rosie shook out the last sheet. Lee's laughter was loud as he ran past her and out into the alley, dribbling the ball, kicking it to his friend. She and Jack had done that.

She turned now. 'Of course I won't say anything but just don't hurt them. Especially Jack. Please don't hurt them.'

Maisie touched Rosie's hair. 'I won't. I promise I won't. I'm glad you know. It will help me to be firm.'

Rosie's magazine didn't take her pieces because they were geared to the American markets, but they thought she had talent and when there was an opening they would give her a chance. They celebrated because Jack came round to say that Maisie was being nice to Ollie again. She seemed more settled, he told Rosie.

'It's strange. I don't know what's happened but something has,' he said.

They went up West and ate in Lyons Corner House while a small band played and then they danced and she felt his body next to hers, dancing in step, always in step, and the evening was warm and long and that night they kissed in the yard, and his mouth was as urgent as hers, and his hands were strong on her body.

'I love you, Rosie. I love you and I want you. But we must wait.'

He drew back and his face was beautiful in the light from the moon and there was the fragrance of Grandpa's roses all around. It was not the place for words, and so Rosie said nothing about Maisie and the man. She could not break her promise.

There was a letter on the hall floor for her next morning, which Norah and Harold had not picked up. They never did, if it was for her.

It was from Nancy enclosing sixty dollars.

Lower Falls

My dearest Rosie,

I do hope that perhaps soon we shall see you. It would cheer Frank up so much. He loved your features. They were published last week. Again to great enthusiasm.

Our local band of defenders against the Commies is in full cry yet again because two Congressional committees have been set up to investigate allegations that 30 US officials belong to a spy ring. Thank God most people don't believe it but there are two men, Karl Mundt in the House and Senator Joe McCarthy, a Wisconsin Republican, who most certainly do.

It would be laughable if it wasn't so serious. A manhole blew up in the street yesterday and Frank yelled, 'It's those Commie bastards.' Some people believed him.

But he is kind of down. He's got himself all worried about Korea now. I keep telling him it's all getting too stupid. He's seeing a new war where there is none. I'm kind of worried about him. The paper's readership is suffering. We have had a brick through the office window, but he won't stop writing common sense. The LA doesn't like that of course.

The Lake was great. Sandra sends her love and that young guy Joe too. Do you remember him? He's doing quite well on the paper now. Wish it could have been you.

All our love,
Nancy

Yes, Rosie thought as she folded the letter and brushed her hair. Yes, she did remember him but like a distant shadow because Jack filled her life now. She put down her hair brush and read the letter again. How serious was all this?

That evening Jack came home, straight to her, his eyes angry, his lip swollen. Jones had wanted him to deliver stolen meat. He wouldn't. He was sacked. He was no longer an apprentice. Jones would inform the Ministry of Labour and the Army would send for him. But when?

CHAPTER 10

January 1949 was cold but there was still no call-up for Jack and so they didn't feel the wind which cut into their chapped skin as they walked to the Palais. Sometimes they walked because it was better to be alone than with either family.

Spring came. The clothing ration ended and there was still no call-up but now, with each day, their kisses were getting stronger, their bodies pushing closer because it could not be long and there was so much love between them, and so much that was beautiful when they were together, so much that was dark when they were apart.

They walked to the rec on the last Saturday in April, when all the plates had been sold, and Ollie had gone to the pub, yet again. Rosie wouldn't think of that as Jack swung lightly, his face tense. Instead she watched the shadows of the clouds scud across the park. There were buds on the clubbed trees. She heard the scrape of his shoes on the earth, the shriek as the chain jolted to a halt, felt him reach out and pull her to him.

'Look after Maisie and Lee for me. Promise me. Promise me,' Jack said as he sat on the swing and she moved to stand between his legs. He always asked her this. He pressed his head against her belly and held her tightly.

'I will, don't worry. It will be fine,' Rosie said, looking at the fence which was being erected around the bomb-damaged houses. Work would begin soon. Then all this would be changed. She hugged him. Everything would be changed.

They'd had a letter from Sam this morning. He had only another six months to go before he came out.

'See, it went quickly,' she said now, listening to the foreman shouting as one section of the fence fell down.

'He'll be home soon. Nothing can happen in eighteen months. You wait and see. It'll all be fine. Maisie and Ollie will

551

sort it out. It's already better.' And sometimes it was, but not always.

She could feel his back lifting and falling with his breathing, feel his body heat, smell him. She didn't need to say that each day for her would be endless without him. He already knew. She didn't need to remind him that there were twenty-four hours in each day, seven days in each week, fifty-two weeks in a year.

She wouldn't tell him that Norah was longing for him to go, so that she would also leave. That Frank and Nancy had written to her telling her to come when Jack had left. But she must stay here for now, alone, without him, without Grandpa, because she had promised him that she would. She would just hold him because he ached at the thought of the future too.

In May his call-up still had not come but the Berlin Blockade ended. Again there was a letter from Nancy talking of Sandra's new hairstyle, Mary's new Hoover. The target on the garage door which Frank had repainted for when Rosie came back out. She mentioned Frank's stress again, but that was all.

The summer was hot and blistered the pavements. The stall did good business and Jack's voice was hoarse at the end of each day but his lips were as soft and warm as always, his hands as gentle, his words of love as tender as they had always been.

And she wrote and told Nancy again that she would not be coming, not yet.

In July the sugar ration was put down to eight ounces a week, the sweet ration was back at four ounces and there was a further cut in tobacco supplies. Another letter from Nancy told her that Truman had tried but failed to dampen the hysteria which was spreading across America after the latest Soviet spy conviction. And had Rosie heard about the attempt to screen all school books by the House Committee for Un-American Activities? Didn't they know that Goebbels had burnt books in the streets? Did this always happen after a war? Boy, is that goddamn Local Administrator having the time of his life!

It's great that Jack hasn't been called up. We're sorry you can't come. So sorry. But maybe later?

But Rosie wouldn't think of this, she pushed it all from her because each dawn so far had brought the knowledge that Jack was next door, so close, so dear and nothing could spoil this love they had. Nothing. Not even absence, nothing.

They went to Southend with Maisie, Ollie and Lee. They ate winkles and she felt the wind in her hair and heard the laughter of the children who pushed go-carts, racing them, screaming as they won, screaming as they lost and she remembered the feel and smell of the old pram which Grandpa had kept and she missed him. But then she missed him every day.

She sat with Maisie, their skirts held around their knees, the wind tugging at their hems and sleeves, and they laughed as Jack rolled up his trousers to his knees, then ducked Lee down into the sea, then across to Ollie, who took him and held him.

Rosie looked at Maisie. 'So, it's all right?'

Maisie took a Marmite sandwich from the OXO tin, squashing the bread together, eating it with small bites. There were teethmarks in the bread. 'Of course it's all right, Rosie. Just you wait and see. You mustn't worry your head about us.'

But behind the dullness of her eyes there was pain. And Rosie did worry. And all any of them seemed to do was wait. She didn't ask about the man. She didn't want to know; all she wanted was for it to be all right.

She watched Jack again, his strong back beneath his shirt, his pale legs in the rolled-up trousers. She wished they could both be by the lake, lying in the sun, tanned. She wished she could see his body. She wished they could lie together and she could feel his hands on her, his kisses on her breasts.

That night she clung to him in the yard, tasting the salt on his skin as she kissed him, seeing the pallor of it clear in the late evening light. She gripped his jacket, searching his face. She never wanted anything to come between them. Their love must never die and pain take its place as it had done with his mother.

'I want to sleep with you,' she said, holding his head close to hers, talking against his mouth, and she felt his arms tighten.

'I want to sleep with you.' His mouth was on hers. 'But not yet. There's time, my love. There's time.'

But there wasn't time. His call-up papers were in the hall when he came down the next morning and in her hall was a letter from Nancy telling her that the last American occupation forces had left South Korea. What would happen now?

She screwed it up and threw it across the yard because Jack

553

was there, beside The Reverend Ashe, reading out his enlistment notice, and what the hell did she care about Korea, or Truman, or bloody witch hunts which were so far away and which had nothing to do with her or the boy who was now holding her, the lashes of his brown eyes throwing shadows on his cheeks?

They both cried, there, within the scent of the rose, and Jack felt he couldn't bear to go and leave her here where he couldn't touch her, hold her, love her. He couldn't bear to go and leave his mum whose pain he could still see deep down but couldn't understand, or Lee who would start school in September without him. What if the shouting began again?

He left two weeks later, on Thursday, from King's Cross. Rosie came, but only Rosie. There were couples kissing, crying. There was the rail warrant in his jacket pocket. There were doors slamming, porters pushing through them. 'Mind yer backs.'

The station smelt of dirt and heat and loss and he held her to him. Breathing in her smell, which drowned out all else, holding her face between his hands, kissing her lips, her eyes.

'Be careful. Come back soon. Come back,' she said, tasting his lips, but the whistles were blowing now and he heaved his case into the corridor, scrambling in after, leaning out of the window, sharing it with another boy, holding her hand, bending to kiss it, but the train was moving and he was leaving and he let her fingers slide from his grasp.

'Stay with Mum. Look after Lee. Promise me.'

She was running along the platform now and her lips were smiling and she was nodding but there were tears all over her face, dripping down on to her blouse.

'I love you, Rosie. I love you, little Rosie. I'm sorry I have to leave you.' He gripped the window. Had she heard?

The station was still busy, there was another train leaving from the next platform, there were whistles, doors, calls, the tannoy, but all she could hear were his words. I love you, little Rosie. And they were Grandpa's words too and now she was alone.

The train picked up speed as it left the station. Jack still waved, though he could no longer see her. The wind was too strong in his face, it made his eyes water. It had made his eyes water when he left for Somerset, leaving his mum behind in the bombs. He was leaving her again, with Ollie. He was leaving Rosie but there was nothing else he could do. He had to go. He had been told to go.

He drew his head back in, pulled up the window. It was quiet except for the voices along the corridor. He rested his head on the window. There was nothing else he could do.

He shoved his case back against the sliding door which was open then eased himself into the compartment, between two other boys. The air was thick with Woodbine smoke. He drew out a cigarette and struck a match, cupping his hands, sucking, smelling the sulphur, trying not to think of the oast-houses, the stream where she had paddled, her legs so slim, so brown. Trying not to hear Lee's laugh, or see Maisie's smile, Ollie confused, angry.

He leaned back, feeling the heat of the conscripts either side, hearing their jokes, their coughs, their laughs, and at last he was talking too, pushing them all down deep inside because there was nothing else he could do. Just nothing and it hurt too much.

And so he listened, but did not really hear, and laughed, but did not really mean it, and talked, but only with his mouth, not his mind. The train lurched and rattled over the points and a boy who spoke with a plum in his mouth sat by the window and told them how he had been a sergeant in the OTC and was going to apply for a commission.

'Frightfully good management experience you know,' he said. The compartment door slid shut, then open again. A boy looked in.

'Seen Joe?'

'Who's Joe?' asked the lad next to Jack, stubbing out the cigarette with his foot.

The boy walked on. There was laughter in the corridor and a packet of cigarettes was thrown past the door, caught and thrown back and still the train travelled on, roaring through tunnels, shafting out into sunlight, further from Rosie, from Maisie. And he didn't want to leave them. Didn't want to be sent to God knows where to do God knows what. He wanted to get on with his own life. But he had no choice, had he? Had any of them? He closed his eyes. There had to be more to life than all of this.

He thought of the sign, ABSOLUTELY NO JITTER-BUGGING ALLOWED. thought of the sign, 12 YEARS AND UNDER ONLY. thought of Ollie slapping Maisie, of himself pulling at his father, heaving him out into the yard, wanting to shout at them all to stop.

But it was all right, he told himself, as he drew on his cigarette, feeling the heat in his lungs, coughing, stubbing it out, leaning back. It's all right, Rosie's there. She's strong, she'll take my place. She'll always love me. I'll always love her.

He shut his eyes, shaking the thoughts from his head, making himself listen to the talk which was flowing past him. Really listen, hanging on to the words, the jokes, the questions, taking a newspaper when it was offered, reading it, passing it on.

He talked to Sid, next to him. He was just eighteen, never left his mum before. Never been evacuated. His hands were shaking. Jack, at nineteen, felt old. But they were all the same. None of them wanted to be here. They all had other lives.

The towns had gone, there was wild free country, not the sloping hills of Herefordshire, or Somerset. He remembered the picture he had unscrewed and sold, the milk chocolate they had been given, the corned beef. He had been sick.

'I mean to say, basic training is absolutely nothing. When you're experienced, as I am, it's a doddle.' The boy with the plum was speaking again.

Sid leaned forward. 'What'll we do then?'

'A bit of marching, a bit of polishing. Getting fit, improving ourselves, you know.'

But they didn't, not yet. All Jack knew was the ache inside, the loneliness of it all, the missing. What was Rosie doing now? What was Maisie cooking for tea? Had his bed been folded and taken from the kitchen? Was Ollie drunk?

The train pulled into the station at a platform which held kiosks selling books and sandwiches and tea, but Jack moved past with the others, his case heavy in his hand, banging against his leg, but this time there was no gas mask.

They hurried along, Sid beside him, skirting through the others, keeping ahead of Nigel, the OTC Sergeant, trying to

556

lose him in the crush. They headed towards the branch line and the train full of conscripts. They tried one door. A boy with a crew cut and no front teeth leaned out.

'Sorry, cock, full up.'

They moved on to the next and the next and by now Nigel was with them again and Sid cursed. Jack winked, opening a door, throwing his case in, Sid's too, Nigel's too. Whistles were blowing, boys were leaning out of windows whistling and shouting, and then they were in but there were no seats. There was singing though, and rampaging up and down the corridor, and Jack remembered how they had pretended to cry on the evacuee train as they passed through stations so that the onlookers got their money's worth.

The moors stretched either side and there was beauty in the sky, in the bleakness of the dales, the scattering of sheep, the heather, the short-cropped grass. But Rosie wasn't here, Maisie wasn't here, and it was fear as well as loneliness that stirred him now because Sam and Ted had told him too much about the Army.

In the station yard there were lorries backed up with their tailboards down. They heaved their cases into these now and Sid lit a cigarette, his hand shaking.

A Corporal pacing backwards and forwards glanced at his millboard, then shouted at Nigel to 'get his bleeding legs working and hurry over'. Then he turned.

'Put that ruddy fag out, you ruddy nig.'

Jack turned, and his eyes met those of the Corporal.

'Got anything to say, nig?' the Corporal shouted at Jack. 'Got any comments to make, any suggestions you would like me to send back to Mother?'

Jack shook his head as Sid stubbed out the half-smoked cigarette, put it back in his packet.

'You see,' the Corporal shouted, stabbing a finger at Jack and Sid, 'we don't like dirty 'abits in the Army. We don't like people bringing their nasty little ways in with them. Put that bleeding fag over there, in that bin.'

He pointed towards a bin fastened to a lamppost over by rusty railings near to the station entrance.

Sid stumbled towards the tailboard, jumped down, ran across, and picked out the cigarette from the packet, but his hands were shaking so much that they all fell into the bin. He reached down, then saw the Corporal, looked again at the cigarettes, and ran back, pushing himself up and into the truck.

'You'd better get yourself back down and go and fetch those cigarettes, hadn't you? You forgotten there's shortages? Or maybe Mummy lets you have hers.'

Sid moved to the tailboard again, hunched down beneath the lorry roof. He ran back, picked the cigarettes out, brought them back. They were stained, dirty, smelling of old fruit.

The Corporal nodded and turned, calling, 'Come along please, Mr Sanders, Mr Nigel Sanders, or Nanny will be cross. Come along. Don't be afraid. You're only leaving civilisation behind. You're not humans any more, you're nigs.'

Sid was shaking and Jack felt anger drown his fear as when the Billeting Officer in Somerset had separated two sisters, sending one to the town, the other to a village. There was nothing any of the children could do. There was nothing he could do now. Nigel hoisted himself up and the lorry rumbled away from the station yard.

They drove into the camp and a wooden barrier fell behind them. Jack felt trapped, lost, but so did the others, he could tell from their faces, even Nigel. They passed bleak married quarters, barracks, squares, huts, black stencilled notices, and then they stopped, jumped out, listened to the shouts of the Corporal, watched the spittle on his chin, the red cheeks which reddened, the eyes which narrowed.

They were lined up, their suitcases still in their hands. They were marched, out of step, to their barracks. They left their cases, turned, marched to the quartermaster's stores.

There were counters, Corporals shouting, battledress, beret, boots – some that fitted, some that did not.

'What a shame, poor little boy wants Mummy to change them? Tough shit. Wear 'em.'

More kit was slapped down and they stuffed it into drab-green kitbags, collected their mattresses, which they draped over their heads, then hauled the bag and blankets to the barracks. Heard a siren. Reported to the cookhouse for tea as their Lance-Corporal ordered. Were sent back for wearing civilian clothes. They changed. The Lance-Jack laughed, standing in the corridor to his room. They were too late for tea.

Jack felt anger come again but it mingled with strangeness, fear, loneliness, all of which he had felt before in Somerset. Rosie had felt it too. Little Rosie.

They marched back again to the barracks, to the thirty wire-framed beds, to the windows which were nailed down and unopenable. To the stove which would have been too small to heat Grandpa's shed, to the tall metal lockers beside each bed, to the stone floor which struck chill into them, although it was August and hot.

They were given pen and paper to write to their families.

'To say that you're having a lovely time,' the Lance-Jack said, walking up the centre of the room, looking them up and down. They were hungry, lying on their beds in prickly khaki, feeling in their pockets for change to go to the Naafi.

Jack wrote home, saying he was having a lovely time, saying his clothes would be sent back, saying it was just like being evacuated and that had turned out all right, hadn't it? No problems, he wrote.

He wrote to Rosie, saying that he loved her, that he would be home for two days at the end of basic training, in two months, that she must look after Maisie, please, and Lee, and herself. Please.

As he, Sid and Nigel walked to the Naafi and bought a sandwich and a beer, he thought of Elsie, the fat farmer's wife in cords who had lit an oil lamp each evening so that he would not be afraid of the shadows in the old farmhouse. The smell of it had eased into his room from the landing. The others were silent too, sipping their beer which dripped on to the formica table. Their thoughts were elsewhere too.

They bought boot polish before they returned to their billet and all night long they bulled their green-corroded brasses, rubbing with emery paper for hours. Their hands grew cramped and stiff, their necks too, from bending. There were Woodbine stubs in the tin ashtrays on the two tables, there was a sourness in their mouths, a loneliness in their eyes which were heavy-lidded, tired, unsure. And always there was the radio playing, but there was no jazz.

Sam, from Liverpool, brought out a candle and a spoon, and heated the handle, rubbing it over the dimples of the boots, squeezing out the oil, rubbing away the waterproofing with it, but who cared? It would make them shine.

He showed them how to spit, then rub the polish which they had all bought in the Naafi round and round. It produced a shine. A bloody shine, and so they all did the same or ironed their boots. They laughed and swore and said they weren't afraid of the Lance-Jack, or the Corporal, or the Sergeant, but they were. Finally at 0400 hours, they slept, though the radio still played through speakers controlled by the Lance-Jack. In their sleep they rocked to the rhythm of the train, to the lurching of the truck, to the voice of the Corporal.

They were woken at 0530 hours. The Sergeant screamed 'Wakey Wakey', and thumped his swagger stick along the end of each bed, swearing, tipping every other metal locker over, standing over the spilled contents, calling them whores who had turned the place into a bordello, telling them their kit would be stacked properly or they wouldn't live long.

Jack shaved in cold water, and dabbed at the cuts which ran red. He thought of Butlins but he didn't smile. Hi-di-bloody-hi, he thought. His eyes were red and sore, his hands and shoulders ached and he hadn't even dreamed of Rosie in that brief hour of privacy, he had been too tired.

Nigel's face was without cuts. He had no need to shave. The cat calls followed him out but he flicked his towel over his shoulder and smiled, walking away, giving a royal wave. They had to fold their sheets and their blankets just right. Put back the lockers, just bloody right.

Then they were out, into air which smelt sweet, into a summer day where birds sang, and Jack had forgotten for hours that anything pleasant existed. They marched with knife, fork and spoon held in one hand behind their backs as the Corporal ordered them to, but were screamed at because they were not swinging the other arm. No one had told them.

'You should have known,' he screamed again.

They marched, out of step, into the cookhouse, drinking sweet thick tea, eating greasy tinned tomatoes, and bacon, then tipping the remains into slop bins whose putrid smell reached out into the steamy hall. They moved along, sluicing their cutlery in the lukewarm tank. Bits clung to the forks and the knives.

Then back to the barracks and the lavatories. The floors were swept, the windows polished. Jack took the ablutions instead of Sid because Sid was shaking and pale. He had called out for his mother just before dawn.

Jack handed him his window cloth, and with Sam from Liverpool hurled buckets down the clogged stinking pans so that the inspecting officer wouldn't complain, wondering all the time how this mad-house could be allowed to exist.

They had their hair cut, the shears pulling and scraping far up their necks. They had a medical inspection in the afternoon, sitting on benches in a building which stank of urine and disinfectant and gleamed with green and white paint. They all passed and all groaned.

That night they blancoed their webbing, pressed their clothing, ironing over a sheet of brown paper which had been wetted with a shaving brush. They breathed in the pungent smell of steam and scorched paper, feeling the heat on their faces, their heads already bursting with the ache of tiredness. There were only two irons between the thirty of them. The night was endless. The music blared. Sid slept and Jack pressed his then wrote to Maisie asking her to send spare pyjamas and underpants so that he could keep the Army issue ready at all times for inspection.

He wrote to Rosie, sitting on the floor because the bed was laid out for inspection. He told her that all he could smell was scorched, damp, brown paper, all he could hear was cursing, all he could feel was the ache of tiredness. The ache of missing her.

'God, I'm bushed,' groaned Nigel.

They spent the last hour of the night on the floor, to avoid messing up their beds, Sid and Nigel too. They were scared, Jack was scared, of the Sergeant with the swagger stick and eyes like bullets and for the second night he was too tired to dream of Rosie.

They were right to be scared. The Sergeant tipped their pressed clothes, their lockers out on to the cold stone floor but they didn't turn and look. They stood to attention at the foot of their beds, their faces set, their minds raw with anger, with despair, with the confusion of tiredness.

561

'You're a bloody shower,' the Sergeant shrieked.

They had their injections that day then they polished the studs on the soles of their boots, the brasses again, the windows, the tables, the buckets, the floors. They polished the words off the lid of the boot polish tin, set it to one side for inspection and bought another for use.

They pressed the military frieze into sharp creases again. They covered everything in newspaper so that nothing would get dirty between the evening and the morning. They moved by numbers, they didn't think, they didn't feel, they didn't dream.

'God, I'm bushed, exquisitely bushed,' Nigel groaned.

'Go to sleep then,' Jack murmured. 'Give us all a break.'

The next day they drilled. The rifles were heavy, their shoulders were sore from them. They marched, they halted, they turned, they about-turned. Sid stumbled on the turn, every time. The Corporal swore. They stopped for a smoke break, Jack, Nigel and the others, but Sid was marched up and down, up and down, and still he stumbled and his face looked like the faces of the sisters who had been separated in Somerset, like Lee's when his father turned from him.

Then they all marched, again and again, and their boots rubbed but they were not allowed to stop for lunch because Sid still couldn't turn and that night Sam cursed Sid, and the others did too, and tipped him out of his bed and threw his locker over because the minutes had ticked away for tea break too, and still he had made mistakes.

'Get out of it,' Jack shouted and Nigel helped him push them away.

They picked up Sid's things, turned their backs to his tears, giving him privacy, shielding him so that the others couldn't see either. They were tired, dog tired, but they laid out their beds for inspection, then Sid's, and walked him to the Naafi though their feet were raw and burned with each step.

'Just a quick one,' Jack said.

'Builds up the sugar level,' Nigel murmured, his lids drooping.

They bought Sid beer and listened as he told them that he got so worried he couldn't think and it was then that he made mistakes and he didn't think he could bear it.

They bought him more beer so that he would feel too ill to think and the next day he didn't stumble or the next, or the next, and he bought them the beers those nights. But the next week the Corporal shouted at him, rode him, cursed him again until he stumbled on the turn again the next day and the beers in the evening didn't help.

Jack watched as the boy's hands began to shake, and the taunts began again as the whole squad was punished, missing lunch, missing tea. He watched as the light faded from Sid's eyes and felt anger above his tiredness.

So when the Corporal lined them up and the Sergeant marched with clipped strides down the ranks, pointing his stick at Jack, he moved it to one side, his eyes hard like the Sergeant's, his hands sweating with the fear he wouldn't show. He didn't want Sid to suffer any more.

He could cope. He was stronger, he was nineteen, a man. Much older than the sister who had been killed by a car when she ran away from the town to the village to see her Sarah. Much older than Lee who had been pushed aside by Ollie.

He was marched away, sworn at, cursed, pushed, his head yanked back by his short hair.

'Got a nice little job for you,' the Corporal said, his voice low, his lips thin. 'You're not going to know what day of the bleeding week it is when you've finished, sonny.'

He was handed scissors and spent the afternoon on hands and knees cutting the grass around the parade ground. The ants scrambled amongst the grass, the dandelions were acrid, their milk spilling white on to the ground. His thumb and finger were blistered. He changed hands. That thumb and finger became blistered too.

He changed again, the sun sharp on his neck. He could hear the Corporal, and the boots.

'Forward march.

'Halt.

'Turn.

'About turn.

'Smoke Break.

'Forward march.

'Halt.

'Turn.

'About turn.'

His thumb and fingers were bleeding, he padded them with grass he had cut. It was cool but with each cut the pain dug deep.

He didn't break for tea. He worked on until the ants and the sun had gone. And then in full kit, he doubled around the tarmacked square on blistered feet which bled warm blood into his boots. But Sid was left alone and that helped the pain of his hands and feet as he lay on the floor all night because there was an inspection in the morning.

The next day he was told to shin up, then jump from gym ropes he could hardly clasp by a sweating instructor who moved the mat as he jumped and laughed as the rope burned his hand and then the mat burned his shins. He laughed as his elbow, then his shoulder crashed on to the hard polished floor.

'Think you know more than the Army, do you?' the instructor ground out. 'Think you can cheek a Sergeant, do you? We'll see about that.'

He was put on fatigues because he was last out of the changing rooms when the instructor hid his boots, slapping his rubber slipper in his hand as he laughed, whipping it across Jack's back. But he wouldn't show the pain, or the anger.

The next day he drilled with raw feet, threw his rifle against his bruised shoulder and held the butt in a hand that throbbed and bled but he showed nothing. There was no smoke break for him and he winked at Sid and Nigel as he marched, looking at the sky, the clouds, thinking of Lee, of Rosie.

He scrubbed the walls in the cookhouse all evening and watched the cockroaches scuttling out from behind the pipes. But none of this mattered. He was tough, he could take it. He was alive. He was nineteen. Rosie loved him. Lee was all right. Maisie and Ollie were all right. Rosie had written and said so.

The next week the Corporal found a speck of dirt on the back of Jack's buckle and grinned as he extended his punishment. He spent the evening syphoning petrol then rubbing graffiti off the lavatory walls with it, tasting it, smelling it. He vomited all night in the latrines.

But he could take it, he told Sid and Nigel who came and stood by him. It was Sam's bloody handwriting.

'How exquisite,' Nigel said.

564

They laughed, all of them, even Sam, who polished Jack's boots for him that night, and bought him a beer, while Sid stayed behind and laid out his kit. Nigel bought him another and because he was such a tight arse Jack wondered why.

'You're keeping that bastard off our backs. We're extraordinarily grateful, you know.'

He didn't understand why Jack laughed, why he laughed even when he lay on the floor beside his bed, and neither did Jack himself, especially in the dead of night when the laughter choked into silent tears and he churned between images of the sisters and Lee and Rosie.

He peeled potatoes when the Corporal decided his locker was a disgrace, though there was nothing wrong with it. He watched the squad run to PE in baggy shorts and singlets, carrying their plimsolls, wearing their boots, their pale hairy legs thickening already from the drill. He thought of Butlins, of Harold, and cut into the potato once more. Rosie had written, she still loved him. Lee was happy. Maisie and Ollie were fine. And he was fine. He was nineteen. He could take it.

Sid shared his food parcels with Nigel and Jack. They were all fitter by the fourth week. The Corporal still shouted, still punished, but Jack hadn't broken. The men were his friends, they cheered as he cut the grass, yet again. They helped him off with his pack after he had been doubled round the square, yet again.

They woke him when he slept too soundly during the education talks in a room thick with smoke as they were told, yet again, of the Empire, and the pox, and they grinned when he winked at them. But he was nearly finished. He was nearly broken. He had no dignity left, no power to save himself. No nothing. Just Rosie's letters and the thought of the hand that had written the words.

In the fifth week the Corporal left his bike outside the hut when the Sergeant had ordered it to be put away and the Corporal left their squad with the Sergeant's language still thick on the air. The men blew up johnnies bought from the barber and let them fly from the door as he passed.

The Lance-Jack took his place, a new stripe on his arm and a voice which was not so loud, not so cruel, and now the fatigues ended and Jack slept at night. At last he slept and had the time and the privacy to dream of Rosie.

In September his squad cursed and swore on the assault course, feeling the skin scrape off their stomachs as they scrambled up and over the nets carrying packs filled with bricks, feeling the straps cutting into their shoulders, humping Sid up before them because last one home got fatigues.

They plunged from logs into murky water-filled ditches, spitting out filth, pushing against the weight of the pack, forcing their heads up and the panic down. They raced and beat the squad from Waterloo barracks in the cross country and the Lance-Jack bought them all beers.

They sat up that night and cheered as Nigel sang and danced and Sam called, 'You'd make a lovely tart.'

Jack wrote to Rosie and told her. They watched new squads arrive and stumble and scramble, and tossed them cigarettes and told them it would be a bleeding picnic.

They shot on the rifle range, feeling the Yorkshire breeze in their hair, the first hint of winter in its coldness, lying full stretch on their stomachs. He wrote to Rosie and told her of the smell of the ground which still had the summer tight in its grasp, of the men, who were now moulding into a team, almost in spite of themselves.

They were paid.

'One pace forward.

'Two, three, salute.

'Two, three, take pay.

'Take paybook.' Open top left pocket.

'Pay and paybook correct, sir.' Place pay and paybook in pocket.

'Two, three, salute.

'Two, three, about turn.

'Left right, left right.' Three bags full. Sir. There were drinks in the Naafi. Only a few days more then a transit camp. Postings came in. Sid was a clerk, Nigel a Sergeant in Education. He didn't want a commission now. He was one of the men. Jack was a squaddie.

The next day, the last before the passing-out parade, they squatted on the grass with the weak late summer sun on their faces around a Sten gun which was taken to pieces by a dirty-fingered NCO.

Jack said, 'Be gentle with the grass, Corp. It's been very carefully cut.' The squad laughed, the Corporal too.

The Corporal put the gun together, then took it apart again. Jack could smell the oil, see it beneath the Corporal's fingernails, and he remembered Ed in that Somerset village. The oil beneath his fingers as he threw the ball to Jack, the drawl as he shouted at him to pitch it higher next time, the sun shining on his red hair. Where was he now? Why had he never written?

The gun was in pieces again. They tried to put it together and failed. They tried again and succeeded and the smell of the oil was heavy and it was the same as the smell on Ed's hand as he had ruffled his hair and asked when his mom was coming down again.

'The aim of war,' said the Corporal, 'is to kill the enemy.'

Sam murmured, 'Don't tempt me, sunshine.'

The others laughed and the Corporal called the comedian out to the front, standing Sam there, pointing to his head.

'Don't aim at his head. You'll miss, and if you hit it, you'll find there's no brain, just air if it's like this specimen.'

Jack pulled at the grass, floating it down in the faint breeze.

'Don't aim at his legs. You won't kill him.'

Had Ed killed anyone? Had he sat in the sun and listened and learned. Ed had needed to. They didn't. The war was over. Frank got over-worried. There was the bomb now. There wouldn't be another war.

'Aim at the body. That'll get them.'

Jack had applied to become a clerk. It was a cushy number but he had been refused. The officer said his schooling was incomplete though his IQ was high and that he would be directed towards the Infantry because his rifle range report had been good. Jack looked at the Corporal and then at the Sten. At least he'd never have to kill anyone. And nothing mattered now, because basic training was over. He was going home after passing out tomorrow. For two whole days he would be home, with Rosie.

CHAPTER 11

The carriage was as full of smoke as it had been on the journey up to Yorkshire, and the floor as littered with cigarette stubs, but now it was different. They had passed out. They would not have to go through anything like that again. Nothing as bad ever again.

They were to be clerks, teachers, wireless operators, or squaddies and then their lives could begin again. And for the next thirty-six hours they were going home. They all laughed again, as Sid won a hand of cards and Nigel dealt another on the table they had made by heaping a coat over a kitbag.

Jack looked out of the window, the cards worn and slippery in his hand. Rain raced down and across the glass, jagged from the slipstream, and he could see little, but as they drew near London the houses grew thicker. There were chimneys belching smoke, there were the same damaged buildings. Nothing had changed in two months. But what about the people? What about his family? Were they all right?

The train was drawing in, shunting, slowing, stopping. They hauled kitbags out on to the platform, then up on to their shoulders, walking in a group. The smell of London was the same but Jack felt as he had done when he returned from Somerset. Strange, different. And his home had been different too. Was it now?

They took the Underground or other trains, waved, slapped shoulders and couldn't say to one another how they felt. This had been a family, and now they might never see one another again. So they waved, laughed, looked away, looked back, and Nigel, Sid and Jack stood still, looked, nodded then drifted into the crowd. What else could they do?

Rosie was waiting at home, at the entrance to his back yard. The rain had stopped, the fog had settled, raw, close. He saw

568

her as he walked down the alley, leaning against the wall, her scarf round her mouth, her coat belted, the collar up. He watched her straighten and run and heard the thud as his kitbag rolled from his shoulders into the drain and then she was there, in his arms. He pulled down the scarf, kissed her warm lips, searched her mouth with his, felt her against him, her arms around him, and the strangeness was gone. She was here. He was home.

'They're all right,' she said into his neck. 'There's been no rows. No trouble.'

Then there was the sound of running feet, panting breath, and Lee was there, clasping his leg, crying, laughing, punching, and Jack picked him up, threw him into the air, caught him, hugged him. He hadn't changed. It had only been weeks. It seemed like years.

Ollie and Maisie bought in beer from the pub, and Rosie ate with them because Maisie said every minute was precious when you were in love. Rosie looked away from the bleakness of her eyes, back to Jack who sat balancing on two legs of the chair. He was broader, fitter. A man. And when he had held her she had felt shy against his strength, against the roughness of his stubbled chin, against the voice which was deeper, stronger.

'Do you still love me?' she had asked.

'More than ever. You are what I dreamed of at night. You are my world. You keep me going and you keep my family safe for me. I shall never love anyone else.'

She had felt the pulse in his throat as she touched his neck and then his hands where the scissors had scarred. She picked up his hands and kissed them.

The two days passed too quickly. Rosie waved from the back yard. He wouldn't let her go with him to the station where they would be pushed and pulled by the crowd, where he would see her face as the train left.

She watched as he walked up the alley, listened as his footsteps grew fainter.

She wrote to him at the transit camp, and then to the Barracks when he moved on there. He wrote to her of guard duty, the inspections, the charging of his friend because of a dirty buckle.

He wrote of the Corporal who read out the Guard Duty orders, issued them with bicycle lamps, whistles and pick-axe handles, allocated the stags, or shifts. He drew second stag – 2030 to 2230 then 0230 to 0430. He wrote of the route they walked, the huts they guarded. He wrote of the hours they spent guarding nothing against nobody.

As November became December he wrote of rifle practice. How he would lie on a groundsheet, feeling the iciness of the earth seeping up into him, seeing his breath white before his face, feeling his fingers hurt with the cold as they held the rifle, then the numbness.

He told of pushing home the ammunition clip with the palm of his hand, seeing a red and white flag for a miss, but more often it was a bull.

He told her he loved her, missed her, and knew that she must love him because she stayed for his sake to help Maisie and Lee, when she could be in America.

On 20 December Rosie made paper chains with Lee, but in Lee's house, not Norah's because Norah would not allow the mess, and she was glad that Jack was lying on groundsheets firing at targets because the British were launching the biggest drive yet against the rebels in the Malayan jungle and that could have been Jack, but it wasn't. Thank God, it wasn't.

She strung the paper chains around Norah's kitchen, though she had not wanted any, but Grandpa had always liked them. She helped Maisie do the same. Balancing the step ladder while Maisie reached up, pushing the drawing pin in, laughing because Lee was laughing, and soon they all were, even Ollie who came through the door with a bottle of wine for Christmas and a message from the pub that Jack was coming home for two days' leave.

They ate the turkey at Maisie's because Norah and Harold were going to his mother's for two days. She looked at Jack, and he at her, and she barely tasted the turkey, because he was back. This year there was no perfume for Maisie, no need for Rosie's lies, and she drank her wine, her shoulders easing, because soon perhaps she could go to Nancy and Frank. 1950 promised to be a good year.

Jack walked her back, into the empty house, up the silent

stairs into the boxroom where ice crept up the inside of the windows and the chill dug even through their coats. He wouldn't let her stay up here where it was so bleak and carried her mattress, her bedding, and laid it where Grandpa had slept, where he slept next door.

She watched the muscles in his back beneath his shirt as he stirred up the fire, straightened the blanket made of cardigans. She watched his arms as he tucked the blankets under the mattress. She watched his face as he turned and held out his arms to her and the bed was soft and warm now as they lay together, and his hand undid her blouse, traced the shape of her breast, and his lips too touched her flesh and his tongue licked her skin and it was the right time where Joe had been the wrong time and the wrong person.

She undid his shirt, pushing it back from his muscled shoulders, remembering the boy who had played flicksies, the boy who had raced in the carts, the boy who had pinched the cheeses, the boy who had been beaten by Jones's man. They were not children any longer. They were nearly twenty.

'I want you, Jack. I love you.' She was breathing in the smell of his body, kissing his shoulders, his chest, his arms.

His voice was soft as he drew her close. 'I want you too, but there might be a baby. We must wait.'

But she was kissing his words away because she was alone and soon he would go and she couldn't bear it.

His kisses were stronger, his leg was between hers, his hands on her skirt, but then he moved, pushing her back, sweat on his face and chest.

'No, not now. Not yet. We must wait.' He stood up and drew on his shirt, turning from her, doing up the buttons, looking into the fire, stooping, scooping out the ash, banking it up. Then just standing, watching the greyness that was all that was left of the smouldering fire.

'We must wait, little Rosie. Wait until we're married.' He turned now and sat with her, pulling up the blanket, wrapping it round her.

'I've never seen your body. I've never felt your skin against mine. I don't need marriage. If you do, we'll marry now.' She leaned against him. Didn't he know what it was like, living with a sister who wanted you to go? The snow would be crisp now in Lower Falls. Frank was under pressure because things had become much worse for liberals in his town. She could go back, lean into Nancy's arms. But more than this, she longed for him and his love.

Didn't he know that, though she had promised to stay for his sake, she was lonely? That the days were long and the nights longer still? But then she looked at his hands, the scars, and knew that it was a time they both had to live through.

January pushed into February and she heard little from Nancy and Frank. She wrote to say that she missed them, loved them, and would have come but Maisie and Lee needed her help and support, but maybe she could come in the summer. Did they understand? Were they angry?

Nancy wrote saying that of course they understood, but they had been a little busy. Mao's victory in China and the friendship pact between China and the Soviets had caused a bit of an upsurge in the Reds under the Bed campaign. McCarthy had launched a true blue Red Crusade, saying that he had the names of over two hundred Communists working in the State Department. Three more of their friends had been fired – one had had his house burned down. Another had killed himself. Frank was still fighting through his paper, through letters to other papers, and he was becoming a target.

But she also said that this was only a wrinkle and Rosie mustn't worry. It was just that it was taking a lot of their time. Maybe it would be better if she didn't come for a while anyway.

Rosie chose to believe her, because there was nothing else she could do. She went next door to Maisie. It was Saturday and they took Lee up West, had lunch in a Lyons Corner House and Maisie held her hand and said, 'It's easy when I have you.' Her smile reached her eyes and Rosie squeezed her hand. What else could she do? And things were getting better for Maisie and Ollie, she was sure they were.

Jack wrote telling her about the trench digging they were doing. And then the trench refilling they were doing, day after day.

In March Norah heard that there was to be a new town built in Corby, Northants.

'If you weren't here then we could go. Why don't you get out and find a place of your own?'

'Because this was Grandpa's house and I can stay as long as I goddamn need to. I don't enjoy it. I just have to stay here.' Rosie sat at the table, watching them both sitting in the armchairs, looking at the space where her mattress had been when they were away, and Grandpa's had been before that. Yes, for now she had to stay here, she had promised Jack.

In April she laughed because customs men raided a liner and seized thousands of pounds' worth of smuggled nylons and Jack wrote to say it was a crime, all those stockings being kept from the streets.

At the end of May the sun was hot and on the first Whitsun since petrol rationing ended Maisie and Rosie took Lee to Southend by train, and walked from the station past streams of cars. Rosie held her face up to the sun. Jack was more than half way through. The sun was out, the world was good today. They would marry when he left and had sorted out a job. He had written and asked her. Soon, all the grey years would be over.

But on 25 June North Korea invaded the South and Rosie wrote to Frank because she wanted to know what it meant. He had always said Truman was afraid of appeasement. Would the United States become involved? Was this the conflict he had dreaded? Come on, Frank, she wrote, tell me what's going to happen. Jack's a soldier now.

She didn't have to wait for his reply because on 26 June President Truman offered military aid to South Korea and Attlee endorsed his actions in the House of Commons. On 27 June the UN backed the opposition to the Communists, making it a police action, not a declaration of war. But did that make any difference? Boys would die anyway, wouldn't they, she wrote to Jack. It was not a question.

The Soviet Union was boycotting the United Nations and was unavailable to veto the motion. On 28 June British ships were placed under the command of US General Douglas MacArthur, the same day that the South Korean capital, Seoul, fell to the North Koreans, and that night she didn't sleep. But so far British troops were not being sent. And anyway the boy at the Butlins fairground had said the only conscripts who went into action were volunteers.

She wrote to Jack in the first week of July, sitting out in the

573

yard as dawn came up, breathing in the fragrance of the roses, sure that England would not send troops into yet another conflict. They had done enough. Yes, here, with the yellow roses unfolding and dew thick on the petals, she told herself that England had done enough.

For God's sake, the houses still hadn't been rebuilt, food was still rationed, unexploded bombs were still being found. Yes, they had done enough. And so she wrote not of the conflict in Korea but of Sinatra's visit which she had written up as a feature and would send to Frank.

She wrote of the new Zephyr that Jones was driving and how she had let his tyres down because of the beating he had given Jack, and the apprenticeship he had terminated. But before she could finish the letter the post came, and a letter was brought out by Norah because it was from America, and not in Frank or Nancy's handwriting.

Norah waited as Rosie peeled it open, looking at the address. It meant nothing to her, neither did the writing. She turned it over. It was from Joe. She looked up at Norah standing beside her. Rosie stared at her, then walked from the yard, remembering his blond hair, his tanned skin, his lips on her breasts, but he meant nothing to her. She leaned against the wall which was not yet warm from the sun and read the letter.

Lower Falls
27 June

Dearest Rosie,

I'm writing to you because I feel you should know that Frank has been ill for some considerable time. It's his heart. They didn't want you to know, which is why they were glad you couldn't get over. The pressure of the last few years, the rise in the anti-Red feeling – though for God's sake Frank isn't a Commie, just a liberal – were giving him problems. They didn't want to tell you. Felt it was better not to.

But Korea was the last thing really. Frank kind of takes all this to heart. He is so scared it will make things much tougher over here for those guys already in trouble with this un-American thing as well as involving our boys in war again. I guess he feels that with MacArthur in Japan it could get real nasty. That guy's such a hot head.

574

Anyway Rosie, Frank has had a heart attack. He isn't well. He could die. He thinks of you as his daughter. I know that it would do him more good to see you than anything else. I work for him now. I know him. Please come if you can. I'm sending you a ticket. Pay me back later if you can. I still remember that summer before you left. It was really great to be with you. Do you remember?

Yours,
Joe

Rosie folded the letter, putting it back into the envelope, taking out the ticket. Hearing Frank's voice, his laugh, seeing his broken pipes, seeing the love in his eyes for Nancy, for her. She mustn't cry. There was no time for tears. She must go now. She had waited too long already. She had neglected them.

'I've got to go, Maisie,' she said, wiping Lee's chin with her finger and licking it. Her finger was sticky. It had been sticky with hops that first summer back here, when her heart was so raw at leaving the lake and the Wallens.

'I've got to, Frank's ill.' She looked at Maisie who was cutting bread, holding the loaf to her body, against her apron, sawing a slice from the top. There were crumbs on the table.

Maisie stopped, her face paling. 'Don't go. Don't leave me. I'm not strong enough.' She threw the knife down. 'Don't leave, Rosie. Don't leave us. Not with Jack gone too.'

She hurried round the table, took Rosie by the arms, shook her, looking at Lee who had gone quiet, and stopped eating.

Rosie smiled at him, at Maisie. 'It's not for long. I have to go. I have no choice. I'll be back. Soon. Hang on. Please, let me go. Promise me you'll stay. Jack loves you so. You and Lee and Ollie. Promise me. If it gets very difficult, I'll come back. Just write.'

Maisie promised to stay, promised to write if it became too hard, and kissed her, held her tight, and there was the smell of lavender on her neck.

Rosie wrote to Jack too. She said that she knew she had promised but she had to go. It was only for a while. You'll understand. He's ill, they've written. I'm needed. I love them but I love you more. Write to me. I love you, I love you.

575

She forgot about Korea. She forgot about everything but informing the office, packing her clothes, posting Jack's letter, taking the train which rattled from the station, and now she cried because she feared that she would be too late.

CHAPTER 12

On the ship, Rosie thought of Jack receiving her letter, reading it on his bed, the only private space he had. She stood by the rail, watching the gulls wheel above the wake as they left Southampton, and wished that he was with her to take her in his arms and tell her that he understood. Surely he would when he knew that Frank was so ill?

She thought, too, of Grandpa standing on the dock so long ago as the children sang 'Roll Out the Barrel' and her voice broke so that no words came from her. Had he heard them as the ship moved out? She would never know now.

As the days went by and England faded, she remembered the leaves on the north shore of the St Lawrence as the ship carrying the evacuees at last drew into Canada, of their colours which she could not believe even now. She thought of the three cheers on deck when they docked, the high arched dining hall where they were taken, the lights in the streets, the food. But most of all the lights because England had been so dark.

On board now, she wrote to Maisie, talking as she would have done had she been there, pulling her back to them all, talking of days gone by; the good times. She would be back soon, she said, and Jack would finish with the Army next year. She wondered to herself how long it would be before Maisie had no more need of their support. They had their own lives to lead, their own love to enjoy. Their futures to explore and work towards.

She wrote to Jack, explaining again, telling of her love, again. She wrote to Norah.

She sat in deckchairs, feeling the breeze on her face, breathing in the air which was free of London smog, free of smoke, thinking of the balls which Frank used to throw to her to catch, the mitt that was warm on her hand, thinking of the balls which he threw for her to hit, the bat which she could swing as well as any boy. Thinking of Jack because she was sailing far away from him and already it was hurting her.

She ate food which was plentiful and fresh and sweet, and felt again the guilt which she had felt as a child a million years ago. But this time she had chosen to come. It was her decision – and she could have made no other. Jack would surely understand that.

She rested in the day because she didn't sleep at night, and each morning asked the purser how much longer, until at last he smiled and said they would dock within thirty-six hours. But she knew that because the gulls were back over the wake again and as they moved along the Hudson River the next morning she saw the cars on the Brooklyn Shore Road, the Staten Island ferries passing the ship. She saw the towers of the city glittering in the morning sun from the starboard side.

She moved to the other side. Here there was the Statue of Liberty, Ellis Island and the low outline of the New Jersey shore. She was back, she was almost home and she was crying.

Merchant ships lay at the piers, steam was surging up from the streets beyond, streets filled with new shining cars. Britain could not afford to keep its goddamn cars, they were exported, and she realised she was gripping the rail, taut with anger.

She took a cab to Grand Central Station and there were no damaged streets, no queues outside the shops, and the tears came again now because she was going home, but she had left home too. She belonged in both, but really she belonged with Jack.

The cab plunged in and out of the shadows of apartment blocks and sped along the double highway of midtown Park Avenue which Frank had said covered the New York Central and the New Haven railroad tracks.

'You a Britisher?' the cab driver asked, his jaws never ceasing to chew gum. He flicked her a piece.

'Yes, but I spent six years here. I'm glad I'm back.'

The gold lettering was still on Grand Central. She walked through the pillared hall, bought a ticket from a booth, thought of all the cleaners, looked up at the zodiac on the ceiling. No, she couldn't see what was wrong with it. She remembered Frank's face and hurried. She didn't stop to look at the Oyster

Bar, or the movie houses, and there was no one meeting her beneath the clock. She felt alone and longed for the feel of Jack's hand in hers.

She moved straight towards the bronze doors, checking her watch. The train would go at one minute past the scheduled time. There were redcaps wheeling trolleys to the silver grey trains, conductors standing by the doors. There was air conditioning on the train. It hummed like the ice-box would hum in the kitchen in Lower Falls. She sat down, she looked at her watch. Come on, for Chrissake. Frank was ill.

But he wasn't at the house. No one was. The blinds were drawn and it looked smaller than she remembered. She walked round to the back. The target was painted as Nancy had said. The rhododendrons were glossy, the lawn was green except where the hose wouldn't reach. There was no jazz sweeping out across the lawn. She stood with her hand to her mouth and longed for Jack because she couldn't bear to think that Frank was dead.

But he wasn't. A neighbour rang the newspaper for her because Frank and Nancy had gone to the lake, and it was Joe who came, driving across in a silver grey Buick which flashed the sun into her face. He drove her to the lake, the hairs on his arm still bleached, his watch still golden against his tan. His voice was deeper, his shoulders broader, but she couldn't look at the hands which held the steering wheel, or the lips which had kissed her breasts.

Instead she listened to the swing music on the radio, and longed for jazz. She looked out at the small towns they were passing through and the petrol stations with their pumps right beside the road and longed for Jack, only for Jack.

'Frank's getting better,' Joe said, reaching forward, pulling out the lighter, drawing on his cigarette. 'He doesn't know you're coming. But I sort of guessed you might use the ticket. I left word with the neighbours.' He was looking at her and she nodded.

'I know. I should have wired to tell them. It was stupid. I was busy getting ready, saying goodbye.'

'Uh huh. So how's little England?'

It was hot, and her legs stuck to the seat. She wound down

the window. There was a smell of petrol, diesel and dust. Heat hazed the distant mountains. She thought of the soft hills of Hereford, the stark dales that Jack spoke of. She looked at Joe's hands now. There were no scars on his fingers and thumbs.

'England's just fine,' she said. 'It was good of you, Joe, to send me the ticket. I'll let you have the money when we get to the lake.'

'Say, no hurry. We know things are tight with you Britishers right now.'

She wound up the window, feeling in her purse. She had the money. It was her savings.

'Things aren't tight with us little Britishers,' she said, putting the money on the dashboard, swallowing her anger. She closed her eyes, pretending to sleep as the next four hours crept by. Pretending to sleep until they drove in amongst the walnut and the ash trees and then the rhododendrons which were purple in June.

Just wish there was still the wild plum and the white oak like my dad knew, she mouthed, as Frank had always done at this stage of the journey, and wondered if Frank had been well enough to do it this time.

She was sitting up now, leaning forward, as the sun went down below the hills and the earth was oozing out the last of the heat. She heard the crunch of the gravel beneath the tyres, saw the wood-lapped house, smelt the lake. Yes, she was sure she could smell it.

She opened the door before the car stopped, ran across and up the steps, opening the door, and then stopped. She hadn't told them she was coming. How different would they be?

But then Nancy was running across the cool pine floor.

'Where the goddamn hell have you sprung from, my darling little Rosie?'

And her voice was the same and the arms that held her, but the face which looked closely into hers was older, so much older, and thinner and the lines were deep from the nose to the mouth and there were shadows beneath the eyes.

'Joe sent me a ticket. I've paid for it. I came. I love you both so much, so I came.' Rosie reached for the hand which was smoothing her hair and kissed it. 'How is he?'

They were walking across the floor and then she stopped and turned, looked back as Joe brought in her bags.

'I owe you, Joe. Thank you.'

He was still so tall, so strong, so tanned, but she longed for Jack, his slighter body, his smile, his pale skin, his drawn face. Her Britisher.

'Thank you,' she said, then turned and climbed the stairs because she had already forgotten the boy who had kissed her breasts after the barbecue.

She sat with Frank all evening, holding his hand, laughing when he chewed his empty pipe, listening as Nancy read him *Gone With the Wind*.

'It makes him fall asleep,' she said.

Rosie sat with him until he fell asleep, then she walked without shoes down the stairs, feeling the coolness of the floors, breathing in the smell of pine from the furniture, from the shellacked logs, from the very air which was cool as she stepped out on to the verandah. She walked with Nancy across the lawn, into the shadows of the trees, and neither spoke as they approached the lake.

She could hear its ripples slapping against the shore, smell it on the breeze, feel the mulch of the woods beneath her feet. She lifted her head. She could not see the star-strewn sky through the branches.

Then they were out on to the shore and the moon lit the air and the water and she dug her shoes into the sand, reaching down, scooping some into her hand, letting it fall through her fingers. Jack would be happy here. She would bring him one day and they would make love here, while the sand was still warm.

She put her arm through Nancy's. They walked down to the water, letting it lap their feet.

'So how is he really?' Rosie asked because they hadn't spoken of this until now.

'Thank God, he's going to be fine. They think anyway, as long as he doesn't get a lot of pressure again.' Nancy looked up at the sky. 'It kind of makes you feel the world's gone mad, Rosie. Here you have a good man, then things change and suddenly there's a suspicion he's a bad man because of the company he keeps or kept. Because of the words of reason he writes.'

She turned and they walked towards the boathouse.

'And what's even more crazy is when that company isn't bad either, but just had or have Commie connections. It kind of makes me want to puke. But it makes me goddamn frightened too because it's happening here, in our "free" country.'

The wind was gentle, there were no waves now, just a swell. It would be a good fishing night for Frank.

'Will he get completely well?' Rosie looked towards the point. Frank had looked older, like Nancy, thinner too. The lines were deep and his eyes sunken. He had no tan.

Nancy hugged her now. 'Sure, honey. Especially now that you're here. He is just so pleased and he knows it must have been hard to leave Jack and Maisie, especially now that they're sending British troops to Korea.'

Rosie drank hot chocolate in the sitting-room, talking about Uncle Bob, about Norah, about Grandpa, watching the moths beat against the glass, hearing their thuds, feeling the cold fear which Nancy's words had brought, but not being able to speak of it, because Frank was ill and needed her. Because Nancy did too.

It was only when Nancy had kissed her at the bedroom door that she could think. She moved to the window, opened it and breathed air which was so different to London. Then she wrote to Jack, thinking of the landlady at Cowes and her son's friend. You only have to go if you volunteer, the man at the fairground had said. She told Jack again now. She also told him again and again that he must not, but then, why would he?

The next day and the next and every day in July and August she sat with Frank beside his bed, with the windows and doors wide open, the drapes billowing in the breeze, playing records on his gramophone. They talked, but never about Korea, or McCarthy or his three friends who now had no jobs, about the 'hate' letters which Nancy said they had begun to receive in far greater quantities since North Korea invaded the South. Neither did they talk about the falling readership.

There were many hours when they just sat silently together listening to the piano of Erroll Garner, the voice and trumpet of

Armstrong, or the record by The Gang, Bob's new band, that had a tension and an urgency which Rosie liked and so did Frank.

She tapped her foot, poured him iced drinks and thought of the reports in the US papers of the American soldiers who were being mauled as the North Koreans pressed home their advance, and of the British 27th Infantry Brigade who were travelling to Pusan from Hong Kong. She thought of all the United Nations troops that were still being pressed back into the South Eastern coastal tip and thought that the world had gone mad.

Each of those days she walked down the gravel path to the mail box and once a week Jack wrote. His first letter was angry – worried about Frank, about Maisie – but she replied, telling him that Maisie was fine. She had seemed better, had promised that if there was trouble she would write and then Rosie would come back. Trust me, she wrote. I'm only here because I had an urgent letter. But she did not tell him that it was from Joe.

After that he sent her love and news of the assault courses they were clambering over, the football match his team had won, and she was glad that his letters were filled with news such as this. Not of battle which seemed to be in every paper that she read.

Nancy and she went to the Club and Sandra screamed and rushed over, her brace gone, her hair permed, her lipstick bright. She was in her first year at College, majoring in English. She was tanned, a gold watch hung loose on her wrist. They sipped vermouth from chilled glasses which stuck to the tables. They slid them to the edge to break the vacuum, and could only talk about the old times because their lives were so different now – Rosie was not at College, she did not have a gold watch – there was nothing between them and all she longed for was Jack.

Nancy held her hand as they walked to the car and Rosie told her then of her love for him, but Nancy knew already.

'Maybe it would have been Joe, if you'd stayed. He's a good man. Pretty ambitious, but a good man. He got you over. That was kind.'

Rosie nodded. Yes, it was kind, but he wasn't Jack. He didn't go back all those years, like Jack. Jack was her childhood, he was England. He was her life.

*

By September the leaves were falling from the trees and Frank was well enough to sit in the back seat while Nancy drove and Rosie looked back at the house as they left, wondering when she would come again. Because she would be back, but next time she would come with Jack.

In her room in Lower Falls her skis still stood, and the Cougar pennant hung as she had left it. The patchwork quilt was still on the bed and she sat and felt the ridges, then traced her hands along the pine headboard which Frank's grandfather had carved. It was the same, all the same, but she had grown.

The next day Mary returned from holiday and they kissed and hugged and Nancy built up the barbecue to catch the last of the mild autumn. As the light faded and the moths were dragged towards the lanterns, Rosie sat with Frank on the glider and listened because now he was home and there had been a stack of hate mail in the box, and he needed to talk.

His words were calm, slow, but his jaw was clenched as he spoke of the fear and suspicion that was rising in America. He wanted to be back where the trees and the lake hid him, but that wasn't possible. Someone had to print some sense.

He gripped his empty pipe with one hand and her fingers with the other, carving points out of the air as the smell of steak rose with the charcoal smoke.

'The fear and suspicion really got going when America heard that Russia was making headway with its own A bomb. Then there was China. How could the nationalists, supported by our wealth, go down to a peasant army? Now there's Korea. The North with Commie backing sweeping us aside as though we were flies.'

He was swinging the glider gently and his voice was calm. Tired but calm. 'They're frightened that another war will take all this wealth from them. Or maybe it's "we", hey, Nancy?' he called. But Nancy shook her head.

'You've never been afraid of poverty. You made all this, you could make it again. You might *have* to make it again if this goes on.' She flipped over a steak and laughed. Frank laughed too and Rosie felt the love flow between them and thought of Maisie and Ollie.

'That guy McCarthy, he's cunning. He wants re-election.

584

He picked out a hot chestnut to get in the papers. He's telling us he knows over two hundred Commies in the State Department. He hasn't named them. He can't name them, but some people want to believe what he says.'

'Steak'll be ready in five minutes,' called Nancy. Rosie nodded and Frank waved his pipe.

'But why?' Rosie asked.

'There was a backlash after the First World War. We had the Ku Klux Klan then. Now we have the Red Menace.' Frank rubbed his face with his hand. There were age spots on the back. 'And it's like I said before; it's hard for people to believe that this great big country of ours can get beaten by Mao, or Korean peasants. Look at our troops in Korea, pinned down by fire power. Cut off, whole battalions surrounded, thousands of our boys captured. It can't be the way we handle things, can it? It has to be betrayal from within. That's the only answer for some.' Nancy called them over now and Rosie helped him to his feet.

'Look at Hiss, a Harvard Law School graduate from a WASP family under suspicion of spying. McCarthy loves that. He tells the people that we are being betrayed by the high-ups within. He tells them that we red-blooded Americans could wipe our boots on the Commies, except for this betrayal.'

The barbecue was hot on their faces, the smell rich and sweet, and it seemed a world away from the harassment and fear of which Frank spoke, but that night there was a phone call, which Nancy took, and it was only when Frank went up to bed, his feet heavy, that she told Rosie that Uncle Bob had just been interviewed by the FBI. He had been reported last week for speaking out at an isolationist meeting back in 1940 and shouting that the Nazis must be beaten. It had been the day after Rosie had yelled at him from the stairs.

The doctor came the following week and now Frank was able to walk down the block, and drive into work for a few hours, and he came home with Joe, who stayed to dinner, his shirt white, his teeth white, his hair bleached. They talked of the jobs Frank had given to two of his blacklisted friends and Joe frowned as he drank from the crystal glass.

'I guess we should be seen to be even-handed,' he said. 'There should be a leader column alongside yours taking a more normal view. We'll be closed if we take too much of a liberal stand.'

Rosie put her own glass down. 'Frank's paper is even-handed.' Her voice was sharp.

Frank laughed. 'He's got a point. I haven't been publishing any of the crazy letters. I guess we'll let them roll. Maybe it'll shake some of these burghers up, make them see what's going on outside their picket fences. And maybe it's time Joe had a column. We'll give it a shot.'

They moved to the sofas and sat in front of a fire which flickered and swept heat into the room, and Rosie thought of the small banked fire, the queues, and Jack. She looked at Joe. He was so big. She wanted to be back in England, to feel Jack's arms around her, his lips on hers, to feel safe. There had been no letter from him last week, or this week, so that night in bed, she read all that she had received and slept with them beneath her pillow.

There was no letter from him the next day either but there was one from Maisie.

> California
> USA
> 7 Sept. 1950

Dear Rosie,

You will see from the letter that I am in America too. I couldn't manage any longer. I love him you see. He came over for me again and this time I had to go back with him. Lee is Ed's boy. Forgive me. Jack left, you left. Ollie is a good man. I've hurt him so much. It was never his fault, always mine. Jack loved Ed too. I wrote to Jack but he didn't write back. Go to him.

> Maisie

She left that day, throwing clothes into her cases, kissing Nancy and Frank, saying she'd come back. She had to be with Jack. She flew. The ship was too slow. Frank paid. She didn't mind. She had to get back to Jack and all the time she cursed the red-haired man and the woman who smelled of lavender because they would bring pain back into Jack's life and he might blame her.

She took a taxi down the narrow streets. They had still not rebuilt the houses round the rec. Why hadn't Maisie written? She would have come back. Rosie had known the man was Ed. Deep down she had known.

She jumped from the taxi, paid, tipped, and ran down between the houses to the alley, her cases banging into her legs. She dropped them in Jack's yard. He wouldn't be there, but Ollie would.

Ollie was sitting at the table, drunk. His face was unshaven. He smelt of stale beer. There were dishes in the sink. Lee's toys were heaped in the corner of the room, broken and hacked apart. Maisie's clothes were with them. There was no fire in the grate and it was cold.

Rosie walked over to him, putting her arms around him, holding him, rocking him, but he didn't cry, he just moaned.

'I'm so sorry,' Rosie whispered. 'I'm so sorry, Ollie.'

He was silent at last, then pushed himself away from her, turning back to the beer, pouring it into his glass, drinking again. She stooped to pick up the clothes, the toys.

'Leave it. I'm going to burn them.' His voice was cracked like an old record.

She moved to the fire then, cleaning out the grate, emptying the ashcan into the dustbin, feeling it in her eyes and throat. She laid wood, then coal, lit it. Held a paper to draw it, heard the crackle then felt the heat.

She boiled a kettle, washed the dishes, made tea. Came and sat at the table with him. She poured him a cup, and one for herself. It was hot and strong. He didn't drink his. He didn't even look. He just drank his beer. She should have stayed in England, but how could she? How the hell could she?

'I knew it was that GI,' he said as Rosie poured another cup. 'Bastard.'

He pushed his chair away, kicking at the toys, standing there, his hands limp by his sides.

'I just knew,' he repeated then he walked into the yard. Rosie followed.

'I loved her, you see. It drove me mad. If I'd been kinder maybe she'd have stayed. But it burned inside me. She wouldn't let me touch her, not after she met him.'

Rosie held his arm. It was dark now. There were lights in Norah's house.

'The boy was his. I knew. It was the hair. They both had the same hair. I used to buy ham off him. I liked him. Trusted him, but only in the beginning. Now they've gone.' He turned and looked at the house.

'Your granddad and me bought these two houses. Things were all right then. Now I've got nothing and he's dead.' He was looking at her now, in the light from the kitchen. 'It's you bloody Yanks. You knew, didn't you, and you never said. Maisie told me. You bloody Yanks, you stick together. Well get out of here. You don't belong. Just get out.' He was shouting, moving towards her, and Rosie backed away from him, out of the yard, because he was right. She had known and there was nothing she could say. But then he called, 'There's a letter here for you. From Jack.'

She stood at the gate, the latch was rusty, there was a slight fog, the dampness made her cough. Why was Jack writing to her here?

Ollie went into the house, came out. The letter was white in his hand. He thrust it at her, then pushed the gate shut. It was dark, too dark to read. She walked to the end of the alley, to the lamppost where Jack and she had swung. She ripped it open.

Rosie,

Norah told me someone called Joe wrote to you. Who the hell is Joe? Is that why you went? Is that why you left Maisie? You promised. You said if I wasn't there, you would be, but one letter from a man I've never heard of and you're rushing back to the Wallens. Was Frank really so ill?

I trusted you and all the time you knew about Ed. She's taken Lee. He was Ed's. You Yanks think you own the bloody world. Go to hell. Go back, you seem to like it so much. Don't let me see you again.

Jack

CHAPTER 13

Rosie spent the night at Norah's. Not speaking to her, or to Harold. She couldn't. She couldn't sleep, eat, think. All she could do was feel.

She travelled to Yorkshire the next morning, her mouth dry. She must see him, talk to him. She must make him understand. The leaves were down from the trees, the wind buffeted the train. There was a view of Harrogate screwed to the wall. What had happened to the one that Jack had taken and sold in Somerset? What had happened to her world?

She turned from the glass-framed picture, from the man who sat reading his paper, blowing his nose. She stood, left her paper in her place and walked up and down the corridor to dull the pain. Everything was dark. There was no colour. He couldn't leave her. He was her life. He was her childhood, her future.

She leaned her head against the window, letting it bang against the glass as the train rushed through long sweeps of countryside, watching the rain jerk down the pane. Yes, she'd known. But she couldn't tell. It would have made it worse. Or would it? She didn't know, for Chrissake. She didn't know. All she knew was that she had promised Jack, and Maisie too, and there was anger added to the pain. Why couldn't people live their own lives? Why reach out and destroy hers? Why, Maisie? For God's sake why?

She changed trains, buying a roll which she couldn't eat from a kiosk, buying stewed tea, feeling it coat her teeth; feeling despair. She had to wait two hours for a connection. This part of the journey was slower, and she wanted it to roar and rush. She had to talk to him.

The camp was large. Squat buildings lined the roads. Nissen huts stood behind barbed wire. White notice boards held stencilled letters. The taxi took her to the duty room. It was six p.m. He was out.

'Where?'

They wouldn't tell her.

She held the taxi, gripping the door as though it would drive off, asking each soldier who passed, ignoring the winks, the whistles. No one knew. But still she waited. Still she asked.

'In the pub, in the village,' a boy with a shaved neck told her. He looked a child.

'Which pub?' She still held the taxi door. The meter was ticking over.

He didn't know. But it was one in Little Somerton.

They drove there along unlit roads. Sheep were huddled on the moors and the trees were stunted and crouched before the wind. Faster for Chrissake, she thought, but she said nothing.

She paid the taxi, standing in the centre of a village which was more like a town and watching it leave. It was dark and cold. The grey stone of the buildings funnelled the winds in off the dales. There were soldiers in the streets and girls who smiled, their lipstick bright in the light from the street lamps and the windows of the houses. There were railings, sharp pointed, newly painted. She could smell it.

Rosie walked up the street, looking at the men, and they looked back, walking towards her, but they were not Jack. She moved on, shaking her head. There were catcalls.

'Give us a knee trembler then.'

She pushed open the door to The Red Lion. It was crowded, full of smoke. Soldiers were playing darts, the juke box was loud. There were girls at the tables, their laughter high, too loud. A man in front turned, he was drinking beer with a cigarette in the hand which held the glass. There was froth on his upper lip. He grinned at her, wiping his mouth with the back of his hand.

'I'm looking for Jack Parker.'

He shook his head. 'Never 'eard of him. What about me?'

She looked past him, at the man behind, the men to the left and right, all of them, but none was Jack.

She turned and left. The man followed, holding open the door, calling after her.

'Come on, sweetheart, I'll buy you a drink.'

590

She didn't turn, she just walked on. She had to find him, had to talk. She couldn't live without him. She couldn't live with this despair. It made her breath shallow, her skin clammy.

In the second pub there was the same smoke, the same juke box music. Lights pulsed from it, on the men, the women, the ceiling, but not on Jack. He wasn't there.

In the third pub there was no music. There was a pool table down one end and dominoes too. There were girls at the tables, soldiers right up to the door.

She pushed through them, looking, asking. Their khaki was rough and damp. It smelt. Was that the smell Jack had meant when he told her about pressing his clothes?

A man caught her arm. She pulled away. He spilt his beer.

'Bloody 'ell,' he said, shaking his head, 'I'm only trying to tell you, Jack's over there.' He jerked his head behind him and she gripped his arm.

'I'm sorry, so sorry.'

Then she was past him, sliding through another group, smelling their beer, their sweat, and he was there, sitting at a table flicking a beer mat over and over, his arm round a girl with blonde hair and black roots, and it was as though she was split apart, jagged and bleeding, as she heard a moan. It was her. It was like the noise that Ollie had made.

But no one else heard. No one saw her. No one was looking. Not the men round the table, not the girl who was leaning into his neck, not Jack whose lashes were still too long, whose face was still too pale, too drawn, so sad.

She didn't hear the others, see the others. Those that pushed her, jostled her, those that sat around his table. They were laughing. Their mouths were open, their shoulders were heaving but she couldn't hear them.

'Jack.' It was her voice. It sounded the same, not as though it came from the pain which was slicing through her body.

She watched as he looked up, his face changing. He moved, then stopped. His face became set, his arm gripped the girl. He turned from her. But for a moment he had loved. She had seen it.

She moved closer. 'Come and talk to me, Jack.'

He was turning to the others, his shoulder towards her, then his back. The girl looked over him, to Rosie, and laughed. There was lipstick on her teeth.

'Talk to me, Jack.' Rosie leaned forward, picked up a glass of beer that the Lance-Corporal who sat opposite him had just put back on the table. It was three quarters full.

'Talk to me,' she shouted and the laughter stopped around the table. But Rosie couldn't hear anything other than her own voice. Now he turned. 'Come outside and talk to me or I throw this goddamn beer over him.'

She nodded to the Lance-Corporal who sat still, doing nothing, saying nothing. There was quiet all around them. She could hear that now. The glass was heavy, and wet. The beer was sticky. The hops had made her hands sticky too.

She said, 'Remember the bines, Jack? Remember how sticky the hops are? How the dust gets beneath your nails? Come and talk . . .' She did not need to go on because he rose.

The girl caught at his hand. He shook her off.

Rosie kept the beer in her hand until he had passed and then she handed it to the Lance-Corporal, but wanted to throw it over the girl. Into her eyes, her hair, her mouth, because Jack had held her and she had leaned into his neck where the smell of him was strong.

She pushed through the crowds, those who were still talking, those who hadn't noticed. The rest opened a path for her, not looking, their eyes busy, and everywhere there was the smell of damp khaki.

She opened the door. It was cold, dark. Jack was down the street, leaning on the wall, his foot up against it, a cigarette in his hand then his mouth. He had done this when she had come home the first time. But then it had been different, he had wanted her.

He watched her come. Her walk, her hair, curling around her face, her neck. Her eyes which were heavy with pain, her lips which were trembling and he wanted to reach out and hold her, love her, but she had gone away. Joe had written and she had gone. Maisie had gone. Rosie had known about Ed, all that time. And now the love washed away and the anger came again, as it had done every day since Maisie had left, frightening him by its savageness.

He turned and walked on, hearing her footsteps behind him, just behind, never at his side because he walked too fast. She would never walk beside him again.

He would never let her. He had trusted her, loved her above all else. But she had rushed to Joe, to Frank, to America, and because of that Maisie had gone to Ed. His heart was full of pain, his eyes too, but she mustn't see that. No one must see his pain again. He pushed it away until only the anger was left.

Rosie followed him, out of the town, to a crossroads where the only sound was the wind, but when it dropped she heard the sheep too. He stopped now, sitting on the rocks off to the left, lighting another cigarette.

'I'm sorry, Jack. I'm sorry I left.' She wanted him to reach out and hold her but he didn't and so she put her hand out. He knocked it to one side and threw his match away. It fizzed in the damp grass.

'I had to go. Joe wrote. To say Frank was ill. He works for him, you see.'

Jack sat slumped on the rock, his head down, his cigarette glowing. 'Is that so? Norah gave me the letter. You left it in your room. You knew him well. You had a summer together. You never told me. Maisie knew Ed well. She never told me either. You knew though. But you didn't tell me.'

Rosie put her hands in her pockets, bunching them. This was all wrong. Joe meant nothing. How could he come into this? How could he touch her life with Jack? This was about Maisie and Ed, not her and Joe. The panic was rising, she wanted to hold him, kiss him, tell him she loved him, only him, but there was such anger in him. It changed his face, now, as she looked at him.

She spoke slowly, carefully. 'It wasn't like Maisie and Ed. Joe works for Frank. I knew him, that's all. Long ago. We dated. He wasn't important.'

Jack didn't look up and his voice was dead. 'I told you about the girl in Somerset. She wasn't important. I wanted you to know. So that you could trust me. So that I could trust you.'

Rosie wanted to reach out, make him look at her, make him see her love. She said, 'I don't know why I didn't tell you, Jack.' But she did know why. It was because Joe had touched her breasts and his tongue had found her mouth and she was ashamed, but how could she tell him that?

He flicked his hair with his hand. It was longer now. She wanted to reach out and stroke it, stroke his face, see him smile.

'Anyway, what about that girl? What about the trust I have in you?' she asked, her hands clenched tighter now, with anger as well as pain. The red lipstick, the mouth, the hair, all in her mind.

Jack shrugged. 'What about her? She's here. You aren't. You went to America. Maisie left. You knew about Ed. You didn't tell me. You deserve nothing better. I thought I could trust you.'

He was standing now, shouting at her, screaming at her. 'Don't you understand? It was Ed. I loved Ed. Ed was like my father. But he wasn't mine, he was Lee's. After all that he's Lee's father and Lee has gone.' He was gripping her shoulders, shaking her until her head jerked backwards and forwards. Then he stopped and turned.

'Tell me you didn't know, Rosie. Please. Tell me it was a mistake.' His voice was tired. The anger was gone in her. She knew his face would be drawn but he wouldn't turn for her to see.

She couldn't tell him. She stood there as the cold wind caught at the trees behind her and at her hair and wanted to be back in Middle Street, back with Grandpa and Jack, back with the roses, with the life they had had. Back where she could understand why this was happening.

'I did know. I saw them. I didn't know it was Ed then, or I didn't think I knew. But when Maisie told me in her letter it wasn't a surprise. She had said she would give the man up. She made me promise not to tell you. I said I would help. I stayed as long as I could. But then I had to go. Frank was ill. I love him.' Her hands were out of her pockets now, reaching for him. 'I didn't tell you because I didn't want to hurt you. I thought it would be all right. She promised when I left.'

He hit her then, turning, slapping her across the face, then pushed her backwards, and again, gripping her coat as she almost fell.

'But you promised me, Rosie. You promised me that you would stay. Then you get a letter from this bugger and you go. What have you done? What has Mum done?'

He was holding her now, hugging her, crying because he had wanted to cry like this when Ollie had rung, when he had caught the train home, gone into the empty house. But Maisie had already gone and Rosie wasn't there and she was his friend and his love and he needed her.

She held him close, though her mouth was bleeding and her face throbbed. She held him because for this moment he was hers again and there was so much sorrow, so much love. 'I did nothing with Joe. I've let you down though. Lee's gone. I can't bear that either but I had to go.'

She felt his breath in her hair, the wetness of his tears. 'I love you. I thought I'd helped. I thought it was safe to go. I had to go.'

But now she felt him stiffen again and tried to hold him as he pulled away.

'I know. You went. Maisie went. Lee went. Over there where Ed is. I trusted you all. I loved you all and now it's just Dad and me.'

He walked back to the road. He could hear the wind in the trees. He could hear his voice, Ed's voice. He had lent him his bike. Ed had given him sweets. They had laughed and talked and Jack had told him that his dad was changing, becoming mean and strange, and Ed had put his hand on his arm. Don't worry, he had said. It's the war.

'And all the time he was laying my mum,' he shouted, laughing, turning to Rosie who was dabbing at her mouth. 'Is that what you were doing with Joe?'

He didn't know where the words were coming from. He didn't know what to do with the anger which filled him, spilled over, made him crazy, made him hurt her. Made his head go round until he felt ill.

Her mouth was bleeding. His Rosie's mouth was bleeding and he went to her again, holding her, telling her he was crazy. He didn't know what he was doing. He loved her, he hated her. He hated them all. He loved them all. She wasn't here when he needed her. She was with Joe, and Maisie was with Ed. He loved her. He loved his mother, and Ed. But he hated them. Christ, how he hated them. They had taken Lee. They've . . . taken . . . Lee.

He was howling now and he could taste the blood on her mouth as she kissed him. She drew him to her, stumbling, falling, taking him with her on to the soft grass, and he kissed her, his tongue in her mouth. He pulled at her coat but she stopped him and, he undid her buttons. Then he ripped at her blouse, he wanted her to tear, to feel his lips hard on the softness of her skin. Had Joe done this too, while Ed took Maisie and Lee from him?

'I love you, Jack,' Rosie said. 'I'm sorry. I'm so sorry.'

He looked up at her then. 'Has Joe done this to you?'

The wind was clawing at the branches, the clouds were whirling across the sky. Rosie looked at him, deep into his eyes, into the pain that all the lies had brought.

'Yes,' she said. 'But long ago and it was not what I wanted. I was confused.' She held his face between her hands, making him listen, making him look into her eyes. 'It was long ago. I love you. I've always loved you. All my life I've loved you.' She was kissing his lips, his eyes, his skin. There was blood on his face and the warmth of it in her mouth and she didn't know that it was hers. Slowly he began to kiss her back.

But the anger hadn't gone. It took hold deeper, stronger. Other hands, American hands, had touched her. Touched his Rosie, the girl who had played flicksies, the girl he had pushed on the swing. The girl he had taken to fetch the cheeses. American hands had touched his mother, taken his brother. Christ, it was all too much. It was all too strong. The rage was too strong.

He pushed up and away, but she pulled him back.

'Don't leave me,' Rosie said against his mouth.

He pushed away again, because he wanted her, but he hated her, loved her, wanted to hurt her, wanted to hold her and the rage was still there; his head felt as though it would burst.

She pulled back at him again.

'Don't leave me,' she said again and now her kisses were on his lips and her hands were on his back, and the wind was all around and he couldn't think, he couldn't see her, and he held her, moved on her, dragged at her skirt, her pants, hauling them down, pushing her legs apart, heaving at his own clothes. He sank down on to her, and she cried out as he tore and entered her. And he cried out as he came because all the love and the hate were still there, and the rage too. And then it was over.

Suddenly it was cold, and they moved, pulled at their own clothes, neither helping the other. Then they sat with their backs to the wind, separate, alone, and he wanted to wipe the last minutes from their lives, but it was too late and he was glad that he was leaving England, taking this rage away from her.

They moved without speaking into the trees where the wind was not as strong. The damp had soaked into their coats. Jack lit another cigarette.

'I'm going to Korea. I've volunteered.'

The branches were cracking, shaking, twisting, and the sheep across on the other slope were moving, baa-ing, Rosie saw them, heard them. He couldn't go. No, he couldn't go.

'You can't. I love you. You can't leave me.' She felt the ache between her legs, the feel of him inside her. He couldn't go. Those were the only words left in the world – he couldn't go.

'You love me,' she insisted, catching at his arm as he lifted the cigarette to his mouth, watching as he drew its nicotine deep into his lungs and then out again, his lips pursed, his eyes on the trees in front.

'I do love you and I hate you and if I stay I'll do what Ollie did. I feel as though I'm going mad inside. Everything's gone bad. I'll destroy us both.' He took her hand. 'I've got to go. I've got to get the anger out of me. It's been building since she went. Ollie cried and I held him and then I held him while he tried to tear the house apart. I wanted to do it too.' He pinched out the cigarette. 'I can't think. There's so much hate. I miss Lee so much. I missed Ed so much.' He dropped her hand.

'I've got to get away. That's all.' His voice was angry again. He stood up. 'Let's get you back.'

He walked in front of her, down the road. There was no train that late so she had to stay in a hotel, alone. He left her there, outside. Not touching her, not smiling.

'I'm sorry,' he said. 'About . . . well, you know. If you're in trouble, let me know.'

She gripped his arms. He couldn't go. Not out there. He couldn't leave her. They loved one another. She knew they did. This anger would pass . . . wouldn't it? But then she thought of Ed and Lee, of Maisie, of Joe, of America and she didn't know.

There was light from the hallway, falling out on to the street, there were soldiers walking past, one being dragged. He was singing 'Roll Out the Barrel' and she wanted her grandpa.

She said nothing. She let her hands fall, made herself watch

597

as he walked down the street, made herself nod as he called back, 'I'll write. When I've sorted myself out, I'll write. If I sort it out. If there is anything worth sorting out between us any more.'

Then he was gone and there was no one left in her life. 'Oh, Jack,' she called, but it came out as a whisper. 'You and your goddamn anger. Your pain. What about mine. What about mine?' She was shouting now but he didn't hear.

CHAPTER 14

Jack sailed from Liverpool at the beginning of October on a troop ship with Regulars, Reservists and National Servicemen, and he was glad to be amongst them, to be leaving England, to be leaving Rosie and the memories. He was glad to be leaving for The Land of the Bleeding Morning Calm as the Sergeant had called it when he marched them up the pier.

He was glad to be on board, to be drilled, to be exercised. He enjoyed the orders, the bull, because it was familiar, like the scar on his hand was familiar. Like the other men were familiar, though he knew none of them. He just knew their language, their style, their habits, because they were like him. He was Army now.

There were no women. There was no tenderness. No betrayal, because if anyone broke the trust, out there on the hills of Korea, they all died.

He enjoyed pushing the ammunition into his rifle, hearing the click. It was cold, final. He enjoyed the storm which lashed the ship for four days, pitching and tossing, throwing him from his bunk, making him sick, making him wheel and fall, because it stopped him thinking and feeling.

He enjoyed the lectures, because then he could not hear her voice in his head. He learned how the North Koreans with Russian-built tanks and weapons had poured across the 38th parallel into South Korea in June.

'Will the West really resist the spread of Communism? is what the Russians will be asking themselves,' the instructor said. 'And I can tell you that we will. They've challenged the UN. They must be stopped.'

Jack listened when Captain Norris said that the Korean War had come when the international outlook was already bad, how the cold war was at its height, how Eastern Europe was under Russian domination. How West Berlin had just escaped this fate. How the Chinese Communists had triumphed in China. He knew all this from Frank's letters to Rosie. But, no, he wouldn't think of her.

He took out a cigarette, smelling the match, thinking of the oast-houses, the fag-ends they had collected as children. But he wouldn't think of that. He must listen to the officer with the moustache now, standing as Captain Norris sat. He must look at the Padre sitting upright, one leg crossed over the other. He must not think of her.

The second Captain was pointing at the board where a map hung.

'In June the South Koreans had a small army, no tanks or heavy artillery and only a small airforce. The North would have conquered South Korea if the United States hadn't had access to their occupation forces in Japan. These, though under strength and ill equipped, were mobilised but were still pushed back to the South East Corner along with our men when they also reached Korea.'

The officer slapped his cane down into his hand. Jack pinched out his cigarette. The Corporal next to him sighed.

'Get a bloody move on,' he murmured. 'I want me bleeding lunch.'

Jack grinned. The Captain was looking at his notes, the men were stirring. The man in front of Jack rubbed his neck. His hair was very short. L O V E was tattooed on his fingers. But there wasn't such a thing, was there?

'As you know, men, General MacArthur launched an invasion in September at Inchon while those in the Pusan perimeter, in the South East, went into the offensive. Now the North Koreans are on the run. We have pushed them back almost as far as their capital Pyongyang. Well over the 38th parallel. The border.' Captain Mackin coughed and looked up as another officer left, papers in his hand.

'It was a hard slog, don't think it wasn't. The harbour was mined, the roads were mined. There are still mines. That took a toll of tanks and men. The casualties have been heavy, but General MacArthur has turned down an order from Washington cancelling their issue of one can of beer a day.'

He stopped for laughter. There was some but the reservist

Tom, on Jack's left, was quiet. He had served in the Far East. He had been a POW at Changi. His war should have been over, he told Jack as they went for food. His wife thought so too.

'It's worse for the girl you've left behind,' he said.

Jack didn't reply. He hadn't left anyone behind, had he? But he didn't want to think about it. He couldn't get past the anger, the hate, to the love. He didn't want to any more. Not now, not yet. It was easier this way.

They sat through another lecture that afternoon and the sea was calm, there was only the vibration of the engines, the smell of diesel, and the Captain's voice again as he told them that the biggest fear was that Communist China would become involved.

But then he swept on quickly, telling them of the country and its people, but all Jack could think about was whether the Chinks would come in, because if they did, it would be tough. Very tough. Tom's hands were shaking and Jack wondered how the Government could send people back into the ring who had already been through so much.

Would the Americans send Ed over here? He had done a lot, hadn't he? They should send him. He should be killed. But he was too old.

'Old enough to be my father,' he said that night as he leaned on the rail and spat into the waves and wondered when the ache inside his head and chest would fade.

The days wore on. They listened, they trained, they wrote to their families, their lovers, their friends, but Jack only wrote to Ollie. He had no lover. But in the darkness of the night, when the only sounds were the grunts of men and the throb of the engines, he felt her warmth, her passion, and turned away from the memory of his own savagery. He wanted to feel love again, as it had once been. But he could not. And so he didn't write.

They arrived in Korea at the beginning of November. It was cold. They could see their breath on the air as they stood at ship's muster. They could see the buildings, the jeeps. They could see the hospital ship too, moored alongside. At Pusan they heard that the Chinese had come in, fiercely, briefly, but everyone knew they would come again. It was only the UN Command who refused to believe it, a Sergeant said as he passed them, grey and tired.

They entrained for Seoul but not before the Red Cross hospital train drew in from the forward battle areas. Tom watched and so did Jack. The red was sharp against the white of the bandages. The orderlies carried the drips beside the stretchers, the nurses checked labels, soothed, gave drinks, listened to a man shout that he could still hear the bugles.

A GI hobbled past. 'Yes, it's the bugles. You know it's them then. It's the bloody Chinese, they attacked us near the Manchurian border. Your turn next, buddies.' He was smiling but it didn't reach his eyes.

'Bloody Yanks,' said Jack. The GI had been big like Ed.

He pushed Tom on. 'Come on, let's go.' But he didn't want to. The Chinese were involved now, up on the border, but they wouldn't stay there. He wanted to go home. This wasn't drilling, exercising, smoking, drinking. This wasn't a scarred hand. This was vivid, stark, shocking. The fear made his voice rough.

'Come on, Tom, get on.'

The wooden seats were slatted, dusty. But he didn't want to go forward. He wanted to go home. This was real. God, Rosie, this is real. He slung his kit on to the floor. The dust caught in his throat. More were heaped on top. Tom was close. He could smell his sweat. But what was there at home any more? Who was there?

Seoul was damaged, bombed like London had been. But Jack wouldn't think of London, only of Korea and the tents they lived in, the mobile Naafi, the mist which changed to sharp cold almost overnight. It was all right, they were told, they weren't moving forward.

They stayed, smoked, bulled, smoked, trained. Felt nothing but boredom. Filled days which went too slowly, watched American troops lurch by in jeeps and Jack felt nothing but hate. In Seoul the hotels were functioning. There were drinks at night, Korean bar-girls who sat on stools with slits up their skirts, but he didn't want them. He didn't want anyone's lips against his. He didn't want anyone near him ever again.

Tom didn't want them either. These girls were Koreans. Koreans had guarded his camp. Their cruelty had been worse than the Japanese and so they bought drinks only for themselves. They sat sipping the beer, watching the flares in the sky. Watching the refugees pulling carts piled high, their faces numb.

The men wore white robes, baggy trousers and straw hats similar to the women who dragged their long hair back into buns. They drank another beer. There had been no more talk of the Chinese and it was 20 November. MacArthur had said they would be home for Christmas. He had to sort himself out before then. He had to write. But he didn't know what to say. He didn't know what he felt.

On the 22nd ten of them were sent north to the forward position as Infantry replacements, along roads girded by frozen paddy fields, and on either side were snow-dusted mountains and hills; shrub-covered, desolate.

Troops were dug in. Smoke rose from the fires. There was a wind. Always a wind and as they travelled the squad talked, but of nothing because they all remembered the boys on the hospital train.

'But the Chinese haven't come and MacArthur said we'd be home by Christmas, didn't he?' Jack repeated.

He shifted on the seat, peering out of the canvas-covered truck, listening but hearing only the wind. He laughed, they all laughed because they had all been listening too. For bugles.

They smoked, looked out at the cottages made of wood and mud and thatched with straw. Three were scorched and ruined. Even in this cold they could smell the human excrement used to feed the soil.

They passed peasants who carried loads on A-shaped frames, women who carried loads on their heads and babies on their backs. The roads were dirt tracks with pot holes which were frozen over. The truck cracked the ice, splintering it, frosting it. Jack threw out his cigarette stub. It arced away, bright in the cold air.

Tom sat, his hands loosely between his knees, his rifle leaning into the crook of his arm.

'I wish I wasn't here,' he said.

'No good saying that when you're sitting on top of a bleeding hill.' The Sergeant opposite nudged his leg. 'You just remember to keep your head down, your eyes open, and pray you get home. You've been in it before. You should know. Help this lot of nigs. Anyway, we're here. Home sweet home.'

The truck stopped at the base of Hill 12. They hauled their kit up on foot, catching on to shrubs, pulling themselves along, slipping, their rifles clattering. A stream ran from the top to the river below and ice crusted the overhang.

The unit they were to join catcalled them at the top. A Lieutenant met them. They saluted. He was grey and lined too, although, they learned, he was only twenty-two. The Sergeant led them to the field kitchen. Others were there before them, warming their hands around their mess tins, moving from foot to foot, nodding as they dug out their tins. At least the beans and stew were warm.

'More shit-diggers. Just what the Chinks want for tea,' a Lance-Jack grinned.

Jack nodded, laughed, and when they had eaten they were shown the hoochies they would sleep in, fight in, shit in. They were shown the machine guns, the mines, the booby traps. That night he and Tom slept in sleeping bags. Dave, John and Simon didn't.

'We've been here too long,' they said. 'You might need to run. Those buggers are like a bloody avalanche.'

The hoochie was heated by an ammunition box into which petrol dripped from a copper tube fed from a can fixed high on the outside. The chimney was made from shell cases, and prodded up through the roof made of branches. It was still too cold for Jack and Tom but there was no firing. There had been none for many days.

But there was the cold and it ate into him. He zipped up his sleeping bag, pulling it over his head, but the cold eased through the ground, the air. It kept the sleep from him and he thought of the ice on the inside of Rosie's boxroom, the damp of the ground when he had held her, driven harshly into her, felt her warmth, her love, and he felt ashamed.

But she had left Maisie, she had gone when Joe had written. Joe had kissed her breasts. Ed had taken Maisie and Rosie had let him and he turned again and again but he couldn't find warmth, he couldn't find sleep and neither could Tom because the Chinese might come. But they didn't. Not then, and not the next day or the next.

'And they probably won't,' Jack said, digging another

perimeter fox-hole, cursing the frost-hard earth, the ice-cold pickaxe.

'Get your bleeding weight behind it,' the Sergeant growled. 'A Chink would shoot your backside off in that pathetic little hole.'

So he dug further and so did Tom, hearing the clatter of stones, looking out across the valley, the river, the hills. Seeing nothing. No Chinese, no birds, just the cold which stabbed into your lungs but didn't stop you thinking. He dug again. He wouldn't think of her. He wouldn't write. He wouldn't write to Maisie either.

On 24 November it was Thanksgiving Day and they watched as trucks brought out turkeys, and planes dropped the trimmings to US troops, and he wondered if Maisie was eating turkey too. He pushed the thought of her from him, but for a moment he stopped and leaned on the barricade he was building from the rocks, not seeing the planes, not seeing the trucks or the snow-frosted world. Just remembering Lee's laugh, the feel of the little boy's arms around his legs in the back alley on his first leave.

Still the Chinese didn't come but there was no sense of ease. Only of waiting. He had spent his life waiting. Should he write? No, he couldn't.

They went on patrol that night as the snow started to fall, heavily, silently. Five of them, the Sergeant leading, Tom second. He knew so much about survival. He had fought the Japs, he had survived the camps. He was quiet, calm, except when his hands shook.

They slid down the slope, digging in their heels, not speaking, not clinking, looking, listening, and Jack's hands were wet inside his gloves and his breathing was rapid.

He was frightened out here, beneath the sky, away from the holes, the others. And no, he wasn't thinking, he was breathing with his mouth open, tasting the snow, straining to hear the enemy, if they came. He was looking, always looking, but what could you see through all this snow which drove in and around him? Christ, he was frightened. These weren't manoeuvres. This was real. And what the hell was he doing here?

He put his feet where Tom's had been, he slipped, recovered. His feet hurt with the cold but that was all right. It was when they didn't hurt that you had frostbite, it was then that you lost your feet.

He looked and listened. His throat hurt from the cold air. There was nothing, just the sound of breathing, and soon the hill had flattened and the going was easier as they crept to the shore of the river.

They set up a listening post behind scrub and rocks where they could sometimes see the river as the snow hurled itself in a different direction and the curtain lifted. Tom linked up a field telephone. They spent three hours watching, listening, feeling the cold bite through their clothes, their balaclavas, their gloves, feeling it stab into their lungs with each breath. It had been minus thirty-five when they left. They could hear the snow cracking the branches of the shrubs and the Sergeant's breath froze on his moustache.

The next patrol came down to relieve them at 2300 hours. They edged up the hill again. Watching, scrambling. Christ, be quiet. Using their hands, shaking the snow which caked their gloves and faces, and always they listened, even as they thawed in the 'warm tent'. But the enemy didn't come and no one relaxed, though MacArthur had said they would all be home for Christmas.

The sound of firing woke them the next night, it was down by the river.

'Thank God, thank God,' he whispered when he woke. 'That could have been me.' Now there were bugles, rattles, whistles and drums, grenades and small arms fire.

But his hands were too cold to unzip his sleeping bag and he wept as John and Dave and Simon ran out, rifles in their hands, ducking and weaving as the Sergeant shouted, 'Take that side and keep your heads down.'

'Christ, I can't get out.' He was going to die. They were coming for him and he was going to die. But Tom was there, calm, leaning over him, unzipping the bag for him, helping him as Ollie had done when Jones's man had beaten him at the warehouse, as Rosie had done with the cheeses. Tom gripped his shoulders.

'It's OK, Jack. You're OK. They're not here yet. Remember what you've been taught and stay with me.' He turned and moved out into the snow. There was firing all round, from the hills ahead and around them.

The fear held Jack still. Dad, where are you? Rosie? He wanted to run. Just run and hide because he could hear screams and shouts and the bugles at the base of the hill and they were getting nearer, the firing was louder. The snow was heavy, and he couldn't see. He hadn't been able to see in the fog either. Dad, where are you?

But the barricades were there. They would keep them away. Jack was out in the open. Following Tom, running, the snow in his eyes, his nose, his mouth. The breath was sharp in his chest. He slipped, scrambled up again, ran to where the Sergeant pointed, heaving the Sten gun up on to the wall he had built, firing down at men who fell as the ducks in the fairground had fallen, but more took their place. For God's sake. More took their place.

His gun was hot. Tom was firing. There were tracers in the air. Flashes from grenades were bright against the snow. Still they came. On up the hill. And he wasn't killing men, he was killing ducks. Ducks which flipped back up, no matter what he did.

They were closer now, scrambling where he had scrambled, firing, blowing their bugles. The Sergeant was behind them. They were much closer.

'Stand your ground,' the Sergeant shouted, but they were so close. He would see their faces soon. They were at the first barricade, leaping over, shooting, stabbing, killing. This was real, for Christ's sake. People were dying. There were screams and groans all round and there was sweat on his face, dripping on to his coat. But he was cold. How could he sweat?

The Sergeant screamed, 'The buggers are through. Over here, you two.'

They crouched and ran back to the next fox-hole. Jack lay down, fired again, heard Tom do the same. It was cold, for Christ's sake. The ground was cold but the Chinese were coming on, falling, dying. Jack fired, Tom lobbed grenades, but more came.

'Where the hell are they coming from?' It was Tom. He was standing, his body exposed. Jack pulled him down.

'Keep firing.' His mind was cool now. It was Tom's hands that were shaking, not his. There was no hate, no love. Just the gun, just the Chinese, and they were closer. For God's sake, they were so damn close.

607

'You've got to hold.' The Lieutenant was behind them, his breath short. He was shouting. 'Got to hold, let Hill 16 complete their manoeuvre. Then we can go, if we have to. But hold.'

John was with them now. They dug their knees in deeper. It didn't matter that it was cold. They wanted to live. They held for five hours.

At 0300 hours the Sergeant slapped Jack on the back, took over the Sten.

'Get out now, over there.' He was pointing to where other men were leaving, stumbling and running, while others still fired, still fought. Jack took his rifle, crouched, ran. Tom was with him, passing him a Luger he had taken from a fallen soldier.

The Chinese were breaking through. They were fighting. He saw arms lifted, guns and knives which twisted and plunged. Tom turned, his head down, his gun up.

'Get out, Jack!' His voice was faint against the noise but Jack heard him, stopped.

'Come on, Tom. Your wife. Get home.' He grabbed him, pulled him, turned him and they ran on together.

They skidded down the hill, ducking and weaving, looking forward, behind, to the side. There were others, friends and enemies. A Chinese lunged for Jack, he dodged, drove home the rifle butt, felt the jolt through his body, but they went on, down the slope, slowing, easing, creeping at the base, sidling off to the side of the road, but there were more and they were firing and Jack felt a punch high up in his arm.

He turned. Tom was down too. There was blood on his chest, on his stomach. He had been shot four times. His mouth was open, his eyes too. He was dead. Snow was already settling. He was warm and Jack took him in his arms, tried to lift him, carry him home to his wife, away from all this, because he had been in too many wars.

But the punch had been a shot and he could only move one arm and the pain was beginning now. He tried to drag Tom, but he had no strength and so he had to leave him, there, in the snow, alone but not alone for there were other dead around him.

Jack felt the anger and the pain rage and he screamed, 'Rosie.'

The Sergeant was there then, pulling, dragging him towards the road where tanks were retreating. He shoved Jack up on to the body of one.

'Hang on or you'll die. Hang on, son.'

There were others clinging, hurting, panting, and he did cling on but not for long because the road was blocked by blazing vehicles and a tank which had lost its track.

He dropped to the road. His coat was too heavy. It dragged at him. He pushed at the tank with the other men but there was too much fire from the hills each side and behind them and so he walked, and another man took his rifle, struggling on ahead.

They passed a soldier on fire from burning phosphorus. How could he burn with so much snow? The flames were so bright. How could he burn when it was so cold? Jack felt as though his head were bursting.

'Shoot me,' the American was screaming. Jack shook his head, stumbled on. Christ, that could have been him. Oh Christ. Dad, where are you? Rosie. He stopped, turned back.

'Shoot me,' the man whimpered now, holding out a blackened claw. 'Shoot me.'

The snow was still falling. The man carrying his rifle had gone, walking on, not waiting. There was just this man here, crying, burning. There was no war, no firing, just the two of them, and one was dying, slowly, and his whimpers seemed so very loud.

Jack did shoot him, with the Luger. The whimpering stopped but pain blossomed in Jack and he cried as he walked because he had shot a man with a blackened, burning body and he would never be free of the smell or the sight of it.

Many others straggled back as the days went by. The UN were in retreat again. He didn't mind the pain in his arm. He didn't mind the throbbing, it was better than being dead. Tom was dead and he had a wife. Jack had no one and he was glad. There was too much pain in loving. Tom's wife would know that now. There was always too much pain. He was glad it took all his strength to put one foot in front of the other. He was glad it took all his mind to breathe in and out. In and out because he didn't think of Rosie, or the burning man, or Tom.

They passed blazing villages, and always the enemy was close behind and to the sides of them in spite of the US airstrikes. There were mortar bombs arcing through the freezing sky. They walked with refugees, then passed a burned out field hospital. A jeep came, doling out hot chow. 'Hurry up. For Christ's sake, hurry up,' the Corporal said, ladling hot cereal and powdered eggs into their helmets because they had no mess-kits any more.

The firing was as close as it had been before, but no closer. Why was the Corporal panicking? He wasn't dead. It was all the others that were dead. Jack dropped his helmet. He was hot, so hot. The food spilled on his boots, into the churned snow.

He sank to the ground. It wasn't cold as it had been when he was shooting the ducks on the hill.

Jack felt the jerking of the jeep, the rattle of the train, and it was like the one that had taken them hop-picking and he knew he must think, he must write to Rosie. But what would he say? He didn't know. He was too tired. Too hurt.

The field ambulance carried him from the train to the ship. A stretcher took him from the ambulance to the gangway. The Medical Officer and Wardmaster lifted the blanket, looked at his shoulder. He screamed as they touched him.

'No gangrene. Those maggots have done a good job,' the Medical Officer said, not looking at Jack, just at his arm. The Wardmaster wrote medical instructions on a label which he tied to Jack's wrist. He was sick of labels. They had tied one to him when he went to Somerset. He wasn't a parcel, he was a person. Rosie hadn't liked hers either. But he wouldn't think of that.

He was carried on a stretcher by South Koreans to the ward on the water line, one deck below the air-conditioned quarters for those seriously injured. They didn't see a doctor on the trip to Japan. There were too many operations needed. Too many amputations because of gangrene.

Jack wouldn't think of the maggots which had been cleaned from his wound. He couldn't bear to think of them in his body. He lay and listened to the throb of the engines, felt the vibration in his wound, his arm which was hot and swollen. He talked to the others as they limped, or sat, arms bandaged, heads bandaged, but they all had their limbs, they all had their lives. Tom hadn't any more and soon his wife would know.

Love hurt.

It was hot. So damn hot. He sat up, but he had no strength, so he lay again. It had been so cold up there on the hill and as they ran away. Pyongyang was burning now. The UN troops were scorching the earth, burning the supplies, stopping the enemy from gaining anything. They were retreating to the 38th parallel. How much further would they go back? Would it all have to be done again?

The trip took three days because the channels could not be guaranteed free of mines and the heat grew worse. The wards were over the main generators. The portholes were secured when at sea.

There were no washing facilities. They were dirty, they were in danger of dehydrating. There were large jugs of water and lime-juice and the boy next to Jack poured him some because he couldn't stand. The ship's engines were so loud. They throbbed in his head, in his wound. All over his body.

He was given more penicillin. He knew there were more maggots but he must wait until Japan to have them scraped away.

An American died and the boy next to Jack told him that they were going to store the body in ice which had to be replenished every two hours, because the Americans returned the corpses to their homeland. Jack turned away from him. They took too many things back to their homeland. They had taken his mother, his brother.

They drew into Osaka and Jack thought that perhaps it was better that Tom was dead, not here with him, because these were the people who had beaten and struck him. These were the people he had hated. As Jack hated Ed. Did he hate Rosie?

The dead went off first, covered with the flag of their country, while the band played. Then the wounded, but not the walking wounded yet. They waited but when it came to their turn Jack still couldn't walk. He was carried on a stretcher and shared an ambulance with a man who had been burned but Jack wouldn't look because he had shot a man with burns. He had been an American. He had pleaded to die.

Jack felt the gun in his hand again. He had shot him. He had looked into a man's face and killed him. Seen the agony go from his eyes, but the light too. An American had asked that of him.

An American had taken his mother. An American had kissed Rosie's breasts, and as the ambulance drew away from the docks towards the hospital he knew he still couldn't write to her.

CHAPTER 15

Rosie walked into the hotel when Jack left, lifting her head and ignoring the gaze of the woman behind Reception, taking her key, climbing into the bed which had not been aired. There was frost on the inside of the panes. He had left her, goddamn him. God damn him. And now she was crying.

Jeeps passed, their headlights flashing into the room, across the ceiling, lighting up the pictures which hung from thin chains. She couldn't sleep. She wouldn't cry. She could scarcely breathe. She lay with her hands on her breasts where she could still feel his mouth.

She wanted to go from the bed, out into the town, to the camp, find him, make him love her, make him push his hate away, her anger, her pain, but she stayed, watching the sky through the window, feeling the throbbing between her legs which had become an ache by the morning. There were drops of blood on the sheet. She sponged them. Each breath hurt. She didn't speak as she paid for her room. She didn't nod. She couldn't.

At the station were the same kiosks selling rolls and newspapers, but she bought nothing, not even tea, and she didn't turn as the train took her away from him. But everything was dark.

She took a Tube and bus and then walked to Middle Street. She walked slowly. She put one foot in front of the other carefully because she ached inside, and she was going home and there was no point to it. And he might come running up behind her, catch her arm, pull her round. Tell her he was wrong. He was sorry. He loved her. But he didn't. And still it hurt to breathe.

She entered the house before Norah and Harold returned from work. The fire was banked. There was a faint heat. She dropped her coat on the floor, her bag too. She dragged the tin bath from its nail on the yard wall.

She smelt the gas before it lit, she heard it hiss as it heated the water in the boiler, she saw the steam beating up to the ceiling, layering the room, clouding the window.

She tipped the water into the bath, poured in cold. There were only two inches. She poured in more cold. Then she peeled off her clothes, leaving them where they fell. It didn't matter that the water was cold. She barely noticed, but she knelt in it, feeling the ridges of the bath on her knees, heaping the water into her cupped hands, splashing it over her body, between her legs, because she had to remove the smell of him or she would die, from anger and from loss.

She splashed again and again, wetting her hair, her body, her arms, her legs, everything. Soaping, rinsing, crying because they had loved but it had not been as she had dreamed. They had loved, but there had been hate, and love without tenderness, only pain. And he might have gone for ever and she didn't know how this had happened. She didn't know how her world could change like this. She didn't know how she could love someone as much without them loving her back.

She dropped her head to her arms, and sniffed. Then to her legs. There was none of him left. Would that help the minutes, the hours, without him? She would not think of longer, of for ever. Now there were more tears, racking sobs which dug deep into her chest and still it was difficult to breathe.

She dressed in fresh clothes, dragged the bath to the yard, tipped the water down the drain. She washed her clothes, hung them on the line where they dripped. She set out the candy she had brought back for Norah on the kitchen table. She hung the scarf she had brought for Harold on the chair and looked at the shirt which had been for Jack, the blouse which had been for Maisie, the car which had been for Lee.

She carried round the bourbon which she had bought for Ollie and left it on the doorstep. What did it matter if he drank it all too quickly? What did anything matter? There was only anger, only pain.

Norah came back at six-thirty and Harold too.

'You're back then. So, how's lover boy? Ollie said you'd gone up there. He said you know all about Maisie's man. Bet

614

Jack didn't like that.' Norah shrugged out of her coat, nodded towards the candy. 'It'll make me fat.'

Rosie made tea, slicing up the tin of ham she had brought back, boiling potatoes, cutting tomatoes into quarters. She put a fruit cake that Nancy had made on a plate in the centre of the table.

She couldn't eat but she made herself put food in her mouth. She made herself chew until the plateful was finished because Norah was watching.

'So, Jack's volunteered?' Norah was smiling, looking at Harold who pushed his glasses up on the bridge of his nose.

'Yes,' Rosie said, and felt Jack's weight on her body, inside her, but she wouldn't cry, not now. Not here.

'Left you, has he?'

'He's going to Korea. For a while. Only for a while.' Rosie took her plate to the sink. Washed it, dried it. She could smell the soda but not him. At least she could not smell him.

'Have you still got your job?' Norah was wiping her plate with bread she had torn off the loaf.

'Leave the girl alone,' Harold said as he stood up, leaving his plate for Norah to clear, moving to Grandpa's chair, opening his paper, stretching his legs out.

Get out of my grandpa's chair, Rosie wanted to shout, but he had been kind. For a moment he had been kind. She stood with her back to the sink. She had given Lee's present to his friend, who had been playing footie in the alley. He was lonely, he had said.

'Don't know why you don't get yourself a live-in job.' Norah pushed a crust that was too large into her mouth.

'This is my home, for as long as I need it. Don't you ever goddamn forget that. I have a right to be here.' Rosie moved to the back door, lifting her coat off the hook, putting it round her shoulders. 'I'm going out.'

'Where to, now Jack has gone?'

Rosie turned the handle, opened the door, walked out into the cool of the evening and the fragrance that still hung on the air from the last of the roses. She didn't answer. She didn't know. Jack wasn't there, nor Maisie, nor Lee. What *was* there, without them all?

As she passed the yellow rose she stooped, smelt its scent,

touched its petals, picked it, held it to her cheek. It was soft, fragrant. Some things never changed.

She walked to the rec. She sat on the swings and heard the laughter of their childhood. She leaned against the chains. His hands had held these. She pushed lightly, her feet rocking against the ground. He had to come back. In spite of everything. He was her life. He must see that. He must see that she couldn't have stopped Maisie. One day his mother would have had to live her own life. Or could she have stopped her? Perhaps she could.

She pressed her forehead against the chain, hard, rocking sideways now, crushing the rose, the stem with its thorns, but nothing helped the pain then, or that night or any night, or the anger.

Nothing helped the panic which caught and held her, pushing her up from the bed, making her walk, rubbing her hands up and down her arms at the thought that he might never want to hold her again. He might never want to look at her smile. How could all that love go, so quickly? How could all that love be pushed aside by hate? How could such anger and pain live inside her too?

The next morning she walked to see Mrs Eaves and thought she saw his head amongst the crowd. But it wasn't him and the pain was too sharp and she turned, looked in the tobacconist's window and cried but the tears didn't make anything better.

The store was bright and warm in a world that was cold, empty and dark. Glenn Miller was being played by a girl with neat peroxided hair and Mrs Eaves saw her, waved, took her by the arm to her office. Her keys jangled as she walked. They talked and Rosie cried again and said that Frank was better but Jack had gone. Hating her, loving her, unable to decide.

'But he'll write. I know he will,' Rosie said, watching as Mrs Eaves nodded, pressing out her cigarette in the ashtray which had Margate written on the edge.

'Of course he will, but it'll take time. And if he doesn't it's not the end of the world.'

But it would be. Rosie knew that, though she said nothing.

She did still have her job, though, and they liked the piece she had written about small-town America. Its fears, its guilts. Its hysteria. They edited it down to half and ran it. For a few days that took her mind from the ship that was taking Jack to Korea but for no longer than that. But now at least she would not hope to see him come towards her as she walked to the bus. Now he had gone but he would be back. She had to believe that, she told Mrs Eaves.

She wrote to Frank and Nancy, telling them that Jack had volunteered, that he was on his way.

She didn't tell them that he might never come back to her because she didn't dare to write the words. She loved him in spite of the pain, the anger. She would never love anyone else and all his love couldn't just disappear, could it?

The day she wrote her letter to Frank she received one from them and read it in her lunch break sitting on a bench in the park.

Lower Falls
26 September

Dearest Rosie,

We miss you so much. How are things? Is it sorted out with Maisie? How did Jack take it? You must not think it is your fault. You couldn't babysit the situation for ever, you know. I trust that Jack understands that.

Here's good news anyway. Frank has had details through of the Inchon landings. It seems MacArthur got it right. He came in strong, surprising the North Koreans but had to ride out a typhoon on the way. They had to time it exactly to land during high tide or they would be wading ashore in mud. As it was, some Marines had to do just that as they attacked Wolmi-do which guards the approaches to Inchon.

There were fierce battles as other forces landed on the mainland but they advanced rapidly, as you will know. Those in the South East are on the offensive too.

This success seems to have quietened down the zealots in our area which is a good respite for us both. Frank continues to do well. McCarthy is still stirring things up nationally.

Come back, my dear, whenever you can, whenever you want to. We love you so very much. We miss you. Give our love to Jack. Bring him too. Joe sends his regards to you.

Nancy

Rosie tore it up, dropping it into the bin over by the seats. She didn't want to read about the war, not now, not ever, because Jack would be there soon. She wanted to go back to Frank and Nancy, to their arms and their gentle voices, but not yet. Not until she heard from Jack. He might write. He would write. He might be injured. She must know. She must stay, and fear began, at last, to dull the anger.

In the second week of October, Sam and Ted were buying a record of Frank Sinatra's in Woolworths when they saw her. They came over, laughing, joking. They were older, much older. They were men but Jack was a man too.

'Ollie says he's gone, the daft bugger,' Sam said, his smile wide but his eyes serious.

Rosie took the ribbon the salesgirl handed her. It was blue and wide.

'Yes, he's gone. He is a daft bugger.'

'Ollie says his missus has gone?' Ted was looking at her now. 'Wasn't your fault. Everyone knew. You couldn't stay with her for ever, you know.'

Rosie touched the ribbon. It was soft and cool. Write to Jack, tell him, she wanted to shout but couldn't. She knew now that he must realise that on his own.

'Come up the Palais. It'll be like old times,' Sam said, looking at the ribbon. 'Not your colour,' he added.

They went that night but it wasn't like old times. Sam and Ted drank beer. She drank sherry. It was too sweet. They danced but Sam and Ted met girls they knew and she was one too many but they had been kind and they knew Jack and for a moment it had been good.

At the end of October she received a letter from Nancy telling her of the UN advance in Korea, and how the North Korean forces had crumbled in the face of the UN forces. In the space of a few short weeks the UN had occupied virtually the whole of Korea.

'Frank is worried that MacArthur cannot now be reined in. He might try to end the threat that Communist China poses to American interests in the Far East by not stopping at the frontier. Truman has to insist that this is a "limited action" against a specific Communist act.

'Maybe it will be over by Christmas. If so, Jack won't fight. He won't be there long enough. Keep hoping, my dear.'

The Features Editor had been working her hard. She typed, took shorthand, read the slush pile, wrote short pieces and slowly the career that she had always striven for was within her reach, and that, at least, gave her pleasure, gave her purpose.

She took the letter into the park and read it again. Even though it was cold she brought her lunch here every day. It gave her some peace. An elderly woman sat next to her, eating ham sandwiches. She wondered where the pig had come from. There was almost no bacon or pork left in the country, or so it seemed. She looked at the snoek between her bread. The Government was pushing these tins of fish at a protein-hungry public but the smell made her feel sick. The taste was rank and salty. It had upset her for days. So had the whalemeat which Norah kept for sandwiches. The taste of cod liver oil was too strong.

The old woman saw her looking, smiled, patted her leg and passed her one.

'Thanks,' Rosie said. 'But no. I'm not very hungry.'

But the old woman insisted and she took it and tasted the fresh ham, but she felt the nausea begin again. She waited until the old woman had left the park, then fed it to the birds, watching as they flapped their wings, listening as they squawked.

The next morning she woke early, eased herself from the bed, put on her coat, crept down, heated the kettle, and ate a biscuit, but it didn't work. She rushed to the privy, leaned over the pan, and vomited. She leaned back against the wall, sweat-drenched, cold; the sickness was in her stomach, her throat. She vomited again and again, but quietly. For God's sake be quiet. She pulled the chain to drown the noise.

She dressed, and made bread and marge for her sandwiches, ignoring the snoek tin with its blue fish, ignoring the whalemeat and the cheese. She worked, and came home through the fog which was sulphur thick. Slept. It was the same all that week and the next but there was no letter from him. Still no letter.

There was one from Frank though.

Lower Falls,
1st November

My dear Rosie,

I got it wrong. I thought things were cooling down a bit. I've been pulled up before the Un-American Activities Committee. Interviewed, hectored, treated with contempt, shouted at until I couldn't think straight. It's this Anti-Nazi League thing and because I know a Hollywood screenwriter who's been blacklisted. You know. You met him.

They wanted me to name friends of his and mine that we knew at College. How can they do this? How can people believe all this garbage about good people? He claimed the 5th Amendment. He hasn't worked for four years as far as they know. But he writes for me under another name. They don't know that of course. Thank God. But am I a coward for saying that?

I thought things were improving. I guess they're not. McCarthy is still fuelling the fire with that goddamn bulging briefcase of his which never actually pulls in any 'spies'. Just ruins good folk. Thank God I don't have an employer. I would have been sacked. People think you're guilty if you stay silent. Have they all gone mad to believe this bunch of lunatics? Haven't we just spent years fighting this in Europe?

Have you heard from Jack? Things still seem to be going OK out there. You are our bright spot. My health is OK so don't worry. I'm just mad.

Maybe you can come out for Thanksgiving, or Christmas? The fighting will be over by then, the troops will be home.

Our love always,
Frank

But Rosie couldn't go. Two days later, on 17 November, she fainted as she shopped at Woolworths, and Mrs Eaves took her into the office and pushed her head between her legs.

'When did you last have a period, Rosie?'

She was stroking Rosie's hair, her other hand was on Rosie's wrist. It was a plump hand, like Nancy's, and now Rosie leaned her head against this woman and wept but said it was only the snoek because that had to be the truth.

That afternoon they took two hours off and travelled by

taxi to a doctor that Mrs Eaves knew. There was a brass plate on the wall, polished so that the letters were smoothed almost to flatness. The bell didn't sound outside but a nurse opened the door, showed them upstairs, and gave them magazines to read while they waited on amber-covered chairs.

Mrs Eaves didn't come into the consulting rooms with her. She went alone. There was a large desk, a letter rack, a blotting pad. There was no ink on it. It was white, pure white. The man who rose and shook her hand was Ollie's age. He had a bald head, a moustache, and kind eyes beneath full, bushy brows. How could someone with no hair on their head have so much above their eyes? Rosie wondered, sitting down, feeling too tired to be here. To be anywhere.

'So, we have a problem, eh, Miss Norton?' The man steepled his hands, rested his mouth on his forefingers, pressed his lip up into his moustache.

'I don't know,' said Rosie, bunching her hands inside her coat pockets. She felt nausea rising. She swallowed, watching the signet ring on his little finger.

'Let's have a look shall we?' he smiled, pointing to the back of the room. 'Just leave your petticoat on. The nurse is there waiting.'

She lay still on the couch behind the curtain at the back of the room, looking up at the coved ceiling, feeling strange hands pressing her. She lifted her legs as he asked. She answered his questions, not looking at him. Tracing the crack which wound up the wall, beneath the coving, then on to the ceiling until it was finished. This could not be happening to her. This man wasn't real. The nurse, who would not meet her eyes, wasn't real.

She dressed, and walked to the chair again.

'Well, my dear. You are almost certainly pregnant. We'll run a test, just to confirm, but there's really no need.'

His hands were steepled again. He tapped his teeth this time. She watched that, listened to that. She didn't think of the words which had been in her own mind for six weeks. It wasn't possible. It couldn't be possible. What would she do? For God's sake, what would she do?

She stooped to pick up her bag from the floor. She said nothing. She couldn't speak. There was too much fear.

'There are things that can be done.' The man was playing now with a paperknife, turning it over and over, the light flashing on its blade. He stopped, looked up at her. 'You aren't married?'

Rosie covered her left hand but then said, 'No.' He knew that already. He had called her Miss Norton. Oh God. What would she do?

'How will you support the child?'

She shook her head. Until those words she had not thought of a child, only of the shame.

'I don't know.'

The doctor hesitated, looked at her, then down at the desk. 'I can help but you realise it must be discreet. It would be quick and painless. Not in a seedy room in some dirty street. But it will cost a hundred guineas.'

Rosie thought of the hop-yards, the sticky smell on her hands, the gypsies who brewed potions. The Welsh girl who had drunk some on a hot and heavy night and then screamed in pain all night but smiled for the rest of the picking because there would be no disgrace, not this time.

But Jack had been at the hop-yard, Jack had smiled and held her. Jack had thrust himself inside her on the cold damp moors and she had wanted him. Not like that, not in that way perhaps. But she had wanted him and she loved him, even if he no longer loved her. This child was part of him. She counted the breaths she was taking, they were in time with the clock on the mantelpiece.

'No, thank you.' Rosie stood up, handing him his consultation fee. The movement made her feel faint. She sat again. He came round the desk, put his hand on her shoulder.

'Will the father marry you?'

'I will be quite all right, thank you,' Rosie said, rising, but slowly this time.

She went to the GP. The next week she collected iron tablets from the chemist in her lunch hour and nodded to Mrs Eaves.

'The baby is due at the end of June,' she said quietly.

Mrs Eaves told her she must sit with her feet up and rest as much as she could at work. She must carry nothing heavy, but a shorthand pad wasn't heavy, neither were the articles she had to sift. Mrs Eaves also said she should go back to America but Rosie said she couldn't. Frank and Nancy had enough to worry about and she couldn't face their disappointment, the ending of all their hopes for her.

'How would Jack find me, when he comes home?' she said and wouldn't allow herself to see the doubt in Mrs Eaves's eyes or acknowledge the same doubt herself.

It was at night that the fear grew and cut the breath in her throat, when she was away from the lights of the office and the smiles of the other girls. It was when she was alone that she allowed herself to think of the child that was growing and she didn't know if Norah would let her stay until Jack came back at Christmas. Because she had to believe that he would, just as she had to believe that he would write. Goddamn it, Jack, write. You must write. Because there was still an anger that swept her as well as fear and love and it helped to keep her strong.

In the first week of December Frank wrote with the details of the Chinese assault which had pushed the UN forces back, slaughtering them in the narrow valleys, even though they marched on only a handful of rice. How Mao's men had marched on through the snow, capturing, fighting. How the British Forces had carried out rearguard duties. How brave they had been. Had she heard from Jack? Was he all right? They would not now be home for Christmas.

Rosie went round to Ollie who opened the door, his face setting when he saw her.

'Is he all right?' she asked because there was no place for anger or her own fear. There was only the thought of Jack and Korea.

Ollie looked at her. 'I'll let you know if he isn't.' He shut the door.

That night she fainted as she stood to take her plate to the sink. Her cheese was still on the plate. She hadn't been able to eat. Harold carried her to the armchair by the fire, Grandpa's chair, and Rosie cried, her head down in her hands, because Grandpa wasn't here and neither was Jack. But Norah was, standing in front of her, her stockings rolled down round her ankles, her slippers trodden down at the back.

'You're pregnant, aren't you?' Norah's hands were on her hips.

Rosie wiped her face with the back of her hands and nodded. 'Does that Jack know?'

Rosie shook her head.

'Then you'd better write and tell him.'

'I can't.'

Norah slapped her face then hard, catching Rosie's hair, jerking her head to one side.

'You're a bloody little slut. Why not? Isn't it his? Is it that Joe's?'

Rosie gripped the arms of the chair. She pushed herself back into it, away from Norah who was leaning forward, her face ugly. She would stay in Grandpa's chair, then she would be safe. It would all go away. All of it. It would roll away to the time before all this.

'Go on then, whose is it?' Norah insisted.

'It's Jack's, but I can't tell him. He's left me. He wants to make up his mind whether he loves me. He'd come back if I told him, but I'd never know whether he wanted to.' Rosie reached out her hands. 'Can't you goddamn understand? I love him. I can't do that to him.'

Rosie looked at Harold now. He was kind sometimes but now his face was filled with contempt.

'So you're alone. Lovely little Rosie hasn't anyone to love her. Now you'll know what it's like.' Norah was reaching down, pushing at Rosie, pulling at her, forcing her from the chair. 'I was left with you and Grandpa. I was alone.'

Rosie clutched at her, she felt sick again. 'But Grandpa loved you, and Grandma. You know they did. Grandma most of all. What the hell are you talking about?' Norah was still pushing her out of the kitchen, towards the hall, and Rosie didn't have the strength to stop her.

Norah shouted in her face now, pulling her back, jerking her to a stop. 'But you had the best. You still have. You go to America, you bring back candy. Push it in my face. You little slut. Well, you've got more than you bargained for out of all this love, haven't you? You're an alley cat.' She pushed her towards the foot of the stairs.

Rosie felt her legs growing weak, her head heavy. The blackness was gripping her again. Sweat drenched her body. She clung to the banister, sank on to the stairs.

'Get out by the morning,' Norah hissed, standing above her, watching.

'I can stay as long as I need to,' Rosie said, anger driving the sickness back, but only for a moment. She leaned her head down on her knees. 'Grandpa said.'

'And what do you think Grandpa would say to this bastard you're bringing into the world? You don't think he'd want it in his house, in his neighbourhood. Where it'd bring disgrace. Where his rose growers would know.'

Norah left her, went back into the kitchen, shut the door. There was no light left. Just darkness. And Rosie knew Norah was right. There were too many memories here. There was too much of the past which needed to be guarded for Grandpa. She must go. It was Christmas in three weeks and it was time for her to go. To find some privacy.

CHAPTER 16

The hospital was clean and white and light. And so cool. Jack was eased on to the bed. The pain was all over him now, sweeping, cutting, and he groaned, turned his head, watched the naval nurse as she smiled. Looked at the bag on top of his locker which contained toilet necessities, playing cards, cigarettes and sweets. There was writing paper too.

He looked away. He wouldn't need that. Not to write to Rosie. Not now, not ever. He wouldn't write to Ollie either. Why tell him?

'You'll be going up to theatre soon. There'll just be a small prick now.' The nurse smiled at him again but his lips wouldn't work to smile back.

It was two weeks before the pain left him and then only in snatches in which he watched the ward, heard the clatter of trolleys, the murmur of voices. But then it claimed him again so that he didn't know which was morning, which was afternoon. He didn't know which was night, which was day.

All he knew was that Korea seemed further away than a three-day boat trip. There were no flares, no bugles. There were no screams. There was no Tom. There was no American dying of burns. No American he had to shoot.

But there was the smell of disinfectant, the gentle hands of the nurses who soothed the boy across the way when he groaned, who soothed Jack when he woke screaming from dreams in which he shot the American, again and again, but the flames kept burning, the hand kept reaching out and the face which called to him was Ed's. Yes, Korea was far away and England even further.

But now the times without pain were longer. He watched the clock move round and the nurses with charts, and smiles, and soft voices, and it was all so clean, so ordered. There were no decisions to be made, no questions to be asked except, 'What day is it?'

'It is December eleventh. Now rest.'

Each morning he was a little stronger and each day and night the dreams faded until at last he did not sleep in the day, or cry out at night.

That morning he ate breakfast, biting into crisp toast, and smiled at the boy opposite who smiled back. There had been no groans from him either.

He watched as the doctor did the rounds, first one bed, then the other. The sheets were starched and correctly turned, the pillowcases too. The Sister coughed, the doctor nodded and then they came to him and he felt the tension rise in him. He was better. He knew that. The doctor would know too. He would send him back, into the battle.

The doctor checked his bandage, talked to the Sister, laughed when Jack said he would be ready to do the town by the evening.

'Maybe next month. Maybe,' the doctor said.

Jack touched the bandage, feeling the tension relax, feeling his face smile. Thank God, he would be here for that long at least. He wouldn't be returning to the snow, the cold, the fear. He could stay here where there was no life outside the ward, outside the cool drinks, and the kind nurses, and the ache of his arm.

The Staff Nurse smoothed his sheets as the doctor moved on. 'A little bit longer then,' she said.

'You knew I was frightened?'

'You all feel the same. Why not? I would.'

'Each day,' the boy across the ward shouted, 'there are letters delivered. I bet my girl sends me one.' Jack had written none. He would receive none and so he turned from the Sister who stopped at each bed but his. Everywhere there were letters, three for the boy across the ward. All his had SWALK written round the flap.

Now there was silence as they read them and further silence as the letters were replaced in the envelopes and visions of home came too close.

He had none of that. He had none of their pain. The ache that he felt deep inside wasn't love. He had told himself that. It

627

was anger. There was no love any more. He knew that. He remembered Tom. His wife must know by now.

He watched instead the Japanese flower girl who came to the ward with a trolley heaped with flowers and foliage. She wore bobby sox, and a skirt and blouse, and she almost looked American, but not quite. There was the golden skin, the lowered eyes, the small steps.

He wished that she wore a kimono like the girls he had seen on the way to the hospital. He didn't want anything American in here.

She took flowers and leaves to the central table. Her hands were small and quick. She undid the copper pulley, and lowered the existing arrangement which hung above the ward's central light. He hadn't noticed it before.

She tipped the faded blooms into a basket, emptied the water into a bucket on the trolley, refilled the vase, arranged the flowers, slowly now, and the foliage, then raised the arrangement back up above the light. That night, a small blue spotlight illuminated the flowers and he dreamed of the hopyards and heard the bees, smelt the hops. Then the scent of roses, the scent of the past, filled the air and he woke crying, but he told the Sister it was the pain.

With each day he grew stronger and the nurses began to decorate the wards as Christmas approached. He and Bill from the bed across the way held the ladders while the nurses climbed and pinned streamers and foliage and the other men whistled and cheered.

That night he dreamed of Rosie making streamers because it was 20 December and in the morning he was running a fever and his wound had become infected. He was too ill to notice Christmas, too ill to open the presents forwarded from Ollie; the tie from Maisie, the letter from Lee, the shirt with no card, which he knew was from Rosie.

'I'm too ill,' he shouted to the nurse and pushed them all from the bed, making her take them from the ward, but keeping Ollie's card and the money he sent and looking up at the flowers which glowed throughout the night.

It wasn't until the middle of February that he was able to move to the convalescent ward and now he knew, they all knew, that though the Communists were pushing them back in the centre, the Chinese supply lines were in doubt.

In the west of Korea US and British troops had recaptured the port of Inchon which had been taken when the Communists carried forward their attack. UN troops were also shelling Seoul which was yet again in the hands of the Communists. On the east coast the South Koreans, supported by naval bombardment, had driven up the coastal highway to the 38th parallel.

They all knew this, but they didn't talk about it. They didn't want to remember, nor did they want to go back.

The next week they had a private in who had been injured when the Allied forces took up positions in a twenty-five-mile arc to the south of Seoul. He told them that Communist resistance had stiffened. That the fourth battle for Seoul was about to begin. That he hoped it would be over before he was returned as fit for active service. He was a conscript. He was nineteen. Jack felt old at nearly twenty-one. He didn't want to go back either, but neither did he want to go to England.

The flower girl came to this ward too while letters were delivered and so Jack heaved at the pulley for her with his right hand. His left was still bandaged, still in a sling which dragged at his neck. Each day he pulled it and smiled and they spoke of the coldness of the weather, the beauty of the flowers, and her voice was sometimes harsh as voices were in the Japanese tongue she told him. But her lips were shaped and gentle, her eyes demure and black. And he didn't have to look at the men opening their mail.

They talked of the summer and the sun that would come and she told him of the giant fish fashioned from bamboo and covered with painted cloth which is launched each July by Toyahama fishermen in honour of the ocean gods. She told him how the Japanese people bore gifts of rice to the dead in the graveyards and he thought of Rosie taking roses to her grandpa, but he didn't want to think of her. She was the past. She was where the pain was.

So he listened again to the flower girl, whose name was Suko, and she told him that their language could mean different things, that their symbols had many meanings. How the white dots of flowering plum and the red dots of camellia keep the

629

Japanese winter from ever being quite dead. He should travel to one of the unbombed cities, she said, when he was more able, and search for the outward signs of the Japanese spirit which had survived defeat and Hiroshima and Nagasaki. The spirit which had sought and found peace.

'For, Jack-san, you have need of that spirit,' she said as she lifted each leaf, each petal, and put them into the bag before pushing the trolley from the ward.

Jack did not help her again. He walked down the corridors, into other wards, talking to the men, looking out at the deep snow, sensing the cold which crackled in the air. He had no need of peace. It was the others who struggled and lashed and betrayed.

In March he took a small Japanese cab into the town and the cold was still sharp in the air. He had three weeks' Rest and Recuperation and would return to a hostel each night, the Sister had said, smiling, unless, of course, he found something more pleasurable to do.

'Sort yourself out, soldier,' she said as he stopped and looked back at her. She was Australian, big and kind, but Jack walked away from her and did not look back. There was no room for that sort of pleasure in his life now.

He looked out from the cab windows at the snow which had been pushed from the road and the pavements. He saw the street walkers, the Cadillacs, the Buicks, the American enlisted men who stood in groups on the street corners, chatting to the Japanese girls, kissing them, linking arms. He turned from them.

He paid the cab driver as they pulled up outside the hotel where he was to meet Bill, and was glad that Tom wasn't here to see this wealth amongst the people who had imprisoned him. Glad that Ollie wasn't here because there were no new cars available in England.

He climbed the marble steps, nodded to the Japanese bellhop, walked through to the bar. Bill was there, he was drunk, and there was beer on the counter where he had slopped it. There was a glass chandelier above them, soft music playing, nuts and crisps in bowls on the bar. Whisky lined the wall behind the barmen. There was no hint of a war being played out on their doorstep. Was there any hint in England?

'Let's eat,' Jack said, taking Bill's arm, steering him through the tables where beautiful people sat, staring.

'Don't you know there's a bloody war on?' Jack said to one girl with blonde hair and a wide mouth sitting with an American Captain. Their hands were linked. They both wore wedding rings.

'Sure, honey, but not in here,' she drawled and laughed. 'And not back in Iowa either.'

Bill lurched and Jack steadied him, walking him through, past the Japanese head waiter towards a spare table. There were flowers on the thick white tablecloth. There was an arrangement carved out of ice up near the stage. A band played a selection of Frank Sinatra's songs.

They ate a steak which was tender and rare and rice cooked in saffron and Jack didn't order wine, only water, and watched as Bill ate and then drank, slowly, carefully, and only when his plate was empty did they leave.

Jack drove him back to his room. Put him to bed, sat with him because the boy was laughing, then crying, and it was only when he slept that he returned to his own bed.

The next day he drank beer in the town with Bill, but not much, and then they walked past underwear shops full of GIs buying lingerie for the Japanese girls on their arms. They stopped at a restaurant which smelt of beer and fried fish.

They climbed narrow stairs and sat on large cushions, cross-legged. There were other soldiers there, laughing, drinking. There were geishas with white corn-starched faces and sticky hair who danced with them when they had eaten the fish which the chef had cooked in a deep pan of oil, swishing it round with long chopsticks.

The Sergeant who sat at the end told them that these girls were 'after the war' geishas who were not trained but who bought a kimono and pretended for the Americans.

Jack left then. He wanted nothing that the Americans sought or had possessed.

He borrowed a jeep the next afternoon and drove to the address that the Australian sister had given him when he called on her first thing that morning. She had kissed him on the cheek too, saying again, 'Just sort yourself out.'

As he drove he looked at the paddy fields pressed up against the tarmac, seeing through the thawed and muddy snow that every space had been cultivated, even the tiny gap between the ditch and a filling station where GIs were buying petrol for their jeep which was full of Japanese girls. He remembered Suko saying that there were too many people and not enough land.

There were no straggling copses, no hedges. In Japan, Suko had said, there were only disciplined, trained trees. There was no space for wanton growth. He passed small paper-windowed houses which soon became jammed together as he approached a village which was more like a town. They were jammed too tightly for fields, too tightly even to breathe it seemed. There were people walking, so many people. As the road narrowed and the houses took the light from the street he looked at the piece of paper in his hand. He stopped the jeep. He asked directions of an old man dressed in black, slowly, in English.

The man pointed. 'Leave jeep. Walk. Ask. Police.'

Jack did, passing tiny shops with paper doors, all with lights which shone through the paper, out into the street. There was a police box on the corner. Jack asked again.

'Keep on. Don't turn. It on right.'

Children ran past in quilted coats, shrieking, laughing. Was Lee doing that in the cold of America?

There were restaurants on either side of the narrow alleys he walked along. One opened on to the street, revealing people eating fish at small tables. So many people and they were all so small, like Suko.

He was there now. He stopped but the door was paper. How did he knock? He couldn't so he called out instead, 'Suko, it's Jack.' He waited, then called again. 'Suko. It's Jack. I've been rude. I ran away from you. In the ward. I'm sorry. I've come to say I'm sorry.'

The door slid back, and Suko was standing there in a kimono, not bobby sox. Her blue-black hair was pulled back. She bowed, three times.

'Jack-san, this is an honour.' She stood to one side. 'Please put your shoes here.' She pointed to the left of the door.

Jack stopped, looked at her. She wore no shoes. There was a Shinto shrine in the room. He stooped, unlaced his boots, placed them next to hers and entered.

He felt too big, too white. He nodded at the old lady who came forward and bowed. He bowed too. Christ, he was so *big*.

They sat on tatami cushions and his ankles hurt as he crossed his legs. Suko laughed, then covered her mouth with her hand.

'You will eat with us?'

Jack nodded and watched the old woman cut each item carefully. The brazier exuded heat, the charcoal had a sweet smell. She tossed and turned the fish and the vegetables, and Jack could find little to say, but Suko didn't speak either. They both watched her grandmother.

They ate with chopsticks and Jack was awkward and clumsy but no one laughed and so he tried again and it was good.

'Perhaps you would come with me tomorrow to find that unbombed town?' Jack said, but Suko shook her head.

'No, Jack-san, that is for you alone. But I take you to see Japan. I take you to puppets, to Osaka with its canals. I take you to the theatre.'

Her voice was soft but the harshness was still there. It always would be. Was there still that faint drawl in Rosie's voice? But what did it matter? She meant nothing to him now.

The next day they drove to Osaka and then along the roads where the piled up snow was melting. Men trudged up and down alleys with wicker baskets on their back. Women passed with babies strapped to their backs. An old battered car passed with Japanese bobbysoxers singing.

What would Tom think?

The next day they watched a puppet show where the Punch and Judy he had remembered from Southend paled into insignificance. These puppets were life-size with their puppeteers alongside, visible. There was no laughter, only tears. No farce, only tragedy, and Jack sat back and waited to be bored. But Suko sat still beside him, her golden skin smooth and pure, and soon the puppets took over the puppeteers and became savage, harsh, too strong, and Jack clenched his hands and believed.

They ate at a restaurant and Suko smiled and nodded and her hands were as delicate with the chopsticks as they had been with the flowers.

As they drove back alongside the fields she told him that in the spring the farmers would pull harrows and the women would dig, then sow. She told him how the farmers had always sold their daughters, in order to have fewer mouths to feed, in order to survive.

'Where are *your* parents?' he asked.

'They were in Nagasaki,' she said. 'They did not survive.'

Jack didn't visit Suko for a week. He didn't know what to say, what to do, but when he called outside her house again she slid back the door and smiled, took him in, gave him green tea. As they sat cross-legged on the floor he said, 'I'm sorry. I couldn't come. I didn't know what to say about your parents.'

Suko nodded. 'I know. One day you will be able to face pain, even that of others. For now you cannot. You must wait.' That was all.

They drove to the theatre, where actors took over the role of the puppets, and Jack listened to Suko explaining as they roared and laughed and cried that the message of this play was blind loyalty, whatever cruel and bloody acts this might require.

Jack watched the disembowelling and could not understand the pleasure it gave the audience, the pleasure it gave Suko. He watched the dancing and was glad when they returned to her small house, away from the colour of the pageant, away from the turbulence, and as he drew up to her house he turned and kissed her mouth. It was soft, small, and so was the body he held and stroked, and so was the hand which smoothed his hair and touched his lips and brought feeling back into his life.

'I've only one week left,' he breathed into her hair.

'You will come tomorrow and we will love,' she said.

Suko's grandmother was not there in the house when he arrived and Suko led him into the room, holding his hand in hers, not kissing him, not allowing him to kiss her.

'Not yet, Jack-san. You are in Nippon now. You must be slow. You must take time.'

He sat down on the cushions and she smiled and bowed, then left the room, and he watched her move with her short steps, one in front of the other. He watched the neatness of her body and wouldn't think of Rosie. She was dead to him now. The ache in his heart was anger, not love.

He drank the saki that Suko had left, first one glass and then another, and then another until there was softness in the room and an easing of his body.

It was then she called.

'Jack-san.'

He rose, his mouth dry, and walked into a small room which was filled with steam from a bath in the centre and the damp heat smothered him, but she was there too, in a white bathrobe, beads of sweat on her face, on her neck, beads which ran down on to her breasts.

She undid his buttons, slipped his clothes from his body, washed him down with soap, her hands gentle, probing, and he wanted her but she kissed his mouth, then pointed towards the bath. He climbed into the water which was almost scalding.

She rubbed his back with soft bark and it was as though there had been no past, there would be no future. There was only the present.

He rose from the water and slid her bathrobe from her shoulders, letting it fall from her body, and the heat he felt was not from the steam, but from within. She was golden, soft and smooth. So small. So very small.

He held her to him, wetting her, kissing her, tasting her sweat, tasting his on her. Then he carried her out into the room where the futon was already laid on the floor, and there, in the heat and smell and the light of the charcoal fire, he made love to her, gently, softly and then with a passion which swept him from the paper house to the cold hillside in Yorkshire, and when he cried he knew why, but he pushed his knowledge away.

He was to spend his last days at Suko's house, she told him. Her grandmother was not there. She had left because Suko asked her to, she told Jack at dawn as they sipped tea from the cups without handles.

'For us to be together, Jack-san,' she said, then set her cup down, took his from him, and they made love again, and again.

Suko worked each morning and wouldn't stay in the village with him.

'I make the flowers bring joy. It is my peace, Jack-san,' she said, her eyes lowered as she stood before him. 'You go to your friends. You return at night.'

635

Jack drove again to the theatre, walking over the bridge, looking down into a stream with ice clusters at the edge. He looked back down the path. There were cherry trees.

An old man stopped. 'In the spring the blossom blooms. Life begins again.'

Jack nodded and made himself walk into the theatre. He sat and listened and shrank from this culture which was Suko's.

They made love that night and the next and there was nothing that was savage, only everything that was gentle. They had four nights left and he whispered that he would come back when the war was over. He would never leave her.

'You're so beautiful.'

Jack held her, feeling her slightness against him, seeing the blackness of her hair against the pillow. She shook her head, then told him of her childhood, of her life with her grandmother as the bombs rained down. She told him of the American who had come with the occupying forces and he stiffened. He could smell the charcoal, feel its heat.

She kissed his mouth. 'I loved him. He loved me. He went back. He died on a plane which crashed as he landed. I loved him. I will always love him. You love someone. You will always love them. We find comfort with each other, that is all, Jack-san. You will not come back to me.'

He was standing now, standing over her, seeing her golden skin against the futon. Had her American seen her like this?

'Has he?' he screamed at her.

She stood now. 'Come and lie with me. We are happy together because we both have a heart which belongs to another. We give comfort.'

She was stroking him now. 'We give comfort, Jack-san. We cast the shadows from our lives for a while, the pain deep inside is soothed.'

He felt her hands, her lips on his chest, his belly, his thighs and knew why he had been back to the theatre. It was there, watching the Kabuki, watching the warrior, his face contorted, his limbs stiff and cruel, that he had recognised the savagery that was in his own heart.

The next day he travelled to Kanazawa, where there was no sign of bombing, where it was as it had stood for centuries. He walked. He stood and looked at the mossy stillness behind an ancient wall. Children were laughing and playing in the distance but he barely heard them.

He walked on to a cottage, and stood in the doorway as a peasant bowed. He smelt the sweetness of the rush matting, and saw the white of an early-flowering plum set as a symbol of stillness in a world which was mad.

He walked in the garden which nestled against the base of the eastern hill. It was walled, self-contained, still. There was an ordered stream, a bridge and no wind stirred.

He could smell again the hops, see the bines, trace the initials on the gate with his fingers. He could see Rosie.

He drove back to the village, back to Suko, back to her arms and her bed and she held him as he slept and that night it was as though he was a child again and the next night, and the next.

He flew back on Monday. His shoulder was stiff but what did that matter? He strapped himself into the bucket seat. All around was the smell of the disinfectant that had been sprayed on the plane's arrival. He clutched the seat belt as the engine roared, swallowed as the plane clawed through the sky. He looked down at the Straits of Korea, and thought of Suko, her body, her sweetness. He thought of the hills he was returning to and then the hills where the bines grew. He had a letter to write.

He looked at the sea again, and heard a distant echo of Chinese bugles.

CHAPTER 17

Norah did not say goodbye the morning Rosie left but Harold came to the end of the yard while Norah dressed in the bedroom. He took Rosie's arm and told her that he would forward any mail if she let him know her address. He gave her two pounds towards her fares.

She took it, kissed his cheek, remembered Butlins and told him that he must keep on with his brass rubbing.

'You mustn't let her take that away from you.'

Now, as she walked to Woolworths, she remembered how Grandma had tried to stop Grandpa's visits to the Rose Club, how Norah had tried to cut down his rose bushes. She dropped her cases and ran back, down the street, down the back alley, into the yard, into the kitchen. Harold was packing his rubbing wax into a grip. He wore cycle clips.

'Harold, what about the roses? Can you stop her?' Rosie was holding the door. She felt the nausea rise but she wouldn't be sick. Not here, not now.

He did up the buckles on the bag, walked to the doorway, then into the yard, strapping his bag to the back of his bike, looking round at the roses then back at her.

'I think so. I like them too. Don't worry. I'll think of something.'

He nodded, pushed his bike out into the alley, stopped, looked back.

'I don't agree with what you've done. With the baby and all that. It's a disgrace. But good luck.' He mounted the bike, then nodded towards Ollie. 'Don't worry. We won't tell him. Norah doesn't want anybody to know.'

He was off then, and Rosie left, looking back, remembering Grandpa shelling peas, his big fingers pushing their way up the pod, her small ones too. And Jack's hands taking five, throwing them up into his mouth. For a moment she could smell Maisie's bread and dripping and hear the echoes of the past.

At the store Mrs Eaves wanted to come with her to look for a bedsit but Rosie shook her head.

'No, I must do it alone but would you ring my office, please? Just tell them I'm ill and I'll be in tomorrow.'

She left her bags though, then caught a bus to Soho because that was where she had been with Jack. That was where the music still played, where there was still hope, warmth. It was a place where she would not be judged as she would be elsewhere, down each street, in each shop.

On the bus she felt sick, she felt alone, because Jack had always been with her before. She took slow breaths, pushing her hands against her mouth, feeling the clammy sweat on her forehead, the cold which swept through her before the vomit. She pushed herself from her seat, out on to the platform, ringing the bell, stepping off, ignoring the shouts from the clippie. She walked into a side street, and leaned against the wall, breathing, counting till at last it passed.

She caught another bus and this time the nausea did not reappear. She walked down Berwick Street where they were putting out the rubbish from the restaurants. She stopped, asked if they knew of any accommodation. They shook their heads.

It was so different in the day. There was no music sweeping out of the cellars, no tarts touting for custom. Instead they were collecting the milk from their doorsteps along with old ladies doing the same. She passed the baker's where people were queuing for their morning bread and barbers who were already open, already snipping.

A violinist played in the alley which connected the two street markets. A man stood opposite shouting that Jesus Saves. He grabbed at her arm, pushed a leaflet into her hand. She dropped it like others had done amongst the rotting vegetables and the woodshavings. She walked along the stalls, listening to the woman in a headscarf shouting.

'Christmas is coming, the goose is getting fat, but what about bleeding me if you don't buy me spuds?' The woman was digging into the money pocket of her apron, she wore fingerless gloves, her skin was shiny from the coins, her nails dirty, and

Rosie turned away. Jack had been able to charm the birds out of the bleeding trees, one woman had said.

She walked along the dirty streets, climbing steps to the peeling front doors of four-storeyed houses, knocking on doors but always there were no rooms. She stopped and had Camp coffee in a café. The teaspoon was chained to the counter. The sugar was clumped on the spoon. It was warm, it was sweet. What more did she need?

She walked in the other direction. It was lunchtime, the pubs were open. Music came from them and laughter. A newspaper seller was packing up for the day.

Rosie was hungry, tired, but she had nowhere to sleep for the night. She walked on past a newspaper shop. There were advertisements in the window. One was for a room to let. She wrote down the address, asked in the shop for directions.

'Just down the road. Second on the left,' the man said, serving a Cypriot with a packet of pipe cleaners.

She found it. Climbed the steps which were crumbling at the edges. There was a basement beneath her, a blanket strung up on a string. The courtyard smelt of tomcat. There were three dustbins. She looked away towards the door which was opening.

A small woman stood there, with neat hair, neat clothes and a smile which she flicked at Rosie when she asked to see the room.

They climbed the brown-painted stairs to a room on the top floor at the rear that looked out over the backs of other houses, pubs, and clubs. But she could see the sky. She took it.

Mrs Eaves came back with her to carry her bags. It was cold and dark as they left the bus but now music was soaring from the basements, castanets from one, swing from another, and Rosie smiled. They used the key that the woman had given her. The light went out before they reached the first landing and they switched it on again but again it went out before they reached her room. Rosie laughed. Mrs Eaves didn't.

'Come to us, Rosie. Please. You can't stay here. You might fall. Does she know about the baby?' She dropped her voice to a whisper.

Rosie felt the laugh die. 'No.'

Mrs Eaves put down the cases while Rosie unlocked the

640

door. 'Well, she said no children on the card. She might throw you out when it begins to show. Come to me then.'

Rosie nodded, but she wouldn't. She was alone now. She would be alone until Jack came back.

There was only a forty-watt bulb in the light and no shade. There was one blanket on the bed but Rosie had brought her jumper-blankets, and her own sheets.

There was a sink and a wooden draining board that was sticky with other people's soap and mess. There was a gas ring and a gas fire which Mrs Eaves tried to light, but the meter had run out. They put money in and it plopped as Rosie held the match to it, flaring blue, then yellow. Its hissing filled the room. There was a table covered in oilcloth, only one chair.

Mrs Eaves took her to an Italian café for tea. She knew the owner and his wife. They had met in the war when she had come here with her GI.

They ate baked beans and chips but could smell nothing but coffee. There were onions hanging against the pine-covered walls but Rosie wouldn't let herself think of Jack and the onion seller in the pub. The other tables were full. Young men with scarves trailing on the floor, wearing old coats, laughing, talking, flicking out rhythms on the tables, talking jazz.

There was a phone on the wall. It rang. The small Italian who had served them threw his teacloth over his shoulder, grabbed the receiver, and, waving his hands in the air, shouted across the room.

'Luke, for you again. You give them my number. Always my number. You all give them my number. I try to feed you. How can I when you make me your office too?' He dropped the receiver, it swung on its wire.

Mrs Eaves laughed and called across, 'Just the same, Mario, eh?'

'Worse, Anne. Much worse.' Mario was shaking his head.

'You need more help.'

'I know, I know. You'll come then, Anne?' He laughed, and walked through to the back.

Rosie moved the Worcester sauce and the salt and pepper into a neat line.

'Everyone is so young,' she said, looking round, moving the sauce bottle behind the pepper then back again.

641

'You're young, Rosie.' Mrs Eaves's hand was plump and warm and Rosie clung to her for a moment and then sat back, watching Luke at the telephone, laughing, putting his thumbs up to his friends at the table.

'We got the gig. Five pounds!'

They cheered.

'Not any more,' Rosie said, touching her stomach.

That night as she lay in the room, moonlight came in through the gap in the curtains which didn't meet. She listened to the noise of the house, the banging doors, the shouting from the room next-door. There was a smell of cabbage everywhere.

She pulled the blankets around her head. The bed was damp. She was alone. But at least she had her job and that would enable her to go forward, to carve out a future for herself and the baby.

There were shadows as clouds passed in front of the moon. There was the faint sound of a trumpet and she thought of his arms around her, holding her. She ran her own hands across her shoulders, held her arms, pretended they were his hands.

The next morning she took the bus back to Middle Street and left her address with Ollie and with Harold, then rushed in to work, travelling back to Soho in the evening. She wrote to Nancy and Frank, telling them she had found a place of her own, giving them her address, telling them she wanted her freedom, telling them she was happy. They mustn't know of the baby. They would be worried and they had enough.

At eleven the next morning, the Editor called her into the office to offer her the job of Assistant Features Editor. Rosie felt the sudden thrill of success, the pleasure which those words brought, but she knew, clasping the arms of the chair, that she would have to tell the elegant woman in front of her that she was pregnant.

'Will it matter, Miss Stephens?' she asked.

It did matter. She was sacked on the spot and told to take her things from her desk and leave at once.

She did. She packed her shorthand pad and her pencils and walked out of the office and it was not until she was walking in and out of the Soho shops, asking for work, that she really believed that her future had been snatched from her and she had to lean against a pub wall and turn her face to the bricks, because it was all too much.

It seemed hours that she stood there, but it was only minutes. Then a man came up and asked her for sixpence for a cup of tea and she dragged one out of her purse, and gave it to him. He was dirty and old. At least, she thought, she was young, and so she pushed herself away from the wall, repeating that to herself.

She asked in more shops, more pubs for a job.

'We need a washer-upper,' said a man with a moustache, flicking his ash on to the floor. 'You'd need to clean the lavs too.'

She said she'd call back. She walked and asked again, crossing Archer Street where musicians were gathered outside the doorways of the agents' and managements' offices.

She stopped outside the Italian café where it was warm and clean and light. It was lunchtime. There was jazz oozing out of a cellar two houses away. She listened, holding the icy railing, putting her hand to her mouth, pushing back the nausea.

The café was full. She pushed through to the counter. Luke was there again, buying coffee for three tables, laughing, throwing shillings on to the counter.

'And one for this girl too,' he shouted to Mario, nodding at Rosie, who flushed. He smiled and she wanted to say, you might not want to, I'm pregnant. But she didn't because there was warmth in his look and in Mario's as he wiped the counter and winked at her.

'I don't know. A bit of success. It goes to their heads.'

Rosie nodded, taking the coffee. 'Thanks.'

She sat by herself on the bench near the counter, watching the ebb and flow of the young men, and young girls. She couldn't join in. She wasn't young any more. How could you be young if you were pregnant? She remembered the contempt in Harold's eyes and in Miss Stephens's too.

Luke sat with the others, then stood up, raising his coffee.

'First gig tomorrow. First bloody gig.' He was laughing, waving to the others at his table to stand. They did. There was a girl with them, long-haired. She hugged a boy with a beard and he kissed her on the mouth and Rosie turned away, burning her tongue on the hot coffee, but it didn't matter.

643

She ordered toast but with no butter. It made her retch. Mario looked up at her.

'Can you wait? We're so busy. It gets worse and worse. You no want a job?'

She did want a job but she leaned across and said, 'Yes, I need a job. But I'm – '

Mario interrupted. 'I know. Mrs Eaves tell me. I no mind. My wife no mind. You come. She say you good worker. I trust her.'

Rosie looked down at the sugar clumped on the spoon. Jack had trusted a lot of people.

She started work on the spot. She walked through the streamers into the back room piled high with old tables and boxes. On into the kitchen where Mrs Orsini smiled at her, her eyes sweeping down her body.

No, it doesn't show yet, Rosie wanted to scream at her, her face rigid as she looked at the small fat woman, not lowering her glance, though she wanted to.

'Oh, these things happen,' Mrs Orsini said. 'Mrs Eaves, she tell us you are a good girl. You love this man. He leave you.' Her arms were folded, she leaned against the table piled high with rolls. Toast was grilling, spaghetti simmering in a large pan.

'No,' Rosie said as she hung her coat up on the hook along the wall and washed her hands, scrubbing them hard, and then scrubbing them again. 'No, he hasn't left me. He's gone to Korea. He'll come back. He'll write. I know he will.' There were tears running down her face but they didn't reach her voice. That was calm, but not calm enough, for Mrs Orsini held her, patting her back while Mario called from beyond the swing door.

'Where my spaghetti bolognese? You women. Where my spaghetti?'

Rosie wrote to Nancy and Frank that evening when the café had closed and she had made tea in her room, that she had taken a job as manageress of a restaurant and that she would freelance for the magazine.

She walked to the window, pushing up the bottom sash, listening to the jazz, to the shouting, to the drunken singing. Her legs ached, her back ached but she had a room of her own and a job. At least for now, she was all right. She wouldn't look into the future, there was no point.

On 20 December she heard from Frank and Nancy.

Lower Falls
December 1950

Dearest Rosie,

Have you heard anything from Jack? We worry about him.

It's been so cold out there. The frost was 45 at its worst. Rearguard duties fell to the new British brigade just arrived in Korea. That would be Jack.

Over here it is cold too. Joe has suggested that Frank writes under a pseudonym. We are losing readers. The reversal in Korea will not help. McCarthy is shouting louder each day. Our Local Administrator has an alarmingly large chest filled with importance. I just hate him.

Let us know your news about Jack. Let us know how the new job is going. It must be good for you to give up the magazine. We understand that you can't leave right now but come when you can. Frank is fit. He's fighting back. He's angry but not strained, if you know what I mean.

All our love darling girl.
Nancy

PS. The enclosed $40 is your Christmas present. It comes with love.

Rosie went into the café early that day and Mario nodded as she asked him about the decorations. She cut strips, coloured them, stuck them and wouldn't think of the fighting. Mrs Orsini helped and it was almost like being with Maisie again. They pinned them up. Customers came in and helped. Luke held her waist, steadying her beneath the holly which Mario had rushed out and bought in the market.

They drank coffee, and ate toast and omelette in the kitchen when the lunchtime rush was over, and Rosie walked to the post office for Mario at three in the afternoon, looking at the people walking past. Looking at the market traders shouting, dipping their hands into their aprons. The religious man pushed another leaflet into her hands and she turned.

'Don't you know there's a goddamn war on in Korea? Tell them all about that instead of pushing paper in people's faces.'

He turned from her, thrusting his leaflet at an old man. She grabbed him. 'There's a war on and nobody cares. Go on, get your mouth round that.'

But he pulled from her and she dropped the letters. An old man helped her pick them up. They were dirty and she was crying, standing in the street crying. The old man patted her hand and walked away. Everyone walked away in the end.

But then Luke came with Sandy, the girl with the long hair, and they walked back with her to the café, and then on home because the tears would not stop, because the world wouldn't stop either. Because life was too difficult.

She lay on the bed, and felt pain sweep across her back, and then her belly. She breathed slowly, and watched Luke boil the kettle on the ring and Sandy put tea into the pot, smelling it brewing, watching the milk being poured from the bottle, and the pain was still there and she was wet between the legs.

They called a doctor. He came and asked what she had taken. Luke held her hand as she thought of the consultant and his brass plate, his hundred-guinea offer. She thought of the gypsies and their brew and knew she might be losing the baby. All this could be over. She looked round the bedsit. She could go to America. She could stay here. Anything. She could be as young as Luke again and free.

Luke was squeezing her hand. It should have been Jack but he had gone, though her love for him had not. It never would. She turned to the doctor, who was standing over her. No one was taking the baby from her. No one had taken her career. She had done that. She had become pregnant. No one had taken Jack. She had helped to bring that about. It was time she got angry. It was time she began fighting again. It was goddamn time.

'I fell. This baby's part of Jack. It's all I've got of him. Just do your goddamn job. Please.'

Luke squeezed her hand again and Sandy smiled but the pain was too bad. She watched as Luke went to phone for an ambulance from the box on the corner, digging into his pockets for pennies, then looking in her purse. The doctor had to give them the money in the end.

She was in hospital, there were more doctors. There was Mrs Orsini and Mrs Eaves and there were days of rest when Christmas came and went and there was no card from Jack, though she had sent a present to Ollie for him back in November. But she wouldn't grieve because she was back in there, fighting.

In January she was back in Soho and Mrs Eaves and Mrs Orsini had put flowers in the room, and the baby was still inside her. She was fit, the doctor said, but mustn't leap over windmills. She had laughed because for now the world was good. Her baby was alive. She was alive and so was Jack because no telegram had come to Ollie.

There was a letter from Frank and Nancy when she got back to her room, and she returned to work knowing that the Chinese offensive had been halted. The United Nations were on the attack, but no one else that she passed seemed to care.

She served coffee, cooked, smiled, and laughed when Mario pushed a chair beneath her as she cut up the vegetables and asked if she had taken her iron today.

'And what about that soldier?'

He banged the pans when she shook her head.

Luke and Sandy made her sit too when she went out with them on a January evening to hear Luke's band's first gig and the warmth of these people made it seem as though the sun was shining through the fog which drifted and froze on the paintwork.

They sat at candle-lit tables in the basement of Chloe's and Sandy pushed her long hair back from her face, as Luke and the band worked their way down through the tables to the small stage.

'They've worked hard for this, all of them.' Her nail varnish was black. It was chipped. She was smoking in quick sharp bursts.

'Are they good?' Rosie asked.

Sandy smiled. 'You wouldn't know about jazz, I suppose. But yes, they're good.'

It was becoming crowded now. Rosie moved her chair closer to Sandy as a young man squeezed another round the table. Sandy was stubbing her cigarette out in the ashtray.

'It's hard, though, for them. They have to work too *and* fit this in. They need more time to practise. They need a place to practise. The flat's too small. The landlord doesn't like it.'

Rosie bought a beer for Sandy, a lemonade for herself from the girl behind the bar. But then the band was playing and Luke blew a trumpet as Uncle Bob had always dreamed. He explored the middle range, digging out melancholic tones, drawing pictures in the air, dredging feelings out of each person who sat and listened.

His eyes were closed, his foot tapped. He blew bends which broke her heart, he played a break while the others rested, improvising, soaring, growling, the sound beginning in his throat and forcing itself up through the instrument and out into the tone of the note. She smelt the steak on Frank's barbecue, saw Uncle Bob moving towards his band and had to turn from Sandy because of the tears in her eyes.

Luke played, Stan and Jim too, the clarinet and the trombone picking up the rhythm, Jake on the saxophone sliding in but he needed to be more mellow, throaty. She made herself listen again, watching the group through the spiralling cigarette smoke from the young man next to her.

Dave played block chords on the piano which was effective in small doses, but Dave knew that, she could tell, because he used it sparingly. Luke played a solo.

'Maybe he improvises too much,' Rosie said to Sandy, who looked at her through the hair which had swung back across her face.

Yes, Jack would think so, Rosie thought, because he liked Duke Ellington. Did he still?

When they broke for a beer and the clapping had died she spoke to Luke, telling him that she thought he used too much verbal agreement on the arrangements. 'It needs to be written out at this stage. It would be smoother, clearer.' And Jake, on the saxophone, needed improving. But the band was good, very good.

She felt the excitement rise in her as Luke looked at her and nodded.

'You know about jazz, don't you?'

'Yes, Frank taught me. Uncle Bob too. And Jack.'

She looked round as the band left to play another set. The excitement was there in everyone. One day they would be good enough for Bob, she'd make sure of that, but there was a great deal to be done before then.

The next day she poured Luke a coffee, Sandy too, as they came in for their lunch, and then she talked to Mario in the kitchen about the back room. She pointed to the packing cases, to the tables, to the extra space that could be used to bring in customers. She spoke to him about a Jazz Night where the bands could practise in front of an audience who would buy coffee and food.

Mario shook his head but Mrs Orsini nodded, slapping him on the back.

'Why not? Rosie knows what she's doing. That young Luke. He is good, is he not? You will hear all bands and decide. OK.' Mrs Orsini looked at Rosie and then at Mario who spread his hands wide.

'I will go upstairs when it starts. I will lie with my head beneath pillow. You are satisfied?'

'Not quite,' said Rosie, putting the dishes in the sink, talking as she washed. 'The boys are getting calls. They are being taken for a ride. They play for too little money. I want to take the calls for them, act as their manager, their agent. If they agree.' She turned.

'So you want to set up another business. Why not? They use my phone already, why not my staff? You would like a small dance floor. You would like me to swing from the ceiling in a tutu?'

Rosie laughed and so did Mrs Orsini.

'Yes, why not?' Mario said. 'For once there is a light in your eyes. Your Jack should see that. And don't forget you have clinic appointment this afternoon.'

Rosie went along. The nausea had almost stopped. There were mothers with young children in the waiting room. They clung to their mothers' legs as Lee had clung to hers and Jack's. As she had clung to Grandpa. She had forgotten that. She smiled at a blonde child and then at the mother, who looked away and tutted.

She was given iron by the doctor and told by the nurse it would be sensible to wear a curtain ring. Her voice was cold, correct. She gave Rosie details of a Home for Unmarried Mothers.

Rosie bought a ring from Woolworths. She went back to her room, climbed the stairs, breathed in the cabbage. Her legs ached, her back ached, but there was still the jazz.

She stood at the window. The sky was grey, full of snow. There would be snow on the mountains of Korea and he hadn't written. She lay on the bed. It was cold. He still hadn't written. She pushed the ring on to her finger. God damn you, my darling love.

She didn't go into work again that day. She lay on her bed but didn't sleep. All she could see and feel were his arms, his lips, his smiling eyes. All she knew was that she loved him. That night she allowed herself to cry, but only that night because she had his child to work for, to protect. A child who would put his arms around her legs. A child she had not pictured until today.

The next day Mario, Luke and the boys turned out the back room, and set up the tables while she and Mrs Orsini wiped the tables, chairs, the walls that she could reach without stretching. Luke would do anything high.

She stood behind the counter and served coffee and tea and food, listening all the time to the banging, the heaving, telling the customers that Thursday was to be a regular Jazz Night. The playing was free, she said, smiling, but the refreshments were not.

Over thirty came the first night and as people left at midnight a man approached Luke to play a gig at Chertsey on 1 March and offered him five pounds. Luke beckoned to Rosie.

'You'd better talk to my manager, Rosie Norton.'

The man smiled. 'Well, Mrs Norton, I'm Tom O'Toole. So, you manage these boys. Strange job for a woman, isn't it?'

Rosie brought out her drawl. 'It runs in the family. You might have heard of Bob Wallen from Pennsylvania.' She didn't wait for him to acknowledge the name which he might or might not have known. 'These boys can't work for that sort of money. Not now. They were offered twice that last week. I turned it down.'

She waved at Mr Orsini.

'Mr Orsini has had to pay ten pounds tonight and he got them for that because I know him well.'

She nodded to Mr O'Toole.

'Give me a ring sometime. On this number.' She handed him a card. 'But I can't stop now. I have to arrange their itinerary with them. Nice meeting with you.'

She shook his hand, and walked past him to Luke and Mario, gathering the boys around her until Jake said, 'He's gone. You've lost us five pounds.' He was smoking grass and she took it from him, and ground it into the floor, taking him to one side. Her back hurt, her legs ached, she had served coffee until the steam had dampened her hair, until she could stand the ringing of the cash register no longer. She was angry.

'If you ever smoke that goddamn stuff in here again you're out.'

'You don't own us.' Jake's head was down, his shoulders hunched, and it was like Sam again in the rec when she had first come home, but this time there was no Jack to stand by her. This time she was alone but it didn't matter, she was still angry.

Rosie looked round, called Luke over. 'He's smoking grass in here. Mario's been good to us. He could be in trouble. I've told him he's not to do it again or he's out. This is your band. Your decision. But if you want to play here again, smoking is out. Right?'

They had no choice. She knew that. They couldn't practise anywhere else. Luke took Jake to one side. She waited. She saw Luke pat Jake on the shoulder then look round and nod. She smiled, and she knew that there would be good days and bad days, but for now, she was strong enough to carry herself through.

'He'll be back. Don't worry. He'll phone. I know he will.'

He phoned back in March when her skirt was too tight to be done up any more. He offered the band twelve pounds to play in Surbiton, expenses on top of that, and so one night Rosie asked Luke to stay late at the café and told him that they must practise much harder. They were in the real world now. They could go on, even to the US, but there was a great deal of work to be done.

She told him that he should write out more arrangements, then maybe he should try the cornet. Luke agreed, kissed her cheek, said he was sending another band along to see her.

The next day the baby moved, for the first time, and a call

came through from Stone's Club near Birmingham. She talked the fee up to fourteen pounds and now she took a ten per cent cut which the band agreed was really not enough, but she wouldn't take more.

That night she wrote to Frank and Nancy and told them of Luke, glad that at least there was one lie less. But as she sat in front of the gas fire which plopped and hissed, the room seemed empty and bare. There had been no letter from the father of the child that had fluttered inside her and no one to share her pleasure.

CHAPTER 18

A truck took Jack straight towards the North. The enemy were in flight, the Sergeant told him and the twenty others who sat either side of the vehicle, lurching and bouncing past refugees and burnt-out tanks from the earlier United Nations retreat.

Jack leaned on his rifle, looking out at the snow which still covered the rice fields. He would write when he arrived. He would tell Rosie that he loved her, that he always had and always would. That he was coming home, when this was over.

'Shouldn't be long before we're home then, Sarge?' he called out to Sergeant Rivers.

'Who knows? Let's hope you're right,' the Sergeant answered.

They travelled for hours jolting along in the wake of the enemy, passing supply trucks returning empty from the forward positions. There were ambulances, too, but they didn't look at those. Jack flexed his shoulder. It was stiff but that was all. He looked out again at the hills splashed with snow. He wouldn't think of Tom either. He had to get home to Rosie.

He lit a cigarette, the match flame was fierce in the cold. He lit Bert's too, then tossed the box along to the Sergeant. There was a heavy smell of sulphur. He and Rosie would go to the hop-yards when he returned. He drew on his cigarette, jigging his feet to keep warm. Christ, it was cold. But it would be cold for the Chinese too.

They reached camp, leaping down and moving in single file off up the track to Hill 81, hearing the revving of the truck, the grinding of gears as it reversed then turned, leaving them, heading back to Pusan to pick up more troops, more supplies.

'Get on up that hill,' the Sergeant barked. 'Might be a bit of nice digging to welcome you back, work you little invalids in before you go running off towards the border doing your good deed for the West.' He was pointing, jerking his hand, his eyes red with tiredness, his voice hoarse. He looked old.

They headed on up the hill, straining their heads forward, carrying their rifles in both hands across their body, then, as the going got steeper, in one hand as they dug in their boots and their rifle butts, cursing, sweat pouring down their backs.

'Great to be bloody back,' Bert groaned in front of Jack, his boots thick with mud where so many feet had thawed the snow. The sun had gone by the time they reached the top. They went straight to the field kitchen, eating where they stood, looking round at the supplies piled up; the ammo, the Stens, the mortars.

There were look-outs on all sides and there was staccato firing in the distance, to the right and left and dead ahead.

'We move out in the morning. Chase the little buggers. Get your 'eads down where you can,' the Sergeant said, pushing past, cleaning his mess tin with a crust of bread.

Jack did the same, then swilled it with water, put it back in his pack, heaved that up on to his back again and headed towards the fox-hole where Bert was standing, beckoning to him.

At least there was no digging. That had all been done on the last advance and their hole was crowded but there was room against the sides. He didn't sleep in his sleeping bag. He had thrown that away. It was cold, bloody cold, but he slept. But not before he had thought of Rosie and the words he would write when the sun came up.

The Sergeant called them at first light and Jack ate breakfast, heaved at his pack, hearing the thuds and clinks all around. He could hear firing and now there were Mustangs high overhead.

'Keeping the pressure on,' an older regular said, nodding at Jack as he wrote his letter, standing up, pressing on Bert's pack, telling him to stand still for Christ's sake, while he told Rosie that he loved her, that he was coming home when his National Service was over. Begging her to forgive him, sure that she would because he knew she loved him too.

'Come on, get over here,' the Sergeant called and Jack stuffed the letter into an envelope, then pushed through the men to the Padre who had held a service as the field kitchen was packed up. He took letters from the men, waving to them as he set off in one direction and they in another, down the hill, taking up the pursuit, heading towards the firing.

It was then, as he dug his heels into the slope, looking out towards the peaks and snow-shrouded shrubs, that he felt a hand grip his shoulder and heard Nigel's voice say, 'Well, you old reprobate, here we are again. Bet you wish you were back cutting the grass with those scissors.'

Jack swung round, stepped out of line, gripped Nigel's arms, wanting to hug him but their eyes said it all and it was enough. Jack saluted then, heard the Sergeant shouting, 'Come along, if you don't mind, Sir.'

Nigel grimaced, and moved on down the hill as Jack fell back into line.

'Catch up with you later, Private,' he called back.

Jack laughed. 'Yes, Sir.'

And it was not until that evening, when they set up camp, bivouacked between boulders, crouching into the existing hoochies, taking two-hour watches, straining their eyes, cursing the men behind who stumbled on old tins left by the previous occupants, that they had time to talk, pressed up against the perimeter look-out.

'Too much pressure, dear boy. Simply had to take a commission.' Nigel was grinning but he didn't turn, he didn't take his eyes from the land around.

'Yes, Lieutenant Sanders. The pips look exquisite. How long have you been out here?'

'Just two weeks.'

Jack knew it could not have been longer. There was no fear in Nigel's eyes and there was still youth in his face.

'We'll soon clear those gooks,' Nigel said.

'Maybe, but they can march on rice, oatmeal, dried peas. They've been fighting with Mao for years. They plan and execute. They're professionals, mobile, take advantage of the terrain. They may be poorly armed but they take weapons from the dead. And they keep on coming.' Jack remembered the bugles, the screams. He remembered Tom and the burning man. 'Just keep your head down, especially now you're leading my platoon.'

They were whispering, listening. There were tracers in the distance. There were flares but he felt better now that Nigel was here, especially with Tom gone.

Nigel looked at him now. 'You're different, Jack.'

'I've been here longer than you and I've grown up a bit. That's all.'

He punched Nigel's arm when their relief came and crawled into his hole, thinking of Rosie, thinking of Suko, thanking her for all that she had shown him.

They set off the next morning as dawn broke. There had been no bugles, but then there wouldn't be. They were the ones chasing this time, weren't they? They marched all day, between hills, alongside paddy fields, the snow and mud clinging to their boots, their thighs sore from the slapping of their wet trousers. Patrols were sent out. The way had been cleared by the troops up ahead. They marched, they slept, they listened.

On the fourth day they were up with the forward troops and the firing was closer and all around. As evening came they straggled through dark hills. There were trees, there were shrubs and large boulders, and Jack looked to each side, straining his eyes.

The Sergeant came along, speaking to them all, but quietly. 'Seems like a good place for a bloody ambush. Keep your wits about you.'

Jack looked ahead to Nigel, who turned. 'Did you tell them, Sergeant?'

'Of course I bloody told them,' the Sergeant said under his breath and then, more loudly, but not too loudly, 'Yes, Sir.'

No one spoke, they were all listening, walking, praying. So far so good. Jack was breathing through his mouth. The air was cold. There was enough light to see his breath. It was crazy. No one would hear his breath over the noise his bloody feet were making. And over the noise the Centurion tanks that had joined them this afternoon were making as they came up the pass behind them.

He turned. He could see their antennae waving. He looked ahead at Nigel, his head turning from side to side. His shoulders were rigid. Jack's were too. Everyone's were.

Then the firing started, small arms thwacking into the ground around them, mortar thudding, screaming.

'Return fire, get some cover. Keep your heads down,' the Sergeant was shouting, waving his arm towards the paddy fields. They were wet, cold. Jack ran, then sprawled down, full length. The tanks were firing, but one was hit by mortar and exploded. The track was slippery and another tank keeled over into the paddy field.

The Chinese were swarming down the hill now, firing burp guns, throwing grenades, and the bugles were blowing. The endless bloody bugles. Jack looked across at Nigel.

'Get your head down, Sir,' he called and Nigel spun round, then ran crouching towards him, throwing himself down beside Jack. Firing as he did so. The rifle butt rammed hard against Jack's shoulder as he fired, again and again, but he couldn't even feel the pain.

The barrel was hot. He reached for more ammunition. Nigel moved along the line of men, talking, helping to reload the Sten. The Chinese were falling but more were coming in their place.

'Don't they know they're supposed to be retreating?' Jack ground out.

Bert lay on his side reloading. 'Bloody little buggers,' he said again and again, but now they were fading. Fewer came to replace them, and Nigel called, 'We're to make our way across the base of the hill on our left. Orders from HQ. Meet up there with a US Infantry Brigade, or what's left of them. Take casualties with us.' He was speaking in short bursts, as though he'd been running, but Jack was panting too. It was fear.

The first squad moved east while Nigel stayed with the rearguard. Jack ran with the first squad, then set up a rearguard under the Sergeant while Nigel and his men broke out, and ran past them. Now Jack, Bert and six others held the Chinese again who faded and left.

'That's what the book says should happen,' grunted Bert.

'Make the most of that piece of perfection then, sonny,' shouted the Sergeant as he passed.

They marched through the night towards the US Infantry Brigade and ate breakfast with men who drawled and looked like Ed, and Jack, though he loved Rosie, could not speak or eat with them.

The UN forces pushed north relentlessly day after cold day and Jack's platoon slept, ate, and marched, forcing the Communists back, seeing the airstrikes on the hills in front, the burning napalm, and he turned from that, feeling sick.

At night he watched the mortar scoring across the cold sky and wouldn't smoke the American cigarettes which Bert had been given.

It became commonplace to storm an enemy-held hill, firing, gripping the shrubs, pulling themselves up, hurling grenades, fighting hand to hand, plunging their rifle butts into heads, hearing screams all round, Chinese and British. Each time they took the hill, they herded prisoners into lorries then sat, their legs weak, vomiting, their stomachs churning from the smell of death. But at least Rosie would soon have his letter and, at least, soon, this war would be over.

At the end of March the Chinese were pushed across the 38th parallel and Jack's unit dug in on a hill which was scattered with the debris of previous battles. They stepped over abandoned Chinese and American equipment, they picked up pay books and identity tags and the Captain sent these back to Seoul which was once more in the hands of the United Nations.

Digging in was difficult in the sandy, frost-hard ground but none the less they tried.

Nigel and Jack talked on watch and Nigel said that the UN and Truman would be looking for a political settlement after throwing back the enemy, but MacArthur wanted to carry the war to Manchuria.

'He'll have to go,' Jack said. 'Or there'll be another war, with atom bombs this time.' He stared across the quiet sky, thinking of Nagasaki, and Suko's parents.

In April they watched the hills bloom with a profusion of colour which he had never dreamed could exist in this land where there seemed only harshness and poverty.

They watched from the hill as the transport became bogged down in the spring mud, they cleared out the fox-holes and cursed it. Their uniforms were wet from the rains, their skin sore from the chapping, but the war was as good as over, they would be going home soon. So they laughed and smoked, leaning on the stone-built barricades, hearing the rain on their tin hats, on their capes, and thought of England. Of its greenness, its rain, its fog, its rationing, and longed to be there.

They heard that the Gloucesters held the most exposed position on the direct approach to Seoul across the Imjin River but surely the Chinese wouldn't come again. They were beaten. There would be peace, MacArthur had been sacked on 11 April.

But they did come again, at the end of April as green was sprinkling the rice fields and new life was beginning all around. They came with their bugles blowing and the Gloucesters saved the left flank of the UN Corps and held up the advance of the Chinese so that the line could be reformed and held. Out of a force of 622, forty-six officers and men returned.

But Jack didn't have time to grieve, because the Chinese were storming his hill, too, and the air was rent with bugles and cymbals and screams, but Jack wasn't screaming, he was lining up the Sten, hearing it clink against the stones of the barrier, and now he was firing it, as the first wave of Chinese rushed up the hill.

How did they move so fast, for God's sake? He heard the gun, felt it judder, concentrated on that, not the bugles, nor the cymbals. He just fired, while Bert fed in the ammunition and threw water on the barrel to cool it as the night wore on, and there was no sense of surprise any more. He was getting used to all this.

He saw four Shooting Stars scream into the valley and bombard the enemy with rockets and cannon fire and napalm and this time he didn't feel sick. He was angry because he should be going home to Rosie. Not firing through showers of mud thrown up by mortar, not lifting a water bottle to his parched lips, not looking at the men he killed, feeling nothing because more would come in their place to kill him and he would never see Rosie again.

They fought all that day, keeping them at bay, waiting for reinforcements but none came. There were too many Chinese storming the whole line. There were supplies though.

'Thank God,' Nigel said as he slapped Jack's shoulder, telling him he would send a relief to take over the Sten soon.

Jack could see the parachutes with ammunition cases dropping amongst the Chinese instead.

659

'Oh Christ,' Nigel groaned.

They fought into the evening. They fought as the sun dropped, brilliant red, behind the hills and now, in the dark, they fired by the light of flares, picking out the Chinese, who were still crawling across the valley and up the base of the hill, getting closer to them now.

Nigel came running out to him, crouching, looking at the rain-sodden maps. 'Can you both hold out for a while longer? They're coming up three sides. No relief teams to spare.'

Jack nodded. 'Keep your bloody head down, Nigel.' He turned. He hadn't called him Sir. They looked at one another and smiled. There was no time for anything but friendship now.

Bullets were thwacking into the mud in front of them as Nigel ran back, dodging, shouting to the Sergeant, 'Get that man down.' But he was too late. Jack saw the radio operator fall, blood spurting from his chest, his radio set blown apart on his back.

There was so much mud flying into the air from mortar explosions, and there was the noise. So much noise and so many Chinese.

At midnight the order came through to pull out, down the hill, deploy six hundred yards to the rear.

They moved, each acting as rearguard, each doing as they were ordered without question, each saving the lives of their friends, and the parade ground flashed into Jack's mind as he skidded down the hill, taking up position as others slid past, then moving again.

They took up positions along the further side of a stream, wading through the water, holding their weapons above their heads, spreading out, flanking the valley, waiting because they knew the Chinese would keep on coming and that their own reinforcements would not.

The enemy came with the dawn. The machine gunners found their targets, and now the British counter-attacked, roaring towards the Chinese as they forded the stream, bogged down in the mud. The rain was in Jack's face, he could taste it, but his mouth was still dry as he ran towards the enemy, firing.

There were no bugles now and the British pushed back towards the valley again, yard by yard, until the day passed and the evening came again but the Chinese rallied and stormed, wave upon wave, as the last of the sun lit the spring flowers, and Bert was killed and Nigel dropped, wounded, his arm useless, and the Sergeant didn't shout any longer, for he was dead.

Jack dragged Nigel towards the base of the hill, ignoring his screams. There were too many all around to listen to just one.

'Break out, all of you that can,' the Captain shouted.

Jack heaped Nigel on to his back, but he was too heavy. He slapped Nigel's face. There was a bullet graze on his forehead and a flesh wound on his arm. He stirred.

'Stand up or die, Nigel,' he shouted, holding his face, looking around, then back at Nigel. 'Stand up, damn you.'

Nigel stirred, groaned. 'Stand up,' Jack repeated. Nigel stumbled to his feet, and Jack slung his arm over his shoulder, taking his weight, moving through the mud, slipping on the stones, but they were moving. At last they were moving.

He dragged Nigel, hearing his breathing, feeling it on his neck. His mouth was still dry from fear and exhaustion. His eyes were sore as he peered into the moonlight. God, Nigel was heavy.

He stopped, and lay down with Nigel beside him at the edge of a paddy field. He could smell the mud, the generations of excrement, and so he thought of the hop-fields, the gentle hills, and when he had rested he moved again. But this time small brown young-looking men loomed up in front of him in the moonlight and the green lush fields of Herefordshire were gone as they shouted and pushed and made Jack walk with his hands on his head in front of Nigel.

When he turned to look at his friend he was prodded with a rifle butt and he was afraid because he had heard of the cruelty of the North Koreans and this is what these men were.

Nigel moaned with every step and Jack breathed in time with his moaning. They could barely see the ground but there was enough light from the cloudless night to avoid the boulders, to stay with the track, and now there were others with them and Chinese soldiers too and Jack breathed more easily.

They were allowed to drop their hands but their fear remained. He stopped and looked back at Nigel, whose feet were dragging, who dripped blood with every step, and the Chinese guard nodded. Jack took his friend's weight and the man behind stepped forward and eased his arm round Nigel's body.

'Let me give you a hand, soldier.' It was a drawl, but Nigel needed help and so Jack nodded but didn't look.

They walked all night and came to a village as dawn broke. They were lined up in the courtyard and there were other Chinese soldiers there. They were given sweetened rice to eat and Jack pushed it into Nigel's mouth, waiting while he gagged, then giving him more.

'Prop him up between us,' the American said, nodding to a cart which was taking other wounded. 'We've heard that they're never seen again. They shouldn't know that he's wounded.'

So they pulled Nigel up, tying the sleeve of his shirt round his arm, needing water to wash the wound, but not daring to ask.

They were searched. Mirrors, scissors, knives were taken by the Chinese who didn't speak and who didn't notice Nigel's arm with the American's jacket slung over it. All the time the North Koreans loitered at the edge of the courtyard, watching.

A Chinese officer came into the courtyard in the cool of the morning sun. He stood before them.

'You are prisoners of the Chinese People's Volunteer Forces in Korea. You have been duped by the American imperialists. You are tools of the reactionary warmongers, fighting against the righteous cause of the Korean people.' He paused, looked around.

Jack tightened his hold on Nigel's good arm. He saw the American clasp his arm more tightly round his body. There were ten men in front of them. Nigel's head was lolling.

'Hold your head up,' Jack hissed and Nigel did.

'You are hirelings of the Rhee puppet government but you will be given the chance to learn the truth through study and you will correct your mistakes. We shall not harm you. At home your loved ones await you. Obey our rules and regulations and you will not be shot.'

They were allowed to sit down and Jack found some shade near the edge of the compound. The mud was deep. It soaked through their clothes but all Jack thought of was Rosie reading his letter, waiting for him, and it gave him strength. But only until a peasant came and struck two prisoners in front of Jack and then turned, hitting him and Nigel with a stick, again and again until blood burst from their lips and heads, because his family had been killed in a raid.

The American, whose name was Steve, stood up and took the stick from the Korean, then the North Koreans moved, pushing through the seated ranks. The mud was in Jack's mouth and nose and he pushed up with his hands and saw the North Koreans take the Yank, pushing him before them towards the edge of the village. He looked for the Chinese but they had gone.

Jack rose, staggered and almost fell but then he was on his feet. He followed Steve and clutched a guard. 'Leave him,' he croaked. 'Leave the Yank.' He was grabbed too. He pulled away but was hit again by the peasant and the blood was running down his face. He turned, called, 'Look after Nigel,' and thought of Rosie as they hauled him, shouting, their breath sour, in his face.

'Hang on, bud,' the American shouted over his shoulder.

They were hauled to a pit, pushed in and there was white blossom on the branch of a tree which hung between them and the sky. Rifles were fired at the walls so that the bullets ricocheted around them, but they were not hit. The North Koreans laughed and the earth smelled of urine, of faeces, but Jack didn't look at the base of the pit, or into the dark flat faces. He thought of Rosie and the bines which swung as though in the sea. And white blossom.

Steve was silent. He stood with Jack, unmoving, until the bullets ceased, and still he said nothing and Jack had no voice with which to speak. Fear had taken it from him.

They were hauled from the pit and a revolver was placed at the American's head.

'Confess your crime, imperialist dog,' the largest North Korean said.

The American said nothing and the hammer clicked but the chamber was empty.

The North Korean opened the chamber and showed Jack. There were two bullets. He spun it, closed it. He held it to Jack's head.

'Confess your crime,' he said again.

Jack looked across the space to the other men, some of whom were visible between the village huts. He thought of Rosie, her mouth, her eyes, and said nothing because there was nothing to say.

But there was no bullet, only the noise of the hammer striking the empty chamber reverberating along the barrel, through the skin into his mind, but Rosie was there, and there was no room for the scream which wanted to leave his mouth.

The Chinese came then, pushing the North Koreans to one side, shoving Steve and Jack before them, back to the village square, and they sat on either side of Nigel and neither spoke because now their legs and their hands were trembling.

They drank the water that the Chinese soldiers passed round and when they had gone Jack cleaned Nigel's wound with the sleeve he had soaked, and dripped water into his friend's mouth, careful not to let the guards see because one man had been beaten for washing his face with the water. He had insulted the guard by using it in that way.

They stayed in the village during the day, pressed up against the hut walls in case the US planes strafed the village. Jack lay listening to the bullfrogs, listening to Nigel's groans, but Steve said little, especially when the North Koreans were near because, he explained, he was American, and the gooks hated them above all else. Jack was glad of his silence. He didn't want to speak to this man.

Each soldier in turn was taken to a hut and interviewed by a high-ranking Chinese officer who asked his rank, name and number, and asked why he supported the Wall Street warmongers who had helped South Korea invade North Korea in July 1950. Jack didn't answer.

'We Chinese believe in a lenient policy to preserve lives so that you imperialist tools can learn the truth. The North Koreans are different. Do not try and escape. They wait for you to do so.'

When Jack came out the North Koreans were there, waiting.

They took Steve too and now they knew that he was American, but there were others who were aircrew and they became the targets of the interrogation instead.

The day passed and at six p.m. the guards came round with

664

sorghum which Jack and Steve ate from cigarette tins because they had lost their hats in the mêlée. A British Sergeant came round too and said that more marching was expected tomorrow and there'd better be a better exhibition than there was today or he'd want to know the reason why.

It raised a smile, it raised morale, and Jack watched the flares and the tracers in the sky, and wondered how this could have happened when they thought they were going home, when he thought he was going home to Rosie.

CHAPTER 19

The landlady stopped Rosie in the hall in March as she searched the wire letter-box for the letter that just might be there. The woman's hair was newly permed and smelt as Norah's had. She wore lipstick and an overall and crossed her arms over her sagging breasts. There was a cigarette in her left hand and the ash drooped, then fell on to the linoleum.

'You've put on a lot of weight. You must think I'm daft. You'll have to leave when that baby you're carrying's due. I wouldn't have that sort of thing here, even if you were married.'

The woman sucked on her cigarette again. There were lipstick marks against the white of the paper. 'This is a decent establishment. No place for the likes of you. You've got to go before it's born.' She exhaled smoke as she spoke, nodded and turned, dropping more ash.

It was the ash that Rosie watched, not the woman who walked back into her room which opened on to the hall. As she opened the front door she watched it blow, then crumble to nothing. She shut the door behind her. She wanted to slam it against the words which she could still hear. Mrs Eaves had said this might happen.

She walked down the steps to the pavement, then turned and looked back at the house, at the peeling balustrade, at the door with its bubbling paint. Where could she go? Fear swept through her. She tugged at her skirt, easing it around her swelling waist where two safety pins were now clasped together. Who would take her and a baby?

The pavement was damp and footsteps were muted all around. She couldn't go to Mrs Eaves; it wasn't fair and there wasn't room. She called in to the butcher's where the smell of meat made her want to retch. There was a queue, there was always a queue, and the woman in front of her wearing a headscarf knotted at the front over her curlers laughed when the butcher brought his cleaver down on to the scarred and stained wooden block and shouted, 'It's 1951 and it'll take three books this morning, ladies, to buy a pound of meat.'

We know that, Rosie wanted to shout. But where can I find somewhere to live and what about the boys fighting out in Korea? Who knows about them, or even cares? And now the Chinese have been routed, will they come home? Oh God, I wish he'd come home. I wish he was safe.

She picked up Mario's order, and carried it to the shop, heaping it on to the table, laughing as Mrs Orsini shouted upstairs to her husband, 'So now the meat is here, Rosie is here, a customer is here, but you are not.'

Yes, she laughed but the laughter was empty because the fear inside her was building, making her weaken and she mustn't do that. She eased herself through the streamers between the kitchen and the café, smiling as she poured coffee for the three young men who stood waiting, knowing that there would be no tips from them. They were in worn coats and shapeless sweaters.

One of them stirred his coffee at the counter. His hands were red and chapped. He looked up at her. His glasses were steamed up and she smiled again as he took them off, rubbed them, replaced them.

'Luke said you might be able to help,' the boy began. 'We play New Orleans style.'

The others at the table behind weren't drinking, they were listening, and Rosie nodded. She mustn't think of Jack coming home, she must think only of fending for herself and the child. 'Tell me about yourselves. What have you done so far? Where have you played?'

As she listened the panic subsided. Yes. It was all right again. She must always believe that Jack was safe. She must concentrate on the new life. That was her job. She must work now, that was all, harder than she had ever done in her life before. She must save enough to tide her over for the birth and a few weeks afterwards and then she would manage. Mrs Orsini hadn't said yet that she could bring the baby to work with her, but she might.

667

But where to live while she had the baby? She pulled herself away from that thought. It was March, she had until June and she must listen to this boy because bands like these were her future. She would be like Bob, manage, guide, but always care. That's where she must put her energy; not into thoughts of Korea, not into fear for herself.

'We're playing at a club two blocks away tomorrow,' the boy told her.

'I'll come and listen.' Rosie smiled. 'We'll talk some more after that.'

She served all morning and in between made bookings over the phone, dropping in her coins, holding a hand to one ear, haggling, always raising the offers to something better while Mrs Orsini clucked and made her eat sandwiches because now she was eating for two.

'But it's too much. I haven't got an army in there.' Rosie smiled at the plump Italian woman. She wasn't hungry but she ate because this was Jack's baby and hers.

After the lunchtime rush she took a bus to Middle Street, slipping down the alley, letting her scarf hang down over her body because no one must know, least of all Ollie whom she was going to see. Perhaps Jack had written and Harold hadn't forwarded the letter.

She pushed open the gate into Jack's yard. Paper had blown into the corners. Lee's old bike was rusted and broken, lying on the ground with the wheel at an angle. The curtains were drawn. The door was locked but she knocked anyway. She wanted to hear some sound, and to touch something that Jack had touched. She wanted to stay where he had been, just for a moment, and hear the echoes of their laughter.

Harold came then, out through Grandpa's yard. He stood at the entrance to Ollie's. 'I thought I heard something.'

He was looking at her body and Rosie held her scarf in a bunch. 'Hello, Harold. I just wondered if any mail had come?'

He looked up at the house where the windows were like blank eyes. 'No. I'd bring it to you, honestly I would.' He was looking at her face now, not at her body, and she believed him, and everything hurt within her. But how could there be so much pain when she knew deep inside there would be no letter? Was she very stupid?

668

'It looks so empty.' She looked back at the house.

'Ollie's gone. He's got a job building the new town outside London. Norah wants to go when it's finished.' Harold nodded his head towards Grandpa's house. 'I don't though. It grows on you.'

Rosie nodded. 'What about the mail, though? What if it comes to Ollie, not to Number 15?'

Harold nodded. His moustache needed a trim. 'She's picking it up. Don't worry. I'll see you get any news.' He turned, then looked back over his shoulder. 'I'd ask you in but . . .'

'She still feels the same then?'

'Yes. Says your grandpa would too.' Harold shrugged. 'You're OK, though, aren't you?'

'Oh yes, no worries. I'm fine.' She walked out of the gate, watching as he turned back into the yard where she could no longer go. She could see that the roses were still there.

'Prune them for me, Harold,' she called softly and he nodded.

'I will. I like them. It's the scent, you know.'

Yes, she did know.

She walked to the rec, sat on the swings and wanted to go to Herefordshire again, paddle in the stream or go back to Pennsylvania and swim in the lake, let it soothe, listen to the ripples, but now was not the time. Now she must work. The wind was cold, too cold, and so she walked back to the bus, past the warehouse where she and Jack had walked with the cheeses and she could hear their laughter again, feel his closed-mouth kiss.

Back in Soho there was music coming from the basement clubs and she pushed her way through to the bars of the pubs which lined the road to the café. She took a job as barmaid three nights a week, starting when the café closed, leaving the other evenings free to listen to groups, practise with them, build up the business.

It would be good for her, she told herself. There would be less time in the bedsit, less time listening to the hissing fire, to her own breathing, to her loneliness. Less time to worry about where she would live, because so far none of the landladies she had asked would take a child.

669

The next night she listened to the new band and the pale young man who played the banjo. She heard its sharp tones cutting through the collective improvisation, through the murmur which continued from the dimly lit tables all around, and later they talked over glasses of beer and he told her that he played the guitar too and Rosie was glad.

'It's more flexible, but keep the banjo too. You can play well. Come to Mario's Club on Thursday. I'll have fixed you a few gigs by then. I take ten per cent.' She looked away as she said this. His coat was so shabby, all the musicians were poor, but so was she, and so would her baby be, unless she charged the rate that Luke said was fair, unless she worked until she dropped.

The boy smiled, and shook her hand, and they sat up talking about the clean and emphatic rhythmic backing that the banjo had always given, about the Big 25 Club in New Orleans where he had always wanted to play. Rosie nodded, her eyes sore with tiredness, but she needed to know her groups, to care about them, to find out their strengths and their weaknesses.

She worked at the bar the next night, pulling pints, smiling, wearing loose clothes to hide her shape, but her legs ached and her arms and her face from the smile that had to be there.

There was a letter in the wire rack on her return but it was not from Jack, it was from Nancy. She read it by the light from the small table lamp Mario had given her, hearing the plop of the gas, smelling it. Sipping cocoa, which was all she could face after an evening of beer-laden breath and nicotine-heavy air.

Lower Falls
March

My dearest Rosie,

Do hope that all is well with you. Your groups seem to be coming along well. Uncle Bob tells us you've written about this guy Luke and his band. Sounds interesting. Maybe if he comes over, you could come too. Perhaps with Jack when the war's over.

I hope to God it comes soon. It might take some of the panic out of things over here. Then 'pinkoes' like us might just be able to get some sleep at night without some nut ringing up and shouting – Reds go home – over the line! Then we might get back to being fifty instead of ninety.

It's not being helped by the Rosenberg trial in New York City. My God, how tempers are rising all around.

It would cheer us both so much if you could come out to see us. But maybe you need to put in time at work, especially when you're just trying to get the restaurant on the road and the groups too. We understand.

All our love,
Nancy

The paper was cold. The heat didn't reach across to the bed and Rosie wanted to read of the maples and oaks at the lake, the target on the garage, the barbecue, Mary. She didn't want to hear of tension, of heartache, because she couldn't go back. All she could do was lie to the people she loved. The people who needed her right now.

Her legs were throbbing, her head ached. She lay down and pulled the knitted blanket up round her head. She wanted to be in her bedroom at Lower Falls, she wanted to be back where Nancy's arms could take away the pain, where her laughter broke into her loneliness. But she wanted to be here more, waiting for Jack, in case he came, in case he wrote.

That night she dreamed that he wrote, but March became April and there was no letter. There was just work, but the money was mounting and she sent in an application for an Unmarried Mothers Home. She was accepted but the letter was cold and the list of garments and equipment required was long.

So she worked on Sunday at the pub also and they said they would take one of her groups on a Friday night, unheard, because her reputation was growing. She slept well that night but couldn't face more than cocoa.

Towards the end of April, the UN forces retreated as the Chinese poured in reinforcements, and the newspaper ink came off on her hands as she read the piece again and again at the Orsinis' kitchen table and cried because now he wouldn't be coming home soon, the UN forces would have to go on fighting and there had been no letter.

She cried and couldn't stop and Mrs Orsini held her.

'He won't be coming home yet,' she whispered as she felt the heat from the older woman's body.

'One day he will. I know he will, if he loves you as we do,' Mrs Orsini said. 'You are a good girl. He cannot fail to love you. You must wait. You must be patient. You must not give up.'

That night as she lay in bed she wondered how long hope lasted. How long she could bear such loneliness. And how could she bear it if he died and she was never told? But Mrs Orsini said that Ollie or Harold would tell her and Rosie knew that she was right.

She worked throughout April, barely noticing the leaves sprouting on the clubbed trees, barely noticing the blocks of ice melting outside the French restaurants along the back streets. She listened to groups, listened to booking managers, and always increased the fees so that the ten per cent she took left the boys with the original offer.

She and Luke spent one evening a week with Jake, coaxing, nagging, drawing him on, because now they were both convinced that his playing could be brought up to the standard of the others, but still it was not quite right. She wrote again to Uncle Bob, telling him that Luke's group was almost ready. That he would want them when he heard the middle range, the melancholia, the dexterity, the heart.

She went to the clinic and they said she was underweight but the baby was strong. They gave her more iron. Mrs Orsini gave her soup, sandwiches, salads, but she was too tired to eat and Mario couldn't understand the circles under her eyes and neither could Mrs Eaves. She didn't tell them about the bar work, they wouldn't understand how necessary it was. She said nothing to Luke either, or to Sandy, who made her sit down now when she phoned because her legs were trembling for much of the day and so were her hands.

She still pulled pints though, in the evening, and it was here one night that Luke found her, pale, tired, bending, stretching, and he waited outside until the doors were locked and the customers had left. He waited beneath the street light, his leg crooked up behind him, until she came out of the side door and for a moment she thought he was Jack and ran towards him, but then stopped.

'Why are you doing this?' Luke said, his arms crossed, his voice hard. 'You're more than seven months pregnant. Are you mad?'

The light cast shadows on his face and Rosie walked past him. She didn't need this. She needed money for her baby. She needed a future. Not this. Not now. She didn't turn but he followed her, grabbing her arm.

'Are you mad or just greedy? Why this on top of everything else? What do you want to do? Go back to America a rich woman? Show off to your friends about how well you've done? You're killing yourself. You're killing the baby.'

She pulled from him. The stars were clear in the sky. There was no cloud, no breeze. She would think of that, not his words.

'I'm going home because for now and for now only it is home. When the baby's born I have to leave. I have nowhere to go, no one to go to.' She wasn't looking at him, she was looking at the sky above the rooftops. 'That's why I'm working. I've got to pay for the goddamn Home, I've got to survive afterwards until I can work. I'll see you tomorrow, Luke.'

She walked on, back to the house by herself, climbed the stairs by herself, but then the baby stirred and she smiled. No, not by herself.

Luke didn't come into the café the next day, or the pub in the evening. Neither did the rest of the group, or Sandy. They didn't play on Thursday night but it didn't matter, because the new group did and the applause was loud, though Rosie had been too tired to tap her foot. Too tired to feel the hurt of Luke's rejection, because that is what his absence meant.

Mrs Orsini was quiet too, and busy. There didn't seem time for her to smile and Mario was in and out. Rosie served coffee, made phone calls, took phone calls, added gigs in the book, totalled up the figures. Served spaghetti bolognese to Mrs Eaves who came and smiled but left quickly with Mrs Orsini, and Rosie told herself it didn't matter.

She served in the pub that night and she had never been so tired. The Chinese and the North Koreans had been held on a line to the north of Seoul and the Han River. Where was Jack? Was he safe? Would he write?

673

As she left the pub she looked towards the lamppost but Luke wasn't there and the walk home was cool and quiet and empty. But the wire box for letters wasn't.

There was one from Frank saying that Joe was coming over to cover the Festival of Britain which had started at the beginning of May. He was also coming to hear Luke's group and to see her, to put their minds at rest that she was well and happy. Frank wanted her to write a feature on the Festival as well since she was doing freelance features in Britain.

Rosie read it again, lying fully clothed on the bed, then she tore it up, into smaller and smaller pieces. How could she hide this baby now and why was there no letter from Jack? And she hadn't written anything since she had left the magazine – her skill had gone, absorbed by the life she now led.

She slept, dragged herself from the bed when the alarm rang at seven a.m. She made tea and toast but couldn't eat, she was still too tired. She pushed her swollen feet into her shoes, and took her coat because the wind was still cool. The landlady was by the front door, holding it open for her.

'Made other arrangements yet?' she asked.

'You've had my rent until the end of May,' Rosie said, pushing past her, buttoning up her coat, knowing that the hem rose at the front and dipped at the back because she was so large.

When she arrived at the café the Closed sign was still up though the door was unlocked. The chairs were still upside-down on the tables and she moved slowly, setting them down, thinking of Joe, working out the letter she would write to stop him coming, the extra lies she would tell, but then Mario came into the room, his white apron smudged, and Mrs Orsini was behind her with Mrs Eaves.

Mario took the chair from her, set it down, took her by the hand, led her behind the counter, through the kitchen, up the stairs. Past the Orsini flat, right up to the top where the attic was. He said nothing and Rosie was too tired to ask.

He opened the door to the rooms which had housed packing cases, old chairs, rubbish. Luke and his band were there, with Sandy too. There were no packing cases any more. There was a carpet on the floor. There were chairs, a table, a cooker. Mario showed her this and the bathroom with the white suite. Light flooded in through the eaved windows.

There was another room with a white-sprigged muslin bedspread draped over a bed. There was a dressing-table. No one spoke. Rosie turned. Mrs Eaves had followed them up and stood with Mrs Orsini.

Luke said, 'This is yours, Rosie.'

Rosie stood but her legs were trembling, and now Luke moved over to the side of the bed where a sheet hung over something. He pulled it back and there was a cot with blankets cut down and freshly ironed sheets.

'And this is the baby's,' he said.

She walked over to the cot, stroked the bedclothes then the headboard. Frank's grandfather had carved the headboard on her bed at Lower Falls out of maple. She heard again the jazz from the open window flowing across the shadowed lawn.

She turned. 'I don't deserve it.' She laid her hand on her stomach. 'I can't take it.'

The sky was blue behind the rooftops and the chimneys. There were white clouds. How strange. There had only been darkness for so long.

She said again as they all stood, silent but smiling still, 'I can't take it.' But how she wanted to be able to.

Mr Orsini spread open his hands. 'Then you look for another job, my Rosie, because the person that works with us now has to live above. It is better for business. We are putting a phone up here.' He turned, the others were grinning now. 'But, you want to leave. You leave. We want you to stay. We want the baby too. We want you live here. Work here, with baby.'

Mrs Eaves came then, took her arm, moved her through into the other room, pushed her towards the chair beside the fire which had been hidden beneath an old sheet up to now. It was Grandpa's.

'We brought it over from Norah's. Harold helped us.'

Rosie sat. She looked at her own hands clutching the arms of the chair which his had held and now she looked up. His books were here too, on shelves along the wall.

'Thank you.' It was all she could say, but it was enough because there were so many tears in her eyes and everyone else's and she wanted to hug them, tell them how much it all meant to her. Mrs Eaves stooped and kissed her head.

'We know, my dear,' she murmured.

675

Mr Orsini clapped his hands and laughed. 'Good, good. Now downstairs, everyone. The café should be open. There is much to do. You too, Rosie, and there will be no more job at pub. There will be no more nasty woman at house. There will be no talk of Home for you and baby.'

He was taking her arm, helping her up while Mrs Orsini nodded and Mrs Eaves smiled. They followed Luke and the group down the stairs and everyone was talking at once but Rosie listened to Mr Orsini. 'You will go now to clinic. You will have baby in nearby hospital. You will come home to us.' He put up his hands. 'No arguments. That is as it should be. We help until Jack comes back.'

Rosie walked to the clinic and there was blossom on the trees, there were children running in the streets, laughing, shouting, as she and Jack had done. As their child would do, and one day they would take her to the hills of Herefordshire and the lake in Pennsylvania.

On 20 May Rosie went to the market for vegetables. She chose spring greens, with the dew still on the leaves, carrots, onions but left the potatoes for Luke to bring later. She listened to the man who sold crockery, dipping his hands into the money pocket of his apron. He wasn't as good as Jack.

She stopped, bought a paper and read of the British and Australian troops who had defended their positions and thrown back the Chinese. People pushed past her. They didn't care that there was a war on. Rosie put the paper into the litter bin and looked up and down the street. Was there fresh spring growth where Jack was? Was there blossom against blue skies as there was here? Was he thinking of her?

She walked on. She knew he wasn't dead. Ollie would have had a telegram and so she thought of him as she had known him, selling his plates, laughing, throwing the cheeses over the wall, and the sun was warm on her face and she didn't see the dog until it was too late.

It ran at her, caught her behind the knee. She fell, the carrots bursting out of their newspaper as her bag fell with her, and for a moment there was no pain, just surprise, just dirt on her hands and in her mouth. Then there were hands lifting her, voices, faces that cared, that were worried, shocked, and now the pain came, passing over her in waves.

'Sit down, missus.' Someone brought a chair out of a shop and an ambulance was called but the carrots were still all over the pavement. Someone must pick them up. The newspaper was lifting and flapping. It was dirty. Her hands were dirty and her mouth. She could taste the grit.

At the hospital she held out her hands through the fog of pain. They were dirty, so dirty, and the Sister smiled and washed them and asked how they could get hold of her husband.

'Jack's in Korea,' Rosie whispered because there was too much pain to use her voice properly.

The doctor tried to stop the baby coming because it was four weeks too soon, but the contractions were stronger, coming too quickly, and Rosie lay on the bed and called for Jack, again and again, because his baby was coming too soon. Mrs Eaves and Mrs Orsini came and patted her hand, soothed her forehead but they weren't allowed to stay.

'We'll be in the corridor. We'll wait,' Mrs Eaves said and there was a smile on her face, but not in her eyes.

The pain came again. 'Don't go,' Rosie called. 'Everyone goes.'

Lucia Anne was born at one a.m. She was small, but strong and beautiful, so very beautiful, and Rosie held her before they took her to an incubator. She stroked the small hands, the perfect nails, the soft hair, the skin. She kissed her cheek. Mrs Eaves and Mrs Orsini saw the baby too and cried when they heard the names because they were theirs.

The Sister came into the ward the next day, her face stern, her lips thin. She pulled the screens round the bed. 'There is no husband, is there?'

Rosie shook her head.

'Then you should have the baby adopted. It would be better. There would be two parents, a settled home.' The Sister straightened her apron. 'You're young enough to start again. Forget all about this.'

'I have a home. The father will come back from Korea. I know he will.' Rosie turned away to face the screen and would say nothing else.

677

At visiting time the husbands came and she looked away, out of the window at the blue sky. She was glad she had been to see Grandpa when he lay in hospital. She was glad she had carried the roses until her hands were raw because there was a loneliness here like no other.

Mario came, and Luke, and then Mrs Eaves and Mrs Orsini and they said they had told Norah. She did not come. The doctor spoke to her the next day about adoption but Lucia Anne was hers, she told him. She loved her.

'But my dear, love is not enough,' the doctor said.

'Love is everything,' she replied.

She took Lucia home and there were flowers in the flat and light, so much light. And there was love. So much love, from them all. But Jack wasn't there.

And Joe was coming soon and what would happen then?

CHAPTER 20

Jack's long march to the 'safe rear' began at seven p.m. as spring edged into the summer of 1951.

'To prevent strafing from UN planes,' the Chinese guard said.

They carried sacks of sorghum and Jack and Steve helped Nigel, who was stronger now but his arm was swollen and stiff. Jack still couldn't smile at the American, because he was a Yank like Ed, but he took the help he gave because the Yanks had taken so much from him.

They marched through mud and the Sergeant at the head of the column set up the rhythm and it helped, it made them feel human after the Korean children had giggled and stared and the North Korean guards had spat.

The mud dragged at their boots, Nigel lost the rhythm. Jack chanted left right, left right, and the Korean guard lunged at him with his rifle butt, screaming.

'OK, buddy, keep your shirt on,' Steve drawled and the guard turned on him and thudded the butt into his ribs.

Jack kept silent because the American had taken the blows which should have come to him. The bruises would have been easier. Steve kept silent too and now Nigel was back in rhythm, they were all in the rhythm, cursing with each step, cursing, counting, cursing, counting, but only in their minds, and Jack thought of this, not Steve and his long loping strides in which he saw echoes of Ed.

Trucks passed them, their lights picking out the road, spewing up mud, leaving the sickening smel of gasoline hanging on the air. Planes sometimes soared above, dropping flares which illuminated the road and adjacent hills, and each time the men had to break and scatter into the roadside ditches, sinking into the stinking mud as rockets hit the hills and the road. Then, as the planes disappeared, they clambered out again, marching on in sodden clothes, which rubbed against their skin. Christ, how they rubbed.

All along the hilltops bordering the roads the Chinese air-raid wardens fired rifle shots into the air when other planes were sighted and again and again they were back in the ditches, cursing the American air crews but cheering them too, if only in their minds.

They crossed bridges and were made to run for the length of them, their breath jerking in their chests, the sorghum sacks breaking their backs, deadening their legs. Jack could hear Nigel groaning but the guards couldn't hear above the thud of boots.

'Better than the assault courses,' he said as they ran. 'Do you remember? Just keep going.' And Nigel did.

Their mouths were dry. There were no drinks, but the guards had nothing either and they carried packs too.

They halted in a village before it was light, crouching in the centre, their bodies cooling quickly in the morning chill. Nigel was groaning but Jack gripped his good arm.

'In your mind, Nigel. In your mind.' Because the prisoners who had been in the Japanese camps in the last war could understand the North Koreans. They understood that the ox-cart which followed them meant death for the injured placed upon it.

Steve checked Nigel's wound. 'It's OK. The maggots are in it now.'

Jack nodded, swallowing. He couldn't have lifted the bandage, seen the writhing mass, but he wouldn't think of that. He would think of his mouth which was dry, of water which had not yet been given. He would think of the stream below the hop-yards, of Rosie standing, letting the water ripple about her legs.

The Chinese officer was shouting at his men and there were bullfrogs in the paddy fields which lay all around them. They were given water to drink and hot watery sorghum to eat, then herded up into the hills before dawn broke and there they lay during the long daylight hours.

They slept on the sandy ground, sheltered from planes by rocks and shrubs, and in the village he could see trees with white blossom bursting from their branches, symbols of stillness. He thought of Suko and the avenues of trees he had not stayed to see in Japan. But most of the time he thought and dreamed of Rosie and hated himself for hurting her.

But then the Chinese would come and sit and talk of their sins, of their crimes against the Korean people, of the right of the Chinese people to Formosa, and all the time the North Korean guards sat and lay on the perimeter, watching the men, fingering their guns, their knives, and no one tried to escape on that first night or day, or indeed the whole journey.

They marched again at seven p.m. when the rain was pouring. It was in their eyes, their fatigues, their mouths and so they weren't thirsty, but tired.

'So goddamn tired,' Steve drawled and Nigel nodded, but Jack looked straight ahead.

They stopped in the morning and this time there was room to stay in village shacks but it enabled the Chinese to talk to them more easily. A smooth-faced lecturer in well-pressed olive greens came by truck and harangued the prisoners as they slumped with knees crossed on the floor, looking out of the door at the blossom.

For two hours they sat and listened and their backs ached, their heads too, and then they were allowed to rest but the children of the village threw stones into the shacks, then beat sticks on the walls so there was no sleep for any of them. They marched again at seven p.m. and the lice were itching.

By ten p.m. they were lying in ditches, scattered before a strafing plane, its roar filling the air which was full of flying cartridge cases. One guard was killed and two prisoners. They were so tired, they barely noticed, but when they arrived at the next village they turned their clothes inside-out and squashed what lice they could between their fingernails.

There had been lice in Middle Street before they'd bought the houses. He and Rosie used to crush the lice there too. Steve checked Nigel's arm again, because Jack could not, and it was then that Jack said, 'Thanks. I couldn't do it.' It was the first time he had said thank you to an American since Maisie had left, but he couldn't look at him when he said it. And it was for Nigel that he spoke, not himself.

That day, they heard a cuckoo call as they lay on the hills

which were drenched in colour. Jack eased himself on to his back and thought of the Somerset village, the hill, the May blossom, the camp he and the other evacuees had made. He thought, too, of the cuckoo which he and Ed had heard. But then he thought instead of Rosie.

Each night they marched, each day they hid, drinking boiled water, eating sorghum, rice. Each day all the prisoners cracked lice and Steve checked Nigel's wound. They listened to the Chinese and wondered how long this would go on for.

For weeks they marched with the ox-cart trundling behind and more prisoners joined them until there were eighty of them. They brought news, but it wasn't good. The Chinese were advancing.

Dysentery had killed fifteen of them after four weeks and still they marched. The heat sapped their energy and now the flies were thick around them as they hid on the hills, resting, lying on the dry ground. They crawled in their ears, their eyes, their noses, their mouths.

When they covered their faces with squares of shirts they felt them crawling on the surface, heard them buzzing, but Nigel's arm was better, the maggots were gone, and he carried his own sack of sorghum. They had no need of Steve now, but he continued to march with them, though Jack barely spoke.

In the second week of June they entered a camp which was set on a peninsula, in a valley between two hills beyond which was the sea. There were barely any soles left on their boots. Their skin was burnt, their hair and clothes were thick with encrusted dirt. Their lips were cracked.

'This is exquisite,' Nigel said, bracing his shoulders, marching in step.

Jack laughed, looking up at the blue sky.

'Hardly exquisite, dear boy,' he answered, looking down now at the single strand of wire which marked the perimeter of the camp, knowing that the geography was the real restriction. He, too, braced his shoulders and marched in step to the huts, then gave news to the prisoners who had been there over the winter; who were thin, bruised, hungry, but who said the regime was kinder now. Indoctrination was the order of the day. It wasn't very successful. Jack looked at Nigel and they smiled. Steve smiled too.

682

They ate corn and millet that evening. They wanted to sleep but were taken out into a large hut and lectured and Jack looked at his thumbs which were black with the ingrained blood of the lice, but still he itched, still he scratched. They all did, but tomorrow they wouldn't march. At least there was that.

In the morning they were put on a wood rota and Steve and Jack went up into the hills with eight others but Jack talked to the others, not to Steve. They collected wood, brought it back, boiled water for drinking, but it was too late for some. Five of their men died of dysentery in the camp that first day.

They were broken down into companies by the Chinese for daily political study sessions. Nigel, Steve and Jack were kept together and there was nothing Jack could do about it. They sat in rows, cross-legged, trying not to listen.

'You soldiers have come here as dupes of the imperialists, the warmongers, the Wall Street big-shots who have tricked you to leave your countries and fight this war to increase their profits,' the lecturer told them. His voice droned on and on.

There were flies everywhere. Jack dropped his head on to his chest and thought of the cool breeze of England, Rosie's soft hands.

They were given paper to write an essay on the lecture they had received. Nigel wrote, and Steve and Jack copied his words. They were all sent for that evening. They stood before the Commandant and confessed their copying crimes as the Commandant insisted they must. But Steve and Jack couldn't write the essays that the Commandant now insisted upon because they had not been listening. They were taken to cells in the village.

The North Korean guards pushed them inside the clay and wattle building which smelled of excrement, urine, and the gasoline which was stored in drums at the end of the passage. There were doors either side. It was dark. Steve murmured, 'This looks kinda fun.'

Jack looked at him now, really looked, because there had been no fear in his voice and he wondered how that was possible. But now he saw the fear in the American's eyes. There was youth too, and kindness, and Jack smiled but then he was pushed alone into a cell.

The uneven dirt floor was soaked with oil. It was dark. So dark. The door opened and he turned. A North Korean guard stood there, a pistol in his hand.

'You come.'

Jack left and Steve called, 'Good luck, buddy.'

He was taken to a wall which flanked the square outside the cells. His arms were tied with wire. He was turned to face the guard. The sun was too bright, the shadows so sharp. For Christ's sake! He was going to be shot. Shot, now. Jack put up his hand. *No*, but the word was silent. There was no time. The guard had levelled the pistol, pulled back the hammer. The gun fired into the wall behind him and Jack's legs shook and he nearly fell.

The guard returned him to the cell and Steve tapped on the wall.

'You OK?'

'I'm fine. Just fine. What else can you do on a quiet afternoon?' But he wasn't OK. He sat on the floor, his arms round his knees, trying to stop the shaking and the tears, listening as Steve in his turn was taken, but he also returned and so the shaking stopped and the tears too. Because he hadn't died today and he wasn't alone.

The guard handed in a blanket, rice bowl and spoon and took their boots, and he couldn't sleep that night because he didn't know when they would come again to take him. The cells were full, and he knew the others couldn't sleep either because they tapped and talked in whispers. So, although there was no light, there was comradeship, and that kept the fear from all their voices.

The next day the guards came and took them one by one, barefoot, to the earth latrine at the end of the passage, then back to the cells. They were made to sit bolt upright from five-thirty a.m. onwards. Jack's back stiffened, burned. He slouched. The guard looked through the grille and shouted. He sat up again, back rigid now, until eleven a.m.

There were no more trips to the latrines. A young American air navigator had dysentery and Steve told the guard, who hit him in the face with his fist, and Jack wondered how he could ever not have liked this man.

The navigator used the corner of his cell.

'That is good. You need to learn humility,' the Chinese officer called through their doors.

At eleven breakfast arrived. They stepped three paces outside the cell to collect the food, but one at a time so they saw no familiar face. Jack forced it down. Boiled water was brought. Jack filled up his bowl, sipped it. Tipped a little on to his fingers, wiped his face, his hands.

At midday the flies and the heat rose. The Chinese bugles blew and the guards shouted that they must lie down for one hour. Jack pulled the blanket over his face, lying on the dirt floor. He heard and felt the flies, felt the sweat soak into the blanket, but it was better than having them in his mouth, crawling heavy and bloated across his skin.

They were then made to sit again, bolt upright, and there was comfort in the knowledge that others were having to do the same. There was such comfort in not being alone.

Each minute seemed an eternity. He thought of Rosie, of the coolness of the bines, the softness of her lips. He didn't think of the cold ground in Yorkshire because it made him feel so disgusted with himself, and so grateful that she could still love him. The shirt had shown that and it was more than he deserved. But at least there had been no child for her to struggle with alone. She would have told him.

At twilight they were ordered to lie down and sleep. They were inspected at nine p.m. A torch was shone in his face. He pretended to be asleep. He pretended to be asleep when Steve tapped, and when he spoke, because the disgust was still with him.

As he walked to the earth latrine in the morning he watched a guard carry a bucket towards a sheet of wrought iron on the ground. He saw him kick the sheeting to one side. An American officer emerged wearing flying boots. He was white and haggard and stumbled to the latrines ahead of Jack.

Jack's guard laughed. 'He not confess to crimes.'

'Good luck, buddy,' Jack called and the man turned, dazed, his eyes deep sunken. He smiled before Jack felt the blow of the rifle, felt it thud into his ribs, felt the dust in his mouth as he fell.

He was dragged back to the cell before he could use the latrine. He was made to sit all day without food, without water, and there was only the corner of his cell as a latrine. But it was worth it to have reached out, for that one moment, to a boy, an American, who was suffering more than he.

That evening, after twilight and after inspection, he talked to Steve about Ed and Maisie and Lee because all the anger and the bitterness were gone. They had disappeared when Steve had spoken without fear and when the American had crawled from the pit.

They were out of the cells within a week and at the end of June the Chinese danced as evening came, swaying in weaving columns to the discordant sound of a drum and clashing cymbals in celebration of a festival only they understood.

'How exquisite,' Nigel murmured and Jack nodded.

'Kinda strange, out here,' Steve said. 'Can't quite catch the tune, but I've heard those cymbals before.'

They had all heard them, but then they had been almost drowned by bugles and guns.

There were fewer North Koreans now and less brutality. They were allowed to wash but there was no soap or towels. They were given anti-malarial tablets and louse powder. They were fed twice a day from the Chinese troops' kitchen. They knew it was all to re-educate them through leniency but by now Nigel had dysentery and none of this helped that.

So each day they listened to lectures, wrote essays, but thought their own thoughts and clung to their own dreams, their own memories, and longed to be home.

In July the Commandant spoke to them. He smoked Dragon cigarettes from China and shouted when Nigel had hiccoughs and couldn't stop.

He told them that some of them were righteous progressive men who were self-consciously learning the truth.

'You are our friends and we will help you to struggle free from the toils of the warmongers.' He looked at Nigel who was still hiccoughing. 'Others of you are semi-righteous, uncertain. You are swayed by every wind that blows. You listen to both sides but cannot make self-conscious decisions.'

Nigel was still hiccoughing, clenching his hands into fists, holding his breath. Men were laughing now, but not the Commandant.

'Others of you are bad men. You believe slanderous things.

You close your minds against the truth. You distract others from learning.' He motioned with his swagger stick to Nigel and the guards came and took him and now there was no laughter.

Steve looked at Jack. 'He's too weak. That dysentery. He ain't fit enough to take that cell, or the pit.'

Jack nodded. He began to stand but Steve pressed him down.

'That won't help. We'll have to wait.'

They didn't take Nigel to the pit though. They took him to the Commandant's hut where he spent the evening writing a self-criticism which he had to read the next day to the camp.

It was clever, very clever, Jack thought, grinning. It was a criticism of the Commandant, not capitalism, but written in a way which made this impossible to grasp. Afterwards Nigel told him that he wanted to go to university when this mess was over.

At the end of the week they were given paper to write a letter home, c/o The Chinese People's Volunteers' POW Corps. Jack wrote to Rosie, telling her that he loved her, that his friend Nigel was here, and Steve, an American. That all the anger was gone, that he would survive. That he was ashamed. That he hated himself for hurting her. That this couldn't go on for too long and he would be back.

They handed them in but an American who knew Korean heard the guards say that they would never be sent and home seemed very far away.

The wood-gathering parties had to scavenge further afield now but suddenly the trips became more popular because Mexican POWs had discovered marijuana growing on the hillsides and now they rolled the leaves between book pages and smoked them to ease the boredom of the days. But Jack and Steve refused to smoke because they needed to care for Nigel who was weaker each day from dysentery and beri-beri.

There were no medical supplies, though there was a doctor who tried to help. The Chinese had no drugs for themselves either.

They still sat through lectures, listening just enough to be able to answer questions, but they also talked to the Puerto

Ricans who knew and understood the herbs which could save lives. Steve and Jack used the remains of the paper which they had been given for their essays to write down descriptions of the plants.

The following week they strayed from the wood-gathering party, searching, picking, stuffing the herbs into the pockets of their trousers, remembering to carry wood under their arms as well. They brewed the mixture up behind the hut and no guards stopped them because boiling up water was common. Nigel drank it from his cigarette-tin and he seemed a little better and they talked of home, and of Oxford where he would go when the war was over.

They did the same the next week, and the next, and then it was the beginning of August and new prisoners said that talks were being held in a tea-house in Kaesong on a ceasefire in Korea. That this must almost be the end, and that day the wood party looked up at the hills, felt the heat and the dust, and because the war would be over soon it didn't seem so important to stretch themselves beyond endurance. They were late mustering, slow in leaving and Jack watched them straggle in on their return. He watched the Commandant too, standing frowning, and waited for what he knew would happen.

The Chinese herded all the prisoners into the square. They were lectured on their negative attitude to labour and made to sit in the sun for the afternoon and Nigel became worse as the heat increased. The herb gatherer had forgotten to gather.

Jack and Steve went out on the wood detail the next morning, even though they were tired and weak and it wasn't their turn, but Nigel was worse. They needed herbs, they needed to make sure the squad were brisk and that Nigel didn't need to sit in the sun again.

They took the sloping paths, lifting the wood which was already hot though it was only eleven a.m. They found the herbs, bitter, sweet. The smell clung to their hands. They moved further from the others, picking, leaning over for wood, glancing behind, checking the guards, picking, always picking. And others did too now for their own friends.

They came out the next day too, and the next, picking for Nigel, and for others, but on the Sunday afternoon Jack and Steve were not cautious enough as they searched and picked.

They didn't check how close they were to the squad. Jack heard the shouting of the guards first, then the warning from Steve, then bullets thwacked into the ground at their feet. There was the sound of running feet and they were pushed face down and kicked, then dragged back to the camp.

They were brought before the Commandant, who accused them of trying to escape. They said nothing. The scent of herbs was still on their hands. Steve looked at Jack who shook his head. They couldn't admit to the herbs in case others were stopped too. In case the marijuana smoking was discovered and men punished.

'You must admit your error,' the Commandant said.

'I'm kinda sick of admitting to errors,' Steve said. 'Why don't you go take a powder.'

The Commandant didn't speak, he just nodded and the guards took Steve across the square. He dropped the herbs on the ground. They were picked up by another prisoner and taken to Nigel.

Jack saw this. He also saw the flies around his head. Then he watched the smoke rising from the Commandant's cigarette and there were no flies near the smoke. Power brought advantages, that was for sure.

'And you. You will admit your error? Your attempt to escape.'

Jack stood to attention. He rubbed the scar the scissors had made. He was tired too, of obedience, of humility. Yes, he was tired and the war was nearly over anyway.

'I have made no errors,' he said.

He also dropped his herbs on the ground and they were picked up too and the soldier who did so said, 'I'll get them for Nigel until you're back out.'

He was thrown into the pit near the latrines and Steve called out from the other, 'You'll like the privacy, Jack.'

He didn't, though, and neither would Grandpa, he thought, smiling wryly. It was dark, it was hot, so hot. The sun beat down on the iron, the guards banged with sticks and he sat crouched, hugging his knees, feeling the sweat rolling off his body. He stripped off his clothes, held his head in his hands while it ached enough to burst.

As the heat of the day beat on the steel covers he took shallow

689

breaths, panting, seeking air, lifting his head, but there was none. He rolled on to his side. The earth was cooler. He buried his face in it but the dust entered his mouth, his nose. He crouched, he wept and the tears were salty and then he sat, still and straight, as Suko had done before the Shinto shrine. He thought of white blossom, of the cool of the stream about Rosie's legs.

They lifted the covers at twilight. He staggered to the latrines, heard Steve's voice as he returned. It was cracked and dry.

'Kinda like a long holiday, eh, Jack?'

Jack slipped down again into the pit. The guard handed him sorghum in a tin and half a can of boiled water. It was warm. They pushed him down. Some of the water spilt. They slid the sheeting over again.

He heard Steve being taken now and when he returned he called out to him.

'Better than a deckchair at Southend, eh, Steve?' His voice was cracked and dry too.

The next night was cold and the morning took so long to come, but then the heat came too and the flies and the noise of the sticks and because they had spoken to one another their arms were tied behind their backs after they had been taken to the latrines. Food was still passed in, though, but they had to bend over and lick it from the tin like animals.

They didn't call to one another again, but they shuffled their feet or they coughed and that was enough. And it was enough, too, for Jack to sit still now and hold his body upright, to ignore the bindings and think of blossom, Rosie and the cool of England.

After two days the guards untied their arms, but pushed them back down again into the pit. There were deep raw grooves in their skin from the rope but these didn't touch the thoughts inside Jack's head, the memories, the echoes of the life he had lived, the people he had loved.

In the second week he pictured the pebbles in the stream below the hop-yards. He picked them from the water. The water was cool, the pebbles wet. He built a pyramid. The pebbles dried. He walked amongst the cool green fountains of hops, and saw the yellow dust beneath his fingernails. He picked the hops, flicking them into the bin. He smelt them, felt them. Kissed Rosie, laughed with Ed, smelt the lavender on Maisie's neck, threw Lee up into the air, heard his laughter. Heard Ollie's too.

In the third week he breathed slowly, emptied his mind, and on each trip to the latrine he coughed with a dry throat, and each time he heard Steve do the same he knew he could go on. They were released at the end of August.

Jack could barely stand. The light hurt his eyes as it had hurt them each time he had walked to the latrine. He was marched back to the compound, through North Koreans who threw stones at him and called him a murderer.

They did the same to Steve, whose beard was dark against his white skin. Jack rubbed his own beard. He watched the stones hit his friend. But Steve didn't notice. He was thin, his legs trembled as Jack's did. They met at the gate, nodded, smiled, held one another's arms.

'The war must be nearly over,' they called to a prisoner who brought them water. They lifted the cans to their lips.

The young boy shook his head. 'New POWs in say the talks will go on and on, maybe for years. There's no truce, only more fighting.'

They felt sick with something deeper than anguish and couldn't move as they watched the boy walk on, his head down, dust scuffing up with each step. The hop-yards were fading. Jack couldn't hold on to them.

They walked towards Nigel's hut but he wasn't there. He had been moved to the officers' camp, another prisoner told them.

'He didn't want to go. He wanted to wait for you, but he had no choice. They're trying to destroy the old leadership system, demoralise everyone, so the officers have been separated from the ranks. He died there last week. We've only just heard.'

CHAPTER 21

Joe came at the beginning of June, when Rosie had only been home a week. He walked into the café as Lucia slept in her pram outside the kitchen door in the small sunswept courtyard. Rosie was talking on the phone to a promoter who wanted Luke at whatever cost.

'Though within reason, my dear.'

Rosie laughed. 'Twenty pounds. Excluding expenses. I don't think I can be more reasonable than that, Harry.' She knew he would take far more in profit for she had been to the function room behind his pub, seen his gold rings, his expensive watch.

Rosie grinned as he sounded her out about a national tour for the band. She turned to write the date in the book. Joe moved and she looked up, saw his blond hair, his tanned skin, his white teeth. She saw the watch which gleamed against his skin. It was new. Everything went quite still and then jogged into motion again as she put her pen down, carefully. There was ink on the nib. It had smeared her finger.

She didn't kiss him but shook his hand, feeling cold, wishing he hadn't come. Her world had been intruded upon. The lies were about to be exposed and she was ashamed. For the first time for weeks she was ashamed.

He grinned, looked around. 'So this is it?'

'Yes, this is it.' She poured him coffee, nodded towards Luke. 'We're on for Saturday. Expenses excluded. Twenty pounds!'

Luke whistled and Joe looked at her. 'From what Frank said I imagined the restaurant would be bigger.'

'Remember you're in little old England now,' she said, wiping the counter.

'You're looking good.' He sipped the black coffee as he leaned against the counter.

Rosie didn't know what to say to this man who didn't belong here. Who shouldn't have come. 'You must meet Luke,' she said, her voice cold and crisp, because she could remember that the hand that lifted the cup had stroked her breasts. It had been a mistake.

Joe arched his eyebrows. 'Have I said something wrong? Burst in on you? I should have rung. I didn't think.' He looked unsure suddenly. She hadn't seen this in him before and she smiled, reaching out her hand, touching his.

'No, I'm just busy. Too much to do, too little time.' She had pushed the thought of his trip away, unable to think of any lies strong enough to make Frank change his plans, too engrossed in Lucia. And now she relaxed. What did it matter? Lucia was with her, safe, beautiful. That was what was important.

'Luke,' she called. 'Meet Joe. Uncle Bob's scout.' She laughed and Joe relaxed, shook hands and passed Camels round while Rosie collected cups, took orders, and passed them through to Mrs Orsini.

She then took Joe out to the yard. There was no point in wasting time but she had to make sure he didn't tell Frank and Nancy.

She walked to the pram, and pulled back the blanket. 'This is my child. Jack's child,' she said.

She watched Joe flush. He looked from the baby to Rosie but said nothing. He just stood, his hands in his pockets, and then he murmured, 'Quite a surprise. No wonder you didn't want to visit Frank and Nancy. They've got quite a bit on their plates already. This might shake them up a bit.'

Rosie touched her child's hair. It was always so fine, so soft, so warm. 'I'll tell them when things are easier for them, but you must say nothing. You must promise me that.'

She waited, wondering whether he would agree, wondering how she could make him, if he refused. But he agreed and she was surprised, but why should she be? He was kind, wasn't he? He had sent her money to go over to Frank. But she was still surprised and didn't know why.

Joe touched the baby, who woke.

'I thought you hadn't heard anything from Jack?'

'I haven't. He doesn't know, but I'll tell him, when he writes, because one day he will.'

He laughed as Lucia gripped his finger. His shirt was so white against the tan of his skin and he had promised he would say nothing. Rosie was grateful. He had touched her child and smiled and she was pleased.

He didn't stay long but came again in the evening to hear the band. Luke played while Joe drank Coke and listened, his finger tapping on the glass. Luke's band played for an hour and the music was good, mellow, haunting, penetrating. They listened to the chord held at the end of the chorus, heard the crescendo as Luke led the band into an all-in section. They heard the growl, heard his improvisation but it was a carefully planned one. He was so good, and Jake was better. So much better, but he still needed to go a little further.

'He'll get there though,' she told Joe. He nodded.

Luke sat with them in the interval. There was smoke in the air and candle wax on the table. Rosie checked her watch. Mrs Orsini was looking after Lucia but she would need a feed at ten.

'Great, really great. This club is good too, better than I expected,' Joe said, and Rosie winked at Luke, who sat back in his chair and smiled. 'You're right, Rosie. Bob'll really go for this. It's what he's been looking for. The guy on sax will have to go though.'

Rosie felt cold. It was as though there was no laughter in the room, no murmur of voices. Hadn't he heard her? Hadn't she just said that Jake would make it? Joe was still smiling, lifting the glass to his mouth, and she could picture him at the Lake Clubhouse, smart, adored, arrogant, ruthless. But he had agreed to keep her secret. There must be some softness there, maybe?

'But Jake is almost there. He's getting better every day,' Luke protested, and Rosie nodded, looking at their clothes, looking at Joe's. But no matter how slick he was, he was wrong.

'He'll make it. I'll stake my reputation on it. I'll pull in favours from Uncle Bob,' she added quietly.

Joe put the glass back on the table, and looked towards the group who were edging their way back through the tables.

'Look, Luke, you're a commodity. Bob can package you but you've got to get rid of the weak link. There's no room for feelings in this game.' He turned to Rosie. 'This is business. You need to toughen up, Rosie.'

Rosie stared at Joe, then at Luke. She waited.

'No,' Luke said getting to his feet. 'Thank you, Joe, but no. We all go, or no one goes. No package without Jake.' His smile was ironic.

Joe shrugged. 'I think you're wrong.'

Rosie put up her hand to stop Luke. She could fight for Luke now that he had made his decision. And she would fight because there was more than one way of doing business. You didn't have to be hard, just fair, and Joe could be fair. He had shown her that this afternoon.

'He's not wrong. Bob thinks of his bands as people. You're wrong, Joe. Think of the group who played at the barbecue, Bob nurtured them. Jake needs confidence, that's all, and a little time.' She wanted to shout at him, but she kept her voice calm. 'Bob wouldn't thank you if you passed this group over and they made it elsewhere, because they will.'

She watched him as he crossed his legs, picked at a thread on the sleeve of his jacket, rolled it between his thumb and forefinger. His nails were short, clean and square.

'Have you a lot invested in these guys?' Joe asked her quietly, leaning forward, talking behind his glass.

'A lot of time, a lot of effort, a lot of pleasure. Why not give them until you leave England? See what happens.' Why did he equate everything with money? She thought of his family. How could he be otherwise? But he could learn. She remembered his hand on her child. She still held on to Luke's jacket.

Joe looked at her and grinned. 'Why not? Bob's in no rush. OK. You got a deal. Just one condition.'

Rosie felt Luke relax, she let her hand drop from his jacket, feeling the relief surge in her too. She nodded. 'What?'

'I've got to write a feature for Frank on the Festival. You're expected to send one back too. Show me round. Let's have some fun.' He was smiling, his voice was lazy again as it had been on the beach by the lake.

She didn't want to celebrate while Jack was fighting, but she nodded. He knew about Lucia. He was going to report to Bob and he had been fair. There was no choice, but they wouldn't be alone. She would take Lucia, Jack's child.

695

But before she went anywhere, with Joe or anyone else, she took Lucia to Middle Street one morning when Norah would be at work. She pushed the back yard gate open, and picked up Lucia, taking her to Grandpa's roses, their fragrance heavy on the mid June air.

She walked along by The Reverend Ashe, took a matchbox from her pocket and tipped out the ladybird she had found, easing it with her finger on to the underside of the bud where too many greenfly were flourishing. Poor Grandpa.

'This will never do, will it, Lucia?' she said softly, bending to kiss the head of the sleeping baby. She heard the back door open and turned. Norah wasn't at work, she was standing in the doorway with a mouth like a sparrow's bum. Nothing changed.

'Hello, Norah.'

Her sister looked her up and down and then the baby in the fine white crocheted shawl which Mrs Eaves had made.

'I heard you'd had it.' She stood with her arms crossed over her breasts.

Rosie moved closer. 'I thought I would bring her to see Grandpa's roses, and now to meet you.'

Norah shook her head. 'I don't want to see your by-blows and now you've fiddled with the roses you can go. That fool Harold spends enough time on them as it is.' Her face was tight.

Rosie gently brushed away a bee that was hovering over Lucia. No, nothing changed. 'I'm sorry I bothered you.'

She reached out and picked the dark red rose from the raised bed. It was loosely budded. She smelt it, put Lucia back in the pram, and laid the rose on her blanket. Before she left she turned. 'There have been no letters for me then? No news for Ollie about Jack?'

Norah shook her head. 'He won't come back for you. You're on your own now.'

Rosie nodded. 'I'm not on my own any more, Norah.' She looked at Lucia, then pushed her from the yard, towards the rec where she sat on the swing with Lucia in her arms and watched the children playing, the mothers sitting knitting, talking. Thinking of Lee and of herself. Of Jack, of Norah. Listening to the echoes.

Norah sat in the kitchen, stirring her tea. The door was shut against the sun and those bloody roses. Shut against the sight of her sister with the baby that she and Harold seemed unable to produce.

Yes, there had been a letter from Jack. She had destroyed it. Yes, there had been a letter to Ollie informing him that Jack was a prisoner of war. She had told Ollie that Rosie had been informed.

She sipped her tea, looking at the space where Grandpa's chair had been, at the shelves devoid of books. How dare she take things from this house? How dare she have a child and a new white shawl? How dare she be loved, because Norah had read Jack's letter before she had burnt it. How dare she be loved when Harold no longer sat opposite her in front of the fireplace, and instead went out rubbing brasses or pruning roses. How dare she?

It was a hot day when Joe and Rosie went to the Festival, and as they approached the South Bank and the Skylon that seemed to hang in the air above them, Rosie said, 'I wonder if this isn't some sort of paternalistic exercise in educating the masses. There are so many exhibitions here which seem designed to present British Society as a family divided, not by class, but by a rift between the imaginative and the practical.'

Why was she talking like this? she wondered. Lecturing and pointing towards the twenty-seven acres which lay between County Hall and Waterloo Bridge.

'Casson and the other architects have laid it out like a miniature wonderland. It's crazy when there's still so much hardship, so much ruin. There's still so much fighting in Palestine and Africa and Korea.'

That was why she was lecturing. Because she was with another man and that man was pushing her child. He had been kind, and it was good to have someone with her, but it should have been Jack.

There were thousands of others strolling with them, stopping, investigating here, by the red, white and blue awning, the role of the British in exploration and discovery. Over there, by the yellow stand, was the geology of the country. Over there by the brown was the history of the monarchy.

697

'This is some kind of a pat on the back, is it?' Joe said, cupping his hand round the cigarette in his mouth, protecting the match from the wind which lifted his hair. He stood with his back to the crowds, one of whom nudged him. He dropped the match. Began again.

'Yes, I suppose so. We deserve it. You just have to look around.' Rosie pushed Lucia on. 'You haven't got this kind of damage back in the States, have you? You don't have to queue for basic foodstuffs. You just call in your loans.'

Joe laughed, drew on his cigarette, flicked the match into a litter bin. 'Point taken. But this really is quite something.'

He was taking photographs now, of the piazzas, the terraces, the murals and modern sculptures. Rosie looked in one pavilion, saw the new design in furniture, the chairs with spindly legs and the spidery staircases rising into the air. They looked as though they would take no weight.

An exhibitor smiled and called her over. 'Come on, madam, try the chair.'

She looked at Joe, who nodded. 'Go on then.' He took a photo and she pulled a face and then another and he was clicking all the time and then they were laughing.

They looked at the plan of the exhibits, following the red dotted line with their fingers, and Joe said they must retrace their steps and start at the beginning or they wouldn't get any sort of an article out of all this.

They began then at The Land of Britain and Rosie took notes on how the natural wealth of the British Isles came into being. She told Joe that she was going to slant her feature by comparing the new architecture – the piazzas, the modern sculpture – with damaged Britain, utilitarian Britain, the Nissen huts, the pill-boxes. He called her a 'goddamn pinko'. They laughed and she waited but he didn't tell her how he was going to write his feature.

They moved along, listening, looking, writing, talking, and he told her that Frank was well, much better than anyone had hoped.

'More important, though, are the circulation figures. They're right up again now that he's started using a pseudonym. The money's rolling in again.'

Rosie looked at him, at his smiling face, his assured manner, the hands which carried his notepad. A woman was in the way of the pram and Rosie stopped, waited.

'Excuse me, ma'am,' Joe called. 'We're trying to get through here.'

The woman turned. Rosie smiled. 'Don't hurry, we're looking too.'

She was embarrassed that Joe had wanted to force his way through. They had all day, there was no panic. She looked at the small models of the Skylon, the symbol of the Festival, which a trader was selling. Rosie bought one, and put it on the end of the pram, and the woman came over, looked at Lucia and smiled.

'You're a lucky couple, she's lovely.'

Rosie nodded and Joe flushed. 'I know,' Rosie said and it was only later as they were looking at the photographs representing the wide range of British manufacturers that she said gently, 'You said that the circulation figures were more important than Frank and that the money is rolling in. I hardly feel that either of these things is more important than Frank. Now I must find somewhere to feed Lucia.'

She looked around. There was a tent for lost children with a red pennant on the top. Her breasts were full and heavy, they were aching. She was angry with Joe.

She pushed the pram into the tent, sat on a folding chair, put Lucia to her breast and thought of the woman who had looked at the baby and said how lucky *they* were. And though she had been angry with Joe it had been so good to pretend for that short moment that she was one of a pair. She looked at the ring on her finger. Was she always going to be alone, or would he come?

They ate sandwiches and tea at a stall and Joe said, 'I didn't mean to say that the paper was more important than Frank. I guess you must know that.'

Rosie ate the moist bread, the Wensleydale cheese.

'Do I?' she replied. 'I'm not sure that I know anything any more.'

Joe put down his cup and asked for coffee because he couldn't drink the tea. It was ninepence. 'Gee, that's a lot.'

He took it and turned back to her. 'It's just that it's everything he's worked for. He loves that paper. I love it. I work real hard now. It's coming up good. It's going to be a good investment.'

'And what about McCarthy? Do you write against that poison, Joe? Do you shout that it's wrong to victimise innocent people?'

Joe bought another coffee and they moved away to let others near. 'Frank writes against it. That's enough.'

They finished eating, then walked further but Rosie was tired and there was something wrong. She was still angry and she didn't understand why.

'I must get back now, Joe. I've some calls to make, some details for Luke's tour to tie up and the other bands too.'

He nodded, pushing a path through the crowds. 'You shouldn't have to work like this, not with a baby. It needs two.'

Rosie shrugged. 'I'm doing just fine.'

'You sure are but it's a lot to handle. You're just swell.' He leaned over and propped the Skylon upright, but it fell over again as she mounted the kerb on their way out.

'Is it still OK for this evening?' he asked.

Rosie nodded. They had planned to go with Luke and Sandy downriver to Battersea Park to see the open air sculptures and then on to the fun-fair. She hadn't wanted to go alone with Joe.

Mrs Orsini looked after Lucia that evening and they took a cab to Battersea Park which exuded so much light that it bounced off the clouds and for a moment Rosie was with Frank and Nancy in New York again.

As they arrived fireworks soared high into the air. They heard the bangs and the whizz and Joe said, 'Guess they knew we were coming and this is the welcome mat.'

Tonight he was different somehow, he talked of Frank's expertise, his kindness. He said how much he respected him, how empty life would have been if anything had happened to him, and Rosie looked at him and smiled, her anger dying.

'I'm glad you feel the same as I do.'

They linked arms with Luke and Sandy and marched in step to the fun-fair singing 'Roll Out the Barrel', and by the time they arrived Joe knew the words.

They sat on painted horses, clutched the spiralling poles, and couldn't talk because the music was so loud, but they laughed. They all laughed and then they swung in boats, the ropes slipping between their hands. They shot ducks and she wouldn't think of Jack. They threw darts and she won a teddy bear and Joe carried it for her. They laughed, sang, drank and she felt young again. So young and the lights were on the river and it was as though she was by the lake. She felt Joe's arm around her, felt his kiss on her cheek.

'It's sure good to see you again, Rosie,' he murmured, and she smiled.

'Yes, it's good to see a friend from America. It's been so long. You were kind to tell me about Frank, and send my ticket over. I shall always be grateful to you for that.' She touched his face. 'Thank you.'

Luke grabbed her, pointed towards a striped tent. 'This we have got to see.' He dragged her off and she laughed and touched his cheek too. It was good to have friends.

They tried to guess the weight of the fat woman in the striped tent and ate candy floss which stuck to their faces in melted strands. They stood and watched the horses again, then had another go, and another. In the hall of mirrors they pulled faces, stuck out their legs, lifted their arms, and laughed until they ached.

They went on to the Fairway of the South Bank and danced, she with Luke, Sandy with Joe. They jitterbugged, and there was no Palais MC to tap her on the shoulder, no forbidding notices pinned to walls.

Joe tapped Luke's shoulder and she danced with him. They jived and his arms were strong as he pulled her towards him, steered her back, moved with her and with the music. His wrists were dark against his shirt. He pulled his handkerchief from his pocket, wiped his face, threw back his head and laughed.

'This is just great.'

And it was. Then the music slowed and they danced cheek to cheek and he told her of the drive-in movies they had in the States now. How kids would drive in, take a bay, honk their horns to bring the girl car-hops to their windows, order their food, which was brought to them on a hook-on tray. How the kids kissed and loved and hooted their horns when they had gone all the way.

She didn't want to hear this. Not from Joe. He was too close. So she talked instead about the growing popularity of jazz in Britain. So many loved it and all the time she could feel his breath on her hair, the heat of his skin as he held her hand. All the time she could remember the feel of his lips and hands on her breasts and she was angry at Jack because he wasn't here. Because he hadn't written and she was lonely.

But then she was angry at herself because she was dancing to music, swaying with the rhythm, laughing, when there was a war on. And nobody seemed to care. And she didn't understand herself.

'The Gloucesters' casualty figures came in as the King inaugurated this Festival,' Rosie said against Joe's shirt.

'Speak up, Rosie, I can't hear you,' he said, quickening his pace because the music was faster now, but they were jitterbugging again and she didn't repeat her words.

They danced until midnight and she wasn't tired but her breasts were full again. They caught a cab, then walked home, all of them, and Soho was still awake and they all wanted to go on to a club, but her dress was wet from the milk and how could she tell them that? She asked them in for a coffee while she checked on Lucia, and asked Mrs Orsini if she would mind staying for longer. Mrs Orsini sat in Grandpa's chair and smiled.

'You look happy. You look twenty-one at last. That is good.'

Rosie said again, 'We'd like to go to a club. I know it's very late, but I'll do the kitchen in the morning.'

Mrs Orsini smiled. 'You feed her now then you go back down and you go to a jazz club with them and we will share the kitchen. I like to see you like this.'

She put down her knitting and held up a hand as Rosie thanked her. 'No. No thanks. You just do as an old witch tells you and be happy. Tonight you are young and you are free. Go and explore yourself. My Mario says the same.'

Rosie picked Lucia up, felt her suck the nipple and she stroked the head of Jack's child.

They went on to the 51 Club. Luke knew the man on the door. Joe bought champagne and the ice clinked in the silver bucket. Rosie ran her finger down it. It was so cold. Joe eased off the stopper with a light thud. He poured the brimming bottle, letting the froth subside in each glass, then topping them up.

'To us all,' he said and they lifted their glasses.

'To us all,' Rosie repeated and included Jack.

They listened to the jazz. The air was thick with smoke and with laughter, theirs included, and Luke said that perhaps there should be dancing at Mario's. It was happening in other clubs. He nodded towards the floor.

'Not enough room, unless we open up the annexe,' Rosie said. 'Still, no reason why not. I'll talk to Mario. But I want to talk to this group first. They're good.'

Luke laughed, but Joe didn't. 'Can't you leave your work behind for one night?'

Rosie looked at him. 'It's work I love. It's work I need. There's Lucia, you know.'

He paused, then smiled, lifting the glass to her. 'I understand,' he said, but she wondered if he did.

She worked her way through the tables, catching up with the saxophonist, a young man with glasses, as he led his group to the bar, and booked them for Luke's tour that she and Harry, the promoter, were organising. She had a full programme now and she and Luke bought the next bottle of champagne because life had been good to them this summer. Rosie nodded, she had eight bands to organise now. It felt good.

They joined the other dancers on the floor and the beat was insistent, the lights revolved, she was young, she was free and tonight she had friends and more than that, she had a partner to hold her, swirl her round, pour her drink, toast her, and the tiredness dropped from her as they danced until nearly dawn.

Joe walked her home, waving to Luke and Sandy, shrugging away their thanks. Rosie was quiet because it was different now that they were alone. It was not so safe, so easy.

The streets were emptying as they walked from one pool of light to the next and there were no ropes hanging on the lampposts. Rosie told Joe that when she and Jack had been children there had been some in Middle Street. They had tied them. She looked at her hands. She could still feel the rope.

He stopped then, caught her arms, held her to him, stared into her face.

703

'He's gone. He hasn't written. He won't come back. Surely you know that now. You must make a life for yourself.'

Rosie pulled away, looking up at the sky where the clouds still hung. 'I don't know that. I don't know anything. If only I knew where he was, what he's doing, what he's feeling, I would know where I was going. No, I don't know anything, Joe, only that I love him.' She wished Luke and Sandy were still here, that they were all dancing and laughing again.

She looked down again at her hands, then at Joe. 'You're going to Japan. Frank told me. See where he is. Find him for me?'

He took her hands in his. He was warm, gentle. 'We were friends, Rosie. It would have been more if you hadn't left. Do you remember the beach?'

She shook her head, but she did. Goddamn it, she did. She said, 'I know he'll write. I know he loves me. Find him for me, Joe.'

She walked back towards the flat, back towards Jack's child. Joe walked with her, his strides long, easy. He said nothing but kissed her cheek at the door.

'I'll be back in December. I'll find out what I can.'

CHAPTER 22

It had been hard to accept Nigel's death, to think that he would never go to Oxford or punt on the river as he had talked so often of doing. That he would no longer wake up in the morning and look towards the hills and say, 'It's quite exquisite.'

Jack and Steve sat against the hut wall together in the baking heat of early September and marvelled that it was still only 1951. It seemed a very long time since they had first arrived in Korea. They felt so old and they were only twenty-one.

As more days passed Steve talked of college, of the history course he would take. His parents farmed in the Mid-West and couldn't understand that he wanted to move to New York, to feel cluttered by the buildings, to hole himself up and write novels.

'They say, get a proper job. OK, so I will, but one day I'll get there.'

Jack threw pebbles at the marker Steve had dropped. He had struck twice. If he did it again it was Steve's turn.

'I've never really thought what I'd do. It was all going to wait until I finished the draft.' He threw again. The pebble missed.

'You got a lot of time to think now, bud.'

The next pebble hit. They heard the click, heard a man rush past them with his arms outstretched, his mouth pursed, roaring like an engine. Two more men came close behind him. They looked at one another and grinned. It was silly time. They stood up, kicked down the pile of stones and joined in the swooping and whirling, dodging in and out of the others. One Corporal became a helicopter.

The guards stood and watched, bemused. But then the planes started making staccato gun noises and the guards moved forward, pushing, shouting, and at a signal from the

Corporal the men stopped dead. Their arms still outstretched until there was another signal, the jerking of a head. They stood to attention, their protest made for today; confusion generated. It made them feel less powerless.

They were made to dig holes as punishment for the gun noises. The soil was dry and stony but they had all done this at basic training. There was nothing new in the world. They were ordered to fill the holes in. They had done this in basic training too.

The next week they watched a tennis match, all the men lining either side of an imaginary court in the compound. They moved their heads in unison, watching a non-existent ball, clapping as the scores were called. This time there was no punishment but it would have been worth it, even if there had been. Jack wrote it down on the extra paper that he stole during essay writing.

'Rosie might be able to make something of it,' he told Steve.

'You make something of it. I'll help.'

Jack shook his head. 'We won't be here *that* long. I'm better suited to the market stall.'

They were still there in November, though, when the cold crackled in the air. By then the ground was too hard for them to dig as punishment and so they were made to stand upright until what little sun there was had gone from the day and frost coated their clothes. A man laughed at the Chinese guards who walked by, holding hands.

Jack allowed Steve to help him draft out an article on the escapade because he wanted to discuss the confusion between cultures, the cruelty of laughter. They knew now that the fighting would go on for a long time and, therefore, they would be here for a long time too. They understood that now and were trying to stay sane, trying not to think of the news the new prisoners had told them when they had been marched into the compound.

The peace talks were being held up by the Communists who wanted all their captured men to be returned, irrespective of whether or not they wished to be. The West remembered Yalta, and would not agree to this. It was insane that they were all kept here, day after day. But they mustn't go insane, they knew that.

'It's like the First World War back there, mate,' a Lance-Jack had told them. 'We're ranged in two lines along a static front lobbing everything we can get at one another, while the politicians talk. It's a laugh a minute. Nice and quiet here, though.'

But that was before he had sat through two hours of indoctrination in Chinese, two hours of translation, then attended interviews, then written essays. They spoke to him two weeks later when he was thinner, bored, restless, longing for a home which was very far away, longing for a letter, though no mail had yet been distributed. No, none of them must go insane. They must have something to work towards, to hang on to.

A new Commandant arrived. He called each of them in for an interview. He smoked but Jack didn't. There was no tobacco any more, only that which was offered by the lecturers, the interrogators, to those who volunteered to give propaganda interviews.

The man had smooth olive skin. His voice was soft. He smiled. Jack smiled. Would it be the same as it had always been?

'What does your father do?'

'He sells vegetables.'

'What does your mother do?'

No, it was not the same.

'My mother does nothing,' Jack said, not knowing now what Maisie did. Was she still laughing with her head thrown back? Did she still make bread and dripping? Do Americans eat that? He must ask Steve. He smiled because it didn't hurt to think of her any more.

'Why you smile? You are proud that mother not work? That mother lazy?'

'My mother is not lazy. I'm smiling at something private.'

'There is nothing private. You are being cleansed here. All is open. Why you smile?'

'I smile because I love my mother.'

The Chinese looked at the interpreter, then back at Jack. Then down at his sheet.

'Why your mother not work?'

'She has a child.'

707

'She could work with your father.'

'Maybe.' Jack shrugged. He couldn't tell this man his mother had gone away with a GI. That she lived in the land where the capitalist warmongers thrived. That she had chosen to do this. He had learned here that truth was sometimes best avoided. Rosie had known that. She had been right.

'How much land your family got?'

'As big as this room.' Jack looked round. 'Yes, as big as this room.'

He could see the shed, the fence, Lee's toys. He could smell Grandpa's roses. Were they still there?

'How many cows your family got?'

'We get milk in bottles.' Yes, he could still smell the roses, and yes they would still be there. Rosie would make sure of that. And no, he wouldn't go insane, not when he had her to return to.

'How many pigs?'

'No pigs.'

'What jewels you own?'

'No jewels.'

'What coins you own?'

'No coins.' But there was the nailer's penny. Did Rosie still have that? He knew she would.

The Commandant wrote, his head down, dandruff on his shoulders, then he sat back in his chair. 'You poor peasant. You should like our ways. You should fight the capitalists.'

Jack shrugged. The questions had begun differently but the end had been the same.

He told Steve not to mention his horses, his acres, his cows. He told him not to be too generous with the truth, not to get angry, not to shout, because he knew his friend dreamed of the pit and woke groaning. Jack did too.

'Don't let him sting you into saying anything,' Jack said.

But the Commandant did sting Steve and he did shout and rage and was dragged to the pit, stripped to the waist when the cold was deep in their bones. He was there while the Americans celebrated Thanksgiving with a service and songs, not feasts.

Jack wrote about the service, about the handfuls of millet which they had cooked to eat that day, and most days. He wrote about the Pilgrims. He drew parallels between the two.

But it was muddled and that was how he wanted it to be because he would need it like that when Steve was released.

He showed it to Steve when he came out. He made him sit and read it, while others threw their jackets over him, and blankets too, all donated by the men who had heated water for him to drink.

'Get away, Jack,' Steve said, pushing the paper aside, trying to curl over. 'Just get away. I've had enough. It's never going to end.'

But Jack had known he would say this. It was what he would have felt and he also knew that if he took the paper away it would be the beginning of the end. So he dragged Steve upright.

'Come on, Steve, I can't get it right. It's confused. You can help.'

Steve was pushing him away again, but Jack came back, shoving the paper in his face. Steve took it, scrunched it up, threw it across the room, and lay down. Rob, another prisoner, brought the paper back to Jack and helped to support Steve.

'Read this, you goddamn give-upper. You bloody Yanks, you're all the same.' Jack wasn't shouting, but his face was close to Steve's. He wasn't angry either, but Steve wasn't going to be allowed to give up. Those who did so died and Jack wasn't going to lose this friend who was so like Ed.

He straightened out the paper but again Steve knocked it from him, and it took an hour to force him to look at it. He stabbed at the second paragraph with a dirt-choked finger.

'Take it out. Who wants to know that garbage? Ain't you got no sense, Jack?' His voice was tired, angry, but he was reading it. Jack rewrote it in the morning and again Steve turned it down and it wasn't until the evening of the second day that he nodded, but Jack didn't care whether it was good or not, Steve was back on side. That was what mattered.

They attended lectures as before, threw stones at markers, as before, and Steve said, 'No more pit for either of us, eh?'

Jack nodded. 'Yep, let's get to the end of all this, then go out and get blind drunk, once in England, once in New York.'

They rose. It was time for afternoon lectures and the young men who filled the camp wondered how the minutes could drag so slowly, how their bones could ache with boredom, but they did. Day after day after day.

The next week they were all called into the big hut and saw a prisoner sitting alongside the Commandant. There were Chinese cigarettes on the table in front of him. The Commandant rose.

'You not have group study this morning. You have morning to self because one has behaved with great satisfaction.' He pointed to the prisoner who stared ahead.

'This man has seen the truth. He will go now from the camp and he will tell the world on the radio of the crimes of the Imperialists. He will tell of the wrongness of his attitude which has given way to correctness.'

There was silence in the room.

'You too can leave this camp. You too can see the truth. Your countries are not interested in you. You are still here. The war goes on. You are behind wire, play foolish tricks while warmongers eat in restaurants. Your wives live well without you. The years pass. Even if you do go home, we can reach you. You are never free of us. It is better to be a friend than enemy.'

He took a cigarette from the pack and gave it to the man, who put it between his lips. He was thin, drawn and his eyes still looked straight ahead. The Commandant lit the cigarette, smoke spiralled up to the wooden roof. Jack watched it disappear.

There was still silence, even when they were dismissed. The words were the same as they had been on previous occasions and there had been silence then. No one booed, no one blamed the man. It was his way of surviving.

'Gets to you, though, doesn't it?' Steve said as they crouched on the ground and threw stones at the marker. Jack had won thirteen games, Steve eighteen. 'Guess the months could become years.'

Jack nodded, looking round at the hills dusted with snow. It was so cold. He looked up at the sky, it was cloud-heavy. There might be snow tomorrow. Where could they throw their stones? It was better to think of that.

But the next week they were told it was over. The guards herded them into columns, the Commandant stood before them, the snow falling on his cap, his pressed olive green uniform, his soft golden skin, as he told them 'All prisoners go home'.

It was too sudden. He could not believe it, but then he felt Steve's hand on his arm. 'We're going to make it, Jack.' And then the joy came, coursing through him from deep inside.

They were dismissed. For a moment they could not move, then they leaped in the air, whooping, cheering, some crying. They were going home, goddamn it, they were going home. Jack thought of Rosie, of running down the alley towards her, of her arms as she came out of Grandpa's yard. Then he thought of the prisoner who had taken cigarettes in return for survival. Would he go home?

Joy pushed the hunger and the cold away. It brought smiles to faces which had stiffened into grim endurance. It brought hope into faces which had been without for too long. They were going home.

They were marched to a train, the snow soaking into their worn uniforms and through the split seams of their boots, but they marched in time, their few possessions slung on their backs.

The Sergeant called out the drill orders. Their shoulders were straight. They took the walking wounded, helping them, bearing their weight, and Jack felt the stones he had thrown at the marker in his pocket. They could be kept with Grandpa's penny.

He turned and looked back at the mountains. 'How exquisite,' he said.

Steve nodded his goodbye to Nigel too.

They were marched to a train. There were no seats but it didn't matter. They would be home for Christmas. They headed south in the last of the daylight, looking out across the country, seeing the ruins, the devastation, the napalm-damaged hills. The people were living in dugouts, hovels. There was nothing but poverty, but they were working, stolidly clearing the snow, cooking over open fires, ignoring the train. Jack wrote about this for as long as the daylight lasted, asking what the fighting had been about, but soon it was too dark to see the page.

There was no light then, no food, no drink. They sat on the floor, moving with the train, huddled together for warmth.

'My mom'll be pleased,' Steve said, his voice a murmur like all the others.

711

'I'll write to mine but first I'll see Rosie,' Jack said.

Before daylight broke they eased into a tunnel and stayed there throughout the day to avoid the air strikes. So the fighting wasn't over, the Sergeant asked the guard, looking uncertain.

'No, you being exchanged,' the guard said.

They had water, they had food, but they were colder now and blew on to their hands, draping old blankets over their shoulders. But did any of it matter? They were going home. They were bloody well going home.

Bob sat with them, talking of the food he would cook on his wife's stove in their prefab.

'I don't know, you retreads. You've all gone soft,' Steve laughed. 'Let her do the cooking.'

Jack laughed too, wondering how reservists could bear to be called up, having already done their bit, and then he thought of Tom. He would not be going back. He thought of Suko too and hoped that she would find happiness.

Bob told them how he would cut the rind off the bacon, fry that until it was crisp, then the bacon, then the mushrooms picked the evening before from fields behind the house. He would take the sharp knife from the drawer, slice the tomatoes, grown against the wall behind the house, and fry them too. He would walk up the ash path to pick the warm eggs from the coop, the straw still on the shells. Soon the whole wagon was listening, hearing the fat spitting, tasting the bacon, the British not caring that it was the wrong season for tomatoes, not caring that bacon was still on ration. It was home, and that was where they were going, and now they cheered and laughed even when the guards swung back the door and said, 'Quiet. You should sleep. Quiet.'

How could they sleep? They were leaving here. The big man himself had said so.

They travelled on south as darkness came. On the fifth night they were shunted into a siding near Pyongyang where they stayed for a week, asking the guards each day when they would be released.

'When Captain come,' they said.

The men used a bucket as a latrine, pushing it far into the corner. They squashed lice which still bit them in spite of the cold, but none of this was for long and so it didn't matter.

On the eleventh day a Chinese Captain slid open the wagon door and they clambered to their feet, pushing towards the entrance. Other guards put up their rifles as the Captain said, 'You go north instead. Prisoner-of-war camp. A mistake has been made.' He smiled and slammed the door shut and there was only darkness, only silence. It had been a trick, but a darker trick than the ones they had played. It was a pitch black trick.

It broke three of the men. It nearly broke all of them. Hope had gone. Hate had come for many of them, but not for Jack. He had had enough of hate. He just wrote it down and Steve helped. They made Bob help too because he cursed and swore, beating the side of the wagon with his fists. He wasn't the only one who came close to despair as the train swept north again. There were tears too, in the darkness of the night.

'Funny trick, eh?' Steve whispered to Jack, his voice full.

'Capped our games in the camp, didn't it? Quick learners, eh?' The tears were dry on Jack's cheeks now, there would be streaks in the dirt. He rubbed his skin.

'The goddamn bastards.'

'Maybe we could try and escape,' Jack whispered. He couldn't bear to think of the train taking him further and further from Rosie. He wanted to break from it, hurl the guards to one side, rush for the South. 'Can't be too far from the lines now, but with each day, it's further. We'll talk as we march.'

A guard had told them they were leaving the train the next morning. They waited, sitting with their arms around their knees, resting their heads, but not sleeping. No one was sleeping. How could they when the disappointment was so sharp, the anger so raw?

They were marched from the train, out into a road cleared of snow.

'To another camp,' the guards said, pointing north.

The Sergeant lined the men up before they left, ignoring the guards who gestured for them to begin. He stood before them, looking as thin as they did, but ramrod straight, his eyes sweeping the men. 'You'll march in step. You'll remember who you are. You'll not let these buggers beat you, or I shall have your heads for my breakfast and your danglies for my lunch. Is that quite clear?'

The men smiled and nodded.

The Sergeant barked, 'About turn.' He ignored the guard who was pulling at his clothes and shouting at his men to hurry. 'Forward march.'

It was only then that the men moved, and they did so in perfect unison. It was only after the first mile that the pace slowed but they were still in time. They would be until they dropped now.

Before Steve and Jack could make their move, two Americans ducked out of the line as it passed between wooded slopes. They sneaked off into the undergrowth. Jack watched them snake across the snow-covered rice field to the base of the hill. They were stark against the white and their footsteps were clear.

Ten minutes later, the alarm was raised. North Korean guards found them two hours later and beat them to death.

Later Jack looked up at the condensation trails behind the shooting stars as the north-west jet streams pushed the planes home and nodded when Steve said, 'Seems kinda pointless. Might as well get through school, buddy.'

They both nodded, still marching, still watching the men in front, blocking out the two beaten bodies which had been thrown into the ox-cart. Those men would never go home now.

They marched until January, through deep forests where all sound was deadened, dragging their legs through thick snow, pulling their balaclavas low. Snow fell from branches, whooshing through the frost-laden air.

'It's quite exquisite,' Steve said and Jack nodded.

Finally, in driving snow, they reached the camp and were pushed into a large barn.

Their Sergeant was saluted by men who were already gathered in the building. One stepped forward.

'Fellow students, we welcome you to this college of correction. I am Sergeant Howe,' he said and bowed.

'How exquisite,' said Jack, bowing back, and they began to laugh, all of them, too loudly and too long, but it was a laugh.

They were given padded overcoats by the Communists which they thought was a trick, but which Sergeant Howe said was part of the 'lenient policy'. They waited in the barn for the interrogation which they knew must come, and then there would be the lecture and the translation.

It came and Jack looked at the Chinese who asked him how much land he had. What his mother did. What his father did. Jack answered him, wanting to ask in return, 'And what have your people just done to our hopes? Did you think it was funny?' but he just answered the questions as they all did, then sat and listened to the lecture, and to the translation, because this was their life now until they left it on an ox-cart or the war was over.

It was eight in the evening before they were released from the barn to their clay and wattle huts which were heated by tiny wood-burning stoves. The floorboards were covered by straw mats with a narrow aisle down the middle.

They slept shoulder to shoulder. The wind swept through gaps in the clay and their breath froze on their blankets, on their lips, as the night hours passed. No one talked, but no one slept either. They had been so close to escape and now they were back at the beginning again.

Early in the morning loudspeakers blared Soviet and Chinese revolutionary music over the compound and Jack leaned up on his elbow.

'I think I prefer Butlins, on the whole,' he said and pushed the despair away, because it was a new morning and he must live each day, if he was to return to Rosie. And he would return.

Before roll-call at seven a.m. the new men, including Jack and Steve, were put on the wood-collecting rota.

'I guess everything's back to normal now,' Steve muttered and he, like Jack, began again. They all did.

They ran across to the lean-to communal latrine in temperatures which were forty degrees below zero and ran back because it was too cold to walk. They had to stand, though, for roll-call and thought that they would die.

Then they did physical jerks as the Commandant ordered. The snow glistened at the edge of the compound and the twilight of the winter morning turned into daylight and the cold air cut into their throats and chests.

One hour before breakfast the squad leader, Corporal Jackson, read a Communist publication aloud in their hut with a guard at the door. He read without pausing for full stops, for correct pronunciation, but used his own. It lightened the morning.

715

Four men collected the food from the camp kitchen where it was cooked in pots, carrying it back to the hut in a large bucket. The men placed their rice bowls and cups round the bucket and millet was spooned out into each. They ate it standing or sitting on their straw mats, talking quietly.

Another four men drew water into another bucket and wash-pan from the kitchens, where there was a gasoline drum full of water which was kept full over a fire which burned from dawn to dusk.

A bell rang at 10.00 hours and they went with the other men of their squad to the lecture room, where they sat with legs crossed on the bare boards and listened while they were instructed on the Marxist philosophy in Chinese, and then again in translation whilst their ears and noses felt that they would drop off with the cold.

They broke at midday, ate rice which contained a few tiny pieces of pork.

'It's a better camp,' Steve said.

'The Commies have officially decided that they'll not convert us all by cruelty. They're trying kindness to turn us into eager little beavers who will spread the message back home, when we get back. Make the most of it. Who knows how long it will last,' the Sergeant said.

They sluiced their bowls, then walked in the compound, taking note of the sentry at the gate and the sentry posts at intervals around the perimeter. They watched the village life which went on outside the wire and Jack remembered the Italian prisoners and how they had given the evacuees apples and showed them pictures of their children. He thought of the hot meal he had eaten. The prisoners probably ate better than the villagers. The whole thing was crazy.

At 14.30 hours they were back in the unheated hall and now the prisoners were made to read aloud from Marxist books and they did so, with no regard for punctuation or meaning.

The lecturer then picked Jack out to give his opinion on the chapter that had just been read.

Jack had listened to the beginning and the end so he stood up and repeated, 'The philosphical basis of Marxism is dialectical materialism which is hostile to all religion. Marxists feel that religion defends exploitation and drugs the working classes.'

He sat down.

'Proper little swot, aren't we?' grinned Bob.

'But what is your opinion of it?' the lecturer insisted.

'Oh-oh,' whispered Steve as Jack rose to his feet.

'Love is an opiate, so is alcohol. They exist. Religion exists. It gives ease as the others do and comfort. Therefore my opinion is that as religion exists so does its use as an instrument of peace and comfort.'

There was silence as he sat.

'Didn't understand much of that,' Steve murmured.

'Neither did I,' Jack replied.

'Neither did he, from the look of him.' Bob was looking at the lecturer who looked at the guards, then shrugged and asked another man for his opinion of Jack's opinion.

The hours crept on and in the evening they were issued with Russian and Chinese papers, translated into English. They used the paper to roll marijuana cigarettes in the summer, the Corporal told them, tearing the outside edge of three of the sheets, but only three, because the guards took the papers back at the end of the evening.

The next afternoon they were issued with paper and pencils and ordered to write an essay on 'Why the unjust aggressor is in Korea'. Jack managed to take two pieces of paper and, writing on both sides of one, he kept the other so his lessons could begin again that night with Steve.

And so the hours and the days slowly passed. Sometimes there were letters though none from Rosie, but then many people had none. They wrote letters too, but doubted that any were sent.

January became February and then it was March which limped into April and the days were still filled with boredom, with hunger, with cold and nothing changed with the coming of spring but the weather.

CHAPTER 23

By mid December '51 Rosie and Mario had extended the club, using the annexe for tables, leaving space in the back room for dancing. Luke and Sandy had left to tour Britain, along with the Larkhill Boys Rosie had met in the club with Joe.

'Bookings are good,' Luke rang to say. 'Full houses everywhere. Harry's bought himself another gold watch. You'll be able to do the same.'

'Or maybe Father Christmas will do that for me,' Rosie laughed. 'See you in January. Take care, all of you.' She put the phone down and looked round her small flat.

The table lamps lit the room softly, illuminating Grandpa's books. He would like it here, not as much as in his own home, but he would like it. There was a small half-knitted cardigan lying on the workbasket. She reached for it, began knitting, listening to the fire which hissed in the grate. She missed Luke and the boys. She measured the length of the cardigan then decreased for the armhole. It was ten o'clock. She was tired. She should sleep but each day and each night she waited for Joe to phone with news of Jack. He hadn't yet.

She finished the armholes, caught the remaining stitches on a holder, cast on for the left front, knitted up to the armhole, but her eyes were dry and sore. Rosie looked at the clock again. Eleven. She put her knitting away and went to bed, hearing Lucia breathing quietly in the cot beside her. The baby hadn't stirred since her feed at ten. She would sleep through until seven. She was perfect.

On 19 December she received a Christmas card from Frank and Nancy together with a present of a $50 bill which she put into the bank with the rest of her money. There would be no gold watch for her. There was a long future to build. She read their letter as she waited for the spaghetti to cook in the café kitchen.

718

Dearest Rosie,

Well, your skis are still in your room, the snow is here but you aren't. We understand though, really we do. Joe told us how busy you are and we can remember how hard we worked when we took over the paper. One day, we'll come to you.

Frank is well. He writes his columns, and edits the paper unofficially, makes his 'pinko' stand for common sense. Two of his friends still can't find regular work but pick up whatever they can. They will never write again, as long as McCarthy can stand up and give the performances that he does.

It is thought that maybe Eisenhower will throw his hat into the ring for the elections. Maybe he will be able to bring him to heel. Enough of that. We survive. I hope it isn't that which keeps you from us? But even as I say that, I know it can't be. Forgive me. It's just that you start leaping at shadows some days, so many friends have turned their backs.

It was so strange, wasn't it, the way the shooting stopped in Korea at the end of November following the establishment of the truce line along the 38th parallel. Joe filed his copy on it, saying no one ordered it, it just happened. For a moment there was peace.

I can't hold out much hope on a full armistice for a long while. The repatriation of the prisoners of war is the stumbling block. Have you heard from Jack? What is that boy playing at? How did you get on with Joe? He's a good reporter. He's sending back some good copy.

Have a wonderful Christmas, Rosie. The house will be empty without you, darling. Dare we say we will see you in 1952?

Your ever loving
Nancy

Nancy did not mention the feature Rosie had written about the Festival. Perhaps there was too much happening with them over there. Rosie wished she could go, but she couldn't.

Mrs Orsini, Mario and Rosie decorated the café and the club the next day, tying together holly with red ribbon bought from Mrs Eaves, pinning it up in corners, sitting Lucia up in her pram so that she could see, stringing streamers across the room. The customers helped. Mrs Eaves helped too and somehow there was enough laughter to wash away another Christmas without Jack, without news even.

On the evening of the twenty-second Rosie cut, coloured and pasted chains for her flat, showing Lucia who banged her rattle on the blanket in front of the fire, turning from her front on to her back, kicking her feet, pushing the rattle into her mouth, dribbling. Rosie kissed her cheeks, they were wet, pure.

She picked up her child and held her, seeing Jack in her movements, in her smile. She carried her to the window, looking out over the rooftops, hearing the jazz, the shouting and the laughter.

'Where are you, Jack?' she called, breath clouding the window.

A telegram came from Joe the next day, while she was serving customers and Mrs Eaves with mince-pies.

'Have news stop Be with you 24th stop Joe'

Rosie put it down. Mrs Eaves read it, folded it, put it away, then asked Mrs Orsini to babysit for Lucia while Rosie came with her to the West End.

Rosie looked at her, then started to put sugar into bowls. They were too full. There would be news tomorrow. It would be Christmas Eve and there would be news. How could she wait that long? Why was it so hard to breathe?

'Come on then, get your coat,' Mrs Eaves said, picking up her handbag and her gloves, pulling them on, pushing up between her fingers. 'Come on, get your coat, I said. Let's get you through this evening anyway. And don't worry. It can't be bad news or he would have cabled you earlier.'

They walked out into the crisp air. There was jazz all around, coming up from cellars, mingling with calypso, with swing. Tomorrow there would be news and she couldn't bear the minutes that had to pass until then.

Chestnuts cooked on braziers, sailors on leave entered the pubs, finding accommodation for their leave, amongst the homosexuals or the girls. Tarts lingering in doorways called, 'Merry Christmas, Rosie. I'll be in later for a coffee.'

Mrs Eaves took her arm and pointed to the Christmas tree outside the pub. There were streamers on it and candles which weren't lit. 'They'll light them at midnight on Christmas Eve, as they always do, now the war's over,' the publican said, as he waved to them from the doorway.

But the war wasn't over. Not the one Jack was fighting and the thousands of other young men.

They caught a bus, singing carols with the Salvation Army band as they waited. They went up to the West End, walked along Oxford Street, then, catching another bus, walked along Shaftesbury Avenue, looking at the billboards; and then they went back to Soho which they both preferred, which they both knew now. At least the evening was passing. There was only the long night to get through and some of the next day.

Joe didn't come until six p.m. on Christmas Eve when the café had closed. Rosie stood at the door of her flat, watching as he climbed the stairs. There was a small decorated Christmas tree fixed into a log in his hand. He held it out. Rosie's breath was shallow again.

'For Lucia,' he said. His mac was open, his belt dragged on the floor. It was dirty, muddy.

Rosie nodded, stood aside to let him enter. The tree smelt of pine. She placed it beneath the window. By the morning the room would smell too. It would be fresh and clean and pure but she couldn't wait any longer. She turned.

'Tell me,' she said.

Joe smiled, shrugged. He looked tired, there were bags under his eyes, lines across his forehead. 'Well, the good news is that he's safe. He's a POW. His father should have been notified. I don't know why he didn't let you know. Something went wrong somewhere. Anyway, Jack is one of the lucky ones. At least he's been named as a prisoner by the Communists. Thousands of them have just been sucked in and lost.'

Rosie turned to the bright sky, to the stars, to the jazz which she could hear drifting up, along with the steam from the clubs and pubs. It was going to be a good Christmas, she thought, as the joy surged within her. He was safe, he was out of the fighting. He had not come back because he couldn't, that was all.

'So that's why he hasn't written,' she murmured, putting her hand to her mouth.

Joe wrestled with his tie, pulling it loose, unbuttoning his collar. He looked around, saw the bottles on the table and asked, 'Can I pour myself a drink?'

Rosie came across the room, poured the bourbon Mario had found for her and then one for herself. Joe could have the crown jewels for bringing that news.

'I've no ice,' she said, feeling the smile broaden on her face.

'Drink up, Rosie. I said that was the *good* news.' Joe swirled his drink round in the glass. It was amber in the soft light. The fire was hissing. She looked at the tree. She shouldn't have smiled, that was it. Or made the streamers. If she hadn't made the streamers it would have been good news only. No, she didn't want to hear any more. She knew the important news, didn't she?

'Take your mac off, Joe,' she said, sipping the bourbon. It was harsh in her throat. The glass was cold. She put it down on the small table by Grandpa's chair, carried the mac across to the hook on the back of the door. It smelt of Joe, of America. It should smell of Korea. Why was it so hard to breathe? Why did her throat ache like this?

She walked back, sat in Grandpa's chair.

'Tell me now, then.'

She didn't look at him, but at the Christmas tree, at the chains she had made, but which would have been better left unmade. Then she looked at the fire as he told her that he had discovered in Japan that Jack had fallen in love with a Japanese girl called Suko. That they had had an affair, that he was to marry her on his return. That he would never be coming back to her and that was why he had never written.

She looked at the glass of bourbon on the table, she pulled it to the edge, tipped it, breaking the vacuum as they had done at the Lake Club when they were so very, very young. There was no vacuum, but what did it matter?

She drank, then looked at the tree, at the fire, at the chains, at Joe who stood there, looking down at her.

He moved towards her, knelt, touched her knee, her arm. 'I'm so sorry. So very sorry.'

'At least he's safe,' she said but she didn't want Joe there. She didn't want anyone there. She wanted to push him away, he was making the room dark. He was taking what air there was. She couldn't hear the hissing of the fire while he was there. She couldn't see the chains. She couldn't see the tree, but it was his tree. He had bought it for Jack's daughter. He had been kind. And there was no pain yet. For God's sake, the pain hadn't come yet.

'Come for Christmas,' she said. 'For lunch. You mustn't be alone. No one should be alone.'

She stood now, keeping the glass in her hand. She walked to the door, took the coat off the hook and gave it to Joe, because the pain was beginning and it was hard to breathe. So hard to breathe.

He left, walking softly down the stairs.

She called, 'There can be no mistake?'

He stopped and turned. 'No, Rosie, no mistake. I can vouch for that.' And what did it matter, he thought, as he moved down the stairs, what did it matter if he had lied. That man didn't deserve her. She was far more suited to him.

The Christmas meal was held in Mario's flat. Mrs Orsini drank sweet sherry and gave some to Rosie because the older woman had heard the news. They pulled homemade crackers and Joe gave her a gold watch and she smiled, felt its coolness against her skin, felt his fingers as he did up the catch. She held it up to the light.

'Luke will be pleased,' she murmured. 'Thanks, Joe.' She wished that Luke and Sandy were here.

She heard her voice from a distance, saw his smile. She gave Lucia Grandpa's nailer's penny, hung now on a silver chain. She pulled her cracker, ate turkey, ate Christmas pudding, found silver sixpences, fed Lucia, sat by the fire, listened to the King's speech but was dying inside.

Joe came the next day and the next and the next, helping, talking, comforting. He played with Lucia who laughed and held her hands out to him. He took the baby to the park, then hoovered the flat for Rosie, typing out his copy, talking to her about her writing, about the Cougars, about the tennis courts at the lake, about Frank and Nancy, about a world which did not include Jack.

She worked in the café, she played with Lucia, she wrote a letter of thanks to Frank and Nancy and on New Year's Eve she stayed up until midnight in the Orsinis' flat and Joe clicked his glass against hers when the clock struck twelve.

'Happy 1952,' he said, and smiled and both their gold watches glinted in the light from the Orsinis' lamps but Rosie wanted her own lamps, her own fire, and could bear all this no longer. She ran from them, taking Lucia, running up the stairs, laying her child down in her cot, stroking the hair that was Jack's, kissing the smile that was his too.

Now the pain broke and she stood at the window, hearing the music. And she cried, great racking sobs, because he wouldn't be in her life again, but how could he not be? He was part of her. His memories were hers. They had swung on the rope tied to the lamppost together. They had smelt the hops, they had stolen the cheeses. How could he do this?

Then she felt terrible rage, searing violent rage. He had shared her life, hated her, loved her, thrust himself into her, torn her, taken her in his confusion and now he had forgotten her and all their years together. Goddamn you, Jack. I hate you, I hate you.

She leaned against the window and hated him, loved him, wanted him, wanted Nancy, wanted the comfort of arms about her. And then Joe came. He held her, his arms were strong, and they had memories too. The lake was there as he soothed and stroked. The lake and the sun and the long sloping lawns where she had known peace and love. Where everything had been so much easier.

He carried her to the bed, he undressed her and undressed himself and she clung to him because he was part of Frank and Nancy's world. He was kind, he was here, he wanted her. Jack didn't. His hands had found someone else's body; his mouth, someone else's mouth.

But Joe was too fast for her, and it was as if they were at the barbecue by the lake again with his lips on her breasts, his hands on her body. She knew she only wanted comfort, nothing more than that, but what did it matter? What did any of it matter? She shut her mind to the face which loomed over her,

724

to the body too close, too heavy. The body which wasn't Jack's and which was entering her, filling her, and now she held him, because passion of a sort was sweeping her too. Passion born of anger, of pain.

In the morning they walked Lucia in her pram across the frost-hardened grass, carving out patterns on the ground. Her hand was warm in his, her lips too, from the kiss he gave her, and it was good not to be alone. But Jack was still everywhere and her love for him was too, and her anger and her pain.

But as the weeks wore on and Joe was seconded to a Fleet Street paper it became easy to be with him. He laughed, he joked, he tossed Lucia in the air and took her back to the time she had shared with Frank and Nancy.

At night she forced herself not to think of Jack as Joe kissed her and held her, because Jack had held another, he loved another. The waiting was over. Their love was over.

But she dreamed of him. Each night she dreamed of him and woke up crying, wanting to clutch at the image, wanting to shake it, hurt it, as she was hurting.

In February the King died and Frank wrote asking for a feature from each of them. Separate ones please, he said, which Rosie thought was strange, because how else would they do it? She left Mario to take any messages and wrote about the black armbands the children were wearing, the adults were wearing, she was wearing. She wrote of the simple oak casket which was moved from Westminster Hall to St George's Chapel. She wrote of the thousands of subjects who paid their last respects to this man who had brought them through war and peace.

The coffin left Westminster on a gun carriage. Big Ben rang out one beat a minute to mark the fifty-six years of the King's life and many of the men and women who stood with Rosie wept. And Rosie wept too.

The Household Cavalry, in ceremonial dress, walked in slow time to Paddington station where the royal train was waiting. As the cortège passed Marlborough House, Queen Mary, the King's mother, stood at the window and bowed her head and the crowd wept again.

Rosie wrote about the woman who turned to her while she was writing and asked who all the words were for. Rosie told her. 'Tell them we loved him,' the woman said.

Joe was covering the story at the Windsor end and when he arrived back that evening he hugged her, kissed her, his lips eager, his tongue searching her mouth. His nose was cold from the frost-full air, and so were his hands as he slipped them beneath her shirt. She laughed and kissed his neck and felt his hands become warm as they stroked her back, her breasts.

'You had a good day then,' she murmured, glad that someone was coming home to her each day, glad that she was becoming used to it, welcoming it, wanting Jack to know that she was not alone either.

Joe kissed her forehead, tucking her shirt back in, moving away, laughing.

'I sure did, so let's have your notes, I'll put this together and then we have the evening left for better things.' He laughed again and reached forward, rubbing his finger around her mouth.

Rosie smiled. It was good to be wanted at last. 'No. I'll write mine. You write yours. That's what Frank asked for.'

She moved to Grandpa's chair and began to write. Joe came towards her. 'Oh, come on, Rosie. Let's put it into one. It'll make a better feature. Won't take me a minute.'

But she refused because George VI had been *her* king, not his.

'Perhaps you should write about the return of the Duke of Windsor for his brother's funeral. That might appeal to the Americans,' she said, wanting to soften her refusal.

'Trying to teach me my job?' His voice was cold.

Lucia called out from the bedroom Rosie had made for her out of the boxroom. She moved towards the door. She didn't want this row. She didn't want any rows. There had been enough struggle already, hadn't there?

'No, you know your job. I know mine.' She didn't want to talk about this any more. She was too tired.

'I still think it would make a better feature. We'll split the fee.'

Rosie stopped. 'Look, Joe. It's not the goddamn money. I don't need the money so much any more. It's just that I have something I want to say from the British point of view. You wouldn't understand.'

Joe moved towards her, pulling her back towards the chairs. 'Oh, come on. I don't give up easy. Let's talk this over.'

'I've told you. No.' Rosie pulled away. He had hurt her wrist. Her watch had dug into her skin. She rubbed it and returned to the door. Now she was angry. 'Goddamn no.' She was shouting. Lucia cried.

Joe left her then, picking up his mac, thudding down the stairs, pushing aside Lucia's pram, scoring the hall wall, and by the time he returned she had finished her feature and posted it. He was drunk. He was sorry. So was she, because he was a good man, a kind man.

Joe knelt by Grandpa's chair and kissed her and she kissed him back because he had soothed her, comforted her, and there was some sort of caring growing inside her for him, though she didn't know how much.

February grew colder and Rosie pulled the blankets up around Lucia's shoulders when they went out. Lucia was sitting up now, pulling herself forward, pointing, her nose red in the cold. Joe never again drank as much as he had on the night of the King's funeral. Instead he talked of the future, of Frank's paper, of the need to keep it in the family, of his love for her.

At night his body sought hers and she liked the feel of his hands and his lips and now she stroked him too, held him, kissed him, and the dreams of Jack were not so fierce. But still they came.

Lucia was pulling herself up, using the table, and it was good to share these moments with someone else. But Rosie still read the news about Korea.

Nancy wrote to say that she was sorry, so sorry about Jack, but it didn't seem like the boy Rosie had loved. Was she sure of her facts?

But Rosie wouldn't allow herself to think about Jack any more, at least while she was awake. She had been working harder in these last few months than she had ever done before. She took phone calls late into the night and made them too, adding to the stable of bands, moving more and more into the

727

promotion side, enjoying the battles, enjoying the triumphs, pushing away the failures.

Joe didn't like it. He didn't like the phone ringing when he was stroking her hair, when he was kissing her mouth. He put on the radio too loud so that she had to strain to hear. But he was so kind and he comforted her, she told herself. He had found out about Jack for her. And it was better than being alone, wasn't it? And after all he had said he would listen to the band again now that Luke was coming home and send his final report to Bob. Rosie planned a party and Joe helped to lay out the drinks in Mario and Mrs Orsini's flat, because her own wasn't big enough. And then Luke was home and the gramophone played Bix Beiderbecke. Luke and Jake kissed her, held her, gave her a package. It was a gold watch.

She took it from the box, held it and couldn't speak but then Joe came up.

'Beat you to it, fellers.' He lifted Rosie's arm, pulled back her sleeve.

Luke and Jake flushed, then laughed, but Rosie didn't laugh. She took off Joe's watch and put it in her bag. She offered her wrist to Luke and he slipped the new one on.

'I'll wear one today, one tomorrow,' Rosie said, knowing that Joe had stiffened. Jack would have waited until he saw whether or not she could cope. But she mustn't think of him.

She took Joe's arm, kissed his cheek, led him away, poured him a drink and told him he was handsome, kind, loving. Soon he was laughing again and asking her to book Luke for Mario's club so that he could hear the group again.

The music was softer now and Luke came and danced with Rosie, holding her. He was familiar and he was safe. She told him that she was sleeping with Joe. She told him that the memory of Jack still hurt so much. He nodded.

'Don't rush into anything. Remember what your grandpa said.'

She didn't rush anywhere. She woke, worked, loved, slept and the days passed, but it always seemed dark. It had seemed dark since Christmas. She was tired. She ached inside. Joe was with her but the loneliness remained.

*

At the end of March Rosie received a letter from Frank enclosing $50 for the article on the King's funeral.

Lower Falls
20th March

Dearest Rosie,

Yes, this is what I wanted. All your own work. I didn't tell you that the paper spiked your feature on the Festival. You copied Joe's ideas about drawing comparisons between the new ideas and the Nissen huts, the austerity etc. I faced him with it. He'd been having some trouble handling domestic features, you know. He told me he had talked his ideas over with you. That you must have 'borrowed' them.

I was sorry you did that but he said things were tough, you might have become confused. I can understand that happening. I've done it myself. I was worried about you. You must have been real upset, real tired, but I guess things are better.

I wanted you to know I love you.
Frank

Rosie waited for the day to pass. Waited until Joe came home. She worked, she phoned, she cancelled one booking because the manager of the theatre was known to pass drugs. Her boys were too good for that. She took a taxi to Middle Street. She walked past 15 and 17 down to the rec. The wooden fencing was still up around the bombed houses.

'Will it ever be finished?' she murmured into Lucia's hair, sitting on the swing, hearing her laugh.

She cooked a meal for herself, not for Joe. Not ever again for Joe.

He came in at seven. Lucia was in bed.

Rose stood by the window. He slung his mac over the arm of the chair, poured a bourbon with his strong tanned hands. His cuff was white against his skin, his teeth white too. His watch golden. He was such a golden boy. He belonged at the Lake Club, not here. He moved towards her, kissed her, put his arm about her.

She handed him the letter, not watching as he read it but knowing when he had finished because he moved away.

For a moment there was silence, and then Joe said, 'I know what this must look like.'

'You must go,' Rosie said, looking at him now. 'You really must go.'

There was no anger in her voice. Just as there was no anger in it when she was dealing with difficult promoters and managers. That was business. This was business. Nothing else now.

'I'm not going. I belong with you. I love you. Together we can do things. We can build up the paper. Take over from Frank. It's all I've ever wanted, you know that. Married to you, that's possible.' He moved to her now, gripping her arm. 'We need each other. Jack's gone. You need me.'

She looked at his hand on her arm and then at him. He dropped his hand.

Rosie said, 'I've packed your bags. They're in the café, by the counter. I'm surprised you didn't see them.'

His lips were thin now and there was no love in his face. There never had been, she could see that now. 'If you do this I'll tell them about Lucia. I'll tell Bob to turn down Luke.' Joe was shouting, gripping her arm again.

Such short clean nails, suitable for the Lake Club. So very suitable. She moved away and again his hand dropped as she picked up his mac. It was still cold, damp and smelt of Joe. It meant nothing to her.

'Get out, Joe. I can't trust you, so there's nothing left.'

'I only wanted you so I'd get the paper.' He was spitting out the words, his shoulders rigid, his hands clenched into fists.

'And I've used you too, and I'm sorry,' Rosie said, holding the door, nodding to him as he stood there, large in this small room where he was now an intruder. 'Please go now, Joe.'

He started to say, 'You're a bitch . . .' but then stopped, shaking his head. 'Rosie, can't we . . . ?'

She shook her head, handing him his mac. He snatched it from her, turned, flung it at the window, driving a glass ashtray to the floor. It broke and only then did he leave, his mac lying crumpled on the sill.

Rosie quietly closed the door, knelt and picked up the splinters. She wouldn't need an ashtray now. She didn't smoke. Grandpa was right. Second best was no good.

She carried the broken glass through to the kitchen in Joe's mac, dropped them in the bin, then stood at the window listening to the sounds of the streets, to a soft cough from Lucia. Yes, he was right, it was better to be alone.

Rosie wrote to Frank and Nancy, telling them that she and Joe had quarrelled, that the report about Luke would be bad, but that *she* vouched for the band. Please would they tell Bob that? She also said that the Festival feature had been her idea. Joe had copied it.

She didn't tell them about Lucia because Joe might not and they had enough heartache now. And she had enough too.

In April she went again to Middle Street and slipped in through the back gate at a time when Mrs Eaves said Norah would be out. She pruned the roses, cutting them back to the healthy buds. She returned to Soho, and bought three rose plants from the market, planting them out in pots in Mario's yard. These were in recognition that the past had gone. There was to be no more waiting for anyone.

In May Frank and Nancy wrote to her, full of love, full of guilt at what they saw as their betrayal of her. They could not write fully until Joe returned from the POW camps where the North Koreans and Chinese were housed. Things were supposed to be bad there, he said. When Joe arrived in Lower Falls in the summer they would tell her what had been decided for that young man.

In the summer Frank wrote to her:

Lower Falls
June 1952

My dearest Rosie,
    We have spoken to Joe. He no longer works for the paper. I now write again under my own name. There has been enough subterfuge. It's time I got out there fighting again. McCarthy can't go on for ever. When the Korean war ends my guess is that he will lose his appeal. All this talk about betrayal by the leadership because of the reverses and then the stalemate is just too easy to spout.

731

God giving that man a mouth was like giving a lunatic a gun.

The report on Luke was bad. Yours has over-ridden it. Bob trusts you.

But now I write about really important things. The first being that I know now that I am a grandfather. Joe told us. How can you think that this would bring anything other than joy? How can you think that it would have made our problems worse? We love you. We shall love Lucia. But your pain is our pain.

Think carefully, Rosie. Joe vouched for the news he brought about Jack's love affair. I have checked the POW list. He is on that but that doesn't mean the rest is true. Give him the benefit of the doubt where love is concerned. Just wait until the end of the war when you will know one way or the other. Please. I know it is what your Grandpa would want.

Incidentally, we are coming over to see you in July.

Frank

CHAPTER 24

The year had passed slowly; tortuously slowly. The lectures didn't change as 1952 slipped into 1953, neither did the nature of the seasons. The cold was extreme, the spring came with its usual glorious explosions of colour.

'Exquisite,' Steve said and they remembered Nigel, but Steve couldn't really see the colour. The lack of vitamins had given him twilight blindness. He groped his way if Jack wasn't with him, and he didn't sleep because he thought he would never write now.

The Doc said he would. That vitamins would reverse the situation.

'But when will he be able to have those, Doc?' Jack had asked.

'When this lot is over.'

But no one knew when that would be. Sometimes they doubted that it would ever happen.

The peace talks continued. New prisoners, conscripts who had not volunteered, told them so. The newcomers told them about the guns which blasted from the trenches and showered shrapnel and earth on to the men of both sides. It was trench warfare again. In this age of great might, they had returned to static trench warfare.

Conditions improved again as the blossom bloomed on the trees. The men were given two larger meals a day, with rice and soya beans. Once a week they had a piece of pork. There was steamed bread, Korean turnip, cabbage leaves which Jack made Steve eat raw because Maisie had always said that cooking boiled the vitamins away. They also had potatoes now.

Jack told Steve how he had picked potatoes in Somerset, how Rosie's grandpa had grown some one year in a bucket in the yard. They had been small and translucent and good enough to eat on their own.

There were no letters from Rosie. Steve had none either though he was sure his mother would have written. Some men had letters, though, and between the news of births and deaths the words which cut deepest were those of everyday life. The sink that was cracked. The bulbs that had been planted before they left. The bike that was rusted.

Jack wrote about all this with a journalist's eye. 'Keep at it. You'll do well,' another American whose father was a Sub-Editor on the *Washington Post* said when Steve showed him.

Each day they threw stones at the marker, because why should they change the ritual of their life, just because one of them no longer saw clearly, Jack asked? He forced his friend to concentrate while he gave him instructions. 'Same direction, not so hard this time.' Jack told Steve that as long as he could still hit the marker he would also be able to write.

'Just you wait and see. You'll use all these months, these years. The times in the pit, the times when the blossom has bloomed and filled us with wonder, and one day you'll win the Pulitzer Prize.'

Steve threw another stone, hitting the target. He aimed in exactly the same direction for his next throw.

'There you are, and just you wait, it'll be over soon. You'll get those vitamins.'

But would it soon be over?

It was for Steve. In April 1953 the North Koreans agreed to repatriate a number of wounded and ill prisoners and they included Steve on the list that they called out at roll-call. They included Bob too because dysentery had taken its toll of the older man and a stomach ulcer was suspected.

Jack scribbled a note to Rosie and gave it to Bob to post. It was hurried because the trucks were already pulling in. The men had thirty minutes to grab their belongings and say their farewells. As the others were being helped to the truck Steve hugged Jack, slapped his back. They held one another and couldn't bring themselves to say goodbye until the guard started shouting at them, pulling at Steve to move.

'See you, bud,' Steve said. 'I almost don't want to go. Don't want to leave you. It's been so long. But I'll see you.'

'You will. You get those vitamins inside you and you goddamn will,' Jack said, helping him up into the truck.

They clasped hands as the truck jerked away. Jack ran along behind waving to Bob, waving to Steve, watching as the mud spun from the wheels, swallowing his envy and his loss, wondering how he could go on without his American who was more than a friend, who had known the horrors of the pit alongside him. Who had defecated in the corner of the same rail-truck, who had washed Jack's rags when he had dysentery. Whose rags Jack had washed in turn.

He turned away as the truck eased into the haze and now the Sergeant shouted at him and the others. He lined them up. Told them that they were a motley shower, a bloody disgrace to their countries and he didn't want to see any long faces. Their friends had left. Soon they would all leave this godforsaken country, and they would leave with their spirits intact, their health intact, even if he had to break their bloody necks.

'And don't you forget it,' he bellowed. 'Dismiss.'

Throughout April the routine remained the same as it always had been and the men stopped looking up each time the Commandant left his house outside the compound. Nothing had changed. They weren't going home, yet.

The days were lonely now for Jack. He threw pebbles at the marker. He sat through lectures, using them to sharpen up his précis. Using them to dream of Rosie. Using them to rest. They were all so thin and tired and more fell ill with beri-beri but no more were shipped out.

Jack remembered the train ride to Pyongyang and feared that the same trick had been played again and maybe Steve would be trucked back. He didn't return though as April turned into May. In the camp they were given sleeping bunks, chairs and tables. Razors, mirrors, combs, nail-clippers, toilet bags, cigarettes, wine and beer. They shaved away the unkempt beards and looked almost young again.

The food had improved so much that the British were more able to play soccer, the Americans to play baseball. Jack wondered if Frank still had the target on the garage that Rosie had told him about.

Each day he threw pebbles at the marker because it was part of his routine and then he squatted in the compound and listened as the Americans threw, batted, ran.

'Now whad'ya gonna do, batter, batter?' was the chant from the supporters.

'Stay loose, baby, stay loose.'

'Whad'ya say? Whad'ya say?'

But solitary confinement still continued too and manual labour outside the compound: hauling logs, unloading trucks, digging channels – and the wood detail, the never-ending chopping of wood.

Peking Radio's English broadcasts continued too, including interviews with those UN troops who had turned, and although most of the men in the camp scarcely listened, the tone of the reports was different and some of them became convinced that the end was near. But Jack, and those who had been with him, could not forget the train journey to Pyongyang and refused to think of home.

On 27 July their Sergeant lined them all up at 1400 hours and, as the sun beat down on the compound square, the Commandant addressed the camp in Chinese.

'The bugger,' breathed Jack, because he knew the Commandant spoke English well. There was a pause.

Then the interpreter said, 'Both sides in the Korean war have agreed to a cease-fire to take effect from now. You will be returned to your own side.'

There were cameramen with the camp staff and Jack knew that they were there to record the scenes of joy, but none of the prisoners moved. They looked at the Sergeant and waited.

He gave his orders. They obeyed. Attention. About turn, quick march. Back to their huts, denying their captors any emotion. Denying themselves any as they sat on their beds and wondered if this was another trick.

One week later, in pouring rain, trucks came and took them to the railhead. They travelled in cattle wagons until they reached another camp. They lived beneath canvas for another two days eating beans and rice. Jack would not believe that he was going home and neither would many of the others.

Small groups departed each evening. Red Cross observers

736

were there now. Jack watched the yellow moon push up over the mountain crest. Where were they going? Back to the camp? Even with the Red Cross he could not bring himself to believe.

But then it was his turn. He pulled himself up into the truck and wished that Steve was here and Nigel, Tom, Bob. And still he couldn't believe. He couldn't feel. A Chinese Captain stood in the rain, urging them to turn from the warmongering capitalists and stay where there was truth.

Jack said, for Steve, for Tom, for Nigel, 'Why don't you take a powder.'

They drove into Freedom Village three days later and passed lorry after lorry taking Communist POWs back north.

There's nothing left for you up there now, Jack thought, the ruined countryside still raw in his mind. It was the people that suffered, always.

They drove into the encampment beneath a 'Welcome Home' arch and slipped down from the lorry. Someone directed them towards doctors who examined them, then on to the interrogators, who examined them. Then on to the psychiatrists who gave them ice-cream, and examined them.

'I just want to get home,' Jack said, because now he believed it and the joy was racing through him. He had been asked to fill in too many forms, been asked too many questions for it not to be the truth. It was over. He was going home. He was bloody well going home.

A woman in WVS uniform came to him as he sat on his bunk. She gave him a shirt and sat and talked to him. It was too long since he had heard a woman's voice, too long since someone had done up the buttons on his shirt, and his eyes filled with tears.

'It's so long since I've seen Rosie,' he said to the woman and then he cried.

The next day he boarded the troop ship, felt the wind in his hair and stood by the rail, with so many others who were too thin, too old, to be twenty-three.

'It was exquisite,' he called out as the ship left, not caring about the looks from those at his side. He was saying goodbye to Nigel and to Tom. 'It was goddamn exquisite.' And he was crying again, the tears smeared across his cheeks.

*

737

The year had passed slowly for Rosie too. Frank and Nancy had come in the summer of '52. They had held Lucia, they had held Rosie. They walked in the park, they looked at the ruins, at the rosebay willowherb which covered some still-unfilled craters. They gazed at the re-building which was slow, very slow. They took her to shows, to restaurants where there was still a maximum price. They went back with her to Somerset but not to Herefordshire because she must go there alone one day.

They travelled through the Somerset lanes, visited Montacute, Martock, Crewkerne, Stoke-sub-Hamdon. They climbed the hill and looked across the Levels. They looked down on the orchard where Ed had camped. They stood outside the school where Jack had been taught. They heard the laughter through the peaked windows and Frank put his arm round Rosie, chewing his empty pipe.

'He'll come back,' he said, but none of them really knew whether he would or not.

Frank and Nancy had left for the States again in August and when they took Luke and the group back with them it was as though they had taken the sun. Winter had come and gone and Bob had sent for the Larkhill Band too. They were all playing in New Orleans which Luke said 'was heaven come early'.

There had been no letters from Jack though she had written. Nancy said that much of the mail did not get through.

In April 1953 Frank telegraphed her: 'Repatriated POWs arriving RAF Lyneham, Wiltshire. May 1st. Meet them. Ask them. Frank.'

He arranged for her to have admittance but when she arrived and saw the plane land, saw the men being helped to the ground, sick, tired, injured, she turned away. This was a time for the families that surrounded her, families that now held back tears that had been falling all morning.

She wouldn't intrude. She would wait. She would work.

Promoters started coming to her with propositions in spite of her youth and because of her honesty, her reliability. On 2 June she covered the Coronation for Frank's paper because it kept her in contact, it kept the paper in the family. She took two-year-old Lucia with her and she sat in the pushchair, waving a flag, turning and laughing at Rosie, with Jack's mouth, his laugh.

738

She wrote of the golden coach, the eight grey horses and wished that Lucia was old enough to remember it all. It was wet and it was cold but wasn't England so often wet and cold? Rosie laughed and so did Mrs Eaves who was with her.

'Will you go back to America?' Mrs Eaves asked.

'It depends if he comes back. And if he does, will he want the stall? It all just depends. Both countries are my home.'

They waved at Queen Salote of Tonga, that huge brown smiling figure whose open carriage, Mrs Eaves said, must have been filled with rainwater.

Each Commonwealth Prime Minister had his own carriage and that led to such a shortage of professional coachmen that, Rosie wrote, businessmen and country squires had dressed up and were now driving some of the coaches. Rosie and Mrs Eaves laughed again and moved to Buckingham Palace where the Queen and the Duke of Edinburgh waved from the balcony at midnight by which time Lucia and most of the other children around them were asleep in their pushchairs.

Rosie said to Mrs Eaves as the crowd roared, 'I missed VE Day. I'm glad I caught this.'

Mr and Mrs Orsini had been watching it on their new television and when Rosie and Mrs Eaves returned they toasted the new Queen in iced champagne which Mario had saved since the beginning of the war. They talked until two, with Lucia asleep in Rosie's arms. Life was good, she thought.

On 15 June the Chinese launched a new Korean offensive and she cried all night because there seemed to be no end to this waiting, this killing.

Then Frank rang her from America. 'It's me. Take no notice. It's these goddamn Commies trying to gain some sort of propaganda success before the armistice is signed. We're close, Rosie, very close. Hang in there, goddamn it. See you. Bye.'

The line was crackling, she had hardly been able to hear. But it was enough.

The roses in the yard behind the kitchen were blooming well by July and Lucia pointed to Rosie's pocket each time they went out, wanting to be shown the matchbox which they always took for the ladybirds.

On 27 July the armistice was declared and a few days later

Rosie rang her jazz groups and her contacts and told them she would not be available for at least two months. Mr Orsini would handle everything. She took a cab to Middle Street and dropped a letter in through Ollie's door. It said:

Dear Jack,
    If you come back and want to see me I shall be in Herefordshire until the end of September. I love you.
                                                    Rosie

She didn't go into Grandpa's yard because Norah was there, the windows were open. She walked to Woolworths and heard Frank Sinatra singing, felt the warmth, basked in the light, fingered the glasses, the jewellery, the same sort of ribbon which she had bought when she met Sam.

'I'm going to Herefordshire. I can't wait here. I shall give myself two months and then that's the end. I've left a letter. I haven't told him about Lucia. He must come because he wants to,' she said to Mrs Eaves, speaking in short sentences because it seemed to hurt too much to speak, to breathe.

Jack's troop ship arrived at dawn on 18 September. He felt better, he had eaten well and there was a little more weight on him now. All he could think of was Rosie and he rushed for the train, sat in the carriage looking out of the window at the greenness of this land. He had forgotten. Somehow he had forgotten how green it was. He leaned out of the window as the train rattled through fields which had been ploughed, through fields in which cows grazed. There was sweetness to the air. He was home.

A woman was knitting opposite. She looked at him as he sat down again. 'Been posted abroad have you? Must have been nice to get a tan like that. I don't know, you young people. Away from the shortages. You don't know you're born,' she tutted.

'I've been in Korea.'

'Oh, that's the one my Harry said was a waste of time.' She was looking at her pattern, tracing the line of instructions. It slipped and fell to the floor. Jack picked it up.

'Yes, you could say it was a waste of time,' he replied and

740

looked out of the window again. So many years had passed, so many men had died. There had been so much waiting, for them all. But there was Steve, there was Bob, and he had learned to write, learned about himself. He shrugged. 'Some of my friends will have thought it a waste of time,' he said. 'They didn't come back. They'll never come back.'

But the woman wasn't listening, she was counting her stitches. There was no point in talking any more. He just sat and watched the country unfold, the towns cluster, the suburbs of London approach. He ran down the platform, out to the taxi-rank. There was a queue. There was always a bloody queue. He was laughing and the man behind him smiled.

'Been away then?'

'Yes.' Jack didn't say where to. 'Going back to see my girl.'

'That's what makes it all worth while, ain't it, mate?' the man said.

Jack nodded, climbing into the taxi which drew up. 'Yes, that's what makes it all worthwhile,' he called back. 'Middle Street,' he said to the cabbie.

He looked out. The ruins were still there, but progress had been made. He smelt the air. It was the same old smoke, the same familiar skyline, the same streets which were becoming narrower. It wouldn't be long now. The taxi was turning into Albany Street, past Woolworths, down into Middle Street. Jack tapped on the glass partition. 'This'll do, mate.' He pushed open the door outside Rosie's house. He paid, tipped, ducked down through the alley, into Grandpa's yard, then stopped. Dropped his kitbag. He was home. At last it was all over. They could begin again, if she would have him.

He knocked on the door, pushed it open, calling, 'Rosie. I'm back.'

There was only Norah there, washing clothes at the sink, her hair permed, her mouth pursed. Grandpa's books were gone from the walls, his chair too. Norah turned from the sink and said, 'Thought you'd be here one day. She's gone. Back to America with that Joe. Gave you up a long time ago. Ollie's gone too, up north of London. Building the new towns.'

Norah didn't watch him go, she just heard his feet run out through the yard. She knew he'd try Ollie's house. She'd left the key there in the usual place but she'd burned the letter he'd got his friend from the camp to post. She'd taken the letter Rosie had pushed through the door. Thought I wouldn't see, I suppose, she thought, scrubbing harder at the dirt ingrained in Harold's trousers from kneeling on those church floors. Well, that'll teach her to tell my husband to go back to his hobby. That'll teach her to take him away from me. She turned back to the sink.

In Herefordshire, the sun was still warm, though it was nearly five p.m. Rosie paddled with Lucia in the stream, taking the pebbles as her daughter handed them to her. They were wet. She carried them to the bank, adding them to the pile of those which were drying.

Two weeks to go until the end of September and Jack had not come.

She looked up at the slopes above her. The bines were half picked. The pickers were using the last of the light, flip-flipping, not looking. Chatting, laughing.

When she had arrived the barley had still been in the fields all around the cottage she had rented. The combine had worked up until the end of August, shaving off the last tuft before the farmer sent in the plough. Seagulls had clustered over the furrows and Lucia had stood with her mouth open, waving at the birds, calling back when she thought they called to her.

Rosie had gone for a walk with her daughter the evening before the pickers came, and climbed the stile into the kale, hearing the partridges as they whickered in the hedge.

They had passed the blackberry bushes, still ripe with fruit, and looked across the sloping fields, down to the stream they were paddling in now. Seeing the thistles, the cows grazing, she had felt the peace of the place, the echoes.

She had waited, then walked her daughter through the bines which swung in the gentle breeze, telling her that one day they would all come and pick hops and then dance like she and Grandpa had once done. She had taken Lucia to the gate, shown her the carved initials. Her daughter had rubbed her hand over the letters her father had cut and laughed.

And each day they had waited.

Rosie turned back to the stream now, easing her feet through the water, over the stones, as Lucia, her dress tucked into her knickers, laughed and held up more pebbles, drips running down her plump arm.

Rosie turned and threw them towards the pile. Yes, they had waited but not for much longer. If he didn't come she knew now what she would do. She would spend half her year in England, half her year in Lower Falls and she would survive and prosper. But . . . But . . .

They waded towards the bank, ate sandwiches which were warm from the sun. Rosie remembered the lake, then Lee at Wembley, and touched the letter in her pocket which he had written, now that he was 'a big boy'. She lay back on the grass, pulling Lucia on top of her, hugging her, rocking gently, hearing the buzz of nearby bees.

There were moths at night, beating against the window, trying to reach the light. Didn't they know it was hopeless? She kissed Lucia fiercely.

'Water, Mummy, water,' Lucia said and laughed, pointing to the stream.

The water was cool against their legs as they waded in again and they scooped pebbles and threw, again and again, and the pile grew bigger as Rosie told Lucia how Daddy had lain on the bank and told her of Somerset and how Grandpa had picked hops that year as though he was a young man again.

Her hand was cold now but the pyramid wasn't high enough and so she threw again.

Another, larger pebble came through the air, hitting the pile before hers did. 'I hit the marker every time now,' Jack said.

Rosie saw his smile, his thin face, his thin hands that he held out to her and to his daughter. Then she was running with Lucia clutched to her, through the water, over the pebbles which bruised her feet, but which she didn't feel. Running as he came down the bank and into the water too, and at last his arms were round them both, his lips were on hers, the same soft gentle lips, the same skin, the same words.

'Mrs Eaves told me you were here. I love you, little Rosie.' And then, into her neck, 'Forgive me.'

'God damn you, my darling love,' was all she said, because the waiting was over.

743